It was impossible to read anything in his eyes except physical longing as Fade struggled to prevent his feelings from rising to the surface. He could not believe this earnest, beautiful, well-born woman was kneeling before him. She was unlike any woman he had ever known before. There was a grace and breeding about her, evident in every plane of her sculptured face and lithe body. Yet there was something more. A vitality, an eagerness to embrace life and hold it fast, a sensuousness he had barely suspected was there. That all this could be his was almost more than he could believe.

Without touching her, he said, "I know I could take you right here..."

Berkley books by Maryhelen Clague

BESIDE THE STILL WATERS
BEYOND THE SHINING RIVER

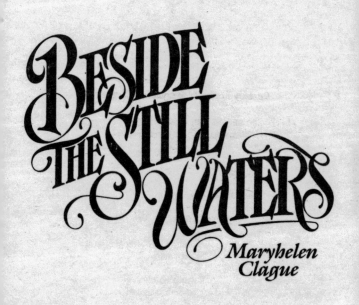

BESIDE THE STILL WATERS

Maryhelen Clague

BERKLEY BOOKS, NEW YORK

BESIDE THE STILL WATERS

A Berkley Book/published by arrangement with
the author

PRINTING HISTORY
Berkley edition/March 1984

ISBN: 0-425-06273-2

A BERKLEY BOOK ® TM 757,375
Berkley Books are published by The Berkley Publishing Group,
200 Madison Avenue, New York, New York 10016.
The name "BERKLEY" and the stylized "B" with design
are trademarks belonging to Berkley Publishing Corporation.
PRINTED IN THE UNITED STATES OF AMERICA

To Bob,

For his never-failing help and support

PART I

Emily

One

LEANING FORWARD in her saddle, Emily Deveroe peered over the sleek neck of her strawberry roan. Down the wooded slope, far in the distance, she could see a solitary rider picking his way through the valley. Settling back, she smiled to herself as she recognized Wilton, her groom, whose distress was apparent even from where she sat. She shrank back quickly as she saw him lift his hand to shield the sun and peer upward in her direction, scanning the trees. Waiting until he looked away, she gave Thor a gentle kick and turned him in a slow half-circle back among the shadows of the pines that edged the hill. Wilton would spend the next hour searching for her, anxiously at first and then angrily as he realized she was hiding from him.

Well, let him, the old woman. It was all Papa's fault for insisting that she ride out with the groom in the first place.

Off in the distance, a sudden burst of gunfire broke through the barrier of thick trees, and her horse raised his head and laid back his ears nervously. Hunters, Emily thought, gently stroking Thor's neck to quiet him. She looked back long enough to enjoy a last perverse glimpse of her groom below. A mischievous smile pulled at the corners of her shapely lips, and with a flick of her riding crop she urged Thor down the other side of the hill toward the brook.

It was not easy for the horse to pick his way through the thick underbrush. Emily let him take his time, enjoying the chatter of the woods around her. She loved this music of the forest. Without the distracting conversation of people, its small noises were heightened: the singing brook, the leaves whispering their secrets, the busy insects, and now and then the startled tympany of some small animal dashing for cover. She loved the solitude, the feeling of being completely at home with nature. Wilton, with his hovering, watchful ways and endless complaints, always broke the spell of her private woodland reveries.

For once she had outmaneuvered him. She would enjoy her hour of solitude; then she'd let him find her and escort her home, scolding all the way.

Another shot rang out, closer than before. Thor jumped again, all poised nervous energy. His frightened eyes searched out the trees and he grew more skittish by the moment. Humming to herself, Emily gave him his head, guiding him only enough to make sure they came out on the side of the hill where the brook cut a long, jagged gash across an open expanse of wild meadow.

They were practically there. She could glimpse the white daylight through a filigree of green leaves. Almost as eager as her horse now for a run across the meadow, she kicked Thor sharply, urging him forward. Just as he broke clear of the wood, the skirt of her riding habit caught with a jerk on the thorns of a wild raspberry bush. Pulling Thor around, Emily yanked at the stubborn serge, cursing the fashion that forced women to ride encased in yards of fabric while men could wear practical trousers. The horse danced nervously while she worked at the skirt, and at last she was able to pull it free. Then horse and rider joyfully bounded through the last stand of trees and into the open meadow.

A burst of sound exploded in front of her, knocking her backward. Clutching wildly at the reins of her rearing horse,

Emily felt a wall slam down on her head. In a horrible burst of pain, the world went snow white before her eyes, then searing red as her body was thrust upward. The red world turned to black, and in the silence the last thing she knew was that she was falling . . . falling . . .

"My God! You're not dead, are you? Please don't be dead. Oh my God!"

Some terrible force shook her body, intensifying the pain in her head. She tried to raise her arm to stop it, tried to cry out, "Leave me alone," but her arm refused to move and the only sound that escaped her lips was a long, low groan.

That seemed to help. The shaking subsided and the insistent voice moved back.

"Bless heaven you're not dead. Thank God."

Struggling to open her eyes, Emily could barely make out the figure bending over her, blocking out the sun. It was the dark outline of a large man, his face indistinct in the shadow. She tried again to speak but could only groan. A strong hand went under her neck, lifting her up.

"Here, try to drink this." A thin trickle of cold liquid ran down her chin. "Can you drink? Open your eyes, for God's sake. Show me you're alive."

"I . . . I'm alive," she groaned. "Let me be. You're hurting me!"

As he laid her gently back on the soft grass, she struggled to remember where she was. Who was this man? Not Wilton, surely. She winced as an icy wet cloth was laid against her forehead, but it dulled the ache a little.

"Thank heaven I didn't kill you. Although you deserve a beating for what you did. Of all the stupid, idiotic, harebrained stunts! I ought to leave you here to take care of yourself."

His gentle hands working at her temples belied the anger in his voice. Emily struggled to sit up.

"What happened? Oh, my head!"

He settled back on his heels, staring at her. She had an impression of anxious dark eyes in a deeply tanned face.

"You came bounding out of the woods just at the moment I was about to shoot a buck I've been stalking for three hours. You ruined my shot, and you very nearly got yourself killed in the process. If I wasn't so relieved to have avoided accidentally murdering you, I might consider doing it deliberately."

"Was I shot?"

His fingers rested on her forehead, lightly touching the skin and smoothing away her hair.

"I jerked the barrel up when I saw your horse, and the ball must have grazed your head. You'll have a devil of a headache for several days, but you'll live. And so will my deer."

The world began to swim around her. Falling backward, she was caught by his arm, and her head rolled against his chest.

"Thor? My horse?"

"He's all right. He's over there enjoying the grass. Here, lean against me for a moment and try to drink a little more of this."

The trickle of brandy that slipped down her throat nearly choked her. "Ugh!" she spat out. "What awful stuff. Oh, my head . . ."

"Drink it. You're probably accustomed to a better quality, but it will make your head feel better."

After holding the flask to her lips once more, he put it to his own for a long draught. *He* certainly doesn't mind the quality, Emily thought, then realized from the shudder she could feel coursing through his body how truly frightened he had been.

"Do you still feel faint? Can you sit up now?"

"I think so. Could I have a little water, please?"

Taking an old-fashioned gourd from his saddlebag, he went to the brook, filled it with cold water, and offered it to her. Emily put the gourd to her lips, using both hands to hold it steady. He watched her drink, settling down on the grass at her side.

"You're Emily Deveroe, aren't you?"

She glanced up at him, seeing his face clearly for the first time. "Do I know you?"

"I'm one of the Whitmans—Fade Whitman. I've been away at sea. You grew up while I was gone."

"Whitman . . . Yes, I remember. You used to work in Papa's stable, a long time ago. You had such a way with horses, Papa said."

He glanced away, a bit embarrassed. "I suppose I did once. But I gave up horses for ships. They're considerably more profitable."

The brandy was beginning to take effect, and the pain in her head had dulled to an almost bearable ache. As her vision cleared, Emily studied the man next to her, trying to see in him the boy who used to hang around the tack room. He was still dark, almost swarthy, with eyes nearly as black as his hair, thick shapely brows, and a wide, generous mouth. The boy had been slight and thin; the man was very tall, with broad muscular shoulders and narrow hips. Glancing around, he saw her watching him and returned her stare so blatantly that she dropped her eyes. Perhaps he was trying to find the girl she had been in the woman she now was. Whatever he saw did not seem to displease him.

"When I think how close I came to killing Josh Deveroe's daughter!"

He said it quietly, almost to himself, but Emily knew what every nuance meant. Josh Deveroe was about as close as you could come in these Republican days to being lord of the manor. The Whitmans, on the other hand, were generally thought of in the village as little better than laborers. Without knowing why, Emily grew anxious to put Fade Whitman at ease.

"Well, I'm not dead and Papa will no doubt give me a good tongue-lashing for bringing this on myself. It's not your fault. I was not supposed to be on this side of the hill at all, but I ran away from my groom."

"That would have been small consolation if my shot had blown away your head. Do you think you can ride?"

Reaching for her hand, he helped her to her feet. Emily stood for a moment before her knees gave out. Then Fade's strong arm caught her once again as she fell back.

"I don't think so."

"Then I'll have to carry you. You wait here," he said, setting her down gently. "My horse is tied over there among those trees. I'll go get him and then attempt to lure that brute of yours away from his grazing. You'll have to ride in front of me."

"I'm sorry to cause you this trouble, but I don't think I could make it alone."

"I know. What you need now is a bed and a doctor. If you can just hold on long enough for the ride back to Southernwood you should be all right."

"Do you know the way?"

His silhouette was blocking the sun, but she could tell he was smiling down at her.

"Is there anyone around here who doesn't?"

Emily was aware of very little during the long ride back except the secure feel of Fade Whitman's arms around her and the pleasure she felt leaning back against his solid chest. By the time they rode into the stable yard behind the great house, her head was throbbing and aching so that even these delights were beginning to fade. Turning Thor over to one of the startled stablehands, Fade rode his own mount up the long carriage drive to the side of the house. He lifted her easily from the saddle. As they started toward the veranda, Emily became aware of people crowding around her. Two of the housemaids appeared from nowhere, fussing and frightened and obviously assuming she had been thrown by her brute of a stallion. At the top of the steps Fade set her down, keeping a supporting arm around her. Emily wavered unsteadily, then looked up to see her father come racing through the double doors, followed by his elderly cousin, Agatha. Both of them were obviously alarmed.

"Emily! What happened? You're not hurt, are you?"

"Oh, the dear girl. She's as pale as a sheet. And look at that wound on her head!"

Emily slumped into her father's strong embrace. She had not been so happy to fall into his arms since she was a child.

"I'm all right..." she began, but the world went swimming around her once more and she could not quite control her tongue. She could barely hear Cousin Agatha issuing orders.

"Chloe, turn down Miss Emily's bed. Faith, run to the stable and tell Joseph to go at once for Dr. Sayre. No, wait," she said, turning to Fade with a question in her eyes. "We should probably know what happened first."

"She ought to have a doctor look at her and I think you should get him here as soon as possible," Fade answered, watching Josh climb the stairs with his daughter in his arms. He was reluctant to discuss the details of the incident in front of the servants. Better to let everybody assume her horse had thrown her until he could clarify the matter privately. Halfway up the stairs, Josh Deveroe turned and threw him a quick glance as though reading his mind.

Fade hovered in the wide downstairs hall while the rest of the group followed Josh upstairs to Emily's room. He could hear them moving about, their voices low and indistinct, and he could make out the hurried steps of the servants as they followed Agatha's commands. He studied the ornate gilt furniture and painted French wallpaper in the hall, waiting uneasily for the moment he would have to face Josh Deveroe. It had been years since he'd stood inside this hallway, and the opulent appointments that had so impressed him as a young boy seemed to have grown a little shabby with the years. Of course, he could leave, and the thought seemed inviting for a moment. But no, something about running away stuck in his craw. It was better to stay and face the consquences. It had been an accident, after all, and one for which the foolish girl must take some responsibility. He only hoped the powerful Mr. Deveroe would see it that way.

Although Josh Deveroe was a large man, his steps on the stairway were so light that Fade did not realize he was there until he heard him speak.

"I think we had better step in here," he said, motioning Fade toward a small back parlor. "Would you care for anything? A glass of Madeira, perhaps?"

"No, thank you." Fade glanced down at his boots, which still bore the mud of the meadow and were tracking up the expensive carpet. Like a fish out of water, he thought, wondering whether to sit or wait to be asked.

"I think I'll have something stronger," Josh said, walking over to a small Dutch *kas* in the corner, its painted designs faded to darkness. He opened the doors, and pulled out a bottle of Allegheny whiskey and a pitcher of water. Josh poured a generous amount of whiskey into a glass, swallowed quickly, then followed it with a little water. He made a face, then set the bottle and the pitcher on a table near the sofa, closed the cabinet doors, and took a seat, motioning Fade to a chair opposite.

"All right, then. You'd better tell me what happened."

"I will, sir. But I wonder if first you can tell me how she is."

Josh appraised the young man sitting across from him before answering. "She's resting. Gone off in a daze, I think. I'm anxious for Sayre to have a look at her head. She was shot, wasn't she." It was more a statement than a question.

Although Fade did not really want to sound apologetic, it was difficult not to be awed by this imposing man. In a few terse sentences he described what had happened—how Emily had come bounding into the clearing just as he fired his gun and how he had brought her home.

"And where was Wilton in all this?"

"Wilton?"

"Her groom. He is supposed to ride with her to prevent just such foolishness. Emily is a headstrong girl, and I have always feared she would blunder into some kind of harm if left alone."

"I think she did say something about evading her groom."

Josh Deveroe crossed his legs and drummed his fingers on his knee, eyeing the other man intently. He was vastly relieved that Emily's accident had been no worse, yet there were consequences he could not afford to ignore.

"You are one of the Whitmans, aren't you?"

"That's right. Frederick. Fade, I'm called."

"Yes. I remember. You worked in my stables for a while. I seem to recall that you were excellent with the horses."

"I've given up horses for the sea. In fact, I've just returned with the *Carolyn Grey* from her last run to Bristol."

"Oh? What rank?"

"Second mate."

"You're very well spoken for a seaman."

Or a Whitman. The unspoken judgment hovered in the air between the two men.

"I've made it my business to learn," Fade said brusquely. No need to mention he'd had a little help from his first mate, who, spotting his potential, had amused himself on the long journey by smoothing out his junior officer's rough edges.

Josh tipped back his large head and studied the young man opposite him through hooded eyes. He was irritated by Fade's arrogance even though he could not help but half admire it. Attractive and self-assured, this young man was obviously a cut above the rest of his family and was no doubt clever and ambitious as well. But he had no business trying to pass himself off as a gentleman in front of his betters.

"So, Mr. Whitman, I must thank you for carrying my daughter safely home. Emily means a great deal to me and I confess . . . Well, no matter about that now. Thank heaven she was not badly hurt. However, there is the other matter of why you were there in the first place. Had you permission to hunt those woods?"

Fade looked him straight in the eye. "No."

"You grew up here. Surely you know it is considered illegal to hunt game on private land?"

"Yes, Mr. Deveroe, I do. And I have hunted these woods all my life. I'm not exactly sure where your land leaves off and that of Mr. Bishop or Mr. Leverett or Mr. Slade takes over. No one has ever made a case of it as far as I know, and no one would have today had your daughter not been injured."

"Perhaps someone should then, before a far more tragic accident occurs."

"Come now, Mr. Deveroe," Fade said. "With all due respect, this is not England and I am not a poacher."

"Young man, do you realize I could have you up before the magistrate? You are very outspoken for someone who could very well find himself in a good deal of trouble."

Even from across the room Josh could see the anger that flashed in Fade Whitman's dark eyes. He also took note of how carefully that anger was kept under control and how the younger man never wavered in his direct gaze, almost daring Josh to follow through on his threat. The arrogant cub!

Reaching out for the whiskey bottle, Josh refilled the glass, his hand trembling so much that the heavy rim clattered against the delicate crystal. Emily's narrow escape had unnerved him more than he cared to admit.

"Well, no matter," he went on. "I am grateful to you for bringing my daughter back. But in the future I'd prefer that you check with my overseer, Daniel, before you go about discharging guns in these hills."

Not bloodly likely, Fade thought. The next step would be a fence around the entire place, no doubt, imprisoning the free, wild woods he had wandered since he was a small boy.

It was almost a relief when the door opened and the elderly woman who had accompanied Emily upstairs entered the room.

"Agatha," Josh said, half rising. "Come and join us. This young man is Frederick Whitman, whom we have to thank both for Emily's injury and her safe return."

Very conscious of his manners in the face of Josh Deveroe's obviously low opinion of him, Fade jumped to his feet as

Emily's cousin walked toward him. He gave her a small bow
and said politely, "Your servant, ma'am."

Agatha Yancy's kind smile was reassuring. "Mr. Whitman,"
she said, nodding.

"Would you like a little something to steady your nerves,
Agatha?" Josh asked. "A glass of wine, or some of that French
brandy perhaps?"

Agatha sat primly on the sofa beside Josh, refusing his offer
with a wave of her hand. "No, no. It's not necessary. Please
sit down, gentlemen."

"And how is our girl?"

"She is conscious and in a great deal of pain. She said most
emphatically that I should tell you the 'accident' was her doing
and not in any way the fault of Mr. Whitman."

The two men exchanged sharp glances. "That was very
generous of her," Josh said.

"What exactly *did* happen, Mr. Whitman?" Agatha asked.
Fade opened his mouth to reply, but Josh launched into his
own account. Absently drumming his fingers against the arm
of his chair, Fade let Josh talk on, taking the opportunity to
study the two people across the room.

They resembled each other very little for cousins. Agatha
was tall but slight, with graying hair that waved back from her
porcelain pale face and a small mouth that fell into a natural
smile. She had a gentle quality about her, apparent in her soft
eyes and modulated voice. Fade remembered seeing her often
in his youth, when her husband, Captain Yancy, was still alive.
Much older than she, Yancy had been a notable river captain
and had spent much of his retirement around the Sparta docks.

Josh Deveroe, on the other hand, was everything his cousin
was not: elegant, imposing, handsome, exuding confidence and
authority. He was large, fleshy, and thick-shouldered, and he
wore carefully manicured sideburns on jowls that grew heavier
each year. His hands were huge, his bearing ramrod straight,
and his clothes were of the latest fashion, impeccable in cut
and fit. He was every inch the squire, Fade thought, suddenly
conscious of his own ill-fitting, linsey-woolsey coat and muddy
boots. As a boy working the stables at Southernwood he had
been terrified of crossing this man. But that was no longer the
case. Perhaps it was because of Deveroe's trembling hands or
the vague look of disappointment in his drooping eyes. Perhaps

it was Fade's own realization of the hollowness at the heart of all this splendor around them. Whatever it was, Fade Whitman no longer feared the great Joshua Deveroe. Right now he wanted nothing so much as to get out of this room and back to the comfortable carelessness of his sister's house.

He became aware that Agatha was speaking, thanking him again. Abruptly he rose, making sure to take her hand and raise it to his lips. On the whole, he was pleased with his performance. No one could criticize him for being ill-mannered.

"You will forgive me, ma'am, if I see to my horse. He was left in your drive unattended."

"Of course, though I feel sure Absolem must have taken him to the stable."

It was easier to make his escape than he had supposed it would be. Josh Deveroe summoned a housemaid to show him out, deigning first to offer him his hand in gratitude for returning his daughter. Agatha invited him to call again, but he took that as an exercise in hollow courtesy. Stepping outside, he felt the warm air welcome him, and he realized he was as glad to be rid of them and this place as they, no doubt, were to see him go.

When he walked around to the back of the house, Fade was startled to see the slim figure of a young man standing beside his tethered horse examining his gun. He had been away so long it took him a few moments to recognize Emily's brother, Garret. The resemblance between brother and sister was so striking he wondered how he could not have known at once. Not only were they of the same height and coloring but Garret's face was so feminine as to make it appear that Emily herself was dressed in Hessian boots, dove trousers, brown velvet riding coat, and high buff stock. The long, wavy hair that Garret affected made the similarity even more striking.

Garret looked up as Fade approached. Suddenly he flipped the gun lightly over in his hand, cocked the hammer, and sighted the long barrel directly at Fade for a few moments, swiveling it aside just as he snapped the trigger.

"This is one of those old smooth-bore muskets, isn't it?" he said contemptuously.

"Yes," Fade answered, annoyed at having his own gun pointed in his face, even if it wasn't primed. "It was my father's."

"How very sentimental—a genuine antique. You keep it hanging over the mantelpiece, no doubt."

"As a matter of fact, I don't."

The disdainful smile on Garret's narrow face said all too clearly that he was enjoying a bit of fun at the expense of this rustic.

"Oh. Too bad—it would have made the whole picture so quaint."

In an effort to control his irritation, Fade reached for the reins and pulled his horse's head around. "If you've finished examining my 'antique,' I'll be on my way."

The touch of annoyance in his tone brought Garret's surprised scrutiny. "Oh my, aren't we proud. You're one of the Whitmans, aren't you?"

"That's right."

"Your fame has already spread. I barely made it into the yard and out of the saddle before being regaled with the story of how you gallantly returned my foolish sister to the grateful arms of our doting parent. I was *so* moved."

Fade was trying to remember what he knew of this strange young man. He barely recalled seeing him during the two summers he had worked at the stables. Possibly Garret had been away at school. Such an arrogant, unpleasant cub would certainly have been past forgetting had he been around. Garret ran his hand over the smooth, worn wood of the stock, deliberately keeping Fade waiting.

"I remember you Whitmans as a dark, scruffy lot. Whichever you are, you're surely the bright star of the tribe. Emily must have swooned at the romance of being carried back in the arms of so dashing a cavalier. How did you ever get her to leave your horse?"

His blood rising, Fade thrust one boot in the stirrup and bounded up into the saddle. Looking down at the slight, haughty figure below, he said, "She was in no fit condition to protest. In fact, she's very lucky to be alive at all."

A sardonic smile played at the corners of Garret Deveroe's thin lips. The sharp downward slant of one side of his mouth was the one striking difference between Garret and his sister. He turned the musket over in his hands again and then, with a sharp, sudden move, threw it at Fade, who caught it with one hand, pulling his horse around with the other.

"Mr. Whitman," Garret called.

Fade pulled up, swiveling in the saddle to look back.

"While you were about it, too bad you didn't do a proper job and blow her head off!"

Three weeks later, on a warm lazy afternoon, Emily sat in a chair underneath a lovely old ash tree on the edge of what had once been Southernwood's formal gardens. With her head resting against the high back of the chair and her eyes closed, she let her thoughts drift. One part of her mind was attuned to the chattering of the birds in the upper reaches of the tree's gnarled limbs, but Robert Slade's level voice, coming from beside her, kept interrupting her reverie.

"I must confess it gratifies me to see you looking so well, Miss Emily. Your color is almost back to normal and the wound on your head is barely discernible. Such a close call..."

Emily stirred restlessly and wished he would go away and leave her to her dreaming. The headaches were much less troublesome now, and were it not for everyone treating her like an invalid she would be off wandering the hills on Thor right at this moment—perhaps stumbling across Fade Whitman again.

"Don't you agree that Emily is looking quite her old self, Mrs. Yancy?"

Agatha, sitting nearby on a bench built around a tree, looked up from her sewing. "Indeed I do, Robert, and if we can manage to keep her quiet a little longer I feel sure this unfortunate accident will have no lasting effects at all."

How like Cousin Agatha. In her quiet way she would see that Emily was confined to a chair until she was convinced of her recovery, even if it took a whole year. Emily's eyes flew open at the terrible thought. Somehow she must convince these people she was completely well. Such a to-do over nothing!

"Nonsense, I am as well as I ever was. It was only a small bruise to my head, after all."

"Yes, but one must be especially careful with injuries to the head," Robert said. "I had an uncle who went quite mad with one."

Emily tossed her tightly crimped curls, looked heavenward, and reached for her drawing pad. What an old woman Robert was; no matter what the problem, he always had a gloomy prognosis. Why couldn't she have a more cheerful visitor? Why

hadn't that Whitman fellow come back to see if she'd recovered? It would have been the polite, respectful thing to do,
and his continued neglect was something of an affront. She
jabbed at the paper with her pastels, making long furrowing
sweeps of color.

Agatha, recognizing the warning signs of Emily's irritation
and impatience, made an effort to change the subject to politics—not a difficult thing to do since Robert was avidly interested in government and intended someday to run for office.

"How do you see Mr. Jackson's future, Robert? Do you
think he will be our next President or will Mr. Adams be able
to overcome his disadvantage and be re-elected?"

Robert Slade leaned forward, his face brightening, ready to
vent an opinion on his favorite topic.

"Mister Adams doesn't have a prayer, Mrs. Yancy. I believe
we are all of us in for a great shock. Not only will Jackson be
President, but he will be such a one as to set Washington on
its ear."

"But this terrible slavery issue . . . I declare, I don't see how
it can ever be resolved. Such an odious business. You know
we never had slaves at Southernwood, or even, I understand,
at West Farms, where my mother grew up. My grandfather did
not believe in it nor did my Cousin Richard, who built this
house, or his wife Celia. Their Negroes were always freemen.
It is a tradition with this branch of the family."

"Since the Manumission Act became effective last year,
there are no slaves in New York," Slade stated. "But one can
hardly impose that rule on the southern states, where slaves
are so closely tied to the economic stability of the region."

"But it is wrong, Robert. To shackle a human being like a
cow or a horse is inhuman. Does not even General Jackson
agree with that principle?"

"He's too cagey to say whether he does or not, yet I know
for a fact that he thinks of Indians as little more than animals.
It would not surprise me to learn that he thinks of Negroes the
same way."

"Well of course you know the situation much better than I,
but . . ."

Emily rested against the chair, scarcely hearing their conversation. She was grateful to Cousin Agatha for talking with
Robert, for it relieved her of the burden. Not that there was

really anything wrong with him. Emily and Robert had been neighbors all of their lives and he was almost like a brother to her. More of a brother, actually, than Garret, whom she had never been able to stomach. It was just that she had no desire to marry Robert Slade, as their families had long ago determined she should. Setting down her crayon, she studied the man—his elegant coat, his carefully arranged hair, his smooth-shaven cheek. His skin was not leathery like a man who worked long hours in the sun. In fact, Robert had something of the soft, pasty look that affects gentlemen who spend most of their time indoors. There was nothing wrong with his physique, if one could discount a tendency to chunkiness, but she could already picture him in middle age: paunchy, with long reddish whiskers, chewing the end of an expensive cigar, gold chains and fobs dangling from his very fashionable wescot. Of course, he was also kind, intelligent . . . and bland. He would offer her a comfortable home and burden her with lots of children who would all look just like him. Perhaps it would not be so bad really. It would make her father extremely happy.

She looked down at her pad, surprised to realize that she had drawn the rough outline of a face—a dark, swarthy, angular face. That hunter again, that Fade Whitman. Why could she not put him out of her mind? Her gaze went back to Robert, who was leaning forward now and waving a manicured finger at Cousin Agatha to emphasize some point.

Robert was like all the men she knew and had always known, like a statue from one of those newfangled machines that stamped out countless copies from the same mold: all quite perfect but all alike. Fade, on the other hand, was like a hand-carved sculpture: unique, a little rough perhaps, but very special. Why hadn't he come to call on her?

"Emily, my dear," Agatha said, leaning forward to tuck the blanket around her legs. "We have been rattling on with no thought to your well-being. Are we tiring you? Would you like to go in and rest now?"

"Please, Cousin Agatha, don't coddle me. I'm perfectly fine. I just don't care a fig about the slavery issue or President Jackson's country manners. Forgive me, Robert, but you know it's true."

"If there is something else you would prefer to discuss . . ."

"Now don't be miffed," she said soothingly. "I know how

important these things are to you, but you know as well how little they matter to me. What I would really like is a turn around the garden. Why don't we do that?"

"But, Emily," Agatha started, "do you really feel up to it?"

Robert was already on his feet and offering her his arm. She leaned on him, grateful, for in truth her legs were not as steady as she wished them to be. That weakness came, no doubt, from long hours spent languishing on beds and couches.

"I should like nothing better. Come along, Robert."

"My pleasure, Miss Emily."

They started down the paths, once elegantly manicured but now carelessly overgrown. Only the most hardy of the roses and other flowers that Emily's grandmother, Celia, had planted twenty years ago continued to bloom among the riotous profusion of wild undergrowth. The lovely pear and apple trees still bore fruit, and the white lilacs and wild dogwood blossomed every spring, but all this occurred with very little help from the hand of men. The great shipping empire built by Josh Deveroe's father, Richard, and his partner, Elisha Yancy, had declined these last years; in truth, it had never really recovered from the War of 1812. Then too, Josh had had so many other concerns that both the house and the grounds had been let go. Emily never walked these paths without picturing her mother bending over the plants, vainly attempting to bring some order back into the garden. Had her health been better, perhaps Morna Deveroe might have succeeded, but since her death two years ago the garden had barely been touched. Perversely, Emily liked it this way—wild and overgrown and filled with tenacious weeds.

"You have a smile on your lips, Emily," Robert said. "Would it be too forward of me to ask what thoughts are giving you such pleasure, especially since I feel sure they are not inspired by my conversation?"

Emily turned and gave him a brilliant smile. One thing about Robert: they could always be completely honest with each other.

"I was thinking about the weeds in the garden, and that reminded me somehow of Frederick Whitman, the gentleman who brought me home."

Robert sniffed. "You mean the man who shot you. And by no stretch of the imagination can one of the Whitmans be described as a gentleman."

"Now don't be boorish, Robert. It was an accident, and he took good care of me once it happened. You must give him credit for that."

"You are more generous than I."

His voice went on while Emily, her hand lightly on his arm, took slow steps beside him. Yet the smile lingered, for a wonderful idea had taken seed in her mind and she was examining it with more enthusiasm than she'd felt for anything since the morning of her accident. If Fade Whitman would not come to her, then why should she not go to him?

"Miss Emily, if'n your papa knew what you were about he'd see you got a good thrashing."

"You are probably right, Wilton."

Of course he never would, Emily thought, knowing full well she could always calm her father's anger, no matter how justified. "But we won't tell him, will we?" she said, casting a wicked glance at her scowling groom. "After all, there is nothing wrong with visiting Mr. Carpenter's store. I've done it hundreds of times."

"Visiting the store, no. But riding right up to a young man's door like a brazen—"

"That's enough, Wilton! You're supposed to protect me from ruffians and accidents. You're not here to sermonize."

"All the same, it ain't fittin' that you should call on this man, and you know it. You were ever a stubborn girl, and your pa should have taken a stronger hand to you long ago. I always said so, I did indeed."

"Oh, for heaven's sake, just be quiet!"

The two horses picked their leisurely way along the dirt track that led up from White Point Landing through the tiny village of Sparta to the old post road. From her high perch on Thor's back, Emily nodded and waved her riding crop at the people walking along the road, many of whom she had known all her life. The small settlement around the landing had existed long before Southernwood was built, and had a vitality all its own and was completely independent of the Deveroes' imposing home. Sparta was an enterprising little community, boasting a town well, store, tavern, fishery, and smithy, and its people were an industrious and independent lot. Small neat homes, each with its own tiny garden and fruit trees, lined the road on either side of the crossing. There was a derelict mustard mill

now eking out its last days near Sparta brook and an old brick-
yard that still filled the air with acrid pink smoke. Marble was
quarried only a mile away, and the recently discovered copper
mine had become one of Josh Deveroe's newest investments.
From the road above the settlement Emily could still catch the
dim sounds of chisels and hammers where convicts worked at
building a new state farm up beyond the quarries. But the
lifeline of Sparta was the river trade emanating from its dock,
where fishing ketches and market sloops set off for regular runs
between Mount Pleasant and New York. One or two of the
better houses in the village belonged to the captains of these
boats, and the boats themselves were now mostly independent
of the great Dolphin fleet that Emily's grandfather, Richard,
and Captain Yancy, had built nearly forty years ago. Although
some ships from the Dolphin yards now ranged farther afield
to Nova Scotia and the West Indies, most of them still plied
the lucrative Hudson River trade, their blue and white flags
proudly flying among the colored sails of the sloops.

Emily pulled her horse to the side of the road in order to
allow a farmer's wagon, loaded with sacks of flour and corn
meal, to lumber by on its way to the dock. It was so white
with dust that she reckoned it must have come all the way from
Connecticut. She had to bend under the thick overhang of the
tulip trees and oaks that crowded the road, yet through their
foliage she could glimpse the house ahead. It was a dark, squat
farmhouse set back behind a low, rough-hewn stone fence. A
twinge of fear stirred in her chest and for the first time she
began to wonder whether she was doing the right thing. But
Wilton's mutterings behind her, clearly audible once the wagon
rolled past, spurred her on. There was no way to back down
now—she would just have to brazen it through. Besides, she
wanted to do it.

She halted Thor before the narrow path that led to the door.
A young boy in a dirty smock was playing in the yard. He
looked up at her, his eyes growing bigger.

"Is this the Whitman farm?" Emily called out.

The child stared at her without answering. Emily was beginning to think she would have to go up and knock on the
door herself when it suddenly opened and a woman stepped
out, wiping her hands on the hem of a long apron. She was
very young, and dark, like Fade. His sister, perhaps, Emily
thought. Or his wife!

"I beg your pardon, but is this the Whitman house?" Emily asked.

The woman stared at her almost as vacuously as the child. "Yes it is," she answered.

"I'm looking for Mr. Frederick Whitman," Emily went on. "Can you tell me if he's here?"

The young woman let her apron fall and smoothed it down with one hand, nervously adjusting the strands of black hair that straggled from her white cap with the other.

"He's round back, cutting wood. Do you want me to fetch him?"

"No, that won't be necessary," Emily said quickly, motioning for Wilton to help her dismount. Catching up the long tail of her habit, she started up the walk, an imposing figure swathed in dark blue cloth with voluminous sleeves and a tall black hat trailing a blue gauze veil. The woman took a step back, retreating before her.

"I'll just step round and see him myself. Is this the way?"

"Yes, miss, under the arbor and straight back toward the barn. But ... I mean, wouldn't you like me to—"

"Thank you, but it's not necessary," Emily interrupted crisply, and started off along the side of the old house, followed by her outraged groom leading the two horses. She could not, of course, escape Wilton, but she'd be darned if she'd have this slow-minded yokel hanging over them.

The Whitman farm was actually neater than it appeared at first glance. A trim arbor in good condition led to a clearing, at the other end of which was the barn—newer than the house and much larger. On either side were small fields of rye and wheat, neatly plowed and sowed, and winter barley almost ready for harvest. Her step faltered as she spotted Fade at the side of the barn, one booted foot on the frame of a ling saw, the long blade in his hand.

He heard her approaching and straightened up. For a moment his look of surprise gave his face the same blank look that she had noted in both the woman and child, but then his expression flashed swiftly to anger. She stopped six feet away, the jaunty air she'd intended to affect dissolving under his furious scowl.

"Mr. Whitman," she began, her voice not quite so composed as she meant it to be.

"Miss Deveroe."

Emily could not meet his level gaze, yet something warmed within her as she glanced at him. He was every bit as imposing as she remembered—even more so, in fact, with his shirt-sleeves turned up to expose the strong arms darkened with black hair, his brown corduroy trousers tightly fitted over muscular thighs, his high boots. She glanced away, conscious of a deep burning glow that flamed her face.

"Won't you ask me to sit down?"

He waved one hand around. "This is hardly a drawing room."

"No, but there is a very serviceable-looking bench against that wall. May I take it?"

For the first time he turned away from her gaze, and Emily recognized the faintest trace of embarrassment in his manner.

"Of course. Please forgive my lack of manners, but you did take me somewhat by surprise."

She settled primly on the bench, trying to smile. "I apologize. I wanted to thank you for bringing me home the day of the accident. I thought perhaps you might come to inquire for me at the house and when you didn't, well, once I felt strong enough I thought it was my duty to call upon you so I could express my gratitude."

He did not answer and she went on, nervously trying to fill the silence. "It occurred to me that you might have shipped out again, but on the chance that you hadn't...The young woman in the house told me you were working back here and—"

"My sister should have come for me. I might have at least met you in the parlor with my coat on."

"Oh, but she insisted." Emily glanced up to catch Wilton glaring at her. "No, *I* insisted on coming round back. Actually, I wanted to talk to you alone. I hope you do not object. It was impolite of me to come at you like this, but after all, it was impolite of you not to call and inquire after my health. Can't we say we're even?"

Fade gave her a long look, then a faint smile twitched the corners of his mouth. Laying down the saw, he walked over and reached for her hand. "You're right, it was impolite of me not to call. I apologize for the oversight and hope that you are completely recovered from your accident." Brushing her fingers lightly with his lips, he stepped away from her. Emily settled back, relieved to know that he was no longer angry at her—and that the young woman at the door was his sister and not his wife.

"I am very well recovered, thank you, Mr. Whitman. And I hope I have learned my lesson. I no longer attempt to escape the watchful eyes of poor Wilton, who is, as you can see, hovering anxiously over there even now, ready to pounce should you not act the gentleman."

Fade glanced at the embarrassed groom. "That is one of the burdens rich young women must bear. In Spain duennas chaperone beautiful young virgins."

"Have you been to Spain, then?" Emily said coolly, inwardly preening because he had all but called her beautiful.

"Yes, briefly, on the voyage before last. It is an interesting country, with a wonderfully temperate climate, but most primitive in many ways. Wonderful wines, though, and lovely women."

"Are you so conscious of the beauty of the women in all the countries you visit?"

"One does tend to notice."

Under his intense scrutiny Emily felt a flush climb her cheeks. There was something between them; she could feel it drawing her toward him, and she was sure he felt it too. It was a feeling she had never experienced before, delicious and warm, with something wild about it. She was not sorry she had come.

"Mr. Whitman, I must ask if you intend to ship out again soon, for if you do not then I have a proposition to put to you."

He was startled, she could tell. Folding his arms across his chest, he seemed to pull away from her.

"I do not know what my future plans will be, Miss Deveroe. At the moment I am debating whether to sign on as a mate with another ship until the *Carolyn Grey* returns or to accept a position I've been offered at the new copper mine. One pays about as well as the other; it is a question of braving the treacheries of the open sea or being smothered by the closeness of the earth."

"You are very well spoken, Mr. Whitman. I like the way you put things."

"For an uneducated man."

"I did not say that. The truth is, my father and I recall how very well you worked with horses and we thought that if you were interested in resuming that vocation once more, we would like to take you on as manager of our stables. I don't know what the job pays, but I feel sure that my father would make it as much worth your time as the mine or a ship."

For a moment Fade could not answer. He was sure that this offer came more from Emily than from Josh Deveroe, for it was a well-known fact that she could talk her father into anything. It was a tempting thought. He would certainly rather work in a large, well-blooded stable than in a mine.

"I understood you to have a head groom."

"That is true, but he is thinking of moving on to become an assistant to Mr. Daniel, our overseer. So we would have to find a replacement for him in any case, you see, and we would rather have someone we know is capable—someone to whom we owe a deep debt of gratitude. Please say you'll consider it."

I wonder how she managed that, Fade thought, studying her upturned face. She had lovely large brown eyes and beautifully modeled lips, strong brows, a determined chin, and a high full bosom tapering to the smallest waist he had ever seen. She was beautiful, strong-minded, a little arrogant, and accustomed to having her own way. She was so far above him in station and wealth, in background and breeding, that it was unthinkable he should be standing here looking her over like one of his horses and discussing his future with her, quite conscious of the strong sexual current growing between them.

He was tempted to say yes right then, but a small voice stopped him. She would draw him into her silken net and he would lose his independence as well as his self-respect. Did he really want this?

"May I think about it and let you know?"

Hooking her fingers around the loop on the tail of her skirt, Emily rose. "Of course. I hope we shall hear from you soon and that your answer will be an aye. Now, I really must get back."

Ignoring Wilton, Fade reached for Thor's bridle. He walked the big horse over to one of the familiar mounting blocks, made of local marble, trying to avoid the nudging Thor was giving his shoulder.

"He remembers you," Emily said, swinging up into the saddle. "He's saying he wants you to come to us too."

Fussing with the girth, Fade made sure of her boot in the

stirrup, handed her the reins, and let his hand brush the fabric over her knee.

"When would you like an answer?"

"Could you perhaps call at Southernwood next Tuesday? Let us say three o'clock. I would be happy to show you around the stables myself—they are considerably changed since you were there last—and then I insist that you have a cup of tea with me. You do drink tea?"

"On occasion. You're going to make sure you get your call one way or the other, aren't you, Miss Deveroe?"

Emily took quick note of the mischievous gleam in his eye. He was not angry with her after all. She touched his shoulder lightly with the end of her crop.

"You'll find I usually get what I want, Mr. Whitman."

Two

WHEN FADE walked back into the kitchen an hour later the effects of Emily's visit were immediately apparent in the half-mocking smile on his sister's face. Though Matilda said nothing, her curiosity filled the room like a scent. Scowling and silent, Fade went about his work; but that evening, as he pulled up a chair to the deal table where the rest of his family already sat, he knew he would not be able to keep the event to himself.

Matilda's husband, Jim—being her second cousin he was also a Whitman—was the first to break the silence.

"Well now," he said, barely suppressing a smile, "I thought as how maybe you'd be too proud to sit with the likes of us."

"Now what's that supposed to mean?" Fade said, bristling.

"Why, only that what with such fancy visitors as you had today, why, we must seem pretty poor company." Quiet, solemn Jim Whitman so seldom made a joke that it took Fade a few moments to recognize he was being teased. By that time his younger sister, Florrie, had joined in enthusiastically.

27

"Goodness me, Matilda, I think as how you forgot to put out the silver. And this ain't the right wine, I'm sure. You must send it back, right now, at once!"

Matilda passed Fade a large bowl of boiled potatoes, ducking her head to allow the shadows to cover her smile.

"That's enough," Fade snapped. "Miss Deveroe stopped by to offer me my old job at the stables and that's all there was to it."

"Oh, o' course," Florrie chimed in, "and old Josh Deveroe couldn't 'ave sent his groom, he must send his fancy daughter to ask you to tend his fine horses. Sure and we believe that!"

"Well, it's the truth and I'll thank you to keep your comments to yourself."

Florrie, usually quite arrogant in spite of her fifteen years, shrank from the tone of her brother's voice. Evidently he had failed to appreciate the humor behind his family's teasing.

Matilda played peacemaker. "Now, Fade. You might as well face it, you're practically famous. The whole of Sparta knows Miss Deveroe came down here to see you today and most would give their right arm to know what she said. You can't do nothin' about people's curiosity, you know."

"I told you what she said. She offered me a job. That's all there was to it, and I'll appreciate it if we can just drop the subject."

Matilda's young son Jeffery wiped a sleeve across his gravy-stained lips and smiled up at his uncle. "I thought she was the prettiest lady I did ever see."

"She's pretty and that's a fact," Matilda said, hoisting the napkin around her son's neck a little higher. "But Florrie's right, you know, Fade. Josh Deveroe could 'ave sent someone else to ask you to run his stables. That Emily Deveroe, for all her bonnie ways, is a mind to herself. She'll be nothin' but trouble for you, I hope you know."

"For heaven's sake," Fade exclaimed, slamming down his knife. "Can we please say no more about Emily Deveroe? She wanted to tell me about the job and let me know that she had recovered from her accident. I'm sure if she had realized her coming here was going to make a scandal she'd have stayed away forever. I wish she had!"

"All right. All right. Eat your supper and we won't say no more about it."

A strangled noise from the room above broke the silence that settled over the table.

"That'll be Ma wanting her supper," Matilda said, rising. "I'll go along and take it to her. Poor soul. She gets more helpless every day."

Jim looked up from his plate as his wife left the room. The yellow light from the tallow lamp threw long gray shadows over his skin, which was still darkened from his day in the mine.

"There's this one more thing, Fade. It happens Isaac Sherwood asked me about you today. Seems his brother, the capt'n, has hurt his arm and needs some help on his boat. He knowed you was killin' time afore the next sail and wondered if'n mayhap you'd be interested in workin' his sloop for a few weeks. 'Course, if'n you're goin' to be up on the hill . . ."

"I didn't say I'd be up on the hill. As a matter of fact I've decided not to accept her offer. The Deveroe stables were all right a few years back, but now I'd rather be on the water. Which is Captain Sherwood's boat?"

"I believe it be the *Oriel*. A trim, high-ridin' vessel, she be too."

"What's her run?"

"Mostly between here and New York, I believe," Jim answered. "Though sometimes she lays into Peekskill too. Mr. Carpenter was telling Matilda the kettles he had in his store came from the ironworks there on the *Oriel*."

Fade studied his plate. In spite of his firm words he knew his feelings were confused. Part of him wanted nothing so much as to take that job up on the hill where he could be near Emily Deveroe. Having her around to talk with, to enjoy her vitality and spirit, to get to know her better—that would make any job worth having. On the other hand, this offer of Captain Sherwood's could not have come at a better time. He would enjoy working a sloop again even for only a few weeks, and it might banish the thought of Emily's dancing brown eyes from his mind forever. She'd be nothing but trouble to him. Witness this very afternoon: one brief visit and the whole village was talking about him. He hated that and he hated the idea of giving in to her high-handed ways.

You'll find I usually get what I want, Mister Whitman!

Well, this was one time she wouldn't. Fade Whitman was

not the man any Deveroe could push around, and she might as well learn that now.

"I think I'll go see Captain Sherwood in the morning," he said, pushing his plate away. "Tell Isaac I'm obliged to him."

On his way home from Captain Sherwood's the next morning, Fade was trudging around the corner onto the post road, staring down at the packed earth beneath his feet and imagining himself at the long tiller of the *Oriel*, when he heard someone call his name.

"Mr. Whitman. Why, isn't this a fortunate coincidence!"

Emily Deveroe was sitting in a small open chaise, a soft rose-colored pelisse with huge sleeves neatly fastened around her shoulders and her face framed in the flared brim of a leghorn straw bonnet decorated with pink and white ribbons and rosettes. In front of her a big Negro driver in a brown riding coat had just pulled the smart, sleek bay horse alongside the hitching post in front of Garrison's Tavern. Without giving the driver time to hop down from his perch, Emily extended one hand to Fade in the expectation he would help her out of the chaise. He had to stop himself from looking around to see if they were being observed before pulling down the steps and taking her gloved hand. With a swirl of satin flounces, Emily swung down and faced him, her eyes bright with pleasure.

"I'm just going to leave this basket with Auntie Garrison. Perhaps you could ride back with me afterward to have a look at our stables. They've gone down so these last few years. Papa has been severely negligent about his horses. It's hard to believe, isn't it, when they were always such a source of pride to him?"

"I much regret that I cannot do that, Miss Deveroe."

"Oh?" Some of the light seemed to leave her face.

"As a matter of fact . . ." Perhaps he shouldn't mention the *Oriel*. It would be better just to let her know he wasn't going to accept Josh's offer.

"As a matter of fact, I have already accepted another offer. I hope you will express to your father how much I appreciate his kindness in offering me the position and how much I regret having to decline it."

Emily glanced away to keep the hurt in her eyes from showing. This fellow disturbed her. There he stood, his dark hair glistening in the sun, his shabby coat barely disguising the strong mold of his shoulders and chest, his black eyes so intelligent and bold for all that he was not quality. Those eyes— they made her breath catch in her chest.

"But you mustn't turn us down so quickly," she declared, tossing her head to give herself courage. "After all, it's a big decision." She gave him a blatantly flirtatious smile. He wasn't going to deny her this.

"You will wait here a moment, won't you, Mr. Whitman? Just long enough to allow me to run inside with this basket of preserves. Auntie Garrison says Southernwood grows the finest peaches anywhere in the country."

"But—"

"I won't be a moment. Then you must at least explain why you are refusing such a generous offer. Perhaps you'd be so kind as to walk with me down to Carpenter's store? Absolem could take the chaise on ahead."

He nearly panicked at the thought of all eyes in the village watching them stroll the lane. "I'm very sorry, Miss Deveroe, but—"

"Oh, come now," she interrupted, laying her hand lightly on his arm and bending into his face as far as the wide brim of her hat would allow. "That's very little to ask of you, Mr. Whitman. Don't you think you owe me that much? I mean, after not calling to see how I got on."

Her nearness was intoxicating. A delicious warmth grew like a flame in his blood and he felt his resolution wavering. To hell with the old biddies of the town simpering behind their hands. He was a free man who could do as he pleased. And this might be the last time he'd have the pleasure of her company.

"Very well, I'll wait."

Emily's brown eyes sparkled. "Good. I'll be right back."

She was onto the porch in a moment, leaving Fade to glance up at the Negro driver, who was trying vainly to hide a knowing grin. "Don't many folks get away from what Miss Emily wants," he finally said sheepishly.

Fade growled and walked around to stroke the bay's sleek neck. Almost immediately his attention was caught. The horse was a superb animal, with good lines and excellent breeding, yet as he looked closer he immediately spotted signs of careless handling. Running his hand down the nose, he pushed back the thick lips and examined the horse's mouth.

"This bridle doesn't fit properly," he said to Absolem. "It's rubbing a sore here. Look."

"Is that a fact," the driver said, jumping down to join Fade near the hitching post.

"Who put this animal to?" Fade said indignantly. "His mouth will soon be ruined if you continue to drive him like this."

"Why, I specks it was one of the stablehands. He was all ready when I gots there after Miss Emily called me to drive her to town. My goodness, I'd of thought Mistuh Foreman would check things better."

"Someone ought to." Kneeling down, Fade ran his hands along the bay's legs, looking for further signs of neglect. When Emily came out of Garrison's and saw what he was doing, she quickly stepped back inside and waited until he had gone over the animal's entire body. Then, hitching up her parasol, she stepped out onto the porch.

"So that's done. I'm ready now, thank you, Mr. Whitman."

Fade turned quickly from the horse with the uneasy sensation that he had somehow been tricked. Before he could protest, she had taken his arm and was starting down the post road back into the village. He decided to allow himself to be led for the moment.

"Though I'm not prepared to accept your father's offer, Miss Deveroe, I'd say he certainly needs someone up at his stables. The man you have now must be very lax."

"I have suspected that for some time, and I'm glad to have you verify it for me. Of course, I haven't given up hope yet that you'll reconsider. You are so quick to see what needs to be done."

"It is quite impossible."

"Oh. That's really too bad. Well, it's too fine a day to discuss unpleasant things. We'll talk about that later. For now, tell me something about yourself, Mr. Whitman."

"There's not much to tell," he answered stiffly.

"Oh, I don't believe that for a minute. Are you quite committed to a life on the sea? What else do you think of doing someday? You do have dreams and hopes, don't you?"

Embarrassed, Fade hardly knew how to answer. "Yes I do, but no one has ever asked me to say them out loud before. I'm not sure I can."

"Then let me help. Do you want to own your own ship, for example? Do you want to be a captain by the time you're twenty-five? Are there islands out there in the sea that you must visit someday before you grow old?"

"Yes." He smiled down at her, beginning to relax. "I'd like to do all those things."

"Or do you want to make a fortune, like my grandfather did, and build a big enterprise that will make you rich?"

"That would do nicely too."

"You are teasing me. Come now. Which is it?"

"I can't answer you, Miss Deveroe, because I'm not sure myself. I'd like to do something that makes a difference, something that would help people remember me, that would make people know I had lived. But what it is"—he shrugged, waving his free hand—"I haven't discovered yet. What about you?"

She lowered her head and he had to bend to catch a glimpse of her soft profile under the brim of her hat. "Father wants me to marry Robert Slade someday. If I do, I suppose I'll end up in Washington City. Robert is very keen on government. But somehow I don't think that's for me."

They had nearly reached the well that stood in the middle of the crossroad. Girls in dirty smocks and boys in loose-fitting trousers ran around it, shouting in a loud game of stone-tag. One or two of the village women stood there leaning on their wooden buckets.

Crossing the dusty street, Emily and Fade stepped up onto the planks in front of Carpenter's store. Emily hesitated, then turned and looked up at Fade with the bright expression that he found so enchanting. Staring down into her eyes, it seemed to Fade as though the whole village had disappeared and only the two of them stood there, alone in all the world.

"And what *is* for you, Miss Deveroe?" he said, sounding a little breathless.

She knew what she longed to answer. The ache within her was so strong it was painful. *You are, you are,* sounded like a silent bell deep down inside.

"I . . . I don't know . . . yet."

How incoherent! He would think she was a stupid, flighty chit of a girl.

The village came crowding back.

Fade coughed, pulled back his arm, and removed his hat once again. "Well, this has been most pleasant, Miss Deveroe.

Please give my regards to your father and tell him how sorry
I am to be unable..."

He was sure the women at the well were watching them and
that the people inside the store were looking out. He was suddenly filled with an urgency to be away.

"Yes, yes, I'll tell him." Did her disappointment show so
much, she wondered. He would be gone in a minute now and
all her chances were going with him. Bowing slightly, he moved
quickly back across the street, hurrying as fast as was polite.
Emily caught her full underlip with her teeth, staring after him.

Oh no. She would not give up so easily. There would be
other chances. She'd see to that.

The tiller on the *Oriel* was eight feet long, a giant arm of
polished wood with a carved hand on the end, its fingers clenched
in a fist. Fade thought there must be nothing in life so sweet
as standing at that tiller, watching the play of wind on the sail
above and the soft ripples on the river ahead, judging and
adapting to the play of its movement. The *Oriel* was a typical
Hudson sloop, about sixty-seven feet long and designed to carry
both passengers and freight. With its immense spread of canvas
and its trim shape, it was able to maneuver beautifully in the
treacherous winds and currents of the river.

Fade was not really surprised when, after a week on board,
he looked up from the helm one afternoon and saw Emily
Deveroe among the passengers on the deck returning from the
city. Nor was he exactly displeased. Through the easy hours
of good sailing she had intruded on his thoughts far more than
he wished. Her lovely profile framed with soft brown curls,
the sparkling glimmer of mischief in her eyes, the delicious
curve of her lips—these images came crowding into his mind,
stirring and unsettling him even as he tried to concentrate on
handling the sloop. When he spotted her that clear morning,
standing at the taffrail looking out over the water, he felt a
sense of pleasure and excitement that far outweighed any dismay.

She turned and looked directly at him. Then, carefully picking up her dainty skirts, she stepped up to the low quarterdeck
where he stood, his arm on the long tiller.

"Why, Mr. Whitman. I heard you were working the *Oriel*
for Captain Sherwood."

Fade touched his cap. "Miss Deveroe. Returning from a trip to the city, are you?" He was grateful she did not pretend this meeting was a pleasant coincidence. They both knew better.

"As a matter of fact, yes. A little shopping excursion." Close behind her stood a small, mousy-looking maid, eying the unfamiliar trappings of the sloop.

"I went down on Captain Jenkins's *Liberty* just a few days ago. Such a lovely little boat she is, too. Papa says she's one of the trimmest on the river, but then she was built in the Dolphin yards, so perhaps he's prejudiced."

Fade concentrated on the sails flapping above them. "She's neat enough."

"What glorious weather for a sail," Emily said, preening a little. "Faith, hand me my sunshade, will you? This heavy sun does very little for a girl's complexion."

The maid opened a parasol, handed it to Emily, and then stepped back to the railing. Well trained, Fade thought, uneasily aware that Emily had probably warned the girl not to keep too close. He was beginning to feel a little self-conscious.

"Have you enjoyed these trips, Mr. Whitman?" Emily asked, settling down gracefully on a nearby sea chest.

"Yes, I have. We've enjoyed good weather for the most part. That makes a big difference."

Far ahead a sturgeon leaped out of the silver river, its body glistening for a moment in the bright sunlight.

"Did you see that?" Emily cried, turning her sparkling eyes back to Fade. "Why he must have been six feet long. Papa says sturgeon that size used to be very common on the river but that they are gradually disappearing. Probably the steamboats discourage them."

"Wouldn't be surprised," Fade answered laconically.

"I'm not too partial to steamboats myself," Emily went on in spite of his lack of encouragement. "They are far too prone to explode, don't you think?"

"They do have a way of blowing up."

"Yes, nothing can take the place of a fine sail, I feel."

When he didn't answer she almost got up to leave, but instead dropped her parasol behind her and turned her face up to the warming sun for a few moments, closing her eyes as she savored its warmth. When she opened them, she found Fade staring at her with an intensity that sent her blood surging.

So he was not quite as nonchalant as he tried to seem, she thought, her hopes flaming into life again.

"Of course, you would feel that even more than I since you have chosen to follow the sea. Where did you go on the *Carolyn Grey* that last voyage? I'd be very interested to hear about it."

Gradually she got him talking, reliving the year at sea and the strange places he had visited. Engrossed in sharing his experiences with her, Fade lost track of time and found it difficult to concentrate on his work. He guided the boat by instinct; luckily, since the wind was soft and the weather excellent, it was not difficult to do. He was almost sorry when the Sparta dock appeared like a dark finger jutting from the shore on the horizon.

Among the figures on the pier he recognized the big black driver he had talked to while waiting for Emily in front of Garrison's. As they neared the landing, Emily excused herself, so he was able to concentrate on the delicate job of bringing the sloop in correctly, a consideration he appreciated. She waved back at him from the shore just before disappearing into the cab of the carriage. Fade saw that the boat was unloaded and safely put to bed before gathering together his things and walking up the hill. Emily had left him as disturbed and confused as ever. Somehow he knew she was as drawn to him as he to her. It was ridiculous and absurd and could mean nothing but trouble and disappointment.

Yet memories of those pleasant moments by the tiller of the *Oriel* stayed with him for many days. They intruded on his consciousness at night, when he wished he could blot them out and go to sleep. They had a way of breaking into his thoughts when he least expected or wanted them. And they were strong enough to raise a warmth in his blood when that was certainly the last thing he desired. He made up his mind: this could not go on. For once and for all he was going to put this girl out of his life, and the sooner the better.

Though Emily did not appear on the deck of the *Oriel* again while Fade was working for Captain Sherwood, he did see her several times around Sparta. She had a way of turning up just where he was, and he knew that with her high-handed stubbornness she had made a point of finding him. Instead of being annoyed by these "chance" meetings, he began to hope that perhaps he would run into her. When he wondered aloud that she had so much shopping to do, she made a point of explaining that her father was anxious to have her build up her wedding chest in preparation for the day she would marry Robert Slade. Fade knew something about the Slades of Tarrytown. They were rich, educated, elegant—gentlemen all. Of course a girl like Emily would marry a man like Robert Slade. It was natural and right. And it made his longing for her more ludicrous than ever. Resolutely he tried even harder to force her from his mind.

When his weeks on the *Oriel* were finally done and he was back working his family's farm again, he had a visit from the overseer at Southernwood, who offered him the job as head groom again. Feeling sure that this was Emily's hand at work once more, he repeated his refusal. It would be torture to be around Emily Deveroe every day.

His growing obsession for Emily made him more restless than ever and when he heard that the captain of one of Aspinwall's merchant fleet was having a brief visit with his family below Tarrytown, he made up his mind to pay the man a call. With any luck he could sign on as mate and be off again in a matter of weeks. It was the only answer.

Darkness had begun to cast long shadows over the post road as Fade made his way back north after a fruitless visit with Captain Warren. Beyond the village his horse grew a little skittish as he worked his way along a path mysterious with the nightcalls of birds and the wavering shadows of tree branches. The wind had picked up, and the air was heavy with the presentiment of a coming rain. Now and then a stray branch was carried on the wind across Fade's path, startling his horse. The hollow through which he traveled had a history of magic, which made the gray bulk of the old Dutch church looming ahead of them seem ghostly and forbidding. Fade was afraid of very little, but he hurried his horse along, eager to get off this part of the road and back to the comforts of the old Sparta farmhouse.

On the far side of the church a black shape, ghostly in the twilight, gave Fade a start until he recognized it as an overturned carriage lying at a crazy angle. A horse stood nearby in the graveyard, its head drooping, and alongside the bank a man and a woman sat dejectedly. Hearing the hooves of his horse on the bridge, they shrank back into the shadows, obviously as afraid of a ghostly specter as he had been.

He called to them, partly to quiet their fears and partly to assure himself that the world was still as it should be. When they stepped out into the road and he recognized the woman, all the dark magic fled.

Emily Deveroe stared up at him, and judging from the genuine surprise on her face, he thought that this was one meeting she had not engineered.

"Why, Mr. Whitman. You can't know how happy I am to see you!"

"Miss Deveroe. What on earth are you doing here? What happened?"

"I'm not sure. We were going along in a hurry, trying to get home before dark, when our horse stumbled, knocking the chaise against the bank. It turned over on its side, dumping us quite unceremoniously to the ground. I think something is broken."

Fade dropped out of the saddle as Emily eagerly clutched at his arm. "I was so hoping someone would come by before it got too dark," she said, and he knew she meant every word. "Robert, come here. It's Frederick Whitman."

The man—a portly figure barely taller than Emily, came hesitantly from the bank as though still not quite certain that Fade was not an apparition.

"Mr. Whitman. Your servant."

So this was the man Emily Deveroe was supposed to marry. Fade removed his hat and reached out a hand. "The same, Mr. Slade. Looks like you got yourself in a rare setting here. Is your horse hurt?"

"No. Checked her over myself. She's a little shaken, but all right. But this carriage . . ."

Emily still gripped Fade's arm, as if unwilling to let go of him. "You'll know what to do, won't you, Mr. Whitman? To tell the truth I wouldn't mind being caught anyplace else. This is just such a . . . ghostly place."

Fade laughed. "You do well to be afraid in this place," he said, deciding to have a little fun. "That bridge yonder is where the headless horseman rides on just such nights as this."

Emily's eyes widened. Then, as she peered closer into his

face and caught the teasing glint in his eyes, she scoffed. "Fiddle-dee-dee. An old superstition."

Robert glanced around uneasily, staring back across the wooden bridge, now almost completely clouded in the gray shadows of dusk.

"No, no, my dear. It's an old legend, but there are many in these parts who would swear to its accuracy."

Although Emily was not quite so assured as she tried to sound, she felt relieved beyond measure now that Fade was with them. "An old story that Mr. Irving blew up out of all proportion. Please, Robert, can't we do something about this carriage? I want to get home. Papa will be worried sick."

"But, my dear, I don't know what. Perhaps this good fellow here would allow me to take his horse back into the village to fetch a smithy. What do you say, Mr.—what was it—Whitman?"

Fade turned his attention to the overturned carriage, examining it carefully, keenly aware that Emily was standing very near him. Then he went to look over the horse standing docilely at the side, nibbling the long grass around the ancient headstones of the graveyard.

"Well, you've broken a thorough-brace. If you can give me a hand to pull the chaise right side up again, perhaps I can mend it well enough to get you home."

"Oh, my good fellow, I can't do that," Robert exclaimed. "I twisted my back when we overturned and I wouldn't press it for the world. Are you sure you can't manage to get it up by yourself? It's very light."

Fade stared at him, appalled. It certainly was not *that* light. "Would you rather spend the night in this place?"

Robert glanced up uneasily toward the bridge. "No. But perhaps if you would allow me to take your horse to my home and bring help."

"For heaven's sake," Emily cried. "I'll help you, Mr. Whitman."

Now it was Robert's turn to be appalled. "Why, that wouldn't do at all, my dear. A lady like yourself . . ."

"Come on, Mr. Whitman. We could have it done in the time it takes to argue about it."

A gentleman would not agree, Fade thought wryly, yet he was curious to see if she really meant what she said. At once

Emily had her shoulder to the cab, and he walked around to
get a hand underneath the wheel.

Fade could not help but admire her determination. "I'll do
the real lifting," he said. "You just give a good pull in that
direction. Between us we ought to get it upright."

They had it up in an instant. Fade crawled underneath to
get a better look at the broken brace, but it was getting too
dark to see.

"Oh my goodness," Robert cried nervously. "I hear something on the bridge."

"Perhaps it's the horseman with his head under his arm,"
Emily replied dryly.

"No, no. I believe it's a carriage."

Providentially it turned out to be old Dr. Sayre driving his
chaise back to Sing Sing. Seeing that he was alone, Emily set
about at once asking him to take them to Southernwood if Fade
would lead the Deveroe horse home. The carriage would have
to stay until Josh Deveroe could send someone back for it.

Before she climbed up into Sayre's reeking leather cab,
Emily took Fade's hand and squeezed it tightly. "Thank you,"
she said simply. After all her machinations it seemed ironic
that fate had taken a hand to help her.

Fade rode back, leading Robert's carriage horse up the long
road toward the hill where the great pile that was Southernwood
overlooked the river, mulling over his own thoughts. Captain
Warren had nothing for him and it might be weeks before the
Carolyn Grey returned. Fate or accident, in truth his resistance
was crumbling. There had been no artifice in Emily's actions
today. Her fright, her happiness at seeing him, the competent
way she'd helped him right the carriage—his admiration for
her was almost getting out of hand.

And, to add to the problem, he now knew the kind of man
Josh Deveroe intended his daughter to marry. Robert Slade
might be a gentleman, but he was not the man for a girl like
Emily. He would be henpecked and miserable in half a year's
time. If this was the caliber of his competition...

What was he thinking of? It was he, Frederick Whitman,
who was no competition for Robert Slade. He did not have a
prayer of winning a rich, elegant lady like Emily Deveroe.

Yet he wanted her more than anything else in the world.
She would never wind *him* around her finger. He could match

her spirit for spirit, courage for courage. She was right for him and he was right for her.

But they came from different worlds. Could so great a chasm ever be breached?

If one never tried, one would never know.

To hell with the sea. He made up his mind then and there to accept the job at the Southernwood stables.

🌹Three

WITHIN A MONTH Fade was settled in a small room over the carriage house. Within another two he had established his authority over the grooms and stableboys, some of whom resented his sudden rise to high places, and had begun the transformation of Southernwood's stables from slipshod carelessness to well-run efficiency. As far as his everyday work went, he had never been happier. Though Josh Deveroe had allowed many of his interests and much of his fortune to trickle away, especially since the death of his wife, he had never lost his taste for fine horseflesh. The animals at Southernwood, from the best riding stallions to the lowliest old graying pony the children had long ago outgrown, were of outstanding quality. For Fade Whitman the care and nurturing of these excellent animals was more a joy than a job.

What troubled him most was his frequent contact with Emily Deveroe, who had taken a sudden interest in the workings of the stables. He was embarrassed that she spent so much of her time hanging around the barns talking with him. Once or twice she had demanded that he join her under the trees for a cool glass of lemonade on a hot afternoon, and several times she had insisted he accompany her on a jaunt around the hills. So far she had not been able to keep Wilton away from these rides, but Fade was sure that would come next. He found her captivating and would have enjoyed the excursions with unbounded enthusiasm, but the dark, wondering looks Josh Deveroe occasionally threw at him, Garret's veiled insults, and Wilton's grumblings were constant reminders of their different stations in life. Nothing but trouble could come out of her interest in him, no matter how much he longed to return it. He liked his new position and he wished it to last, but he could not escape the feeling that a deep pit was looming just ahead and he was walking straight toward it.

The first misstep came on a beautiful clear day when Wilton came down with the ague and Emily insisted that Fade ride out with her in his place. They left the house and headed inland for the wildest section on the hills, both of them sensing an undercurrent of excitement that quivered beneath their careless small talk about the blueness of the sky and the signs of a dying summer. At the highest point overlooking the silver river Emily dismounted and strolled to the edge to admire the view, pulling out her long hat pin and throwing off her tall black silk hat with its long blue veil. The wind caught the gauzy material and laid it like a cloud over her shoulder while she shook her hair free.

Fade stood by his horse watching her, longing to walk over and put his arms around her. He had never seen anything so lovely.

"Isn't it beautiful! How I love this sight—the river, the distant hills, the wonderful open sky. Up here I always feel like a god looking down on the world."

"Goddess."

She threw him a brilliant smile. "Do you ever come up here, or is this your first time?"

"Not the first."

"I come often. I have ever since I outgrew my pony. Wilton hates it—complains all the way up and all the way back about how it will ruin the horses' legs and bring on his rheumatism.

But I adore it." She glanced over to see Fade's dark eyes boring into her and felt a flush climb her cheeks. How she wished he would come closer.

"You love Southernwood, don't you?" Fade said, never moving from his position next to the grazing horses.

"Yes I do. I always have."

"I think you are the only one of your family who does."

"That's very perceptive of you. Mama always disliked it—said it was too big and too grand. Papa . . . well, I think Papa only came back to live here because both his parents were gone and he wanted to keep it in the family. And Garret . . . Garret has no warm feelings for anything or anyone, especially since Mama died. He hates Southernwood just because Mama did."

"Then how did you come to care for it so?"

"I don't know. It's just a feeling I've had all my life. I love the house, the grounds, these hills, the river. They all seem to be part of me—in my blood, so to speak. This land has been in our family for a long time, you know. It belonged to my great-grandmother, long before my grandfather built the house."

"It's strange, but I remember the house as much more elegant than it looks now, though maybe that's just because things seem more grand to children than they do to adults."

"Oh no, it has grown shabby from neglect. Papa squanders money on a new venture every week. The latest is this terrible copper mine, which doesn't seem to be paying off at all. Besides, he simply doesn't care that much for Southernwood. He'd rather spend his money on things that interest him. I sometimes wonder what will happen to the old place once I leave and only Papa and Garret are left to care for it."

"Are you so certain to leave?"

Emily shrugged, her smile fading. "Oh, I suppose I shall have to marry Robert Slade and move farther south, near Tarrytown. I shall keep an eye on the house, but that is not the same as living there. The funny thing is, I can hardly imagine anywhere else feeling like home."

Turning her head, she caught his dark scrutiny once again. Their eyes locked, and Emily was unwilling to be the first to let go.

"Why are you looking at me like that?"

For a moment he did not answer. Would it be better if the words were never spoken? Would something be changed and lost forever, or would something be gained? If he never spoke, how would he ever know?

"I was thinking how much I want to make love to you."

Emily gave a short gasp. Her startled eyes held fast to his while her mind searched for a reply.

Throwing her hat and riding crop on the ground, she swept up her skirt and walked over to stand before him, so close that her breast, under the tight bosom of her riding habit, brushed against his coat.

"Fade . . ."

There was anticipation as well as anxiety on her face, a look that said she was glad to have it out in the open at last.

"Do you want me to apologize?"

"Apologize! Don't you dare."

For a moment he stared, astonished, and then he threw back his head and laughed in spite of himself. Standing so close, he began to notice little details about her face he had never seen before: tiny freckles, barely visible, that dotted the bridge of her nose; flecks of amber that lightened the pupils of her dark, sparkling eyes; little shadowy lines that crinkled at the corners of her thickly lashed eyes when she smiled; the even whiteness of her teeth just visible behind the dusky curve of her parted lips.

His laughter slowly faded and, very gently, he pulled her against his hard body and kissed her lovely mouth. It began as a light, affectionate gesture, but as his lips began to move insistently on hers, a wave of feeling caught them in its grip. With the touch of their bodies a gulf was breached and a longing, growing ever more intense, cried so strongly for satisfaction that reason and sense were eclipsed beneath it.

Accustomed to the polite, tepid advances of young men she had known all her life, Emily was lost before the passionate masculinity of the man who held her, demanding with his hands and his lips and the pressing mold of his body on hers a consummation wilder and freer than anything she had ever imagined. It frightened and overwhelmed her at the same time. It grew within her like a flame, forging into an all-consuming fire, filling her with exquisite delight. She wanted everything he wanted, just as strongly and just as completely. When his lips released her, she gave a joyous moan and, throwing her arms around his neck, returned his kiss with an abandon that was as much a surprise to her as it was to him.

Fade's resolution to be sensible wavered and was drowned under the shock of her wild desire. His lips bruised hers, then turned to seek the sweetness of her neck, the curve of her cheek, the valleys and hills of her ear behind the long rope of her hair. He wanted to tear open her habit, cup his fingers around her breasts, and taste their delights. He longed to throw her down right there on the grass, rip away the yards of confining fabric, and lay her body bare, then envelop and possess her, make her completely and thoroughly his.

What was he thinking of? He raised his head, tore away his hands, and stared into her face with such a look of horror that Emily recoiled before it.

Her hand went to her throat as she cast about, confused and disappointed, wondering what she had done to turn him away. Was she too wanton? Too inexperienced? Too lacking in the skills of love?

Deliberately Fade stepped back from her and dropped his hands to his sides. "This is insane," he muttered, and with relief she realized it was not her fault.

He walked over to the edge of the hill and dropped onto the grass. He was still stunned by her reaction and his as well. He had held many other women in his arms, but never, never had he so desperately wanted to possess one. He was shaken by the awareness of how much this daughter of Josh Deveroe had moved him. She had made him vulnerable, and if he didn't watch his step there would be nothing but trouble ahead for him.

"Crazy . . ." he murmured almost to himself. Then, looking back at the mystified Emily standing behind him, he tried to explain. "I'm not going to ruin your life and mine simply because of a little lust."

Lifting the long train of her skirt, Emily ran to kneel before him, joyous in the new freedom that allowed her to slip her arms around his waist.

"It is not simply lust, Fade. I know it is not. I've felt from the first that there was something between us, and you've felt it too. I know you have."

"There can be nothing between us, Miss Deveroe."

"Not Miss Deveroe. I'm Emily. Your Emily."

Her lips brushed his cheek. He yanked her hands away, setting a distance between them.

"This is impossible. I am a groom in your father's stables.

Remember the difference in our stations, our backgrounds."

Emily devoured his face with her eyes. He was head and shoulders above all the young men she knew. Athletic and virile, he had none of the foppish manners affected by the *ton*. It was not just his dark good looks that captivated her. There was something about him that said he had been out in the world and had conquered it. He knew it well, all its joys and its terrors. He was *real* as it was real, in contrast to so much of her world, which seemed mannered and affected.

Except for his obvious physical longing, Fade's eyes betrayed nothing of what he was feeling. He could not believe this earnest, beautiful, well-born girl was kneeling before him. She was unlike any woman he had ever known. There was a grace and breeding about her, evident in every plane of her scupltured face and lithe body. Yet there was something more: a vitality, an eagerness to embrace life and hold it fast, a sensuousness he had barely suspected was there. That all this could be his was almost too good to be believed.

Without touching her, he said, "I know I could take you right here. It's what we both want. But I will not do that to the daughter of Josh Deveroe. I will not do that to you."

Emily sat back, recognizing the wisdom in his words. She did not especially wish to be initiated into the joys of love while rolling about on the grass, worrying that someone might be peering out at them from the dark woods. It would be grand now, but how would she feel when she returned to the house and had to look her father in the eye?

"All right. I know what you are saying. But listen to me, Fade Whitman. I want you more than I've ever wanted anything in my life, and I believe you want me too. Station and background and wealth or lack of it have nothing to do with anything. We will have our time together and it will be right. I will see that it is."

Her hand reached for his and he clasped it firmly. "I am almost tempted to believe you will."

"Now, kiss me again, and hold me for a little until we have to go back."

His arms went around her and his hands roamed over her back while his lips nibbled at her ear. He could hear the deep lusty laugh that rose in her throat.

"You siren. You beautiful, enchanting siren."

And into the pit he fell.

* * *

It wasn't easy to get Wilton out of the way, but in the weeks that followed Emily became adroit at inventing excuses to be alone with Fade. Those stolen minutes they spent out riding or in a dark corner of the stable were more precious to her than anything else in life. As it became clear that Fade found them equally precious, she grew more determined to find new ways to be alone with him. The crucial thing was not to let her father know about their relationship until the right moment. Impatient as she was, she waited, confident that in the end she would be able to convince Josh Deveroe that her entire life's happiness rested on being married to Fade Whitman.

On a particularly wet, miserable day, when spells of sporadic rain finally gave way to interludes of dark, scudding clouds, Emily pulled a heavy wool cloak over her head and made a dash to the house from the stable, where she had spent a quiet hour with Fade. Most of that time had been spent talking and giggling, with only a few quickly stolen kisses behind the door of the small tack room when she was sure no one was watching. Once they had been interrupted by the arrival of her father's chaise rolling hurriedly into the barn, but Emily had managed to keep out of sight and Josh had been too preoccupied to take any notice of Fade's unusual nervousness.

As she entered the wide hall of the house, handing her drenched cloak to the housemaid, Chloe, her father called to her from the dining room. Emily caught her breath, wondering for a moment if Josh had seen more than she thought in the stable, but when she entered the room her fears subsided. Josh Deveroe obviously had something on his mind, but she was willing to bet it did not concern her.

"Papa, let me do that," Emily said, taking the decanter from her father's hand, which was trembling so that the heavy glass threatened to drop. "It would be a shame to break that crystal goblet," she said, sitting down at the table. "There are not too many left of the ones Grandmother brought to this house."

"It's this infernal shaking," Josh said, sinking into a chair opposite her. "Perhaps you have noticed it's got worse of late."

Emily handed her father the glass. "Nonsense. It's just that you are working too hard. A good rest and it will go away completely. I've told you over and over you spend too much of yourself in these ventures you love so."

Josh smiled at her with something of his old assurance. "Those *ventures*, as you so disdainfully call them, keep you in style, my girl, and don't you forget it. Where have you been? You look damp enough to catch your death of cold. Haven't I told you not to go walking about these grounds on days like these? You'll take a chill, for sure."

"Nonsense, Papa. I'm strong as a horse. A little rain would never hurt me. And you drink too much wine for your own good. You really ought to take better care of yourself."

Josh looked away absently. "You'll take a chill like your mother. She was always taking a chill."

"Mama had a poor constitution. It's your health I'm worried about."

He looked back at her sharply. "It is strange you should say that, Emily. I called you in here because I've just seen old Dr. Sayre down in the village. You see, I wondered that this trembling did not go away—it's held on for a devil of a long time now. So I thought to get his opinion. He feels . . . he feels my health is not all that it should be."

Emily felt the blood drain from her face, but she answered with assurance. "Dr. Sayre? That old woman! What does he know? You might at least have seen the younger Dr. Sayre, although the son is too much under the influence of his father to be trusted."

"Well, there are better doctors, and rest assured I shall seek other opinions. But I feel I should tell you what he told me. You might as well be prepared."

"Papa!" Emily reached across the table for her father's hand. "Please don't go on like this. You look so . . . so serious!"

"If Sayre is right, it is a serious matter, my dear. He thinks I have the shaking palsy."

"What is that? I never heard of it. Besides, it can't be true. Look at you; you're as fit and strong as you've always been."

"Emily, my dearest girl, you must not argue the point with me. I know it is only Dr. Sayre's opinion right now, but if he should be correct, then it must be faced squarely. The palsy is a progressive disease and a very slow one. I'll not be a cripple for a long while."

"Papa!" Running around the table, Emily knelt by her father's chair, clasping him around the waist as though to shelter him from the things he was saying. "This cannot be true. Not you. You can never be a cripple."

He stroked her hair away from her forehead, looking into her worried eyes, her youthful face so full of promise and beauty and so dear to him. More dear than anything else in his world.

"My darling girl, I need your strength now. You are the only one I can count on."

Emily could tell from the look in his eyes how deadly serious he was, and she felt as though a hot knife had been plunged into her chest. "What about Garret? Shouldn't he know too?"

"You know I cannot count on Garret for anything. You have always been the stronger of the two and now I must rely on your strength."

Emily laid her head against his vest, oblivious to the heavy gold watch chain scratching her skin. She knew too well how undependable Garret was and did not try to argue the point with her father. She was just not sure of her own courage right now.

"I am thinking of the future, Emily," Josh went on. "I believe you should marry Robert very soon. You are eighteen and of an age. It might be possible for Robert to become involved in the Dolphin interests. I have very little hope of Garret ever being able to run things."

"Oh no!"

He continued as though she had not spoken. "It would comfort me to see you well established. Robert is a good man and will be successful, I believe, in whatever pursuit he chooses. He will take care of you, and that is more important to me than anything else in the world."

"Oh, Papa. Please, can't we talk about this later?" She struggled to keep the panic out of her voice. "After all, Dr. Sayre could very well be wrong. You must go to New York and let the doctors there examine you. Sayre is nothing but a village quack."

"He brought me into the world, Emily, and my parents depended on him most of their lives. Over the years I have found him to be right more often than wrong and that is why I take what he said today seriously. Very seriously."

"All the same, you cannot be ill, Papa. Not you. You cannot."

"My poor girl. I've upset you. You always were one to try to force the world to be the way you wanted it to be. Well, some things just . . . happen and we must learn to accept them."

"I'll never accept this! Never!"

She clung to him while Josh, resting his chin on her head, gently stroked the long strands of hair from her face. She would come to accept it in time, as he would. She was strong and capable, as unlike her weak brother as possible. She was the one he must depend on, not Garret.

He kissed her white forehead and wiped away the tears streaking down her face. She was like him, this precious daughter, this child of his soul, whom he treasured above all the people on earth. How sad that she could not have been the son. If it was the last thing he ever did, he would see her safe and provided for. Then let this disgusting disease do what it would.

Agatha spent most of that rainy day working on a spencer with an embroidered collar that she intended to send to her daughter-in-law in Boston. It was the sorrow of her life that her only child had married a girl whose ties to Cambridge were so strong that she refused to live anywhere else. Now her son's ship kept Boston for its home port and they spent their lives so far away that she seldom saw them. These little gifts she fashioned with her own hands were a symbol of her longing and her love, yet she felt sure they ended up in a drawer. "Another of your mother's efforts," she could hear Annette say when the latest gift arrived. But she would send it anyway, the product of long hours, a little piece of her talent and her heart for those she could not be near.

Needing more wool, Agatha laid aside the board and headed downstairs to her sewing table in the back parlor. As she stepped to the landing that looked out over the hall, she saw Garret standing near the dining-room door. His back was to her and he was bent forward in a way that suggested he could only be eavesdropping.

Agatha gave a quiet cough that brought Garret around suddenly. He had the grace to look flustered for a moment as he stepped away from the door, pulling down his vest.

"Cousin Agatha. You do come and go quietly, don't you?"

"I was not attempting to be quiet, Garret. It is only when someone has something to hide that they care who is approaching."

Garret's youthful face broke into a lopsided smile. "Touché. However, I should point out that one honored with a confidence has no need to stoop to eavesdropping. In this house that honor is reserved for one person only and that is certainly not you or me. Is it, Cousin?"

Agatha looked at him sharply as she headed for the parlor. To her dismay he followed her.

"I must say, Garret, that it doesn't bother me. One of the most admirable qualities in life, I believe, is the ability to mind one's own business."

He sprawled on the gold sofa, watching as she fussed among the silks in the table. "How deadly dull it would be if everyone lived by that maxim. Come now, Cousin, confess. Aren't you just a little interested in hearing what I might have picked up? It does concern you, you know, and me as well. And we're bound to learn eventually anyway."

Agatha looked at him as though he had suddenly turned green. "I'm sure Cousin Josh will tell me anything he wishes me to know in his own good time."

"Agatha! What a goody-two-shoes you are," Garret snickered. "Well, I don't intend to wait to be told what is of vital importance to me. Papa should know that by now. However, Papa has a singularly blind eye where I am concerned."

"Oh, Garret, why can you not be more pleasant. I declare, I don't understand you at all. I never did."

Languidly Garret picked himself up off the couch and pulled the lapels of his fashionable riding coat. Trying to communicate with Cousin Agatha was a bore. He had better things to do.

"Well, don't say I didn't try to let you in on the great secret. Good day, Cousin Agatha."

Agatha watched him through the door, shaking her head. Such a strange boy. Morna had always spoiled him terribly— that must be it. Ah well, he was very young. Perhaps he would turn out all right in the end.

Though it was still raining off and on, Garret decided to go out anyway. All the while he was having the chaise harnessed, he engaged his father's head groom in small talk, ignoring Fade's obvious distaste and smiling to himself as he thought of his destination. For, unknown to this handsome, arrogant, lowbrow groom, he intended to pay a visit to the Whitman home in Sparta. It was a neat little bit of deception that tickled his fancy all the way down the hill and across the old post road to the small settlement near White Point where the Whitman farmhouse was situated. He was not exactly sure why he was doing this, but then he often did things on impulse with a feeling that it might pay off later. He felt certain that there was something going on between his sister and this Whitman cub, but had not yet been able to determine how serious it was. It would not hurt to get a glimpse of this family on its home ground, and it just might give him a few aces up his sleeve for later.

The rain had slackened by the time he pulled up in the yard near the low clapboard farmhouse. Off to the side there was a stone well and, as luck would have it, a girl was there working the bucket gears. She was younger than he and dressed in country style, with an old oil slicker thrown back over her shoulders. Her long hair was braided into a rope that hung down her back, and even from here her ripe figure was apparent. He fastened the horses to a tree and started across the yard, oblivious to the mud that splattered his boots.

"Hello."

She turned suddenly, straightening, the heavy bucket in her hand. Her features were round and coarse; her full breasts, swelling the tight blouse underneath the slicker, were highly developed for one so young. She gave him a long, appraising look, and a coquettish smile spread over her face.

"Why, hello. It's Mr. Deveroe, ain't it? Fancy that."

"That's right. Garret Deveroe. And you are . . . ?"

"Florrie. Florrie Whitman." Her look grew increasingly coy. A real flirt, Garret thought, and about as subtle as a plow ox.

"Well now. And what might you be wanting, Mr. Garret Deveroe? Would you like a drink of water? Or maybe a glass of buttermilk?"

"Never touch buttermilk, thank you. And I'm not thirsty. I'd just like to talk a little." He looked around the yard, trying to observe if there was a face at any of the windows. "I'm looking for Fade Whitman. Is he at home?"

"No, he's up at your big house on the hill, as you ought to know. He works there now. There's not anybody to home right now but me. Matilda's up at the store near the dock with her little boy, and Jim, her husband, is working the mine. So there's just me—that is, if you don't count Ma, who's bedridden and so gone in the head that she don't know if it's daylight or dark."

"Are you Fade's sister, by any chance?"

She hoisted the bucket, shifting her hips provocatively. "That I am, as I'm sure you would know if you was to ask him."

Garret reached over and took the bucket from her. "You're a very saucy girl, Florrie. Where can we go to talk?"

"Well now..." She hesitated, feeling very sure that this swell had more than just talk on his mind and quite willing to oblige him in any way he might wish. "There's the barn...?"

"I'd prefer the house. You do have a parlor, don't you?"

"Yes, but the kitchen would suit better. The parlor's all closed up. Come on."

She led him into a large room with a huge old-fashioned fireplace that was now almost wholly obliterated by a tremendous black iron stove. After the cold rain the warmth and dryness of the kitchen seemed inviting. Garret set down the bucket and pulled a ladder-backed chair up to a plank table that stood in the center of the room. A little disappointed but still hopeful, Florrie threw off her slicker and plunked herself on a corner of the table, leaning closer, the better to show off her ample expanse of bosom.

"So it's talk you want. Well, that's as good a place to begin as any. What would you like to talk about?"

Half an hour later Garret left, having learned a good deal about Fade Whitman and his useless brothers, his senile, bedridden mother, and his elder sister's demanding family—and having successfully fought off Florrie's eager willingness to be taken advantage of. In the end he grudgingly gave her a few coins and a kiss; on her part, it was wildly passionate and on his barely tolerated, but it was worth it. He had long ago learned that the more one knew about a person, the less one had to fear him.

It was raining heavily again, big drops pelting the cover of the chaise and drenching the back of his horse as he struggled to pull the vehicle up the muddy rutted roads. Deep inside the womb of the carriage Garret smiled to himself. How fortunate for him that Emily had developed such a consuming interest in this Whitman fellow.

Within a week the land had dried out and was decked with the full brilliance of autumn colors. The air was nippy and crisp—perfect, Emily thought, for a long ride among the hills behind Southernwood. As luck would have it, Garret had spoken for

Wilton that day, saying he needed the groom to look over some horses in Tarrytown that were for sale. With a singing heart Emily, followed by Fade, began the climb toward the highest point overlooking the river.

After an hour's ride they finally reached their favorite spot and dismounted, sprawling on the velvet grass. It was impossible not to fall into each other's arms. Emily pulled away the buttons at her collar so Fade could kiss her throat; she would have opened them all the way down but he stayed her hand. She knew it was out of love that he refused to take advantage of her on these occasions, yet it was becoming more and more difficult for them both to put a rein on their desperate desires. Finally she broke away from his embrace and sat up, brushing the grass from her dark blue riding skirt.

"I don't know how much longer I can bear this," she cried. "We must find an answer. We must."

Fade lay back with his arms under his head and looked up at the cloud-smothered sky. "There is no answer for us, Emily, my dear," he said bitterly.

"I don't believe that. I don't. There must be a way. If only I could find the right time to talk to my father."

"Your father is ill and he is pressing you to set a date for your marriage to Robert Slade. How in heaven's name do you hope to persuade him to let us marry? I have nothing to offer you. I'm far beneath you socially. I'm in his employ, for God's sake. It's hopeless, Emily."

"It's not! It can't be. I don't want to marry Robert and I do want to marry you. That ought to count for something. Father simply has to be convinced. And he will be as soon as I can find the right time."

Fade rolled over onto his side, resting his head on one arm. "My darling girl. I wish it could be, too, but I'm wiser than you. The only answer is for me to go away again the next time the *Carolyn Grey* takes port. Until then at least we have a little time to fashion dreams that can never come true."

Emily looked down at the dark thin face she knew so well. How could she ever bear to lose him? It would break her heart. She leaned down, pushing him over on his back. Sprawled over his body, her arms tightly entwined through his, she covered his face with kisses. Fade's arms tightened around her and he rolled Emily under him, his lips hard on hers.

What did the future matter? This moment was all.

The afternoon sun was beginning its long westward descent when they finally rode into the cobbled stable yard, and Emily knew she had missed the family dinner. She hoped her absence had not created any concern, but her happiness was so great that she barely cared. This glorious euphoria would carry her through the next few days before it faded, leaving her vulnerable to a growing despair over their future. Glancing quickly around to make sure no one was watching, she blew Fade a kiss and started for the house.

Faith, her maid, met her in the hall, taking her hat and crop and almost twitching with nervousness.

"Oh, Miss Emily, your father has been asking for you. He's in a rare taking. He wants you to come right away to his study."

"Is he ill?" Emily asked. A small twinge of trepidation began to grow in her chest.

"I only know he's in a rage such as I've never seen, not since I came to work here at Southernwood." Her eyes filled with tears. "He yelled at me, he did, something terrible. Said I was to wait here for you and the minute you stepped foot in the door send you directly up to him. Please go quickly, miss, or likely he'll think I didn't do my duty."

Emily looked up the wide staircase as though for an answer. What could have happened? Josh Deveroe was not given to tyrannical rages. Had his illness begun to affect his mind?

She calmed her maid and started up the stairs, anxious for her father. His study was behind his bedroom and it took her only a minute to reach the doorway. Josh stood in the center of the room. When he saw her he advanced, his arms upraised. On his face was a look she had never seen before.

"So there you are!" he bellowed. "You wicked, ungrateful child. After all I've done for you. All I've given you. All the trust I put in you!"

"Papa, what's the matter? What have I done?"

"Carrying on behind my back with a low-born whelp of a fisherman. Out on the grass rolling around with the hired help! Giving yourself to that . . . that two-timing snake I took in as an act of charity."

Emily shrank back against the door frame. How had he learned? Who had seen them? Her father loomed over her and for an instant she thought he would strike her. Then he began to tremble, a shuddering that racked his entire body.

"Papa, please, you'll hurt yourself. You're ill."

"I'm not so ill as to let this disgrace pass unattended. You'll see!"

She reached out to grab Josh's arm as he staggered past. When he pulled away from her, her view was no longer blocked, and she saw Garret leaning against the window sill, his arms folded across his chest, a barely disguised smirk of triumph on his face.

 *Four*

THE OFFICE of the Westchester Copper Mine Company was little more than a clapboard lean-to thrown up beside the salt grass in front of the bluff that hid the mine itself. There was just enough room inside to allow Josh Deveroe and the thin foreman, Henshaw, to bend over a high table covered with an assortment of papers—plans, statements, bills, and manifests. As he shifted a large roll of plans, Josh's fine beaver hat fell in the dust on the ground. He retrieved it hurriedly, brushed it off, and set it back on his head to prevent any further damage.

"It doesn't look good, Henshaw. I tell you it doesn't look good at all," he said, rolling up one large sheet of plans in order to inspect another underneath.

"I wish I could say you were wrong, Mr. Deveroe, but in truth I cannot. We've gone well over five hundred feet into that cliff and found nothing to match the original vein. Of course—"

"There's always hope for the next shaft," Deveroe finished for him. "Humph! That's the way of miners. There's always gold around the next corner. Might as well pour money down a well and hope it comes up in the bucket. I tell you, businessmen must have a little more assurance in order to keep investing in such a venture."

"That's all too true, Mr. Deveroe. I know well what you mean. It's only that the original vein was so promising."

"Yes. Well, promises are one thing. A healthy return is another."

He bent over the paper and studied the thin, spidery lines that covered it. Outside, the rhythmic clanking of the pump kept up its singsong repetition in counterpoint to the noises of the dock not far away. A thin, cold upriver wind carried the stink of the fishhouse a few yards to the south. Josh rolled up the plans and looked wistfully over at the dark entrance to the mine. No getting around it, he was disappointed. Another disappointment.

"What does Mr. Kemeys say?"

Henshaw coughed and looked away. He had tried to appear confident and assured, but the facts no longer supported his optimism and it would do no good to pretend they did. Deveroe would learn that soon enough at the next board meeting.

"This morning he was saying as how the funds were getting too low to continue."

Josh tried not to reveal his dismay in front of the foreman. The truth was he had invested heavily in this copper mine, sure that it would be the means of reviving the Sparta dock community. He could do nothing about the competition from the dock at Sing Sing, two miles upriver. Once the turnpike road was rerouted away from the landing, the death of the village became almost certain. How he hated the thought! He had grown up here, his father's sloops had used this dock since he and Elisha Yancy first started in business. The Dolphin shipping interests had grown from the landing and prospered until now they covered the great oceans of the world. Perhaps it was sentiment, but he had desperately wanted to help bring a new prosperity to the community that had been so much a part of his life. And once again he had failed.

"We did everything we could, Mr. Deveroe," Henshaw was saying. "It just appears the copper was all on the surface and there is no richer lode in these rocks. I've seen it happen many times before."

"I'm sure it's not your fault, Henshaw. I know little of mining, but it seems to me you've been an excellent foreman. Though it is hard on those of us who invested heavily in it, it must be harder still on you and those other Cornish miners who came over with you. What will you do now?"

Looking out into the distance as though the answer lay somewhere on the blue river barely visible through the willows, Henshaw said, "I don't quite know yet. Some of us will return to Cornwall, in the spring. Some will stay. There might be work in the marble quarries, what with the new state farm being built up there, but unfortunately a miner can rarely turn to any other form of work. It's too bad, for there appears to be a lot of opportunity over here. With a bit of land a man could make a place for himself."

"If only the silver mine had been successful," Josh said, laying a hand on the man's shoulder. "We don't seem fated for mining in Sparta, do we?"

"It seemed like such a rich vein," Henshaw muttered, looking back toward the mine entrance. "It's just a bloody shame."

Directing Absolem to drive the chaise up the hill from the dock, Josh brooded during the short distance through the village to the Whitman farm on the old post road. He dreaded this interview, yet he knew it was necessary. Given a choice, he would never set eyes on Fade Whitman again, much less confront him on his own territory. Those Whitmans had always meant trouble. The father, Ben, had drunk himself to death after terrorizing and abusing his poor wife and children for years. One of the girls seemed solid enough, but that younger one was already the talk of the village with her wanton ways. God, he hoped he wouldn't run into her! There were several other brothers, as he remembered, all of them serving in some menial capacity at the fish house or the dock. None of them were enterprising enough to make anything of themselves, and all of them had the reputation of being slovenly and lazy. And now rumor had it that the mother was so crazy she had to be tied to her bed half the time. Probably the result of knowing she had produced such a family.

Turning the corner at Garrison's Tavern, Josh glanced nervously toward the small farmhouse at the end of the road. He had to admit that Fade seemed to have some small hint of promise. If things had been different, he might have even been persuaded to help the young man along a little, offer him a few opportunities and see if he used them correctly. But that was before he knew how the bastard had taken advantage of his daughter. Now there was only one thing to do: get rid of him forever—and the sooner the better. The yard was still banked with snow in places, but behind the house, near the barn, he could hear the thud of an ax hitting wood. With any luck he would find the fellow there and avoid the rest of the family altogether.

Fade Whitman settled back in one of the Windsor chairs that graced the seldom-used front parlor of his mother's house and studied the man who sat opposite him. Mr. Deveroe was obviously nonplussed to find himself ushered like an honored guest into this chilly, shabby room and offered a glass of ale. Such courteous treatment was not what he would have preferred, and Fade knew it well. That was why he had donned his coat, and insisted that Mr. Deveroe step inside, offering him the best chair and refreshment and politely introducing him to his sister Matilda.

"I take it you have not found other means of earning a livelihood since leaving my employ, Mr. Whitman," Josh began uncomfortably.

Fade's eyes narrowed but his voice remained remarkably pleasant. "That is really not your concern anymore, Mr. Deveroe."

"Come now. Your dismissal had nothing to do with the quality of your work, you know that. I was greatly pleased with the way you were managing my stable. It was unfortunate that you had to leave as you did, but I think you can understand there was no alternative."

Fade watched the older man over his steepled fingertips, noticing how Josh gripped the arms of the chair.

"As a matter of fact, I understand the *Carolyn Grey* is due in port sometime in the next two months. I intend to sign on again as a mate if the captain will have me. Until then, I make do with odd jobs here and there."

From upstairs a horrible scream pierced the silence. Fade's

face went white but he quickly regained his composure knowing Matilda would see to his mother.

Instinctively Josh tightened his grip on the arms of his chair—a habit he had developed lately to cover the trembling in his hands and arms.

There were several more garbled screams from above, hurried footsteps, a door slamming, and then quiet again. As he intently studied the braided rug at his feet, it occurred to Josh that Fade Whitman bore more of a burden than he had ever suspected.

"This has been a difficult winter to be without work. I have a better offer for you if you are inclined to take it. I can get you on board one of the Dolphin ships in New York immediately. I have in mind the *China Comet*, mastered by Oliver Shields, as fine a captain as you could want. She's a good, trim ship and very fast. She's in port now and, as luck would have it, in need of a seasoned first mate. A word from me and you could sign on tomorrow."

"And bound for China, I gather?"

"Eventually, yes. She will touch at several other ports en route, all of them interesting and profitable. You would have a share in those profits."

God, it was tempting. A glorious vision swam before his eyes. One year's sail and there would be enough to take care of his family for years, yet it stuck in his craw that Josh Deveroe should pull the strings of his life. He could not bring himself to say yes, but he could not say no either.

"Perhaps you would like some time to consider. If you could get word to me by this afternoon, I would send a letter down to you this evening. Then tomorrow you can go into New York and—"

"In a mighty hurry to get rid of me, aren't you, Mr. Deveroe?"

Josh flinched. The ungrateful bastard! "Yes, I am. I want you away from Mount Pleasant and unable to influence my daughter. Emily is headstrong and willful and once she decides she wants something it is difficult to dissuade her from it. But time and separation will do the trick—that and her marriage to Robert Slade. If you are hanging about down here in the village, it will be that much more difficult."

"Are you so sure she will give up? Perhaps our feelings for

each other are stronger than you suppose."

"Poppycock! She's only a girl. And your feelings, I suspect, cannot help but be affected by her wealth."

Fade's voice was quiet but cold as ice. "How dare you, sir!"

"Come now, you would be less than human if they were not. I do not hold that against you. Emily is quite a catch and I am sure she has encouraged you to some small degree. But she is the dearest thing in the world to me, Mr. Whitman, and I will not have her future ruined. She *will* marry Robert Slade and you will go away and leave her alone forever, I am determined."

Careful to maintain his composure, Fade rose. "I thank you for your offer, Mr. Deveroe, but I must refuse it. And now I think you had better go."

"You cannot refuse. I'll double the salary. Why, you would be making nearly as much as Captain Shields himself. And perhaps you could have a larger share of the profits. Think about that, Mr. Whitman. It could amount to more hard cash than you are likely to see in your whole lifetime. Think what you could do with it."

Fade turned and opened the door, waiting for Josh to leave. "Good day, Mr. Deveroe."

Underneath his heavy sideburns Josh's face began to grow purple. He stood up, leaning on his cane, his whole body threatening to turn to quivering jelly with the trembling in his legs.

"Don't be a fool. The world is filled with women, Mr. Whitman, and one of them will do as well as another. You hardly know Emily. This is all just a silly girl's romantic dream."

Fade's dark gaze was unflinching. "You are right, Mr. Deveroe. I love Emily but I know her little. And if I really loved her enough I would go away from her for her own good. But it is not because of Emily that I refuse your very *generous* offer."

"What then, for God's sake?"

"As rich and powerful as you are, you cannot control my life. I will not sail away on your ship just to put your fears at rest. Marry Emily off to Robert Slade if you can, but you will have to do it without my help. All I will give you is my promise not to encourage her on my behalf. Now, please go. I have several chores to complete."

Josh stood in the doorway looking long at this dark young man who had defied him. Another garbled scream from upstairs forced his gaze momentarily to the ceiling. Then, clapping his hat on his head, he stumbled furiously out the front door and down the path to the road.

The young fool! The stubborn, pig-headed young fool!

Fade looked nervously around the tiny room that served as Mr. Garrison's taproom. Narrow and long, with a large fieldstone fireplace covering the wall at one end, it was as grubby and shabby as the local tenants who gathered there almost every evening to buy a jug of ale or porter, sometimes even Allegheny whiskey, all served by Mr. Garrison without benefit of a license.

"Emily, you little fool. What can you mean coming here like this!"

Across the table from Fade, Emily lowered her head to hide her face under the sloping brim of her cabriolet bonnet. "I had to see you," she whispered. "No one will suspect anything. You know I often call on Auntie Garrison to bring her some delicacy or other from our pantry. And Faith is sworn to secrecy. She won't tell anyone I ran into you here."

She leaned closer across the plank table. "Come, Fade, I've known Auntie Garrison my whole life. It will be all right, I promise."

"Just the same..." He ran his fingers up and down the wooden tankard and glanced furtively at the door. "You never know who might come in."

"Not at this hour. Besides, Faith will warn me if it's Papa. I simply had to see you, Fade. I know what Papa has been trying to do. I know that he tried to bribe you into signing on to one of his ships and that you refused."

"Now, how...?"

"Garret told me. He's a born sneak and he has a way of always knowing everybody's business. Besides, Papa is putting great pressure on me to marry Robert Slade at the first possible moment. He has already decided whom to invite to the wedding, where it will be, everything except a date, which I have absolutely refused to set."

"Perhaps you should marry Robert Slade," Fade said grimly. "After all, your father may be doing this for your own good.

I've told you many times I have nothing to offer you."

Emily's shapely mouth settled into lines of stubbornness. "Some girls might allow their fathers to ruin their lives while they stand meekly by, but I am certainly not one of them. I'll die if I cannot live with you, Fade. I'll drive a knife into my chest right at the altar in front of Papa and Robert and everyone."

He smiled at her. "That is just the kind of melodramatic thing you would do, you wild little creature." Reaching across, he took her hand and pressed it quickly to his lips. "I hope I get to see it."

"Don't tease me, my love. I'm deadly serious. I will not marry Robert Slade, ever. I won't marry anyone but you. That is why we must do something right away. If Papa is to be stopped, we must act very soon."

"Emily, what are you thinking of now?"

Her voice grew very low and she leaned so close to him that the satin ribbons on the brim of her hat grazed his hair.

"We must go to New York. I can easily arrange to pay a visit to one of my cousins or to the theater—something like that—and once there, we can meet and be married. By the time Papa finds out, it will be too late for him to do anything."

"But your age . . ."

"I'm nineteen now. I don't need his consent. We'll lie about the circumstances, and surely we can find some poor cleric who will believe us. It's our only hope, Fade, our only hope."

He knew Emily well enough to realize how serious she was. In the silence he could hear a low hum coming from the lean-to kitchen, where Auntie Garrison fussed about, letting them know she was not listening. Fade's mind was a jumble of conflicting thoughts and emotions. Part of him wanted to jump at the chance to marry Emily and yet he was reluctant to take a step that might ruin her life.

"How would we live?" he finally said. "You would never be able to come back to Southernwood or see your father again. Have you thought what that would mean?"

She looked down again, determined that he should not see the look of dismay his words brought to her face. "Yes, I've thought of that. I love Papa and I love Southernwood, but I love you more. If I have to choose between them, then I choose to be with you. As for how we could live, what does that matter? We'll manage somehow."

"But, Emily, you are used to fine things, servants, anything you want. Do you know what it would be like, having to make do on a few pennies a week? You would hate it and one day you would come to hate me, too, for bringing you to it."

"Never! Of what use are fine things if my heart is breaking? I love you, Fade. You are all that matters to me. I can make do with any kind of life as long as you are there to share it with me. We could live in the city, or if you want, we could strike out for the frontier. Many people do and they have great adventures while making their fortunes. I'd go anywhere with you."

Fade felt his resistance crumbling under her singleminded determination. The frontier had always held a lure for him. He loved Emily and the last thing he wanted was to leave her. Besides, the idea of getting the better of Josh Deveroe was appealing. It was quite a gamble, but then he had never yet flinched before a throw of the dice.

Pushing away the tankard, he reached for both her hands, gripping them in his own. "All right. I'm not saying I'll agree; but tell me how you plan to bring this off."

Getting Josh's permission to go into the city proved to be even easier than Emily had anticipated, once she hit on the idea of telling him she was actually going to shop for a trousseau and wedding gown. Reasoning that pretty new clothes would help mitigate her opposition to marrying Robert Slade, Josh readily agreed, provided she stay with one of her cousins and take along her personal maid and groom.

"Oh, Papa, please. Cousin Dexter drinks too much and Cousin Christy is such a bore. All she ever talks about is who wore what to which party. Can't I please stay at the City Hotel? I've been there hundreds of times and they know me well and will look out for me. Please, Papa."

What she said was all true, of course, and the hotel was right downtown near the shops. Christy and Dexter lived farther out among the fields and woods of Greenwich Village.

"Oh, very well, then," Josh sighed. "But I expect you to be careful and to use your common sense. The city can be a dangerous place, what with all the world's riffraff arriving there every day of the week."

Throwing her arms around her father's neck, Emily kissed

him on both cheeks. She supposed she ought to feel guilty, but her heart was singing. Once ensconced in the hotel she would find some excuse to send Wilton home while Faith, of course, would remain her willing accomplice. For the first time, marriage with Fade seemed a real possibility.

Emily knew she could not pack too much without arousing suspicion. With just enough boxes to look practical, she kissed her father good-bye at the Sparta dock, where a launch waited to take her to the steamboat anchored in the channel. It was the most difficult parting Emily had ever endured. But attitude was all, and if she was not to arouse suspicion, she had to pretend a nonchalance she was far from feeling. She carried it off well, and as her launch pulled away, it was a happy and confident Emily that her father saw waving from the deck. Only when she turned to the river did she give way to the tears she had choked off.

Once Emily arrived in the city, all her optimism came bounding back. She checked into the hotel, had Faith lay out all her bottles and brushes in her comfortable room, and nervously waited for the supper hour, when Fade was to meet her in the dining room. Over a meal of fried oysters and pigeon pie they laid their plans. Fade had already located a clergyman who, retired and infirm, was agreeable to performing a quiet ceremony without asking too many questions. All that remained was to send Wilton home. After the wedding they would move into a boardinghouse near the new Park Theater until they could locate more permanent lodgings in a better area or until they decided to take the coach south for a trip to the western lands.

"I have a little capital, Emily, but it will have to last us for a long time. I hope you are prepared to face that."

"It's no worry. I brought nearly fifty dollars with me and several good pieces of jewelry. Some are worth quite a lot of money. I'll sell them if need be."

"I hate the thought of you having to sell your jewelry. Surely I'll find work before we're reduced to that."

"Don't worry. The pieces that are important to me are the least valuable ones—a topaz and some pearls which belonged to my grandmother. The others are better sold if they will help us to be together."

Fade sat back in his chair and studied the woman he was going to marry. Emily was looking lovelier than ever, her face glowing with excitement and happiness. Her hair was crimped and curled in the latest fashion and entwined with a rosette of artificial flowers and narrow satin ribbons. Her white shoulders glowed like cream in the soft candlelight, and the broad *V* of her neckline, covered with masses of lavender ruffles, barely disguised the sweeping fullness of her breasts. He had never loved her more than he did at that moment, yet he was uneasy, made afraid and guilty by the furtive way they must go about obtaining the one thing they both wanted so desperately.

"Emily, are you sure . . . ?" he said hesitantly. "I am so afraid that you will find yourself stuck in a life you have never known and may well come to hate. I wish it didn't have to be this way."

Emily looked up at him and he could read all she was feeling in her expressive eyes. Fade had already learned that all her emotions were perfectly mirrored in her face. He could recognize each one, from the bright animation of joy to the strained lines of depression or anger. Now he knew from the stubborn set of her mouth and chin that it was useless to try dissuading her, and he was not even sure he wanted to.

"I wish it too," she answered, "but better this way than not at all. Oh, my love, why won't you believe me? As long as I can be with you I won't mind how I live, or where."

"I shall take leave to remind you of that someday," he said, smiling.

She took his hand and squeezed it hard. "If I change my mind, you have my permission to do so."

The next morning Emily sent Wilton back to Southernwood on the pretense that she needed Thor brought down and stabled nearby so she might ride every day. He put up a strong argument, reminding her that horses were available for hire should she require one, sure that Josh Deveroe would be angry with him for leaving her unprotected in the city. But Emily prevailed, and full of misgivings, the groom set out for the steamboat landing to catch the eleven o'clock boat upriver. Unfortunately, he forgot his tobacco pouch and, finding himself a little early, went back to the hotel to pick it up. As he entered the lobby he spotted Fade Whitman, neatly attired in a wool tweed suit and tall broadcloth hat, sitting uncomfortably on one of the velvet benches.

Sure that Fade had not seen him, Wilton ducked behind a large potted plant and waited. Soon Emily came down the broad stairs and ran straight to where Fade sat. She kissed him quickly, then they walked off, arm in arm.

Wilton was not a quick-witted man, but he had heard rumors about the reason for Fade's sudden dismissal, and the sight of these two together here with no one but Miss Emily's maid for chaperone filled him with anxiety. He considered not going back to Westchester in spite of Emily's orders, but on second thought decided Mr. Deveroe should know what was going on and the sooner the better. He almost ran the short distance to the boat landing.

"Really, Garret, I do think you might give a little more attention to matters of business," Josh said, thrusting a sheaf of papers across the table toward his son. "The Dolphin interests will be yours someday. That ought to inspire you even if concern for my feelings does not."

"I do try, Papa, but you really don't care a fig for my opinions. Why should I put myself out?"

"Now, that is not true."

"Haven't I suggested over and over that you break your sentimental ties with the Sparta dock and move your business to Sing Sing? You continue to ignore me, and every year you lose a few more customers. The future is upriver, not here at this isolated backwater village."

Josh rubbed a hand across his chin. "It's difficult to break the ties of a lifetime, and if we pull out, so will the others. I do not want to be the man responsible for bringing down a town."

"Business is business, Papa. Besides, the engineer who re-routed the post road is responsible for isolating Sparta. Now the Dock Association clings to their scurvy little tariffs when it is cheaper and more convenient for the farmers to bring their produce to the Sing Sing dock. They are writing their own death warrant."

"A businessman owes some responsibility to the people he serves."

"There, you see. Why do I even try? You won't listen to me, and then you berate me for not talking. It's your business. Do with it what you will."

Josh started to make an angry retort, but he was stopped by the sudden appearance of a figure in the doorway.

"Wilton! What are you doing here?"

Wilton, nervously turning the wide brim of his hat in his hands, took a timid step into the room.

"Excuse me, Mr. Deveroe, but there's something as you should know."

"Is Miss Emily with you? What brought her back so quickly?"

"No, sir, she's not with me. She said I was to fetch Thor. But I think the real reason she sent me back was so's she could meet that Fade Whitman again. I seen him with my own eyes, waitin' for her in the hotel lobby, so I come on up here to tell you of it fast as I could."

With a strangled cry Josh jumped up from the table. "By God! You left her in the city with that lowly fellow? What were you thinking of? I ought to have you horsewhipped."

"I couldn't do nothing about her, Mr. Deveroe. You know how Miss Emily is. I thought it was you who should take care of it."

Furious, Josh turned to his son, who sat smirking at them both. "Did you know about this?" he shouted. "Did you help her deceive her own father? I should have known!"

"Why, Papa," Garret said innocently. "This is the first I've heard of it. You know as well as I that Emily needs no help when she sets her mind on something."

"Put the horses to immediately, Wilton. I'm not waiting for the boat. If I don't get down there and stop her she'll be ruined. Damn! That my own daughter would do this to me!"

He was out of the room and down the stairs as fast as he could go, while behind him Wilton went tearing toward the stables. In the quiet room that served as Josh's private office, Garret bent down and began methodically stacking the strewn papers, smiling his lopsided smile.

It had worked. All he'd had to do was supply a little information here and there and the foolish girl had done the rest. For the first time Garret could really believe that someday everything Josh owned would be his.

Emily's room at the City Hotel was actually a suite, with a large sitting room adjacent to a smaller but exquisitely decorated bedroom. After supper at the nearby Shakespeare Hotel, she returned there with Fade, throwing her cloak to Faith and snuggling up next to him on the velvet plush settee. It was difficult for him to put his arm around her since his best coat was cut in the latest fashion, fitting like a second skin. Somehow he managed, tucking her head under his chin and enjoying her favorite scent, attar of roses. She herself looked like a rose in her pink corded silk dress with its short puffed sleeves and full flowing skirt.

Emily leaned against him and sighed with contentment. "Eleven o'clock tomorrow and all the waiting and hoping will be over. Are you sure everything is ready? Nothing will go wrong?"

"As sure as I can be. The parson is sufficiently bribed, the license is in my pocket, and today I purchased the ring. Not a grand one with diamonds as you ought to have, but a serviceable plain gold band. The diamonds will have to wait until I make my fortune."

"I love the idea of a plain gold band."

Hesitating, he traced the line of her cheek lightly with his fingers. "You can still back out, Emily. Are you really sure you want it this way?"

She reached up and kissed him lightly on the lips. "Oh yes, except that I feel badly that Papa will not be there. I never imagined myself getting married without him. But if this is the only way I can have you, then this is the way it shall be. I do think you might have acted a little less of the gentleman, though, and stayed the night with me."

"Now, we've been over that again and again. I will not bed you before it is legal, much as I would like to, and you might as well accept it."

Emily played absently with his watch chain, a thin silverplated thing worlds away from her father's rich heavy gold fob. Soon it would be replaced with the lovely gold one she had bought him as a wedding gift, inscribed with their names and tomorrow's date. The thought made her warm with happiness. "When I first met you I had no idea you were so moral, Mr. Whitman."

"Oh yes you did. And it's not morality. It's the idea that I'd be doing just what your father would expect, and I refuse to give him that satisfaction. I'll take you honestly or not at all."

Emily looked wistfully toward the door of her bedroom, which Faith had carefully closed. They had been over this before, but she wanted him so much. Just as she opened her mouth to reply, the door to the hall burst open and Faith came rushing in, white-faced and flinging her arms about.

"Miss Emily! It's your father. He's here! Here in the hotel..."

Emily fell forward abruptly as Fade jumped to his feet. "He can't be," she cried. "It's impossible."

"No, no. It's true. I saw him down in the lobby and he's coming up the stairs! Oh, Miss Emily, what will we do? He'll kill us all!"

Fade had turned very pale but was holding on to his composure. Looking from his face to that of her frantic servant, Emily struggled for a minute, seeing her beautifully laid plans going down in ruins.

"No, he won't!" she exclaimed furiously. "Fade, get out of your coat. Hurry. And Faith, help me with these buttons. Hurry, you clumsy girl, hurry!"

Twisting and tearing at the fabric, she began pulling off her dress while Fade looked on, horrified.

"For God's sake, Emily, what are you doing?"

"Don't ask questions. Just get that coat off and hurry, please, please. Oh, these horrible fashions! Why do they have to fit so tight!"

Squirming around, she worked the dress down around her ankles while Fade, thinking he must be crazy to follow her example, struggled out of his tight-fitting coat.

Grabbing up the dress in a bundle, Emily tossed it across the room. "Faith, throw open the bedroom door. Hurry! And turn down the bed covers. Better yet, muss them up, make them as rumpled as you can."

"Oh, but Miss Emily, he'll kill me."

"*I'll* kill you if you don't do what I say at once! Hurry up!"

They could hear Josh Deveroe's enraged voice as he advanced down the hall and toward the suite. Faith ran off to the bedroom, throwing the bedclothes every which way while Fade, finally divested of his coat, stood grinning at Emily in waist and shirtsleeves. With one furious snatch she tore away the exquisite folds of the high stock he had so carefully fashioned earlier in the evening and, just as Josh came storming into the room, threw herself at him, sending them both careening backward onto the settee in a cloud of ruffled petticoats.

Josh stopped dead in the doorway, unwilling to believe his eyes. "You bastard," he bellowed at Fade, tearing Emily away. "I'll have your head for this!"

Resolutely Emily thrust herself between the two men. "It's too late, Papa. I'm ruined!"

"Emily!" The horrified look on Fade's countenance was a perfect match for Josh Deveroe's. "For God's sake, Emily, tell him the truth."

"God damn you," Josh yelled, raising his cane above his head.

Emily grabbed at her father's arm. "Don't hurt him, Papa, it will do no good. You're too late!"

Fade stood his ground, very calmly taking Emily by the shoulders and pulling her back.

"I know how this looks to you, Mr. Deveroe, but it is only one of Emily's tricks. We plan to be married in the morning and until that time I certainly have not and will not take advantage of her."

"Don't believe him, Papa. I'm telling you the truth."

"She is not . . . Emily!" Fade said sharply. "Stop this playacting. I tell you, Mr. Deveroe, I do hope to marry Emily, but I have not bedded her."

Josh looked from one to the other, his arm wavering. Which one to believe? He could almost swear Fade was telling the truth, and yet if appearances were to be believed . . . His knees began to tremble, and cursing his affliction, he edged himself down onto the settee. "Faith," he said curtly. "Bring your mistress her dressing gown."

With timid steps Faith carried out Emily's blue velvet gown and helped her slip it over her chemise and petticoats before dashing back to the safety of the bedroom. Silently Josh studied them both. He had to control his rage.

"So you're not yet married," he finally said, his voice trembling with anger.

"No," Emily replied, settling in a chair opposite her father. "But the ceremony is set for tomorrow morning."

"Well, it's set no more. You're coming home with me tonight."

Emily's jaw set into its familiar stubborn lines. "That I will not do, Papa. I'm staying here. If you won't allow me to marry Fade, then I'll live with him in sin. But I won't go back with you and I won't marry anyone else."

"This fellow only wants your money, Emily. Why can't you see it?"

"Because it's not true."

Fade stepped up beside Emily, laying a possessive hand on her shoulder. "I know you don't believe me, Mr. Deveroe, but I do love Emily and I don't want her money or yours. I intend to make my own fortune someday, and until then I can certainly care for her, if not in the grand style she has known, certainly in a comfortable one."

Emily reached up and gripped his hand. "And all I want is to be with him, Papa. I don't care about money."

Josh ran his fingers through his long hair. He had never felt so defeated. If only he wasn't so ill and weak all this would never have been allowed to happen. He would try a different tack.

"Listen to me, my dear. Romantic notions never outlive the first flush of youth—I know that very well. Believe me, your dreams won't last beyond a single month in a grubby flat, sweeping floors and eating watered soup. You've alway had the best, Emily. You'll never get used to the kind of life he can offer you."

"You are wrong, Papa. I know it. I am truly sorry to hurt you because I love you very much, but all I want in the world is Fade."

It was a long hard moment before Josh could answer, the hardest and longest of his life. He was going to surrender his beloved daughter to a man who at that moment he almost hated. But he knew it was inevitable; he would never have the strength to stop her from something she wanted so much. He rested his hands on the gold tip of his cane and looked fiercely into Fade's eyes.

"You will never get a penny from me. She will have no dowry at all."

"Fine. I'll earn her one myself."

That was a surprise. Turning back to Emily, Josh made one last plea. "Robert will be so hurt . . ."

Her fingers tightened around Fade's. "Robert Slade has always been a good friend to me, Papa, and I hope he always will be. But I don't want to be his wife. I would only make him miserable."

Josh had to admit that there was some truth in that. For all his good qualities, Robert was too amiable and easygoing to bridle a spirited mare like Emily. He looked back at Fade Whitman and saw the fine chiseled face and determined mouth. At least he might offer his headstrong daughter some opposition, though in the end she would no doubt have her way with him too.

"Very well, then," he said bitterly. "Have your marriage tomorrow, but it shall be without me. However, I shall spend the night in this sitting room to prevent any recurrence of the sorry spectacle that greeted me a few moments ago."

"Oh, Papa, thank you! Thank you!" Emily cried, throwing her arms around her father's neck and kissing him on both cheeks.

He took her firmly by the arms and pushed her away. "And you shall not come back to Southernwood. I'll have no more to do with you."

"Oh, Papa, surely you don't mean that. Give us a chance to show that we can make this work, please. Never to see you again is too harsh a punishment. It will break my heart."

"Then we are two of a kind, for you are breaking mine."

Slowly getting to his feet, Josh turned away from his daughter to conceal the hot, undignified tears that had suddenly welled behind his eyes. Stumbling a little, he started for the decanter of claret provided by the hotel.

Behind him, Emily took Fade's arm and walked with him to the hallway. They talked softly for a while, then said good night with a quick kiss and a long embrace. When she returned to the suite her father was sitting in a chair near the window with his back to her. She wanted so much to go up and put her arms around him, but his anger and hurt had created a barrier she could not cross. She stood watching him for a moment, wishing he would turn, then moved silently, sadly to her bedroom and closed the door.

Five

IT WAS a full year before Emily was reconciled with her father. During that time she stayed in the city and concentrated all her energies on building a new life with Fade, trying not to remember how much she missed her father and her old home. Once during the first six months Garret paid her a short surprise visit, but aside from furnishing her with some idea of her father's health—"He grows more feeble every day"—nothing satisfying came of his call. Indeed, Emily envisioned him carrying back all the details of her small shabby home without any mention of the happiness she and Fade had found there.

At the end of those six months she wrote to her father—a cheerful note describing her active life and, she hoped, indicating her contentment. Of course there was no answer but, undaunted, when his birthday came around she sent him another letter and a small quilted lap robe she had made herself. The quality of the work was deplorable—her sewing had always been laughable—but it came from her hand and it was sent with heartfelt feeling. This time her efforts produced a terse note of thanks, which raised Emily's hopes that eventually her father's anger would run its course. Then, one day shortly after their first wedding anniversary, Josh appeared at her door. Even Josh himself never knew why. Perhaps it was the sense of contentment and joy he read between the lines of his daughter's letters, or because no requests for money had been forthcoming, as he had been certain they would be. Or perhaps he was prompted by his own failing health and the bleakness of a life spent rattling around in a huge old house with a son he despised. Whatever the reason, finding himself in the city on a particularly bright, sunny day, he rode an omnibus to the modest district where his daughter lived.

Strangely enough, just the night before, Emily had dreamed of Southernwood—a cloudy dream from which no details emerged except a poignant longing for the home she had known as a child. When she answered the door and saw her father standing there, for an instant she thought she was back in her dream. Then the shock of the reality drained the strength from her legs and she nearly fell. Throwing her arms around his neck, she kissed him and clung to him with such joyous fervor that all the barriers Josh had thrown up between them crumbled to dust, never again to rise. At the end of an hour he left, still unwilling to see Emily's husband but convinced of both her happiness and her ability to manage in reduced circumstances.

And she was happy. Shortly after their wedding she had learned something about Fade Whitman that she had not known before, something that convinced her she had been right to throw her lot in with him. He had accumulated a fair amount of capital from his long voyage with the *Carolyn Grey* and had set it aside as a foundation for his future prosperity. So they were not destitute as her father had assumed and as she herself had feared they would be. She also learned that he had strict notions of how this capital was to be used, one of them being that it was not to be frittered away in luxuries. Reluctantly agreeing, Emily threw herself into the business of getting by on a budget, something she had never in her life done before.

Fade was a worker, and he wasted no time searching out a job. Drawn to the docks, where the great ships lay with their long bowsprits and jibbooms jutting out over the broad cob-

blestone quay that was South Street, he was hired on as a clerk
in one of the wharfside counting houses. Although he was
beginning at the bottom and competition was fierce among the
men hoping to rise through the ranks to the exalted heights of
merchant, Fade was quickly spotted as a mature man with a
firsthand knowledge of ships and a nose for practical cargo.
Anxious to make a name for himself, he was up before dawn
and down at the docks in order to be the first one to open the
store. He did everything that was asked of him, no matter how
lowly. His duties included sweeping floors, running errands,
entering goods at the Custom House, delivering goods sold,
and accounting cargoes received from ships. He also spent long
hours copying figures into the books. Because the coal stove
was at the opposite end of the long room from where the
miserable clerks sat at their tall desks, Fade's fingers would
often be so icy and numb he could barely move the quill. But
his enthusiasm paid off and he was quickly promoted. Soon
he was spending most of his time in the storage lofts and
managing orders for the inland and southern merchants who
crowded the showrooms in the spring and fall, or—what he
loved best—dealing with the captains and the cargoes unloaded
from their great vessels.

While Fade was establishing a niche in the mercantile world,
Emily kept herself busy turning a bare, shabby four-room house
on Provost Street into a home that was both attractive and
comfortable. For the first time in her life she whitewashed
walls, stitched and hung curtains, and hounded the markets for
secondhand furniture. Though she hired a widow, Florence
Allen, as her cook, she did the cleaning herself and for a time
took some pleasure in it. But wielding a broom and dustpan
soon lost its allure, and finding herself with time on her hands
and without the means to fill it, she found a position as a
teacher at the Infant School in the basement of the Presbyterian
church on Greene Street. The modest salary was enough to hire
an additional servant for the house, but the real advantage of
Emily's work was the insight it afforded her into the changing,
fluid, teeming metropolis that was New York.

If at times both Emily and Fade grew tired or discouraged
by such long hours of work for so very little return or the lack
of luxury or graciousness in their lives or the dreadful situation
of the ever-growing hordes of poor that filled the city, all their

troubles seemed insignificant in the quiet moments, when Fade would take her into his arms and they'd lose themselves in the joy of being together. Emily waited, almost holding her breath, for the magic of those times to disappear as everyone had said they would. Instead they grew stronger, deepening the bond between them.

Needing nothing from her father freed Emily to reach out to him and attempt to heal the breach between them, not in the hope of what he could do for her but simply because she loved him.

One evening shortly after her father's visit, Emily was sitting in her small parlor trying to mend a petticoat by the light of a sputtering oil lamp when she heard Fade come in through the front door. It had been dark for several hours and she was relieved to have him home, for the streets of the city grew daily more dangerous, filled as they were with disappointed men just off the ships, speaking no English and desperate for a drink of whiskey. When she looked up he was standing in the doorway, one hand on his hip in a devil-may-care attitude, his long sideburns setting off the mischievous smile on his lips, and on his head the strangest piece of attire she had ever seen.

She quickly put aside her sewing, ran to the door, and threw her arms around his neck.

"What on earth is that thing you're wearing?"

"Make a guess. What do you think?" With one finger he deftly pushed the brim up in a rakish angle.

"Well, it's obviously some kind of a hat, but it looks as though it had been stepped on by a horse. And what is it made of? Where on earth did you find such a thing?"

"You are correct, my lovely wife: it is a hat. And mark it well, for this hat is the beginning of our fortune."

Emily stood back, admiring him and laughing. *"That* thing! If I did not know better, Fade, I'd think you had been stopping over at the grog shops on your way home."

With one arm around her shoulders, he walked back to the sofa, handing her the hat to inspect.

"No, my dear, there is more of logic than spirits in that statement. These are palm-leaf hats, Emily, made in the islands of the West Indies, and they are going to be the coming thing. When I read of the new tariffs on leghorn and straw, it occurred to me that these palm hats might be the very thing to take up the slack. So I ordered a shipment of both the hats and the leaves they're fashioned from—a shipment that just arrived today. Of course, I'm not the only one to think of it; there are several other enterprising gentlemen importing palm right now. But we few are in on the beginning and I am sure we'll all do well. At least for a time."

"Aren't you clever! Why, you have talents I never dreamed of!"

"Mr. Collins, my employer, says I have 'a nose' for business."

"You do, and I love it," Emily said, kissing him there, "as I do all the rest of you."

"Hmm . . . some parts more than others, I suspect."

"Please, sir. You shock me."

Pulling Emily to him, he locked his arms around her, then kissed her forehead, her nose, her chin. "If I did not know you for such a hot-blooded wench in bed I might believe all that ladylike modesty."

"Fade!" Laughing, Emily pulled away from him and picked up the hat, turning it over in her hand. "It is a funny-looking thing, you know. Do you really believe they will be popular?"

"I'm certain of it. I've already promised the entire shipment of finished hats to one of the shops in the city, and a hat manufacturer in Westchester is interested in buying the undressed palm. Using one sample as a guide, he thinks he can have his workers turning them out within a month. All I need is a place to store the shipment until he is ready for it, and I've already hired a loft in Mr. Wilkins's warehouse near the Old Slip."

"But, Fade, won't that be terribly expensive?"

"I'll use the money from what I've already sold to expand—new products, new shipments. I see myself as a kind of man in the middle between the ship's cargoes and the store merchants who come to buy at the docks. I'm going to be rich myself someday, Emily, and all on my own terms."

She settled back in his arms. "Yes, I think you will be. Does Mr. Collins know that one of his clerks is about to become his rival? You had better be careful he doesn't fire you."

"One or two more shipments like this and I won't need Mr. Collins at all. I'll hire a shop and set up business for myself.

Of course, it will take a long time to create an enterprise as large as Collins and Thompson, but someday . . . someday I'll be the one to sit on the platform or in the back office and bark out the orders that will send twenty young men scurrying. What a satisfaction that will be."

"Dearest Fade, and you will do it, I know you will. And all because of a palm-leaf hat!"

"Well, it's a first step. Now, what about my supper? I'm starving after running around South Street all day and then walking all the way uptown tonight."

"I'll get it for you," she said, moving out of his arms. "It's a pigeon pie Mrs. Allen left warming for you." She paused for a moment beside the door and looked back at her husband, who was smiling to himself.

"You know, Fade, my father's firm, Westover and Jones, would no doubt—"

"No! If I wouldn't ask them for a job I certainly will not ask their help in distributing my merchandise."

"But—"

"We've been over this before, Emily. Whatever success I may have in the world of commerce is not going to be dependent on your father. I'll do it on my own, if for no other reason than to show him he has misjudged me."

"But it makes it so much harder on you." She devoured every detail of his lean, dark face. How dear he was to her, more than she could ever have imagined when marrying him was only a wild dream. She admired the very spunk and determination which kept him from asking her father for help.

"I'll get your supper," she said, and turned toward the kitchen.

"And how was your day at the Infant School?" Fade inquired as they sat together at the small table in the parlor, enjoying the pigeon pie and trying to keep warm in the heat of an anemic fire.

"Oh, much the same. I am concerned about my young monitor, Bridget. She has not appeared for three days now and I am afraid she might be ill. I thought perhaps tomorrow, since I have the day off, I might walk around to her home and inquire about her."

Fade looked up sharply. "Do you know the address?"

"Yes. Something called 'Cow Bay' off Worth Street."

His knife clattered as he threw it down. "For God's sake, Emily, that's right in the middle of the Five Points! You certainly will not walk there. Why, that's one of the worst areas of the city."

"But it is not very far from here."

"All the same, you might as well cross the Red Sea for the difference between this neighborhood and that. Don't you know that the flood of immigrants who arrive in droves every day at the wharfs head straight there to find a place to live? It has become a tenement shantytown and I won't hear of you going into it."

Emily jabbed at the pastry with her fork. "I know Bridget comes from a poor family, but she herself is a lovely girl. I care about her, Fade, and I hate to think she might be ill with no one to help her."

"If she lives down there, she probably has twenty people to help her, all living in the same room. I mean it, Emily, you are *not* to go into that section of the city, alone or with anyone else. I don't give you many orders, but that is one I certainly must insist upon."

"Oh, very well," Emily said grudgingly. "Let's talk about something more pleasant. I had a letter from Father today and he has actually invited me to come and visit him at Southernwood. However, he didn't say anything about you coming too, so I don't really think I should go."

"Nonsense. It will be good for you and for him. I have no wish to go, but it would please me to know that your family ties have not been irrevocably broken. Besides, you could take some money to Matilda for me and bring back word of my mother."

"Do you think so? I confess I would like to go back. It's such a dear place to me."

"By all means, go. I shall be so busy selling my palm hats I shall hardly miss you."

She began gathering up the plates. "In that case I shall not go at all."

Reaching up, he pulled her down and kissed her squarely on the lips. "You don't really believe that, do you?"

Emily smiled at him. "No. But you are so euphoric over those ridiculous hats that it just might happen."

Fade placed the palm hat back on his head and admired it in the mirror just across the room. "They will be the rage, I promise you."

With a swish of her skirt, Emily carried the tray of dishes

to the sideboard and picked up the small glass servant's bell. "You'll probably wear that thing to bed tonight!"

It was late spring before Emily finally returned to Southern-wood, and what she found there disturbed her greatly. On her second day home, she went searching for Garret, determined to have a few moments alone with him. Though he was on his way out, he grudgingly agreed to a brief talk on the bench near the orchard.

"I do think you might have let me know how ill Papa was, Garret. I would have come up here without waiting for an invitation if I'd had any idea of the extent of his deterioration. He certainly was not this bad the last time he visited me in town."

Garret Deveroe slouched on the bench and stretched his legs out in front of him, tipping his chin so the sun shone full on his face. He had such a pounding headache that it was difficult to concentrate on his sister's complaints, so he simply tuned them out as he had long ago learned to do.

"He shakes so now with the palsy," Emily went on, "that I don't think he could walk even a short distance."

"His frailty is deceiving," Garret answered, "as you will soon discover if you want something from him that he does not wish to give."

Emily watched her brother without attempting to hide her contempt. "What have you been trying to do? If you've been badgering him..."

"Did he say that?"

"He told me a little."

"No doubt."

"You should not upset him, Garret. Not now of all times."

"Did he explain to you that what I'm trying to do is not at all unreasonable? He clings to the hope that the Sparta dock will grow prosperous again when half the county is using the new dock at Sing Sing. All I want him to do is to face reality. But no—he must always make the decisions, and his opinions are always the right ones. He complains that I don't help him with the business, but when I try to, he dismisses my ideas as so much nonsense. He is impossible!"

Emily adjusted her straw hat to keep the sun from her eyes. There was some truth in what Garret said, she knew. "Perhaps if you could just humor him a little, not be so adamant about what you think should be done."

"Humph! I can see you doing that if you had any opinions about the business. But with you, of course, he would listen attentively, do as you recommend, and then tell everyone how clever you are. Bah!"

"Oh, Garret, that's not true. You have always exaggerated my relationship with him. He gets just as annoyed with me as with you."

"Oh yes. He disowned you when you married Frederick Whitman and here you are, just one year later, back in his good graces."

"But I wrote to him first, remember."

Garret stretched and stood up, straightening his fancy velvet riding coat. "He was ready to take you back the day after the wedding. Heaven forbid I should try something like that. I'd never see the inside of this house again. But no matter. The business will be mine someday—if there is anything left of it. We'll see then if my opinions are worth anything."

"Where are you going?"

"To the village to have a jug or two. Your company is delightful, sister dear, but only for so long. Then one must be about the serious business of the day."

"Papa says you are drinking far too much."

Garret's eyes flared with anger, but his thin lips twisted in a smile. He looked down at his sister with cold eyes. "I'm sure he thinks so."

Emily watched him as he made toward the stables, noting the fashionable cut of his fine clothes and his self-assured walk. Garret was an enigma to her. She wished she could understand him. He had intelligence and talent, but he never seemed able to free them from the heavy burden of his jealousy and bitterness. Now that she had returned to Southernwood, she was more concerned than ever about the situation here. Her father's illness had progressed so much more rapidly than the doctors had expected that now when he walked across a room he had to stop frequently to regain his balance. As his physical condition grew weaker, his stubborn anger against Garret seemed to grow in strength, whetting their longstanding antipathy. She was too far removed now to be of any help to either man, and so found herself standing by helplessly as the situation worsened. If only Josh would allow Fade a place in the family! She felt sure her husband could help, as a buffer between father and son if nothing else. But though her father was prepared to forgive her, he was not yet ready to go that far. Nor did Fade want any such concession.

Closing her eyes, she leaned back and listened to the quiet sounds of the country around her, drinking in the heady aroma of the fruit trees mingled with the fragrance of the lilacs and wild white dogwood her grandmother had tended so long ago. Soon her father would wake from his daily nap and she would join him for tea, pouring from the fine old pear-shaped silver teapot, taking sugar from the polished bowl, sipping from fluted Worcester cups.

Oh she did love it here. It was home and it was beautiful and it was dear. It was perfect until she remembered the shabby little brick house on Provost Street. But a warmth stirred within her when she thought of Fade coming home to that house. No, Southernwood was not perfect and it never would be unless he was there to share it with her. *Perfect* meant being with him, no matter where.

❧ Six

BY THE NEXT year Fade's small business had done so well that Emily was able to hire Bridget away from the Infant School and take her on as a personal maid. By the following year it was successful enough to allow Fade to quit his job with Collins and Thompson and set up his own small shop. In place of a corner on the top floor of Wilkins's warehouse, he now held the entire floor and it was jammed with a collection of merchandise as varied as it was practical, moved in from the docks and out to the stores of New York's outlying communities with a rapidity that stunned its enterprising manager. Using his "nose for business," as he continued to call it, Fade picked his cargoes with an uncanny instinct backed up by a careful reading of the political and economic scene. When he chose wrong, as occasionally he did, he wrote it off quickly and sold the merchandise at a reduced price, sometimes hiring out vendors to hawk it on the streets if nothing else worked. For the most part, the profits he made went into more and varied products, allowing a small but steady growth in his business. The one concession he made to Emily was to allow her to look for a house in a better neighborhood, but even then he kept a strict rein on her decorating budget.

By the fourth year they were settled in a lovely old house near St. Paul's Chapel, which Emily had fitted out in a style that was gracious and comfortable. Her joy was complete when, after longing for so many years to have a baby, she at last found herself pregnant. When she miscarried in her third month her disappointment took all the joy from her life for a time, but she soon recovered her natural good spirits and resolved to try again.

"At least now I know I'm not completely barren," she said resolutely to her husband, and went back to filling her life with charity works, concerts, lectures, and frequent trips to the Park Theater.

By 1835, when she celebrated her sixth wedding anniversary, Emily was convinced that Fade was going to prosper in a way she had never dreamed possible when she fell in love with him. Her pride in her husband's achievements was the crowning touch to her love for him. When Josh himself, sick and infirm in body but still mentally alert, began to make guarded compliments and even went so far as to admit that perhaps he had been a little hasty in his judgment of Fade Whitman, Emily knew she had won. She looked to the future with confidence, sure that eventually a warm relationship would grow up between her father and her husband. Now, if only she could also have a baby, her happiness would be complete.

One warm afternoon that spring Emily was surprised to see her husband walking up the street toward their house at a time when he should normally be busy at the docks. Beside him was a tall, cadaverous man with a thick black beard and the angular stride of one who is more at home in the woods than on a city street. When they entered the parlor and Fade introduced him as his brother Jesse, her shock almost took her breath away.

Jesse Whitman resembled his brother only in the darkness of their skin and hair. He was so tall that his lanky, angular frame seemed to fill the low parlor. Although he wore the fringed-leather sumac-colored shirt of a frontiersman and spoke in the uncultured accents of the Whitmans in Sparta, Emily found herself warming to him as they talked around the supper table. He was honest and unpretentious and he had the look of a man who has known many adventures.

"I tell you, Fade," he said, lounging in his supper chair and gripping a tankard of beer, "you ought to chuck all this merchant's life and head for the west. A man can be a man out there with no one to tell him he's better nor worse than the next fellow. And there's fortunes to be made as well. Big fortunes."

"I'm doing all right here, Jesse. Better than anyone else in the family ever has."

"But this is pennies. I'm talkin' about dollars. Why, you could spend a few years there and come back and sit at your father-in-law's table without battin' an eye. Excusin' the reference, ma'am."

Emily muttered something in reply. She was acutely conscious that Jesse was having some trouble with the idea that Fade's wife was Josh Deveroe's daughter, and he seemed to feel she had brought herself down in the world by marrying him. The fact that in all these years her husband had not once been invited to sit at his father-in-law's table did not help matters.

"There ain't no aristocrats out there, Fade, like back here in New York. Old Hickory Jackson has helped put snobbery here in the east to rest somewhat, but it ain't gone completely and won't be as long as there's old money to cling to. It gives some men the idea they're better'n others and nothin' will change that. It's un-American."

Fade glanced at his wife, sharing something of her discomfort yet intrigued by his brother's description of frontier life. "But that is changing, Jesse. Why, in just the last few years I've seen men make great fortunes in manufacturing. I may be only a small merchant, but there are plenty of others who could buy and sell me."

"Yes, by working the sweat off'n poorer men."

"That's true, and that's why I don't care about getting into the business of mills and factories. But at least allow that those who do sometimes make themselves very rich."

Jesse threw back the lapel of his leather jacket and scratched at the checkered shirt underneath with a long finger. For an uncomfortable moment Emily wondered if this outdoorsman was bringing into her house creatures she did not really wish to have there.

"And they'll set themselves up as aristocrats in time, mark my words. The whole system back east is rotten. Give me the clean air and free movement of the west anytime. You can be anything you want out there. An enterprising fellow like you would end up king of the hill, mark my words!"

"Come now, Jesse. You exaggerate. My education is severely limited and what I do know is mostly self-taught."

"So? You have a way about you that men look to, and that's all you need out there. Why, in time, I've no doubt they'd even send you to Washington City to the Congress."

"Won't you have some more beer, Jesse?" Emily cried, jumping up from the table and growing more and more uneasy at the enthusiastic fire in her husband's eye. "And there's more mutton left. How about another slice?"

"No, no, I've plenty, thank you, ma'am," Jesse answered, looking as though he had just remembered she was there. Moving restlessly around the room, Emily fussed with the fire, then refilled her husband's glass.

"Surely you aren't telling us the whole story, Jesse," she said tentatively, settling back at the table. "I've heard horrible tales of savages and wild beasts and towns where law is unknown. Is there no truth in those stories?"

Jesse stroked his thick beard in long, slow pulls. "Yes, there is some truth in them stories. Savages there are a'plenty and one of the first things a man has to learn when he comes across them is how to behave in such a manner as to keep his scalp. Even then..."

He coughed, as though made uncomfortable by the memory of scenes too horrible to tell. Emily glanced at Fade, who was leaning forward, hanging on every word.

"As for wild beasts... well, one gets to know the forests pretty quick. Sometimes it's a friend and sometimes it ain't. As for the towns, they may be rough at times, but if you learn to hold your liquor and to use your fists proper, why you're respected soon enough. And what man would want to be respected for anythin' more?"

Fade watched his brother without really seeing him. His

mind was far away in the free, open hills of a country where a man could really be a man—strong, unbridled, independent. Suddenly his world of counting houses, merchandise, and account books all seemed grubby and confining, a dark constrained world where a man choked out his life in endless bondage to the clink of coins.

"How long will you be staying with us, Jesse?" Emily broke in, forcing her eyes away from her husband.

"Oh, just the night, thank ye, ma'am. I thought to take the steam packet upriver tomorrow and stay a few days at the house, just to say hello to Matilda and Florrie and see how Ma is gettin' on."

Emily could barely hide her relief. "Did Fade tell you? Matilda has three children and her husband, Jim, has a job working on the new aqueduct."

"What about Florrie?" Jesse asked his brother.

Fade's eyes shifted to his wife. Florrie was a subject they had avoided discussing since the girl's unfortunate marriage at sixteen, when she was already six months gone with child.

"As wild as always. A husband and two children have done nothing to tame her. We might as well accept the fact that she'll always be a disgrace to the family."

"She wants a good beatin'. She always did. Trouble was Ma got sick when Florrie was still too little to learn her better."

"Well," Emily said, trying to make her voice light, "perhaps we should be thinking of bed. Fade has to rise early, you know, to open the shop."

She rose, hoping, but both men kept their seats. "Why don't you go ahead, dear," Fade finally said. "I don't often get a chance to talk to Jesse and I'd like to hear more about what he's been doing these last years."

"But you'll be so tired tomorrow."

"I'll be up soon."

Fighting to keep down her fear and irritation, Emily turned away, leaving the two men looking after her. Somehow she sensed it was important that Fade not let her win in front of his brother. "Very well, then. Good night," she said, and left the room. She knew they would talk long into the night and Fade would be exhausted all the next day, but he would recover from that soon enough. What really concerned her was his look of growing interest and involvement with each new description of the frontier. If not for her, he would be off tomorrow; she knew that now. It frightened her to think that his ties to her might not be strong enough to hold him here against every other inclination of his heart.

Carrying a single candle, she walked slowly up the stairs to their bedroom, that special place where she and Fade had known so many happy hours of passion and intimacy. She set the candle down on the dressing table, where it threw a soft halo of light against the darkness, and began to pull absently at the buttons of her dress.

Tomorrow she would write to her father, and if that did not work she would go and see him. Somehow, soon, she would see that Fade was drawn into the Deveroe business. It was the only answer and it must be done. The sooner the better.

The following day Jesse Whitman left for Mount Pleasant and with his departure some of Emily's worries subsided. As the days passed and no more was said about the delights of the frontier, she began to think her concern had been exaggerated. Fade himself never mentioned it again, and indeed he seemed more involved than ever in his small but substantial business. By badgering her father Emily did at last manage an invitation for both of them to visit Southernwood, but it did her little good. Fade absolutely refused to set foot in the place.

"But Papa wants you to come. And you're my husband. You deserve to be there."

Laying down his quill, Fade studied her face across the open pages of his ledger book. Her large, expressive eyes were filled with earnest pleading. No doubt she sincerely believed she was thinking of his own good, but he knew her well enough now to realize when she was determined to win her point. This was one he would not concede, however, and she might as well learn it now. Old Joshua Deveroe might forgive him for marrying his daughter, but it would be a long time before Fade would forget that the old man had called him a bastard and accused him of wanting only the Deveroe money.

"No, Emily. I will not. Don't keep badgering me about it, for my mind is made up. You can go visit your father as often as you want, but leave me out of it—and that's final."

Emily turned away, biting her lip. Damn him. He could be so stubborn sometimes. All right. She would have to drop the subject for now, but she was determined to raise it again. She'd find a way to tie him to Southernwood somehow, if it was the last thing she ever did.

From their house near St. Paul's Chapel the strident sound of the alarm was clearly audible. Fire was so prevalent in New York that Fade at first did not bother to look up from his book as Emily walked to the window and pulled back the heavy drapes. Though she could see nothing at all on their narrow street in the cold December night, the cacophony of bells from Broadway had a frantic quality that suggested this was no simple one-family house suddenly aflame. When the big bass church bells began to add to the clamor of the alarm and to echo from points all around them, they both sensed that something out of the ordinary was happening.

Fade was already pulling on his heavy, three-collared greatcoat to have a look, when there came a frantic banging at the door. Emily pushed past him to open it, finding a stammering young boy on the step, almost incoherent.

"It's Jamie Dann," Fade said behind her. "One of the Wilkins's apprentices."

"God bless. Mister Whitman, come quick," Jamie cried, yanking off his woolen cap. "It's fire—the worst I ever seen!"

"Not the warehouse?" Fade's face had gone suddenly white. He threw Emily one worried glance and was out the door, followed on his heels by the Dann boy. "Wait!" Emily called, grabbing for her heavy cloak and bonnet. "I'm coming with you."

Paying her no attention, they set off at a run down the street, leaving Emily to keep up as best she could. As soon as she reached Broadway, she became part of a crowd streaming toward the docks, a running, noisy mob filled with curiosity and a swelling excitement, jostling each other with mindless urgency. Emily strained to see Fade's hat bobbing ahead of her and pushed her way around others who were as eager as she to reach the blazing scene. As she came nearer to the wavering red nimbus that filled the night sky, Emily felt the hairs rise on the back of her neck. It was obvious from the long fingers of flame thrusting high into the air that this was no ordinary fire.

It had started on Merchant Street, a narrow, crooked alley

between Hanover and Pearl lined with tall, newly built dry
goods and hardware stores. But by the time Emily and Fade
arrived, the flames were leaping like lightning in every direction. They had already leveled the buildings on Merchant and
spread to the closest stores on Pearl, turning the street into one
long wall of flame. Merchants were trying frantically to save
their stock by pulling their wares from the flaming buildings
and piling them into the narrow roadway. Around these mountains of goods people massed, getting as close as they could
bear the heat: merchants, their wives and children; mechanics,
some of whom showed open delight at the ruin of those richer
than themselves; solemn onlookers trying to help the harassed
firemen who struggled to get water from frozen hydrants.

Emily wrapped her shawl tighter around her shoulders and
looked on helplessly as yet another row of stores and warehouses flashed into life under a wall of fire. When she was
able to make her way through the crowd to the Old Slip she
found Fade there, running in and out of Wilkins's trying to
salvage all he could of his valuable stock. Emily eagerly joined
the group of apprentices, friends, and sympathetic strangers
who were helping to empty the warehouse. Then she took her
turn standing guard over the growing pile of goods, hoping that
somehow the fire would be stopped before it got this far and
trying to discourage the ominous-looking men in ragged clothes
who eyed the bolts of cloths and bales of spices and teas,
looking for an excuse to begin looting. Near her, some of them
had already broken into the crates of wine and champagne
pulled from the burning buildings, and several were roaring
drunk. Emily could hear them laughing and calling: "This will
make the aristocracy haul in their horns . . ." and recognized
the cant with which the Tammany politicians fomented unrest
among the city's poor. Yet the dismay on her husband's face
soon drove away any indignation. It had been a hopeless task
to try to empty Wilkins's warehouse, for the fire, restlessly
sweeping in all directions, was carried by the wind toward the
huge mounds of valuables piled in the streets. Fade saw his
entire stock disappear in one great mountain of flame. He
cursed, he pleaded with a silent God, he very nearly wept; and
try as she would, there was nothing Emily could do to comfort
him. If there was any consolation to be had in seeing other
men go down with him, Fade might look for it there, as street
after street in the first ward was enveloped by flames.

They stayed all night, watching with sick horror as the fire blazed: from Pearl Street to Coentis Slip, Wall Street to the river, all of South and Water Streets, Exchange Street including Post's stores and Lord's beautiful row, William, Beaver, and Stone streets—all utterly destroyed.

There were some scenes of awesome beauty that Emily would never forget: the graceful statue of Alexander Hamilton, only a few months on its pedestal, silhouetted against a yellow sea of flames before it fell, crushed under the collapsed dome of the new Merchant's Exchange; the dome itself, outlined for a moment against the night sky, caving in like a jelly sculpture and crashing into the building below; the bright gold ball and star above the Rev. Dr. Matthews Church on Garden Street gleaming brilliantly in a planetary explosion just before they disappeared into the chaos below.

The fire raged on into the next day, leaving behind streets of scorched, blackened ruins. Wandering among them the following day, Emily was struck once again by images she would never forget, not for their beauty but for their stark despair: a mountain of ruined coffee at the corner of Old Slip and South Street; bales of worthless tea; stacks upon stacks of half-burned silks, prints, laces; mud, streaked with a blend of indigo and rich drugs, oozing in the streets.

Every hour the crowds of spectators grew, as did the hordes of looters picking through the ruins for anything of value. Companies of soldiers and patrols of private citizens were called out in an attempt to keep away the worst of the crowds, but the enormity of the disaster was too great to prevent all but the most flagrant from taking what they wished.

A few days later, Fade and several other grim-faced associates sat down with Mr. Wilkins to review the extent of the damage.

"Everything's gone," Wilkins began, his face looking as though it had been carved out of flint. "The goods, the buildings, the stores, the records—nothing was saved."

"But the insurance . . . ?" one of the men ventured hopefully.

"Gentlemen, I won't try to delude you. Over six hundred buildings were totally destroyed in this fire and property and goods of at least fifteen million dollars. The collective capitals of all our insurance offices are recorded at less than twelve million. We'll be lucky if they can come up with fifty percent on the losses, and I'm not likely to get that much since I pared my insurance costs three years ago to cut overhead. It was a risk—a gamble—and I have now lost. If you are ruined, so am I, for whatever consolation that offers."

"Brown and Hone, John Schermerhorn, Samuel Howland, the names would fill a book," the gentleman sitting next to Fade broke in, leaning his head in his hands. "This is the most terrible calamity in the history of our city."

Fade stared down at the table, growing sicker inside by the minute. Hone, Schermerhorn, Howland—they could all rebuild. They had friends, connections, other resources. But everything he had was tied up in this fledgling business that now lay among the ashes and rubble littering the Old Slip. How would he manage to purchase the goods to fill orders for which he had already received a commission? He would have to borrow on his house just to return the money.

"Well, the stockbrokers will get nothing; perhaps they are worse off than we," he heard another voice say, grasping at a crumb of consolation.

What did he care about stockholders? He only saw years of scratching and scrambling to get that first foothold again, tied to ledgers and manifests, entombed in the dark recesses of the counting house for the rest of his life. His stomach turned over at the thought.

Next to him, Isaac Jones, who had lost the entire contents of his dry goods store, drummed his fingers on the table.

"I still can't believe it," he exclaimed. "Nineteen blocks. The whole first ward. It's worse than the great fire of 1776."

"Much worse. That involved mostly homes. This was the whole of a merchandising community."

"We shall have to rebuild, that's all," Wilkins said grimly. "We must throw off despondency and begin working to redeem this terrible loss."

Fade could not answer. At that moment he wanted only to die.

"How bad is it?"

Emily was almost afraid to ask, seeing the bleakness in his eyes. Fade reached for the glass of rye whiskey she had just poured him and gulped it down, wiping his arm across his mouth. Absently she thought she had not seen him make that gesture in many years.

"As bad as can be. Wilkins was not able to save anything—not one piece of his total inventory."

"But surely the insurance . . . ?"

"He had very little. It was a cost-cutting risk I knew about and shared in since it cut my costs as well. Some owners will get at least fifty percent, but he'll be lucky to receive ten. There's a committee attempting to raise a fund for the merchants, but they've already announced that they must be selective."

Emily clenched her fists in her lap. "I can get your name at the head of the list. My father knows Mr. Hone well, and Mr. Schermerhorn."

"No! I don't want any favors because you are a Deveroe. If they won't do it for Fade Whitman, they'll not do it for Emily Deveroe."

"But, Fade, it's your future. Your life."

Slamming down his glass, Fade rose and moved to the window, looking through the curtain without seeing the street at all. "It's not my life. I still have my life and my health. I'll start over, that's all. That's what everybody else is doing."

"But, my dear, with what? When you first began you had at least a little capital. There is none of that now. Oh, how I wish I had not spent so much furnishing this house."

"It doesn't matter. We'll put together something. There are a few things left to mortgage or sell—my watch or some of your jewelry. Or I'll go back to Mr. Collins. He never wanted me to leave in the first place."

The tone of his voice as he spoke those words tore at Emily's heart. She knew that was the last thing in life he wanted—to be imprisoned once again in a counting house, laboring long hours to add to another man's prosperity. She went to him, slipping her arms around his waist and then leaning against him.

"We'll think of something, my love. There must be a way out. All we need do is find it."

For once he did not even smile indulgently at her brave words.

For the first few months after the fire Fade tried valiantly to rebuild from the ashes of his former business. Because he would not accept help from Josh Deveroe, who for once was willing to offer it, or any of the Deveroes' wealthy friends, his task was that much more difficult. As the weeks went by he began to realize that this attempt to rebuild his business was unfortunately coming at a time when the nation's economy was growing more and more unstable.

"It's President Jackson," Emily raged at each new discouragement. "If he hadn't started this disastrous war on the bank we would not all be in this mess. That crazy old man!"

"He knows what he's doing," Fade answered quietly, not really believing his own words.

"You always defend him because he sides with the rabble. He wants to break men who have money, who know how to handle it, who have always known how to handle it."

"The aristocracy, you mean."

"Now you sound like that mob, the rabble that roams and riots in the streets."

"They riot because they cannot afford the price of bread. Neither can we. At times I think the only answer is to go crawling back to Mr. Collins, yet when I think of the ten dollars a week I would earn, I know we could not live on it in these inflationary times. I tell you, Emily, I don't know what to do."

And then the answer came, an answer Fade in his secret heart had waited for. His brother Jesse returned to New York and this time, when he spun tales of the opportunities of the frontier, there was nothing to hold Fade back. Nothing except his wife, who thought her heart would break at the prospect of his leaving.

"You can't love me and do this," she cried, clinging to him. "You are my whole life and yet you will turn your back on me and walk away, leaving me alone."

"Emily dearest, it is only for a short time, I promise. Jesse has an idea that I could do the same kind of thing I did here, but without the competition and the enormous capital needed in New York. I know I could make it work again, and as soon as I get a little money together, I'll send for you. You know I will."

"And what will I do in the meantime? Live here in New York? Without you?"

"Of course not. You'll go stay with your father at Southernwood. That won't be so terrible, will it? You know how you love the place."

"Not without you," Emily wailed. She could not believe he was doing this to her. It was too much to bear.

Breaking into tears, she threw herself down on their bed, hiding her face with her hands. He knew he should go to her, hold her and reassure her that this was for the best, yet something held him back. He did not really wish to analyze this feeling, for he sensed there was something of anger in it—anger because she refused to see the wisdom of this move; and something of fear—a terrible fear that she would somehow work her wiles to get him to change his mind.

Well, he was not going to change his mind. He was determined to go, convinced it was his best hope. It might cost her something, but all these years of struggling in the moneyed world of the city had cost him something too. Now it was time he put his own wishes first.

Emily wept, feeling the gulf between them. This was the first time her distress had not brought him running to comfort her. A cold knot of fear grew deep within her at the thought that she was losing her power over him. With every fiber of her being she longed for him to hold her in his arms and tell her how much he loved her and wanted only her happiness. Instead he stood across the room like a statue.

"There is no need for you to carry on so," he said quietly. "I'll send for you just as soon as possible, or if it turns out I can make some quick capital, I'll come back here for you. For God's sake, have a little trust in me."

She felt as if there was a lump of heavy, uncooked dough swelling in her chest, choking off her breath. After all the disappointments of the past year—the fire, the hard work, the poverty of their lives—this was too much.

"Let me at least go with you," she cried. "Don't leave me behind. I don't care what the difficulties are as long as we can be together. Take me with you, please, Fade."

He looked away. This was the most difficult plea of all to answer. There would be danger and there would be hardships, but he knew her well enough to know that she could probably deal with both as courageously as he. It was not fear for her safety but something far more insidious that held him back. It was the siren call of freedom, the guilty longing to do exactly as he pleased and go anywhere his fancy took him, unencumbered, even by love.

"No. No, it would be far too dangerous. Give me time to find the right place for us to live, one that will not be too difficult or too primitive for you. Then I'll come and get you, you know I will. You have my solemn promise, Emily."

Sensing something of what he was feeling, Emily wiped her eyes with her handkerchief and steeled herself to accept what she could not change. He had to have this time, much as she hated to give it to him. He had to work this western fever out of his blood. She had seen the seed planted during Jesse Whitman's first visit to their home and she had guessed then that someday Fade would follow this star.

"All right. At least I'll be able to take care of Papa."

For the first time a smile flitted across his lips. "That's my girl."

"And you'll write to me, often. Lots of letters."

"All the time. Long letters full of my adventures."

"Oh, Fade. You will be careful? It's so dangerous."

Moving to the bed, he sat down beside her, slipping his arm around her shoulders. "I'll be careful, I promise. All I'm interested in is making a future for us, not taming the wilds of the frontier."

She leaned her head against him, slipping her arm inside his coat, exulting in the feel of his strong hand on her neck and the gentle whisper of his lips on her forehead. He loved her, she knew that. And he would come back, she knew that too. But oh, dear God, keep him safe while they were apart and let them be together again soon. For without him, her life was not worth living.

In the following weeks Fade and Emily sold everything they owned that could be converted into quick cash, except for a few pieces of old jewelry that Emily refused to part with. Part of their capital went into supplies needed for the trip and a small store of stock. The rest went into hard specie with which to finance both the long journey and the business opportunity that might lie at its end. Fade insisted that Emily set aside one hundred dollars for her own use even though she would be living in her father's house. Recognizing his need to provide for her, she reluctantly agreed. He was anxious to take her up to Southernwood himself, but she absolutely refused.

"I've taken the packet upriver so many times I could pilot

it myself," she said. "Bridget will be with me, and no doubt Absolem will be waiting at the dock with the gig. Besides, you'd only have to turn around and come back to New York again afterward. No, my dear, I'd rather say good-bye here in the place where we've been so happy."

"Not good-bye. This is only a temporary separation. I want you to keep remembering that."

"I'll try. I promise I'll try."

Emily kept a tight hold on her emotions when she was around him, though in private she frequently gave way to a grief that threatened to choke the breath out of her. Her determination to be strong was helped by Fade's obvious enthusiasm for the trip. If she sometimes felt that their impending separation was less painful for him than it was for her, she laid it to the fact that he was facing a new adventure while she was going back to a place she knew well, where her primary role would be to deal with a sick father and an unpleasant brother. In all honesty she admitted that if their positions were reversed it was possible she might not be exactly overwhelmed with grief either.

Her husband knew what she was feeling. Sometimes in the still hours before dawn, when anticipation kept sleep away, Fade would stand at their bedroom window looking down at the darkened street and thanking his stars for this opportunity. Oh yes, there was guilt—guilt that he should be so happy and she so miserable; guilt that his life promised adventure and excitement and hers bleak drudgery. But down in the deepest recesses of his soul he knew, too, that he was glad of the chance to go away and be on his own once more.

Something inside Fade turned over, making him feel sick. He walked away from the window, determined to go downstairs and look over his invoices once more. He heard Emily stir and sigh before drifting off again into a soft, silent sleep.

How could he wish to be free of this woman, the dearest thing in his life? Leaving her behind would be like leaving a part of his own body behind. No, this trip was a necessary step toward rebuilding their fortune, so that he could establish her once more in the comfortable life she had always known. He was doing this for Emily, and just as soon as it was practical and possible, he would see that she was there to share it with him.

*   *   *

On an overcast day in late August, Emily said good-bye to her husband on the landing at the foot of Barkley Street where the North River steamboats took on passengers for the trip upriver. From the deck of the sloop *Cornelia* she watched him standing on the dock, waving his hat to her until he became an indistinguishable blur in the crowd of people milling around the pier. She tried to etch into her memory the lean face with its long sideburns, its wide, shapely mouth and dark eyes. Her heart was breaking but she stood firm and smiling, waving her white handkerchief with as much brave cheer as she could summon.

As the *Cornelia* moved up the Hudson and left the city behind, Emily turned and went downstairs to the salon. There she found a chair in the corner where she could face the window and pretend to be absorbed by the river view while silent tears ran like raindrops down her white cheeks.

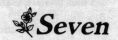

Seven

GARRET DEVEROE yanked on the reins, snatching his horse's head sharply back and pulling the flying hooves to an abrupt stop. Hearing the clatter on the bricks in the yard in front of the stables, a boy came running out to take the halter while Garret swung himself out of the saddle.

"Damned ruffian, I'll teach you to defy me," Garret cried, and with a *whump* brought his crop furiously down against the beast's sleek neck. Shrieking with fright, the horse sheered back, dragging the boy, who was clinging to the halter and trying at the same time to avoid the blows of the whip.

Whoosh, whoosh, whump! Garret flailed the terrified animal again and again until finally, his rage spent, he threw the crop across the yard into the shrubbery lining the stable walls. By then Wilton had come running out to help the stableboy, who was fast losing the battle to manage the terrified animal.

"Saints alive, Mr. Garret," Wilton sputtered, pulling the

horse under control, "that's a blooded animal you're raising welts on. If Mr. Josh could see ye, he—"

"Hold your tongue, you useless old man, or I'll take the same whip to you." Hoisting one boot onto the mounting block, Garret scraped at the encrusted mud. "That wretched animal tried to throw me. If I had my way I'd shoot it right here and now."

Wilton ran his hands over the welts rising on the horse's neck. He knew he should keep quiet, but abusing one of his horses was very nearly an unforgivable sin, even for old Josh's only son.

"There now, old dear. Quiet, now, quiet," he crooned softly, stroking the horse's neck. Anger rose in his throat like bile.

"Look at him, now, Mr. Garret. Covered with foam, his mouth all cut up. God knows I taught ye better."

"Mind your own business," Garret shouted, turning on the old man. "They're my horses and I'll treat them as I please. And you're my servant and the same goes for you. My father might put up with useless, nagging retainers, but I assure you I never will."

Wilton clamped his teeth together and glared murderously at Garret. If he was turned out now it would be difficult if not impossible to find a similar position. That fact tempered his longing to thrash this spoiled, abusive young cub within an inch of his life. The fine horse on which he had taken out his spleen was worth twenty Garrets.

Just at that moment Emily came riding into the yard on Thor and quickly took in the situation. She knew the horse to be spirited, but nothing he could have done should have earned him the state he was in. A little more of this harsh treatment and he would be ruined.

Ignoring the block, she slipped easily off her horse, hitched up her skirt, and waited for the stableboy to come and take Thor's reins.

Garret glanced over at her, standing so cool and poised, silently condemning him for his childish behavior.

"You had an excellent ride, I trust," she said coolly.

"No, I did not." He straightened up, adjusting the wide leather belt at his waist. "But obviously you did. Why, Emily, I'd wager that even when you are so daring as to risk a gallop, never a hair comes out of place."

"Oh, stop it. I take things slowly now because I haven't been doing much riding, but there was a time when a good gallop was my favorite thing."

"Oh, yes. That's how you came to meet the great Frederick, was it not? You, boy, what's your name?"

The young stablehand who had returned to take Thor stopped abruptly, afraid to look into the fierce, scowling face of the heir to Southernwood.

"John, sir."

"John what?"

"John Orser, sir."

"One never knows which of the river families the newest urchin represents," Garret muttered to his sister. "Well, John Orser, go over there and retrieve my riding whip for me."

Unsure, the boy looked at Emily, who was still waiting beside her horse.

"Go on, you brat, or I'll use it on you!"

She nodded. Relieved, the boy ran for the whip, quickly handed it over, then hurried to lead Thor away.

"My, Garret, you do enjoy bullying the weak, don't you?" Emily said, starting for the house.

Garret fell in step beside her. "It does them good. I learned very early that you can't let servants or horses get the upper hand. You ought to have heard Wilton a moment ago; that worthless old man attempted to scold me for the way I handle my own property. If I had my way I'd turn him out this very afternoon."

"He knows us both too well. After all, he's seen us grow up. He gave us our first riding lessons."

"What does that signify? Sentiment has no place in a business. I won't be like Father, who let that useless old Negro, Vestal lie around here for years after he was too infirm to work, simply because he had lived through the Revolution with Grandmother. I'd have had him out the minute he couldn't earn his keep. That's what's wrong with everyone around here: the estate is going to seed and the business is drying up, and all because of useless sentiment."

Emily tried to ignore Garret's complaints and enjoy the beauty of the grounds through which they walked. The brilliant fall colors had passed their zenith and were beginning their long descent into winter's bleakness, but there were still enough splashes of orange, red, and yellow to make the world seem a painter's palette. Dried leaves crunched deliciously under their feet and the heady scent of apples added a sweet pungency to the air. It was so beautiful; how she wished Fade were here to share it with her!

The thought of her husband brought tears welling to her eyes. She quickly glanced back at her brother's profile, shutting her mind to the memory of the face she loved so well. There was little about Garret to move one to tears. His youthful countenance was fast becoming set in lines of discontent, as though he were always noticing the faint odor of something rotten in the air. She wished she could understand the growing brutality and arrogance that led him to hurt animals and those beneath him. He was not unattractive, he had wealth, he had talents. Why was he not happy? The only answer she could think of was his strained relationship with their father. If she spent one day walking in Garret's shoes, always under the dominating thumb of a parent who made no secret of his dislike, who knows—perhaps she might wind up beating horses and intimidating servants too.

"Where did you go today, Garret?" she said, sounding a little more sympathetic. "Your horse was very winded."

"I was in the village, that's all. Perhaps I took him up the hill a trifle too fast, but the disgusting animal tried to throw me."

And what were you doing, she wanted to ask.

"You must have had something disagreeable happen in town."

"Indeed I did." Garret sniffed. "I ran into George Slade, Robert's father. From what he tells me—and he ought to know—we are on the verge of a panic. I've tried my best to get Father to sell off some of his worthless interests for hard cash, but of course he ignores me as always. He continues to invest in stocks that rise and fall with President Jackson's spleen, and worse yet, he stubbornly insists on accepting notes of credit from men who are 'friends of long standing.' A worse excuse for risk I can't think of. He never pays any attention to my suggestions, and now, if George Slade is right, we may be in a fair way of losing everything."

"Surely it cannot be that bad," Emily said. Garret was inclined to pessimism and in a question of business she would trust her father's instincts over her brother's any day.

"It will be, mark my words. Hard times have already hit New York—as you ought to know."

"That's certainly true. When I left the city I had never known prices at the market to be so high. Beef had gone up to twenty-five cents a pound and a small turkey cost as much as a dollar and a half. But I felt it was not bound to last."

"It will probably get even worse. There has been too much speculation and debt. Real money is more and more scarce. We could take advantage of the situation if that stubborn old man would only listen to me."

"How do you know so much about it?"

"I keep abreast of what is happening. And I have good instincts—damn it, I know I do, if I were only allowed to use them."

They had reached the porch, where Emily paused to look out over the shining river far below. It was a view she loved and never tired of seeing. To her surprise Garret paused, too, and looked out over the long, sloping hill, but his eyes were veiled to everything but his own concerns.

"It was the same with that useless copper mine and the outworn Sparta dock. He clings sentimentally to useless ventures and gets involved in crazy local speculations. Even the Dolphin yards continue to put out old-fashioned sloops and paddle steamers when it is speed everybody wants. Do you know that Captain Cobb has nearly finished building a steam packet to cross the ocean? We should be taking chances like that, not throwing good money after bad on ventures that have no chance of paying a good return."

"But you know how he loves the river boats and the old dock. They've been part of his life for so many years, he doesn't want to see them ruined because people desert them for new things."

"Bosh! That kind of sentiment is all right for songs around the drawing-room piano, but it's got no place in the counting house or office." He drummed his fingers absently against the worn old wooden column supporting the roof. "I could make this family wealthy again, I know I could. If George Slade is right and a panic is about to hit, mark my words: many men will go under. We could come out on top, if we only played it right."

"At the expense of other men's failures! Papa would never

do that. I am surprised that you would want to. By the way, did Mr. Slade speak of Robert? I have heard nothing of him for several months."

"He's very busy now since he was appointed to serve as an aide to our distinguished congressman from New York. He's enjoying Washington City—all the parties and the glamour. Imagine! Prim, proper Robert. No doubt he's the toast of the town belles."

"He has never married, then?"

"Not yet, but you can be sure someone will grab him. He has all the proper qualifications to suit the grandes dames eager to marry off their luscious little vestal virgins. It's only a matter of time."

"Oh, Garret, you are so cynical. Don't you ever enjoy anything?"

"Seldom. Most people have some kind of ulterior motive behind their pleasantries. I prefer honest, unadorned hostility; it's easier to deal with. Oh God, speaking of pleasantries, I think I hear old Agatha's voice inside. She must be paying the patriarch a visit."

Emily gathered up her skirt to enter the house. "How nice. I always enjoy Cousin Agatha."

"Then you may do the honors for us both," he said, starting back down the steps. "I'll escape up the side entrance to my room. Don't let on you've seen me."

Emily looked after him, shaking her head. Then, hearing Agatha's soft laughter, she eagerly opened the door and stepped into the hall.

There was a fire going in the back parlor, and the tea things on the table were a welcome sight. Carrying her riding hat, Emily moved to kiss her father, who was ensconced in a chair near the hearth, a plaid woolen lap robe over his knees. Then she crossed the room to greet her cousin, who was sitting on the sofa.

"Cousin Agatha, you look positively blooming today. And you've even got Papa smiling. What's the occasion?"

"Oh, Emily dear, I've had some wonderful news. I'm so excited I hardly know where to begin."

"I'm glad you're home, Emily," Josh said, smiling up at her. "Even if it means I have to hear it all over again. At least now we'll have the sound of someone else's voice in the room."

"Oh, Josh," Agatha said as she poured Emily a cup of the hot tea. "Have I bored you terribly with all my concerns? And here you are, a captive audience."

"Nonsense, Cousin Agatha," Emily said, taking the cup and sitting beside her on the sofa. "Papa loves company. You know he would throw you right out if he didn't enjoy you so much. Tell me your news."

"Well, I've had a letter from Annette, Nicholas's wife; he's taking her abroad on one of his sailing trips. They'll be gone nearly a year, and she has asked me to keep Claes, my grandson." Her voice bubbled in its happiness. "Isn't it wonderful? I'll have him with me for a whole year. Children keep you young, you know. Oh, I'm so sorry, I—"

"That's all right," Emily broke in, fastening her gaze on her cup. "I have quite recovered." With her father present she said no more about the miscarriage she had suffered in New York. Now that Fade was gone she wished more than ever that she had a child to console her, but there was no use in dwelling on hopeless thoughts. "I'm happy for you, Agatha. And for myself too. I will enjoy having Claes around as much as you will."

"He is only three and a half, you know, and will no doubt be a trial at times. But I won't mind. I'll be so happy to have him with me."

"Nicholas must be losing his faculties," Josh said, "to take his wife on such a voyage. Women don't belong on ships."

"It's done though, I understand, by some of the merchant captains when they have to be away for long stretches. I suppose it is a consolation for them. I could never get Elisha to take me with him, although I often longed to go."

"We will see that your young grandson has a wonderful time in Mount Pleasant," Emily said, setting down her cup. "And we must find a pony for him. I know just the one. I'll teach him to ride."

"Oh, not for a while, please. I don't want him to get hurt."

"Nonsense. Three years is just the right age to begin learning. He'll have no fear at all at that age."

"*She* had no fear at all," Josh said, laughing. "Emily took to a saddle like Nicholas to the deck of a ship. But here now, my girl, Agatha was not the only person today to receive an important letter."

Emily looked sharply at her father. He gave her such a teasing look that she was almost afraid to guess his meaning.

"What..." she began. Josh reached under the robe and pulled out a heavy folded envelope. He held it toward her, his hand trembling.

Emily came near to knocking over the tea table as she flew across the room to her father's side. It was from her husband, just as she had hoped, the first word since their separation.

"Oh," she cried, torn between wanting to tear it open on the spot and to save it for a private moment.

Her father seemed as pleased as she. "Why don't you take it upstairs and read it in your room? Agatha can tell me some more about how wonderful it will be to have Claes living with her for a while."

Clutching the envelope to her breast, Emily said, "Would you mind, Cousin Agatha?"

"Not at all, dear. Please go. Your father, in his good-natured way, has castigated me so much that I shall be embarrassed to mention my grandson's name. But since he has already made the mistake of asking me to dinner, I shall only promise to stay off the subject until then."

Josh lifted a weak arm and laid his shaking fingers on Emily's hand. "Perhaps then you can tell us something of what Fade writes. Go along now and read your letter."

She kissed him lightly on the top of his thinning hair. "Thank you, Papa," she said, and fled the room.

The letter had been written weeks before, at Harrisburg, just before Fade began the great passage west over the Alleghen Mountains. For Emily, even Fade's almost indecipherable scraw was dear. Although skimpy on specific details, his letter expressed an excitement and anticipation she could not help bu envy even as she devoured every word. The trip so far ha been uneventful: Philadelphia—"a beautiful city, so muc neater and more clean than our New York"—to Lancaster b coach and thence to Harrisburg, where Jesse was to meet him The farther west he went, the more strange and unreal he foun both the country and the people. "It is difficult to imagine whe you have lived near a great city all your life what an enormou and empty country lies just a few hundred miles away. S many of the people are from Europe, but for a New Yorker does not seem so strange to be surrounded by a body of men all speaking other languages. Some of them, the Germans particularly, have set up their own little fatherland out here on the edge of the wilderness. It is a strange feeling to be among them in your own native land and feel a foreigner!"

He was especially impressed by the Indians. "You remember, Emily, those poor, starving remnants of the Algonquian nation we were accustomed to see in Mount Pleasant? These men are as different as night from day. They are tall and dignified, even proud! They look at you as though they could easily take your scalp right there and never feel a qualm, which no doubt is true, for although they make an attempt to deal with the settlers, their enmity lies just under the surface. While waiting for Jesse, I spend a part of every day practicing with my rifle, for I suspect one's instincts for survival out here ought to be honed to a very sharp edge.

"So far there's been no chance to track the wilderness, but I suppose that will come once we leave the rivers behind. I cannot get over the land here in the west—great quantities of it—rich forests, mountains, wonderful rivers, thousands of acres of forest, and barely a town or settlement in between. There is opportunity here, I know it. One has only to find the means. There are also thieves and rascals and fellows like me who are searching out their fortune, as well as not a few violent men trying to escape their past. I keep my money well hidden, I assure you, and I look behind me at all times."

"I miss you, my dear, and a thousand times a day long for you to be here sharing all this with me. Yet the dangers you would be exposed to are far too great to satisfy such a selfish wish. It is a comfort to me to know that you are safe and comfortable with your father."

Over and over Emily read the last sentences, hoping they were true. It was not difficult to see that Fade was enjoying his journey so much he surely could not be thinking of her very often. And as welcome as his letter was, it had been written weeks ago. Where had he gone since? There was not a single line about his final destination or even the next stop on his journey. How frustrating it was to always wonder!

She kissed the pages and cried over them, rejoicing that she had them. It was at least a small link with this man who meant the world to her.

* * *

During the next two weeks a subtle change was felt at Southernwood. Emily could not put her finger on what was happening, but it seemed as though a dark cloud now hovered over everyone. Perhaps it was because Agatha had left for Boston to spend some time with her daughter-in-law before bringing her grandson to the estate. Or, as Emily mused to herself, perhaps it was her own melancholy—the aftermath of Fade's letter. Her father seemed withdrawn and her brother was more caustic and unpleasant than usual. Once she heard the two of them quarreling bitterly in Josh's study, more like embittered enemies than father and son. She was about to intervene when Garret stomped out and flew from the house in his gig.

"Papa, couldn't you attempt to get along better with Garret?" she asked Josh the next day as he leaned on her arm, shuffling down the walk to sit in the garden. He was more feeble than ever, as though the scene the night before had drained what little strength he had left.

Josh's pale face hardened at the mention of his son. "There is no way to get along with that boy. Sometimes I wonder if he is not a changeling and no son of mine at all." Gasping for breath, he fell into the chair Emily pulled up for him. She settled a rug over his knees and sat down on the bench opposite, drawing her cloak around her against the nippy air.

"His mother always spoiled him," Josh went on, staring out at the river, "and now he drinks too much and keeps terrible company. He has no pride in being a Deveroe at all. He makes our good name a scandal in the village to satisfy his own pleasures. I have given up on him, completely!"

"But perhaps if you had a little more faith, if you showed him that you do believe in him . . ."

"But I don't," Josh said, his voice rising. "He has given me no reason to. I've had nothing but disappointment from him, and now I am past caring."

"But, Papa, sometimes Garret's ideas seem sound. At least to me."

His dark eyes flashed. "Are you going to turn against me too?"

"Of course not. I only mean that what he says sometimes makes sense."

"And what I say does not? I have run this family's business for thirty years and now, because I'm afflicted with this cursed trembling, I am supposed to retire and lie around in an easy chair all day while that foolish boy tries all manner of crazy, newfangled ideas. I tell you, he has no sense at all. He will ruin us in a month if he has his way. He is not . . . he is not natural!"

Emily wanted to protest, but her father looked as though he was about to choke. Concerned, she drew her cloak closer around her shoulders and said quietly, "Papa, please don't upset yourself so. We won't discuss it anymore. I'm sure you know best."

Josh reached out a trembling hand and Emily grasped it tightly. She did love her father so, yet he seemed to have a stubborn blindness where her brother was concerned that she could not understand at all. It was difficult to feel much affection for Garret, but surely he could not be as bad as her father believed. No one could.

"Don't you desert me," Josh said, and Emily was appalled to see his eyes fill with tears. "It is hard enough to have to live like a cripple—" His voice broke and Emily reached over, putting an arm around his shoulders. "You don't remember, but I was a man who once thought he could handle anything," Josh went on. "Now . . ."

"I do remember, Papa. And you are still that strong, capable man you always were. Your body might not work as well, but inside you haven't changed. You must remember that."

He clung to her almost like a child holding tightly to his mother for comfort.

"My dearest girl. You don't know what it means to me to have you here."

She stroked his hair, keeping her arm tightly around his shoulders, her thoughts flying across the mountains to the western frontier.

Perhaps Fade had been right after all.

In mid-January Agatha returned to the village with her grandson, Claes, a chubby, sandy-haired boy of nearly four, who immediately won Emily's heart. Finding him curious, shy, and well mannered, she took great pleasure in doting on him. But her joy in having Claes near her was overshadowed by the general gloom that accompanied the opening of 1837.

Rich and poor alike were experiencing the hard times. Even Emily, who had never paid any attention at all to the manner in which her father conducted his affairs, took to reading the papers and discussing the state of the economy. She was somewhat influenced by the suffering she saw everywhere around her, but for the most part her interest was fueled by the fierce quarrels between her brother and her father that now occurred with increasing regularity. Her new efforts helped her at least to understand Garret's frustration, for she soon realized how Josh kept a tight cocoon of secrecy around all his financial affairs. No matter how she prodded, he stubbornly refused to give her anything more than his casual assurances that everything would be all right. Small hints were all that she could pick up to indicate how the family business was faring. The workers at the Dolphin yards, after much bitter discussion and a threat to strike—though without resorting to rioting, like the mobs in New York—finally agreed to a fifteen percent cut in pay. How they were going to manage when the prices of the simplest commodities were constantly rising, Emily could not imagine. On her trips to the Sparta dock she was struck by the inactivity there. Where the wharves used to be crowded with stocks of bales, barrels, chests, and boxes, now only a forlorn scattering of goods was to be seen. The road once thick with farmers rattling to and from the dock in their loaded wagons now had its silence broken just a few times a day. According to Garret, the business at the Sing Sing dock was better but by no means what it used to be.

Even Southernwood suffered. Horses were put up for auction, and one of Josh's prized barouches was sold to Mr. Slade, who had always admired it. Yet life continued to be comfortable and Emily lacked for nothing, not even a new frock when she expressed an interest in one. So, trusting in her father's judgment, as she always had in the past, she put from her mind the worries that could be read in the faces of so many men.

With the coming of spring, the economic disaster that had loomed on the horizon for the past several months erupted in full flood, engulfing the country in desolation. The month of March saw the failure and bankruptcy of numerous established concerns in New York. Money dried up, stocks rose and fell disastrously, men who a year before had thought themselves rich now sold their expensive furniture on the city's sidewalks. Immense fortunes that had been accrued through the wild spec-

ulation in real estate and internal improvements melted away
into nothingness. By May the banks had begun to fail, overwhelmed by the panic that brought subscribers, big and small,
scrambling to their doors to remove their money. One by one
the banks suspended payments, not only in New York but in
Philadelphia, Baltimore, and then the rest of the country.

Although Emily was not aware of it, the economic structure
of the entire nation was near collapse, and the specter of depression reached out to engulf the far reaches of the western frontier
as well as the agricultural south and the mechanized north. She
liked to imagine that Fade, somewhere out in the vast land of
opportunity that was the west, was managing to turn these
terrible times to his advantage. A second letter, written shortly
after the first, from Pittsburgh, had been optimistic and full of
wonder at the new experiences he was enjoying every day.
Since then she had heard nothing, and, except for a brief reference in the Pittsburgh letter to St. Louis as the doorway to
the great far west, there was nothing to indicate where he had
gone from there.

Yet, in spite of her own comfort and ease during that long
summer of 1837, Emily was aware that these disastrous times
were taking their toll on her father and brother. While the one
became more secretive and withdrawn, the other grew daily
more sullen and argumentative. There was an I-told-you-so
implied in Garret's every utterance. Emily grew weary of the
struggle they both seemed almost to enjoy, and her only defense
was to ride off on Thor; daydream among the beautiful lavender
and white lilacs her grandmother had planted, write to her
husband long letters which she had no idea how to address;
and spend much time with bright, cheerful, uncomplicated Claes,
who was a great comfort to her.

The September rain beat heavily on the dining-room windows,
whose surfaces had been turned to mirrors by the darkness.
From the table candlelight flickered and danced on the silver
and translucent china dishes that covered the cloth. Emily sig-
naled Chloe to remove the dishes, and then laid down her
napkin. The meal was over and now she supposed that she and
Agatha would be forced by tradition to leave the room, even
though she longed to stay and hear the conversation that would
follow their departure. Across from her, Garret slouched in his

chair and toyed with his glass. He had already had far too much to drink, yet the way he eyed the port bottle on the sideboard suggested he was ready for more. On her right, Mr. Slade sat back in his chair and patted his rather large paunch, barely able to wait for the ladies to leave so he could light up a Spanish seegar. She looked down the table to where her father sat hunched forward in his chair. He was dreading this, she knew, since he was no longer able to lift his glass without help. His eyes, still bright, glanced up to catch hers, and he nodded for her to rise. Disappointed, she pushed back her chair.

"Come, Cousin Agatha. I suppose we may as well leave the gentlemen to their smoking, though I would far rather stay and hear the latest news about our financial calamity."

"Not suitable at all for a young lady," George Slade said paternally. "You mustn't worry your pretty head with such matters. They will all be handled in good time by men who know how to deal with them."

Emily bit back the retort she longed to make. Although Robert Slade was her good friend, his father had always impressed her as a pompous bore who took the attitude that women had nothing in their heads but cotton wool. How fortunate it was that he had not become her father-in-law. They would have never spoken a word to each other after the first month!

The door had no sooner closed behind them than Garret started in. "You don't seem to be suffering too badly in this panic, Mr. Slade. Tell us your secret. We could use a little help."

Slade solemnly shook his head. "My boy, it is all an act. Why, in one day's transactions I was twenty thousand dollars poorer, all because of the drop in stock prices on the Delaware and Hudson. I own extensive real estate, it is true, but I have no way of raising hard money on it, no more than your father here. We are all going to end up poor men before this is over, mark my words."

"Why should you want to raise capital on your holdings," Josh said, "with the rate the usurers charge! Hold on to it. This thing has to pass."

"That's Papa's standard answer," Garret said, rising to take up the port decanter. "A glass, Mr. Slade?"

"Thank you, yes, my boy." George Slade picked up one of the candlesticks and lit his seegar, puffing it into life. Releasing a great blob of smoke, he sat back contented. Garret watched the smoke, which hung like a small cloud over the table before drifting away, and then he reached over to pour his father a glass.

"Has to pass," Josh repeated. "Help me with this, Garret."

Reluctantly Garret helped steady his father's hand long enough to raise the glass to his lips. A thin dribble of wine ran down the old man's chin, gleaming like blood.

"It's the ruin of the country, all this mechanization," Josh went on, wiping at his chin with a napkin. "It dehumanizes people. It takes away the dignity of every man working for his own family. It destroys nature and gives any poor fool who can acquire passage to these shores the idea that he can make himself a fortune. Now it has brought us to utter collapse."

"Bosh!" Garret exclaimed. "Why, how do you think your fortune was made, Papa, but at the expense of little men working for you? And, if I remember right, Grandfather started out with very little himself after the war. If he hadn't been so clever with those government securities, we wouldn't be sitting here in this grand house today."

George Slade made a clucking noise with his tongue. "Come now, you are too harsh on your father, Garret. I've done very well with my mills, it's true, but they are not for everyone. The owner must make conditions profitable for himself while at the same time see that they are conducive to the well-being of his workers—no mean trick, I assure you."

"Well-being!" Josh interrupted. "Twelve hours a day at a loom, breathing cotton dust, ears blasted by the unnatural clang and incessant clatter of machinery. Women and children spending their lives in such a manner! And for a dollar a week. It's unnatural!"

"Why, sir, I'll have you know that many of them are happy to get it, very happy indeed."

"Perhaps so, but it is still an abomination. They were better off in the clean air of the farm or the river."

"Once a Jeffersonian, always a Jeffersonian." Garret smiled at George Slade, who looked uncomfortably from father to son. "Papa hates progress."

"And speed!" Josh added petulantly. "Hurry, hurry to the next reckless venture; over the next hill lies the golden goose. It's the sickness of this country."

"Nevertheless, it's the way of the future."

"Railroads," George broke in, "now there's the future. These canals will run their course, but the railroads are going to bring the whole country together in a way that's never been known before. Canals are too expensive to build and basically impractical. Believe me, when I have ready cash again, every penny is going to go into rail stocks."

Garret leaned forward on the table. "I couldn't agree more. I've tried for two years to get Papa to invest in the railroads but he won't listen. Maybe you can talk to him."

"I don't need your advice, either one of you!" Josh thundered. "The river will be a useful highway when these crazy railroads are a thing of the past."

"Don't upset yourself, Josh."

"It does upset me! I don't wish to talk business at all. You, with your smug pride because you made a few good choices, and Garret here, who has no sense at all about anything, trying to tell me how to run my affairs."

Garret's face went dead white. "You have no right to say that."

"Oh, don't I?" Josh turned on his son, his whole body trembling. "And who has more right? Who knows more what you are, eh? Answer me that!"

Sitting rigid in his chair, Garret gave his father a black look.

"Papa is not feeling well," Garret began, his voice very controlled.

"Papa is feeling fine," Josh shouted. "Don't lay your own failings at my feet. Don't try to make me the cause of your . . . your . . ."

Garret jumped to his feet. "If you'll excuse me, Mr. Slade," he said, then bowed briefly in George's direction and headed for the door.

"You wastrel!"

The door slammed behind him and George Slade, his amazement exceeded only by his distress, reached for the bottle of port.

"You are very hard on the boy, Josh."

"Humph." Josh slouched back in his chair, gripping the arms to control his shaking body. "If you knew him as I do . . ."

Once in his room, Garret took a bottle of Allegheny whiskey from his clothes cupboard, where he kept it hidden. Then turning the oil lamp up to a low wavering flame, he sat down at the table and consumed half the bottle's contents over the next few hours. He could hear the rhythmic chiming of the standing clock on the landing, and other sounds told him when Agatha and Slade left, when Emily helped her father up the stairs to his room. Finally, quiet settled over the house. Several times he debated rousing himself to go down to the nearest tavern as was his usual custom after these unpleasant scenes, but somehow tonight he could not find the energy. Sleep was impossible though, so he sat and drank, slowly slipping into a foggy stupor.

A few minutes after the clock had struck two, he was surprised to hear a shuffling sound in the hall. Coming suddenly awake, he raised his head from the table and started up, more curious than frightened. He had long ago thrown off his shoes, and his stockinged feet made the barest of sounds as he moved across the rug, opened his door, and looked out on the hallway.

He was surprised to see the stooped figure of his father, holding a flickering lantern with one hand while he gripped the rail near the top of the broad stairway with the other. Crazy old man, Garret thought, trying to go down those stairs by himself when he cannot even hold a glass steady.

He stepped out into the hall. "For God's sake, Papa, let me have that lamp before you set the whole house on fire."

Moving silently, he took the lantern from Josh's hand. The old man looked up at him, and Garret shrank back from the angry fire in his eyes.

"You've been drinking. I can smell it from here. That's a fine solution to your problems, isn't it?"

"Where are you going?" Garret answered, trying to keep his words from sounding too slurred. "Do you want help?"

"Not from you, sir, thank you. No, sir."

Shuffling along with his hand on the rail, Josh moved onto the first step as Garret stood watching.

"And why shouldn't I drink?" he muttered. "Precious little help I get from anywhere else."

Josh turned and looked up at his son. "I have about finished with you, Garret. I know what you are, you see. I've known it for several years. You may be my son, but I want no part of you. The very sight of you is offensive to my eyes. I want you out of here."

Garret struggled to take in his father's words through the fog in his mind. "You don't mean that."

"Oh yes, I mean every word," Josh said dispassionately. "I might as well tell you, I have decided to leave everything I have to Emily. I'm a sick man, but I'm still good for a few more years if the doctors are right. You will be provided for, but the control of everything I have shall be left to Emily, and to Fade if she chooses to let him help her. You will never be allowed to squander her livelihood on your . . . your unnatural weaknesses."

Fury clouded Garret's eyes. "You wouldn't! You wouldn't do that."

"Oh, but I would. I've been thinking about this for a long time. Tonight I asked George Slade to send round his solicitor early next week."

Garret stared at the bent figure, took a step forward, and looked deep into the dark, angry eyes as if to verify the truth of his father's words. As he drew closer to his father, Josh almost visibly shrank back.

"Get away from me," he spat out. "I hate the sight of you. You contaminate everything you touch. You should not even be allowed to live in the same house with your sister, that pure, good creature."

It was too much. The mention of his sister acted like a tinder to Garret's rage. It swelled up in him, a black cloud of wrath, blinding him with its intensity. With his free arm he swung out furiously and struck his father.

Surprise, shock, and sudden fear flashed across Josh's face for an instant before his body went crashing backward, arms flailing. He lay there balanced precariously on the stairs, struggling to move, staring up at his son, his mouth working in silent gasps.

The hot rage subsided, and with cool deliberation Garret looked down at his father lying on the stairs below him. Carefully putting out his foot, he shoved with all his strength, sending Josh's body tumbling down the whole length of the stairway.

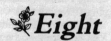

Eight

"Cousin Emily, play with me and my new boat, please."

Emily reluctantly tore her gaze away from the mesmerizing flames of the fire and reached out to stroke Claes's blonde hair.

"Not right now, dear. Why don't you let it rest for a while and look at one of your nice picture books. Cousin Emily is very tired."

"Don't bother Emily, Claes," Agatha said, laying aside her knitting and awkwardly pushing herself up from the sofa. "I'll help you. Why don't you draw a lovely picture of your new boat for Cousin Emily."

"Oh, perhaps I could . . ." Emily half-heartedly made to rise.

"No, dear. You stay by the fire. Come along, Claes, darling." Taking her grandson's chubby hand, Agatha led him, still clutching his sailboat under his arm, across the room to a table covered with books, pastels, and a large sketch pad. Emily watched as Agatha sat the boy down and arranged the paper and crayons in front of him. She supposed Claes could not

121

understand why his friend Emily no longer had the heart to play with him as she used to. She wished she could explain to him that the death of her beloved father had changed her world, but she knew he was too young to understand her loss. Claes had missed his mother very much when he first came to live with his grandmother, but in only a few short weeks that memory had been diminished by the new and enticing world he had discovered and the doting devotion of these two women.

Where was *her* comfort? The husband she longed for was off, God knew where, in the wilds of Ohio or Missouri, if he was alive at all. She could not even be sure of that, not having had a letter in over a year. The father she loved next only to Fade was cold in the earth, leaving her to live in a barren house under the domination of a brother who considered her his chattel. Her life had become so bleak that she could no longer even enjoy the pleasure of Agatha's delightful grandson.

"That should keep him busy for a while," Agatha said, breaking in on Emily's gloomy thoughts. She gingerly lowered herself back into her place on the sofa near the fire's warmth. "I don't know whether or not I should thank you for giving him that sailboat for Christmas, Emily. Ever since he laid his hands on it he has wanted nothing else. He cannot understand at all why the ice on the river should prevent him from sailing it. Of course, what can you expect with the father and grandfather he's had—both of them with the sea in their blood."

"I'm so glad he likes it," Emily answered absently.

Agatha picked up her knitting and leaned toward the fire. "I shall probably have to spend every day by the shore of the river once the weather warms up again. At least I won't have to worry anymore about what the sun will do to my complexion. That is one of the benefits of old age. When I was a girl my mother would never let me sit in the sun without a wide-brimmed hat, parasol, and white paste. All to prevent the horrors of a freckle."

The quiet of the room made small sounds seem louder: the fire snapping in the hearth; the click of Agatha's needles; the soft whispering strokes of Claes's crayons on the paper.

"I do hope the weather breaks soon," Agatha went on, glancing up at the ice-encrusted windows. By the middle of January it begins to seem as though winter has been here forever. Of course, I suppose that is what makes spring so welcome."

When there was no answer from the silent figure opposite her, Agatha gave up trying to make casual conversation and declared, "Emily, my dear, when I invited you for tea today, I did not intend to lecture. But you cannot go on like this, grieving and withering away over your father's death. Josh has been dead now for nearly four months. I loved him too, and I miss him terribly. But life must go on."

Emily turned an angry and bitter face toward her. "I'll never get over it! Never."

"But you knew he was ill. Surely you must have expected that someday you would lose him."

"Yes. And had he died in his bed perhaps I would have been able to accept it. But falling down the stairs and breaking his neck! There are too many questions. Why was he trying to go downstairs in the middle of the night? Where were the servants? Why didn't I hear him?"

"But, Emily dear, you know Faith said she had caught him doing the exact same thing twice before. I blame his stubbornness. He simply would not admit that he was too weak to maneuver the stairs alone and it hurt his vanity to ask someone to help him. That was his way, you know. Even as a young man Josh always had so much vitality. Nothing had ever defeated him before and he could not admit anything could now."

"I don't believe it. He knew how ill he was. If only someone had heard him."

Over the rim of her glasses Agatha studied the girl's sad figure. The taut lines in Emily's body, the bitterness with which she looked out on the world, worried her. She was so different now from the vivacious, cheerful girl she had always been.

"You must accept what is, my dear. I know that you have the strength to do so. Now you must make a home for Garret and yourself."

"Ha!" Emily spat it out, more a curse than an exclamation. "You don't know what it's like living there now. Garret treats me like a servant—an unpaid servant at that. In his warped mind he has decided that since my husband has disappeared and my father is dead, he is now the sole guardian of my body, soul, and property."

"Why, that is nonsense! I know that Josh must have left you well fixed."

"I have a comfortable annuity, but everything else is Garret's—the house, the yards, the stocks and shipping interests, everything. I don't care about any of it except Southernwood. I had hoped that would be mine. I'm the only one who really cares about the place."

"Surely Josh must have been aware of your feelings. I'm surprised he did not consider them."

"I think his will was made long ago, when I married Fade. I know he intended to change it, because he told me so. Once he knew he could trust Fade, he meant to divide everything between Garret and me, but he must not have got around to it in time."

"But you are comfortably fixed?"

"Yes, except Garret controls even that." All but the hundred dollars Fade left me, Emily thought to herself, and no one was going to know about that. She had managed to keep the money hidden and untouched all these months, and now it was her only security.

Shaking her head, Agatha laid her knitting in her lap and pulled her shawl closer around her shoulders. "Josh probably counted on Garret to take care of you . . ." she began.

"He never would have done that. Papa knew my brother better than anyone and he must have guessed what Garret would do with no firm hand to control him. And he was right! Every suspicion has proved correct."

Agatha was startled at the fury in Emily's voice. "Why, my dear, I know the young man is headstrong, but surely his heart is in the right place."

"Oh, Cousin Agatha, you don't know what you are talking about. He is a monster. He doles out just enough to me to buy a few ribbons or laces if I should need them, excusing his penury by saying that times are difficult and there is no more. He turned out, without a penny, four faithful servants who have lived at Southernwood most of their lives, just because they were old and infirm. He is filling their places with common immigrants right off the boat, and the worst kind of people. He will not allow me a glimpse of the books—he is even more secretive than Papa in that regard—and I suspect he is raising loans on the property and the house while I can do nothing about it.

"And he has grown so arrogant. I am not allowed to leave the table until he gives me permission. Imagine! He constantly threatens to sell Thor because he is twelve years old now and not so strong as he used to be. He tells me that every thread on my back is only there because he allows it to be, and the worst of it is, that is legally true. I have no rights, no property, no home except by his charity. It is too much!"

"Why, Emily, how appalling!" Agatha spluttered.

"And that's not all. He drinks too much, often going down to the quarters of those Irishmen he brought here and getting drunk alongside them. He is sometimes gone for days at a time, in the city or roaming about the local taprooms, making a spectacle and a scandal of himself. I don't object because I am so happy to be relieved of his presence, but then when he comes home he is worse than ever. Oh, if only Fade were here!"

"Why, I am surprised at Garret." Agatha reached for her handkerchief, expecting Emily to burst out crying at any moment. But her cousin's anger was far too deep and consuming to dissolve into tears.

"But I won't give in to him," Emily went on, clenching her hands in tight fists. "He would like to drive me away so he can have everything Papa built up, but I won't let him do it. He can have all the business, but he will not have Southernwood as long as I have breath in my body."

"My poor girl. You are always welcome to come and stay with me."

Emily managed a wan smile. "Thank you, Cousin Agatha. I shall remember your kind offer if things become too distasteful. If Papa had only changed his will as he planned I would have had Southernwood and none of this would be happening."

"Well, if life gets too difficult, at least come and visit Claes and me for a while. We will help you restore your equilibrium."

"Ah, well. Perhaps things will improve next week," Emily said, staring again into the fire. "A friend of Garret's is coming to stay with us—a German Baron, from the Grand Duchy of Baden. That ought to put Garret on his best behavior. I know he thinks highly of the man."

"I hope so, my dear. I hope so."

And perhaps if I try hard, Emily thought, I can forget to hope that there will be a letter on the table in the hall when I get home today.

For months now, Garret had been telling Emily about Baron von Arensten, his new friend, describing him as "very pompous and dignified until he has a few glasses of champagne, when he becomes the most suave, gracious gentleman you could ever hope to meet." Garret had made Emily cringe by insinuating that she might be interested in the man. Although it was true that she hadn't heard from Fade in a very long time, he was still her husband and she knew that someday he would come back for her.

According to Garret the baron had seen and admired Emily on her trip upriver from New York. Hearing about this imposing man and his secret regard for her, Emily had concluded that anyone Garret thought so highly of must inspire instant dislike. But the baron proved to be a surprise.

When he stood before her, very straight, his manner all charm and suavity, she was impressed in spite of herself. He was of middle height, with a strong jaw and cool blue eyes framed by thick auburn lashes. He had a neat, pencil-thin mustache above his full upper lip and spoke perfect English, with only the barest hint of an accent. He was impeccably dressed in a brown velvet coat of lustrous softness that had huge shoulders and a tapering waist, the style that was the rage among the fashionables. He was younger than she had expected, yet obviously more mature than Garret. During that first elaborate meal they shared, Emily found herself wondering what could possibly have led him to form such a strong friendship with her brother.

She was fascinated to hear him describe his beautiful homeland and all the wonderful places he had visited, and devoted most of the dinner conversation to asking him about Paris, London, Vienna, and Rome—cities he seemed to know intimately.

"Oh, how I should like to see Westminster Abbey, the Louvre, the palaces and gardens of Europe," Emily exclaimed, her eyes shining. "How lovely it must be to know them as you do, to have such wonderful sights just a few days distant instead of weeks away across an ocean. It surely must be one of this country's worst drawbacks to be so far from Europe."

The baron leaned across the table, smiling at her. "It would be my greatest pleasure to show you these wonders," he said, startling Emily with the blatant admiration in his eyes. "You would grace them all."

Suddenly uncomfortable, Emily laid her spoon by her plate and looked away. "Someday I hope to visit them with my husband," she said pointedly. "Perhaps you will be our guide."

"Of course, of course. I should delight in it."

"But first your husband must be lured back from the wilds of the far west," Garret put in with a smirk. "He seems far more interested in Indians and woodsmen than the civilized capitals of Europe."

The baron frowned at Garret before turning a kindly smile on Emily. "Garret tells me your dear husband is seeking his fortune in the old French territory of Louisiana. I was at New Orleans once, a very interesting city if somewhat primitive. Has he gone there by chance?"

"Why, no. I believe he has gone to St. Louis," Emily said, grasping at the only clue she had from Fade's two letters.

"Oh, yes. That is a thriving place from which I understand emigrants set out on the Oregon Trail. No doubt it offers many opportunities for an enterprising man to begin a trade."

Although there was a condescending tone in his mention of trade, the baron knew more about the western lands, Emily thought, than she did. New Orleans and St. Louis were only names to her, vague and dimly perceived as wild, riotous, primitive places no civilized person would want to go near. Perhaps she should make an effort to discover more about them.

"When do you expect him to return?" the baron asked.

"I'm . . . I'm not sure, but it should be soon. He has been gone many months."

"I suspect he must write you wonderful letters, full of exotic descriptions. I myself should welcome the opportunity of visiting the west; it sounds so utterly fascinating."

Emily glared at her brother, daring him to speak. "Oh yes," she said, "his letters are most interesting. And such a comfort."

Garret came forward in his chair, all at once very businesslike. "I suspect it is time you retired, Emily, and left us to our port. We shall see you in the drawing room later."

Her deception over the letters had stirred into life the pain of not having heard from Fade in over a year and the grief it caused her. "Please, Garret," she said quietly, "I have such a headache. I would appreciate it very much if you would excuse me."

Her brother's eyes hardened with sudden anger. "I expect you to pour coffee in the drawing room and—"

"Nonsense, my dear friend," the baron broke in soothingly.

"I wouldn't hear of Mrs. Whitman waiting upon us when she is not well. By all means, my dear lady, take your rest. We will manage very well, Garret and I, be assured we shall."

Garret's expression softened. "Oh, very well then. Go on to bed. But we shall expect you at breakfast."

Emily threw the baron a swift look of gratitude and rose from the table. Perhaps with von Arensten around life at Southernwood would become a little more pleasant.

"By the way, Madam Whitman," the baron added, jumping to his feet before she could turn for the door, "I understand you are an expert horsewoman."

"Not expert, but I do enjoy riding."

"I was most struck by the beauties of your very excellent estate. Would you do me the honor of riding out with me some morning and pointing out the more pleasant trails? I should be so pleased if you would."

"Why, of course, Baron. I should be happy to."

"Ah, that has made my day, lovely lady. Now please, have your rest."

Emily looked from one to the other: her sullen brother, struggling to hide his annoyance that for once she had won a point; and his sophisticated friend, all graciousness and concern.

"Good night, then."

"Good night."

The door closed softly behind her as the baron resumed his seat and pulled out a long Spanish seegar. "Well," Garret said, reaching for the decanter. He poured the ruby liquid into his glass, where it glinted like jewels in the lamplight.

"She is everything I hoped for. Every promise I saw in her on the deck of the steamer so long ago has proved true." He puffed at the flame, then blew a thick white plume of smoke into the air. "She is utterly charming."

Garret smiled as he took a long draught from the glass.

"Good!" A wave of hair fell forward over his brow and the shadows from the candles made crevices in his thin cheeks, heightening the almost feminine features of his face. Running his tongue over his lips with relish, he added enough to his glass from the decanter to fill it again.

Baron von Arensten lounged back in his chair and threw Emily's brother a hard, brittle glance. "You will please control yourself as regards strong liquor while I am around."

"Why, I just enjoy a little wine after a good meal. It's common practice, you know."

"I know well. I also know you have little control over your deplorable appetites and I have no wish once again to drag you from under the table and carry you to bed."

Annoyed, Garret angrily set his glass down on the table. "You of all people should understand my 'appetites.'"

"Exactly. And if you wish to have them fulfilled with any regularity, as I expect you do since I am now your honored guest, then you will please to control the drinking. I detest drunkenness!"

Von Arensten blew another puff of white smoke toward Garret's face.

"But you like my sister," Garret added, waving it away with his hand.

"I like her very much indeed."

"Then we must see what we can do about satisfying *your* little 'appetites,' mustn't we?"

The baron's smile held none of the charm he had turned on Emily. It was more of a satisfied grin, sinister and calculating.

"I am glad we understand one another so well," he said.

The first two weeks of von Arensten's visit brought a much-needed lift to Emily's spirits. The baron went out of his way to show her every consideration, a solicitousness she had not enjoyed since Fade's departure. She reacted with a warm politeness calculated not to encourage him yet not to send him away either. The truth was, the improved atmosphere in the house, due in no small part to his presence, made her feel grateful to him.

Yet there were many miserable hours when she sat alone in her room weeping after still another day had passed with no word from her husband. She had written to everyone she could think of who might be able to get information from the frontier, particularly Robert Slade. With his position in the government, she had reasoned, he must know the people who came and went between Washington City and the wilds of the western territories. He had answered her politely, assuring her he would ask anyone who was going west to look out for Frederick Whitman. That had been four months ago, and so far all she had received was one note from Robert saying he had not yet been able to locate Fade but that he would keep trying.

Meanwhile she continued to send her own letters to Pittsburgh, the last place he had written from, marked "To be sent on." The silence was like a wall isolating her in a prison of worry and frustration. Under it all lay the thought that surely if Fade were alive and well he would have written to her. She was sure of that. But to imagine him lying ill in some primitive hole or, even worse, dead and buried in an unmarked grave was too terrible to consider. She must hope. She must continue to write. Someday word would arrive.

With the coming of Spring, 1838, economic depression gripped the country, laying a dark pall over the land. Times had never been worse. Though prices fell along with stocks, there was no ready cash anywhere with which to take advantage of the situation. Garret was full of a scheme to convert everything their father had left to cash and invest it in the railroads—particularly the one planned for the Hudson Valley. It took Emily only a week to realize that his hospitality to Baron von Arensten was tied to this scheme, though just how she was not sure. Obviously the baron had money and Garret intended to get his hands on some of it to bolster the Deveroe interests. For Emily, the whole question could hardly have mattered less.

The baron, who was interested in every aspect of Westchester life, persuaded Emily to accompany him on exploratory visits to mills, factories, shipyards, and quarries in the surrounding districts. At first reluctant, she soon found that she was as avidly interested as he in these enterprises. Her father had always hidden the particulars of the business world from her and now she began to realize how fascinating they could be. For the first time she was struck by the fact that well-to-do young ladies like herself were actually very unproductive creatures—especially if they had no children. Running a house, producing a family, and doing a fine job of tatting was the most that was expected of women, even educated ones. It was rather a shocking and pleasant surprise to learn that a whole world existed beyond her front door, a world where one's mind and imagination could be put to good use.

While Baron von Arensten smiled indulgently on her enthusiasm, Garret grew more and more furious, accusing her of nosing into things that did not concern her and that were most unladylike. Emily concluded he was both fearful that she would somehow learn too much of how he was handling their father's business and more than a little jealous of all the time the baron was spending with her. Gradually the pleasant-mannered Garret who had emerged during the first days of the baron's visit gave way to the Garret of old: surly, arrogant, and foul-tempered. Emily decided to ignore him and simply enjoy the broader view of life which von Arensten had opened up to her.

One clear, lovely spring day the baron invited Emily to ride up with him to view the progress of the work on the great Croton Aqueduct, one of the most ambitious ventures yet attempted in Westchester. Emily was glad to go, both for the pleasure of the ride and because she had been following the growth of the waterworks with great interest.

They were returning in the gig at midafternoon when they came across George Slade riding his sleek black gelding down the post road toward Tarrytown. He invited them to his home for tea, and so instead of turning off at the winding uphill road to Southernwood, they continued on to the grand Georgian villa overlooking the river where Mrs. Slade laid out her best tea service for them.

The Slades were brimming with news of Robert's wedding, which had taken place in Washington the previous winter.

"Not so grand as it should have been," Jeanne Slade said almost with a sigh, "since times are so difficult. But it was a fine affair nonetheless. I was so sorry you could not be there, Emily."

"Garret felt he could not take the time," Emily murmured, making much of stirring her tea, "and I did not want to go alone, of course." The truth was her brother had decided that sending a suitable gift was easier and less expensive than making the trip, particularly when Emily would certainly have demanded a new dress for the occasion.

"Robert seems happy," George said, sitting next to Emily on the settee. "She's a very nice little thing, delicate, perhaps a little plain but from a fine family in Virginia. Lots of money."

Emily stirred her tea listlessly. She remembered trying to convince her father that she was too strong-minded and determined for Robert. And now he had married a delicate, plain "little thing." Well, she hoped he was happy.

"You have such a lovely view of the river, Madam Slade," the baron exclaimed, breaking into Emily's reverie. "I wonder if we might have a closer look at it. Your river reminds me much of my home. I never weary of gazing on it."

"The Hudson has often been compared to the Rhine, Baron," said Jeanne Slade. "By all means you must take a stroll on our terrace. Emily, won't you join us?"

"I've seen it many times before."

The baron held out his hand to her. "Ah, but your presence will make it all the more lovely. Please do come."

A little embarrassed, Emily laid down her cup and rose. She hoped the Slades understood that von Arensten's flowery compliments were only part of his European manners.

Offering an arm to each of the women, the baron escorted them through the terrace doors and out onto the flagstone porch, down a few low steps to the sloping lawn. At the edge of the green expanse several stone benches were set in front of trellised frames heavy with newly green vines. They were halfway down the lawn when Mrs. Slade was abruptly called back to the parlor to attend to some household crisis. Sending them on, she bustled back into the house, promising to join them again in a few moments.

Laying a hand on her arm, the baron led Emily to one of the benches where, in the seclusion of the trellis, they could look out over the sparkling river, its surface patterned with colorful sails. Not really eager to make light conversation, Emily gazed out at the shadowed hills across the river, reflecting on her life and her loneliness, wondering once more where her husband could be. When the baron broke the long silence, she realized with a sinking feeling that he was not making light conversation either.

"My dear Miss Emily, I cannot express to you how I have come to love this place."

How she wished he had not fallen into the habit of calling her Miss Emily, as though she had never married. No matter how many times she corrected him, he never seemed to remember she was Mrs. Whitman.

"I am happy that you enjoy it so much, my dear Baron. I feel the same way about the Hudson Valley. There is no place in the world I can imagine loving any more."

Reaching out suddenly, he took her hand, gripping it so strongly that though she moved away from him on the bench she could not reclaim it.

"You must know that it is your presence more than anything else which has made this place so pleasurable for me."

"Baron, please..."

"No, please, let me speak for once. I have been silent for so long. All this time while you sat beside me in the gig or across the table at dinner I have kept my lips closed. Now, in the beauty of this place, I must say what is in my heart."

Inching away from him on the bench, Emily tugged at her hand. "Mrs. Slade will be coming back at any moment. Even now she must be able to see us. Please. Let go of my hand."

To her consternation he moved even closer to her. "We are quite hidden. And it is so beautiful here, just as you are so beautiful. All of nature is heightened by your loveliness, yet overshadowed by it as well. I myself am overcome."

She had reached the end of the bench and felt the thick vines of the trellis digging into her back. To Emily's horror, he laid his free hand against her cheek and traced a light pattern down her face to enclose her neck in his hand.

"Baron! I am a married woman. Please remember yourself!"

His face was so close to hers she could feel the faint tickle of his mustache against her skin. His breath held no trace of the smell of tobacco, so common on all the men she knew, and in fact had a light, not unpleasing odor of mint. Yet she grew more distressed by the moment when it became obvious that he was going to kiss her. Pushing against his chest, she tried to wriggle free of his embrace, but felt herself crushed against him.

"Baron!"

His lips closed hard against hers. For what seemed long minutes he held her, the strength of his embrace enclosing her in a vise. She couldn't breathe; she couldn't move. Her fury grew with every second that passed.

When at last he released her, she gasped for breath and, swinging her hand with all the force she could muster, gave him a ringing blow on the cheek. She wanted to flee as fast as possible, but when she jumped up, he gripped her arm and stood in front of her, blocking her way. Emily saw that the passion in his eyes had given way to a cold fury. For a moment she thought he was going to strike her; instead he visibly struggled to bring his emotions under control.

"Perhaps I deserved that . . ."

"Perhaps! You most certainly did and more. How dare you force yourself on me!"

His voice was like ice. "Never again lay a hand on me or you will certainly be sorry."

Emily's rage left her gasping for words. How dare he be affronted! "Never lay a hand on me, Baron, or I assure you you will regret it, as well. If my husband were here . . ."

"Ah, but he is not here and has not been for some time. In fact, if I understand correctly, you have not even had a letter from him in many months. A woman bereft of a husband for such a length of time ought to welcome the advances of a man like myself."

"I suppose you think I should be flattered," Emily spluttered.

"As a matter of fact, yes. Why not? I have much to offer a woman. I give you my undisguised admiration and for it I receive a blow to the face. My pride is considerably offended, Miss Emily, considerably."

"Your *pride!* Baron, you are unbelievable. You force yourself upon me and your pride is hurt because I take it as an insult. I don't know how the women in Germany are brought up, but I assure you that American women are not accustomed to such unseemly behavior. Now, please, let me pass."

He did not move aside but turned to face the river.

"Very well, perhaps I am not well enough acquainted with your American ways. Please excuse my thoughtlessness and be assured I would not have purposely offended you for anything. I apologize, *Madam*. You would do me a great honor to accept my apology and put this regrettable incident from your mind."

Emily was still so angry that she wanted nothing so much as to run from this man and never set eyes on him again. Yet he *had* apologized, he was a guest in her home—or her brother's home—and with any luck he would soon leave and she would never have to face him again. Her good breeding finally won out over her fury.

"Very well, Baron. I accept your apology. We will say no more about this and I shall try to forget it ever happened. Now, if you will excuse me, I should like to go home."

"Of course. We shall go back to Mr. Slade's lovely house and make our farewells. How unfortunate that Mrs. Slade was not able to rejoin us."

He offered her his arm, but Emily refused, fussing instead with her shawl as they walked back up the lawn. She had lied to Baron von Arensten about one thing: she would not mention this incident again, that was true, but she would never forget that it happened—never!

"Well, I hope you're proud of the way you botched things," Garret said to von Arensten after Emily had left the men to their port that evening.

"Botched?"

"Yes, botched. You noticed, I suppose, the way she barely spoke a word to you all through supper. Why, she hardly looked in your direction. My guess is she cannot bear the sight of your lecherous face. This has set back weeks of work and I for one don't know how we are going to patch it up."

"Lechery, my dear friend, is a far cry from the kind of impassioned embrace I gave your sister this afternoon. Why, any German woman worth her salt would have got down on her knees and thanked me."

"Baron, your arrogance is going to ruin us both. Bah, this port—might as well drink rainwater. Where's the brandy?"

While Garret rummaged through the bottles in the cellarette, the baron lounged in his chair, taking long draughts on his seegar and studying the stains on the tablecloth. He was not quite so assured as he pretended to Garret. That unfortunate incident this afternoon had been brought on partly by his honest desire for a beautiful woman, one whose constant presence was eating away at his patience. He wanted her more every day and he was going to get her, one way or another. But the combination of the sparkling afternoon, the sight of the river in all its glory, so reminiscent of Germany, the heady closeness of Emily's body, and the loveliness of her sculptured profile as she gazed out across the Hudson—all had overwhelmed him, eliciting one of those impulsive gestures he always regretted later. Yet he would find a way to make it right again. He was determined.

Carrying the squat brown bottle back to the table, Garret prepared to attack its contents. "Weeks of work," he muttered.

"I don't know why you even want her anyway. She's skin and bones, conceited, and too damned self-willed by half for a woman. If you ever get her, you'll regret it forever."

"I don't want her forever. But since the day I first saw her standing on the deck of the steamer I have felt a desire for her. And as you know, my dear Garret, I make it a practice to satisfy my desires. Your sister has become something of a challenge."

"Yes, well, I don't see how you can win this 'challenge.' You've thrown up one obstacle too many."

"I do not have to clear away the obstacles, my friend. You do."

"Me! It's too much to expect me to rectify this."

"Very well, then. I shall pack my trunks tonight and be gone by tomorrow. And your little hopes of making a fortune on the railroad will go with me."

Garret paled. "Now let's not be hasty. You know I don't want you to go. It's just that Emily is so stubborn."

"But you have several holds over her to which you can always resort. Just keep remembering our bargain: I help you if you help me."

Swirling the brandy in his glass, Garret stared at it sullenly. "I haven't forgotten. But, damn, you've made it blasted hard. Sometimes I wonder if it's worth it."

With a well-manicured finger the baron flicked the ash of his seegar onto the rug. "You are going to drink too much of that potent brandy, my friend. How do you plan to spend the night? Lying drunk, face down on the table?"

Garret looked up quickly, but the baron's face was impassive and revealed nothing. "Why should that matter to you? Perhaps I'll walk down to the back quarters and get swilled with Mick. There's nothing like a good roaring drunk to clear the mind."

"It is beneath the dignity of a gentleman to get drunk with servants, especially immigrant servants. I am feeling unsettled tonight. The encounter with your sister has left my emotions stirred up."

Garret ran his tongue across his thin lower lip. "Are you inviting me to drink with you?" he said quietly.

"Why not? I shall go up now," the baron said, jabbing the stub of his seegar against the plate. "Come along when you like." His hand on the doorknob, he turned back to look at the slight figure hunched over the brandy bottle, the face, even when seen from this distance, all anticipation.

"But don't be long."

All the next week Emily avoided the baron as much as possible without openly insulting him. If he entered a room she soon left. When he invited her to ride out with him, she was prepared with an excuse. Once a meal was over she was up and away from the table, and for several days she managed to miss tea by visiting Agatha during the afternoons. Though her manner was polite and her excuses always plausible, by the end of the week it was obvious to all that she did not want to breathe the same air as the baron. Outraged, von Arensten vented his spleen on Garret and began making plans to depart Southernwood. Garret sought out Emily and pulled her into their father's small study.

"You are ruining me!" he began, his face growing ruddy with anger. "I've gone to a great deal of trouble to entertain this man and now you go and spoil it all. Damn it, Emily, you must know how important he is."

"I don't know what you mean," Emily began, thinking ignorance was her best defense.

"Don't play coy with me," Garret cried. "You know very well what I mean. Why do you think I asked that man up here? Because he has the money to help me put this family back on its feet again. All I have to do is bring him around to investing it for me. I was very close to that, and then you had to go and enrage him with your arrogance until now he's threatening to leave!"

Emily stared at her brother open-mouthed. "He tried to kiss me! He made advances that no gentleman would. If you think I am going to put up with that kind of thing just to help you with one of your business schemes, you might as well think again."

"You ought to be flattered that he tried to kiss you. He's an attractive man and God knows you haven't had one around in long enough time."

"Garret!"

"Well, it's the truth."

"I should have known you would react like that," Emily said, her outrage matching her brother's. "It would be expecting too much to imagine you would defend your own sister."

"Oh stop the maudlin histrionics! Your virtue hasn't been impaired. What's one little kiss when thousands of dollars are at stake?"

"It's the principle of the thing. I'm a married woman who happens to love her husband very much."

Garret threw up his hands. "When will you accept reality, Emily? You haven't heard a word from Fade Whitman in well over a year. He's probably dead somewhere, scalped by Indians or mauled by some wild animal."

"Garret, stop it," Emily cried.

"Or perhaps he's taken another wife. That's common on the frontier, I understand. Men just disappear, assume new identities, and leave their old lives behind forever."

"Fade would never do that!"

She began to cry and Garret, sensing he had hit a soft spot, leaned toward her, and said mockingly, "Oh, wouldn't he? Was he so happy with you, then? I saw you together and I'd bet there were many times he longed to be free of an overbearing wife who made demands on him. Our dear Frederick had a mind of his own and was always one to value his freedom."

Emily turned from him, fighting to hold back the tears. "That's not true. We were very happy together."

Her voice broke and she put her hands to her face. How many times in the dark of the long nights had she agonized over these same questions? Smiling to himself, Garret let her stand a few moments, then laid a hand gently on her shoulder.

"Emily, I'm only trying to help you face facts. Suppose Fade never comes back? You must think of yourself. Here is a wealthy, attractive man who is ready to offer you the world if only you will reach out and accept it."

"But I don't want him! Even if Fade never comes back for me I shall always be his wife. Not for ten barons with all the wealth of China would I consider myself a widow and marry another man, not if I grow old and crippled waiting for Fade to return."

It was too much. Clenching his fists, Garret turned away to keep from striking the stupid woman. "Then for God's sake sleep with him!"

Emily gasped and turned to face her brother. She could hardly believe she had heard him correctly.

"What harm would it do?" Garret went on. "He's used to getting his way and you've piqued him by your refusals. You might even enjoy it, and you'd be doing me a great favor."

"You . . . you rotten skunk! That's why you had him come here, to get me in his bed. I always knew you were vile, Garret, but I never suspected you were this vile."

"Oh, spare me your righteous anger. Here is someone with something I want—money; and I have something he wants—you. It could be a great bargain."

Emily started from the room. Jumping ahead of her, Garret barred the door.

"Oh no you don't. I want you to understand all that is at stake here. Baron von Arensten is ready to buy four thousand shares of stock in the Hudson Railroad in my name. It would support this house and this estate you claim to love so much for the next fifty years. It would rescue the Dolphin yards from bankruptcy and help us hold on to some of the better investments Papa made until they can begin paying again. We need this money, Emily. Desperately!"

"I don't need anything in the world that desperately. I'll starve first or even sell Southernwood."

"That's a jest. You won't even sell Thor, that useless old hay burner. You'd do anything to save this house. You know you would."

Emily gave him a long, bitter look. Her anger had turned cold, leaving her disgusted and sick. "No, Garret. Fade is still my husband, and I will never, never so debase him or myself. Now, please. Let me pass."

Garret looked deeply into her dark eyes. God, how he hated her, the self-righteous prig. She had twisted their father around her little finger and now she was setting about to ruin the promising bond between the baron and himself. He had never wanted anything so much as he wanted to close his fingers around that slender white throat and choke the life from it.

"You're being very stupid," he said in a voice thick with hatred.

"Let me pass, please."

He moved from the door and she swept out of the room, her heels clattering on the landing as she ran to her bedroom. Let her closet herself away there for the rest of the day, he thought; he'd make some excuse to the baron. But it was all too obvious now that he had laid his cards on the table and they had been rejected. With her stupid principles and loyalty she was never going to cooperate. All right, then, he'd just have to find another way to get her into the baron's bed. He had no doubt at all that he could.

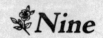

Nine

BARON VON ARENSTEN, gentleman that he was, liked to sleep well into the morning. Garret, on the other hand, no matter how dissolute an evening he'd spent the night before, was up early and about the business of the day. Determined to see her brother privately, Emily was up before the servants were stirring, dressed and with her portmanteau packed.

She found Garret at the breakfast table staring sullenly into his tea, his chin resting on his hand. His long hair fell over his forehead in a boyish wave not at all in keeping with the pasty skin and shadowed lines of his face.

"I want to go visit Cousin Agatha for a few days," she started, not troubling to sit down at the table. He looked up at her without moving, his eyes full of hostility.

"There's no need. Von Arensten is going down to New York for a few days. You'll not be troubled by him or me either. The less I see of you right now the better."

141

"I'm offering you an opportunity to see nothing of me at all. I have an open invitation from Cousin Agatha and I would enjoy the change of scenery."

"And company, too, no doubt."

"I won't deny that."

Garret looked back down at his cup, longing to lace it with a big helping of whiskey. "How can you stand to be around that dull old woman, always blathering on about the way things used to be and what a great man Papa was. You'll be bored to tears."

Emily shrugged. "I don't mind Agatha, and I enjoy Claes very much. Besides, Garret, you care as little to have me around as I care to be here."

"For heaven's sake, sit down. I can't stand to have you hovering over me like that."

Emily perched stiffly on the edge of a chair. "May I go?"

He waved a hand without answering.

"Thank you." She hoped the sarcasm in her voice was not too evident. No point in starting another argument now, when all she wanted was to get away.

"Ask O'Flannery to drive you. He's not needed today."

"I'd rather have Absolem."

"Oh, all right. What does it matter? With you and von Arensten gone, at least I'll have a little peace and privacy for a few days."

Emily rose to leave. She could well imagine how he would use his privacy.

"The baron will be back next Tuesday. I want you home by then," Garret called after her. His imperious tone made Emily furious, but she pursed her lips and said nothing.

Emily had known her driver, Absolem, all her life. Of all the servants left on the estate, he was the one she trusted most. His grandfather, Vestal, had been with the Deveroe family even before Southernwood was built. She settled behind him now on the leather seat for the drive to Agatha's house, feeling like someone just released from prison. As the carriage went bouncing down the drive and past the small gate house, they passed a man on horseback just entering the grounds. He wore an old-fashioned round hat and a short blue workman's woolen tunic. Emily twisted around for a second look as the carriage rolled down the drive.

"Wasn't that Cornelius Foley?" she asked.

"Yes, ma'am," Absolem answered, flicking the reins over the bay's back. "He probably come to see Mr. Garret. He come a lotta times to see Mr. Garret."

Emily settled back against the seat. Cornelius Foley was Florrie Whitman's common-law husband. A big man with hands like hams, he was a known troublemaker. She wondered what business he would have with Garret. Perhaps he had some news of her husband and she should have Absolem turn back? But no. If there was any news of Fade surely it would be she herself who would hear, not his slatternly sister. Besides, it would be foolish to run the risk of having Garret change his mind. Better to keep silent and enjoy her few precious days of freedom.

"Oh dear, I do wish I had known you were coming."

For a moment Emily was afraid Agatha was going to send her away. The older woman was visibly distressed, rubbing her thin fingers up and down her gaunt cheek. "It is a little . . . that is, it might be . . ."

"I'm sorry, Cousin Agatha, if I've caused you any inconvenience. You did say I could come when I needed to . . . and, well, I need to now."

Emily sank down on Agatha's tufted velour sofa, and began pulling off a glove. It looked as though there would be no point in removing her bonnet and pelerine. Her heart began to feel leaden in her chest.

"No, no, my dear, it's no inconvenience." Agatha reached over to take Emily's gloves from her. "I sincerely meant it when I invited you to come, and if you need to, then that's all the more reason you must stay. It's just that I'm . . . that I have an engagement."

"But I won't be in your way. You must go on about all the things you'd normally do. I'll stay here and keep company with Claes."

"There's no need for that. Here, take off your bonnet." Agatha herself untied the ribbons and laid Emily's hat on the table. Then, a little nervous but determined, she took her hands.

"You might as well know the truth, Emily dear. I am delighted to have you visit me for just as long as you wish to stay. If I seem a little flustered it is because I am deeply involved right now with the Justice League and we are holding a very important meeting tomorrow evening in the village. I have been working on it for weeks."

"The Justice League. But that's an—"

"Exactly. An abolitionist club. I did not want you or Garret to know about it, but I have put myself, body and soul, at their disposal."

Emily laughed with relief. This was nothing that could not be handled. "Why, Cousin Agatha, I never knew you felt so strongly about slavery."

"I never used to, to my everlasting shame. But I know better now. Slavery is a blot on the conscience of the country. It is a disease, a canker, and it must be rooted out at the core or we shall all die of it."

Emily untied the buttons on her pelerine and settled back on the sofa. "But the Deveroes have not owned slaves for years. No one in New York is allowed to anymore. Why should you care so much?"

Agatha's round spectacles slid down her thin nose and she lifted her chin to peer at Emily through them.

"Oh, Emily," she said, pursing her narrow lips. "I fear you are a very shallow creature at heart. Not that it's your fault. You have just been too pampered and babied all your life to appreciate how other people suffer. Don't you know anything about what's going on in this country?"

"Well, I know the subject is in the papers now with much more regularity than it used to be. And I know that every time the Whigs and the Locofocos wish to malign each other they use the term *abolitionist* as a kind of insult. As for being for slavery or against it, I don't suppose I ever thought about it much."

"Well, you should think about it! No man should be in bondage to another, colored or white. It's not Christian or Republican, and how a country that calls itself both has managed to live with it for so long is beyond me."

"That's easily answered. It's because this country puts greed before either Christianity or Republicanism. After all, slavery is a perfectly logical economic reality in the south. If we lived there we should probably resent the abolitionists too."

"I can see you need educating in this matter, Emily dear. The abolitionist movement is one of the strongest forces in the country right now. There are clubs in every major town and speakers who do nothing but travel between them, attempting to prod the consciences of unthinking people like yourself. I have here in the house several pamphlets which I shall see you read at once. Then tomorrow you must go with me to the meeting. One of the most forceful men in the movement, Mr. Owen Ward, will be there to speak to us. He's coming to supper here at my house first, so you will have an opportunity to talk with him privately as well."

Emily laughed. "My goodness, Agatha, are you going to make all this a condition of my being allowed to stay?"

Agatha managed a sheepish smile. "No, dear, of course not. But I am thinking that perhaps it was God's will that you came to me right now."

"I can see I shall have to resist mightily lest I become the newest convert to the Justice League. Very well, Agatha. I promise to listen to your arguments. Meanwhile, I can't tell you what a blessing it is to be here."

Agatha pushed her glasses back up her nose and got to her feet. "Now, I'd better go tell Ruby to prepare a room for you."

"Yes," Emily said, rising, "and I'd better let Absolem know he can drive the carriage back. When you first saw me arrive, you were so obviously distressed I was afraid to have him leave."

Agatha smiled and laid a thin arm around the girl's waist. "Forgive me, my dear. You should know you are always welcome in my house. My devotion to the cause made a shambles of my manners, but we'll make up for it. I promise you."

Owen Ward proved to be as interesting a man as any Emily had met since leaving New York City. He was barely up to her height and given to plumpness, but his flashing dark eyes in a head too large for his body were so arresting that one quickly forgot his unheroic figure. He had a mane of thick white hair and long sideburns that reached nearly to his shaven chin, and when he wanted to read from one of his pamphlets, which he did rather frequently during dinner, he pulled out a pair of tiny spectacles and perched them halfway down his nose. Emily thought he was the personification of a country schoolteacher until he launched into one of his fiery quotes and was instantly transformed into an Old Testament prophet. Inspired by his logical diatribes, she found herself examining the issue of slavery with a concentration never before imagined.

"Professor Dew of Virginia and John Calhoun of South Carolina, as well as many other southerners, will try to tell you that slavery is not a national evil, that it is for the benefit of the country. What they really mean is that it is for the benefit of the south. It is a moral evil. A blot on the conscience of this country. A crime against the Savior they so piously profess to accept."

Agatha, her fork poised over her plate, was leaning forward, engrossed in every word. "Won't you have a little more blanc-mange," Emily asked, hoping to lighten the conversation and fill in for her hostess's lapse of manners.

"You seem to be an intelligent woman, Mrs. Whitman," Ward said, waving away the dessert. "Do you know that the college I attended, Oberlin, is the only school in the country to admit Negroes? Education is the best means of loosening the Negro's chains. There are those who will tell you that if you educate a black man you only make him more conscious of his inferior place in society and thus more unhappy. Not so! Those who would claim such a doctrine have only one goal in mind: to keep things as they are. They fear an educated black society because it means an end to their tyranny and repression."

"But surely, Mr. Ward, they have some reason to fear. If your way of life rested on the service of an inferior race, would you want to have it wrecked? And I have been told that slavery is not so abhorrent to some blacks, that in fact they are inclined to be rather contented under it."

Ward looked at Emily as though she was feebleminded. "Mrs. Whitman," he said, shaking his large head, "I fear that you are typical of the unthinking, unenlightened masses in this country who, rather than face the truth, would prefer to believe a man in chains is happy. Would *you* be happy? Do you have any idea of the suffering and degradation the slave endures? Right now there is a man having supper in Mrs. Yancy's kitchen who will speak at the meeting tonight from his own experience in bondage. The things he will tell you are shocking and terrible to hear, but I hope you will listen carefully and sear them on your heart."

Emily stirred in her chair, uncomfortable under the imposing glare of this fiery man. She had come to Agatha's hoping to escape the depressing troubles of Southernwood, and suddenly she felt as though she had jumped from the frying pan into the fire. Of course slavery was evil and certainly *she* had no wish to hold any man in bondage. Had not her father often said that a freeman made twice as good a servant as a slave? But her own small world was difficult enough to handle right now and that left her with no enthusiasm at all for changing the larger world. All she wanted was privacy and peace, not a crusade.

"Mr. Ward," Agatha spoke up, "is it true that Oberlin College also plans to allow women to study for a degree in higher education?"

"Why, madam, the first woman enrolled as a student three years ago. And that should be another lesson to you, Mrs. Whitman," Ward said, turning back to Emily, "for most women are also held in bondage."

"Oh, come now, Mr. Ward, that is going too far."

"No, Emily my dear, what Mr. Ward says is all too true. We women are too prone to accept the shackles men force upon us. I myself had a good and generous husband, but I know many women who do not and their lives have certainly been lives of bondage. And aside from marriage, I have often thought that many fine intellects have been wasted for no better reason than that they belonged to the wrong sex. Why, you yourself, my dear, have an inquiring and enterprising mind. Think how you might have benefited from a better education."

Flustered, Emily fussed with her napkin, crumpling it on the table. "Why, I really never wished . . ." But she thought back to some of her early outings with the baron, remembering what a shocking but pleasant surprise it had been to realize that a whole world existed beyond her front door, a world where one's mind, imagination, and hands could all be put to good use. Perhaps it was true that well-to-do young ladies like herself were actually very unproductive creatures, that what was expected of them was very little indeed—to run a house, produce a family, and do a fine job of tatting. But, surely, to call this bondage was extreme. And besides, it had so little to do with her . . . The delicate chimes of a fine old clock on the mantel interrupted these thoughts, much to her relief.

"Dear me," Mr. Ward said, rising from the table. "The time is getting on. I must collect Nathan from the kitchen and move along to the meeting hall. Thank you for such an excellent dinner, Mrs. Yancy."

Agatha was already on her feet. "We'll all go with you,

Mr. Ward. Our chairman, Ted Erving, will be here any moment to escort us in his carriage. I'm sure you will want to have a look at the hall before people begin arriving. Emily?"

"Of course, Cousin Agatha. Just let me get my cloak."

Like a lamb being led to the slaughter, she thought, arranging her bonnet over her side curls and Grecian knot. Her face, peering back at her from the hall mirror, looked thin and wan in the lamplight. "I wish we could stay home with a good novel," Emily said, speaking to her reflection. "But we must instead go redeem the world! High-ho! Let's get it over with, then."

The old meeting house was a dilapidated building on the outskirts of the village. It consisted of one large room, lit by old-fashioned whale-oil lamps set at intervals along the wooden plank walls that cast a ghostly gloom and set shadows dancing across the ceiling. There was a small raised platform at one end, decorated with a large spray of evergreens and a flag. A pine table sat in the center of the platform, and behind it three straight-backed chairs awaited the principal speakers.

The room filled up quickly, and Emily was surprised to recognize many of her neighbors. She'd had no idea that so many prominent members of the village cared about abolition at all, much less that they belonged to the growing ranks of crusaders. It was this spirit that put her off the subject, she decided, thinking back to the supper conversation. An issue is one thing, but when it becomes a crusade crying out for martyrs, sacrifice, and choices—that was too strong for her taste. She took a chair near the back and sat down to endure the evening.

Yet after Mr. Ward began to speak, his hands gripping the table while his whole body, poised on the balls of his small feet as though ready to spring, leaned forward, Emily was spellbound in spite of herself. He was a masterful speaker, haranguing them one moment, soothing them the next. There was almost a religious fervor about Owen Ward, and Emily found her emotions being played like a violin.

When Mr. Ward had finished, he turned and brought forward a stooped coffee-colored old man with white hair crowning his blunt face. Nathan was the escaped slave Mr. Ward had mentioned at dinner. Even from the back of the room Emily was struck by the vitality and spark in his eyes, and when she later learned that he was not nearly so old as his white hair and stooped shoulders suggested, she was not really surprised.

With a warm handshake and a pat on his shoulder, Ward turned the podium over to Nathan, who began to speak in a soft voice, thick with the dialect of the south. The feeling beneath his words as he quietly began his story had the people in the room hanging on his every word.

And it was a terrible story: of forced separation from his parents as a child and later from his wife and children; of harsh floggings and brutal punishments; of being forever at the mercy of other men for no better reason than that they were white and he was black. As his quiet voice detailed horror upon horror, Emily was moved almost to tears. I never knew, she wanted to stand up and shout. I never thought... Then she caught herself and thought, Remember, this is what they want. Mr. Ward would like nothing better than to go on to the next meeting in the next town bragging about how he made a convert of the callous Mrs. Emily Whitman.

She sat back in her chair, fussing with the folds of her pelerine and forcing herself to watch the rapt faces of the people around her.

A sudden crash shattered the window at the end of her row. Emily gasped, rose, and scrambled with the people around her toward the center of the aisle as another window and then another was broken, sending splintering glass in all directions. At the rear of the hall the doors were slammed open and several men rushed through, their faces blackened with soot, some wearing black hoods with huge eyeholes. They all carried rifles or pistols and several had bags of eggs from which they began pelting the speakers at the front of the room. It was utter confusion—women screaming and people clambering over one another to reach the shelter of the side aisles as missiles flew the length of the hall and spattered the walls. The room was filled with the sour, nauseating odor of rotten eggs. One of the masked men ran up behind Emily and shoved her against the wall. For the first time she could make out what they were yelling.

"Damn abolitionists! Nigger-lovers!"

"It ain't fit for a black man to stand on the same stage as a white!"

"Drag 'em off. String up that nigrah!"

"Troublemakers. We don't want you here. Get back to the swamp where you belong." A heavy thud cracked the plaster on the wall beside her and Emily realized that rocks had been added to the eggs flying through the air. Several of the lamps broke, dousing people with hot oil and sparks and throwing the room into a dim grayness, which added to the confusion.

"Look out," Emily screamed to the woman nearest her. "Your skirt's on fire!"

Flames streaked along the edge of the worn carpet while the woman, yelping in fear, dashed aside, flaying at her skirt. Her husband, shoving Emily out of the way, yanked off his coat and began beating at the fire, quickly putting it out. By now the whole fury of the mob was focused on the front of the room, where a hailstorm of rocks and eggs were thick in the air. Emily tried to work her way toward the stage, hoping to find Agatha and somehow get her out the back way. When she finally got close enough to the front of the room she understood why Mr. Ward had wanted to inspect the hall before the meeting began. He and Nathan had disappeared through a door painted to blend into the wall, conveniently placed near the stage. But Agatha, trembling with horror, stood rooted to one side below the platform, her hands to her face. Pushing her way through the crowd, Emily managed to grab her cousin's arm.

"This way," she cried, pulling Agatha toward the rear.

Agatha looked at her, her eyes huge and blank.

"Come on!" Emily said urgently. With one arm around Agatha's shoulders and the other bent to make a battering ram, she worked a way through the screaming crowd until the rear doors were in sight. Ducking through them, she was appalled to see that several other members of the mob were outside the building, riding their horses back and forth and shooting their pistols in the air.

Emily stood frozen on the porch. Up until now these men had been only the faceless members of a mob. All at once there was something familiar about one of them. It was Cornelius Foley! Throwing her cloak over both of them to shield their faces, Emily pulled Agatha across the porch and down a side alley toward the other end of the building. If they could find a dark, quiet place to hide, this mob would probably disappear as quickly as it had come and they could make their way back to the Yancy house. With any luck Garret would never learn they had been there that evening.

To Emily's surprise Owen Ward was barely perturbed by the evening's violence.

"This has happened before," he said, standing in his shirt-sleeves beside Agatha's kitchen table while Ruby worked to wash the filth from his coat. "And no doubt it will happen again. I am becoming rather accustomed to it. Poor Nathan, though, is severely shaken."

"Would you care for a small glass of wine, Mr. Nathan?" Agatha said to the trembling Negro. "It sometimes helps to steady the nerves."

"No thank you, ma'am," he answered, visibly attempting to control himself. "But a little whiskey—that'd be nice."

"Oh dear, I'm afraid I never keep whiskey in the house." Agatha looked apologetically at Owen Ward.

"It's all right, Mrs. Yancy. Nathan will get used to this too if he intends to make the circuit with me. Unfortunately, the worst of this violence is always directed at the black man. But you will be protected, Nathan, I promise. Did you notice tonight how several of the men in the room crowded around the stage in order to allow us to escape? There are those who care, Nathan. I hope in time you will come to believe it."

Mr. Ward laid a steadying hand on Nathan's shoulder. Standing there in his shirtsleeves, his stock awry, and his hair wilder than ever, Emily thought he looked as little like a blazing reformer as any man could. Yet there was a power and a presence about him that impressed her. He had courage and zeal, and she possessed little of either just at that moment.

"Dear me, Mr. Ward," Agatha said, her voice still shaking, "you will want a washing up, I suppose, before you settle in for the night. Can I have Ruby heat some water for you?"

"Thank you, just enough to clean my face would do it. Though I deeply appreciate your offer, I don't think it would be safe to stay here in the village tonight. Somewhere between here and White Plains we shall find an inn where we are not known. I can always say Nathan is my slave." He smoothed back his wild mane of white hair. "What a world we live in!: we are allowed peace and a night's lodging as long as we preserve the relationship of master and servant, but let us profess to appear as brothers and friends and we will be driven from the door!"

There was a sad truth in that, Emily thought, even as she felt relieved that Owen Ward and Nathan were leaving. The idea of a mob descending on Agatha's house was too terrible to contemplate. Theodore Erving, who looked somewhat relieved himself to have the troublesome guests out of his village, nevertheless offered to escort them part of the way. By the time they were ready to ride off an hour later they had been joined by three other men from the village, all committed to seeing the spokesman of their cause safely out of Mount Pleasant. Emily watched them canter off in the darkness, impressed that these men whom she had always thought of as ordinary citizens with no other concerns but their own, were actually committed to an unpopular cause—and for no other reason than that they believed it to be right and just. Perhaps her own little problems and the safe cocoon of her small world *had* blinded her to the greater issues and more profound problems of the times.

The first stirrings of Emily's public conscience were quickly dispersed the next morning, when Garret stormed into Agatha's sitting room, tracking mud on her carpet and slapping the table with his riding whip.

"How dare you! How dare you appear at such a gathering, dragging our good name through the mud! Making yourselves the laughingstock of decent people! I won't have it!"

Agatha broke in furiously. "Garret Deveroe, this is my house and I'll thank you not to come in here acting so ugly. And stop beating my table. You'll scratch it up."

Garret turned on her, his face dark with fury. "Keep quiet, old woman. You are responsible for this. My sister comes down here for a visit and in one day's time she's mixed up with a bunch of fanatics. It's all your fault, I have no doubt. Get your things, Emily. You're coming home."

Agatha laid an arm around Emily's shoulder. "You don't have to, Emily. He's your brother, not your father or your husband."

"You'd better be glad I'm not, for it I were, I'd beat you half to death for last night's foolishness."

"Foolishness!" Emily cried, her eyes crackling with anger.

"That mob was shooting and throwing stones at defenseless men and women. I suppose you approve of that."

"What I think is my concern and none of yours. That sentimental rabble was asking for just what they got. They were lucky to get off as easily as they did. If you don't get your things together and come home now, you'll never find the door open to you again."

"Don't let him bully you, Emily dear." Agatha laid her hand on Emily's arm. "You don't have to go. You can live here with me."

Emily looked from one to the other. She knew Garret's threat was not an idle one. He would love nothing better than to push her out completely.

"I think I'd better go back," she said quietly.

Agatha threw up her hands. "And you think women don't wear shackles! Emily, when will you wake up?"

A little surprised at the easy capitulation, Garret ordered her to hurry about the business of packing. He had hoped she might choose to stay away, and yet this reassertion of his authority was not unpleasing.

"I haven't really unpacked," Emily murmured, picking up the few belongings she had scattered around the room. "It won't take me but a few minutes."

"You have an hour. I'll send Absolem down for you. And you be ready because I don't want him gone too long. He's needed in the stables."

Garret stalked from the room, slamming the door behind him. Emily could barely meet her cousin's eyes for the pity and sadness she saw there.

"Don't you see," she almost cried, "if I don't go back, Garret will say I've forfeited any claim to Southernwood. It's more mine than his and I refuse to let him take it away from me."

"You don't have to explain anything to me, dear," Agatha said sadly. "Garret seems to destroy everything he touches. You do what you feel is right, Emily. You know I am here if you need me."

Emily threw her arms around Agatha's thin shoulders and hugged her close. "Thank you, Cousin, for understanding. You know, you're the only person in the world right now who is a comfort to me."

Looking into Emily's earnest brown eyes, Agatha smoothed back a wayward strand of hair from her temple and thought how much she resembled her grandmother, Celia. There was the same sweetness about her and a softness that appeared when her face was not set in stubborn lines of determination, as it often was.

"Claes will be disappointed," she murmured.

"Tell him I will come back tomorrow for the day and we'll go to the river. Perhaps we can prevail on Captain Sherwood to take us out on his sloop for a short ride."

"He'd love that. Now, you go get your things together. You mustn't keep Garret waiting."

When Emily returned from her excursion with Claes the following afternoon, she was surprised to see a familiar figure standing at the edge of the lawn overlooking the river.

"I thought the baron was away," she said to Absolem, not even trying to conceal her dismay.

"That gentleman, he go to New York but he come back today. It almost be like he thinks Southernwood's his home, Miss Emily. I don't believe he is ever goin' to leave."

Though Emily was inclined to agree, she discreetly kept her feelings to herself. Inwardly she was dismayed. She had been looking forward to spending a few days at home without the baron's company.

She was in her room laying out her brushes on the dressing table when a soft knock and a courteous "May I come in" announced that Garret was at her door. He was all charm as he entered and welcomed her back.

"I understood von Arensten was away," Emily said, knowing full well why her brother was making such an effort to be sociable.

"He went to New York briefly to take care of some financial business, but soon found the pleasures of our peaceful country life more enticing than the jaded city. I trust you will be pleasant to him."

"I think I would rather avoid him. Can't you make my excuses for dinner? After all, I did come home as you asked. Isn't that enough?"

Garret settled in the room's one comfortable chair and idly fingered the fob at his waist.

"I don't know," he said, showing great restraint. "See here, Emily . . ."

"No, you see here," Emily said, her hackles rising.

"Emily, I did not come up here to start an argument. I simply want to ask you to make an effort to be pleasant to him—nothing more. All that other business is forgotten, dead, buried. The baron will treat you with the greatest deference and respect and all you need do in return is show him the same courtesy you would any other guest."

Emily sank down on the edge of her bed and crossed her arms over her chest, eyeing her brother suspiciously.

"Are you saying he wants nothing more from me than a few pleasantries?"

"Absolutely. My word on it."

"I don't believe you."

Garret struggled visibly with his growing irritation. "All right, then, perhaps you will believe me when you are in his company. At any rate, I expect you to appear for meals and not be sullen when you do so."

Emily looked away from the smiling, deceitful face to her window, through which sunlight was spilling bright gold over the carpet.

"There must be something in it for the two of you. What is it, Garret? You might as well tell me or I swear to you I will be the most *un*pleasant company anyone ever sat down with at a table."

"I'll be happy to tell you. The baron made a draft of five thousand dollars yesterday which he plans to loan me for the purchase of shares in the Boston-Albany Railroad. It's a fine opportunity to get into what will surely be a lucrative business someday. Without this loan I shall have to pass up the chance."

Emily studied her brother, trying to see behind his enigmatic features. "Why doesn't he buy the shares himself if they are such a good investment?"

"Because he isn't interested in investing in an American business. Soon he will be off to Europe again, and he has no idea when he will return."

"And I am to believe that he is doing this for you with no expectation of reward? That friendship alone is now the motive behind such generosity?"

"Believe it or not, it is true. You will be doing me and,

incidentally, Southernwood, a great service by humoring him."

All at once the light in the room was blinding. Emily rose and briskly pulled at the blinds to diminish the glare.

"Oh, very well. I shall try to be polite to the man, though it's going to be difficult. In spite of what you say, I still don't trust him."

The next two days almost convinced Emily that her judgment of Baron von Arensten had been wrong. No one could have been more politely attentive or less forward. By the third day she risked taking a short ride with him and returned convinced that Garret must have, for once, been telling the truth. The baron made no advances, no sly remarks, never so much as touched her even to help her off her horse, and seemed in every way politely remote. By the fourth day his impeccable manners had almost driven away the memory of that afternoon in Tarrytown, and the atmosphere of the house had drifted into a pleasant tranquillity. Garret seemed in better humor than she had seen him in years.

On the fifth day Emily put aside her fears and decided to pamper herself. There was to be a late supper party to which Mr. Slade and his wife, Jeanne, had been invited. Though the affair was mostly to be a business get-together for the gentlemen, Emily decided to make herself as pretty as possible, wearing her best rose silk frock with the wide blond lace and balloon-shaped sleeves. She curled her hair in long spirals on either side of her cheeks and carefully drew the back up in a Grecian knot. Pearls at her throat and an artificial camellia at the crown of the knot were just the right finishing touches. She went downstairs to greet their visitors feeling prettier and gayer than she had in weeks. It does something for a lady's self-esteem, she thought, to dress up now and then, even when it is only to preside at a table.

When she entered the parlor she found only Garret and von Arensten sitting before a flickering fire which had been laid in the hearth against the dampness of the evening.

"The Slades are not here yet?"

"They're not coming," Garret replied, pulling a chair forward for her. "A note arrived only a few moments ago explaining that Mrs. Slade is ill and George felt he was needed at home. I suppose they are afraid of the cholera which is so prevalent in the county right now."

"May I say how lovely you look this evening," the baron said from across the room. "On such a chilly night it warms the heart to see so much summery beauty."

Disappointed, Emily nodded an acknowledgment of the baron's compliment. She had been looking forward to a change of faces and to the company of another woman.

"Well, we must make the most of the evening ourselves," Garret said gaily. "Baron von Arensten has been saving a bottle of fine old champagne, Emily, which we planned to sample tonight. Now it will have to be three of us rather than five. So we'll each have more."

"It is of the highest quality, Mrs. Whitman," the baron added. "I'm sure you will enjoy it."

"I'm sure," Emily murmured. And so would Garret. A thin sliver of anxiety intruded on her happiness. Her brother had been on his good behavior lately, which meant that he had tempered his drinking. All at once she envisioned him in a drunken stupor by the night's end. So much for a convivial evening.

Her first suspicion that something was wrong came when she tasted the wine. There was a hint of an odd odor she almost recognized but could not quite place, and the taste seemed faintly bitter for so fine a champagne. Watching Garret, all good humor and overflowing with fellowship, her distrust began to flower. The baron, who seemed in as high spirits as Garret, kept up a cheerful banter that made it easy for her to disguise the fact that she was not drinking. When they rose from the table to go back to the parlor, she carried the glass with her and poured its contents into a vase of flowers in the hall. Holding the glass so that her hand covered the bowl, she pretended to sip at the contents. Perhaps she was being very foolish and overly suspicious, but she wasn't taking any chances.

As the hours passed, the drowsiness and blurred vision Emily experienced convinced her that her suspicions had been correct. The two men kept eyeing her and asking solicitously if she felt sleepy or ill. At first she denied that anything was wrong, but then Emily decided to affect great dizziness and torpor and see just what their game was.

Leaving the baron and her brother in the parlor, she dragged herself heavily upstairs, allowed Faith to remove her clothes and brush her hair, and fell gratefully into bed. Never had it felt so good.

Their voices woke her, though they were barely more than whispers. By half opening her eyes, she could make out the dim light of one candle and the shadow of her brother's form bending over the bed.

"I tell you she didn't drink it," Garret hissed. "It's too dangerous."

"But how can you be sure? She seemed drugged to me."

The baron's voice came from the other side of the bed. Emily struggled to rise up in indignation, but her limbs refused to move. She groaned and stirred and felt the two men freeze. That would not do. If she wanted to know what they were up to, she must pretend to be asleep. Lying very still, she tried to make her breathing even and slow though her heart was pounding.

"You promised!" the baron hissed.

"I know. But not now. Unless she's really drugged there'll be hell to pay in the morning. Come on. I'll make it up to you."

"Bah! I will not wait much longer."

Garret's voice was conciliatory. "We'll try again tomorrow and I promise I'll find a way. The taste is too easily detected in wine. It has to be in the food."

Their voices were receding now; they must be nearly out of the room. Emily heard the faint click of the lock and opened her eyes to the darkness, the hairs on her neck standing stiff as with an electric shock. Obviously Garret had planned to drug her so that the baron could climb into her bed. She was filled with horror, anger, and disgust at the thought. Forcing her legs over the side of the bed, she dragged herself to the window, fumbled with the latch, and threw it open. The cold air helped clear her head as she forced herself to walk back and forth across the carpet, willing her reluctant limbs to function.

How could he do this to her—her own brother? Had he so little regard for her, not to mention common decency, that he would use her to fulfill the lust of a man she despised?

It took her nearly half an hour to gain control of herself. This was absolutely the last straw. She knew she ought to wait until morning to confront Garret, but she felt she would surely explode with rage and indignation before then. Drawing her robe around her shoulders, she put on her slippers, lit the lamp beside her bed, and marched down the hall to Garret's room.

There was no light under the door. He was probably already asleep or, if not, lying in the dark trying to think of new ways to abuse her. Well, she would wake him up soon enough!

Rapping sharply on the door, Emily did not wait for an answer but walked boldly into the room, ready to strangle her brother with her bare hands if he gave her the opportunity.

The scene that met her eyes seared itself on her mind for the rest of her life. Facing her, his back arched against the bedpost, was her brother, the lamplight gleaming on his naked shoulders, his head thrown back as if he were in an ecstatic trance. His hands rested on the muscular shoulders of the baron, who was on his knees before him, his bare buttocks to Emily, his head working energetically against Garret's thighs, one hand clasped tightly around his waist.

It took her a moment to realize that the bobbing shadows, so intent on what they were doing, were two men, and a moment more to understand. Nausea rose like bile in her throat as she stood rooted in the doorway, staring.

At her horrified exclamation, Garret's eyes flew open. Slowly, almost curiously, the baron looked around, then rose to his feet, fully baring to Emily a torso laced with thick, black hair.

Not a word was spoken. As quickly as she could make her feet move, Emily turned and fled down the hall to her bedroom, slamming and locking the door, gripping the edge of her dressing table in an attempt to still her trembling.

So much was clear now. How blind she had been all these years! This was what had turned her father against Garret. For his only son to indulge in such an unspeakable perversion must have been a terrible blow to a man like Josh Deveroe. Now she understood why Garret never seriously courted any woman, why he never even considered the idea of marriage. Now his close friendships with men like von Arensten and the drunken servants in the shacks out back made sense. Now she knew why he avoided normal men like Fade and Robert.

Garret was her brother, but he had contaminated Southernwood with his unnatural sickness. It was no longer the home she had always loved. Now it was a prison, a den of nightmares. She would not stay within its walls one day longer.

Rushing to the small mahogany desk opposite her bed, Emily located the secret drawer where she kept the money Fade had given her before leaving New York. It was almost all still there—nearly one hundred dollars in cash that would buy her her freedom. In a frenzy she began piling her clothes on the bed, adding two small miniatures, one of her father and one of Fade, and a few pieces of good jewelry to the heap. She would take everything that mattered away with her and leave nothing behind to show she had been witness to this depraved scene.

There was a loud banging on her door.

"Emily!" Garret's voice. "Emily, open this door. I want to talk to you."

"I don't want to talk to you," Emily cried. "Go away!"

The handle of the door rattled vigorously. "Emily, I warn you, open this door or I'll have it torn down. This is still my house!"

She longed to cry out angrily that he could go to the devil, but something warned her that he would make good on his threat to break down the door. Keeping silent, she waited until he spoke again. This time his tone was conciliatory.

"Come on, Emily. I can explain everything. It's your fault, you know, for walking into my room like that. Let's just talk it over and get the whole matter settled right now."

Emily forced herself to sound more hurt than furious. It was the only way to buy some time.

"I'm very upset right now, Garret. Can't we wait until morning? I promise I shall listen calmly to your explanations then."

Garret took time to weigh this suggestion. "Very well, if you promise to try and understand my position."

"I promise." She forced her voice to betray nothing of her disgust.

Emily heard Garret's footsteps receding down the hall and a low murmur of voices before his door was shut.

Let him think she would lie here crying and distraught until morning. He would learn soon enough that she had taken herself out of his influence forever.

It took considerable self-control for her to wait until she felt sure both men were asleep. Then she quietly dragged her portmanteau from the downstairs closet and carried it back to her room. As she packed her belongings she plotted her next moves. If she returned to Cousin Agatha's house Garret would be down there by tomorrow afternoon to drag her back; she would not willingly involve anyone she knew in this sordid affair.

No, she was finished with Southernwood and Mount Pleasant. There was a great, wide world out there and somewhere in it was the only person she wanted to be with. Though she had heard nothing from Fade in all these months, Emily knew with a deadly certainty that she would never be able to build a new life until she discovered what had become of him. If her husband was still out there, she was determined to find him or die in the attempt.

Captain Sherwood's market sloop would leave the Sparta dock at first light and Emily knew she could talk him into carrying her to the city. Quietly stealing from the house, she shook Absolem awake. His eyes seemed to grow larger when he saw her box. He started to exclaim but she quickly shushed him. His voice dropped to an outraged whisper.

"Miss Emily, you cain't go down into the city like this—sneakin' off and nobody knowin' where."

"Keep your voice down, Absolem. I have to go. All I ask is that you drive me to the dock."

"But, Miss Emily, it ain't fittin'. Why, you got no maid nor woman with you. What your Papa think about you goin' off like this?"

"Papa's dead and it doesn't matter anymore. I'm going, Absolem. I'm going to look for my husband and nothing you or anybody else can say will stop me. Now hurry and hitch up that horse."

"Miss Emily, I knowed you since you was a babe, but I ain't never knowed you to do anything so crazy. You can't go runnin' off cross the country like this. Why, it's wild out there—Indians, outlaws, crazy mens. An' you settin' out without even a maid!"

"If you don't go hitch that horse I'll walk to the dock!"

"All right. All right. But it ain't fittin'!"

All the way down the hill to the village Absolem grumbled while Emily sat next to him terrified that she would turn around and see Garret thundering after her. She would not know a moment's peace until she was on the boat and in the middle of the river.

It proved simple enough to bribe Captain Sherwood to take

her along. She piled her boxes next to the stacks of crates and
barrels on the deck, and finding a spot on a huge wicker chest
near a pen of bleating sheep, she settled down for the journey.
As Absolem returned to the shore, Emily took one last look at
the dark green hill where, far up at its crest, the home she had
always loved was bathed in shadows. Then, amid the familiar
cries of the captain and his deckhand and the screeching and
swooping of the gulls, the sloop pushed off. The orange sail
caught the wind and the boat glided smoothly toward the middle
of the channel. Too miserable to cry, Emily fastened her gaze
intently on the river, broad and slow and the color of mud in
the growing dawn. A cough behind her brought her sharply
around.

"Absolem! What on earth are you doing here?"

"Ah'm goin' with you, Miss Emily. You got to have someone to watch over you, and I knows that if Mr. Josh could look
down from out of heaven this minute and see what you're doin',
he'd say as sure as anythin', 'Absolem, you go take care of
my little girl.' And that's just what I'm goin' to do."

Emily knew she should be annoyed, but she felt only relief.
"But Mr. Garret will be very angry with you. And what about
the carriage?"

"Dat little Orser boy, he'll take it back up the hill. And Mr.
Garret—he not such a good boss to work for anyhow. Besides,
I thinks maybe it might be time I saw something more of this
big world."

Emily laid her gloved hand on his thick dark arm. "You're
a good man, Absolem. But you must <u>understand</u> this will not
be an easy trip. I don't know what I'm going to find or what
difficulties lie ahead. And there's probably a good chance that
some part of my journey will take me into one of the slave
states. You're not afraid?"

"I'm not afraid of nothin'—you know that, Miss Emily."
He smiled broadly, showing even white teeth. "When we gets
to those terrible places, we just start tellin' folks I'm your
slave."

Emily squeezed his arm in a warm gesture. "Thank you,
Absolem. I confess I do feel much more confident having you
along."

She turned back to the river, thinking with pleasure of Garret's rage when he discovered both of them gone. With Ab-

solem to protect her and money in her purse, with the warm free winds of the river caressing her face and the darkness that had become Southernwood slipping away in the distance behind her, she felt sure she had done the right thing.

Ten

EMILY HAD visited Washington City years before, when as a little girl she had accompanied her father on a pleasure trip. She remembered it as a town in the process of becoming, with the smell of new wood and fresh plaster everywhere. Now, years later, it still looked unfinished. With the exception of the imposing marble houses of government, the city was a collection of low one- and two-story buildings, dusty wide roads that a wet dew could churn into a sea of mud, and weed-choked lots marked out for the next thrust of expansion.

She went straight to Gadsby's, the only boardinghouse she knew about. One look at its prices and she knew it was much too dear for her purse, which would have to be opened many times in the weeks ahead. Nevertheless she decided to take a room for one night, because it would afford her both the opportunity to look for a cheaper residence and time to pay a call at the Capitol in search of Robert Slade.

The next morning she went straight to the Capitol. Robert was not expected for another hour, so she left Absolem to notify her when he arrived and took a seat in the ladies' gallery, from where she could watch the Senate at work on the floor below. During her wait Emily listened to a long, boring diatribe by the Senator from Rhode Island which was enlivened only once, when he referred derisively to a fellow congressman as a "jackal." That gentleman, seated across the room at the time, took offense at this designation. Bounding over desks and chairs, he began pummeling his opponent with his fists. The fight that followed was quickly broken up by cooler heads in the chamber, and once decorum was restored, the speaker straightened his stock and coat and droned on, interrupted only by the frequent *twings* and *twangs* of tobacco streams clanging into the spittoons that cluttered the floor.

Observing the government in action was not her favorite pastime, Emily decided, just as Absolem finally appeared and motioned her from the gallery. She followed him down a long marble corridor, to a small office where she saw Robert Slade sitting behind an expanse of oak desk. He rose to greet her with a warm cry of welcome, taking both her hands and ushering her to a leather upholstered chair. She was certain he was glad to see her, though when he discovered her purpose some of his pleasure turned to dismay.

"You can't mean to go traipsing out into the wilds of Tennessee and Missouri by yourself! Why, Emily, I've always known you for an independent young woman, but this is pure folly."

Emily leaned forward in her chair, purpose evident in every line of her body. "I must do it, Robert. I must find my husband. There's no way I can go on like this, wondering where he is or even if he is alive. You'll help me, won't you? For the sake of our friendship."

Robert studied her for a moment before answering, weighing his chances of changing her mind.

"I don't approve, Emily, and I'm concerned for your safety. But you are almost a sister to me and I never could deny you anything. Of course I'll help you find Frederick."

Jumping up, Emily impulsively threw her arms around his neck and hugged him tightly. "Oh, thank you, Robert, thank you. I knew you wouldn't fail me."

Her embrace had disturbed the neat cut of his reddish whiskers. Smoothing down the damage and straightening his perfectly tied satin stock, he pulled up a chair opposite hers and became very brisk and businesslike.

"We'll have to plan an itinerary. I leave for St. Louis myself in another month; it should be easy enough for you to accompany me. In the meantime we must find you comfortable lodgings. And you must dine with us tonight. You've not met my wife, Gaby, have you? She'll be so pleased to make your acquaintance; she's heard so much of you from Father and me."

Emily let him ramble on, grateful for the invitation, but knowing that she was not about to cool her heels waiting a month for Robert. But how to tell him that without losing his help? Watching him, with his every hair in place and scarcely a spot to be found on his perfectly fashioned clothes, she realized again that fond of him as she was, he reminded her of nothing so much as a figure on a wedding cake. But right now he was her only hope, and for Fade's sake she must curb her old tendencies to take charge or tease him about his dandified ways.

Robert settled back in his armchair and crossed his legs, resting one well-manicured hand on his knee.

"But where is Garret? I should think that it would be a brother's responsibility to accompany you on this journey."

Emily felt her cheeks grow warm and hoped her discomfort was not too obvious. "Oh, he wanted to, of course, but there were pressing matters at home. Business affairs. You know how difficult the times are right now."

"I do indeed. The difference between Garret and me is that I was blessed with a father who early on recognized the importance of wise investments. It is unfortunate that Josh did not do the same."

"Garret often urged him to diversify, but he wouldn't listen. Papa had grown to love the old ways and hated to abandon them. I think he was afraid of newfangled inventions like the railroads. And when he did branch out, so many of his investments failed that it made him even more wary."

"There's more to it than that, Emily. Your father never trusted Garret's judgment. It's really too bad; my father has said many times that Garret has a good nose for business and, given his head, would be such a success as to make the rest of us sit up and take notice."

"Papa had good reason," Emily said quietly. "And I have not seen Garret accomplishing any great miracles since Papa's death. We are worse off than ever before."

"That's because your father left him saddled with too many debts and bad investments."

Pushing down her irritation, Emily fussed with the clasp on her short cape and made ready to leave.

"Well, perhaps we can talk more at dinner this evening. Let me say once more, Robert, how grateful I am to you for helping me with my journey and how much I look forward to meeting your new wife."

"But we haven't yet discussed your trip," Robert said, jumping up.

Emily gave him her hand. "We'll work it out tonight. At what time should I come?"

"I'll send my carriage for you at seven. Gadsby's, right?"

"For the moment. And, Robert, no party, please. I'd as soon not advertise that I am in Washington at all."

"There won't be another soul, I promise. Gaby and I want you all to ourselves," he answered. He walked her to the door and lightly kissed her fingers.

Emily gave him a grateful smile and left his office, wondering if Gaby would be as interested in the exclusive pleasure of her company as Robert supposed.

Gabrielle Slade turned out to be a very tiny woman with an unfortunate tendency toward mincing words and gestures. There was more than a small tinge of jealousy and suspicion in her manner, and with her first greeting Emily was made aware that the new Mrs. Slade had indeed heard of her and, furthermore, knew she had once been Robert's intended.

Almost everything Emily said and did seemed to provoke Gaby's displeasure, particularly her announcement that she intended to leave immediately for Pittsburgh. "Pittsburgh!" she cried, making quick birdlike flutterings with her tiny hands. "Why it's such a wild, barbaric place, I'm told."

"Nevertheless," Emily answered in a firm voice, "it's the last place I know Fade visited. It seems logical that if I am to pick up his trail that would be the place to start."

"But, Emily," Robert said, trying to hide his dismay, "you cannot go on to Pittsburgh without the protection of a husband or a gentleman friend. It would not be safe."

"I have Absolem. Surely his size and strength will discourage anyone who would try to take advantage of me."

"But you don't even have a woman with you." Gaby echoed her husband's misgivings.

"You asked for my help, Emily," Robert said irritably, "yet I don't see how you need it. If you plan to set off like this on your own, there is nothing I can do to stop you and little I can do to help you on your way."

"You can give me information," Emily answered, anxious to appease him. "Where would Fade have been likely to go after Pittsburgh and how would he have gone? I know almost nothing of the western country. Help me to plan the best route, one that he might have followed. You know so many people; perhaps someone returning from the frontier has heard of him. That's how you can help me."

Gaby spoke up. "Why don't you hire a detective who knows the west to find Frederick for you? Surely that's the proper way to pursue your search."

Emily turned and stared coldly at Robert's wife without even deigning to answer her. Robert, knowing only too well that once Emily had made up her mind heaven and earth would not deter her, did not especially care for the growing contempt he sensed in her manner toward his wife. Perhaps it was just as well that Emily would be leaving Washington at once.

"I'll agree on one condition," he finally said. "Promise me you'll be in St. Louis in two months' time. I'll meet you there and see how you're getting on. If you've found Fade, that's all well and good. If you haven't, you'll come home with me and do as Gaby suggests—leave any further searching to people who are more capable of handling it. After all, I don't think your father or mine would countenance your gallivanting off to the Indian territories of New Mexico or joining a wagon train along the Oregon Trail."

Emily turned his proposal over in her mind. What if she found that Fade had joined one of the trains to the northwest? Of course she would follow him, but there was no need to mention that now. Let Robert and his proper wife think they'd won their little victory.

"Very well. I agree."

Robert sat back on the settee and crossed his legs, content that his good judgment had prevailed at least once. Opposite him, Gaby fussed with an antique fan of painted chicken skin and dabbed at her white throat with a lace handkerchief.

"I do so wish I could join you in St. Louis," she said petulantly. "If it were not for my condition I most certainly would take advantage of this opportunity to see something of the western states."

Robert reached over and solicitously patted her hand while Emily's eyes flew simultaneously to his wife's middle. Gaby's low-cut dress of lemon taffeta indicated no sign of pregnancy, but then she had been careful to keep her shawl crossed over her waist all evening. They had only been married a short time and already . . .

"I wouldn't hear of it, my dear," Robert was saying. "It is far more important that you take care of yourself."

There was a glimmer of triumph in the glance Gabrielle Slade threw Emily. It did not go unnoticed. She had won something after all. Emily was only sorry that she let it bother her.

Emily's stay in Washington turned out to be a brief one. Two weeks at a modest hotel did not place much of a demand on her purse nor did it involve her very often in social visits with the Slades. She shopped for a few items she was told were difficult to find on the frontier and—on a brief foray into Virginia—witnessed her first slave auction, a horrible experience that brought back memories of Owen Ward and Nathan. Before she set out for Pittsburgh, Robert's wife arranged for one of the young girls of her household to accompany Emily as her personal maid. Emily was deeply grateful. Josie Briggs was a quiet, mousy-looking creature, barely more than fourteen years old, but she seemed efficient and sufficiently awed to be taking such a trip as to accept Emily's authority unquestioningly. Though Emily was quickly irritated by her childish ways, she was more relieved to have her along than she wished to admit even to herself.

She began her journey on a morning gray with overhanging clouds; Robert accompanied her to the stage office. In addition to a welcome loan of twenty-five dollars, he had also provided her with the names of several people in finance and government on whom she could rely for assistance, as well as a list of lodgings where a woman traveling alone might stay with propriety. She was surprised when he pulled out two more folded papers and pressed them into her hand.

"What is this? No more loans, I hope. I assure you I am very well provided for in that respect."

"No, no. I'm going to take your word for that. No, this is something else I only thought of last night. It took some fancy footwork this morning to have these papers drawn up in time, but I thought you might need them."

Emily glanced at the first few lines, impressed with the authority of their legal language.

"They are documents declaring Absolem to be a free black," Robert explained. "You are going to be in slave territory and you may well need to prove that he is not a runaway. Believe me, his stature and strength are impressive enough that many a bounty hunter will want to cart him off to the south."

Emily stared at him incredulously. "You can't be serious! Why, his family has been with ours for generations. They haven't been slaves since Samuel Deveroe's time. Surely if I explained that—"

Robert shook his head. "Emily, you know so little of the world that I wonder at my stupidity in letting you set out like this. Of course Absolem is a freeman, but if you think you have only to say so in order to verify that fact, well, you are going to be sadly disillusioned. Put one copy safely away, and give the other to Absolem. He must never be without it. At least then I shall rest a little easier."

The seriousness of his expression was enough to convince her, and she quickly tucked the documents into her reticule. "Very well, Robert. I admit you are wiser about these things than I. I will do as you say."

"It is not only for Absolem's sake I do this, you know. Where will you be if you lose him?"

Emily smiled up into his worried eyes, suddenly touched by his concern. "Please don't worry about me, Robert. I'm going to find my husband and nothing will deter me; not slavers, not savages, not anything. I can take care of myself; I'll be all right."

He studied the determined lines of her face, the anticipation in her eyes that suggested her eagerness to be off. She was not his responsibility, so why should he worry? It just seemed so improper for a gentlewoman to make such a journey alone— but then Emily Deveroe had never been an ordinary woman. Reaching down, he kissed her lightly on the forehead.

"I think you will be. Heaven help the frontier! Now go, and God speed."

Emily threw her arms around his neck and hugged him tightly for a moment. Then, without looking back, she climbed up into the swaying, odiferous cab of the carriage and settled into the largest space left, next to a woman in a huge coal-shovel hat with a large basket on her lap. Josie wedged in beside her. In a few moments there came a loud ceremonial cracking of the whip and a noisy "yehaw!" at the horses, and the carriage jerked forward and rolled down the street.

The bouncing and swaying of the cab sent the ruffled brim of the coal-shovel hat knocking against Emily, who soon realized that before they reached Baltimore she was going to have a stiff neck from trying to lean out of its way. Uncomfortable as she was, her heart was light and her hopes high. At last she was *doing* something, not just languishing and waiting. She knew with every fiber of her being that if Fade was still alive out there she would find him. She was going to be with her husband again, somehow, somewhere. Of that she had never felt surer.

At Harrisburg she took a room in a small, pleasant hotel where the mention of Robert Slade's name set the manager bowing. Early the next morning she went immediately to book passage on the canal boat to Pittsburgh, then began making the rounds of the town's many inns, trying to locate one where Fade had stayed.

Absolem followed along behind her, grumbling all the way. "T'ain't fittin' a lady should cross over the door of these low-life places, Miss Emily. I don't know why you don't let me do the askin'. I know how to talk to these tavern men. T'ain't fittin'."

"I'm not turning you loose in this town, Absolem," Emily answered. She was more conscious of Robert Slade's warning than she ever thought she would be. And the more she saw of Harrisburg, the more she did not want the big servant out of her sight, for she was as daunted as he by the crudity of some of the town's hostelries. A few were so filthy that she felt sure Fade would have never stayed there, and those she passed by without entering. Sometimes she had to grit her teeth and stiffen her spine before stepping across the threshold, only to be surprised at the deference and respect she received even in the rowdiest atmosphere.

At the seventh hotel the owner remembered Fade; he had stayed there nearly three weeks, waiting for his brother to appear to accompany him on his way west. Though the man told Emily at some length what a fine gentleman her husband was, he knew only that Fade had intended to go on to Pittsburgh and nothing about his future plans. Even so, Emily left with her heart singing. It was her first real contact with Fade after so many long months. Here was someone who had talked with him and seen him; somehow that helped bring him closer. She could barely contain her eagerness to be off again.

The canal boat was little more than a barge with a long house perched on the deck, and it was crammed to capacity with passengers and their boxes. The overflow was piled on top of the cabin roof. Happy as she was to leave Harrisburg, Emily's enthusiasm for the journey was soon blunted by the primitive conditions aboard the vessel. Inside the cabin was a long room separated at one end by a red curtain to make a sleeping section for the ladies. The walk outside was so narrow as to invite a dunking in the canal, yet the crowded interior reeked so of stale tobacco and assorted cooking odors that the danger of drowning seemed preferable to that of asphyxiation. With cloudy weather or the coming of night, the air outside became so brisk as to drive everyone indoors, the ladies crowding around a fat iron stove at one end and the men around a similar one at the other. To her surprise Emily soon found that she was not the only woman passenger unchaperoned by some male family member. One young woman with a baby was on her way back to her husband in Louisville, while a pair of thin, tight-lipped older ladies turned out to be spinster sisters traveling to St. Louis to join their brother. There were several other women and a few young girls, all of whom had husbands or fathers sleeping on the other side of the red curtain. Most of them were too absorbed with their own concerns to be curious about Emily, much to her relief.

Supper was laid for the passengers on a long table placed down the center of the cabin. On the evening of the second day, Emily looked up to find one of the men watching her intently. He had a pleasant face with light brown whiskers down the side of his cheeks and narrow lips unadorned by any facial hair. Catching her glance, he smiled at her and, picking up a wooden trencher, leaned forward across the table.

"Might I offer you some more of this black pudding, ma'am?" he inquired politely.

"No, thank you," Emily murmured, fixing her gaze on her fork.

"Oh, do try some more. It's most tasty, and I have traveled often enough on this canal to know how unusual that is."

"Thank you, sir," Emily answered coolly, "but I am not very hungry."

"I'll have some of that," said a very large man sitting two seats down the table. Reaching across with a huge arm, he took possession of the bowl and began piling pudding on a plate already loaded with shad, liver, steak, potatoes, sausage, and pickles.

Emily looked up to see the first gentleman giving up the bowl with a wink in her direction. She concentrated on her food during the rest of the meal.

The passengers had to leave the boat for a short trip by rail across the Alleghenies. Waiting next to Josie on the platform, Emily was disconcerted when the gentleman who had offered her pudding approached her and, removing his white beaver hat, spoke to her directly.

"I trust the trip over this great mountain does not frighten you, ma'am," he said. "I have made the journey several times and I can assure you that for all the dangers it seems to entail, it is quite safe."

"Sir, I am not afraid. I have taken trips by rail before this."

"May I be so bold as to introduce myself? Jonas Sutter, ma'am, from Baltimore. I could not help but notice you are traveling alone save for your servants, and I thought perhaps I might be of some small service to you."

Aside from a few politely distant conversations, this was the first man to take a direct interest in her since she had begun her trip, and Emily found herself more than a little wary. Yet, when she thought about it, what was there to fear? They were surrounded by forty other travelers, living as close together as a family of immigrants in a Five Points cellar. Surely it would not be inviting disaster to show him simple good manners.

"I am Mrs. Frederick Whitman, from New York," she answered, giving him the briefest of smiles. "I thank you for your very kind offer, but I am well cared for. My husband will be meeting me at... at the end of my journey, and in the meantime Absolem watches over me quite well."

"Absolem? Oh, you mean your Negro servant. I've always felt that one can only trust Negroes so far, but I'm sure Mr. Whitman would not have entrusted so lovely a piece of property as yourself to his keeping without good cause."

"That is correct," Emily answered, bristling at being labeled "property." "Excuse me, but I see it is time to find a seat. Come along, Josie."

Without waiting for an answer she pushed her way into the rail car and found a place for the two of them next to the young lady with the baby. Although the child had shown a deplorable tendency to wail at all hours of the day and night, right now anything was preferable to continuing her acquaintance with Mr. Sutter. In the crowded car as in the canal boat, Emily drew her solitude around her like an invisible cloak. It was both her protection and her consolation, discouraging any overtures of friendliness.

There was another night and day to be endured before the distant glow of fires and the dim echo of clanking hammers warned that they were approaching Pittsburgh. They boarded a second canal boat on the far side of the mountain, and it carried them through country that Emily found more interesting with every mile. Behind the huge dense forests stood distant hills that breathed vapor from the recent rains. They drifted past new settlements of log cabins, windows patched with paper or old clothes, clustered around fields of wheat thick with the blackened stumps of felled trees. As the ponderous boat glided past mile after uninterrupted mile of splendid forest, Emily decided there would never be enough people on the whole earth to fill up these endless acres.

Pittsburgh surprised her. It was a bustling town already on its way to becoming an important city; the industry there would have done justice to a great port like New York. On the hills above the town, the fancy houses of the more successful citizens were already rising. Under a canopy of ever-present smoke from the ironworks in the heart of the city and near the junction of the two great rivers, neatly laid streets, shops, public buildings, and modest homes revealed the mighty hand of civilization at work in the middle of the wilderness.

Emily took rooms in a clean but unpretentious inn far enough from the waterfront to ensure peace but close enough to allow her to visit all the others. For three days she went from one hostelry to another, Absolem in tow, trying to find a landlord who remembered serving her husband. When none did she turned to the shops and banks, but again found not a trace. When Enos Porter, the chief clerk at one of the banks on Robert Slade's list, learned that she was a friend of the Slades, he went out of his way to assist her. He called on her in the parlor of her small hotel three days after their first meeting, genuinely concerned that he could not be more helpful.

"I regret, ma'am, that I have been unable to come up with anyone who remembers your husband. You are quite sure he came to Pittsburgh?"

"Yes, I'm certain of it. He must have stayed somewhere, bought supplies, talked to people. I cannot understand why someone doesn't recall him."

Mr. Porter sat back, crossed one knee over the other, and steepled his fingers. "That's really not so surprising, considering the numbers of people who swarm through this town every week. Of course, most of them have to cool their heels waiting for a boat south, but it is just possible that your husband and his brother made unusually quick connections and went right off again. That does happen occasionally."

"Oh dear. What rotten luck. He waited in Harrisburg three weeks and here, where he was bound for heaven only knows where, he takes right off again."

For a moment Mr. Porter was afraid the lady was going to burst into tears. Instead she resolutely set her jaw.

"What do you suggest, Mr. Porter?" Emily asked. "I'm not sure where to go next. Living here as you do, have you any idea what his next stop would most likely be?"

"Oh yes. Nine-tenths of the people who come through Pittsburgh take the steamboat on to Cincinnati and St. Louis. I think it is quite plausible that your husband did the same. The choices you will face in St. Louis will be much more difficult: from there one can strike out for Oregon or head south to New Orleans. Of course he might have gone to Youngstown, or Charlestown, Virginia. But the route to one is overland and dangerous, while the other lies through the mountains. No, my guess is he would follow the river. Certainly that is what I would suggest you do."

Emily rose. "I believe that is excellent advice, Mr. Porter, particularly since I have promised to meet Mr. Slade in St. Louis next month anyway. I shall book passage right away."

Enos Porter took her hand and smiled at her. She had lovely eyes, he thought, and a fine figure. A pity they were being wasted while she ran around the country searching for a husband who did not value either enough to stay home.

"Be careful in your choice; steamboats blow up at the rate of about one a week. I would suggest the *Morovia*. Her captain is experienced and has never had an accident. I should be honored if you would allow me to make the arrangements for you."

Emily gave him a grateful smile. "Why, thank you, Mr. Porter. I would appreciate that very much."

She watched him leave the hotel; when he reached the door, he looked back and raised his hat to her. How nice to find someone so pleasant so far from home! It made her feel a little less adrift in a hostile world. I've been foolishly fearful, Emily thought, and I have let my fears hold me back from making new friends and acquaintances when I desperately need both. From now on I intend to be the most sociable person on board!

The *Morovia* was a grand affair compared to the primitive canal boats that had brought her to Pittsburgh. The city docks were lined with steamboats, smoke belching from their twin black chimneys and fire flashing from their depths, ready to convey a steady stream of homesteaders into the frontier territories.

Emily had a berth for herself and Josie in the ladies' cabin, which though comfortable enough was not quite up to the elegance of the small staterooms opening off of it. She wished her purse might allow for that kind of luxurious privacy, but decided it was wiser to conserve her funds. By the end of the first day on board she had begun to feel hopeful again. By the third, the sound of the boat's creaking machinery, the ever-clanging bell of the lookout as he spotted great trees rising from the water, the slap of the paddles, and the slow panorama of the wilderness drifting leisurely by all had blended into a comfortable routine. Some of her anxiety had been left behind at Pittsburgh and with every passing mile she felt more sure that she was nearing the moment when she would be with Fade again.

On this trip she made a determined effort to get to know her fellow passengers. Some of them had been with her on the canal boat: the two spinsters with faces like dried apples; the fat gentleman who loved to eat and his gaunt wife, the woman with the baby. Mr. Sutter appeared again but did little more than lift his hat and smile when he passed her on the deck. Among the newcomers there was the captain's wife, a friendly, loquacious woman with a bubbly sense of humor, and a lonely young girl of barely fifteen who was bright and curious and whose innocence drew everyone around her like moths to a flame. There was a woman, Rose Marley, several years younger than Emily, who had been married only two months and was traveling with her husband, Mordachi, to settle a homestead in the prairie country. She was a timid creature, easily awed by the world. Welcoming Emily's friendly overtures, she latched on to her as though grasping a lifeline, never realizing that the self-contained Mrs. Whitman felt equally unsure of herself in this strange wilderness world.

Of course there were many more men than women crowding the boat, but Emily had little to do with them. They treated her with a politeness that almost bordered on reverence when she was in their company, while out of it they paced the decks or sat by the stove chewing and spitting.

Belowdecks were te immigrants, mostly English and Irish, on their way to make their fortunes in the fabulous new world of open land and endless opportunity. Though Emily had heard them singing, the only time she actually saw them was when a small group, loaded down with boxes, chests, and an occasional chair, would leave the boat for some settlement on the shore, waving good-bye as the boat drew away. She wondered at their courage in facing that great emptiness and made up her mind then and there that she was not cut out to be a pioneer.

Early on the morning of the fifth day, Emily was standing by the railing near the bow when she was overcome by such a longing for Southernwood that she all but burst into tears.

All at once home seemed a world away, and as long as Garret was there she could never return. But what would she do? Where could she go? She had dwelled for so long on the single goal of finding her husband that she had never faced the question of what came afterward.

"Good morning, Mrs. Whitman."

Startled, Emily turned to see Jonas Sutter smiling down at her, his white beaver hat in his gloved hand.

"Oh, Mr. Sutter. Good morning."

"I hope I do not disturb you?"

"No, not at all. I was only watching those people who just went ashore and thinking of the homes they have left and how hard they will have to work to make new and comfortable lives."

"Ah, but they have probably left nothing behind but miserable hovels. Who otherwise would wish to strike a homestead in these barren forests?"

"I expect that is true. Pioneers most likely do not come from comfortable homes. I know I could never be one."

Leaning against the rail, Sutter gave her a look that was almost bold in its sensual appraisal. "That is precisely my point. You have the look of the patrician, Mrs. Whitman. One does not search for fine porcelain in a forest; one keeps it in elegant houses to grace exquisite mahogany tables. Earthenware and pottery—they are the stuff of the common man."

Emily raised her eyebrows. "You sound like a patrician yourself, Mr. Sutter."

He seemed surprised but pleased that she had not cut short the conversation. "I like to think so. I am from South Carolina and accustomed to gracious ways."

Emily gave way to a mischievous urge, although her smile never faded. "That explains it! I believe there are no more refined people anywhere than those from South Carolina."

"Exactly."

"In fact, I was so impressed with South Carolina manners while I was in Washington City that I thought to see some redeeming effects of them in your slaves. I have been sadly disappointed. They do not seem to benefit at all from the refinements of civilized society."

"Of course not," he exclaimed, looking at her as though she had lost her senses. "They are blacks and inferior in every way."

"Indeed?" Emily said. "Their faces are among the most hopeless and forlorn I have ever seen. I wonder that your fine sentiments can be so blunted to their misery."

For the first time there was a brusqueness in his manner. "Madam, are you an abolitionist?"

Emily laughed. "Not at all, Mr. Sutter. It happens that I have rarely thought about the problem at all. It is only that we have not had slaves in my family since before the Revolution."

"Like most northerners, ma'am, you are judging the problem from one perspective without seeing the whole picture."

Emily knew enough about the slavery issue by now to recognize Sutter's prickly defensiveness as a typical southern reaction. Wishing to avoid a confrontation, she attempted to change the subject. At once he grew more amiable and after several minutes raised his hat, bowed politely, and left her by the rail. She was not sorry to see him go.

On the whole, her new openness made for a much more pleasant journey than she had expected, and by the time the boat reached Cincinnati she had almost begun to enjoy traveling. Once there, she found a room at a cheerful hotel with a beautiful garden and then turned all her attention to scouring the city in search of someone who might remember Fade. Though she tried to keep her hopes high, she was terribly conscious that she now had less to go on than ever before. He might not have even come this way from Pittsburgh, but this was the gamble she had taken, and now that she was here there was nothing to do but try to see if she'd made the right move.

Cincinnati was a pretty town with neat streets and gaily painted houses, each with its own carefully tended garden. Making the rounds of the hotels and shops, Emily soon grew discouraged when no one could remember two brothers passing through over a year before. Then, just as she was about to reserve a berth on the steamboat to Louisville, Absolem came running up the steps of the hotel veranda waving his round hat, the tails of his black serge coat flying behind him. One look at his broad smile and Emily knew he had unearthed a clue.

"Good news, Miss Emily," he cried, nearly dancing around her chair. "I found someone who remembers Mr. Fade. Ole' Absolem found the man, he did."

"Absolem, be still! Stand still, for heaven's sake, and tell me."

Forcing down his exuberance, Absolem stood before her, turning his hat in his thick fingers.

"There's this gentleman, Mr. Reynolds, he's called, a great big man with a face like a fry pan, and dirty—dirtiest collar I ever did see."

"What about him?" Emily cried. "Get to the point."

"Well, the captain down at the wharf, he tol' me to see this Mr. Reynolds. He thought he remembered that two men—two brothers—came through this here city, but all he knows for sure is that they took this Mr. Reynolds's coach and went off in it."

Be careful, Emily thought. It could be someone else. "Absolem, that's very helpful. Did you see Mr. Reynolds? What did he say?"

"He say he remembers these brothers all right, but he can't tell their names. But they went in his coach, he knows that for sure."

Her hopes rose in spite of caution. "Where? To St. Louis, surely?"

"No, ma'am, to Columbus. Mr. Reynolds, he drives the mail coach to Columbus regular. He says he knows he took two brothers, white mens with black hair and one of 'em with this big beard. He remembers clear. Ain't that good, Miss Emily?"

"It's wonderful, Absolem, wonderful. But that means we must change our plans. Do you know where this coach has its office? Can you go back there right away and book us a ride to Columbus?"

"But don't you wants to talk to this Mr. Reynolds yourself? I told him you'd come right away."

"No, I'll take care of the bill here and speak to him when we leave. Be sure he's our driver. You've done a good piece of work, Absolem, and I'm grateful to you."

The pleasure he felt was evident on his broad face. "I take care of you, Miss Emily, just like I told you back on the Sparta dock. We'll find Mistuh Fade, don't you worry."

He went bounding down the steps while Emily headed into the hotel to see the landlord about her bill. After so many disappointments she almost allowed herself to believe Absolem was right.

*   *   *

Joseph Reynolds had, as Absolem described, a face as broad and flat as a pan. In addition, he had a bulbous nose, yellow teeth, shrewd little eyes, and the typical reticence of a driver. Yes, he remembered two brothers, one of them a wild and unkempt woodsman, the other a regular gentleman, completely out of place in the backwoods. He threw Emily's box high up on the boot, gave her a hand up the steps to the broad swaying cab, gave Josie an indifferent boost, and then promptly forgot them both, entirely absorbed in driving his team.

Emily did not mind, so completely was she convinced that she'd finally stumbled on Fade's trail. To her surprise a macadamized road had been laid between Cincinnati and Columbus, so although the trip was boring, it was more comfortable than most coach rides. Except for a brief stop at a dingy wayside inn to water the horses and the dozen passengers, the coach drove straight through. By the time it finally pulled into Columbus twenty-four hours later, Emily was cramped and exhausted. She longed for nothing so much as to stretch out on a comfortable bed.

She quickly found a neat though unfinished hotel and slept fitfully until early afternoon. Then, too excited to try to rest longer, she decided against waking Josie. She dressed herself, put her bonnet over her braided hair, and went downstairs to begin her search. As she walked through the hotel toward the portico and veranda, she fantasized how wonderful it would be if Fade had set up a shop in this town and all she had to do was walk through the door and into his arms again. That tantalizing idea was quickly dismissed, for it was certain that Jesse Whitman would not have followed his brother to Columbus simply to set up a store.

The veranda looked out onto a sweeping field that still bore the burned stumps of cleared trees. Some careful hand had laid out several beds of young flowers and small bushes. How typical, Emily thought, to find both the cultivated and the wild side by side in these new towns.

"Mrs. Whitman."

Looking up, she saw the landlord of the hotel hurrying toward her. He had taken off the frock coat in which he'd greeted the passengers on their arrival and was in his shirtsleeves, with tight bands above the elbows.

"Mrs. Whitman, coachman Reynolds tells me that you are

looking for those two brothers who came to Columbus last year. It is providential that you arrived just at this moment. Providential indeed."

Emily suddenly felt her breath catch in her throat. "Why? Do you know them? One of them is my husband. Can you tell me where they can be found?"

"Why..." There was something about the look on his face that made Emily step back.

"Your husband..."

Emily leaned closer, her gaze fixed on a bead of sweat that inched its slow way from under the rim of his round glasses which were perched halfway down his nose.

"I'm sorry. I didn't realize." He yanked out a red handkerchief, pulled off his glasses, and ran the cloth over his face. "I thought perhaps you would be able to claim the body."

Emily froze. "The body?"

"My, this heat is fierce, ain't it? Goin' to be a terrible summer for sure if it's this hot so early."

"The body?" she repeated in a voice like ice.

"Well now, I didn't mean to be so heavy-footed and I'm that sorry. I hope you won't hold it against me. Truth is, one of those brothers was brought in just last week, mauled by a bear. He was in pretty bad shape and he died just last night. That's what comes of city folk thinking they can handle the wilderness when they don't know a darned thing about it. We get 'em all the time, scalped by the savages, torn up by wild animals, sometimes even shot with their own guns. Not to mention those that never come a back at all."

His voice droned on. Emily's knees began to buckle and she reached out for the nearest chair to steady herself. The landlord caught her arm and helped lower her slowly.

"Forgive me, ma'am. I can see I've shocked you considerable."

"My husband's brother is a skilled woodsman. I don't see how..."

"We don't understand it neither. The two of them was livin' in the woods out Tiffin way, trappin' beaver I believe. This fellow, he comes draggin' in to the nearest neighbor half dead and they load him in a wagon and carry him here to the doctor, but it's too late. Nobody seems to know where his brother went."

"It might not be my husband," she said, looking up at the man with wide unseeing eyes. "I'm not even sure he came to Columbus. It was only on a chance that I came here myself."

He patted her arm gently. "That's true. These fellows weren't long enough in town to be known, even by name. But I recollect it sounded like Whitman. And there's a *W* engraved on his watch."

"His watch?"

"Yes, he had a watch—and worth something too. It might help you identify the body. The only other way is to have a look."

"Oh no!"

"I can't say as I blame you, ma'am. He's not a pretty sight."

"Perhaps if I could see this watch it might at least tell me something."

"Yes, I believe that would be best. If you'll just sit here and compose yourself, I'll get my coat and hat and take you round to the undertaker's. You're sure you're up to it?"

Emily fought to get a grip on herself. She could not know anything for sure until she saw that watch. She knew Fade had left with the one she had given him when they were married and was never without it. One look and she would know for certain.

"I'm up to it. Please, please hurry."

He left her sitting in agony on the veranda and though he was back almost at once, it seemed an eternity to her distressed mind.

They set off down the paved walks that had looked so inviting only a few moments before. It was not a long way to the undertaker's, but once inside the tiny frame building it seemed to Emily that all the cheerful brightness of the town had suddenly turned gray. She was introduced to a gaunt, solemn-faced gentleman in a severe black suit who sat her in a red velvet tufted chair, then went to a desk and pulled a small package wrapped in gray paper from a drawer.

Emily took the package as though it were poison. Carefully unwrapping the paper, she laid bare the heavy gold watch, elaborately decorated with a scrolled *W*.

How many times had she watched Fade take it out and wind it in his strong hands? How she had loved the sight of the thick gold chain across his waistcoat, the look of elegance and refinement it had always given him.

"Yes. It's my husband's watch."

Her words were barely audible.

"You're quite sure?"

"Yes. I'm certain. I gave it to him myself when we were married." She handed it back to the undertaker as though she could not bear to touch it. "If you'll look inside, underneath the second lid, you'll see 'from Emily.' Open it."

Emily waited, her eyes closed, praying she was somehow wrong. She heard the sharp click of the lid opening.

"Yes, I see it is there. It must indeed be the same watch. Very well, madam, if you will just tell me how you would like us to dispose of the body, what kind of marker . . ."

He went on, brisk and businesslike, while Emily fought to keep from screaming. What did she care what happened to the body? She would never see Fade again. Never feel his strong arms around her. It was too much to bear.

"We have only a small cemetery, but I'm sure you will find it a satisfactory last resting place."

"No!" Jumping to her feet, she faced the two men, her eyes wild. "No. I won't let you bury him until I've seen him for myself. Even if this is his watch, I must see him. It's the only way I'll know that he is really dead."

Appalled, the hotel proprietor tried to take her arm. "But, madam, he has been horribly hurt. You will be exposing yourself to a terrible pain, and it is not necessary, I assure you."

Yanking her arm away, Emily turned on him in fury. "I've come all the way from New York to find him. I must be sure. I won't allow you to bury him until I've seen him for myself."

The undertaker touched her elbow lightly. "The body is reposing in the back room, madam. If you will follow me."

Disgusted, the other man turned away. "This is madness. For a lady to view such a sight is beyond all decency. I ask you to reconsider, Mrs. Whitman."

Emily threw him a stubborn glance and started after the undertaker. After a short hesitation the landlord followed, more interested in the spectacle than he wanted to admit. Besides, he reasoned, the lady would probably faint and he'd be needed to help carry her out.

They entered a small dark room whose air was already thick with the heavy scent of death. In the gloom Emily could make out the shapeless lump of a body underneath a dingy sheet. She stopped on the threshold, wondering if she had the will to get through this.

Stepping up to the body, the undertaker lifted one end of the sheet into the air, beckoning her forward.

Two steps closer, enough to see: dreadful jagged scars patched with something that resembled biscuit dough; heavy coins weighing down the eyelids; a glimpse of white teeth behind the slightly open lips; dark hair spilling around the pasty white face like a black halo.

Her knees buckled and she fell senseless back into the landlord's waiting arms.

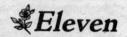

Eleven

SUNSET WAS the only time of day when the Mississippi River looked beautiful. Emily stood by the boat's taffrail and watched as long bars of red and gold shimmered over the broad sweep of water, flaming the tops of the dark vegetation lining the banks. The interminable frogs were blasting at full bellow just as they had all the way from Louisville, and the mosquitoes had all but driven her indoors. Yet she stayed, watching the slow darkening of the desolate landscape.

For someone used to the Hudson River Valley with its sweeping vistas and high hills rising out of the water, with its gorgeous colors of blue, silver, and foam-laced slate, the Mississippi River seemed to be a piece of creation that God must have made just before the Sabbath when he was too tired to care. Choked with jagged, deformed stumps, the gray-brown sludge lined by marshy banks thick with half-grown stunted trees, it was simply a roadway, and the sooner they reached their destination the happier Emily would be. But what would she find this time? Where should she go? There were still several weeks to be got through before Robert Slade would arrive in the town. How would she pass all that endless time?

A painful pinch on her neck interrupted her thoughts and she slapped at a mosquito the size of a New York ant. The sun had almost disappeared and darkness was closing in. Taking one last look at the threads of golden light fast slipping underneath the black water, she sighed and turned back to her cabin. For this trip she had indulged herself by hiring a single small stateroom and she had not regretted it. The privacy had done much to restore her equilibrium after Columbus.

"Miss Emily, you want I should take up your box now?"

Absolem's dark bulk was barely discernible in the gloom.

"Not yet, thank you, Absolem. I still have to put a few things away. Give me another half hour."

"Yes, Miss Emily."

He turned and slipped away toward the lower decks. Emily thought once again how invaluable he had been to her all through these last few days. Josie, after her first energetic attempts at efficiency, had soon given up the struggle and lapsed into a lethargic depression which Emily suspected was largely a case of homesickness. It soon became too much trouble to tell the girl ten times to do the simplest task and Emily finally gave up and did everything herself. She had already made up her mind to send the child back with Robert when he returned to Washington. No doubt she could find someone better in St. Louis, even if she had to buy herself a slave. It would be some satisfaction, Emily thought, to purchase a black girl and then give her her freedom.

"Good evening, Mrs. Whitman."

Emily looked up to see Jonas Sutter blocking her way, holding his hat in his gloved hand.

"Mr. Sutter." Surprised as she had been at first to find him aboard the *Messenger*, she had to admit his good manners and excellent conversation had made her trip much more enjoyable and had done much to calm her after the horrible trauma of Columbus.

"So we arrive tonight. It will be a relief to get off this steamboat, will it not?"

"Indeed yes. And a relief to know that we arrived here

without its blowing up. I confess that when we struck that great tree this afternoon I did not have much hope of ever seeing St. Louis."

He fell into step beside her. "These boats are accustomed to maneuvering around floating timbers and sawyers. Tell me, will your husband be meeting you at the dock?"

Emily hesitated. She had been careful to reveal almost nothing of her personal situation and she was reluctant to begin now. There was something about Sutter—the way he eyed her sideways, as though he was always trying to size her up—that made her distrust him despite his excellent manners.

"I don't expect him to."

After a pause Sutter tried again. "Your journey does not end in St. Louis, then?"

"Why . . . I'm not sure." How flustered she must sound. Blast the man for being so insistent; it was really none of his business.

He went on: "I only thought . . . that is, you once told me that he would be meeting you at the end of your journey, so I inferred that would be St. Louis. You will find traveling beyond this point very primitive—especially for a woman of your delicate sensibilities."

Emily fought down her irritation and turned to give him what she hoped was a pleasant smile. "Please have no concern for me, Mr. Sutter. I am very well able to take care of myself."

"Of course," he said, recognizing a dismissal. "And you have that fine black servant to help you. I must ask you to forgive a blundering fool whose only motive is concern for your welfare."

"You are a very kind gentleman, Mr. Sutter, and I appreciate your generous feelings. Good night."

He bowed briefly and left her at the door to her stateroom. Emily closed it behind her, wondering if she had insulted him. Well, no matter. They would be arriving within another hour or two and there were far more important concerns to be faced than Jonas Sutter's tender feelings.

She could not wait in the stifling cabin, so she went outside in spite of the mosquitoes and watched the lights of St. Louis draw near. The boat had barely docked before a great rush of people clambered aboard, each searching for a husband, relative, or friend. Emily tried to turn her gaze from the warm embraces and excited cries of the people all around her, hugging each other and laughing and calling as they spotted some familiar face. Even the spinster sisters, standing beside a tall man with a crinkly black beard, allowed a suggestion of affectionate animation to tinge the severity of their long faces. As she watched many of her acquaintances on the boat joyfully greeting loved ones, she realized she had never felt so alone in all her life.

As she left the boat, Josie and Absolem following behind, she glimpsed Mr. Sutter standing to one side in deep conversation with a man who had obviously come to meet him. Emily did not want to see Sutter again and she quickly made for the wharf where several cabs stood waiting. This was a welcome sign of civilization and, she hoped, an indication of other comforts to come. The driver took her to the Planter's House, a large, pleasant hotel, where she engaged a room. Feeling a little better, she took off her dress and her stays, had Josie brush out her hair—one of the few chores the girl did not object to doing—splashed some water on her face and neck from a rose-colored porcelain pitcher and bowl, and fell onto the feather mattress.

She was here, the last place she knew to look. All she wanted now was to rest, but images of the undertaker's back room came unbidden, crowding her mind. She yanked the quilt over her head, clenching it in her fists. She could still smell the odious reek of death in that room, and she could not blot out the horrible vision of that butchered face.

But it had not been Fade's face, of that she was certain. Even with the disfiguring wounds she could tell that the man was not her husband. Who he was, how he had come to have Fade's watch in his possession, she had no way of knowing. All she knew was that he was not Fade Whitman.

After regaining consciousness, she had fled the undertaker's establishment. Dragging Absolem and Josie from their beds, she'd flung the three of them back into the first available coach and torn madly back to Louisville. She could barely remember the details of that trip. All she had wanted was to leave Columbus behind forever.

Now at last she was here in St. Louis. From here Fade's trail would be next to impossible to pick up; he might as well have gone to the stars. If she could not find a trace of him here, there was nowhere else to look.

But at least he was not lying dead in the grubby back parlor of a Columbus mortuary. Nothing worse than that could happen now, she thought, before falling into a fitful sleep.

Later Emily would look back and rue that conclusion, for just when you think nothing worse can happen, it usually does.

Her first two weeks in St. Louis gave her no cause for worry. She found the town more interesting than any place she had visited on her trip. It was a city of great contrasts. Settled originally by French immigrants, there was still an old French portion of the town with quaint, run-down, turreted houses. Around it had been thrown up a sea of new buildings, the wood still raw. Strongly Roman Catholic, it boasted a cathedral and a hospital that dispatched a steady stream of missionaries to the Indians; it also had a strong Unitarian and several Protestant communities. There was evidence of culture in its marble-fronted stores, its dignified homes, and its halls for lectures and concerts, yet its real vitality lay in commerce. The grubby shantytowns were teeming with men, women, and children, all en route to the west. Huge wharfs, warehouses, and cattle stations handled more people and livestock in a year than Emily remembered ever seeing in all her time in New York City.

She found that, more and more, she was enjoying all this variety, caught up in the excitement of each new day. There was a leisurely air to her daily visits and inquiries, and when she found no trace of Fade she did not despair. She had to wait until Robert Slade arrived anyway, so there was no reason to hurry her search. She began to relax, almost to enjoy her excursions, fruitless though they seemed.

And then Absolem disappeared.

Emily did not miss Absolem at first. He had accompanied her that morning to a small hotel on the outskirts of town. Her landlady recommended she visit the place since it was frequented by trappers and mountain men, one of whom might know something of Fade. It took them an hour to find the hotel, which provided no more useful information than any of the others. Returning to her own hotel, Emily decided to spend the afternoon in the comparative coolness of her room. Later she had supper in the dining room, and then with nothing better to do, decided to attend a lecture that was being given in the hotel's parlor. There she heard Dr. Angus Sourby give a long, boring monologue on phrenology. The evening was cool, but the ever-present assault by the mosquitoes kept her from venturing out to enjoy it. She retired early, studied the shape of her skull in the mirror over her dressing table, trying to identify some of Dr. Sourby's telltale characteristics, then went to bed and read a little in one of Mrs. Radcliffe's romances.

She read too long and slept too late the next morning. It wasn't until she was finally dressed and ready to tackle another series of hotels that she discovered Absolem's absence. It turned out that no one had seen him since the morning before, nearly twenty-four hours ago.

She searched for him all morning. By afternoon her calmness gave way to a growing sense of anxiety that something was very wrong. Early that evening she went to the tiny room over the servants' quarters Absolem had shared with another Negro man. When she found his free papers lying far back in a drawer of the one chest in the room, panic overwhelmed her.

"He was supposed to keep these on him always!" she exclaimed.

The man shuffled in front of her as though he expected to be blamed for Absolem's disappearance. "He tol' me he don't need those papers," he said. "He say he a freeman and eve'body knows it. He don't have to go round tellin' peoples he be free."

She crumpled the papers in her fist. Such a little precaution for him to take. Why couldn't he have done it?

"Do you have any idea where he might have gone?" she said, trying not to intimidate the man, yet longing to shake him until his teeth rattled.

"No, ma'am, 'cept I did see him leave yesterday with a buckra gentleman. But I see'd him do that before too."

Her head shot up. "A gentleman?"

"I don't know his name but he very smart dresser, even in dis heat. He wear a tall white beaver hat and he have hair like this on his cheeks." He brushed his hands along the sides of his face.

Jonas Sutter!

There must be hundreds of men in St. Louis who wore sideburns and white beaver hats, yet something told her that

Sutter was involved in Absolem's disappearance. And even if he wasn't, he was the one person who would be most able to help her.

It was too late in the day now to do anything more than inquire whether Sutter was staying at her hotel. Finding that he was not, Emily went up to her room and to bed.

Early the next morning she was up at the first sounds of traffic on the road outside her window. Clutching Absolem's free papers, she took a cab straight to the dock. She could remember Sutter saying something about how his business dealings involved shipping, but in the maze of warehouses and merchant houses near the river she was afraid she would never be able to identify his establishment. If luck was with her, the *Messenger* would still be at her berth on the wharf and perhaps the captain would know more about Jonas Sutter's enterprises.

Her first stroke of good fortune was to find the boat still docked and the captain aboard. He was able to direct her to a warehouse which Sutter had told him he often used. Emily sent the cab hurrying to the place. Feeling completely out of her element there, she wended her way around mountains of bales and boxes, sweating laborers heaving barrels onto racks and carts, and harried men in shirtsleeves clutching stacks of papers, pencils stuck in the bands of their straw hats. Weaving among them were bankers and merchants in fashionable coats with gold stickpins in their elegant cravats, overseeing the teeming activity. When they realized there was a lady present, several gentlemen politely raised their velvet-smooth beavers and offered her their assistance.

After three fruitless inquiries she finally found a merchant who directed her to a stuffy little office at the rear of a dusty building under a long, sweeping tin roof. Sutter sat behind a desk, writing in some sort of ledger. As he looked up, the shadow of a frown momentarily darkened his face, but then he smiled broadly and rose to welcome her.

"Why, Mrs. Whitman. What a pleasant surprise," he said, reaching for his coat. "Do come in and sit down."

Pulling a rickety straight-backed chair up to the other side of the desk, he offered it to Emily with a flourish.

"Mr. Sutter," Emily said, not allowing his good manners to put her off her guard, "I am in the greatest distress and I need your help very badly."

"Why, dear madam, I am so sorry. Of course, if there is anything I can do to be of service—"

"Absolem has disappeared," Emily interrupted. "He has been missing now for over twenty-four hours and I hoped you might have some idea of his whereabouts."

"Me? How would I know?"

"He was seen leaving the hotel with a man who resembled you."

There was a brief hesitation in Sutter's indulgent smile. "Why, I haven't seen your servant since you left the *Messenger*."

Embarrassed, Emily looked away. She had been so sure . . . "I'm so afraid something terrible may have happened to him."

Sutter was all sympathy. "My dear lady, I can understand your distress at losing such a valuable servant, but it does happen rather frequently, I'm told."

"Can you help me find him? I don't even know where to begin looking."

Sutter's eyebrows knitted together in a frown. "Oh dear . . . But no, of course I shall help you. My problem is that matters here will detain me the rest of the day. However, first thing tomorrow morning we shall begin making inquiries. I know a few places where we might ask about him, although frankly, Mrs. Whitman, he will be very difficult to find. You see, there are so many possibilities."

Emily's heart sank at the thought that she would have to wait so long for his help. Tomorrow morning might be too late. Without really knowing why, she felt sure that time was important.

"What kind of possibilities?"

He gestured with his hand. "Oh, brawls, accidents, kidnapping . . ." Sutter seemed to be choosing his words very carefully.

"Kidnapping?"

"Well, you see, many kinds of people pass through St. Louis every day. Some are simply good folk going farther west to begin a new life. But many are criminals trying to leave the past behind. Absolem might seem to them a valuable piece of property which could be offered for resale."

"But he's not a piece of property. He's a man."

"Perhaps back in the idyllic world of your New York Hudson

River estate, Mrs. Whitman, but you are in the real world now. There are no illusions in a town like St. Louis, just hard truths." Sitting back, he smiled at her indulgently. "However, I do not mean to alarm you. He probably is just sleeping off a drunk behind some saloon. I'm sure we'll find him tomorrow and bring him home, hanging his head."

The reasonableness of Sutter's observation made Emily wonder if she was not letting her hysteria get the better of her good sense. Glancing up to see Jonas Sutter's sympathetic expression, she even wondered that she had mistrusted him; he understood this world so much better than she.

A man in shirtsleeves materialized at the door to speak to Sutter, who excused himself and stepped outside the office to discuss some piece of business. Emily sat and waited, twisting her hands in her lap.

Her instincts told her there was something wrong here. She could swear Sutter had not really been glad to see her, and his offer to help had had a ring of insincerity about it. Glancing up, she made sure that the two men had their backs to the office door and were engrossed in a sheaf of papers, then reached out and turned the ledger on the desk around so she could read it. Running her thumb along the page, she found references to several names among the figures and "dittos". Mentally she listed them for recall: Howard Corbin; James Bush; Temperance Crowe; Oliver . . .

Sutter's voice rang in dismissal. Twirling the ledger around, she sat back in her chair and gave him a pleasant smile as he entered the office.

"I can see that you are very busy and I am disturbing you," she said, rising. "I shall go back to the hotel and wait until tomorrow before looking any further into this matter."

If Sutter was relieved he kept it well hidden. "That would no doubt be best. Please try not to worry about your servant. I am confident we'll find him. Shall I call for you tomorrow at, say, ten o'clock?"

"Would nine be convenient? I should prefer to begin early."

He took her hand politely. "Nine o'clock, of course."

"Thank you, Mr. Sutter, for your assistance. You don't know how much it means to have a friend you can turn to in a strange city."

Murmuring a few polite responses, he escorted her outside

and into her cab, giving the driver directions back to her hotel. Emily smiled and waved, trying to look relieved and confident until they rattled down the wharf and turned the corner onto the broad street that led back to town. Then, leaning forward, she tapped the driver on the shoulder and in her most authoritative voice directed him to take her to the sheriff's office.

"Mrs. Whitman, you don't have one chance in a hundred of finding that Negro."

Sheriff Lauder leaned back in his chair and ran one finger along the curve of his ample mustache. What a nuisance! With all the real worries of this Godforsaken town, now he had to deal with a northern belle all tears over some worthless nigger.

"I don't believe that."

"Be reasonable, ma'am. He might be drunk, he might be shot, most likely he's already been shipped south to be sold as a slave on some plantation in Louisiana or Texas. It happens every day."

"But Absolem is free. He has papers, legal papers saying so."

"Did he carry them?"

"No. He was supposed to, but I found them in his room."

"Probably wouldn't have made no difference if he had. Free niggers are kidnapped all the time. They can holler as loud as they want about being free, but a few chains and the strap soon takes the starch out of them."

"The strap? Oh no!" The tiny little room grew close around her.

Lauder shifted his big frame back in the chair and rested one boot against the desk. "I'd like to help you, missus, but the chances are pretty slim. Besides, big strong buck niggers are easy to replace. There's an auction right here in town next Friday. Why don't you just go along there and pick up another?"

Emily glared at him. "You don't understand, Sheriff. Absolem is not just a 'buck nigger.' He's a family servant. His grandfather helped my grandmother survive the war with the British during the Revolution. I've known him all my life. His family has been with my family for four generations."

"He still comes from Africa, don't he? And his granddaddy was a slave. They did have 'em even in New York, as I recollect. One slave is as good as another so long as his health is good."

Emily could see she was getting nowhere.

"Very well, Sheriff," she said, picking up her parasol and reticule. "I'm staying at the Planter's House. If you hear anything about a black resembling Absolem, please let me know."

"I'll do that," he said. But he did not even bother to get to his feet—a terrible breach of etiquette, Emily thought contemptuously.

In the cab again, she decided to make one more desperate try. Directing the shocked driver to a street of notorious saloons, she steeled herself to walk through one after another of their swinging doors and inquire if the barkeeps recalled a black man wandering through. Though Absolem would not have been allowed to step up to the bar and drink with the whites, he might have bought a bottle to drink outside.

It only took two attempts before she lost her nerve. As she entered the first saloon and approached the bartender a brawl broke out. One of the men drew his pistol, sending the people in the room scurrying like rats before a light. Emily was jerked down behind a table, ostensibly for safety's sake, but before she regained her feet a hand had gone up under her dress. Shocked and outraged, she fled as soon as the ruckus was over without asking any questions at all.

The second saloon was even worse. It was full of women with gaudily painted faces and tawdry costumes. The men wore boots and dingy shirts and many had holsters with large pearl-handled pistols. Seeing Emily enter, they immediately concluded she was a lady of quality down on her luck and ready to sell the only marketable thing left to her. Emily was propositioned twice before she even got to the bartender. When a bearded drunk slobbered against her cheek, she fled back to her cab.

The driver snapped the reins and moved smartly off into a more fashionable neighborhood while Emily tried to calm her nerves. Her panic and fear threatened to get the best of her. What would she do without Absolem? He was her only protection and she depended on him for so much. She felt an obligation to him, too, along with a real affection. He had never been mistreated in his entire life; how would he survive as a slave? The very thought of chains and whips sent shudders down her spine and brought tears to her eyes, yet it was already past noon and she was no closer to finding him than when she started. Her only chance was Sutter, a man she could not really trust. What in the world was she going to do?

Fighting back a lump in her throat, she started across the hotel lobby, ruling out lunch. She felt too sick to look at food.

"Emily!"

Absorbed in her thoughts, Emily barely heard her name being called.

"Emily, where have you been? I've been waiting all morning for you."

With one foot on the carpeted stair, Emily paused and turned to look up into the blue eyes of Robert Slade. Unbelieving, she stood there, her mouth agape.

"Yes, it's me," he said, laughing. He opened his arms to her.

And it really was. Robert, with his elegant velvet coat and buff trousers, not a hair out of place in his carefully coiffed mustache and sideburns; Robert, with his sympathetic eyes. With a cry of joy Emily fell into his arms and burst out crying.

They sat at a small round table covered with a spotless white linen cloth, which was barely discernible under a multitude of dishes. Emily had moved most of the food around on her plate while Robert consumed a portion of each of the fourteen dishes with his usual gusto.

"Now," he said, sitting back in his chair and wiping his mouth with a napkin. "I've had a good lunch even if you've barely touched anything. You really should eat, Emily. Things always look less bleak on a full stomach."

"I'm not hungry," Emily answered, thinking of the gaunt yellow-faced women she had seen in the saloon.

"Well, at least have some more tea," Robert said, waving to a waiter. "You must have something to keep you going."

An aproned waiter appeared and refilled Emily's cup. The tea was welcome even if the food was not and Emily sipped it gratefully.

Robert pulled out a tobacco plug and broke off a corner of it with his teeth. "Now, let's see what would be our best way of finding Absolem. Or of attempting to find him, at any rate."

"You don't sound any more hopeful than that sheriff."

"Well, the truth is it looks very bad. I don't think there is much question that he was kidnapped by slavers. Absolem never struck me as one to get involved in brawls or to pass out with a bottle of whiskey behind some saloon. On the other hand, he's a fine, healthy, strong Negro man. They're the most valuable commodity in the slave trade."

Leaning her elbow on the table, Emily rested her chin in her hand. "Oh, Robert, the thought of that poor creature in chains makes me almost ill. What a terrible thing!"

"Yes, but unfortunately it occurs every day. I warned you of this, you know."

Emily looked away. "Yes, you did. We both grew careless. I suppose I just could not believe that such things happened. That is, I knew it happened to poor blacks in Africa, but not to free men from free states. It just seems past belief."

"Emily, when are you going to start looking squarely at life? You've never been concerned about anything that doesn't touch you directly. The world is bigger than Southernwood!"

"That's not fair, Robert," Emily cried. "I really care about Absolem, and I'm afraid he is being terribly hurt somewhere. I want to save him. I must save him."

Robert reached out and squeezed her hand. "Forgive my harsh words, Emily. Like most of us, you ignore the big issues while you care greatly about the single individual. We'll do our best to find him, and if he has not already been sent south, I think we can. It sounds as though this Sutter will be no help at all. In fact, I would not be surprised if he was somehow mixed up in Absolem's disappearance. Do you have any other names to go on?"

"I saw some names in a book in Sutter's office: Howard Corbin, Temperance... let's see, Temperance Crowe." Her brows creased in concentration. "James Burns... no, Bush. James Bush. That's all I was able to see."

Robert folded his napkin and laid it carefully on the table. "Very well. I think the next thing to do is go back and see that sheriff. Right now, without wasting another moment." He rose, then came around to Emily's side and helped her to her feet.

"But he was no help at all. Why, he all but told me to run along to the auction Friday and buy a replacement for Absolem."

Placing a light hand on her shoulder, he directed her toward the lobby. "Ah, but that is because you do not understand southerners and frontiersmen, and Sheriff Lauder sounds as though he is both. Did you happen to notice if the good sheriff owned a horse?"

"Yes. A beauty, obviously part Arabian. My driver pointed

him out to me as we were leaving. But I can't see what that
has to do with anything."

"You will, my dear. You will."

Half an hour later she was back in the sheriff's stuffy office
watching in amazement as Robert presented himself as a high
public official from Washington with great influence in government. Sheriff Lauder now sat straight in his chair, his manner guarded but respectful, listening intently. When Emily
recalled the cavalier way he had earlier barely tolerated her
presence, it filled her with rage.

"This Negro comes of good stock," Robert was saying. "We
have known his family line for several generations and his
blood is of the finest African. He is immensely strong, in good
health, has excellent teeth and some intelligence. In short, it
would be a great loss for him to be shipped south to be wasted
on some cotton plantation and would be a severe loss to Mrs.
Whitman's estate."

He might well be describing a horse, Emily thought, yet
his practical words obviously impressed Sheriff Lauder far more
than all her protestations about affection and loyalty.

"But, Mr. Slade," the sheriff said in his slow drawl. "You
might as well look for a needle in a haystack. If this black man
has not been shipped out of St. Louis already, there are fifty
places he might be hidden. And that's just the ones we know
about. I wouldn't even know where to start."

"What were those names you saw in Sutter's ledger, Emily?"

Emily repeated them, hoping she had remembered correctly.
They were all obviously familiar to the sheriff.

"Now, that helps a bit," Lauder said, stroking his mustache.
"Temperance Crowe you can forget. He's been in jail for the
past week. Howard Corbin is a cattle merchant. He might be
doing slave trade on the side, but I've never got wind of any
such thing. Our best bet is Jim Bush. He's a nasty one, into
every kind of low deal, and he hates niggers. I know he's done
flesh peddlin' in the past."

"Can you question this Bush?" Robert asked.

"He'd only lie. The best thing is to surprise him. I know
where one or two of his pens are and if we catch him off guard
we can search them."

Turning to Emily, he said, "It's a long shot, Mrs. Whitman.

I don't know all the places Jim keeps his contraband, and even if I did, he could spirit your man away while we're in the process of looking. And that's if he hasn't already sent him south."

"I understand," Emily said, "but at least it's something."

"You've got those papers?"

"Right here, safe in my pocket."

Sheriff Lauder rose. When he unbent his long frame his head nearly touched the ceiling.

"All right, then. Let's go have a look."

Emily stood in the damp darkness of the hallway twisting the ribbons of her sarcenet reticule around her fingers while Bush flipped through a ring of keys. She felt sick. Try as she might, she could not blot out of her consciousness the sights she had just witnessed in James Bush's slave pen. The spectacle of half-naked men, chains dangling as they slouched on the hot ground or against the confining walls, coarse, thick ropes around their necks like oxen in the fields. Their eyes revealed the gamut of emotions—from stark terror to such terrible muted anger as made her shrink before them. And these were only the men. She had glimpsed the companion pen, between whose slats women's and children's faces had peered out. Bush angrily shook the heavy ring and glared at the two men with exasperation.

"I tell you, I ain't got no more. You've seen everything. You got no right to—"

Sheriff Lauder reached out and grabbed the heavy man by the collar, leaning into his face. "You find that key, Jim. I don't want no trouble from Washington and neither do you, so if you're smart you'll open this door. We know you got another nigger in there, and more than likely it's our man. If he is, he's a free black and you're in big trouble."

"How was I supposed to know that? I was told he was a runaway from Georgia."

"Who told you that?" Emily said angrily. "If it was Mr. Sutter, he knows very well that Absolem is my servant."

"Did I mention Sutter?" Bush retorted. "I'm not sayin' it was Sutter and I'm not sayin' it wasn't. I only know he identified this here slave as a runaway. That's breakin' no law that I know of."

"You're a damn liar," Lauder said, jerking on Bush's shirt collar.

"Wait a moment, Sheriff," Robert interceded. "We have no need to resort to violence. It is possible that Mr. Bush here made a very natural mistake. It is even possible that the man behind this door is indeed a runaway from Georgia. Our only concern is to make sure he is not Mrs. Whitman's servant, or if he is, to restore him his freedom as the law rightfully allows. I'm sure Mr. Bush would not wish to obstruct justice."

Jim Bush glared at Robert Slade. Damn bigwig politician butting his long nose into what was none of his business. How was he supposed to know this woman had such influential friends? Now his hard-earned two hundred dollars was flying out the window. Sullenly he flipped through the keys until he found the correct one, slipped it into the lock, and pushed the door open.

Even from the hall the cell reeked. Emily put her handkerchief to her nose and started in, but Robert gently pushed her aside.

"You wait here."

"She stood aside as the men entered, then peered around the door. The mound of raw flesh across the bare cell seemed barely a human being at all, but when Robert reached down to turn the man over on his side, the face looking up at him was all too familiar. With a cry Emily started forward. Absolem was staring up at Robert, disbelieving, too weak to manage more than a wan smile.

"Why . . . Mistuh Robert? Why . . . I didn' 'spect to . . . see you till . . ."

Emily ran to the cot, peering over Robert's shoulder.

"Miss Emily," Absolem said, his voice just above a whisper. "I knew you'd come. I knew you'd save old Absolem."

"Hush, Absolem. Don't talk. We're going to get you out of here. Everything's going to be all right now."

"I knew . . ."

"Can you stand, Absolem?" Robert asked. "Can you walk?"

"Don't . . . know . . ."

Furious, Robert turned back to Bush. "Get these damn manacles off right away. And get us some kind of wagon. We've got to carry this man back to the hotel."

"I need to see his papers, Mr. Slade," Lauder broke in. "Just to be official, of course."

"Here," Emily cried, digging them out of her purse. "They're all right here. His name is Absolem Devoe and he was born and lives at Southernwood in the Hudson Valley of Westchester County, New York. Mr. Slade and I both can identify him as my servant."

"You won't mind if I just have that identification drawn up and signed."

"Not at all. The sooner the better."

It took both men to drag Absolem's heavy body up the stairs once he was free of the chains. A wagon was waiting outside; they laid him on his stomach with a burlap sack over his raw back to keep off the flies. While Robert hailed a cab to follow the wagon back to the hotel, Emily stood waiting silently beside Lauder and Bush.

"Well now, that worked out all right," the sheriff said, breaking the silence.

Emily turned on them both, her face livid with fury. "No thanks to you! When I came to you alone, you did nothing to help me. If Mr. Slade had not happened along, Absolem would have been sent south to spend the rest of his life in an unjustified and illegal servitude. And you"—she turned to Bush—"you wretched peddler of other men's agony!"

"Come along, Emily," Robert said, taking her arm. "Sheriff, thank you for your cooperation. When the papers are ready, bring them around to the Planter's House and we'll sign them. Good day . . . gentlemen."

The cab pulled away behind the lumbering wagon.

"How could you be so pleasant to those two!" Emily cried, still fuming.

"What's to be gained by insults? We got what we wanted. There simply is no way to put Bush out of business in a slave state like Missouri. The most we can do is rob him of his commission on this one man."

"But they're evil, the sheriff as well as that loathsome Bush. He didn't do a thing to punish him."

"Calm yourself, Emily. He enforced the law for us. He made sure our rightful property was returned. Without him we would never have found Absolem."

He was right, of course. As her anger subsided, relief at having found Absolem flooded over her. It would be weeks before his back was healed, but at least he was where she could take care of him. Thanks to Robert.

She looked up at Robert from under the brim of her hat. "What would I have done without you, Robert?" she said sheepishly. "Thank you."

He smiled at her. "Anything for an old friend."

"Robert, with all the excitement I forgot to ask why you're here early. You were not supposed to be here until next month."

For the first time since he had stopped her in the lobby of the hotel, there was a glimmer of mirth in Slade's eyes.

"I came to find you," he said, "and my reasons were twofold. One, I bear a letter from your Aunt Agatha, and—"

"Aunt Agatha! How nice to have news of home." On second thought, she hoped it would be nice. It had been a long time since she'd given Garret any thought and now the idea of being drawn back into his world was a little dismaying. "And what was the second reason?"

Robert grinned and drew her arm through his. Ahead of them, the wagon lumbered to a stop as the road filled with lowing cattle being pushed into the intersection by two men on horseback. Dust swirled around them, momentarily blotting out the other carriages on the crowded roadway.

"Because, my dear Emily, I think I have located your Fade!"

✿ Twelve

IT HAD BEEN almost two years since Fade stood on the landing at the foot of Berkley Street waving good-bye to Emily as her steamer pulled out into the North River. During those long months she had often pictured the rapturous moment when they would be reunited. The details varied: sometimes he came striding, strong and purposeful and full of vitality, onto the porch of Southernwood while she flew through the door and into his arms; other times she waited at the Sparta dock, searching him out among the figures standing on the deck of the launch bearing him toward shore as he waved his hat to her in welcome. More recently she had envisioned herself jangling the bell of a shop door in some dusty frontier town, where, from behind the counter, he would look up, shock and surprise and, hopefully, joy lighting his face.

What she had never imagined was that she would follow the soft, gliding footsteps of a sister of the Sacred Heart, whose voluminous robes billowed gently like a sail around her, down the close, dark corridors of the new Roman Catholic hospital in St. Louis.

She never pictured herself hesitating beside one of the cots while the sister checked through her papers, afraid to step closer, fighting down the raging excitement in her chest, trying not to hope that the emaciated figure underneath the blankets might truly be her husband.

A nod from the sister and Emily flew to kneel beside the bed, pulling the edge of the blanket away from the man who lay with his head turned away from her. He was drifting in a dream but at the movement of the covers he turned toward her, slowly, achingly, straining to see.

"Fade? Oh, oh, Fade!"

Confusion, then a glimmer of recognition. His lips struggled to form her name. At last he managed an unbelieving, hoarse whisper: "Emily!"

Emily glanced back over her shoulder at Robert Slade, who was standing at the foot of the bed, his hat in his hand, smiling at her. The look she gave him was a mixture of triumph, gratitude. Then, reaching across Fade's wasted body, she grasped his thin shoulder and buried her head against his neck. With slow, strained movements his arms encircled her, gripping her shoulders. She was hardly aware of his embrace, for she was too busy sobbing with happiness.

With Robert's help Emily found rooms in a new boardinghouse with brightly painted window boxes filled with red geraniums. They moved Fade there right away, for Emily felt sure that the loving care she could give him would be far superior to any he would receive in a hospital. Within two weeks Absolem would be well enough to join them, and she would have her whole family together.

As Fade grew stronger and was more able to talk, Emily began putting together the pieces of their lives that had been fragmented since his departure. Fade did not know how long he had been ill, only that he had contracted swamp fever soon after reaching St. Louis. It seemed to come and go after that, with varying degrees of intensity. He thought he had been in the hospital two or perhaps three different times. During one of these times his presence was noted by the new congressman from Tennessee, who was visiting local facilities and who later, when he met Robert Slade in Washington, recalled a gentleman from Mount Pleasant, New York, ill in a St. Louis hospital.

"I don't think I would have ever thought of visiting the hospital," Emily told Fade. "You are so seldom ill it just wouldn't have occurred to me."

"Perhaps it was Providence. I didn't plan to stay here; I was going to go on down to New Orleans. But somehow every time I thought I was ready to leave, this accursed fever would strike me down again. This was an especially bad spell, Emily. If you hadn't come when you did, I think I might have given up trying to fight it."

Emily pulled the blanket up around Fade's lap as he sat near the bedroom window and kissed him on the forehead.

"Then thank God and Robert Slade I did come. I nearly thought to find you dead in Columbus. I don't think I could have survived having to identify your corpse a second time."

"What a strange coincidence that was! I lost my watch to that man in a poker game back in Louisville. He was a gambler—I never had a chance."

"If he had not been traveling with his brother perhaps I wouldn't have been so misled. I really believed it was you and Jesse I was following."

Fade leaned back against the pillow braced on the high back of the chair. Even talking seemed to tire him. Would he never regain his old strength?

"I was never traveling with Jesse. He sent word to me at Pittsburgh that he couldn't come."

"I wish I'd known that. I went about it all wrong."

He smiled at her through his weariness. "My darling, you thought I was traveling as a gentleman. You would have done better to ask about a peddler."

"Fade! You could never be a peddler."

"Give me your hand."

He grasped her fingers tightly, holding them like a lifeline. She was so strong, so capable. Imagine her coming halfway across the country like this to find him. He reveled in her strength, the comfort of her help. The pleasure he had felt at his independence and freedom was diminished now by fatigue and weakness, and by his terrible memories of being alone and ill in a strange city where no one cared whether he lived or died. The old restlessness might return someday—he could not swear it wouldn't—but for now it was good to lie back, rest, and let her take care of him.

In the excitement of finding Fade and getting him settled, Emily paid little attention to Agatha's letter. But as her husband began to regain his strength and show more interest in the world around him, she found herself brooding over its contents, asking herself over and over what it meant. Agatha was obviously upset, for the ship bearing her son and daughter-in-law had not yet returned. No one knew if it had been lost or was simply delayed. Yet it was not her own concerns that had prompted her to send the letter with Robert Slade—it was the situation at Southernwood, which was rapidly deteriorating under Garret's care.

By now she knew that Fade had written her from every stop along his route, and although he said he had often wondered why some letter from her did not catch up with him, he had put it down to the erratic nature of his life and continued to send her long descriptions of his journey. Obviously, Garret had kept Fade's letters from her, trying to convince her that Fade had either died or abandoned her for someone else.

Emily waited until she felt Fade was stronger, then hired a carriage to take them upriver to a pleasant little inn on the banks of the Mississippi. There, after a good meal, she broached the subject of their future. At her first words she could sense his reluctance.

"Do we have to think about this yet, Emily? It has been so pleasant here with you and without the worries of the everyday world to interfere."

"I know, dear," she said, determined to be patient. "But our money will soon be running out and we'll have to make some kind of a decision about what to do next. Have you thought about it at all?"

"I wouldn't mind staying on in St. Louis to try to get a business going. Or perhaps we could go down to New Orleans, as I originally planned. I'm told it is a trading center where prospects are good for new ventures and that it is a fascinating town. I know you'd enjoy it."

Fade groaned inwardly as he saw her catch her underlip with her teeth. That usually meant something was coming that he would rather not hear. Beckoning to the innkeeper, he called for another glass of champagne.

"I had a letter from Aunt Agatha..."

He felt a sinking sensation in his chest.

"She says that things are very bad at Southernwood. Garret has gone completely off—drinking too much, filling the house with his terrible friends, letting Papa's business rot on the vine to pay for his foolishness. She suspects that he is addicted to laudanum, too, and that can be a very damaging habit."

"I thought Garret had a little more to him than all that suggests. What on earth changed him?"

"I don't know. But Agatha says he intends to sell Southernwood—the house, the land, everything. It will pass out of the family, and all to support his degenerate ways."

Gripping the stem of his glass, Fade swirled the golden liquid. "And...?"

"Southernwood is my home, too, you know," she answered, leaning toward him across the table. "And yours, too, Fade, since you are my husband. You don't wish to see your fortune disappear, do you? I know I don't want to lose Southernwood."

"It is not a fortune I ever wanted."

"I realize that," Emily said, still trying to sound patient and amiable. "But, nevertheless, it is yours. Papa's business may not be totally ruined. It only needs a strong hand at the helm. You've got it in you to take over and make it a success again. I know you do."

The earnestness in her voice dismayed him. "You don't really expect Garret to just sit back and say, 'Here you are, Fade, you run things now,' do you? He's still the head of your family, Emily, not I."

She sat back very straight in her chair. "I've thought about that. If things are as bad as Agatha says, I intend to have Garret declared incompetent by the court. Then they could make you Papa's executor. You're the perfect choice. You can bring order into this mess, Fade. I know you can. You can save Southernwood."

Fade was suddenly conscious of his tight grip on his glass. "Southernwood!" he said bitterly. "That's what really matters, isn't it? It's what you care about before all else."

A flush spread over Emily's face. "That's not fair, Fade. You always come first, you know that. If you say no, very well then. We'll go to New Orleans, or find a house here in St. Louis. I'm only asking you to consider this as one of your choices."

He studied her face, the strong, stubborn lines, the pleading in her dark eyes. She was holding her breath, waiting for his answer, he could see that. She was right, of course. Southernwood was a plum just waiting for him to pluck. He would be an instant success—no struggle, no poverty, no failure.

But what of his own hopes? What of a man's pride in his accomplishments, the feeling of having broken the world and tamed it to his own desires? Was his integrity as a free man worth bondage to the Deveroes? He loathed Garret. Just the thought of having to deal with him again was enough to drain his tenuous strength. He disliked Southernwood and all its pretensions. He hated the thought of having to live on that hill while down near the docks his own family made bitter comments about his good luck.

On the other hand, if he did this he would be in a position to help them. And God knows Garret needed someone to bridle him before he wasted everything old Joshua Deveroe had built. Hadn't he always deplored useless waste? Emily was staring down at her hands, her lovely face clouded. She expected him to refuse.

Reaching over, he squeezed her hand. "Let me think about it," he said quietly. "I'm not quite prepared to give up the dreams I brought with me. If we go back now, I may never have the chance to prove myself again. I promise you, if I feel I cannot succeed, we'll go back to Southernwood."

Emily considered his words. There was still a chance that he might decide their future lay in New York. He deserved this opportunity to try to make it on his own; if he left now just to please her, he might spend the rest of his life resenting the choice. And in any case, at least she was by his side again. She could face any kind of future as long as he was with her.

She raised his fingers lightly to her lips. "Thank you, Fade. That's enough for me."

Fade's worst problem was now regaining his strength. The last bout of swamp fever had come close to doing him in, and the sweltering heat of St. Louis did nothing to improve his condition. But he was out on the streets a little longer every day, visiting the merchants, nosing around the stockyards, exploring the flats where hordes of itinerant families were readying themselves to set out on the western trails. He took all the odd jobs he could find that were light enough not to bring on a relapse of the fever. After three disappointing efforts he finally located a semipermanent position with Joseph Salter, a storekeeper whose stock was popular among the people outfitting for the wagon trails. Though the work was hard and the hours long, Fade's prowess at remembering inventory and his pleasant way of dealing with the public soon made him indispensable to Mr. Salter. His wages were enough to keep them in groceries if not in luxuries, and he felt that eventually Salter might even consider making him a partner.

Worrying about his future, he earnestly sought conversations with the men who wandered into the store, trying to learn as much as he could of the choices that lay open to a man like himself. Did he have the strength to face new hardships and carve out a foothold for himself and his wife in a wilderness? More and more he found himself remembering Southernwood as a haven of peace and security.

Still, he had almost made up his mind to stay in St. Louis when two conversations discouraged him. One was with his doctor, who told him frankly that another bout with swamp fever would probably be his last; and living on that mud-brown river with its eternal heat and mosquitoes, there'd be no escaping swamp fever.

The other, with Salter, occurred a few days later, just before the store closed. He had walked onto the porch with the last customer of the day and was standing there savoring the cooler air of the street after the closeness of the shop. Beside him, Salter sat exhausted on a chair tipped back against the porch window. Offering Fade a plug of tobacco, he indicated the barrel next to his chair and Fade lowered himself onto it, glad to be off his feet for a few moments. From one of the saloons farther down the street they could barely hear the tinkling of a piano and an occasional howl. A farm wagon lumbered by with two brown and white cows tied to its rear gate, stirring up the dust.

Salter worked his jaws and sent a stream of tobacco spewing onto the porch floor. "There goes another yokel," he drawled. "Seems like there's more of them every year."

"You must have seen this town change a lot since you've been here."

"Oh, I seen changes all right. When I first come to St. Louie I never thought there was this many people in the whole of the western world. Now I've seen 'em come and I've seen 'em go. Some stays out there forever with the Injuns and the prairie dogs and some show up again, goin' back to where they came from. They go out with big plans but they come back with their tails between their legs, just grateful to still have their hair. But more keep comin' all the time. Don't see how there can be too many left back east by now."

Fade was struck by a sudden thought. "How long have you been out here, Mr. Salter?"

"Ten years. Ten years, come next Septembry. Seems like fifty!"

Mentally Fade inventoried the shabby store behind him, its shadows bathed in the gray dusk of descending night. Ten years of commerce and this was all Salter had to show for it: a collection of calico and kettles, flour and beans. Ten years beside this flat, ugly river and he would sit like Salter, his face creased with worry and pale from imprisonment in dark rooms, spitting tobacco juice onto a sawdust floor.

A protest rose within him. He had a vision of a blue river flowing peacefully between rising bands of green, gulls squawking as they gracefully danced above its surface, the salt smell of the great sea. A vision of a white house with painted shutters, fragrant apple trees in a nearby orchard, flowers growing along winding paths.

He came home that evening deeply unsettled, to discover Emily crying beside the round table in the parlor, a letter crumpled in her hand.

"I'm sorry. I didn't mean to do this in front of you," she said as he put his arms around her and pulled her tightly to him.

"What's the matter?"

"It's another letter from Agatha. It came yesterday, but I wasn't going to tell you about it. When you were late getting home I sat down to read it over again and it just tore at my heart." She wiped her eyes with the hem of her apron. "You must be hungry. We can talk about it over dinner."

Fade washed his hands and face while Emily set out a cold

supper and coffee. Sitting opposite him, she described Agatha's letter while he picked at his food.

"Nicholas's ship never returned, and they presume now it's lost at sea. Poor Agatha is so upset. She says that her only comfort is that Annette's mother is too ill to take Claes and has agreed to let her raise him. It's the only thing that has kept Agatha going since she finally gave up hope of seeing her son again."

"Isn't she rather old to be taking on such a small child?"

"Yes, but she has a good heart and a young spirit. I think she'll be good for the boy." She carefully made no mention of how Agatha had expressed the hope that Emily would come back to help her care for Claes.

"Was that all she said?"

Emily ran her finger absently along the polished wood. "No. She says Garret is still as bad as ever . . ."

Fade looked up.

". . . and that he's put Southernwood up for sale."

He leaned back in his chair. It was no more than he'd expected. "Does he have any buyers?"

"Not yet. It seems money is as hard to come by back east as it is here."

"But of course he'll find someone in time."

"Of course." Emily's voice was full of despair.

She twisted her napkin through her fingers, her lashes casting feathery shadows on her cheek.

"Would you still like to go back, Emily?"

His voice was so hushed she almost could not believe she'd heard him correctly. "Not unless you want to."

Fade tried to sound nonchalant. "Well, I've been giving our future a lot of thought. According to Dr. Lantry, St. Louis is not a healthy place for me. If I live long enough and stay with Mr. Salter, in another ten years I might be the proud proprietor of a store like his. Somehow that idea does not seem to hold the attraction it once did."

"But the frontier? It's what you've wanted for so long."

He pushed his plate away. "Now that I know it well, I find it is not all I had hoped it would be. Oh, it has excitement and great possibilities. But I'm tired, Emily. And to be honest, I'm a little more intrigued now by the possibility of stepping into a business that's already been built. Why should we let Garret throw away everything your father and grandfather worked for?"

"Oh, Fade. Do you really mean it?"

It was almost worth giving up the last of his youthful dreams to see the look of unabashed joy on her face. *Did* he really mean it?

"Yes, I mean every word. How would you like to go home?"

In an instant Emily was kneeling before his chair, clasping him in her arms.

"Oh, Fade, my darling! It's what I want more than anything in the world. You won't be sorry. I know you won't."

He hugged her tightly, drawing from her strength. No, he would not be sorry. He had made his decision and he would never look back.

The trip home would have been fascinating to Emily under any conditions, but to share it with Fade was, after her long, lonely venture west, a supreme happiness. Instead of retracing the overland route they had both taken to St. Louis, they traveled by canal boat downriver to New Orleans, that thriving and most French of cities, then boarded a two-masted schooner, the *Gaspé*, for the cruise around the Florida territory and north to the lively harbor of Charleston. They traveled by stage to Richmond and then to Washington City for a few days' rest and a visit with Robert and Gabrielle Slade and their young son, Ethan.

Though the Slades insisted Emily and Fade stay with them, Emily used Gabrielle's baby as an excuse and booked rooms at one of the hotels. The hint of relief in Gabrielle's quick acquiescence confirmed her hunch that Mrs. Slade cared as little as ever for her company.

Emily loved playing with Ethan. She could spend hours holding him, crooning meaningless sounds, grasping his tiny fingers.

"He's an aggressive little thing, isn't he?" Robert said one afternoon. He was peering over her shoulder as she sat in the Slades' family parlor cradling the baby. "I think he's going to have a mind of his own—just like my father."

As if to justify his papa's remarks, Ethan's muted fretting began a crescendo into a full-force wail.

"I think he wants his supper," Emily said, handing the baby to his nurse, who was waiting to take him away.

Gabrielle was lounging on a nearby sofa, propped up in front of a mound of pillows. She welcomed her husband home from the Capitol by tilting her head up for his kiss. "When Ethan is hungry he lets you know in no uncertain terms. He's already a very determined little creature."

"I think he's lovely," Emily said. "You must be very proud, both of you."

"Is it so obvious?" Robert asked, beaming as he pulled up a chair to join them. "But, come, how are you enjoying your visit? You are looking very fit, Fade. Your stay in Washington City must be doing you good."

"I feel better every day," Fade answered. And he did, except when he thought of how near they were to Southernwood.

"I have talked them into staying for supper, Robert," Gabrielle said, handing her husband a glass of wine. "I think Emily would like to play with Ethan again after his nap."

"Are my thoughts so transparent?"

"They are written all over your face." Robert smiled at her and settled back in his chair. "My, I'm glad to be home. The amount of traffic in the streets this afternoon was beyond anything I've ever seen. It took me all of twenty minutes to get here! This city is becoming too crowded; I won't be sorry to leave it. Thank heaven the President's term is over soon."

"How can you be so sure that the Locofocos will lose the next election, Robert?" Fade said. "You might well be here another four years if President Van Buren is reelected. You talk as though the outcome is already certain."

"I believe it is. The economy is just too depressed. Many people feel that only a change in administration can bring things back to rights, and I'm not convinced they are wrong. At least it is worth trying a new direction. And when a good Democrat like myself is willing to venture the thought, you can be sure there are many others who think the same. All the Whigs have to do is come up with a popular candidate—which will probably be Henry Clay—and they can sweep the country. And when Van Buren leaves, I go too. I can't even say I'll be sorry."

"The thought of living in New York fills me with dismay," Fade said almost to himself. "It's been so long . . ."

"You'll find it very changed. I'm told that gangs of hoodlums roam the streets of the city, making it unsafe for honorable

gentlemen to go abroad. Riots, knifings, unbridled crime—
they are all more common every day. The genteel society we
used to know has almost disappeared."

"It's all that riffraff they allow to come swarming into the
ports every day," Gabrielle exclaimed with some feeling. "They
are the dregs of Europe and their countries are glad to see them
go. If we do not close our doors they will ruin this great land
for the rest of us, mark my words."

Emily paid little attention to the conversation around her.
By telegram and letter she had informed Cousin Agatha of her
intention to come home and had begged her to do anything in
her power to prevent Garret from selling the house before she
got back. But she had heard nothing in reply. Now, with the
last leg of the journey before her, she knew she would soon
have to face her brother again. The image of Garret as Agatha
had described him kept intruding upon her thoughts, blotting
out the careful plans she must form. With her cousin's help
they might be able to surprise Garret in a state that would allow
them to petition the court to declare him unfit. It was her only
hope.

Gabrielle sank back on the pillows, out of breath after her
vehement declaration. Where was her strength, she wondered
for the hundredth time. Ethan was over four months old and
she was still lying about like an invalid. Not that Robert seemed
to mind. In fact, he loved her weakness and dependency. What
troubled her was the frequent waves of nausea that came and
went every time she thought about food. She had heard of
women who barely rose from one childbed only to lie down
again in a second one. Surely she could not be with child again
so soon after the first. It was so . . . unseemly. So unladylike.
She would be the butt of little jokes and the sly smiles of her
friends behind their fans.

It was Robert's fault. He simply must learn to curb his baser
instincts. If, in fact, she was with child a second time, she
grimly set her mind that it would never happen again this
quickly—not even if she had to lock her door at night. And
how she wished these tiresome people would be on their way
and get back to New York.

". . . long to live by the Hudson again," Robert was saying.
"Perhaps if you settle at Southernwood, we shall be neighbors
after all. Won't that be nice, my dear?"

Gabrielle started. "What? Oh yes indeed, it shall be the best of all."

Emily looked away. When donkeys fly, she thought.

A maid in a starched white apron and lace-edged cap appeared at the French doors, announcing the meal. Rising, Robert helped his wife from her lounging chair, then offered his arm to Emily.

"And tell me, Emily my dear. How is Absolem doing these days?" he asked as they started into the dining room.

"He was so frightened by that terrible experience in St. Louis that he will barely allow us out of his sight now. He wears his free papers in a leather bag around his neck night and day and he can hardly wait to get back to Southernwood."

"He had good reason to be frightened. It was only by the grace of God that we were able to save him."

"And through your help."

Robert nodded in appreciation and pulled back her chair at the table. "This slavery issue grows more intense every day. The abolitionists are just as extreme as the southerners. Between the two of them I can only see disaster ahead."

Fade seated Gabrielle, then took his place, laying his napkin in his lap with a flourish. "I heard a lot of talk in Missouri about how the south is ready to secede from the Union if the government tries to infringe on their right to hold slaves. At first I laughed, but by the time I left I perceived there was little to smile at."

Gabrielle looked away as the servant placed a bowl of steaming green soup in front of her. Please God, she thought, don't let me get sick now!

"Slavery is wrong," Emily said vehemently. "Now that I have seen it firsthand, I agree completely with the abolitionists. It is an evil blot on our country."

"But an economic necessity in some parts of it," Robert added.

Fade smiled at his wife across the gleaming mahogany table, so polished that the glow from the silver and candles was reflected in its brown depths.

"Emily's new crusade against slavery is confined to the south, you'll notice. In fact, I don't hear much from any abolitionist about the kind of slavery Negroes endure up north."

"That's not fair!"

"Isn't it, dear? It's true you gallantly rescued Absolem, but he is still your inferior. Would you sit at a table with him? Would you allow him to board at your inn? Has he a chance of ever being anything more than a servant?"

"Fade! You make it sound as though what I did was selfish on my part. I genuinely care about Absolem. It hurt me to think of him chained and suffering. He . . . they . . . Negroes are like children and we must care for them like children."

"Exactly. It's still the old master-servant relationship. You don't allow black men to vote, to attend schools, to have any of the same opportunities for advancement in the world as white men do. You would be horrified at the thought."

Emily was beginning to feel very distressed. "Fade, I never heard you talk such nonsense. What's happened to you?"

"Perhaps I've changed," he said. "Or perhaps it's because I too was once considered an inferior in the sight of people like the Deveroes."

Amused, Robert looked from one to the other. Fade Whitman had always been the only man he knew who could stand up to Emily Deveroe. "It's going to be very refreshing, Fade, to have you as a neighbor. Now, my dear Gabrielle, would you ask them to bring on the fish."

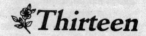

Thirteen

ONCE FADE made up his mind to return to Southernwood he then had to consider the problem of how to handle Garret. Emily had spared him none of the details of her life in Westchester or of the scene that had finally driven her to slip away in the night.

"I can understand how it horrifies you," he said, trying to sound sympathetic, "but truthfully, it doesn't surprise me. I always suspected Garret might lean more toward men than women."

Emily swelled with indignation. "Well, I never thought of such a thing. It's not normal. It's evil and...perverted!"

"My dear, if you knew more of the world you would be aware that Garret's particular type of perversion is far more widespread than polite society wishes to admit. I saw many instances of it while we were living in New York."

"It makes my skin crawl. It's like lifting a rock and seeing all manner of loathsome things come crawling out into the daylight. Ugh!" She shuddered. "I don't know how I will be able to look him in the face again."

"I'm sure you'll manage," Fade said dryly. "But the important thing now is how to get the upper hand before he realizes what we are about and tries to stop us."

Emily was for sweeping down on Southernwood and announcing her intentions in no uncertain terms until Fade pointed out that the single most important element in their favor was surprise. Unless Agatha had told him of her letter to Emily— and that was not likely—Garett should have no idea that his sister and her husband were anywhere near New York.

So it was that they went up the Hudson by steamer to Peekskill, then took a carriage back down to Agatha's house, arriving unannounced late in the evening. After a reunion full of joy and tears, Agatha sat them down and described in detail Garret's dissipation, which was even worse now than when she had first written. The next morning they were up before dawn for the trip to White Plains, where the three of them sought out Judge Jonathan Ward, and laid the problem before him. He allowed that a court injunction could be obtained declaring Garret insane, but his condition would have to be verified by a doctor. The process would not be easy, and it would certainly not be pleasant.

"Is there no other way?" Emily asked.

The judge looked her over with piercing eyes set well back under thick white brows. He turned back to Fade as though the question had come from him.

"You might be able to have him declared incompetent by reason of habitual drunkenness, but that would only prevent his involvement in managing the property and estate belonging to Joshua Deveroe. There's some precedent for such an action, but it might not stand up in the appellate court. If you want to get him out of the way completely, I would suggest you have him designated insane. Of course just the threat of such a suit might be enough to make him turn legal control of the property over to you."

Fade glanced at Emily's pleading eyes. He knew they were both thinking the same thing. Garret was no crazier than they were, yet his behavior was erratic enough to give them ammunition for such an action. As a last resort his distasteful sexual preference could be dragged out into the light of day, too, though Emily prayed things wouldn't go that far.

"I think the first thing we ought to do is to try to frighten Garret into cooperating." Fade said. "With any luck, no further steps will be necessary. What we need from you, however, is some kind of a letter so he'll know we are serious about our intentions. Can you do that for us?"

"Of course. I'll write it up as though it were the first step in the procedure. If you can come back in an hour I'll have it ready for you."

"Thank you, sir. We ought to be getting on up there this afternoon before he hears that we're back. Come along, ladies. We can get lunch at the hotel dining room while we're waiting."

Later, after picking up the letter, they settled in Agatha's barouche for the drive to Mount Pleasant. None of them relished the confrontation that lay ahead. Emily's lunch was lying like a dead weight in her stomach. Even the sight of the familiar well-loved shrubbery, and graveled drive curving upward toward the house on the hill filled her more with dread than delight. Suppose he was not there. Or what if they found him sober? She pictured Garret, his shotgun pointed at their collective heads, daring them to dismount from the carriage. If he ever pulled himself together enough to understand what they were about, he would move heaven and earth to stop them.

As the carriage rolled briskly toward the side entrance to the house, Emily could see the results of Garret's neglect. There were no hands at work in the fields and no sign of activity anywhere. Even the stables seemed abandoned. The only signs of life were a few men lounging on the ground near the out-buildings and the well that served them. They looked up inquisitively as the carriage rolled past. By the time it pulled up to the porch, one man had risen and was striding toward the rear of the house, wasting no time. Fade bounded out to hand the women down.

Emily stared aghast at her beloved home. It had grown more derelict than she had remembered. Paint was peeling from its walls and several long boards had been pulled from the flooring of the porch, leaving jagged holes that opened onto the ground beneath.

Inside, it looked as though no one had been through with a broom since the night of Emily's departure. She looked up to see Chloe standing on the stairs, staring at her open-mouthed, as though she had seen a ghost walk through the door. Her apron was dirty and her straggly hair hung like Spanish moss from under her dingy cap.

"Miss Emily!" the girl gasped.

"Where is my brother?"

Chloe turned to the tall figure behind Emily. "And Mr. Fade . . ."

"We want to see Mister Garret," Fade said briskly, "and at once."

Chloe's fingers gripped the stair rail. "I'll . . . I'll just go tell—"

"No! We'll announce ourselves. Where is he?"

"Why, he's upstairs in his room, I do believe. Asleep. Yes, he's asleep. He often sleeps in the afternoon, he does. Often."

"No doubt."

Fade's sarcasm was lost on the obviously frightened girl as he swept past her and up the stairs. Emily followed close behind him, while Agatha pulled the housemaid around and headed for the seclusion of the parlor.

"Get to the kitchen, girl, and heat me up some water for tea—if you can find a clean cup in this horror of a house, that is. Go, at once!"

Emily and Fade stood in the doorway of Garret's room, trying to adjust their eyes to the dim light that filtered through the shuttered windows. The heavy breathing in the area of the four-poster told them he was lying on the bed. Motioning her to stay where she was, Fade walked forward to look at the man lying face down on the unmade bed.

"Out cold," he murmured. Walking over to a washbowl near the window, he picked up a pitcher half filled with water, then went back to the bed and poured it over Garret's head. Spluttering and coughing, Garret finally came to, half rising to peer at them through bleary, outraged eyes.

"Get up!" Fade barked in a voice Emily had never heard before. Garret's eyes flickered back and forth between his sister and her husband.

"I don't believe it . . ."

"It's true," Fade answered angrily. "Get up and see if you can clear your head. We want to talk to you."

"Don't have to talk . . . and especially not to you two," Garret muttered sullenly, wiping his face with his sleeve. "Got a nerve, coming in my room like this . . . Get out! Get out before I throw you out!"

Moving quickly, Fade grabbed him by the collar and yanked him to his feet. "You couldn't throw out a cat right now," he said scornfully. "We're going to have a talk, Garret, so you'd better get the fog out of your head long enough to understand what we say."

Garret's legs buckled under him. "All right, all right. Take your hands off me, you bully. Always a bully. All you Whitmans . . ."

Fade left him sagging on the damp bed while he went to close the door, motioning Emily toward a seat near the window. Pulling up a straight-backed chair, he straddled it and crossed his arms over the top.

"Listen to me, Garret, and understand what I say. You are a drunkard, a wastrel, a laudanum addict, and a pervert."

Garret looked daggers at him, his crooked mouth curling into a sneer. "You do me too much honor, sir."

"These are vices for which witnesses can be found, as you well know."

Garret's angry glare swept from Fade across the room to Emily.

"So you found him after all. What did it take, Emily, sister dear? How did you persuade him to leave his other women?"

Emily started forward, but Fade waved her back with a motion of his hand. "Don't try to sidetrack the conversation, Garret. Emily and I have come back to Southernwood with a court injunction to have you declared insane . . ."

"That's a lie! I'm not insane and you know it."

". . . if we must. With a little cooperation we will be willing to change 'insane' to 'incompetent.' It's not a bad bargain when you consider what life at the Bloomingdale Asylum is like."

Garret was becoming more alert by the minute. "You're bluffing. You could never get away with it."

Fade pulled out Judge Ward's letter and handed it over. Grabbing it, Garret unfolded the heavy paper and strained to make out the writing in the poor light.

Studying her brother as he frowned over the letter, Emily wondering that a man so young and once so attractive could in this short space of time become so haggard. His face was yellow, and there were bags under his eyes, creases down his cheeks. His hair looked as though it had not seen a comb in weeks and his clothes as though he had slept in them for several days. There was a stubble of blond beard on his chin, and his eyes were empty and dark as always, like pools of stagnant water. Yet behind them she could see that his intelligent mind was working. He was struggling to grasp the full meaning of this sudden intrusion, much as a cornered animal tries to assess its best means of escape.

Garret threw the letter back at Fade. "You could never get any court in this county to find me insane and you know it." His speech was interrupted by the stomping of heavy boots outside in the hall followed by a loud banging on the door.

"Are you all right, Mr. Garret?" a muffled voice cried. "Do you need any help then?"

Garret smiled over at Fade. "That would be Micky. He's a big man, Micky, and very strong. I could ask him in, you know, and have both of you thrown out on the porch like the baggage you are."

Fade's stare was unflinching. "Try it. This is Emily's home too. We'd be glad to add assault to the list."

Garret seemed to consider this as the banging grew louder. "Go on back, Micky," he finally called, "and stop beating down my door, damn you. I don't need your help."

The banging stopped, but they could tell the man had not moved. "You're sure, then?"

"You heard me! Go away, you damn Cork bastard. I don't want you up here. Go out back where you belong."

Garret turned once more to Fade, ignoring Emily. "What is it you want anyway? What did she promise you, my inheritance?"

"It's my inheritance too," Emily said, speaking up for the first time.

"There isn't going to be any inheritance, Garret, the way you're going. We're here because we intend to save something of all your father left the both of you. What we want is for you to give me power of attorney. I'll manage the property and the business, you'll receive a handsome allowance per annum, and we'll all be better off."

"You! What do you know about managing property or a business?" Garret said bitterly. "You Whitmans are nothing but fishermen and loafers. Why don't you go string out your seine nets in the river like all the rest of your kin. Oh, I take that back. Your sister isn't stringing nets. She's far too busy hopping into the bushes with everything that strolls by in britches."

Emily gasped, but Fade kept his level gaze on Garret. "No matter how I manage the Deveroe interests, it has to be better than the job you have done. You have a choice: you can agree to our terms or we can take you into court. The details of your way of life should delight the local gossips."

"You wouldn't dare." Garret turned to Emily. "You would never be able to show your face in public. The scandal would damage you far more than it would me."

"I would dare, Garret," Emily said coldly. "And I would tell everything—everything about you and your friend von Arensten. If it killed me I would do it. I would do anything to save Southernwood."

"Bah! This rotting hulk of rubble? If anyone is insane it's the two of you."

He was weakening, they could tell. Fade went on in his even voice, pushing home his point.

"It's not a bad deal, Garret, if you think about it. You will be free to live where and how you like as long as we are free to run Deveroe Enterprises. The way you're going, very soon you will be completely without money. This way you'll be subsidized for life."

"Assuming you don't run everything into the ground. Besides, what if I choose to live here?"

"No!" Emily cried angrily. "That's my one condition. I get Southernwood for my home. You can live anyplace else."

"How lovely," Garret answered sarcastically. "You get the house, he gets the business, and I get an allowance." His face twisted in fury. "This is nothing but blackmail. Unmitigated, villainous blackmail."

"It will be a most *generous* allowance," Fade said quietly.

Garret ran his fingers through his unkempt hair. "I'm not agreeing. I've not said one word about agreeing."

Rising, Fade pushed back the chair and reached for Emily's hand. "We'll be downstairs. We'll give you an hour—then we start back to White Plains."

"You can't do this! You don't have a leg to stand on."

They walked from the room and closed the door behind them. Emily's knees wobbled as she followed Fade down the stairs and into the back parlor, where they found Agatha sitting on the gold brocade sofa. Absently Emily noticed a long tear in the back where the cotton wadding was working through.

"I've had some tea brought up," Agatha said. "You both look as though you could use some."

Emily fell into an upholstered chair near the hearth. "I certainly can."

"Forget the tea," Fade said, sitting heavily opposite her. "Get that maid in here and tell her to find some whiskey. Quick!"

They had given him an hour. After forty-five minutes, Garret appeared, his hair combed, his face gleaming from a recent wash. He was far more sober than he had been earlier, and his mood was even more vicious.

"Get out, old woman!" he snapped as soon as he saw Agatha.

Her eyes flashed, but she looked to Emily for verification before rising and picking up her ever-present tatting. "Your manners grow more gracious with every passing year, Garret! I'll wait for you in the garden, Emily. At my advanced age yet another family scene is one too many."

The door had barely closed behind Agatha when Garret, leaning against the mantel, crossed his arms over his thin chest and got right to the point.

"I intend to call Micky in and have the two of you thrown out bodily. But before I do, there are a few things I want to say. The nerve you have displayed walking in here like this and threatening me—"

"Don't make the mistake of thinking this is an idle threat," Emily broke in.

Fade motioned her to silence. "Can we assume you are sober now, Garret?"

"Sober enough to know what the two of you are. And to see you thrown off my property."

"You can call in your brawny Gaelic friend and have us evicted, Garret, but I want you to be very clear about what the consequences will be. We have already sought the counsel of a judge. We can make application to the Court of Common

Pleas in the county, charging that you are a habitual drunkard and are incapable of handling your real and personal estates. You have made enough enemies that we will have no trouble finding people who will testify against you. Your estate can be taken from you on that basis or, if we want to go farther back, on the premise that you are incapable of standing as executor of your father's will."

"That's a lie. No law allows for such a thing."

"Oh, but it does. It comes under Title Two in reference to lunatics, idiots, drunkards, and those convicted of an infamous crime."

"And don't forget, Garret," Emily added, "I could testify to your unnatural relationship with Baron von Arensten, which, unhappily, I witnessed. You could be convicted of a 'crime against nature' and spend as many as ten years in prison. Once convicted, all your estate would be forfeited anyway."

The look he gave her was terrible in its unrestrained hatred. "You would never have the courage."

"Oh, but I would. I told you upstairs I will do anything to save Southernwood. If Papa had changed his will as he intended, it would have been mine at his death. I will never let you sell it off as long as there is breath in my body."

"This is . . . criminal! Vindictive, hateful . . ."

"That is not true, Garret," Fade answered. "If all we wanted was to steal from you, why would we have come here first? We are offering you the chance to live as you want."

"What does that mean? If I agree to this robbery, will you put it in writing that you will not prosecute me?"

Emily and Fade exchanged a look. "As long as you keep to your side of the bargain," Fade said.

Turning his back on them, Garret thumped his fist lightly against the marble mantel. What to do? He hated the thought of giving in more than the thought of losing this wretched house and crumbling business. Everything had gone downhill since von Arensten had left, taking his money and his solace with him. Let Fade and Emily have Southernwood—as long as he got more than his share for doing nothing.

"I'll need at least a week to consider," he said.

"Oh no. You make up your mind right now, or we go straight to White Plains."

"That's unconscionable!"

"Nevertheless, that's part of our terms."

Garret's eyes flickered back and forth between them, looking for one last out. He might still call Micky in. It would be a great satisfaction to see these two manhandled. On the other hand . . .

His words were barely audible. "Very well. I agree."

Emily felt her body go slack with relief. "Oh, Garret," she began, "you won't be sorry—"

"Just shut your mouth!" he said, turning on her viciously. "You've got the better of me, you two, and I suppose it makes you happy. But you'll live to regret this, I promise you. I'll get even with you if it takes me the rest of my life!"

Fade rose and moved to Emily's side. "Perhaps your comfortable life may help to soften your need for revenge, Garret. Let's hope so, anyway. We are going to have our boxes brought up from Mrs. Yancy's. You will be good enough to tell us which rooms you want us to occupy at least for the moment. Then if we can scare up some supper in the kitchen, perhaps afterward you and I might begin to go over the books."

Storming over to a gilt secretary against the wall, Garret slammed down the lid and drew out a long brass key from a drawer, throwing it down on the table in front of Fade.

"Go over them yourself. They're your worry now. I'm going into the village and get drunk!"

Within a week Emily and Fade were established at Southernwood. Emily took firm control of the house, giving notice to most of the servants, who had adapted themselves to Garret's slovenly ways, and hiring new ones who could be more likely to do as she expected. The entire house was cleaned, the kitchens scoured and stocked. Regular hours were established for meals, except for Garret's—Emily made it plain that he would keep his own hours and was to be served as he wished. She set about looking for someone to manage the stable and grounds, someone who would see that, even by starting late, a harvest was brought in the following fall. It was a lot to handle and, at times, a worry, yet she found that the joy she felt at having Fade beside her in her beloved home made all the problems manageable. Her long-cherished dream had come true at last.

Fade spent his first weeks poring over ledgers and record books and visiting the Dolphin shipyards every day. He knew that once he was familiar with the financial state of Deveroe

Enterprises he would have to make a trip to New York to visit lawyers and bankers and then begin his inspection of the various businesses in which Josh Deveroe had invested. Through Garret's mishandling, these had now dwindled to two fulling mills, a local lumberyard and sawmill, some shares in an ironworks at Peekskill and the Delaware and Hudson Canal Company, and several tracts of real estate scattered around the county. According to the books, none of these efforts was producing much income, while Southernwood itself was a dark hole down which money ran, never to be seen again. Whether or not he could pull all this back into some kind of order was a question he did not like to ask himself. Yet he was stimulated by the idea of trying, and he certainly could do no worse than Garret, even had he been to the manor born.

Fade had not seen his family for more than two years. So before he made his first trip to the city, he shored up his nerve and took the short ride down the hill. His mother was dead now, but as far as he knew, Matilda and Jim still lived in the clapboard farmhouse near the old post road; he felt he must at least do them the courtesy of announcing his return. Though it had to be done, he dreaded this task more than any other that awaited him. He wasn't sure of anything about the Whitmans except the reputation of his sister Florrie, which had grown even more notorious since he went away.

The house looked shabbier and smaller than he remembered—perhaps he was just getting accustomed to Southernwood's grand scale. Matilda recognized him at once and came running across the yard, her apron flying, her cap askew, to throw her arms around his neck.

"Look at you! The grand gentleman! Oh, Fade, you must have done wonderful well out there in the western lands. Come into the kitchen and have some of my cider and tell me all about everything. How is Jesse? What did you do out there? Did you see any of them fierce Indians and what did they look like? You never got close to losing your scalp, did you?"

He let her take his arm and lead him into the kitchen, chattering all the way. It was the same cluttered, grease-spotted, homey room, warm with the smell of freshly baked bread and dried apples. Seating himself at the table, he laid down his hat and riding crop and loosed his stock.

"Now then, you look more like the Fade I remember,"

Matilda said, running her rough palm along his cheek. "You haven't really changed so much."

"Nor have you," he answered. That wasn't really true. Hard work had made Matilda look older than her years. She had something now of that leathery, strained look that he would always remember when he thought of his mother.

"I don't know how Jesse is, and no, I never came close to losing my hair. The closest to death I came was when I caught the swamp fever, though that nearly took me off all right. Three times I came down with it, and on the third I don't think I'd have ever got up again if it hadn't been for Emily."

A shadow fell across Matilda's round, homely face. "I heard you was up on the hill in that grand house. Can't say as I blame you any."

"It's not like that, Matilda. I know I said I'd never live there, but if Emily and I don't step in and save the place, it's going to be lost to the Deveroes. And, think of the good I can do for all of you."

"Humph. I don't want nothing from up there. It's a scandal the things that go on up there, leastways since Mr. Josh died. Why everybody in the county knows—"

"It's going to be different now," Fade broke in. "But let's forget Southernwood. Tell me about the family. How is Jim? And your kids? And Florrie?"

Matilda rose to take a loaf of bread from a cupboard and cut a slice for Fade. "Shame on me for forgettin' my manners. Here now, would you like some cider with it?"

"Thank you, yes."

Filling his glass from a wooden pitcher, she took her seat across the table. "Jim is doin' fine. He's working on the aqueduct. Has done much better there than ever he did down in that worthless mine, and it's better for him. My Jeff is sixteen now. The youngest, Jesse, he's a real dear, a lot like you was as a youngster, and the others are coming along. They're most of them in school, 'cept for Jeff, who works with his father. Florrie . . ." she began, then looked away. "Florrie is a worry, I'll tell you, Fade. She just went all to hell when Mama died, maybe even before. She never had no one to keep a hard rein on her, you know."

"I'd heard as much."

"Anyhow, she's left Foley and she's took up with that scrawny no-count Gus Merrick and she lives with him in some little shack down near the state farm. I took two of her babes to raise—they're both asleep upstairs right now. I suppose I'll get the next one too. She drops 'em like a mother rabbit."

"Some women are lucky that way."

Matilda's pale eyes darkened. "You never did have a babe now, did you, you and Miss Deveroe."

"Matilda, she's been Mrs. Whitman for ten years now. Can't you learn to call her Emily? She is your sister, you know."

Looking quickly away, Matilda smoothed a strand of hair under her braided knot. "I'll never be able to think of such a grand lady as a sister, Fade, no matter what you say."

"No, we've not had children, though Emily lost one in the early stages. It just doesn't seem to come as easily to some women as others."

"Humph, I wish I'd been one of them. Seems like all my Jim had to do was hang his britches on the bedpost for me to get with child!"

Fade smiled at his sister, all at once feeling very warm toward his family. She was only slightly older than he, but she had always been a kind of keel for the others, very steady and quietly dependable. Uneducated, she never struck him as particularly quick-witted, yet her simplicity and earthy goodness had been a comfort when he was young, and was even more appreciated now.

He sat for nearly half an hour with her before straightening his stock and reaching for his hat to leave.

"Will you be back soon?" Matilda asked, her voice eager.

"No. I must take an extended trip to look over old Josh's investments. But I'll come see you when I get back."

"I'll look forward to that." Timidly she reached up and kissed his cheek. "I'm glad you've come home, Fade. You were always the special one in this family."

She walked her brother to the road and waved after him as his horse turned up the hill. Her words echoed in Fade's mind all the way home. For the first time he was grateful he was living near his family.

✿Fourteen

CHRISTMAS OF 1839 was brightened for Emily by the presence of the Slades and the delight Agatha's grandson, Claes, took in the many gifts a doting family showered upon him. The small boy had by now grown accustomed to living with his grandmother, and though he often spoke of his parents, it was more as a memory from another life than with a sense of loss. All of Emily's frustrated maternal feelings were lavished on the child, and he seemed as fond of his Cousin Em as of his grandmother.

Robert Slade and his family had moved back to Tarrytown in late September, and in spite of her dislike for Gabrielle, Emily found comfort in having them as neighbors. They had two children now, boys barely a year apart in age. Emily thought the older, Ethan, was a delight, but the tiny new baby, Wesley, was quiet and sickly and reminded her too much of his mother. Yet it was good to hear the laughter of children

that Christmas in the old house on the hill where it had not
been heard for so long. Emily threw herself into decorating the
rooms downstairs with ropes of holly and fragrant pine and
overseeing the sumptuous dinner of puddings, roast meats,
oysters, pies, sweetmeats, and pastries. When it was over and
all the guests had gone, she looked around the messy parlor
and thought it had been one of the happiest Christmases she'd
known in years.

Even Garret's presence had not dampened her good spirits.
Although he had sworn to anyone within hearing that he would
never go near Southernwood again, he'd appeared suddenly
just before Christmas dinner, half drunk, sullen, and argumentative. Expecting the worst, she'd invited him to join them
and was surprised to find that he stayed reasonably well mannered, though he left immediately afterward without a word of
thanks.

On the first day of 1840 Emily insisted that Fade join her
in calling on their friends in the neighborhood, a New Year's
custom that was very popular in the city and one she was
determined to observe as a tradition in Mount Pleasant as well.
In the beginning it was something of an ordeal for Fade; most
of the people they called upon were old friends of the Deveroes
and he suspected they looked on him as an intruder. But his
good manners, the admirable judgment he had already shown
in his handling of Josh Deveroe's estate, and his wife's obvious
devotion impressed all who met him and he came home feeling
for the first time that he might actually belong in Emily's world.

Nor did Fade forget his own family. Matilda and Jim, her
silent, rough-mannered husband, their children, and Florrie,
who had now left Gus Merrick and was back living at home,
had a Christmas such as they hadn't known for years. Jim was
a proud man and adamant about not accepting charity from
Fade, but Matilda and Florrie had no such scruples and they
saw the comforts Fade's position had brought them as a sign
of a hopeful future.

On a bitter January afternoon Fade entered the side door at
Southernwood and nearly crashed into Emily, who was just
leaving the pantry, a stack of table linens in her arms and a
set of keys jangling at her waist. He had been in New York
on business for nearly a week and her cheerful domesticity was

as welcome as the snug warmth of the house itself. Setting the cloths on a chair, Emily greeted him with delight, offering a quick kiss before helping him unwind his long scarf and slip out of his greatcoat.

"You look tired, my dear. Was business so bad then in the city?"

"No, it's just the cold," he answered. "Everything went well, but I had to make some decisions and I'd like to talk them over with you. Have you a minute?"

"Of course. Just let me ask Chloe to send in some tea. You would like a cup, wouldn't you?"

"I'd prefer a brandy and water."

A quarter of an hour later he was sprawled in his favorite chair, his feet before a substantial fire, and the glass of brandy in his hand, feeling less frozen every minute. Perched on the brocade sofa across from him, Emily waited expectantly.

"I've had several months now," Fade began, "to look over all your father's investments and try to determine the best way to handle them. You know I've never been much of a business manager, Emily—"

"That's not true," she interrupted. "You did an excellent job of building your own import firm before the fire wiped us out."

"Well, a small import firm is not quite the same thing as handling stocks, factories, shipyards, and the other cozy little enterprises wealthy men use to make themselves rich. Nor does it initiate one into the niceties of high finance. I've tried as hard as I can, and damn it, I still cannot understand all the details of the country's economic condition, although clearly it's very bad."

"I could have told you that from the prices at the market."

Loosening his stock, Fade sighed. "The times are very hard, that's for certain. If you talk to the Whigs they'll tell you it's all the fault of General Jackson and his vindictive war on the banks. If you talk to the Locofocos, they'll tell you that it's all the fault of the banks and the wealthy merchants. But wherever the fault, there's no denying that there is very little specie in circulation, stocks have fallen, rents have been cut in half, taxes are punitive, and trade is practically at a standstill. Why, cotton has almost ceased to move at all and real estate is a drag on the market."

"My goodness," Emily cried. "You make it sound as though doom is just around the corner."

"That's how the men I talked with made it sound. But there are a few gleams of light in the gloom. For one thing, I have learned that businessmen *always* talk as though the country were on the verge of bankruptcy. Another thing is that more and more of those merchants who still have money want to invest it in building houses out here in the country, close enough to town to still get there easily by rail. And that is to our advantage."

Emily glanced out the window. A light snow was beginning to frost the paths curving away toward the stables in the distance. She found she was almost holding her breath for fear her husband had decided to sell some part of Southernwood.

"Now, I am no authority on building ships, but it doesn't take much intelligence to see that through these last few hard years the Dolphin yards have been the only investment to pay their way. They have continued to turn out sloops and barges at a modest pace that was still enough to make a small profit. So we must hold on to them at any cost."

"I'm glad to hear you say so. That was the first business my grandfather started when he moved to Mount Pleasant, and I should hate to see it go out of the family."

Fade leaned forward in his chair, resting his hands on his knees, his dark brows creased with the earnestness of his thoughts. "It would help if we could take on a partner. I've approached Mr. Wilkerson with the proposition that we merge our lumber yards with his at the farmers' dock. He plans to enlarge the dock, which I think is a fine idea. Garret had already moved most of his shipping business from the Sparta dock and this will simply expand that operation. What do you think?"

"It sounds like a good idea, but you would understand it better than I." She realized she was twisting her hands in her lap, still waiting for some mention of the estate.

"I intend to sell off most of the shares in the fulling mills," Fade went on briskly. "There are larger operations in Connecticut and Massachusetts which do that kind of thing infinitely cheaper and better. I thought to hold on to the stock in the Delaware and Hudson Canal Company, and if and when things get better, buy even more in similar types of utilities. Coal steam, iron—they will be needed as the country turns more and more to factories and railroads. But meanwhile, more immediate action is needed if we are to survive."

Emily held her breath.

"I want to get rid of as much real estate as the market will take. Garret ran up some huge debts and they must be honored if our credit is to be reestablished. We shall keep the smaller holdings that bring in a little rent, but I thought we'd sell a parcel of Southernwood."

"Oh no!"

"Not the house—not even any part of the estate that you would miss. Just some of the outlying land. Mr. Bishop would like twenty acres to the south in order to build himself a new house. We'd never miss it; it's mediocre grazing and hunting land, but it will bring a pretty fair price. I could pay off Garret's debts and have enough left to invest in the best deal I've yet seen—something which is sure to rebuild the Deveroe finances."

Emily breathed a sigh of relief; that did not sound so bad.

"Now look here," Fade said, reaching over into his pocket for a piece of paper which he spread across Emily's lap. Slashed across it was the outline of something that resembled a ship's hull but was far more elongated and sleek than the usual cod's head and mackerel tail shape.

"While I was in New York I visited Smith and Dimon's shipyards. They have a clever young designer there, John Griffith, who showed me an innovative idea he has for a new type of vessel that could well turn out to be the fastest thing afloat. You should see it, Emily. It's a whole new concept: long, slender hull, graceful as a feather; sharp, jutting bow; and a full stern to cut drag. She'd carry topgallant, royals, maybe even skysails and moonrakers—a whole cloud of sail, and three masts. She's the most beautiful thing I ever saw."

"But I don't understand," Emily said, looking quizzically up at him. "Is this something the Dolphin yards could build?"

"How I wish it was!" Fade leaned yet closer toward her in his enthusiasm. "No, we're much too small an enterprise for that, but someday, when she is built, I'm determined to have shares in her. Griffith believes she'll be so fast that she can make the trip from China in as little as ninety days."

"Ninety days! Come now, Fade. That's fantasy. Nothing moves that fast."

"Well perhaps it will go a little slower, but not much, and think of the cargo that can be brought back and forth in two trips a year instead of one! She's the vessel of the future; someday there'll be a whole fleet of ships like her sailing the seas. Mark my words!"

Affectionately, Emily rose and kissed him. "Why, Fade. You have become a visionary. I always knew you could handle Papa's business better than Garret. Go ahead, my love, and sell those twenty acres, and when the time comes invest in your marvelous ship. But no more than twenty. Agreed?"

Clasping Emily around the waist, he pulled her to him. "Agreed. You won't be sorry, dearest. I promise you."

He rested his head against her breast and she ran her fingers along his brow. "My darling Fade. Nothing you've ever done has made me sorry. You should know that by now."

Spring passed quickly for Fade, engrossed as he was in his work. When time could be found, he took the schooner to the city to visit the yards of Smith and Dimon to study the model of Griffith's beautiful ship, *Rainbow*.

Despite the scarcity of hard cash, he was pleased that he had achieved almost every one of his main goals. Yet, looking around him, Fade could see that even in these hard times, great fortunes were being made by others. Old John Jacob Astor in New York sat parsimoniously on his fifteen million, but his son William was already well on his way to surpassing that. The enterprising Captain Vanderbilt had cornered the steamboat business on the North River and was expanding his realm farther every year. Henry Brevoort, dealer in real estate; William Aspinwall, merchant prince; Gardiner Howland, shipping magnate—there was a long list of men who were turning the depression to their advantage.

The future of trade was wide open, Fade concluded, and the man who owned and ran a fleet of more efficient merchant ships could not help but amass a fortune. It was even possible that someday the Dolphin yards might actually be turning out such vessels. They would probably have to move to New York in order to do it, but that was not impossible either. Perhaps one day they might merge with one of the larger, more established firms in the city like Williams, Brown and Bell!

So he dreamed while he worked diligently to make his

visions come true, and as the first year at Southernwood drew to its close he could see real signs of progress. He was very satisfied with himself.

When Fade walked into Matilda's kitchen on a sunny day in early June 1840, she knew at once that some great happiness was swelling within him.

"It's been some time since you came down from the hill," she began; then, not wanting to sound as though she was annoyed with him, she quickly added: "I'm that glad to see you, Fade, I missed you."

Since his return to Mount Pleasant, these short visits had become something of a comfort to Matilda, not only because he always left her a little money but more because he talked to her as a friend and an equal. Much of her life was spent with her taciturn husband, whose conversation, except when he was reading from the Bible, was mostly monosyllabic, and Fade was a welcome relief from the monotony.

Fade laid down his hat and pulled up his usual chair, reaching for the wooden cider pitcher that always sat on the table. He liked Matilda and respected her understanding of the gulf that lay between their two worlds. She had never tried to take advantage of the fact that he was better placed than she.

"You look like a cat set loose among the pigeons," Matilda said now, setting a tankard in front of her brother.

"It's Emily," he said, his face shining. "She's with child, and much farther along than the other time. She did not even realize it, we've grown so accustomed to accepting our childlessness. The doctor says he thinks she has a good chance of carrying to term this time if she's very careful and takes plenty of rest."

"Why, that's grand news, Fade. I'm so happy for you."

"We're happy too, Matilda, only trying very hard not to let our hopes run away with us. She would love a child so much. Even now she showers affection on Claes and that little Ethan Slade as though they were her own."

"And I don't suppose Fade himself cares one way or the other about it," Matilda said, her eyes twinkling.

"Of course I care. But one grows used to disappointment. Anyway, perhaps this time it will be different. We'd both love that."

"This time it *will* be different," Matilda said with conviction. "I just have a feeling, and my feelings are usually pretty good. I knew the night when old Mrs. Ackerman was going to die just as sure as a voice from heaven had told me. And I knew when Carrie Shaffer was carrying her third that it was not going to be right when it was born. And the night that Captain Orser's sloop, *Boxer,* run up on that rock—"

"Heavens! Stop, please. We want a joyful outcome, not a disaster!"

"Well, I can tell those too," Matilda said earnestly. "This is going to be a good healthy baby, Fade, I feel it in my bones. You'll have your son, just wait and see."

"I hope you're right. In the meanwhile, next time you go to one of those 'shout-em-up' camp meetings you and Jim love so much, say a little prayer for Emily, will you?"

"I'll say several. As a matter of fact, we've got a visiting preacher coming next week, Reverend Archibald Knight, and he's supposed to be a real Bible thumper. A good man, I understand, and a whiz-bang, regular hellfire and brimstone preacher. I'll make sure you're both remembered, and the baby as well."

Fade reached over and gave her hand a squeeze. "Thank you, Matilda." How different her bony, leathery hands were from Emily's soft ones! But then his sister had married at fourteen and since then had known nothing but hard work and childbearing. Jim was a good man, less given to drink than most, and he worked hard; he expected nothing less of his wife. A different kind of woman might have taught him a thing or two, but Matilda had always been compliant, quietly accepting what fate brought her. These emotional religious revivals seemed to be the only occasions when either she or her husband allowed themselves to shed their self-imposed restraints.

"You ain't seen anything of Florrie now, have you?" Matilda's question broke into his thoughts.

"Why no, I seldom do unless she wants something. Does she still live in that shanty near the dam with that sorry Michael Burke?"

"Yes, but they're having a hard time of it. I'm surprised she hasn't come asking you for help. He'd probably beat her if she did and he found out!"

"I've no doubt."

"He's all right 'cept when he starts on the demon whiskey. That turns him into a wild man. There's a lot of drunken fighting that goes on among the workers, has been ever since they started that aqueduct."

"But where do they get it? I thought it was against the law to sell those men whiskey."

"Oh, come on now, Fade. Why, every farmer that lives close enough and has room to turn around in his kitchen has made his house into a grog shop. And those foreigners—they love to hate each other, you know."

"Well, the aqueduct is all but finished now," he said. "That should help the situation. And it certainly is a marvelous accomplishment."

"Humph. May be, but what happens when that work is done? There's bad feeling among them now. What's it going to be like when there's not enough work to go round?"

"Is this something you and Jim worry about?"

"Jim does, I'll tell you for sure. 'Course Jim is a Christian man, but there's plenty as lets their resentment spill over. Not just against the Irish, but the Scots, the Norwegians, the Swedes—all those fellows who've squatted here now and won't go back. Our second son, Avery, is fourteen now and he has to find work. They don't like it when jobs they might have had go to these people. It ain't fair."

"You know Jim need never worry about work," Fade reassured her. "I'll find something for him, and Avery too. Just tell him to come round and see me."

"That's very decent of you, Fade, but he'll never do it. He's proud, Jim is, and he hates the idea of taking charity."

"But it's not . . . oh, very well. You keep me informed then, and if the need arises I'll make sure he gets an offer. Meanwhile, here's something for you and something for Florrie. You'll see she gets it?"

"I'm obliged, Fade. Florrie will be too. She drops in nearly every other day."

He rose to put an arm around his sister's shoulders, giving her a warm hug. "Don't forget that prayer," he said. "We need all of them we can get."

Although Emily, too, was delighted at the prospect of a child, she was a little afraid to believe it, having been disappointed before. Most of the women she knew, rich and poor, suffered through a pregnancy every year. Having lost one infant almost before she knew it was expected and then having gone so many years without conceiving at all, she had finally made up her mind that there would never be any children for her. And now this!

Though she felt better than ever before in her life, Emily was still far beyond the age when most women carried their first child. And her family history was not encouraging. Her grandmother had had only one child and her mother two. But now that there was hope, she was determined to be as careful as possible, to pray diligently, to prepare nothing for the baby's arrival until at least her seventh month, and to never lose sight of the possibility that something would probably go wrong. At the first sign of any weakness, she went to bed. She lifted nothing and did not exert herself in any way that might be too strenuous. Her housekeeping routine began to slacken, but she did not care; the servants could easily be brought back into line once she was safely delivered of the child.

As the months went crawling by and nothing happened to terminate her pregnancy, Emily gradually let loose of the tight hold she had kept on her imagination and allowed herself to dream. It was exhilarating to realize that at last she might be able to give Fade the son and heir all men wished for. Surely that would cement the love he felt for her. By December, her eighth month, it was almost impossible to curb her soaring joy, and she finally allowed herself to prepare for the baby's arrival.

During the weeks before Christmas Garret appeared at Southernwood regularly, almost always drunk. On one particularly horrible afternoon, he showed up wildly waving a pistol and ranting on his old theme of how they had tricked him out of his inheritance. Fade sent Emily to her bedroom and called Absolem; between them they got the pistol away and Garret off the grounds. The next day Fade went to see his brother-in-law at the house he kept in the village and, finding him sober, told him that should he ever reappear on the hill with a weapon he would be shot dead on the spot. It was difficult to know whether this threat made any impression on Garret's clouded mind, but thereafter he confined his unpleasantness to taunts and vague threats.

Christmas Day passed without incident, though Garret drank

enough gin toddys for three men and passed out under the table; Fade had him carried home.

"He gets worse every day," Emily sighed, relishing the peace of the back parlor. "He's younger than I am, but looks ten years older," she went on, almost to herself. "I wish I knew of some way to help him."

"I don't know why you should want to help him at all. He's a bitter, twisted man, who has never done anything except try to hurt you."

Frowning, Emily folded her hands protectively over the bulge under her loose satin sacque. "He always resented me. I don't know why, unless it was because Papa showed me so much approval and Garret so little."

"Yes, well now we know why, don't we?"

Emily shuddered, thinking of the child she carried. Of course he would be perfect, would grow up to do great things and be a person the world would esteem. Wasn't that what every mother hoped for her son? How did it happen then that innocent children became men like Garret?

Seeing her shiver, Fade got up to move the needlepoint fire screen from in front of the flames. It was a cold night and there was a wet drizzle, half rain and half snow, falling outside. In the soft light of the whale-oil lamp Emily's face looked wan and drained. He was filled with concern for her. If something should go wrong now, when they were closer than ever before . . .

"Feeling all right, my dear?"

"Oh yes." Emily smiled up at him. "A little weary, that's all, and anxious now to be relieved of this burdensome weight. One of the first things I am going to do once our son is born is to go back to riding every day. I've missed it so, and there's nothing better for keeping one's shape."

"Emily, you mustn't be so certain this baby is a son. It could be a daughter, you know, and then you'll be terribly disappointed."

A sudden flare from the fire cast shadows over the fine planes of her face. "Oh no, if the baby's healthy, that's all that matters. I would prefer a boy, of course, but a daughter would be nice too."

Reassured by her words, Fade returned to his chair and took up his pipe. Beside him, Emily stared into the flames, mes-

merized by the choreography of light and shadow dancing around
the logs. She knew that her words had been spoken for Fade's
benefit. As far as she was concerned, a daughter would be
small consolation compared to the joy of a son and heir, a little
Fade to be molded and guided by herself.

Yet the choice was fate's, not hers, and she had not completely lost sight of that fact. If the child turned out to be a
girl she would love it, but oh, she did so want a boy.

By the end of December snow, in some places nearly eighteen
inches deep, blanketed Mount Pleasant. Then the new year
came in, bearing with it a sudden spell of balmy weather. Emily
saw it as a symbol of the blessed arrival expected at the end
of January and her joy soared with the temperature. She felt
sure now nothing could go wrong.

In the early hours of January 1841, the pleasant weather of
the past few days gave way to a rain that, as it grew heavier
and steadier, showed all the promise of developing into a full-
fledged storm. The warmth of the air kept the rain from turning
to snow, which was at first a relief to everyone. But as the
torrent continued all Tuesday, all Wednesday, and on into
Thursday, relief turned to anxiety. The heavy snows melting
under the downpour were added to the water running off from
the storm and the ground began to soak and weaken before the
onslaught. By Wednesday afternoon Fade had every available
man at Southernwood out working to hold back the heavy
waters that threatened to damage the buildings and fields. By
early Thursday morning, with the torrential rain continuing and
the ground no longer able to absorb any more, every weak spot
had been shored up, drains dug where they would do the most
good, and all perishables moved to higher platforms. Looking
around, Fade felt reassured: since they were on a hill, they
were not likely to suffer as much damage as the small homes
and farms on the lower ground near the river.

As it happened, the rain heralded more than the danger of
flooding. That Thursday morning when Emily took her first
step out of bed, she knew something was wrong. Clapping a
hand to her side, she groaned under the sharpest, most cutting
pain she had ever known. It couldn't be the start of labor—
that was impossible; it was too soon. She dressed with difficulty, ate a little breakfast, and sat most of the morning waiting
to see if the pains would come back. For a while she was able

to hope that they had been only a momentary discomfort, but as the hours wore on that proved to be a vain wish. Throughout the morning the stabs returned, and by noon she was truly concerned. Staring at the clouded, weeping window pane, she decided that when Fade came in for dinner she would have him fetch the doctor. It was probably nothing, but it would not hurt to be sure.

One long, branch-encrusted arm from the top of the ancient half-dead ash tree, a casualty of the storm, had fallen half across the shed adjoining the barn. With his oil slicker fanning out around him and his hat dripping gently in a sudden drop of the wind, Fade was just thinking to finish this salvage job and go up to the house for dinner when he heard his name called and looked up to see Robert Manning, one of the apprentices and the son of the foreman at the Dolphin yards, riding up.

"Pa sent me to fetch you, Mr. Whitman," Robbie called, trying to hold his streaming horse steady. "He's worried about the Croton dam. Reservoir's already near eight feet high and still rising."

Leaving the broken limb to the other men, Fade hurried over. He had been down to the Dolphin the day before to make sure all precautions against flooding had been taken, but if the river went out of control, there was no telling how much damage might result. The yards were not as low on its banks as some of the mills and houses, but they were close enough to cause concern.

"How bad does it look?" he asked, grabbing the bridle to steady the wet, miserable horse.

"Bad enough. They got crews at the dam trying to shore it up with sand and rocks but he says to tell you that if'n it goes, all hell goes with it."

"All right. I'll come down at once."

Calling Absolem to saddle his horse, he sent word up to Emily without bothering to go back to the house himself. The loss of the Dolphin yards at this point in their financial recovery would be a disaster such as they might never survive. Southernwood itself, he thought, was secure enough now to be left to the farm workers. His place was down near the raging river.

While Fade was hurrying his mount down the hill, dodging the fallen branches and trying to avoid the deepest mires of mud,

Emily sat forlornly in her house, wondering what to do and wishing he was with her. She had no doubt now but that some activity was seething inside her womb, and the sooner she got help the better. There were two midwives in the village but she really wanted young Dr. Sayre, the son of their old family surgeon, who had helped her through the long months of her pregnancy and in whom she had great confidence. But should she drag him up here in such weather for what might be a false alarm? She had never dreamed she might have her baby without Fade around for moral support, and it seemed impossible now that this could be happening at such an inconvenient time, especially when she supposedly had another three weeks to go. But might that not in itself be a sign that something was very wrong? All of a sudden she was filled with panic at the thought that some mishap might yet cause her to lose this precious child. It no longer mattered if it was a son or a daughter, as long as it was born healthy and alive. Heaving herself up, she ran for Faith and ordered her to call in Absolem immediately. He was to go fetch Dr. Sayre as fast as his legs could carry him, and if the doctor was not available, then one of the midwives. Maybe even both of the midwives!

Robert Manning had been the foreman at the Dolphin yards since shortly after Elisha Yancy turned over the entire business to Josh Deveroe. As a young man, Fade had often seen him around the village but had only come to know him well since taking Garret's place as head of the firm. He knew Bob for a quiet, capable, and unflappable man, personality characteristics that made the restless anxiety with which he now greeted Fade all the more disturbing.

"We've done about all we can here for the present," Manning said, standing under the protruding tin roof of a storage shed, "but the dam's in a bad way. They give it only a few more hours to hold."

Fade looked around the yard, at the newly laid keel on its ribs, the wooden outbuildings and warehouses, the storage sheds, the furnaces, the old unused pit saw, and the stacks of trimmed timbers. Even his ancient two-story office, part of the works when Richard Deveroe originally bought the place from Jonas Stewart, seemed suddenly rickety and insecure. The rain had already worn narrow threads through the mud of the yard and water stood in tiny pools, dull gray under the glistening rain.

The storm itself might not do too much damage, but if the dam broke and a wall of water came rushing through, it would be sure to carry everything with it. Yet there was almost nothing they could do to prevent that from happening.

"Well, Bob, what do you think?"

The foreman rubbed a calloused finger along his jaw and stared out over the yard at the thundering rain, characteristically thinking through his answer before speaking. Fade waited patiently.

"Well now, Mr. Whitman," Manning finally said, "I figure we're possibly far enough from the path of the river to miss the main thrust—if we're lucky. It depends on how far she spreads."

"I tend to agree," Fade answered, "but there's always the chance we're both wrong."

"Yes sir, that is true. But if we throw up some kind of barricade in front of the yards and we get no more than the edge of the flood, we might be able to deflect the worst of it."

"No barricade on earth is going to help if the full force of that river comes through here."

"Yes sir, that's correct. But then again it might help if it don't!"

It was their only hope. "How many men can you put to work?"

"About fifteen including my own boy, Robbie. Most have already gone up to watch the dam, but there's enough left."

"Good. Let's get about it, then."

On into the night the rain continued, slackening briefly only to swell again with renewed fury. For the next three hours the crew at the Dolphin struggled to dig a ditch, then fill it with tree limbs, rocks, and sand before the rain drowned it in water. The heavy winds fed them plenty of debris, shattered branches, whole small trees, and even floating logs churned up by the storm. Cold and soaked to the skin, Fade worked alongside the men, stopping only now and then to realize how bone-tired weary he was from nearly two days of rigorous effort.

It was in the early hours of the morning, when they were in the last stages of shoring up the wall, that the dam finally broke and a thundering torrent of furious water swelled the Croton River, slashing with murderous force down three miles to the mouth at the Hudson.

They could hear the roar inside the yards. Most of the men

who had been working on the barricade threw down their tools and scrambled for the higher ground behind the buildings. Refusing to leave, Fade, Bob Manning, and his young son climbed the stairs to the second-story office, where they stood by the window and strained to see through the darkness.

Fade tried to smile. "If this building looks as though it's going, Bob, I'm telling you now, I get the roof!"

"I always wanted to ride down the Hudson on a raft," Manning answered with a short laugh. It was a relief at least to be out of the rain.

"I've done it," young Robbie said, his eyes gleaming, "but I don't think I want to do it in this!"

They could hear the water approaching long before they saw it. Like one huge wave crashing toward the shore, it came straight at them, a devastating wall of river carrying with it all sorts of objects that surfaced and disappeared under its voracious tide. Through the growing light they could make out the white-tipped edges sluicing over grasses and trees. Fade found himself gripping the window sill, trying desperately to judge its distance and force, wondering if he should make for the roof while there was still time.

Beside him, Bob said coolly, "I think we're going to get the edge."

"Wow!" his son cried, his face pressed to the window. "Wow!"

The wall spread, flattening itself out like a lake fanning its banks. It hit the barricade with a roar, drowning out the creaking strains of the flimsy structure trying to hold it back. With a loud swoosh the lake swallowed everything in its path and came sweeping into the yards, carrying timbers, broken trees, and flotsam from far upriver along with sections of the barricade itself.

The office swayed and trembled as water swirled over the yard. Gripping the sill, Fade looked at Bob as if to ask, *Now?* before scrambling out the window onto the roof.

The building groaned and shuddered with the effort to remain standing. Then the two men could almost feel the slack as the water found its level and slowed, leaving only the thump of the flotsam that jarred against the building.

"I begin to hope . . ." Fade said quietly.

Manning's lips creased in what passed for a smile. "It's

going to hold. I can tell." Beside him, Robbie looked almost disappointed.

The light was growing stronger as dawn struggled through the gloom of the rain. Looking down, Fade saw that the yard had been submerged in what he guessed was about three feet of water. It had swelled rapidly to that level and then eased off, leaving behind the cluttered remains of its trip downriver. He allowed himself a brief sigh of relief that their luck had held. It would take days for the water to slack off and the mess to be cleaned up, but at least the yards had not been destroyed. For that he gave up a silent prayer of thanks.

He stood by the window long after dawn turned to daylight, watching in fascination the watery plateau around the Dolphin yards where farms and fields had formerly existed. It was now choked with the debris left by the river's destructive path. Fade recognized piers from the bridges higher up—Pinesbridge and Wood's Bridge. Timbers and jagged sections of houses and roofs floated in the new lake. Pieces of buildings—one of which he would swear was part of Bailey's wire factory—dead animals, great hunks of ice, whole trees, and mounds of mud and silt poked their grotesque heads out of the wet valley floor. How many men might have also been carried away underneath this disastrous torrent he could only guess.

But the Dolphin yards still stood firm. God be thanked for that!

Once Fade knew the danger to the Dolphin was past, he gave way to the most debilitating weariness he could ever remember and headed for home. The rain too had worn itself out and now, having done its worst, had finally begun to slacken. By the time he stumbled up the back steps of Southernwood—dirty, clammy, his chin dark with a two-days' growth of beard—only a light drizzle fell, turning the daylight to cream.

Since the mud that covered him from head to foot was too much for Emily's elegant hall, he entered through the kitchen and there ran straight into their cook, Absolem's new wife, Glory, who was standing in front of the big black cast-iron stove that dominated the room. Her eyes widened when she looked up and saw him.

"La, Mr. Whitman, look at yourself!"

"I know, Glory. Heat up some water for me, will you. I

want nothing in the world so much right now as a good bath and a soft bed. And tell Mrs. Whitman I'm back, will you."

"Why, Mistuh Whitman, I can't do that. Why she's in bed herself. You done missed all the 'citement round here."

Pulling up a chair, Fade began peeling off his boots. "I've had excitement enough to last me for the rest of my days. Don't tell me something else has flooded."

He had one boot off on the jack when something about Glory's dancing eyes aroused a suspicion.

"What are you talking about?"

"Why, nothing, Mistuh Whitman, nothing at all, 'ceptin' that Miz Whitman, she done had her baby while you was off fixin' that dam. Nigh on about two hours ago."

Still holding the jack, Fade jumped to his feet. "What do you mean? She wasn't supposed to . . . Why didn't I know about this? No one told me, sent me any word . . ."

"Why, you was so busy with all that flood water, Miz Whitman, she say to let you alone. But we took care of everythin', me and old Granny Stead, the midwife. And now you got a fine baby daughter. As pretty a little chile as ever I see'd."

Fade went hopping toward the stairs on one stockinged foot. "Emily—how is she?"

"Why, she's just fine too, Mr. Fade. We done took good care of her."

It was only later that he realized what a sight he must have seemed bursting into Emily's bedroom, hovering over her pale form under the bedclothes, calling her name, stroking away the long strands of dark hair that spilled around her on the lace-edged pillow.

She had been drifting off into the sweet oblivion of no pain and the joyous knowledge that she was a mother, even if the baby was a daughter instead of the longed-for son. When she opened her eyes to see Fade bending anxiously over her, she was overcome with happiness. Lifting her arm slowly, she laid a hand against his cheek and smiled glowingly up at him.

"Fade, you missed . . ."

"I know. Can you ever forgive me?"

"Of course. I wouldn't let them call you. You were so busy."

"The yards are safe, Emily. If only I'd known, I'd have come home even though I might have had to let the whole crew drown!"

"No, that wouldn't do at all. It's all right. Have you seen your daughter?"

He glanced toward the small cradle under a crocheted lace canopy, where Faith stood proudly watching.

"Go look," Emily whispered.

Weariness overcame her as he moved away and she closed her eyes, drifting off into a few moments oblivion. When she opened them again, she saw that Fade was standing across the room, one leg still incased in its muddy boot, the other in a damp stocking, cradling the baby in his arms and looking down into the child's face with such a blatant expression of wonder and love as to send a stab of pain through Emily's chest. All at once she felt afraid. It seemed as though an invisible door had closed between her and her husband, shutting her out. There was something between Fade and his daughter that she was not a part of. She was merely looking on, a witness to this happiness she could not share.

Closing her eyes, she turned her head away. It was only a momentary pang—it would be forgotten with one night's decent rest. A silly figment of her overwrought imagination.

But, oh, how she wished the baby had been a son.

PART II

Damaris

*Fifteen*

"EVERYBODY DUCK."

Bending over so that her head almost touched the seat in front of her, Damaris Whitman sucked in her breath to make her eleven-year-old body lighter. Wesley Slade's asthmatic breathing seemed suddenly loud in her ear. Overhead, the low bridge of the railroad crossing blanketed the sun, casting a tunnellike shadow over the skiff. Then, gliding easily through the inky water, the skiff slid out of the tunnel and into the sun-dappled mouth of Sparta Brook and five heads were raised as one, four light-haired and one dark.

Stretching her legs out as far as the crowded skiff would allow, Damaris settled back on the seat and dipped her hand into the indigo water, rearranging the patterns of light on the surface. In the front of the skiff, Jesse Whitman, her cousin, rose to one knee and pushed on the slim oak pole he was using to propel the boat.

"I wish a train had come by while we were under there," Ethan Slade said wistfully from the back of the boat. "I love to go under the trestle when a train is passing."

"I don't," Damaris replied firmly. "The whole thing shudders like it's going to fall in. It's much nicer this way."

"Look at that," Jesse called, pointing toward the shore. Along the bank stood a long wall of narrow poles stacked neatly together. In front of them lay huge mounds of netting dyed the color of oak bark and squat cones of coiled rope, like giant beehives shimmering in the dappled sun.

"They've brought in the shad nets," Jesse said almost to himself. "I thought there was another week. At least that's what Pa told me, and he ought to know. He's been up working one of the seine crews on Crawbucky Point every night for the past month."

"How far up the brook are we going?" asked a timid voice from behind Damaris. "I don't like it where it gets narrow— the trees make it so dark."

"Oh, Corrine," Damaris said scornfully, "you are the biggest fraidy-cat I know. Everything scares you."

Ethan, who was sitting beside Corrine, turned to her eagerly. "You do right to be afraid, Corrine. When it's dark and the trees hang over the boat like this, sometimes wild animals jump out at you right into the skiff. And bats!"

"Oh, oh . . ." Corrine cried.

"That's right," Damaris joined in eagerly. "And big crawling bugs drop right into your lap. Not to mention pirates with long knives, just waiting . . ."

Corrine began to cry.

"Now stop it, you two," Wesley said, looking back over his shoulder at the small girl. "They are just trying to scare you, Corrine. There's nothing dangerous in here. It's very cool and pleasant."

"Stop worrying, Corrine," Jesse added in his quiet, sensible voice. "We can't go very far up anyway because the brook gets too narrow."

Damaris sniffed. "Good heavens, Corrine, I don't know why you should be scared. Jesse can handle anything on this river, you ought to know that by now. How I ever got such a scairdy-cat for a sister is beyond me. You should have stayed home with Winnifred if you didn't want adventure."

"Winnifred is a baby," Corrine pouted.

"Well, what do you think you are?"

"Oh, let her alone, Damaris," Wesley said. "She's all right."

The small cove they had entered from under the bridge channeled into a narrow brook, blue and shadowy under its canopy of overhanging trees. Here the banks, sloping gently upward, began to be wild with an overgrowth of moss and rocks. Through the thick trees they could now and then catch a glimpse of the rear yard of one of the houses on Hampton Street.

Damaris, accepting Wesley's admonition without argument, stretched her long neck back, savoring the coolness of the shadowed brook after the hot sun and white glare of the river. As Jesse had said, they could not go very far, for the brook soon became too shallow to take the skiff, yet she loved floating along under the trees this way. Behind her she could imagine Ethan's brooding face, looking restlessly from one side of the bank to the other as though he were viewing it for the first time; Corrine, timidly eyeing the shadows and scrunching close to Ethan on the seat; Wesley, his usual joking banter not in evidence today; and ahead, thrusting the pole gently into the soft underbelly of the brook, Jesse, his knowledgeable eyes seeing the myriad living things beneath the water's surface.

Above them the birds squawked and chattered almost as loudly as they did outside her open window at dawn, when their screeching woke her every morning. She wondered why people spoke of birds as "singing." Now and then you might hear a collection of warbles that resembled the musical notes of her mother's pianoforte, but mostly it was just a constant cacophony of chatter and complaints, a lot like the parlor when all the family came visiting, and especially when Uncle Garret happened to be there. She could hear the lowing of cattle and an occasional neigh of a horse, even the clatter of a wagon lumbering down Hampton toward the dock, and in the distance a woman's voice, a child's screech, the soft clinking of the hammers at the quarry, though that was so far away she really had to strain to hear it.

Jesse began humming a soft tune—one of those gospel songs he had learned at a camp meeting. He had a gravelly voice, not really very pleasant, and Damaris wished he would be quiet so she might listen to the sounds of the woods and the brook, which seemed to her infinitely more lovely, and in a way more religious.

"I want to go back now," Corrine whined.

Her reverie shattered, Damaris looked around in disgust. "I wish you had stayed home. You spoil everything."

"Mother wouldn't like me to be here," Corrine answered, goaded to defiance. "Papa either."

"Papa won't mind."

"My shoes are getting wet and there's mud on my dress. Mother will be angry."

"Papa will take care of it. He grew up here. He told me he used to spend hours on the brook when he was younger than you, fishing and playing. Stop worrying about your clothes."

"But you know how Mother doesn't like us to get dirty."

"Pooh!"

"Look," Ethan broke in, "there's the back of Uncle Lew's yard. And his old horse is in the pasture. That's funny, because I know he's working up at our house today."

Uncle Lew Bird was one of the free blacks living in Sparta. The tiny house in which he and his family somehow crowded together had a long sloping yard that reached down to the brook. Over the years he had cleared it and built a series of rickety, worm-eaten wooden fences, which he had subdivided into small pens for his livestock. Uncle Lew was known to have the oldest horse, the laziest cows, and the meanest goats in all the village.

"Pull up, Jesse," Ethan said. "I want to get out."

Damaris looked around to catch the mischievous glint in Ethan's amber eyes. She was sure his fertile mind was thinking of something exciting, and if Ethan was up to anything, she wanted to be part of it. "Me too," she said quickly.

Jesse obediently pushed the skiff toward the bank, and Ethan jumped out, his boots sinking into swampy mud half an inch deep.

"I'm coming too," Damaris said, rising to set the boat rocking.

"Your shoes..."

"Oh, bother my shoes." Resting a hand on Wesley's shoulder, with a quick motion she pulled off both shoes and stockings, heaved up her skirt and petticoats, and stepped out of the boat into the mud. It oozed deliciously between her toes.

"Come on, Wesley."

"No. I don't feel like it. You go."

That was unusual. Most of the time Wesley was as eager to follow in his older brother's shadow as Damaris. But Ethan was already halfway up the bank and Damaris hurried after him, not worrying about the others. Let them sit there and miss the fun. She caught up with Ethan at the back fence, where Uncle Lew's ancient chestnut horse lifted his head and stared at them curiously. Making a soft clucking noise, Ethan lured him nearer the gate.

"What are you going to do?" Damaris whispered, even though there was nobody around to hear.

"Oh, I don't know. I just thought it might be interesting to open old Lew's fences and then sit back and watch the fun."

"Ethan, we'll get in trouble."

"So . . . ?"

Like Ethan, Damaris gave only momentary consideration to the thought. "Do you think anybody will see us?"

Ethan looked around. He loved these pranks, but he wasn't so careless as to carry them out in plain sight. "I don't see anyone. If we work fast and keep quiet, I bet we can open everything and be gone before anybody knows a thing about it. Want to try?"

"Sure. But I don't want to go anywhere near that mean old goat."

The old horse had lumbered up close enough to the fence to nudge them with his nose. Deftly, Ethan pulled up the bar and swung the gate open. The horse stared at it stupidly, then moved cautiously closer to inspect this curious phenomenon with its promise of freedom.

"I'll get the goat pen. You take the cows."

"What about the chickens?"

"That's pretty close to the house. Everybody in Lew's family works somewhere, but you never know if one of them stayed home. Beside, there are always chickens and pigs wandering around the village. That's nothing unusual."

He was off quickly, hunched over just in case anyone was in the house, working his way toward the goats. Damaris scrambled behind him, keeping close to the fence until she reached the gate to the cow pasture. Nearby four somnolent brown-and-white cows huddled together, lazily lifting their heads as they spotted her. She opened the gate and started to run back toward the brook, then decided that was only half doing it. The real fun would be to shoo them out. The patchy sod hurt her feet, but she managed to get behind the animals and swoosh them toward the open gate by flapping her skirt. Three of them were already out, waddling toward the road, when Ethan caught up with her.

"Damaris, you idiot! Do you want them to see you!"

"I was just trying to make sure they left."

"Well, you're going to make sure we get caught! Come on, let's go back to the boat."

Grabbing her hand, he pulled her after him into the shelter of the trees. By the time they reached the skiff they were giggling, picturing the havoc Lew's livestock would create wandering freely through the village.

The boat rocked and swayed as they climbed back in. Corrine, noticing Damaris's dirty feet and the muddy hem of her dress, groaned to think of the scolding she was bound to get. In spite of the bullying she took from her older sister, she felt genuine pain when Damaris earned their mother's punishment. She knew it was her sister's own fault and none of her concern but somehow she couldn't help responding to everyone's suffering as though it was her own.

"Did you let the goat loose?" Damaris said, turning toward Ethan.

He smiled broadly. "Yes, but not before that damned horned devil tried to bite me. He doesn't even have sense enough to know when someone's doing him a favor."

"I think we'd better get back to the river," Jesse said, pushing off. "If you two get in trouble for this, I want no part of it."

"Oh, Jesse," Damaris answered, "just because you're older than us you act like some kind of old man. It's just a little fun."

A flush spread over Jesse's homely features. "It's not that. My pa would thrash me within an inch of my life if he thought I was doing something like this. Your pa ought to give you a good hiding now and then, Damaris. It wouldn't hurt."

"My papa would never do anything like that to me!"

The same thought flashed through four other minds in the boat. That was certainly true. Damaris could wrap her father around her little finger any time she wanted, and he loved it.

They entered the wide pond and headed toward the low railroad bridge.

"I hope you don't catch it from your mother," Wesley said sympathetically. Like Corrine, it hurt him to see anyone suffer.

Damaris shrugged. "Oh, I'm always catching it from her anyway. It was worth it, wasn't it, Ethan?" She smiled back at him.

He glanced down at her, his eyes dancing at the thought of the mischief they'd made. "It will be if Jesse will hurry up and get us back to the dock. If we run up the street, we may be able to see what's happening."

"Bridge coming up," Jesse called. "Everybody down."

When Damaris and Corrine got back to the house, Damaris received a royal scolding from her mother over the condition of her shoes and dress. But that was nothing compared to what happened later that evening, after Uncle Lew Bird paid a visit to her parents.

Even Fade was horrified, though his rage was nothing compared to Emily's. She had the sisters hauled from bed to face her in the parlor, looming before them like a warship with all guns blazing.

"What on earth am I going to do with you? How could you do such a thoughtless thing?"

The two girls stood facing their parents, Damaris with her hands behind her back, staring defiantly at the floor, Corrine at her side crying quietly.

"How could you be so naughty? Do you realize the damage you caused?"

"It was just a prank." Damaris spoke up.

"A prank!" Emily shouted. "It took Lew Bird three hours to catch that stubborn old horse again, after a day spent doing very hard labor in Robert Slade's hay fields. Those cows stomped through three gardens, eating the vegetation and plowing under the rest. And that horrible goat! He tore the wash right off Mrs. Acker's line! She doesn't know yet how many of her clothes are ruined!"

Damaris had to stifle a giggle at the thought, but she knew mirth had little place in the face of her mother's anger. Nor was her Papa's severity tempered by any appreciation for the humor of the situation.

Emily turned to her other daughter. "And you, Corrine. I'm shocked that you could take any part in such a thing. It's not like you at all."

Corrine sniffed louder but said nothing. Watching her, Damaris thought the little ninny wasn't even going to exonerate herself. Well, she would not allow Corrine to be a martyr for her sake.

"Corrine didn't do anything. It was all me and . . . well, it was just two of us."

"You needn't attempt to defend Ethan Slade," her father broke in sternly. "We know he was involved and I would not be surprised if the whole thing was not his idea. What shocks and hurts me is that you would go along with him so readily."

"When did she ever *not* go along with Ethan and his wild schemes?" Emily cried in exasperation. "I tell you, Damaris, this is too much. If you will not learn to act like a lady and curb your wildness, I shall just have to send you away to some kind of boarding school."

Damaris's eyes flew to her father, who was looking at her mother with a curiously defiant gaze, though he said nothing. This was an old threat and the one she most dreaded. Surely her father would never allow her to be sent away.

Fade turned to his daughter and said sternly, "You certainly will be punished for this, Damaris—for the damage and trouble you caused old Uncle Lew. He has a hard life and he doesn't need this kind of added irritation. Now, both of you may go. We will continue this discussion in the morning."

"If you hadn't already had your supper you certainly would do without tonight," Emily added as the girls turned to go. When the door closed behind them she moved to the window, twisting the handkerchief she held in her hands.

"What are we going to do with that girl? She is more trouble than the other two put together. I simply don't know how to curb her wild spirits."

Fade settled back in his chair. Now that his daughters were out of the room he couldn't help imagining Lew's goat pulling down old Mrs. Acker's wash. "She's just a child," he said with a slight smile. "She'll grow out of it."

"She's eleven years old! Small wonder I can't make a lady of that girl when you always try to protect her from the consequences of her rash actions."

"You exaggerate, Emily. She's just full of high spirits—a few more years of maturity should temper that. Besides, it's really Ethan. He's a devil if ever there was one, and he's always leading her into some mischief. I wish she didn't idolize him so."

Emily looked around at her husband. She was fond of Ethan in spite of his habit of involving Damaris in his highjinks. "Why won't you let me send her away, then?" she asked stubbornly. "A good ladies' finishing school might be just the thing. At least she would be away from these friends who have such a deplorable influence on her."

An invisible door slammed between them. She could see Fade's countenance darken.

"And break her heart in the process. No. We've discussed this before, Emily, and I absolutely refuse to allow you to send her away from Southernwood. She'll outgrow this kind of trouble."

You refuse to allow her to be sent away from you! How she longed to shout these words into his stubborn face, but as always, she held her tongue. This was the one subject they could never discuss without rancor.

Fade, as anxious as his wife to avoid that kind of confrontation, rose to lay a hand on her shoulder. "Come on, Emily. We've two daughters who are angels. One high-spirited child is not too much to handle."

"Winnifred and Corrine are only children."

"They're nine and six. What really matters is that they have a different temperament. Damaris was always willful and strong-minded. She loves fun and she likes to have her own way. But she's a good girl at heart."

He longed to add that of the three she was the one who was most like her mother, but as Emily had left dangerous thoughts unspoken, so did he. He knew that he was too quick to come between mother and daughter, but neither of them realized how alike they were and how that very similarity was the source of most of their conflicts. If only they could accept how much he adored them both.

Emily reached up to grasp his hand. "Very well, but we cannot let her go unpunished. What do you suggest?"

"Oh, I don't know. Two days restricted to the house? A week without visiting Wesley and Ethan?"

"She might go and stay with old Cousin Agatha for a week. That would keep her out of mischief."

"Hmm. That's not such a bad idea. A week of enforced boredom would be a terrible punishment indeed for Damaris."

Emily squeezed his hand, then turned and went toward the door. "Very well. I'll make the arrangements."

Ordinarily Damaris would have wept for hours at the thought of spending a week with Cousin Agatha. The poor old lady, sweet as she was, required endless reading to and waiting on, and the enforced seclusion in her small house seemed more like a prison every day. Even when Claes was there he was little pleasure. All he cared about were his boats and what was happening at the dock, and since she could not accompany him or share in his interests, he was no help at all. Now and then she might talk him into playing a game of cribbage in the evening, but that was about the extent of his companionship.

Worst of all, she hated being around her Uncle Garret. He was temporarily renting a room in Agatha's house and was in and out all hours of the day and night. When he was drinking she avoided him, having learned years ago to hide in her room or a closet or anywhere he might not spot her. But when he was sober, it was even worse: he would talk on and on about the disappointments he'd suffered, and he would make nasty comments about her parents. She had often thought of confiding in her papa about Uncle Garret's strange behavior, but something told her that would only make things worse. And, after all, Garret was harmless enough. He was just slimy and he made her flesh crawl and she detested him.

As it turned out, this time she was spared Garret's company altogether. The very next morning, even as the housemaid was packing her portmanteau for the trip, Damaris crawled into her bed feeling ill and feverish and unable to swallow. By the following day she was burning with a high temperature and her face was flushed and swollen.

Emily could not help but remember the rumors about a new outbreak of scarlet fever running through the county. The yearly epidemic had not yet reached Mount Pleasant, but this might be the vanguard. From Tarrytown came word that Wesley Slade was down with an even higher fever and the doctor was very concerned. Emily had Dr. Sayre brought hastily up the hill and began watching the other girls for any symptoms of illness.

Her anger at Damaris was forgotten in the week that followed. While the girl lay feverish and miserable on her tester bed, Emily stayed by her, placing cool cloths on her hot forehead, trying to get liquids down her painfully sore throat, watching for any sign of a break in the disease's fearful progress. Fade came and went anxiously, almost unable to bear the sight of his daughter so ill.

Toward the end of the week when the fever diminished and the swelling subsided, a restless Damaris became impatient to be out of bed. Then Corrine came down with the same thing, though much less severe and not nearly as debilitating. Emily nursed Corrine as she had Damaris, never leaving her bedside until she felt sure the child was safe.

From Tarrytown came word that Wesley too had survived his illness, though he was still very weak and sick. Emily was thankful, for Wesley was a lovable boy. And even though the years had not mitigated the quiet dislike she felt for Gabrielle Slade, she had no desire to see Robert's wife suffer. How ironic, she thought, that it was Wesley who lay ill and not Ethan. Yet she had to admit that Ethan was the more vigorous and attractive of the two boys and she rather admired the high spirits that got him into trouble. Somehow that was more acceptable in a boy than in a girl. Now, if Damaris had been a son . . .

The final irony was to learn that the children's illness had not been the dreaded scarlet fever after all, but a simple case of the mumps. And so they were spared the worst.

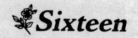

Sixteen

"Blast it, Damaris. If these hoops you young girls wear get any bigger we won't be able to sit in the same chaise together!"

Pushing aside the mountain of fabric that spilled over his legs, Fade flicked the reins over his bay's back and guided the carriage deftly around the sharp curve that led onto Main Street. Beside him, Damaris pulled in the ruffled skirt that swelled like a globe around her.

"It's the fashion, Papa. Besides, I thought this one was very pretty."

And it was, Fade thought. Fashioned from a small flower pattern in lavender and pink printed on muslin and tiered in large ruffles, it gave his lovely nineteen-year-old daughter the freshness of a summer's day. With her dark hair falling in long coils from under the wide leghorn hat that was tied with a lavender satin ribbon, she was a sight to draw the eyes of the loafers lounging around the saloons and store entrances as they rolled smartly by.

"It is very fetching, my dear. But every year the skirts grow larger. It's getting out of hand."

"Oh, look. There's Wesley."

Damaris waved one net-gloved hand at Wesley Slade, who had just walked out of Jonas Walker's solicitor's office. Spotting them, he removed his tall brown silk hat and waved enthusiastically back.

"Pull up, Papa. I may as well get out here. Wes can take me around to the stores I want to visit."

"You'll have to watch your shoes. The mud is worse than usual today."

"I'll walk on the planks."

Delighted to see the Whitman carriage stopping near him. Wes hurried over to hand Damaris down.

"This is an unexpected surprise," he said, caught in a swirl of lavender and pink as he helped her from the chaise. "I was just going down to the American Hotel for some 'tea and fixins.' You'll join me, won't you?"

Stepping safely onto the planks and out of the mud, Damaris drew his arm through hers. "Oh, no. First you must take me around to Barlow's and then to Mr. Holmes's. I have a long list of things to buy for Mother and Corrine and a few things of my own to find. Oh, and the bank. I really should stop there too. Then perhaps we'll have time for tea."

Wesley smiled up at Fade. "I can see my afternoon has been rearranged for me."

"You are doing me a service, Wesley, to take her off my hands. I have business at the dock, and I feared I'd never get around to it, squiring this demanding young lady around town. You're sure you have the time?"

"It will be my pleasure," Wesley answered.

"I'll meet you at the hotel in an hour, then," Fade called, snapping the reins.

"Two hours!" Damaris called after him.

The two young people set off down the flagstone sidewalk shaded by a canopy of oaks and elms.

"And how is everyone on the hill?" Wesley asked, feeling a quiet contentment to be walking arm in arm with his favorite girl, enjoying the admiring and friendly nod of the many acquaintances who passed them on the street.

"Oh, the same as ever. Corrine reads and sews and hardly

ever says a word. Papa talks all the time about his beautiful ships, and Mother, well, since Papa put his foot down and forbade her to take part in any more women's rights shenanigans, she has done nothing but think up projects for me. Sometimes I wish he had left her alone."

"Your mother is a very enterprising and intelligent woman. She probably needs these crusades as an outlet for all that energy. She is good at it too, for in spite of all the turmoil she caused around here, she was responsible for some real gains in improving the lot of women."

"That is very perceptive of you, Wesley, and you're right. She threw herself into it and she did a good job. I think the fact that women in this state now have limited control over their own property is partly due to her efforts. But you know Mother—she overdoes everything. And when she started insisting that unmarried women refuse to pay their taxes, well that was just too much. Papa felt she was going to ruin him before she got through. My goodness, Wes, you must let me retie that neckcloth before we leave. Now that you're working in a lawyer's office, you really ought to take more care about your appearance."

As always, this familiar admonition rolled right off his back. He smiled good-naturedly and raised his hat to the widow Morris, meanwhile guiding Damaris around a goat who was nudging at the garbage in the street.

"You've been telling me the same thing ever since you were ten years old, Damaris."

"Yes, and you never pay any attention to me. All the same, I tie Papa's cravats regularly and I do it well. I shall never rest today until I get my hands on yours. Good afternoon, Mr. Shannon. How is your little daughter feeling?"

"Afternoon, Miss Whitman, Mr. Slade," said Shannon, a thin man in a shabby black suit. "She's doing right poorly, I'm sorry to say. T'would be nice to have little Winnifred come and play with her sometime. T'would raise her spirits, I'm sure."

"I'll tell Mother you said so," Damaris promised. "Meantime, my best to her."

"Thank you, Miss Whitman. Thank you quite sincerely."

They passed on and Damaris leaned closer to Wesley. "Mother will never allow Winnifred to go near that Shannon child again. Why, her home is the grubbiest place, and I'm sure the girl has lice. No wonder she's always sick."

"More likely it's because her house backs on Kill Brook. It's an open sewer, you know."

"Well, democracy can only go so far! Ah, here is Barlow's store. Now you read off the list and I'll hunt for the items."

Straightening a limp iris, Emily gave the last touches to a bouquet of fragrant flowers she had just brought in from her garden. As she stood back to admire it, she caught her reflection in the gilt mirror over the hall table and leaned closer to inspect her face, running her hands along her cheeks to draw the skin taut.

How depressing that age loosened everything so badly! Her brown hair, salted now with gray, was still thick and lustrous and she fancied her eyes were as interesting as ever. But oh, the chin and neck, the puffy sacks under the eyes . . .

Enough of this, she thought, tossing her head; Fade still likes the way I look and that is all that matters.

As she turned away, she was all at once aware of a commotion outside: footsteps running on the path, voices calling, and surely there was a carriage coming up the drive. Pleased with the thought of visitors, Emily hurried to the porch, where the afternoon sunlight filtered through the overhanging lilac bushes. A carriage was approaching, the driver smartly putting the dark horse though his paces. She could see Corrine coming up the path, too, her hat bouncing behind her, petticoats and skirts lifted up and out of the way of her flying legs.

Corrine! Of all people to be so excited. Focusing on the carriage, Emily recognized the driver. Ethan Slade! He was smartly dressed in a black frock coat and leather driving gloves, his tall hat at a rakish angle, as self-assured and elegant as ever. Hurrying down the stairs, she stood on the first step and watched as he pulled up.

"Good afternoon, Mrs. Whitman," he said, smiling down at her with a roguish glint in his brown eyes and a teasing grin on his face that recalled for Emily the mischievous little boy she had been so fond of.

"Ethan Slade, where on earth did you come from?"

"Straight off the packet from London. Just got home an hour ago and took the first moment free from Mama's embraces to drive over and pay my respects."

Ethan bounded down off the seat and handed the reins to a stableboy, who had outraced Corrine. Clasping Emily in his arms, he gave her a warm hug. "You look as beautiful as ever. A year away hasn't made a particle of difference."

Emily stood back, her hands on his arms, looking him over. "And you are as full of blarney as when you went away. How good to see you, Ethan. Come in, come in."

With a flurry of her skirts, Corrine came running up beside them, gasping for breath. Laughing, Ethan reached out and lifted her off the ground, swirling the eager young girl around once before setting her down and kissing her lightly on both pink cheeks.

"And, Corrine. Look how you've grown. Quite the young lady you are."

"I was in the orchard when I saw your carriage go by. Oh, Ethan, I'm so glad you're back. We missed you so much."

Taking his arm, Emily led him up the stairs and into the house. "I'm sorry, Ethan, but Damaris is not here at the moment. She went into the village with her father, but I expect them back any time. You must sit with us and have a cherry punch. I want to hear all about your trip and your year in London. How exciting it must have been!"

Corrine followed the two of them into the parlor, wishing her mother had not mentioned Damaris. Settling quietly on a chair across from the sofa where Ethan and her mother sat chatting, she studied him avidly. He looked heavier than he had when he went away, more solid and muscular. The sideburns along his cheeks were thicker and longer and flecked with gold. In spite of England's famous gray weather, his lean face was tan and healthy looking. As always, he exuded vitality and authority.

"And are you a full-fledged physician now, Ethan?" Emily asked, unaware of her daughter's scrutiny.

"Full-fledged and accredited. Ready to hang out my shingle. Of course I expect you to come to me with all your ailments."

"Oh no," Emily teased. "I have known you since you were a baby and I will never be able to think of you as a seasoned doctor. I think I shall stay with young Dr. Sayre for a while longer."

"*Young* Dr. Sayre who's older than my father! Madam, you cut me to the quick. How will I ever establish a practice if everyone distrusts me because of my youth? It's not fair."

"I never could understand why you chose medicine in the first place. Why not the law, like Wesley, or perhaps the church?"

Even Corrine giggled at that.

Ethan looked over at her, his eyes dancing. "Why, Mrs. Whitman, as many times as you yourself have called me a rascal and a scalawag, do you really think I would be the appropriate person for the church?"

"Now, Ethan, you did have a knack for getting in trouble, but you know that in spite of that I have always been especially fond of you," Emily said, beaming. "If you had not always dragged Damaris into your pranks, I would have probably been the only one to defend your high spirits."

"A willing accomplice, you must admit."

"Oh, I admit it. You two are a pair if ever there was one."

Corrine turned away. In truth, Emily had always defended Ethan at the same time that she was hardest on her eldest daughter for committing exactly the same "crimes." It was an old pain for Corrine, that wish to be as recklessly daring as Damaris. She herself almost never earned her mother's stern disapproval, but then she never did anything mischievous or naughty.

"Oh my goodness," Emily cried, getting abruptly to her feet. "I think I hear them coming now. How fortunate Damaris has returned while you are here."

Ethan followed Emily into the hall and waited there until she returned with Damaris in tow, followed by a bright-eyed, excited Wesley and a more sedate Fade.

"Ethan, you scoundrel," Wesley cried, pumping his brother's hand. "You were expected next week. How good it is to see you!"

Ethan threw an arm around his brother's shoulders before turning to hug Damaris. "The packet arrived earlier than expected. A miraculous event, I'm told. Damaris Whitman, you grow prettier every time I see you. How grown up you are. What a difference one year has made."

His enthusiastic hug had knocked off her hat, and with her black curls askew, her eyes glittering with excitement and delight at seeing him, her shapely lips forming a glowing smile, Ethan thought she had never looked more beautiful. He felt a possessive surge of desire for her that surprised him with its force.

"Oh, Ethan, you are still the smooth talker," Damaris replied, laughing. "How wonderful to have you back. You look as though England agreed with you."

Once the three of them backed off a little, Fade moved forward to shake Ethan's hand. "Has it really been a year? Welcome home, Ethan. Come sit down and tell us all about your experiences abroad."

There was so much affection among this small group of young people, Fade thought as he ushered them into the parlor. They had grown up together so closely that they were almost like brothers and sisters. Or they would be if no more complicated emotions arose to disrupt their lives. He poured out three glasses of Madeira, handed one to each of the boys, then sat down, fingering his own glass and contentedly observing the scene: Ethan still with that touch of arrogance, holding court as though it was the most natural thing in the world; Corrine adoring and quiet; Damaris flirtatious, her eyes unusually bright; Emily beaming as she looked upon them—he knew how much she hoped to have Ethan for a son-in-law; and Wesley, who instead of being jealous of all this affection lavished on his brother, willingly and happily joined in the celebration of Ethan's homecoming.

Ethan had just finished describing his lectures at the College of Surgeons and his hours of practice at the London Hospital when he turned unexpectedly to Fade. "So tell me, sir, how do things go here? Is the shipbuilding business prospering?"

"It's going very well," Fade answered, pleasurably surprised at his interest. "The Dolphin yards continue to turn out sloops and steam packets for the Hudson run as well as a few schooners for the West Indies trade. We also now own shares in two beautiful clippers, as fast as anything that was ever under sail. They can make the trip from China in less than three months— unheard of ever before. With luck the voyage to San Francisco now takes around ninety to one hundred days. Every year they grow more fleet. Wonderful ships!"

"There was much excitement in England about iron ships. Have they been experimented with over here as yet?"

"Oh yes, there are always fools who will fiddle around with crazy ideas. I admit the screw propeller and the steam boiler are probably here to stay, but an iron ship can only sink to the bottom. It'll never replace the clipper."

"Ethan, you haven't told us anything about London as a city," Damaris interrupted. "What was it like? Did you see the Crystal Palace? The queen? What about the latest fashions? Are hoops as large over there as here?"

"Damaris, be still," Emily said harshly. "Ethan will tell us all about the London scene when he has time. Right now he's talking with your father."

Reluctantly Damaris sat back and folded her hands, wishing her mother would stop treating her like a child.

"I kept abreast of what was happening in the States by reading the papers regularly over there," Ethan went on, "although they are not exactly unbiased toward America. I got the impression that business was prospering."

Fade nodded. "I would say so, yes. After the disastrous forties, the fifties were a welcome change. Everyone hopes the sixties will be even better."

"If war can be avoided . . ."

"Did you read of that over there too?" Emily asked, surprised. "Has it gone so far?"

"It appears to be expected even though no one can quite believe it will really come," Ethan answered.

"I would say that was an accurate picture of us, as well," Fade said. "Everyone expects it but no one really believes it can happen. Unfortunately, it probably will."

Wesley said, "Do you really think so, sir?"

"I hope I am wrong, but it seems as though our southern states are bent on a course of secession that will make a war to preserve the Union inevitable. And if Mr. Lincoln is elected, there can be no other answer."

"There is much sympathy for the southern states in England."

"There would be, especially since the south supplies so much of the raw cotton for English mills."

"War!" Damaris almost spat out the word. "What a terrible thing. But at least it should not touch us."

"Slavery is a terrible thing," Emily answered her. "If it takes a war to do away with it once and for all, then perhaps that will be a good thing."

"My abolitionist mother!"

Emily turned a stern eye on her daughter. "I've seen slavery firsthand, which you have not, my dear. It is a scourge on society."

"I agree with you, Mrs. Whitman," Wesley said. "And if war does come and there is a regiment from New York, I intend to join it."

"Oh, they'd never take you," Damaris scoffed. "Your health is too precarious. You'd be home in a week with typhoid or dysentery."

"Perhaps, but at least I shall have tried. What about you, Ethan?"

Ethan stared into his glass. "It might be interesting to treat battle wounds. And the army will need surgeons, I suppose."

"Slavery is one issue," Fade added in his serious, steady voice "but there are others. Free enterprise, the solidarity of the Union, an agrarian economy at odds with an industrial one. There are no easy answers. Frankly, I don't envy Mr. Lincoln taking over at such a time."

"Ethan, of course you'll stay to supper—you and Wesley both," Emily said, steering the conversation away from the serious turn it had taken.

"Thank you, ma'am, but I'd better not. I have said hello to Mama, but Father was not there. He's expected later this evening and I know he'll want to see me."

"Tomorrow, then—I insist. And tell Robert and Gabrielle to come along too. But for now, it is so very lovely outside, I think it would be very nice for you to have a stroll round a good American garden. Damaris, why don't you take Ethan outside? It will give him a chance to tell you all about those English fashions."

Uncomfortable, Damaris glanced at Wesley, sure that he would not wish to see his brother lured away. But he seemed engrossed in talking to Corrine.

"But, Mother, Ethan's only just arrived. I'm sure he'd rather visit with all of us."

"Nonsense, my dear. It's been a whole year since you two have had an opportunity to be alone together. Now go, I insist."

Ethan was already on his feet. "I agree with your mother, Damaris. After nineteen days on a packet ship, a stroll around the garden would be just the thing. Come along now."

His obvious enthusiasm filled her with joy. Ignoring for the moment her mother's imperiousness, she took Ethan's arm and let him lead her out of the room. By the time they had reached the graveled walk, he was well into an amusing description of the London scene and her laughter was echoing back through the open windows of the parlor. Emily heard it and smiled smugly across the room at Fade.

Winnifred Whitman thrust out her full lower lip and narrowed her cat's eyes, glaring at her mother.

"I don't see why I can't take part in the dancing like Damaris and Corrine. I'm almost fourteen years old and I'm still stuck upstairs with Felicity Webber and Elizabeth King, staring down at all the fun through the railings. It's not fair!"

Emily smoothed her youngest daughter's long honey-blond hair, thinking how much she looked like her father when she was feeling angry or frustrated.

"Just a little longer, my love. Don't be in too much of a hurry to grow up. After all, you are my baby. When you're as old as your sisters, I'll have no one left."

"I don't want to be a baby or a schoolgirl. I want to be a lady."

Pushing Winnifred aside, Damaris peered into the glass and pinched her cheeks to make them pink. "Then you'd better start acting like one instead of running around the halls giggling at the beaus in their ruffled shirts. The last time we went to a party I was embarrassed to death, you made such a sight of yourself."

"That's not true! We were only laughing a little at Stephen King. He looked so funny with his hair all curled up and his big front."

"Well, he was horribly chagrined. He thought he looked the rage of fashion."

"Mother, have you seen my white gloves?" Corrine asked as she entered Emily's bedroom from the hall. "One of them is missing, and I can't find it. I know I had them the last time we went out to that party at Mr. Ward's."

Winnifred looked from one to the other of her sisters, admiring their softly colored billowing dresses and masses of long tight curls enhanced with artificial flowers and lappets of fragile lace. Then she glanced down in disgust at the old-fashioned pantaloons that showed a good four inches beneath the hem of her dark blue skirt. Her mother would not even allow her hair to be curled but insisted it hang long and wavy down her back like some little ninny from the nursery. It was maddening to be forced to remain a child when one longed so to be a mature, gorgeous young lady.

"You've probably just misplaced it," Emily said, looking with admiration at her three girls. "Take one of mine."

"But it will be too large."

Damaris twirled around to admire the way her star-bright yellow bouffant skirt spread out around her. "You don't have to wear it, silly. Just wear one and carry the other. No one will ever know the difference. Here, Winnifred, help me fasten this bracelet."

Winnifred's stubby fingers groped at the clasp of an ornate circlet of worked gold set with tiny colored stones. How she wished she could wear something so fine.

"Now let me see," Emily said, standing back to look the three of them over. "Winnifred, straighten your collar. Damaris, you look lovely, but that décolletage is simply too low. Here, put a handkerchief there—so. The lace will cover a little bare flesh."

"Oh, Mother!"

"Corrine—pretty as always. That soft pink becomes you very nicely. Yes, I think the three of you will do. After all, this is the first party the Slades have given since Ethan came home and we do want the Whitman girls to shine."

Throwing a soft French lace shawl over her own dress of dark burgundy, she ushered them from the room, still giving orders: "Now, Damaris, I do not want you to spend the whole evening with Wesley Slade. This is Ethan's party and you must make him feel very special. And stay away from Stephen King— he's nothing but a coxcomb and he always tries to monopolize your whole evening. Winnifred, Damaris is right. If you do not behave yourself upstairs I shall ask Gabrielle to make you sit in the kitchen."

"Mother! You wouldn't."

"And, Corrine, you mustn't sit quietly in a corner all evening like a little mouse. You are as pretty as any girl who will be there. Make the gentlemen notice you. Talk to..."

They had reached the landing on the stairs. Below stood Fade, looking up. The four of them stopped momentarily under his admiring scrutiny.

"The most beautiful women in the county—all four of you," he said with pride.

Emily beamed as she glided down the stairs. "And the most

handsome escort. I do hope you'll grant your wife one waltz and not spend the whole evening in the card room talking politics and business."

He reached up to take her hand. "And drinking and gambling . . ."

"Well, heaven knows what goes on in there since you men always prefer it to the ballroom."

"I promise you at least one dance. Now hurry, girls, and get your wraps on before our barouche leaves without us. We're already sure to be among the last arrivals."

Damaris clicked her tongue as the housemaid draped a velvet pelisse over her shoulders. "Papa, one should never arrive early. It's *de rigueur!* After all, we don't want to appear eager."

Fade hurried them through the door and down the steps to where the large enclosed carriage waited, the coachman in elegant livery perched on the cab.

"You mean you don't want Ethan and Wesley to think you're eager. Though why you should go through such a charade with two galoots you've known since you were in your cradle—"

"Papa! They're not galoots!" Corrine objected.

Fade helped Winnifred into the carriage, then stepped in after her, both of them having to search for the seat under the mounds of crinolines.

As the carriage pulled away, Corrine smiled to herself, thinking how wonderful it was going to be to have a whole evening in which she could watch Ethan Slade.

Robert Slade's Tarrytown house was one of the most elegant in the county. He had enlarged and improved the modest structure built by his parents forty years before until it was more a showplace than a home, and it was never set off so well as when the Slades were entertaining their friends. Tonight, soft yellow gaslights twinkled from the windows and colored lanterns gleamed like a bright necklace of stars along the drive and paths that rambled toward the hill overlooking the river. The lively music of a small orchestra could be heard as the Whitmans approached the house. Servants in old-fashioned satin coats and white wigs stepped forward to hand them down. Damaris thought this party—in honor of Ethan's return and graduation—must be the most lavish the Slades had ever given. All their old friends and neighbors were there as well as many people she didn't recognize—probably Robert's political friends from Washington and New York.

The upstairs bedroom that had been set aside for the ladies was crowded with excited, giggling young girls. Damaris stayed only long enough to throw her cloak on the bed and, after a superstitious glance to see if her mother was looking, whisk the lace handkerchief from the neckline of her dress.

She barely made it back to the foot of the wide staircase before she was surrounded by young men eager to fill in her dance card. Fending off Stephen King, for she had as little wish as her mother to let him dominate her time *this* evening, she waited expectantly for Ethan to speak up and claim her. He stood a little apart, on the fringes of the group, watching her with a look of detached amusement on his handsome face. Damaris began to fear he was not going to claim her for even one dance when at length he shouldered into the group and took her card from her hand.

"Since I'm the guest of honor, I ought to at least have the prettiest girl at the party for my partner in the waltz."

Damaris gave him an arch look to hide her pleasure. The waltz was the most coveted dance of them all. When her mother was a girl it had been considered quite shocking, since the man actually had to hold the girl in his arms. The thought of Ethan holding her and swirling her around the room made her almost dizzy.

"Now, Damaris," Wesley said, "if you don't go in to supper with Ethan, then I claim the honor. Agreed?"

"Well, I don't know, Wes. He hasn't asked me yet."

"Oh, come on, Wes," Stephen cried, fingering the gilt buttons on his cream-colored waistcoat. "You two brothers can't have all the good fortune this evening."

Ethan seemed to be giving his full attention to the parade of young women coming through the door of the ballroom, and for a moment Damaris thought perhaps he had not even heard this exchange. When he turned back to her it was with that same detached air.

"I don't know. Since the party is in my honor, I really must keep my time free to partner as many of the guests as possible."

Damaris laid her hand on Wesley's arm and gave him her most brilliant smile. "I should love to take supper with you, Wes. Here, write it in right now."

Without another glance at Ethan, she allowed herself to be led into the ballroom, where the orchestra was noisily tuning up for a round of quadrilles. Let him keep his time free. He could consider himself fortunate to get one waltz with her!

Damaris quickly lost herself in the pleasure of an evening she felt sure she would remember for years. She and her friends had a gloriously silly time, laughing and giggling at the slightest provocation, flirting outrageously, all with a good humor that seemed especially fitting on this occasion. When she saw her parents dancing together, Damaris found herself feeling very proud: her mother had never looked prettier nor her father more handsome. They were obviously still so in love with each other that it was a pleasure to watch them.

By the time Ethan strolled over to claim Damaris for the waltz, she had forgotten her irritation with him and as they whirled around the room she fancied that her happiness was apparent to everyone looking on. There was something special about Ethan's strong arm around her waist, his lean face close to hers, his eyes, full of suppressed amusement, looking down into her own. The thrill it gave her to be so close to his virile, masculine body was almost disturbing.

The music finally came to a close and they stopped, breathless before the open terrace doors; she was surprised when he pulled her through them and led her outside.

"Let's stroll for a moment," Ethan said, guiding her down the low steps to the garden path, which was dimly lit by lanterns swaying gently in the evening breeze.

"Let me catch my breath," she cried, pausing for a moment beside one of the marble statues Robert Slade had brought back from Italy. "The waltz must be the most exhausting dance ever invented!"

She stood breathing heavily until she looked up and saw him studying her. All at once embarrassed, Damaris fluttered her fan, then slipped her arm through his and started off down the path. The cool, quiet night air was a welcome change from the glare and noise of the ballroom, and having this time alone with Ethan made her happier than she cared to admit.

"Have you come to be used to being home again?"

Their steps crunched lightly on the graveled walk. "Oh, I suppose so, though it is very quiet after London. I don't think I'm really suited to the rural life. The idea of starting a practice in a small village like Sing Sing or Tarrytown and spending the rest of my life lancing boils and dispensing pills is just too boring to contemplate. With every day that passes I feel more sure I cannot do it."

"What do you think of doing in its place then?"

"I thought I'd try New York, at least at first. I would rather practice in a city, or perhaps even a hospital. What I'd really like to do is teach in a medical university, but I must get some practice in before attempting that."

Her disappointment grew with his every word, but she was determined not to let him know it.

"Your mother will be quite distraught to see you go off again so soon. So will mine, for that matter. You were always her favorite."

"New York is not so far, you know," he said, pausing beside a bench that overlooked the sequined river. He pulled her down beside him, clasping her hand. "I expect to be back in Westchester often. And I expect my family and friends to visit me in the city. There's no reason why we should lose touch with one another."

The touch of his hands set her skin tingling. "No, I suppose not. Isn't the river beautiful tonight? How fortunate that nature itself gave you the right setting for your party. If I didn't know better I'd say you had influence in high places."

He smiled down at her. "You know that any influence I might have would be more likely to come from considerably lower!"

"Oh, Ethan. You always try so hard to appear wicked and you're not, you know. Mother says you just have high spirits."

"Little does she suspect. I must tell her sometime about the dark side of my life abroad."

"Now you intrigue me. Just what was it like?"

"Naturally I can't shock a young lady with such details."

Damaris tapped his arm with her fan. "Pooh! You won't shock me. I know all about the ladies of the night who roam London's streets, and even something of the dens they inhabit. New York has them too, you know."

"Now I'm shocked. How did you learn of such things?"

"I read. I look. I ask questions, only half the time the men I know won't answer them—or the women either, for that matter. But I have ways of finding out."

Throwing back his head, he laughed delightedly. "Damaris, you're wonderful. Most of the young ladies I know would go into vapors at the mention of such shameless subjects. But I don't know why I should be surprised. You were always the most daring creature alive."

"So tell me, then. How do the whores of London rate? Better than those in New York?"

"Damaris! You may not be a lady, but I'm too much of a gentleman to answer such a question. Besides, how would I know?"

"You know. I *know* you know."

"Why don't you ask Wesley? He's such a special friend to you."

She did not miss the edge to that comment. "Wesley wouldn't even want to think about such matters. He's a dear in every way, but he's much too pure to be interested in whores and gin rooms."

"That's true enough. Were he any less of a good fellow he'd be unbearable. But come, enough of this. We'd better be getting back."

Jumping to his feet, he pulled her up beside him but made no move to start back. Damaris waited, fluttering her fan, highly conscious of the closeness of his body.

"Speaking of good fellows," she said, talking too fast and too furiously, "do me a favor and save one dance for Corrine. She admires you so and she's far too retiring to elbow through the flock of women who have surrounded you all evening. It would give her so much pleasure."

"I've already put my name on her card."

She glanced up to see him staring down at the swell of her breasts. Breathlessly she waited, wondering why he didn't start back down the path to the house and whether her heart was beating so loudly that he could hear it too. Then, moving quickly, he pulled her to him, lightly brushing her cheek with his lips before searching out her mouth.

The world seemed to shift around her. After the first few startled seconds, she gave way completely and let her arms steal up around his neck, clasping him to her with the same possessiveness with which he held her.

It was a long kiss, not very tender, but hard and full of fire. When he finally released her, Damaris swayed for a moment, struggling to gain control.

Ethan stepped back, dropping his hands. "And did that make your evening?"

His words were like cold water dousing all her warmth and pleasure. She turned away from him angrily.

"Ethan Slade, you arrogant...egotistical..."

His chuckle only provoked her more.

"How dare you take advantage of me!"

"Come now, Damaris. I meant no offense. You are very beautiful in the moonlight. I could say my senses got the better of me, but that would not be true. I wanted to kiss you and I enjoyed every minute of it. So did you for that matter."

"You are no gentleman!"

"Perhaps not, but what does that signify? We're old friends."

She stepped back and the outraged anger on her face both surprised and dismayed him.

"I meant no offense by that remark either."

"I suppose you think there's not a woman in that house who would not give her soul to have you kiss her in the moonlight. Well, I'm not one of your adoring simps, just panting to have you throw me a few crumbs of your sacred attention! I don't need you. I can have any man in that room back there that I want."

As annoyed now as she, he reached out and grabbed her arm. "Damaris Whitman, you irritating girl! Why do you always misinterpret everything I say? Why must we always argue?"

"Why must you treat me like...like one of your whores?"

"That's a stupid remark, even for you! Listen to me. You are mine. You were always meant for me and you always will be. I don't care how much you flirt with those other coxcombs or how many of them are your friends as long as you remember that you belong to me."

She was too furious to do anything more than stammer. Pulling her arm away, she struggled to get out a coherent sentence. "I don't belong to you, Ethan Slade, or to any other man, and you'd better remember that!" Then, turning on her heel, she ran back toward the house.

Ethan stood staring after her, wondering how it happened that what he'd intended as a pleasant, warm moment had somehow been turned inside out and taken on shades of darkness.

"I cannot stand it any longer!" Winnifred cried, grabbing Felicity Webber by the hand. "I won't stay locked upstairs all evening and miss all the fun. I won't."

"But, Winnifred, your mother said . . ."

"I don't care what Mother said. I won't miss all the dancing."

Before Felicity could protest any further, she was pulled into the second-floor hall toward the great landing above the wide curving stairway. The music grew more glorious with every quick step.

"But if they see us . . ."

"They can't see us on that little balcony. Besides, I wouldn't care if they did see us," Winnifred answered, pulling Felicity along. "If I can't dance myself, I will at least watch the others."

The two girls were followed by Elizabeth King, two years younger, her tight long blond curls bobbing as she ran. When they reached the end of the hall, they hovered in the semi-darkness. The three of them clustered together and peered cautiously around the wall.

"Can you see anyone?" Elizabeth whispered.

Winnifred poked her head a little farther out, for she knew from experience that there was usually a traffic of ladies making to and fro from their withdrawing room.

"No, not at the moment. I think it's safe."

One last look to make sure no one was coming up the stairs and Winnifred bobbed out into the landing. Giggling as they ran, the other girls followed her and made it swiftly to the far side and down the hall. Winnifred stopped abruptly as she saw that the door to the balcony stood open.

"What's the matter?" Felicity asked, peering around her friend.

"I don't know. There may be someone there already."

"Let's go back, then. Come on, Winnifred. My papa will be so angry with me if he finds out."

"No, I won't go back," Winnifred said stubbornly. This was the one thing she had looked forward to all evening. "At least let's see if anyone is really there or not."

"I don't like it," Felicity cried, looking around.

"Both of you wait here," Winnifred answered. "I'll go take a peek. If it's empty I'll call you."

Felicity looked up and down the hall, somewhat reassured by its emptiness. "Go ahead, then, but hurry!"

Winnifred scurried up to the door, keeping close to the wall. Cautiously she peered around it, straining to see into the darkened interior of the small balcony. A figure sat there hunched in the corner, half hidden by the draperies, staring down into the ballroom below. In the shadows it was difficult to make out who it was; then all at once she knew.

"It's only Claes," she called back, motioning to the other girls before slipping around the door and scrunching up next to her cousin.

Claes Yancy shrank back in surprise until he recognized Winnifred's bright face. "You gave me such a start! What are you doing here?"

Winnifred leaned forward, attempting to peer over the railing of the balcony without being seen from below. In the glow of the lights the whirling figures of the dancers were a kaleidoscope of gay colors.

"What are *you* doing here?" she whispered. "I have to hide in order to see anything, but you could be down there dancing."

Claes slid closer to the wall as the other two girls followed Winnifred into the shadows of the balcony. He was rather glad of their company once he'd gotten over the shock of being found out.

"Oh, I feel more comfortable up here than down there." He shrugged.

Winnifred looked up into her cousin's face. A well-built young man in his mid-twenties, he had the suntanned, weathered look of a sailor and even she, young as she was, could sense how ill at ease he was in formal evening dress. Still, it was incomprehensible to her that anyone would willingly pass up the opportunity to be down there amid the music and lights.

"Don't you like to dance?"

"Well, yes, I do, but I'm not very good at it."

"That doesn't matter. A lot of young ladies aren't either, but I bet they'd love you to ask them."

"No, I don't think so. Besides, I'd hate it if I asked them and they refused."

Why, Cousin Claes is very shy, Winnifred thought, understanding for the first time in her young life that adults could suffer some of the same terrors that plagued children.

"I know how you feel," Felicity whispered. "I think I would love to go to a ball, but then I think that if none of the gentlemen asked me to dance how terrible it would be."

"That's nonsense," Winnifred sniffed. "Why, your father would ask you if no one else did."

Claes smiled down at Winnifred, reminding her all at once

of his grandmother, her old Aunt Agatha, who had died two years before. "Yes, Winnifred, but you don't understand that that can be a humiliation all the same."

"No I don't, for I should be very proud to dance with my papa."

"So should I," Elizabeth chimed in, not wishing to be left out of the conversation.

The music swelled and for a few moments four rapt faces turned toward the dancers below. Then Winnifred grabbed her cousin's arm. "I tell you what, Claes. You can dance with us. Right here in the hall. We can hear the music just as well as down there and if you have any trouble with the steps I can show you how they go. I'm a good dancer."

"Oh, Claes," Felicity cried. "Would you? Please?"

Elizabeth scrambled forward almost into his lap. "Please do, Claes. We should love it. Please."

Claes Yancy looked down at the girls' faces staring pleadingly up at him. "Well, why not." He smiled. "It would give me a chance to turn a few steps."

They pulled him up and in an instant were back out in the hall. "I'm first!" Winnifred said, claiming her cousin's arm.

"I'm next," Felicity chimed in before Elizabeth could speak.

"This is a polka, Claes. Do you know how to do it?"

"Why it's next door to a sailor's jig. Of course I know. Madam, if you would do me the honor," he said, bowing formally before Winnifred. Giggling, she grabbed his hands and was off in a swirl of skirts and bobbing blond curls, while the other two girls stood on the side jumping up and down in anticipation of their turn.

That was the way Damaris saw them as she came up the landing toward the ladies' withdrawing room. For a moment she almost interrupted but then thought better of it. She knew her shy, silent cousin suffered from painful feelings of ineptitude in most social situations and the broad grin on his face as he twirled her young sister up and down the hall suggested he was better left alone. Besides, it kept Winnifred from pushing herself forward and causing comments.

Nor did she have the heart to interrupt someone else's joy when she felt none herself. She was more upset than she wanted to admit by the scene with Ethan. It both thrilled her to remember his words—"You belong to me"—and at the same time drove her into a fury of frustration. How dare he make such an assumption? The arrogance, the selfishness of it!

As she passed the clock in the hall she realized it was almost time for supper. Well, good enough. She would tidy up her hair, splash on some cologne water, pink up her cheeks, then go and find Wes. He was always good company and a comforting presence. And she would not give Ethan Slade so much as a glance for the rest of the evening!

The party had gone so well that Emily was beginning to let herself relax and enjoy it. Fade had danced with her three times and so far, at least, had not allowed the company of the other men to monopolize his time. With her black hair and her dark, flashing eyes, Damaris was certainly one of the most beautiful and popular girls here, and when she danced with Ethan, they were so attractive a couple as to draw all eyes. And she was sure she had not imagined the look of possessiveness with which Ethan had held Damaris and looked at her. Emily herself had only sat out two sets and that was out of breathlessness, not for lack of partners. How irritating it was that as one grew older one could not continue to do all the things one used to.

Then, just as she was beginning to feel there would be no flaw in the evening, she heard a familiar voice and her stomach gave a sickening lurch.

Turning quickly, her worst fears were confirmed as she saw Garret standing under the arched doorway, looking around the room, no doubt searching for her or Fade. Though he was dressed in formal evening clothes, Garret somehow still managed to look unkempt. His effeminate good looks had long ago given way under the ravages of drink and laudanum and his resentful eyes no longer disguised his sullen anger at the world. She was relieved, however, to see that he appeared almost sober. Spotting her, he came straight across to her chair, wobbling only slightly.

"I didn't think you would come here," she muttered, looking around to see if any of her friends were watching them.

"You mean you hoped I wouldn't," Garret answered, smiling and bowing with obvious overemphasis at someone he recognized.

"You won't cause any trouble?"

"Why, my dear sister, I wouldn't think of it."

"That's a lie. It's why you came, isn't it—to embarrass me?"

"I came to dance with my charming nieces and to welcome back the gallant Ethan, just like the rest of the community. My, he does make a striking figure, doesn't he? All the girls must be positively swooning."

"You leave him alone, Garret. This is his night and you will not spoil it for him. Just this once try to think of someone besides yourself."

Just then Garret saw Damaris returning to the ballroom through the terrace door and his eyes narrowed in appreciation. She was a handsome girl all right—she had her father's dark good looks. In her bright yellow dress and with the daisies in her black hair, she was a lovely sight. Glancing at his sister, he read Emily's thoughts as clearly as if she had spoken.

"You have him all staked out, don't you?" he said, noticing at once that he'd hit a nerve. "She's too good for him. She could have anyone here. Why throw her to that arrogant egotist?"

Fury brought a rush of color to Emily's cheeks. "You don't know what you're talking about," she said angrily, keeping her voice low. "Mind your own business."

Garret gave a sly chuckle. "I can read you like a book, Emily dear. You'd just love to have your beautiful daughter marry the catch of the county, wouldn't you? It would be the pinnacle of your ambition. Of course, he's only a lowly doctor now, but who knows? Someday he may change over to politics like his nose-in-the-air father. Senator—even President, eh? And there will be Damaris beside him, and you whispering directions over her shoulder. Why, just think, you might even be running the country from behind the throne!"

Fluttering her fan, Emily fought down the anger she felt. The truth was that, except for imagining herself running the country, all those other thoughts had occurred to her. Ethan had the talent, good looks, breeding, and money to go as far as he wished in any field. Her dearest dream was to see her daughter standing beside him on that illustrious journey.

"Garret, you shall not ruin this evening for me," she said, smiling grimly. "Please go about enjoying yourself, get drunk, fall on the floor, insult whomsoever you please. I shall take no responsibility for what you are or what you do and I shall not be hurt by it. Just remember that."

"Well, I do admit that would remove some of the fun. But I shall struggle to enjoy myself all the same. Now, if you will excuse me, I think I shall go have a conversation with my beautiful niece."

She watched him wobble across the hall toward the supper room, knowing how dismayed Damaris would be to see him here yet feeling sure the girl could handle her uncle with aplomb. He does all these things to embarrass me, but this once, Emily thought resolutely, no matter what he does, I will not be embarrassed. But oh, I hope it isn't anything too bad!

Damaris looked up from the supper table to see her uncle crossing the room toward her and suddenly the food on her plate lost its appeal. Beside her, Wesley Slade saw both her reaction and its cause and placed his hand on her arm.

"It's all right. He'll behave himself or I'll take him out."

Garret sat down next to them, smiling his twisted smile.

"Aren't you having supper, Uncle Garret?" Damaris said cheerily. "It's very good."

"I have all the supper I want right here," Garret answered, holding up his punch cup. "You young people can eat all those sweets. It helps you keep up your strength for dancing."

"You look as though you could use a little strength yourself. You're thin as a rail. Do you not intend to do any dancing yourself?"

"Only with my favorite niece," he answered, leaning forward and smiling unctuously at her. Damaris moved back in her chair and looked to Wesley for help. Coming to her rescue, he managed to sidetrack Garret into a conversation in which Damaris was politely ignored until at length Garret had had enough and induced Wesley to go and refill his glass. Once they were alone, he turned his full attention on his niece.

"That's a very nice boy. Boring but nice. You like him, don't you?"

"Of course I like him. We're very old and good friends. Why, I suppose he's the closest thing I have to a brother."

"Not like that other one, eh? He'd never be a brother to any woman."

In spite of herself Damaris felt her face grow warm. "Why, I don't know what you mean."

"Oh yes you do. You don't have to play games with me,

my girl. I'm your old Uncle Garret," he said, digging his fingers into the bare flesh of her arm. "You're a spirited one, like me. Not a bit like that mousy Corrine. Winnifred, now she's got spirit too, but she's still a baby. But you—you're a corker, you are."

"Please, Uncle Garret, you're hurting my arm."

Quickly he removed his hand. "Oh dear. Can't have that, can we? Bruises on your fair skin. But you mind what I say. That Ethan, he's not to be trusted. He'll take advantage of any girl he can get near and leave her the worse for it. He'll take advantage of you if you let him."

Growing more uncomfortable by the minute, Damaris searched the room hopefully for a sign of Wes returning. "Uncle, I think you have had too much to drink."

"Of course I have. That's not the point, my girl. Mark my words, your mother intends to give you to that lecher; and what your mother wants, she gets. You don't belong with him. You'd do better with Wesley."

Giving him a sharp glance, Damaris curbed the urge to tell him to mind his own business. "Really, this is nonsense and not a proper conversation at all. I must ask you to—"

"La dee da and fiddle dee dee," Garret mimicked. "Not a proper conversation! Well it's the hard truth and you'd do better to look at it now before you find yourself falling between two stools. She'll ruin your life just like she has mine if you don't stop her. Mark my words."

Two bright spots of color on Damaris's fair cheeks told him he had struck his mark.

"That's not true."

"Isn't it? Just you wait and see."

Relieved, Damaris spotted Wesley carefully weaving his way through the crowd, trying not to spill the punch. Just as he reached the table Garret rose and took the glass, then gave them both a polite bow before wobbling off.

"Is everything all right?" Wesley asked, resuming his seat. "I hated to leave you alone with him, but I could see no way out of it."

"It's all right. He was just spouting the usual nonsense. He's already half-intoxicated."

"I'll ask John Butler to keep an eye on him. If it looks as though he's going to cause a scene, the servants can gently ease him outside."

"I don't know why I should care," Damaris said bitterly. "There's not a person in the room who doesn't expect him to make one. He's done it often enough!"

It was nearly dawn when the Whitman family returned home and fell into their beds. After the pleasures and rigors of the evening, sleep did not come easily to any save Winnifred, who, despite happy memories of skipping up and down the hall on Claes's arm, was so exhausted that she fell immediately into a deep slumber.

Fade lay looking up at the ornate plaster ceiling of his bedroom, his thoughts on the conversation he had shared with the visitors from Washington over brandy and cigars in the library of the Slade home. War was inevitable, they felt, especially if Lincoln won the election, which he was almost sure to do. The southerners were intransigent. Issues had so crystallized by now that neither side could back down even if it wanted to. The issue was no longer just slavery or even tariffs and free trade: it was nothing less than the preservation of the Union itself. If the southern states were allowed to secede in order to form another nation, it would mean the end of Federalist democracy as the Founding Fathers had established it and the beginning of a collection of minor sovereignties like Europe. He was appalled at the thought, yet he was even more appalled at the thought of young men actually dying to keep it from happening. For the first time he was glad that his three children were all daughters.

Beside him, Emily stirred and smiled to herself, recalling an image of Damaris and Ethan twirling around the ballroom. Afterward they had strolled outside and stayed away for quite a long time. She wondered what had happened. Had he perhaps said something of his intentions? How could she find out? No use asking Damaris, who'd never say. But she'd find a way to nose it out somehow. After all, she was as anxious as her daughter to have this young man declare himself.

In the room she shared with Damaris, Corrine struggled to get to sleep, all the while going back over every detail of the evening, wondering what she could have done to make it better. To her surprise she had not lacked for partners all evening, but it was the memory of her dance with Ethan that lingered most sweetly in her mind. How kind he had been to her. How gentle. And how he had eclipsed all the other men at the ball.

Across the room, Damaris heard her sister sigh and settle
under the covers. She lay staring at the ceiling, thinking back
over her conversation with her Uncle Garret, her thoughts seething. The memory of Ethan's hands tightly gripping her arms,
the long, hard crush of his lips against hers . . . It sent a thrill
through her just to think about it. Uncle Garret's ridiculous
words: "Your mother intends to give you to that lecher." Ethan
was not a lecher, though certainly he was experienced. But
what was wrong with that? It was his calm assumption that she
belonged to him without even so much as a by-your-leave on
her part that was unsettling. Ethan's arrogance and her mother's
willful determination—where did they leave her? What about
her intentions? Her determination?

She flounced over on her side, setting the bed creaking.

"Your mother intends to give you to that lecher . . ."

Well, we'll see about that!

❦ Seventeen

WESLEY SLADE stepped out of the grocery store opposite his office on the corner of High and Spring streets and surveyed the road before him. Rain poured down in a steady stream, pelting the tin roof that stretched over the walkway. In the street itself the rain had transformed the usual dust into a slate batter of mud. He was contemplating wading into it to cross the street when he saw the carriage.

It was moving up Spring Street, the big roan horse maneuvering smartly in spite of the slush. From underneath the hood of the gig Ethan waved at him and guided the horse skillfully toward the porch so Wesley could hop aboard.

"I don't think I've ever been so glad to see you," Wesley said, adjusting his hat to allow for the moisture seeping through the calash top.

"The weather wasn't quite this bad when I started out, but as it got worse I thought you might welcome a ride home. I was actually coming to town to give Dr. Sayre a hand in his office, but the weather discouraged me."

"I can drive home if you want to stay."

"No. Thank you anyway, but I've lost my taste for it. Just getting around these streets would be the ruination of my boots."

Wesley hesitated. "Was he counting on you?"

"Now, brother," Ethan said, laughing, "don't get your conscience worked up over me. I told him I'd be in sometime this week, and tomorrow will certainly do as well as today. Besides, it's a most depressing business. One I'd just as soon put off."

"Why, I thought you medical men were all aflame to solve the ills of the world. Isn't that why you chose the profession?"

Ethan frowned. "In a way, I suppose. But I find country ailments like boils, pneumonia, chilblains, and scarlet fever very mundane. I would prefer to handle the more difficult diseases, not simply to treat them but to search out the causes. There is so much we don't know. I keep wanting to ask 'Why, why?' And these old fellows like Sayre only know how to lance and patch. They never ask why. They are satisfied simply to treat."

Wesley studied his brother's profile as the gig lumbered along the rutted roads. Ethan had always been a fine-looking man and now his intelligent, virile face was made even more attractive by long, carefully groomed sideburns. Wesley admired the way his brother seemed so confident and self-assured, so knowledgeable about the world, so unflinching in the way he sought out that knowledge and made use of it. Beside him Wesley felt like a gray nonentity.

"What would you really like to do, Ethan?"

His brother looked at him, startled, then broke into a thin smile. "You'll be shocked."

"Tell me anyway."

Ethan turned his concentration back to his driving, for they had entered the post road with its heavier traffic. "I would like to have a human corpse to dissect," he said.

Wesley felt his stomach turn over. "My God, how different we are. That's the last thing I'd want."

"Of course it is. But I wish it more than anything else. All mine. To cut apart and see how it works, taking all the time I need. With no restrictions and no moralizing clergymen or magistrates standing over me to see I don't abuse the dead."

"But didn't you get enough of that in London? I understood it was part of your training."

"Oh, it was. But I had to share it with several others and there were strict time limitations. My appetite was more whetted than satisfied. You see, Wes, deep inside of me I know that I could be a fine surgeon. I just know it. And that's what I really want. There are some exciting things happening once you get out of a backwater place like Tarrytown. Chloroform has changed the whole nature of surgery. We no longer have to wait for the patient to faint in order to get him to be still. We can go in and do what we need and he never knows anything. It's wonderful."

Wesley studied the corn fields, limp from the rain, along the road. "You're not going to stay here at home, are you, Ethan?"

Ethan flicked the reins over the bay's back, his wide, finely shaped lips pursed in a stubborn line. "No, I'm not. I can't, Wes. I'd shrivel up and die in this country town. I want to be in a city—in a large hospital."

"Have you told Mother and Father yet?"

"No, but I shall soon. I thought I'd go to New York first. If nothing works out there, I'll try Philadelphia. But it's got to be one or the other. And after all, neither is as far as London. I'll get home often enough."

They rode in silence for a while. They were nearly to the dip in the hill before the old Dutch church when Wesley spoke again. "Will you take Damaris with you?"

Ethan looked up sharply. "Damaris?"

"Well..." Wesley shrugged. "You two...that is...I just thought perhaps you meant to ask her to marry you. You've always sort of taken her for granted, haven't you?"

It was Ethan's turn to shrug. "I suppose I have. And yes, someday I'll marry her, no doubt. But right now it would be foolish to saddle myself with the responsibility of a wife. And Damaris is so tied to this place. She'd do her damnedest to prevent me from leaving, I know it."

"Aren't you going to speak to her at least? Form an engagement?"

Ethan stared ahead. "I don't think so. I'm not really anxious to be tied down right now in any way."

Wesley turned to stare at his brother, his gray eyes widening.

"Don't you think that is a trifle unfair? I'm sure she's expecting you to speak for her."

"You mean her mother is expecting it. Damaris knows my intentions. She'll wait."

Wesley felt a surge of anger at his brother. Ethan had always had a strong self-serving streak, but this was too much.

Ethan went on, unaware of his brother's feelings. "Besides, the future is very unsettled. If Lincoln and Hamlin are elected in the fall, the southern states are sure to raise a ruckus. There might well be a war. And who wants to be tied down with a wife and family in the event of a war?"

"Perhaps Douglas and Johnson will win the election. Then there'll be no war."

"Do you really think so? Things are at too high a pitch over this abominable slavery issue for either side to back down now. Personally, I don't think Douglas has a chance."

Wesley gripped the side of the chaise as it swayed down the hill. "Either way, Ethan, the real point is that you are not willing to commit yourself to Damaris right now. Perhaps you never will be. Have you thought of that?"

"Oh, I'll get around to it someday."

For years Wesley's good nature and uncompetitive spirit had made him tolerate his brother's selfish ways, but this was the last straw. During those same years he had become so close to Damaris Whitman that she was almost like a part of himself. It had taken him a long time to admit that he wanted her for his wife as much as he wanted her for a friend. He was outraged by Ethan's cavalier assumption that she would be standing around waiting for him whenever he decided he was ready. But to actually challenge Ethan—the fair son, the capable, the well-beloved—he could barely imagine such a thing.

"You're her good friend," Ethan said flippantly. "You can hold her hand if she gets impatient."

That did it. Wesley turned on his brother, fighting to keep his rage under control. "You won't object, I trust, to other men putting forward their suits while you are away pursuing your own concerns."

Ethan looked up in surprise. "Other men? Why, you don't mean you'd ask to marry her yourself?"

"I would like to, yes."

Ethan laughed and Wesley barely suppressed the urge to

knock him off the seat. "Go ahead, brother dear. Let her choose between us. I have no qualms about the outcome."

Unfortunately, neither did Wesley. But as he absently watched the gate posts of his father's house loom nearer, the turmoil within him grew ever stronger. Whatever Ethan's motive, he was treating Damaris shabbily. This both hurt and infuriated Wesley, who resolved then and there that he would speak to her. He would at least offer her the consolation of a second choice and if by some miracle she should accept him, he would be the happiest man alive. But, he caught himself quickly, of course that would not happen.

In spite of his sudden determination, Wesley said nothing. He stood by and watched as Ethan set off for New York two weeks later after having faced their mother's tears and their father's stern warnings to stay out of the tenth ward. He could detect under Damaris's gay, carefree attitude small signs of hurt and perplexity, and no wonder. He felt sure Ethan had told her nothing of his long-range plans. It would be more like his brother to just leave, assuming everything would stay as it was until he decided to come back and claim what was rightfully his.

By November, when Lincoln and Hamlin won the election, it was clear to all that some kind of terrible confrontation between north and south was bound to come. On December 20, 1860, South Carolina voted to secede from the Union and the terrible and unthinkable became reality. Events seemed to pile up, one on top of another, hurrying to a conclusion that no one really wanted but that no one seemed able to prevent.

In the village stores and barrooms the men who sat around stoves smoking their pipes and sucking on straws began placing bets as to how long the war would last. Six months was the most popular estimate, though some were convinced that the country's troubles would be resolved peaceably once Lincoln took office, and some at the other extreme believed it would take a lot longer to bring the southern states to their senses. There was already talk of raising a militia unit from the village, just in case it was needed.

Once Ethan had left for New York, he might as well have gone back to London for all Damaris heard of him, and she was confused and hurt by his behavior. She fancied that her mother was even more disappointed than she, and the look of bewilderment in Emily's eyes every time Damaris caught her staring at her only added to the turmoil she felt. She knew her mother was blaming her, as if it were Damaris's fault that Ethan had not settled matters.

Then she received a letter from him, filled with descriptions of his activities at the hospital and his dissatisfaction with the place. He now had his sights set on the Jefferson Medical College in Philadelphia, and as soon as he could arrange it, he planned to take up residence there. He never mentioned their future or his feelings for her, but the maddening assumption that she belonged to him lay underneath every word, and it drove her to a fury. Some days later, Emily, sure now that her hopes were dashed, made some unguarded remarks, hinting that Damaris should have done something to force a commitment, backed him into a corner, used her feminine wiles. Damaris could only marvel that her mother understood her so little, for she would die before she let Ethan Slade know she was languishing one moment for him. And she certainly did not intend to marry anyone who had to be trapped into asking for her hand.

Christmas went by without a visit from Ethan, much less a proposal; he merely sent her a short note and a small gift. She hoped he might make an appearance for her birthday, but once more she was disappointed. By the middle of February she was so angry and hurt that had he gone down on his knees and begged her in tears to marry him she would have refused.

And then Wesley decided to speak his mind.

"There is almost certain to be a war," he said quietly to her one evening as they sat alone in the back parlor, "and I intend to go with the first regiment that is raised. It would mean so much to me to think I had you to come back to."

Damaris was stunned when he took both her hands and very gently kissed her. His lips felt tender and soft and his kiss both warmed and comforted her.

"I love you with all my heart, Damaris. I've always loved you. You are my best friend and dearest companion. It would make my world to have you as my wife too."

Companion . . . friend. Yes, they had been both since childhood. Yet in all that time she had never thought of Wesley as a husband or a lover. Looking up into his familiar face, it was almost as though she saw him for the first time. The thick lashes that framed his gray eyes, the wide forehead above his heavy brows, the generous mouth, always smiling, the rounded cheeks so in contrast to his brother's lean, long face. She began to realize how very dear he was to her.

"If there is someone else . . . ?" Wesley went on questioningly, almost as though he expected her to refuse him.

Well, why not? Let Ethan Slade look elsewhere for some woman to come running at a movement of his finger. She would make her own happiness.

"I'll marry you, Wesley. And I'll make you a good wife. I promise."

They spent the rest of the evening making plans. Once her father gave his permission, they would announce their betrothal. They would not set a date for the wedding until they knew more about what was happening in the country. If war came soon, he would go with the local regiment and they would be married when he returned. If it dragged on or never materialized, they would marry in August. By the time he left the parlor, Damaris had not only accepted the idea of Wesley as a husband, she was even looking forward to planning the wedding.

Her excitement lasted until she broke the news to her mother the next day.

"You cannot do this!" Emily cried. "I won't allow it."

Stammering, Damaris could barely find the words to answer. "I'm over eighteen, Mother. I can marry whom I please."

"You must not marry Wesley," Emily exclaimed, striding up and down her bedroom in distress. "You will make yourself miserable for the rest of your life. Can't you see, he's not for you. You can do so much better!"

Damaris calmly sat down on the edge of her mother's bed and watched her pace the room. Only the clenching of her hands betrayed her inner fury.

"You mean Ethan, of course."

Emily stopped and faced her. "Well what if I do? He intends to marry you, I'm sure of it. What will he think if you—"

"I don't really care what he thinks," Damaris broke in, jumping to her feet. "He has treated me shabbily. I never see him, seldom ever hear from him, and he has given me absolutely no indication of his intentions. I don't have to take that kind of treatment. He had all the women of the county hanging on his every word—let him be so cavalier with them. I don't need him or want him!"

"You don't mean that, my dear," Emily said, struggling to curb her distress. "You know you have always admired Ethan. You two are meant for each other. You're so well suited."

"Mother, that is all in your imagination. I am far more suited to Wesley, who is neither arrogant nor high-tempered as Ethan and I both are. He will treat me kindly, and he loves me— and what is more to the point, he has *asked* me. And I intend to marry him."

Throwing up her hands, Emily turned away. "You will regret it the rest of your life!"

"Well, Mother, it is my life, after all," Damaris said, moving swiftly to the door.

"Damaris!" Emily halted her daughter as her hand was turning the knob. "Ethan is anxious to get himself established before he takes a wife. At least wait a little longer. Give him a bit more time."

Without a word, Damaris stalked through the door, slamming it after her. She would not give her mother the satisfaction of knowing that her marriage might well have to wait on the war.

On February 20, 1861, the President-elect's train came through Westchester on its way to Washington for the inauguration. Damaris and Wesley joined the crowd that waited near the tracks for a glimpse of Mr. Lincoln, who was making it a habit to stand at the end of the train and wave to his supporters, sometimes even to stop and address the crowd. Even though the majority of Westchester voters had cast their ballots for Douglas, many people, out of curiosity if not affection, thronged the tracks in the towns along the train's route. Perhaps the grim events that had taken place in the south since Lincoln's election had solidified sympathy and support for the new President.

Wesley had decided their best view would be from the gig, and he edged it as close to the fringes of the crowd as possible. The train slowed as it passed through the crowded station area, and a band struck up a patriotic tune. Old Howit, the local howitzer and a relic of the Revolutionary War, blared forth its ear-splitting shot, and the crowd cheered and waved banners and handkerchiefs. Getting one good look at President Lincoln by standing up in the gig, Damaris was struck by the pleased expression on his face. Obviously he was grateful for these signs of support.

"I did not realize he was so tall," she said to Wes, settling back in the seat.

Wesley, who had been standing at his horse's head holding the bridle in case the nervous animal suffered a panic at the noise of the cannon, came back to join her, waiting for the crowd to disperse before taking to the road.

"Could you see him very well? I couldn't."

"Yes, I got a good look. He's very tall and thin and his face is rather homely. But he's impressive all the same."

"He'll need to be impressive where he's going. I wish him well, but I cannot help wishing it was little Douglas we were cheering. At least we would know what we had. Whether this man can bring about a reconciliation with the southern states and restore the Union is anybody's guess."

Damaris slipped her arm through Wesley's as the buggy started up Water Street. "All I hope is that he can prevent war from coming. Look, there's Jesse. Can we give him a ride?"

Standing by the side of the road, Jesse Whitman saw them at the same time they spotted him. Working his way out to the buggy, he stood smiling up at them, his freckled face full of triumph.

"Wasn't he great? Weren't you impressed? He's gonna make a wonderful President."

"Well, we know where your sentiments lie," Wesley said. "Come on up. We'll give you a lift up the hill."

"No thanks. Two's enough for a gig. I don't mind the walk, and besides, I want to go back to the opera house and hear the speeches. Might even make one myself, I feel so happy."

"But, Jesse," Damaris said to her cousin, "Mr. Lincoln's no gift from God, you know. We don't really have any idea whether he can prevent a war from coming or not."

"Prevent? By God, I hope he doesn't! I'm ready to go right now. I already told Pa that when they ask for the subscription I'm gonna be the first man in line, and I don't care what state the crops are in."

"I'll be the second," Wesley said quietly.

"No you won't! Oh, you men. All you can think of is fighting and glory, and we poor women must stay behind and worry. Aunt Matilda feels the same way about you, Jesse, I'll wager."

"No, there you're wrong. Ma and Pa both know that if it takes a war to stamp out the evils of bondage, then it's my Christian duty to carry the sword. And that I'm ready to do."

Wesley, who was beginning to feel the cold, pulled the rug up over their laps. "Damaris is just jealous," he said to Jesse. "If she were a man, *she* would be the first in line, having just stomped over your prostrate body."

"Oh, that's not true at all."

Waving to Jesse, Wesley started the buggy while Damaris sat quietly brooding. It *was* true, and how typical of Wes to see it. She hated the thought of being left behind, and if only she'd been born a man instead of a useless woman she would be off at the first call to revel in the excitement and glory of soldiering. The travel, the new experiences, the challenge and thrill—how wonderful it would be!

And yet that was not the way life was. She would have to see the people she loved go off to experience those things. And, after all, war was dangerous. They might get hurt. They might even be killed.

Clutching Wes's arm, she nestled closer against him in the gig. But that was unthinkable. There probably would never even be a war. That tall, ungainly, ugly man on the train would stop it from happening, she felt sure.

By April, though, events in the world outside Southernwood had begun to take on an aura of unreality. Damaris felt as though she was living in some kind of strange state somewhere between dreaming and waking, as though everything around her was not really happening. She spent her days making wedding plans, sewing, searching through *Godey's Lady's Book* for dress patterns, but it was like playing some game. In a rare moment of clear-sightedness she realized that she did not really expect this wedding to take place; it was all make-believe, a child's "pretend." Then all her planning became perfunctory. And Wesley, because he himself felt unsure about the future, did not press her.

On April twelfth the first guns were fired by the newly

formed Confederacy against a small federal fort in Charleston harbor. On the thirteenth, Fort Sumter was surrendered to the South and on the fourteenth was evacuated. On the fifteenth, President Lincoln called for seventy-five thousand militia to serve for three months, and the following day the New York Legislature passed a law providing for thirty thousand volunteers to serve for two years in addition to the state quota under Lincoln's call. On the seventeenth, Virginia—a pivotal state—seceded from the Union to join the Confederacy. And on the nineteenth, United States troops marching through the city of Baltimore were attacked by a mob of secessionists; a riot ensued in which four soldiers and twelve civilians were killed. It seemed as though the whole world had gone crazy. Even then, the truth of what was happening did not become real until one day in early May when Damaris stood with the crowd on Main Street, waving and cheering as the first all-volunteer company of ninety men marched south to join the New York Seventeenth Regiment of Westchester Chasseurs.

Everything that could make a noise was being used: drums, tin lids clanging together, homemade whistles and flutes, wooden spoons on iron pots, all the noisy cacophony of the band. Women wept and older men cheered as young men marched away looking near to bursting with pride and excitement.

True to his word, Jesse was in the first ranks, walking alongside the farmboys and fishermen he had grown up with, each dressed in his best and carrying a complimentary supply of Dr. Brandeth's pills from the local factory. Damaris felt a constriction in her chest as she watched him and her other dear friends march away to fight in the war. Wesley came by on his fine bay stallion and stopped beside her. He reached for her hand and pressed it to his lips before continuing on. Abandoning her mother and sisters, Damaris impulsively broke away to follow the soldiers down the slope of the hill toward the water, where they were to take the boat for the city. Fade went after her, catching up quickly and the two of them fell into step beside Wesley's horse.

When Wesley smiled down at her, Damaris knew he was pleased and proud of her gesture, yet she had to fight to keep from grabbing the bridle of his horse and telling him to stop this nonsense and turn around and go back home with her. It wasn't until they reached the foot of the wharf, where he leaned down to kiss her quickly before guiding his mount toward the dock, that she really believed he was going. Damaris fought to keep back the tears as her father put his arm around her.

"He'll be all right," Fade said soothingly. "You don't have to worry about Wesley. His sound good sense will see him through anything."

She could not answer, for she didn't know herself why she wanted to cry. Her tears were not exactly tears for a lover but rather for a dear and treasured friend. Mostly they were tears of frustration, because events had gone far beyond what she could control, catching them all up in some terrible nightmare she wanted no part of.

"I don't want him to get hurt," she sobbed.

Fade pulled her head against his shoulder, patting her as he had when she was a child. "He won't be hurt. He'll come back. You'll see."

His words were prophetic. Within a month Wesley was back in Westchester and out of the army forever. In the dampness and harshness of camp life, with its unsanitary conditions and taxing schedules, he had contracted a severe case of camp fever complicated by dysentery. After a short time in the hospital he was sent home.

Damaris hovered over him with a solicitude that was part genuine relief and concern and part an attempt to cover her uneasiness over the fact that now she must really make up her mind about getting married. Although Wesley said little to her, she knew he was as aware as she that there was no longer anything standing in the way of their wedding if she was still of a mind to go through with it.

Damaris struggled with the issue until she felt sure that Wesley was well enough to expect some kind of answer. She knew he would release her if she asked him, for he was acutely conscious of his loss of health and deeply shamed by what he considered the fiasco of his attempt to become a soldier. All she need do was speak.

Searching her own heart, she decided to go ahead. Nothing had changed in her world since February, when she had agreed to marry him, so there was really no reason to wait. Her mind was made up, and this time her commitment was real. With a new enthusiasm she went about putting her plans into motion: setting a date, July 28; sending invitations; planning a reception;

finding a place for them to live after the marriage. And her enthusiasm acted like a tonic on her future husband, bringing back a glimmer of the old good humor and satisfaction with life that had always been second nature to him but had been temporarily dimmed by illness and shame. More and more Damaris was filled with a pleasurable glow of happiness as she looked forward to her wedding day.

And then Ethan came home.

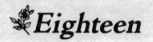**Eighteen**

HE COULDN'T believe she was serious. Weeks earlier, when he had read the beginning of Wesley's ecstatic letter announcing his engagement, Ethan had been ready to throw some clothes into a valise and take the first train to New York. But then he had come to the part about waiting on the war, and that had changed everything.

Ethan, more of a realist than some, felt sure that the war would be no six-week affair but rather a long, stubborn, bitter contest. He knew the south and southerners better than his brother and the Whitmans, whose lives had been largely confined within the bounds of Westchester and New York City. He knew their pride, their regional devotion, their love of the land and the past, and their aristocratic pretensions. They would not give up easily unless the very first battle went decisively against them. If that happened Wesley might come home very quickly, but Ethan was betting it would not and that Wesley would spend the better part of a year or perhaps several years involved in the struggle for the Union. There would be plenty of time to bring Damaris to her senses.

Although he was renting a room in a neat house in Philadelphia and had made a few halfhearted efforts to seek a position either at a local hospital or with an established physician, Ethan's real interest lay elsewhere. He was drawn to the growing conflict between the states like a moth to a flame. The lure of tending battle wounds seemed to him infinitely more interesting than the treatment of mundane illnesses that was the daily routine of an ordinary physician. When he heard the news of the civilian rioting against the Sixth Massachusetts in Baltimore, he left Philadelphia at once. As it turned out, by the time he arrived there, the wounded had gone on to Washington with the rest of the regiment and without any hesitation at all Ethan hurried after them.

By the end of April he was settled in Willard's Hotel, caught up in the fever of a city arming itself for a civil conflict. He found everything about the vibrant, half-formed town fascinating. Offering his services to the Medical Division of the War Department, he was soon busy visiting the growing number of army camps scattered around the city, treating dysentery, heatstroke, camp fever, and an occasional gunshot wound. Although he was not yet ready to join the army, he found the routine of the huge encampments exhilarating.

Several letters arrived from home during June, but Ethan left them lying around carelessly until he found time to open them. Most were from his mother. She informed him of Wesley's return due to camp fever and supplied all the uninteresting details about his recovery. The fact that she barely mentioned the wedding plans led Ethan to conclude that nothing much was happening on that score. He could not really believe anything ever would. Damaris would never do such a silly thing, certainly not without first seeking to know his mind on the subject.

As the Army of the Potomac grew in numbers and strength, Ethan became so engrossed with what was happening around him that he completely forgot about Westchester. In June he offered his services to the newly formed United States Sanitary Commission and was soon caught up in provisioning field hospitals and improving the poor conditions of the army camps across the Potomac. A battle was certainly likely, especially since the Confederacy had voted to move its capital to Richmond, only a hundred miles south of Washington itself. A large Confederate army had formed, one part of which lay between Richmond and Washington and the other, in western Virginia, near the arsenals at Harper's Ferry. U.S. General Patterson was keeping this western force occupied while across the Long Bridge in Alexandria General MacDowell's Federal forces prepared themselves to overrun the Confederate army near Manassas, sweep down on Richmond, and end this rebellion once and for all.

By early July, Beauregard's Confederate forces were strung out along a stream called Bull Run, with headquarters in nearby Manassas, only thirty miles from Washington. Although MacDowell still did not believe his army was ready, Congress was clamoring for him to march out and destroy the Rebels before they—unthinkable thought—surprised him and stood before the gates of Washington itself. It was then that Ethan received the fancy, engraved envelope that contained his invitation to the wedding of Wesley Slade and Damaris Whitman, set to take place on Sunday, July 28, at four o'clock in the afternoon.

For the first time he realized that if he did not do something quickly this foolish affair was actually going to occur. Reluctantly he packed a few clothes, assured his superiors that he would be back in a few days, and took the train to New York.

Damn her, he thought, staring out the window at the sultry green woods sliding by. How like her to push him this way until he was forced to interrupt his life and handle the mess she had created. How mean of her to lead Wesley, his good-natured, trusting brother, on like this, then dash his hopes at the last moment. It was all really too much. He just hoped it would not take too long to set things right.

Damaris looked up from a copy of the Republican newspaper she was reading when she heard a horse approaching on the path. It was so hot in the house she had sought the shade of the thick maples behind the orangery, where in the comparative coolness she could read about the distressing events taking place to the south. The news grew more terrible every day. There was bound to be a clash between the two armies sometime soon but, thank God, Wesley would not be involved in it.

Ethan was down there somewhere, but his father had said he would serve only as a physician and would not be involved in the fighting. There were so many others, though: Jesse, Stephen King, Arthur Acker, Will Terry—so many of her friends.

She did not see her visitor until he was almost upon her; then her breath caught as she looked up and recognized Ethan striding across the lawn, characteristically slapping his riding crop against his thigh.

Silently she put down her paper and waited, her heart thumping in her breast. Her first swell of pleasure at seeing him quickly faded as he stalked up to her and angrily threw the wedding invitation in her lap.

"You little fool. What do you mean by this?"

Pursing her lips, Damaris fought down her urge to throw it back in his face. "Why, hello, Ethan. Welcome back. I've been quite well, thank you."

"Don't play coy with me," he said, sitting down on the stone bench opposite her. "I've had to leave the army at a most sensitive time in order to chase back up here and straighten this thing out. The least you might have done is write and tell me of it before matters went so far."

"I wrote you several times, I believe," she said coldly.

He stirred under her relentless gaze. This was not quite the welcome he had expected. "You mean last winter. But that was before this . . ."

"Even so, you barely troubled yourself to answer once, as I recall. Why should I have continued when you were obviously uninterested in my life?"

"Now, that is not true and you know it. I've been very occupied. It was difficult for me to be concerned with letters and such trivia when my whole life had to be planned out. I thought you would understand that, you of all people."

"I do not consider it trivia to speak with those about whom we care and to be spoken to by them. You never came to see me. What was I supposed to think?"

"For God's sake, I told you last summer you were mine. You knew that. Why must I continually repeat it!"

Damaris clutched the paper in her fists. "Oh, Ethan! Really, your arrogance is beyond belief. You make a statement like that without ever asking my mind on the subject, then you go on assuming it is true without ever even having the courtesy to answer my letters or pay me a visit. How could you think I would just sit here waiting for you to throw me a crumb of your attention? How could you know me so little?"

"It never seemed that way to me. I had plans for us."

"When you finally got around to them, and heaven knows how many years that would be."

Ethan leaned forward, resting his elbows on his knees, twisting the crop in his hands. "All right, then, I'll move my plans forward if that will satisfy you. We can be married sooner than I planned. Perhaps even before I'm established."

Damaris watched him, smiling smugly. She knew what that concession had cost him.

"How kind of you. And the war? Even before the war?"

"That would be impossible. There's about to be a fight between the southern and northern armies. It may resolve things, but then again it may not. They need surgeons with the army and you might as well know I'm extremely keen on having the experience."

"That does not surprise me."

"But it probably won't last too long and then, I promise you, we'll be married at once. Surely that ought to satisfy you."

Damaris leaned back against the tree, her eyes closed. Her anger was gone, dispelled by the absurdity of the situation. For the first time in her life, she almost felt sorry for Ethan; it was so uncharacteristic of him to have to give in to someone.

"Why did you come here, Ethan? Why come back now? What do you expect to accomplish?"

He looked up, startled. "Why, you must call off this foolish ceremony. Tell Wesley you made a mistake and you are deeply sorry for causing him any hurt."

"And then languish here waiting for you to come back again whenever you're ready? Do you really think I'd do that?"

Letting the crop fall, he reached for her hands. "You must, Damaris. It's what I've always planned for us."

Her eyes flew open and he blanched before the dark fury in them. "How can you believe I'd treat your brother so shabbily—that decent, good man who loves me so much? And who loves you, for that matter."

"You'll never be happy with him, Damaris. He's far too tame for you."

She could almost feel the heat rising in him. Swiftly she pulled her hands away. Above all else, she knew, she must not let him touch her. "I intend to marry Wesley, Ethan, and you might as well accept it."

"You can't!"

In a swift movement he was beside her on the bench, clasping her in his arms. Filled with panic, Damaris pushed against his embrace until she finally managed to jump up and flee behind the bench.

"I can and I will. Don't try to stop me, Ethan."

He could not believe this was happening. He stood facing her, his cheeks flushed and his eyes dark with fury. How dare she treat him this way!

"I can see you are in an unreasonable frame of mind. We'll talk about this again tomorrow."

"No! Don't come here tomorrow. I don't want to see you again. Go back to the war and treat your wounded soldiers. I mean to find my own happiness and it certainly does not involve spending my life waiting for you to honor me with a few moments of your attention!"

Flinging down the newspaper, she turned and, skirts swirling, ran up the path toward the house. He looked after her, filled with rage and chagrin yet at the same time aware of how beautiful she looked. She was like a filly, all grace and spirit, who needed breaking to his hand in order to serve him as she was meant to do.

Jamming his hat on his head, he reached down for the riding crop lying on the grass. Picking up the paper as well, he smoothed it out and thrust it under his arm. He'd look at it later.

By the next morning Ethan was sufficiently disturbed to give some very deep thought to Damaris Whitman. The meeting the day before had gone very badly—even he could see that. A methodical examination of the facts was needed if he wanted to regain her. Why he should want to was beyond him: she was a stubborn, pig-headed, fiery little fool and hardly worth all this trouble. He could have any number of women. Why waste all this time and energy on one who made his life so difficult?

Because he had always meant her to be his. Because she was fascinating and beautiful and more intelligent than any other ten women he knew. Because it galled him to think of her giving herself to his spiritless brother when she could have him!

Yet, hard as it was to admit, he saw that he had gone about it all wrong. He had been too harsh, too angry. Instead of bringing her to her senses, he had made her more stubborn than ever. That was the wrong way to handle Damaris, and he ought to have seen it before. Very well, then. He would make a supreme effort to be agreeable, affectionate, enticing. She would never be able to resist that.

He thought of Wesley, good-natured and kind but as romantic as planked shad. A woman like Damaris had a lot of passion underneath her ladylike exterior, and a tepid fellow like Wesley would be the last to arouse it. While he, on the other hand . . .

Ethan had known many women and had long ago learned what they liked. And for all her protestations, he knew Damaris felt a strong physical attraction toward him. All he had to do was tap it.

It ought not to take more than a week.

The next day Ethan showed up at Southernwood and proposed that he and Damaris spend the afternoon together. Much to Damaris's surprise, her mother urged her to go. This happened again the next day, but by the third afternoon Damaris realized that Ethan and her mother were coconspirators, and she ordered him to stay away from her. Yet in spite of her angry words, Ethan could sense that her resolve was weakening. Her insistence seemed to him more a sign of panic and fear than irritation, so solicitously and pleasantly he agreed to leave. He would wait for the right moment to press her for a decision.

From a distance, Wesley watched Ethan's scheming with dwindling hopes. After giving some consideration to the idea of speaking frankly to his brother, he decided it would be better to say nothing. He was by no means sure that, forced to make a decision, Damaris would choose him. He also knew that Damaris needed to get Ethan out of her system if she was to be happy with him; and if she could not, then it would be better for all concerned to know it before the wedding. The good sense of this, however, could not keep away a sick fear that all his hopes were about to be destroyed by his brother's conniving.

Ethan's chance came on the fifth day. Strong cool breezes

from the north pushed aside the July heat. There was a brightness and sparkle to the world that heightened the silver-blue
of the river and the deep, lush green of the trees and shrubs.
Blue periwinkles and yellow daisies that had drooped in the
oppressive heat now swayed prettily in the wind. The sky was
like a clear globe with the depth of lapis in its color. Early that
morning Ethan appeared at Southernwood on his black stallion,
determined to take Damaris out riding for the day if he had to
throw her on her horse.

Damaris had ten reasons—all of them good ones—why she
should not waste her time, especially with Ethan. Yet underneath them all she wanted to go as much as he. It was too fine
a day to spend indoors. Her mother would take care of most
of the afternoon's scheduled chores, and a day's leisure would
be a welcome break from the stress of wedding preparations.
Besides, she thought as she pinned on her hat, Ethan would
be gone soon and who knew when she would see him again.
There could be nothing wrong in having this one last time
together.

It was late morning by the time they got started. They rode
for several hours, stopping frequently to rest the horses and
admire the sweeping river view. They raced across fields and
level ground, stopped to visit briefly with farmers they had
known all their lives, waited for flocks of sheep to cross the
trails, dismounting at shallow brooks choked with stones to let
the horses drink.

By midafternoon, they found a plateau overlooking the river
far in the distance and there spread out a picnic that Ethan had
brought along: cold fowl, fruit, cheese, and a bottle of wine
with two tin cups. Their horses grazed nearby while they devoured the lunch, cleaned up the crumbs, then stretched out
on the grass in complete comfort. Damaris had long ago removed her hat to let the wind catch at her hair, and since her
riding habit had made her uncomfortably hot under the afternoon sun, she also undid the top buttons of her jacket to bare
her throat.

They talked and laughed and reminisced, then fell silent as
drowsiness took over. Rolling onto her side, Damaris gave way
before the sluggish air and warm sun, the fatigue from the ride,
and the fullness of the meal and fell soundly asleep.

It was numbness in the arm on which her head rested that

finally woke her. She sat up and stretched it out, rubbing hard to revive the feeling, and noticed that Ethan was close beside her, still sleeping soundly. Her arm back to normal, she lay down again on her side and watched him, his face only a few inches away.

A warm feeling swelled inside her just to observe him so closely. His thick eyelashes fluttered slightly against his face and a muscle in his mouth twitched. How brown his skin was. How shapely his brows. What bliss it would be to trace the outline of the fine curve of his lips...

His eyes fluttered open and he turned his head slightly, smiling quickly at her. She wanted to draw back, sit up, make some inane comment, but she was mesmerized and too lazy to move. His eyes caught hers, and she was unable to pull her glance away. For a long moment he held her without touching her, then very slowly he reached out, cupped his hand around her neck and, pulling her toward him, brushed his lips against hers.

It was so light, so gentle, so lovely. She gave way to the pleasure of it as he moved his mouth lightly back and forth against her lips. He slipped his arm under her head and she lay back against it while his lips worked over hers, ever more seductive and insistent.

Closing her eyes, Damaris let herself drift away on the delight of pure feeling. Gently his lips began to search out her face, the outline of her nose, her brows, her eyes, her cheeks, and again her lips. Then they were on her neck, sending a burst of pleasure through her body. This was something she had never known before. She wanted this incredible delight to go on, never to stop. Of its own accord, her body moved sensuously under his in silent assent and his hands grew more demanding. His tongue explored the inside of her ear, sending shock waves up her spine, and it was almost with joy that she felt his hand working at the buttons of her habit.

With an abandon as surprising to her as to Ethan, she helped him tear aside the fabric of her riding dress. She arched her back as he sought her breast and freed it from the confines of her shift to take it in his mouth.

She was wild. On fire. Burning up. He moved suddenly against her, thrusting his hand under the skirts of her habit and she never even cared. Abandoning herself to her willing flesh,

Damaris writhed under him, feeling Ethan growing as frenzied as she herself. Confining clothes were thrust mindlessly away; nothing mattered but the mad consummation of this spiraling, hot desire. When he finally went thrusting into her, she welcomed it, not even minding the pain, wanting only to feel him inside her, consuming her, devouring her with his body.

At the end she was a raging torrent of feeling, hovering on the edge of a high precipice. Then, falling away on ecstatic waves of satisfaction, Damaris was suddenly aware that she had been seduced. Gasping over her, Ethan saw the sudden panic that filled her eyes and, clasping her to him, rolled over on his side, holding her close.

"My darling. My darling Damaris. My love," he said, smoothing back a curl from her damp forehead. He knew he must be gentle now of all times or she would never forgive him.

"Ethan," she cried, her body beginning to shudder.

"I never meant that to happen," he said quietly, "but I'm glad it did. It was always supposed to be this way, don't you see? We were meant to be together like this."

She buried her face in his shoulder. "What have I done? What happened to me?"

"Only what every woman should enjoy with the man she truly loves. It was a good thing, Damaris. It was beautiful. Now you know how much I love you, and now you are really mine."

She could not hold back her tears. With them came the release of all the heightened feelings she had experienced. Yet, in spite of her tears, she heard his words gladly. He had been right all along. She did love him and always had. He was her true lover in a way that Wesley could never be. Why had she fought it for so long?

He wiped her wet cheeks with his fingers and kissed her again. "My darling Damaris. My dearest love."

They stayed there long afterward, full of wonder at the depth of what they had experienced and talking about all it meant. Damaris had refastened her jacket and sat with her arms around her drawn-up knees.

"How can I tell Wesley now, at this late hour, that I've made a mistake?" she groaned. "I'd rather die than hurt him.

He's so good. He doesn't deserve this."

"I know my brother. He'll understand and forgive you just because he's Wesley. Besides, I think he always believed you would marry me. No one was more surprised than he when you said yes."

"But I feel so rotten."

"I don't like it either, but I did try to tell you, you know."

"Oh, Ethan. Do you really want me? Can we be married soon? In spite of what's happened today I still am not willing to spend my life waiting around for you. You must understand that."

"I do. Truly I do. It will be soon, I promise."

Damaris shaded her eyes with her arm. "Look at the sun. It must be getting on to late afternoon. We've been gone most of the day."

"Everyone will be scandalized."

She laughed. "We ought to be getting back. It's been such a heavenly day, though, I dread to see it end."

He lay on his side, his head resting on his hand, looking up at her. "Happy?"

"So happy."

Reaching up, he pulled her down again. Opening the front of her dress to bare her breasts, he traced them with his lips. Damaris stirred under him, filled with the first intimations of warm delight.

"Ethan. We ought to go back," she said reluctantly.

"Yes. But there's something we must do first."

Desire burst in her like a flame flaring in a gust of wind. Let it be late. It didn't matter. Nothing else on earth mattered but this.

It was almost dark when they got back to Southernwood. Ethan left her at the stable with a swift, possessive kiss, and Damaris floated across the walk, into the empty hall, and up the stairs to her room. Emily appeared there moments later, her eyes bursting with questions.

"My, you had a long day."

"Yes, I did, didn't I, Mother," she answered, preoccupied with removing her hat and veil, hoping there was nothing in her manner to betray the fact that she had crossed the gulf separating girl and woman that very afternoon.

"How was it?"

Something held her back. Her mother was so expectant, would be so delighted, would be so . . . so smug about having known it all along.

"Oh, it was pleasant enough."

Emily studied her daughter as she fussed with her habit. She could tell something had occurred, something decisive. How like Damaris not to confide in her. She felt an urge to grab her by the shoulders and shake it out of her, but that would only make her more stubborn. Deliberately she went over and began helping her daughter with the laces of her skirt.

"Wesley stopped by late this afternoon. He had word from his cousins in Albany that they would be down for the wedding and he thought you would like to know." She did not miss the sudden tensing of her daughter's thin body.

"Oh? That's nice."

"I saved your supper, my dear," she said, forcing herself to sound indifferent. "Change into something comfortable and come down to the dining room. Willa will put it out for you."

"Thank you, Mother. I appreciate that."

Emily closed the door, smiling to herself. It would take a little time but eventually she would know. Damaris was too full of her feelings not to blurt them out sooner or later.

Ethan managed to get into the house and up to his room without seeing anyone but servants. Pulling off his grass-stained clothes, he washed his face and hands at the stand, slipped on a brocade robe, and pulled the tasseled sash tight around his waist. He felt very pleased about the way the day had gone, yet when he thought of telling Wesley that Damaris was lost to him, all his pleasure turned a little sour. He truly did not want to hurt his brother, who he suspected was a much nicer person than he himself would ever be. But facts were facts and must be faced. The sooner he got all this straightened out, the better.

There was a polite cough at the door and he looked up to see John, the head butler, standing there with a small silver tray in his hand.

"Excuse me, Mr. Ethan, but a telegram arrived for you while you were out."

A telegram! Turning it over, he saw it was from Washington and, with a surge of excitement, tore it open. It was from

Richard Pollack, one of his fellow surgeons assigned to the army. It informed him in a few terse sentences that General MacDowell had marched out that morning to meet the Confederate army at Manassas and his services were needed at once.

Ethan could hardly contain his excitement. At last, a real battle! And he might well miss it if he didn't hurry.

He caught John halfway down the hall and dragged him back, ordering him to arrange for a carriage at once and to send Talbot, his valet, to help him pack. Speed was essential. The robe was on the floor and he was halfway into a newly pressed shirt when Wesley appeared at the door, glancing curiously at his brother racing around the room and Talbot searching through the pile of discarded riding clothes scattered on the floor.

"What in the world . . . ? Are you off again?"

Ethan threw himself onto a chair and began pulling on his boots. "MacDowell's army has marched out to Manassas. There's bound to be a fight and they want me to be there. I suppose they expect to have a few wounded."

Wesley, who had sought out his brother half planning to ask about the ride with Damaris, forgot it completely. "So they are finally going to get this business settled. How exciting! How did you find this out?"

Ethan threw the telegram across the room. "Talbot, for God's sake, come and help me with these damned boots. I can't get them on alone. And hurry, you lazy fellow! We have a long ride ahead of us."

In an instant the harried servant was on his knees. "Yes sir, we'll make it. Never fear."

"Well keep at it, then. What do you think, Wes? Isn't it great news?"

Wesley crumpled up the paper in his hand, fighting down a surge of envy. Had it not been for that damned camp fever he would be down there now marching through Virginia. How galling to have Ethan go off and to be left behind.

Then he remembered the wedding. Well, that was surely a consolation. To marry Damaris he would gladly forgo all the battles in the world. "I hope you'll be back in time for the ceremony next week."

Ethan paused for a moment, remembering, wondering if he

should say something to prepare his brother for the news. Yet wasn't that really up to Damaris? There was no time right now for a discussion. He had to get going immediately.

"I'll do my best. This business shouldn't take too long." Pulling on his coat, he raced to the chest of drawers for another pair of riding gloves and his crop.

"I've laid them on the bed, sir," Talbot said with a trace of triumph. "And the crop has been washed after today's ride."

"Talbot, you're a jewel. I'll write you all the details, Wes. Everything that happens."

"Yes, please do that."

Ethan was halfway out the door. "Talbot, I'm going to say good-bye to Mama. You have five minutes to get this valise and yourself to the carriage."

The man did not even look up from his work. "I'll be there, sir."

"Ethan!" Wesley followed him into the hall. "Take care of yourself. Even doctors can get hurt if the shelling turns out to be heavy."

"Oh, don't worry about me. I'll probably spend most of my time in a field hospital well behind the lines. If we have any wounded at all, that is."

"No you won't. You'll be right up there on the front trying to see everything that's going on. You won't admit it, but I know you."

Pausing, Ethan looked into his brother's anxious, honest face, thinking that Wesley's concern ought to be for himself. Only Ethan knew what further loss lay ahead for Wes, after the disappointment of not being able to go with the army. In a sudden surge of genuine sympathy for his brother he walked back to lay an arm around his shoulders, gripping him tightly.

"I'll be careful. You take care of yourself."

Fifteen minutes later Wesley stood in the driveway and watched Ethan's carriage disappear behind the gentle curve of trees lining the path to the post road.

"God speed, Ethan," he muttered. If, as some men expected, all this turned out to be a brief business, Ethan would be back very quickly. But somehow Wesley felt in his bones that it would be a very long time before he saw his brother again.

When Ethan stepped off the train from Washington he found the city in turmoil. After several visits to livery stables in a vain attempt to rent a horse, he gave up and went back to claim his old room at Willard's Hotel. The lobby was jammed with people, mostly congressmen, political hacks, and hordes of newspaper reporters, judging from their conversation. There was a conspicuous absence of military uniforms, most of the officers now having moved on with MacDowell's forces.

Pushing his way through the crowd, Ethan careened straight into an old friend of his father's, Congressman Ely from New York, standing cheek to jowl with two men he vaguely recognized, Benjamin Wade, the Senator from Ohio, and a reporter with the *Evening Star*. Ely's face broke into a wide smile when he recognized Ethan.

"My dear boy," Ely bubbled, clasping Ethan's hand. "You must come have a rum toddy with us in the bar. Momentous news, is it not? I tell you the whole city is thrilled. We'll soon have this unpleasant business settled once and for all."

Ethan managed to pull his hand away. "Thank you, sir, but I really must be on my way. I was in Westchester when I received the news that MacDowell had finally moved out, and I'm anxious to get to the camp."

"Ethan here is a surgeon," Ely explained to his friends, "and a good one too. They'll be needing you, my boy, from the look of things. There's going to be a major confrontation, I'm convinced."

"Humph," Senator Wade replied, his eyes glistening under his heavy brows. "I shouldn't think he'd be much needed in this battle. Why, if it lasts fifteen minutes I'll be surprised. Those southerners are all bluster."

"Now there you are wrong," Ely answered, stroking his beard. "These farmboys from the south might not know much about the business of an army, but their officers are aristocrats raised in the saddle. They won't be so easy to subdue. It's going to take the better part of a morning, mark my words."

Ethan suppressed a laugh. "Gentlemen, our army is made up mostly of farmboys too, remember."

The reporter, a thin fellow with a heavy growth of black beard that partially covered his pockmarked skin, pulled a card from his coat pocket and handed it to Ethan.

"With my compliments, sir. I can think of no one who deserves it more than one who is hurrying to serve his country in a time of crisis."

Turning the card over in his hand, Ethan stared at the elaborate engraving. "Why, this is an invitation to a ball in Richmond! Are you serious?"

"Never more so," he replied pompously. "They are all over Washington. Hang on to it, Doctor. When that ball is held, these will be the most popular invitations in the country."

"I shall keep it then," Ethan said, pocketing the card. "But I wish I shared your optimism. I cannot even commandeer a horse to catch up with MacDowell."

"I can explain that," Ely replied, gripping Ethan's elbow and urging him gently toward the wide doors opening on the bar. "These greedy livery stable owners are saving their horses for carriages which they offer at a thousand dollars a day to ride out to watch the battle. You should have asked for a chaise. But don't worry about it. I am riding out to Centerville in the morning with some friends in my hired carriage to see these Rebs beaten. You can go along with us."

Ethan looked incredulously from one to the other. "Is this allowed?"

"Allowed?" cried the Senator. "Why, sir, there is no government business to be done in Washington City because half its citizens are out there already. There is not one but wants to be on the scene when this business is settled once and for all. I myself would not miss seeing these cantankerous, arrogant southerners receive their comeuppance for anything in the world. I have longed for it these thirty years past."

Forcing his way through the crowd, Ely pushed Ethan into the bar. "You shall certainly ride out with us tomorrow. It will allow you to arrive in plenty of time. I had it from the best sources just an hour ago that General MacDowell does not plan to move against the enemy before Sunday at the very earliest. So that's settled. Now come along and have a bourbon and water. Willard's has the best boiled crab legs in the city, and I want to hear about your good father. It's been months since I saw him last."

Reluctantly Ethan allowed himself to be led up to the bar, shaking his head at the way there seemed to be no distinction between civilians and soldiers in the business of conducting this war. Perhaps this was a characteristic of civil confrontations, but it was like nothing he had heard of before.

It was well into the next afternoon when they reached Centerville. The trip had taken a long time because, in addition to the supply wagons, white-topped ambulances, caissons, sutler's carts, last-minute troop reinforcements hurrying to join their regiments, the road was filled with pleasure carriages containing men and women in a festive mood, who were bent on seeing with their own eyes how the south would finally be brought to its knees.

The one wide dirt street of Centerville, lined with simple stone and clapboard structures, was awash in a sea of men bivouacked on the ground, and supper fires lit up the landscape like sparks from a firebrand. The atmosphere at the camp was somewhat subdued; the men were sobered by the realization that they were all sitting within reach of the Confederate guns, and the order to march at two-thirty the next morning had already been issued.

Ethan's first order of business was to commandeer a horse for the morning's march, and after a few false starts, he claimed an aged gelding whose spirited eye suggested there was some wind left in him but whose appearance had made him unattractive to the officers in the camp. After hobbling his horse, Ethan spent an hour with Dr. Pollack looking over the stone church that had been converted into a hospital and checking out medical supplies and ambulance wagons. Then he took a blanket and climbed into an empty wagon for a short rest.

There was an electric excitement in the hours before dawn as column after column of marching men set off down the Warrenton Turnpike toward the winding stream called Bull Run where the Confederate forces had redrawn their lines. It was heightened by the quiet with which the march was begun, for the officers had emphasized that surprise was one of the conditions of success in this enterprise. No drums or bugles were heard, only the soft grinding of wagon wheels and the muffled tread of boots and horses' hooves and gun carriages. Falling in with a New York regiment under Colonel Porter's Second Division, Ethan was struck by the way the men spoke to each other in subdued voices at the beginning of the march. Some of this careful rectitude wore off as, after marching only two or three miles, the columns were halted to begin a long wait while General Tyler's First Division advanced to make a feint attack on the Rebel front line. As dawn grew toward daylight, Ethan, impatient with the inactivity, rode back to where a small brook called Cub Run crossed the turnpike. There, on each side of the crest of a hill, were all the carriages from Washington, filled with the civilian spectators and flanked by assorted camp followers all waiting expectantly for the battle to begin. Riding down the lines, Ethan spotted Congressman Ely and some of his friends sitting on the ground in front of their barouche, enjoying a breakfast of cold chicken, preserved fruits, bread and butter, doughnuts, hot coffee, and champagne. He did not need much urging to join them.

"What's going on up ahead?" Ely asked, handing Ethan a plate piled with food.

"Nothing at all. We've been sitting for nearly three hours waiting for Tyler's advance force to reach a bridge over Bull Run. I'm beginning to think we may not see any action today after all."

"Oh, you'll see some action," Ely said, pouring him a cup of coffee. He leaned closer and whispered, "I happen to know that MacDowell plans to make his main attack by a left flank. I suspect the columns you're with will be marching around to do just that. In fact, as much as we enjoy your good company, if I were you I'd not tarry long."

The hot coffee tasted good even though the day already gave promise of becoming sweltering. Ethan gulped down his breakfast, thinking it unlikely that Ely should be the recipient of such privileged information yet unwilling to take a chance on missing the action.

"Gentlemen, my thanks," he said, rising and donning his hat.

"We'll share supper in Richmond tonight," Ely said jauntily. "Or tomorrow by the very latest."

Ethan smiled and climbed back into the saddle, turning his horse down the turnpike toward Bull Run. He wished he could share the congressman's confidence, but he remembered too well the Union soldiers he had seen since leaving Washington. Many of them were only young boys, and even on this simple march they had clearly showed that they obeyed no authority but their own. They had stopped to rest and refill their canteens at every stream. The road was littered with haversacks, blankets, and boxes of army rations they had dropped along the way; every blackberry patch was an invitation to stop and gorge themselves. If this was an army—and it was true he had never seen an army close up before—God help the Union!

When Ethan rejoined the lines, he found that Porter's di-

vision had already started off down the country road jutting
north from the turnpike that was to carry them around the left
flank of the southern forces. Hurrying his horse along, he finally
caught up with the last of the column as it neared the end of
its twelve-mile trek. Here, the thunder of heavy artillery sig-
naling the arrival of Tyler's advance force shattered the morning
air, sending dark clouds of terrified birds and a thick fog of
ominous gray smoke high over the trees. Wild animals, rabbits,
squirrels, all kinds of small game, came bounding in terror
through the woods, fleeing the terrible noise. Even an hour
before there would have been a scramble to catch some of them
for supper, but now the weary men ignored them and continued
on their way through the underbrush toward Bull Run.

The line halted near a shallow stream called Sudley Springs
Ford, and the hot, hungry, exhausted troops fell to the ground.
By now the dust raised by the troops and wagons lay like a
red pall over their entire route, a certain sign to the Rebels that
they had come. Crossing the stream, Ethan spurred his weary
horse forward across Sudley Stream, where General Burnside's
brigade was already deployed over a long front, moving cautiously forward five paces apart.

Tying his mount at the rear of a line of trees, Ethan hitched
a medical pack across his shoulders and ran to the slight shelter
offered by a grassy knoll. In the distance he could make out
Confederate forces forming a line, bringing up their batteries,
mounted officers shouting directions as they rode furiously back
and forth. Fascinated, Ethan suddenly realized he was part of
the front lines and, scurrying forward, placed himself behind
a solid trunk of a pine tree and watched as the Federal skirmishers on either side of him moved cautiously, nervously,
through the fields and thickets. The thickets around him gave
out onto a slight depression which sloped upward to a ridge
where the Confederate brigades were drawing up. Ethan clearly
recognized two six-pound cannons turned on his own lines and
could spot the colorful jackets of the infantrymen positioning
themselves around patches of brush. It gave him some feeling
of confidence to see two Federal batteries being readied, men
scurrying around preparing the guns.

All at once came a rattle of musketry and bright jets of flame
spouted from bushes, trees, and fences as skirmishers began
their volley. An answering roll spewed across the field, leaving

smoke and the sulfurous stink of gunpowder hanging in the
air. At first the action was not as startling as he had expected.
Then it began to grow in intensity; the noise of musket added
to light artillery swelled to an ear-splitting roar. When the big
close-range artillery fire began booming, the whole scene took
on the character of a nightmare. In just a few moments a
choking fog had covered the area and Ethan could barely see
two yards ahead of him. Then it dispersed momentarily, and
he made out the crumpled body of a young infantryman. Instinctively he ran forward, crouching down out of the line of
musket fire, to where the boy lay face downward on the grass.
Twisting his medical bag around, he grasped the soldier's
shoulder and turned him over on his back, ready to drag him
back to the shelter of the pines. With a sudden lurch of his
stomach, Ethan saw that half of the boy's face was blown away.

"God!"

He pulled back, stunned, while on either side of him came
the sharp sound of musket balls whipping into the dirt, plowing
up the ground. A shadow moved beside him, and Ethan saw
an infantryman moving in a crouching position toward the
Confederate battery. Just then there came a roar of cannon fire,
and as Ethan watched in horror, the man's head went flying
off his neck, tumbling along on the ground behind him. Ethan
caught a quick glimpse of rolling eyes and a jaw still working
up and down before he threw his hands over his head and dived
into the grass.

"My God!"

He couldn't move. He was frozen fast in the grip of a
paralyzing fear that turned his bones to liquid. It wasn't supposed to be like this! It was supposed to be exciting, glorious,
noble. This was all noise, horror, devastation. Would he ever
get away from this field alive? Would it be his head next?

With a heavy thud a body fell on top of him and, terrified,
Ethan rolled over and looked up into the eyes of a young private
half kneeling on the ground, one hand clutching his rifle, the
other gripping his thigh where a red stain slowly spread.

"Damn! I think I've caught a ball in my leg," he cried,
grimacing in pain.

An automatic instinct brought Ethan to the soldier's side.
The moment of paralyzing fear was past; he felt his strength
coming back. "Let me see," he said, pushing aside the boy's

hand to run his fingers over the leg. "I'm a surgeon."

There was a loud scream behind them as a wounded horse reared and fell to its side, throwing its rider. Looking frantically around, Ethan spotted the brace of pines he had left only minutes before.

"Can you make it back there?" he yelled.

"I don't know."

"Lean on my shoulder." Struggling to support the injured man, Ethan managed to half drag him back to the shelter of the woods. He hastily bandaged the man's leg, then ran back to the field. The smoke from the cannon was so thick he could barely breathe, much less see, and the pounding of the artillery was punctuated by the horrible screams of the wounded and dying. As his eyes adjusted to the fog, the scene around him began to register: men were falling, clutching themselves, twitching convulsively. He ran from one to another, trying to assess quickly the extent of their wounds. Some, lying in grotesque positions or in the last throes of death, he left where they lay, seeing there was little hope. Those who were still alive he dragged back to the trees. As the choking smoke grew thicker and the deafening noise screamed around him he ran back and forth, dodging the mangled carcass of a dead horse, stepping over corpses. He seemed to exist in a nightmare of hissings, screamings, howlings, explosions, wild shoutings, smoke, and debris.

Ethan was hardly aware of what he was doing, so obsessed was he with the need to carry from the field any who might still be saved. Spotting a group of men lying clumped near a shattered oak, he ran forward, closer to the end of the line than he had been before. He reached them just as an artillery shell tore across the top branches of the tree, shattering what was left of it and showering its broken limbs. The mangled corpses of five men had left a sheen of blood and gore over the grass, and Ethan slipped, falling to the ground just as one of the limbs from the tree fell on top of him. It grazed his head, leaving him dazed and half-blind. A man rode up to him, bending over from the saddle of his horse. Suddenly there was a shot and the horse screamed and jolted sideways, falling and throwing its rider, who landed half under it. Though his vision was blurred, Ethan thought he recognized Captain Hansen from the New York regiment he had set out with that morning. Trying to force his body to move to Hansen's aid, he watched groggily as the captain managed to pull himself out from under his horse, holding his left hand to his thigh.

"For God's sake, Dr. Slade. You don't belong here. Get to the rear!"

Ethan managed to sit up, his head reeling. An aide came running forward leading another horse as the captain grasped the reins and, using his good leg, tried to swing up into the saddle. On the third try he made it. Looking down at Ethan, his face black with smoke and powder, his eyes flaring, he said, "Goddamn it, we've set up a dressing station back beyond the springs and you're needed there. Now get the hell off this ground!"

Ethan stared up at him stupidly, trying to stand and unable to make his limbs obey.

"Orderly," Hansen called, circling on his frightened horse. "Take this man back to the field hospital at once. He's a doctor."

Ethan was pulled roughly to his feet and toward the brace of pines where he had stood earlier. Too dizzy and groggy to object, he plodded along, letting himself be led. By the time they reached the shelter of the dressing station, nearly half a mile behind the fighting, he was almost glad to be there. Now the noise was more bearable, the smoke a little thinner, and his head had cleared enough so he could walk on his own.

Under a canvas canopy, Pollack looked up from where he was bent over a makeshift table, working on a wounded man.

"Where the devil have you been, Slade? Get to work, for God's sake! I need help here."

His head was clear again. Ethan noticed Pollack's arm was red up to his elbow, sweat poured off his face, and his operating coat was stiff with congealed blood. Stifling an urge to run, he pulled off his coat, rolled up his sleeves, and grabbed an apron. The orderly had had the foresight to bring along his medical bag and, thrusting it open, Ethan pulled out the scalpel, saw, and probes, while an orderly threw a long plank over two wooden supports for a table.

All sense of time was lost. The pounding of the guns was broken now and then by wild cheers from the distance at some victory that had been gained. There was a lull of unnatural quiet after the noon hour, and sinking to the ground, weary as he'd ever been in his life, Ethan thought perhaps the end had come at last. But the noise soon picked up again and the carnage, judging by the men brought into the hospital, was worse than before.

There seemed to be no end to them—the bloody, horribly torn bodies that came to his table in a steady stream. His old wish for a cadaver to examine had come true with a vengeance. Never had he seen so many inner organs suddenly exposed nor felt so helpless in his poor attempts to put a body back together. So many mangled arms, legs, hands, and feet had to be amputated that the gory pile of discarded limbs grew to monstrous proportions. There were men with holes bored right through their heads, still living, looking blankly out at the world in startled frozen horror; men with parts of their shoulders, diaphragms or pelvises torn away, some of them clutching at their insides in a futile attempt to keep them where they belonged. Where there seemed some hope the doctors worked furiously to cut, ligature, and suture, but where one look told them it was futile, they swiftly moved the patient aside to die. There was no time for the dying while the living clamored so loudly for help.

By the middle of the afternoon ambulance wagons were carrying the wounded back to the church in Centerville that still served as the main hospital. The drivers returned with horrified stories about the dead bodies stacked waist-high outside its walls, but by this time Ethan was beyond being upset by anything. Earlier that afternoon word had swept through the field dispensary that the Rebels had been pushed back and victory was imminent, but the continued fighting had dampened his hopes that this was true. Judging by the noise, the battle had grown even more fierce, Ethan thought as he stepped away to wet a rag with cold water and hold it to his parched face. Turning back to his table, he saw yet another soldier had been placed on it. One leg was gone just below the knee while the man's right arm, grotesquely angled in a blood-soaked sleeve, told Ethan that underneath he would find the same jagged wound he had seen so many times this day. The soldier groaned and with a start of recognition Ethan leaned closer into his face.

"Jesse! Jesse Whitman. It's Ethan."

At the sound of Ethan's voice, Jesse's eyes flew open and he turned his head. Recognizing Ethan, his eyes widened and the fingers on his good hand clawed Ethan's bloodstained apron.

"Ethan! Ethan, save my arm. Save my arm, please Ethan!"

Something sickening churned inside Ethan. All the others had been so faceless, so anonymous. But this was his boyhood friend. They had grown up together, known each other all their lives.

"I'll do all I can, Jesse. You just hold on and let me take care of everything."

"Save it, Ethan. For God's sake . . ."

Cutting away the soggy cloth, Ethan suppressed a groan. The arm was mangled beyond help and would have to come off. Thank heaven Jesse seemed not to realize yet that half of one of his legs was gone as well. Someone on the field had tightened a makeshift tourniquet around it with a bayonet and belt, so Ethan was able to give his whole attention to the arm, cursing because the supply of chloroform had run out long ago.

The fingers of Jesse's good hand clutched so tightly at Ethan's apron that he had to fight to untangle them. Swiftly bending away, he reached into his medical bag, pulled out a flask of whiskey he had been jealously hoarding, and slipped his arm under Jesse's head.

"Here, Jesse. Drink this. It'll help."

"Don't take it off, Ethan. Please don't . . ."

Jesse's voice faded as though he realized his plea was useless. Gulping down the searing whiskey, he fell back, his eyes tightly closed, muttering to himself: "Out of the deep have I called upon thee, O Lord . . ."

"Jones," Ethan barked to one of the more competent orderlies. "Come help me with this."

"Lord, hear my voice. O let thine ears consider well, the voice of my com . . ."

Jesse fainted cold away with the first incision, much to Ethan's relief. Ethan had his arm off just above the elbow and the stump sutured and bandaged before Jesse awoke. Then swiftly he saw to the stump of the leg, grateful that someone on the field had given it competent care. As Jesse was carried off on a stretcher toward the church, Ethan walked away, leaned against a tree, and gulped down the rest of the whiskey.

Dear God, would this day never end!

It was nearly four o'clock when they began seeing the first signs that the battle had gone against them. It started with a scattering of stragglers making hotly for the rear of the lines and back down the road toward Centerville. Soon there was a flood of men hurrying away from the hard-fought ground, still clutching their muskets, their uniforms layered with powder, dust, and sweat, their faces black and grimy, their eyes wide with shock. When officers rode on their heels, frantically berating them to turn and get back into line, Ethan suspected that a rout was developing. Within half an hour the entire Federal army was in full retreat. The men in the dressing station stayed as long as they could, but when it became apparent that they would be captured if they remained any longer, they too began to pack up and strike for the rear.

Ethan was one of the last to leave and, too tired to walk, he commandeered a seat on one of the ambulance wagons carrying the wounded. He expected that once they left this road for the Warrenton Turnpike they would be swiftly away, but something about the unnatural noise as they drew closer to that road told him that it was not to be so. When the congestion on the trail grew so thick they could go no farther, Ethan jumped out and fought his way forward to see what was causing the trouble. The sight that met his eyes was almost beyond belief.

After a lull during the first part of the retreat, Confederate guns had resumed shelling the retiring Federal army. They struck one of the pleasure carriages trying to cross Cub Run and overturned it, blocking the bridge. Word had spread that the Rebels were in hot pursuit of the retreating Federal army, and in the ensuing wild panic soldiers, civilians, carriages, wagons, caissons, horses, and mules had all merged into one churning mass of confusion and fear, struggling to ford the stream and make their way back to the safety of Washington. Around them frantic officers and some civilians harangued the men to turn back and form some kind of orderly line. They might have saved their breath. They were completely ignored as men and screaming women sought to find a way out of the melee in search of one thing—safety.

Near the rear of the line Ethan stumbled across Congressman Ely, his carriage long since overturned and trampled, running doggedly in and out of the ranks, urging the men to go back and save the day. Ignoring him, as the soldiers were doing, Ethan quickly decided there was no way through that frantic, congested mass. Trudging back down the side road to the ambulance, Ethan grabbed up his bag and the coat he had discarded so many hours before.

"What should I do, sir?" the driver asked, beginning to feel the infectious urge to run.

"Stay here with the wounded. You're safe enough and the road will clear eventually."

"But, sir, suppose them Rebels come up?"

"Don't panic. It looks as though they're not pursuing. They probably have too many problems of their own right now. I'm striking out through the woods. Whatever you do, don't let anyone take those mules."

"Who'd want 'em?" the driver muttered dejectedly.

"They're cutting loose anything that moves down there trying to get away. You shoot anyone who tries that. That's an order. Your job is to get these men to a hospital in Centerville. Understood?"

The driver nodded, looking longingly after Ethan as though he'd like nothing better than to follow him.

Ethan was gone in a few moments, swallowed up by the underbrush. Knowing little except that he was moving in the general direction of the east with the sun at his back, he was driven by a searing, all-consuming compulsion to be away, anywhere away from this terrible place.

It was raining the next morning when he trudged, weary and bone tired, across the Long Bridge into Washington, one of an endless procession of exhausted, footsore, dirty, and dejected men.

Finding his old room at the hotel still free, Ethan sank to the bed without even removing his bloodstained clothes. He had been up since two o'clock the morning before, had marched nearly forty-five miles, and had endured first the terrible reality of battle and then long hours trying to repair the carnage left in its wake. He wished he could sleep forever. Yet the next day, after a bath and a shave and a change of clothes—he left his bloodied garments to be burned—he felt sufficiently himself again to visit the city's makeshift hospitals and see to the wounded and sick men who had been brought back from Bull Run.

As the week dragged by, he found that he could even take some comfort in his work again—something he feared he had lost forever that terrible Sunday before. He saw Jesse just once, lying on a cot clutching a worn Bible in his only hand, staring blankly at the ceiling. Ethan tried to talk to him, but though Jesse turned and looked at him, eyes like dark empty pits, he would reply to none of his questions. Ethan wasn't sure if the shock of losing two limbs had left his mind incapacitated or if Jesse was refusing to speak to him because he blamed him for not saving his arm.

Well, at least he would go home, back to Sing Sing, where his mother and cousins would dote on him and care for him. He'd probably be called a hero and the town would turn out to give him a rousing welcome. Not that that was any real compensation for a leg and an arm, not by any means.

Damaris would be one of those whose sympathy and concern would help Jesse begin to face life again. Damaris! It was the first time he had thought of her since that fateful moment when he'd opened Pollack's telegram.

At that same moment Damaris stood swathed in folds of antique satin and lace, watching Wesley slip a plain gold band on her finger. Suddenly Ethan's face thrust itself into her mind. Ethan, to whom she had given her heart and her body, who had taken her gift and then gone off without even saying good-bye. She forced his memory away. He'd been nothing but trouble and pain and would never be anything else. She heard herself repeating the vows of the ceremony and thought how unreal her voice sounded. She belonged now to this decent, kind man standing beside her, this man who loved her so dearly. As Wesley, smiling and radiant, bent to kiss her gently, softly, on her lips, she closed her eyes and willed herself to receive all he had to give. He was offering her so much warmth and love, while with Ethan there was only bitterness and longing and cold.

It was a bitterness she knew she would carry in her heart till the day she died.

❦ Nineteen

"THIS MAN could have returned to camp three days ago. He's nothing but a malingerer."

"Now hold on there, Doctor. My head is still poundin' somethin' fierce, and every time I stand up the room spins like a wind-jenny. If'n you send me back to camp, you'll kill me for sure!"

Throwing a contemptuous look at the hefty specimen of young manhood lying on the cot, Ethan snatched at a piece of paper fastened to the wall above his pillow. "You're with Colonel Davenport, I see. That explains why you don't wish to go back. He'll work the devil out of you."

"Well, the colonel is a hard man, there's no doubt about that. I've seen many a fellow strung up by his thumbs just for questioning an order."

"And you think it's safer here in the hospital. Well, sorry my friend, but the fever's been gone three days and your bowels are back to normal. You are well enough to return to camp and we need that bed for the truly ill. So get your things together. The orderly in the front room will make out your dismissal form."

"Now wait a minute, Doc. My back! Did I tell you about my..."

Ethan had already turned away, annoyed and disgusted. It seemed as though the men in this hospital came in two varieties: those who were too sick to go back to camp but who nevertheless, had to be restrained from staggering out the door and those who would much rather continue lounging on a comfortable cot in a cold ward than return to the damp huts and endless drills of the Arlington cantonments. He was bone tired of both.

Although there were stoves at both ends of the long ward, they did little to disperse the chilling draft from wet December winds that seeped through the shuttered windows. The old Union Hotel in Georgetown had been converted into this hospital, which housed the sick and wounded from the military camps surrounding Washington City. A drearier place, Ethan thought, could not exist. It was even more depressing than London Hospital in the Whitechapel slums: the worn carpets and peeling wallpaper; the damp, tortuous passages, and lack of water closets, sinks, or even a dead house; the decaying woodwork and undrained cellars that added their odors to those accumulated over the years from a long stream of humanity, and now the fetid miasma of sick men. It was all beginning to get to him, and he was suddenly obsessed with the need to get away, to escape all this dark misery. Pulling his white medical coat closer around him, he picked up his surgical bag and headed for the old lobby, now the admitting room. At least there was a roaring fire there in the huge old hearth and by standing close enough to it he might temporarily remove the chill from one side of his body at least. It was this inactivity, he thought, as he walked back through the ward, ignoring the men's cries. Of course, it was winter and you could not expect a campaign, but nevertheless, the new commander of the Army of the Potomac, General McClellan, was taking his own sweet time whipping his regiments back into fighting shape. Ethan was not the only person in Washington who felt McClellan might have made some move against the Rebels before the full force of winter blew in. Instead he kept his huge army drilling and marching outside the city, always preparing for the strike that never came. So the infirmaries ended up half filled with sorry men making excuses to lie around the wards while the more enterprising soldiers debated whether or not to simply walk away and go home.

"Excuse me, Dr. Slade."

Ethan was so absorbed in his thoughts that he had not even noticed the approach of the gaunt soldier who, because he was nearly ready to be discharged, had been acting as a nurse in the wards.

"There are some visitors waiting to see you. I put them in the dispensary at the end of the ward on the first floor. They said they wanted someplace private-like."

Surprised, Ethan thanked the man and hurried down the dark stairwell to the first floor, wondering if this could be another group of congressmen eager to tour the hospital. On opening the door he was startled to see his father's pudgy figure jump up from a chair to greet him with an outstretched hand and a delighted smile.

"My dear boy, how are you? It's been so long since you were home that your mother and I decided that if we wanted to see Mohammed we would have to come to the mountain ourselves."

Ethan quickly masked the irritation he felt at the thought of entertaining his parents. "Mother? She's here too?"

"Yes, back at the National Hotel. Not a bad place now that the southerners have abandoned it. The ride down was strenuous for her and she decided to rest rather than venture out in this cold. But here, I've brought along someone else for company."

He stepped aside and Ethan saw a girl standing near the stove, a long fur-lined cloak billowing out around her, the hood thrown back over honey-colored curls.

"Corrine. How pleasant to see you," he said, kissing her hand lightly.

Corrine colored and looked shyly away. "It's good to see you too, Ethan. My family sends you their regards."

"You must tell me how they all are. Well, well, how nice to see you both. Come sit down and . . ." His words trailed off. Actually this was a damnable interruption of his carefully ordered routine, but there was nothing to do but put a good face on it. "Did you really come all this way just to visit me?"

Corrine settled on a worn leather settee. "Well, not completely."

"Actually, we are on another errand," Robert Slade added, sitting down beside her. "The ladies of Sing Sing have been working their fingers to the bone to put together a few things that might be helpful to your dispensary. We decided to deliver them firsthand rather than send them off willy-nilly and hope they would eventually get to you. Isn't that so, Corrine?"

"Indeed it is," she said in her quiet voice. "We have quite a number of bandages, some linens and clothes, and a huge amount of keepsakes, most of them from the silly young girls, who hope they'll receive a letter in return from some handsome young private."

"These silly young girls cannot be much younger than you," Ethan teased. "Would a few of these romantic missives come from your hand?"

Corrine blushed and fastened her gaze on her muff.

"She's much too serious a young lady for such nonsense," his father interrupted, "and she's here on a much more serious mission. She wants to be a nurse."

"Oh?"

"Yes, I do," Corrine said. In spite of her shyness she was not willing to have Robert Slade speak for her on so important a matter. "I want to help with the war more than anything in the world. I'm a good nurse, Ethan. At home I'm always the one everyone wants when there's a sickness, from the field-hands to Mother herself. I know there are some volunteer nurses working in the hospitals here and I want to be one of them. I'm sure I have something to contribute."

"You don't know what you're asking, Corrine," Ethan scoffed. "First of all, we're taking care of men, not children and old women. Second, mending a few scratched knees and festered sores is a far cry from handling the wounded in a field hospital. I went through that and it was a nightmare, I assure you. You are much too gentle and refined even to think of such a thing."

"Well, of course she wouldn't go into a field hospital, Ethan!" Robert exclaimed. "What are you thinking of? But I agree myself that in a hospital such as this, where wounded men

come to recuperate after a battle—assuming we ever have
another battle—Corrine might be of good service. We thought
you could find a place for her as a volunteer on the staff here."

Corrine ran her fingers nervously along the soft fur of her
muff, struggling with her hurt over Ethan's cutting remark and
her strong desire to persuade him to help her. "I have handled
worse cases than you think, Ethan," she said quietly. "I've set
bones, patched broken heads, tended a gangrenous leg..."

"I'm surprised that Emily Whitman would allow you to be
around such things."

"She is a very competent nurse herself, and she taught me
a great deal of what I know. I am aware that Miss Dix is
recruiting women to serve as nurses for the army, but she insists
they be over thirty years old. Yet there are some women working as volunteers in Washington. Miss Schuyler at the Women's
Central in New York told me about them: Clara Barton, Miss
Alcott, Mrs. Griffin—I know I could be of as much help as
they. Won't you consider taking me on?"

Robert Slade reached over and tapped Ethan's arm. "I've
known Corrine since she was born, Ethan, and I tell you that
underneath that gentle exterior is a core of hard strength. I
admit I was reluctant at first to suggest such a thing to you but
she has won me over. Think about it, for her sake and for
mine."

Abruptly Ethan rose and went to stand next to the black
iron stove, staring down at its hot circular plate. Damn this
chit of a girl, coming here like this to interrupt his life. She
was so namby-pamby, she'd probably faint dead away at the
first sight of an amputated limb. Why couldn't it be Damaris
sitting there asking for a place to work beside him? Damaris!
Just to think of her made the bile rise in his throat.

"How is the family at Southernwood, Corrine? Your mother
and father? The newlyweds? How do they do?"

Taken aback by the abrupt change of subject, Corrine
searched for words. "Why, they do very well, thank you. Papa
is hoping to obtain some new contracts from the government
to build ships with which to implement the blockade of southern
ports. Mother is as busy as ever organizing the Ladies' Union
Relief Association to help win the war. And Damaris and Wesley seem very happy. They are living at Southernwood, you
know, but so far that seems to have worked out very nicely

and we all get on famously. Of course, we are all excited about the coming baby."

Ethan's hands clenched into fists. "Damaris is expecting a baby? So soon? They certainly didn't waste any time, did they?"

There was such bitterness in his voice as to earn him a hard look from his father. "That is to their credit," Robert said. "Wesley is almost beside himself with joy, and I believe he will make an excellent father. Since this will be the first grandchild in both families, it could not be more welcome."

"No doubt it will be spoiled beyond hope within a year," Ethan said, making an effort to seem amiable. Abruptly he turned to Corrine, saying, "I'd like to help you, Corrine, but it's really not up to me. You must apply to Mr. Olmsted at the Sanitary Commission. I am sure that if he feels you are capable of serving as a volunteer nurse he'll sign you on, even though you are too young and too pretty. If this war ever picks up again you might well be needed. Judging from what I saw last July, it is going to be no swift or easy matter to bring these Rebels to their senses."

A flush of pleasure diffused Corrine's delicate skin at the thought that he had all but called her pretty. "Oh thank you, Ethan. I shall do so at once."

Silly twit! "Perhaps you would like to do a turn with me around the wards. We've mostly camp fevers and stomach disorders right now, and the usual assortment of civilian illnesses. I was only half through my rounds when I was called away."

Corrine glanced at Robert, beaming with anticipation. "Do you think it would be seemly, Mr. Slade?"

"Of course. It's what you want, isn't it? Go ahead, my dear. Ethan will take good care of you."

"Keep your cloak on and carry your muff," Ethan said, striding toward the door. "The wards are chilly beyond belief."

Corrine happily followed him into the hall, her heart singing. She was not going to feel the cold at all.

When Damaris learned that Ethan would not be coming home for Christmas that year, she was the only person in two families who was not disappointed. At this point he was the last man on earth she wanted to see. In fact, the thought of Ethan Slade was perhaps the only thing that could shake the dreamy contentment that had been hers ever since the wedding. Wesley was proving to be such a pleasant and easy companion, a tender and able lover, a solicitous and devoted husband, that most of the time she was able to drown all thoughts of what might have been in the comfort of what was. The knowledge that she was going to have a baby was the crowning of her joy. Wesley was beside himself with happiness. There was something in him that responded eagerly to the idea of being a father, as though it was a vocation marked out for him before all others since the day he was born. And his delight was contagious.

What if, on occasion, some small shaft of pain cut through her joy—some sharp stab of doubt, some not quite audible voice wondering if this was not perhaps Ethan's child? With a furious determination she would push the fledgling horror quickly down, determined not to even think of such a possibility. It was not likely anyway, for there had been only that one brief afternoon with Ethan compared to many nights of love with her husband, especially in the first joyous intimacy after their wedding. If she looked at the possibility frankly and honestly, she had to admit there was perhaps a slight chance that this was Ethan's child. But it was much more likely that it was not. And in the last analysis, she could never know for sure and therefore she saw no use in even considering such a thing. A lot would depend on what the baby was like, but even then one could never be certain.

She forced the terrible subject from her mind and found herself thinking less and less of Ethan Slade as his brother made her life happy and serene. Until Corrine came home full of talk about Ethan and his work, and smiling her secret smile at the thought of going back to Washington to serve at his side.

Thus, against her expectations, Christmas was very difficult for Damaris. She sat at the table, groaning under its load of dishes, festooned with ropes of holly and glimmering candles, surrounded by Whitmans and Slades, listening with downcast eyes as Robert Slade launched into another glowing description of Ethan's hospital, Ethan's thoughts on the war, Ethan's critique of President Lincoln, his cabinet, and his generals, and she felt the old fury and bitterness grow within her like a choking weed. All her contentment began to crumble, her happiness to crack like shattered glass.

The long meal was almost over, sweetmeats, blancmange,

and Christmas puddings were at last being served, and she forced herself to keep a check on her feelings until she could get out of the room. It didn't help that from the opposite side of the table Uncle Garret kept his ferrety eyes glued to her face. Every time she looked up, she caught him studying her as though he could read her every thought. But that was nonsense. He had consumed enough wine to be almost beyond reading anything, and there was only one other person on earth who could possibly imagine what she was thinking. Thankfully, that person was far away.

Emily, sitting at the foot of the table, fixed her gaze on her eldest daughter. Emily didn't like the way Damaris had looked these last few days. It was too soon, this pregnancy; it was almost unseemly to have a baby right off like that. Heaven knows, she was as delighted as everyone else at the thought of a grandchild, but she did wish they had waited for two or three months at least. Damaris was a healthy girl, but this was a lot at once—marriage and pregnancy, and then the care of a new baby. From the first she had watched Damaris carefully for any signs that her health might suffer, but all of Emily's fears had seemed foolish in the face of her daughter's glowing contentment. But now she began to wonder if it was all beginning to take its toll. She must make sure that the girl got more rest. Damaris was always doing too much. They practically had to threaten to lock her in to keep her from riding out every day on that spirited horse of hers. She would speak to Wesley about it first thing tomorrow. Wesley hovered over Damaris so. If he thought she was risking herself or her child, he would move heaven and earth to keep her well. The only question was whether or not he could control her.

Emily looked around the table. Fade, at the other end, elegant and distinguished with his new short beard that had barely a speck of gray, bending forward in his eagerness to make some point about the southern blockade to Robert Slade. Robert, at her right, also straining forward to carry his point the length of the table. Robert was getting very plump now; how fortunate that she hadn't married him! And on her left, Winnifred, looking very grown-up in her new pink satin gown, bending around Garret to carry on an animated conversation with Claes Yancy. They had become good friends, those two, in spite of the disparity in their ages. Between them, Garret sat and glared around the table with contempt for them all. Next to Claes and on Fade's right, Gabrielle Slade wafted her lace handkerchief to her dainty nose at intervals. Gabrielle always had a chill of some sort. Her poor health was the most constant thing about her. It had been a concession on Emily's part to place Claes between Gabrielle and Garret, since the two of them could not abide each other.

Emily knew Gabrielle thought Garret was invited only to annoy her. There was some truth in that, she thought, smiling to herself, yet it was not the whole reason. Garret was her brother, and despite everything, she clung to a hope that some glimmer of family affection might someday break through the wreck he had become.

". . . commissioned the conversion of several steam packets into gunboats to patrol the waters outside Charleston," Fade was saying. "They'll be more of these, mark my words. It's our only hope of cutting off the British cotton trade and thus stabbing the Confederacy in the jugular. If we don't do it right away, we run the risk of Great Britain coming in on their side and that would be disastrous."

"But surely, Mr. Whitman," Wesley broke in, "you don't expect old sidewheelers and second-class sloops to maintain that blockade effectively. Already the south has several blockade runners who evade these old scows as easily as flies on a side of beef. Even your beloved clippers are simply too large and ungainly to do the trick."

"That's true," Fade said grudgingly, "they are fashioned for long, fast voyages." But to imagine that our best hope lies in vessels encased in iron is just an absurdity. They'll sink. Mark my words, they'll sink to the bottom."

"Fade, you have been saying that for years against every proof of a successful iron-clad," Robert Slade answered, his voice rising in his enthusiasm for an argument.

Emily barely listened as he went on, citing his friends in Congress as well as naval personnel and shipbuilders to make his point. Robert loved bringing important names into his conversations, as though reminding himself that his past glories in Washington were real. Across from Gabrielle, Emily saw Corrine delicately dip her spoon into her pudding and absently raise it to her lips. Everything about her second daughter was delicate, Emily thought: her small oval face, framed in wisps of fine honey-colored hair; the small nose and tiny lips that curved lovingly into a secret smile. Only her eyes were large, although they probably only seemed so in her small face.

Self-contained, that was Corrine. One never knew what she was thinking or feeling. Quietly, pleasantly, dutifully, she went about her business, willing to help when asked, turning back into herself when the request was done. Emily knew she had deep wells of compassion for suffering anywhere she found it. As a child she had never even been able to swat a fly or slap at a mosquito. A hurt dog or sick horse reduced her to tears. The worst incident in her entire childhood, Emily remembered, was when her hound, Keeper, had been killed by Mrs. King's fancy chaise and four. Yet when it came to helping Emily with one of the many illnesses or accidents that occurred around the estate, Corrine was a steady, strong nurse. The girl was filled with happiness at the thought of serving in the hospital in Washington and Emily only hoped she was doing the right thing in letting her go.

"Ethan thinks the war will not be won by the blockade at all," Robert was saying. "It's the battleground that counts, he told me, and I cannot help but think he's right."

"But there isn't any battleground," Wesley said. "And certainly if the first contest was any indication, we might as well hope for the war to be won somewhere else."

"Well now, that is not so true either. Ethan told me all about Bull Run, and it was not quite what we read in the papers."

Gabrielle spoke up, rising to the joint defense of her beloved eldest son. "It is only a southern lie that we suffered a defeat that day. After all, when you consider the odds—ninety thousand Rebels against only fifty thousand of our boys . . ."

"Oh, Mother," Wesley said, sitting back in his seat and laying an arm along the back of his wife's chair, "that's what you read in our local paper. The truth is very different. It was more like thirty-one thousand of them and twenty-nine thousand of us. And it was a rout, you can't hide the fact."

"Yes, but Ethan told me himself that we had all but won the day when some mistaken idea of southern reinforcements sent the Union soldiers retreating. Up until then they had fought brilliantly."

"And the retreat was an orderly one," Corrine startled everyone by saying, "until the confusion caused by the panic of the civilians, who should never have been allowed near the battlefield. Ethan said so himself."

"Our resident expert," Garret muttered. "How fortunate he was there to enlighten us."

Ignoring Garret, Wesley leaned across Damaris and questioned Corrine further about Ethan's description.

Emily thought how well Wesley was looking. He had gained weight since his marriage, and he exhibited a new flair and elegance in his appearance. She had always found Wesley to be something of a bore—pleasant and good-natured but not particularly interesting. Even now she still thought that Damaris and Ethan would have made a more handsome and well-matched couple. In time, she feared, Wesley would probably turn her spirited daughter into his own counterpart: homebound, family-centered, plump, and content—in short, a bore. Yet there was no mistaking the love he had for his wife. It was an all-consuming, adoration, as though he found his whole reason for living bound up in the person of Damaris Whitman Slade.

Gabrielle's strident voice cut through Emily's thoughts. "Corrine, considering the terrible descriptions dear Ethan gave us of that day at Bull Run, I hope you have reconsidered going down there to serve at the hospital. It really does not seem the proper thing at all for a young well-bred girl of your sensibilities. I confess I am surprised that your mother and father would even consider allowing it."

Emily bristled, but Corrine spoke before she could open her mouth. "We have discussed it at some length and they want only what will suit me. Obviously I shall be in good hands there. I'm not at all afraid of serving in any way that will be helpful."

"Corrine is a first-rate nurse," Fade added, not quite able to keep the irritation out of his voice. "You may be sure we will see that she has every protection. If it makes her happy to help the war effort in this way, then we shall endeavor to aid her. She asks for very little."

"Here, here," Robert joined in, for Corrine was a great favorite of his.

"I only wish I could join her," Winnifred said, pouting. "As usual, I'm too young to do anything exciting."

"And Corrine has a lot of strength underneath that gentle exterior. I've always said that," Robert added.

"I hope you will delay leaving until after the baby arrives," Wesley said. "We are counting on your skills to help us through those first weeks."

Corrine smiled her appreciation. A deliberately loud belch from Garret at that moment broke the sudden silence. "Your pardon," he muttered.

Gabrielle tore her revolted gaze from him and with magnificent disdain pretended he was not there. "Have you any idea yet when you might be going down?" she asked Corrine.

"No, not exactly. I had a letter from Ethan two days ago and—"

Damaris's wineglass went over, sending a burgundy stain over the white cloth. A thin stream of it cascaded down the table and onto her velvet skirt.

"Oh dear," she said, as Wesley jumped up, drew her away, and mopped at the mess with his napkin.

"Don't let it go to waste," Garret said, suddenly awake; trying to make a small joke, he leaned across the table, sending his glass over too.

"Really, Garret," Emily said through clenched teeth, "I think you've had enough."

Garret recognized vaguely that his pride had been stung. "In that case," he said, wobbling to his feet, "you'll excuse me if I withdraw!"

"Please do."

With great aplomb, Garret took a full minute to fold his napkin into a small square, lay it down beside his plate, and stumble down the length of the table. He paused near Gabrielle and, to her horror, reached out a hand.

"I'm sure you'll excuse . . ."

Drawing away, Gabrielle sniffed in a barely audible voice, "Indeed."

Garret laughed, and it was apparent to everyone that his contempt for Mrs. Slade was in every way the equal of hers for him. By the time the door closed behind him the wine had been cleaned up and the unsightly stains covered with clean napkins. Damaris resumed her seat and toyed with the dish of blancmange before her while she pretended not to hear Corrine's description of Ethan's note. She had never dreamed the friendship between the two of them would go this far.

"My dear, are you feeling all right?" Wesley whispered, his fingers closing over hers on the table.

"Yes, thank you. I'm fine. Really."

"You must lie down after dinner is over. A rest would do you good. The festivities, all this company, it's been too much for you."

"I'm all right, Wesley. Really. Don't fuss over me."

The interminable meal went on for another half hour before the ladies finally withdrew, leaving the men to their cigars and port, an ancient custom which Emily, who had been raised on it, insisted they maintain. By the time Damaris followed her mother, sisters, and mother-in-law into the elegant front parlor, her irritation had swelled to such a point that she wanted nothing so much as to find a corner and weep. She feigned a headache, and Emily suggested she go upstairs and lie down.

In her room Damaris's maid helped her get out of the heavy velvet gown and the petticoat and hoops that extended it like a barrel around her legs. Once her stays were loosened and her corset off—she was almost to the point where no corset was possible, heaven be praised—she slipped on a loose nightgown over her chemise and a soft blue brocade dressing robe over that. Then, unpinning her braids, she dismissed the maid and stretched out on a chaise, hoping that a rest and perhaps a brief nap might sweeten the sourness in her stomach, the result of too much rich food and too much wine.

The dyspepsia that had caused her so much discomfort in the first months of her pregnancy showed signs of returning now, and all her muscles were tensed. After twenty minutes of fruitless effort to relax, Damaris gave it up and went downstairs to fetch a book her mother had given her as a Christmas present. As Damaris walked through the hallway, she could hear the men arguing in the dining room and the women talking softly in the front parlor. She moved quietly ahead to the back parlor and shuffled through the pile of gifts there until she found the book she wanted. Looking through the window, she saw that it was snowing—fat, heavy flakes that gave the gray landscape the silver sheen of a fairyland. She put down the book, stepped to the window, and pulled aside the heavy gold drape to enjoy the beauty of the evening. With one hand against the curtain and the other resting lightly on the bulge under her robe, she felt a sudden sadness wash over her. Her eyes filled.

What's wrong with me, she thought, mentally scolding herself, crying when I have every reason to be happy? And I was happy until Corrine went down to Washington and raised this terrible ghost. It's jealousy, of course. That Corrine should see Ethan, talk to him, work alongside him. She's such a mousy little thing; Ethan is doing this only to hurt me. He's a monster, not worth thinking about, not worth a single tear. He's so much less a man than his brother—I ought to thank my stars I married Wesley instead of him. He would never have married me anyway. He would have kept me dangling along, waiting and hoping until I had no youth left and no other chances. How can I still cry over him!

There was a flutter under her hand as the baby in her womb stirred. Her fingers smoothed the soft cloth and her tears spilled down her cheeks. *Oh, Ethan, is this your baby?*

Letting the curtain fall, she turned back and picked up her book. It was then she saw the figure standing in the doorway.

"Uncle Garret! You startled me."

Did she imagine that his body loosened into a relaxed attitude from some taut concentration that had been there before?

"Sorry, m'dear," Garret drawled, sauntering into the room, his large satin tie half undone and his coat hanging like a sack on his gaunt frame. Clutching a large crystal wine goblet in one hand, he extended the other to place it on her arm in a gesture she supposed was meant to be affectionate. The alcoholic cloud of his breath was enough to raise the old nausea. Pulling back, she endured his horrible embrace for a few seconds, then fled to the door.

"I don't feel very well," she muttered. "I just wanted my new book before lying down."

"Yes, you're ready for bed, aren't you?" Garret said. "You look lovely—s'always."

"Good night, Uncle."

"Yes, yes." He raised his glass in her direction. "Good night."

Hurrying up the stairs, Damaris fought a vague sense of unease. How long had he been there? She hadn't heard a sound, but then Uncle Garret always moved lightly on his feet, turning up where you least expected him. Of all people to walk up behind her like that!

If only she could be sure she hadn't been speaking out loud.

Twenty

DAMARIS'S SON was born on April 24, 1862, a healthy, nine-pound baby with none of the wrinkled redness of a newborn and bearing unmistakably the stamp of his Slade forebears.

"I declare, the only thing about him that suggests Whitman is his black hair," Emily repeated proudly to all the friends who came to call. "He's already the spitting image of Robert—Robert when I first knew him as a small boy. The same fat cheeks and cherubic mouth. He's a Slade all right, but we'll claim him for ours all the same. I helped deliver him and I know!"

Such comments did not endear Emily to Gabrielle Slade when they got back to her—as Emily knew they would—but since the joy in the Slade household was every bit as great as that at Southernwood, Gabrielle decided at this point she could forgive Emily anything, even the unpardonable sin of having known her Robert as a small boy.

Unfortunately Corrine was not there to help in the care of mother and child, having left three weeks earlier for Washington. She wrote long, chatty, happy letters and in one of them she mentioned that she seldom saw Ethan since most of his time was spent at the army camps. While Damaris pretended to herself it did not really matter, this little piece of news somehow helped her to think less about Corrine and to lose herself almost completely in the joy of her child.

They named him Frederick after her father.

"We can call him Freddy," she said to the baby's proud papa, "so there shouldn't be any confusion. Fade is such an old-fashioned nickname anyway."

Any name Damaris chose would have pleased Wesley, who did not really care what they called their child. He looked from his wife, radiant with happiness, to his small son, pink-cheeked and beautiful in every way, and he thought, Was ever man so blessed as I? He had never felt that life owed him anything, and now he was all the more surprised and delighted to find that he had been freely handed all the riches of a happy man. He had a wife he adored, had found in the law a vocation that kept him interested and busy, and now, as a crowning achievement, he had a son to love and raise. What more could he ask?

Now that she could hold the baby in her arms, now that he was a person with a recognizable countenance and burgeoning personality, Damaris laid to rest all the doubts that had plagued her through the past months. If anything, Freddy resembled Wesley more than his lean-faced, square-jawed brother. And what did it matter anyway? He was himself, that was all. Never again would she even consider the possibility that he might have been conceived on that dreamy, unreal summer's afternoon on the hill overlooking the river. Wesley was Freddy's father. It was Wesley he would call Papa and Wesley he would love. And that was as it should be.

Fade stood at the window of his dingy office looking out on the quiet, whitewashed world. A light snow had frosted the jagged raw planks and rotting bones of the abandoned hulks scattered about the Dolphin yards. He could make out the clatter and snap of hammers and saws in the huge warehouse, the men shouting back and forth, their busy activity in sharp contrast to the desolation of the yards. Thank heaven they had received this limited government contract to convert two paddle boats into war steamers or they'd have had no work at all over the winter. What was happening to the demand for river boats—the ceaseless need for sloops and steamers to support the heavy traffic on the Hudson that had made the Dolphin prosper all these years?

The damned railroads, of course. That had to be it. Smelly, vile things that destroyed the beauty and peace of the landscape and shattered the old, comfortable patterns of living. Iron and steel, belching boilers and smoke, where once there had been the quiet peaceful dignity of sail and sleek hull slipping through the green water.

"Fade?" His sister's voice broke into his pensive mood.

"Oh," he said, startled. "Forgive me, Matilda. The snow has a way of mesmerizing me."

Matilda pulled her heavy wool shawl around her shoulders and shrugged as though she expected nothing less of the world than that it should ignore her. "I jest ought to be getting back, I suppose, before it gets any worse. I don't want to intrude . . ."

"It's no intrusion," Fade said, walking back to his chair. "I'm glad you stopped by. We don't really get a chance to visit much anymore, even though we live so close."

Matilda lowered her head, hiding under the wide brim of her poke bonnet. Neither of them wanted to recognize the truth by speaking it aloud—that Matilda and her family refused to visit the big house on the hill while every year Fade grew more reluctant to drop by the farmhouse, as though he had finally become ashamed of his origins. It had taken Emily Deveroe many years, Matilda thought wryly, to make her brother over into gentry but it looked as though she had finally succeeded. Now that his daughter was married to a Slade and all the nabobs of Westchester society were to be found at their table, Fade was finally more Deveroe than Whitman. But then, what else could one expect?

"I tol' Jim I'd be back by noon," she muttered to fill in the silence.

"And so you shall be. I'll have someone drive you back in my carriage. Now don't object—it's beginning to snow rather hard and I'll not have my own sister walking so far in such weather. Surely Jim can raise no objections to an act of kindness."

Matilda could not look at her brother, but in her secret heart she was relieved to be spared the long walk back in the cold. Arthritis made her poor bones creak and groan more each year.

"He's a proud 'un, that's for sure."

"Too proud if you ask me. But there, we won't go over that ground again."

Matilda, who was every bit as stiff-necked as her husband, caught her thin underlip with her teeth and steeled herself to tell her brother what had brought her here. Watching her struggle, Fade knew that at last she was nearing the point. Taking his time to light his pipe, he waited patiently.

"There's this one thing," Matilda muttered, so softly he could barely hear her. It was so seldom that this sister asked him for anything that he hesitated to speak for fear of sending her right out of the room before she came out with it. He assumed it was money, since the winter had been a harsh one and the kind of odd jobs Jim did best were difficult to find right now.

"It's Jesse," Matilda blurted, her voice suddenly forceful. "I'm that worried about him, Fade." She turned her pale serious eyes on her brother and he was surprised at the depth of feeling in them. They were usually so veiled and unrevealing.

"All he does is sit around and brood, reading his Bible and saying never a word to anyone. He's worn the pages that thin, but it brings him no comfort. When he does talk it's to say he's not a man anymore. A vile cripple—that's what he calls hisself—no use to anyone. I'm fearful for him, Fade, that he'll do hisself some harm. He was always the best of my chicks, could take care of hisself and was good about caring for others too. Now he's only full of his own grief. I don't know what to do about it neither."

Fade scolded himself that he could have ever thought Matilda would ask him for money! Yet this was almost a worse problem. He realized that he'd barely thought about Jesse since his first euphoric welcome home a year and a half ago—the parade, the speeches, the hero's laurels. The one or two times he'd visited the house in Sparta he had taken for granted the gaunt figure slumped in a corner of the kitchen thumbing the pages of a Bible.

"It is a terrible blow, Matilda, to lose an arm and a leg both at once. It would be to any man. You must expect him to take some time to come to grips with it."

"But that's just it!" she cried. "He's *not* coming to grips with it; he's letting it destroy him. He doesn't think he's a man anymore no matter how much I tell him that he's still the boy he was and what if'n he did give an arm and a foot honorably for his country. Nothing helps him look at it any different. He can't spend the rest of his life like this. It ain't right!"

"Does he ever leave the house?" Fade asked.

"Only to go with us to camp meetin'. Even that don't give him no comfort, and when any of the girls or fellers he used to know come round to speak to him, he won't say a word and he hobbles off inside to hide from them. The rest of the time he just sits in the kitchen. And he's a young man, Fade. A young man!"

Her face crumpled and the tears slid down her cheeks. Embarrassed, Fade pulled out his handkerchief and handed it to her, asking gently, "What would you like me to do, Matilda?"

She dabbed at her eyes, then folded the cloth neatly and handed it back to him. "I don't rightly know. I just thought you might be able to help some way. Talk to him, try to help him get out and find somethin' to do that will make him like his old self again."

"I'm sure I can find work for him somewhere, either here or at the house, if he'll let me. But none of you have ever allowed me to do that."

"I know," she said, defeated. Jesse had not changed that much and certainly Jim had not, even though he was just as worried as she about his favorite son. "I don't know what you can do, Fade. I just know he needs somebody to do somethin'."

"Yes, I think he does too. It's a damned shame that a man should be broken by his country and then thrown aside to wither on the dung heap. We cannot let that happen, Matilda, not to one of our own. I'll see that something is done. I promise you."

Matilda fixed her gaze on her hands. "I'd be that grateful to you, Fade. I truly would."

Coming around the desk, Fade gave her thin shoulder a squeeze. "Now, you sit here a moment and help yourself to some of that sherry on the table over there while I go and tell Samuel to get the gig ready. I'll be right back."

She wouldn't touch the wine of course, but a few minutes alone would give her time to compose herself again. He didn't want her going home suffering agonies of embarrassment because she had for once revealed some inner pain to her well-heeled brother. In all these years he had been married to Emily, how often had Matilda asked anything of him—once, maybe twice? Not like Florrie, who always had her hand out. He determined then and there that he was going to help Jesse for her sake if he had to move heaven and earth to do it.

The next week Corrine, now at the new Campbell Hospital on Boundry Street in Washington, received Fade's letter describing Matilda's problem and asking for her suggestions. "You must have seen many men in similar predicaments," he wrote, "and judging from the letters we've had from the doctors who know you, you've been of great help to them. How did you do it? I confess I am at something of a loss. Jesse is such a proud fellow. When I went to see him, he acted as though I were offering charity to a poor relation and would barely speak to me. I came away profoundly uncomfortable, both at the sight of that poor maimed creature and at my inability to convey any of the very real concern I felt. Any suggestions from one so experienced would be much appreciated."

Corrine read her father's letter over and over, straining by the light of the tiny lamp in the hospital cubicle she called her private quarters. Her heart ached for her cousin Jesse, the quiet, capable boy who had always known how to do everything so well. It was Jesse they had looked to through the years of her childhood, Jesse who could explain the mysteries of how things worked, what made them grow, or why some things prospered and others died. It was Jesse who understood why some shad fishermen strung nets on poles while others were drift netters; who knew how to attract sturgeon with burning pine knots and harpoon them with a spear; who could point out the intricacies of every brook, hill, forest, field, and glen between King's Ferry and Tarrytown. The thought of him drying up and dying by inches for want of spirit hurt her terribly.

Yet how to answer? It was nearly a year now since she had come to Washington as one of the volunteer nurses for the Sanitary Commission, and though she could not count the number of men who had come through the hospital maimed and crippled from battle injuries, most of them had moved on quickly, before she could witness the kind of hopeless despair that would eventually set in when they realized what the rest of their lives would really be like.

There was little time to dwell on it anyway, for her days were long and arduous and she fell into bed at night so exhausted she had little time for writing letters to her anxious parents. Looking back, she felt some pride in the fact that she had contributed to the improvements so evident in the new hospital. The dark, fetid wards of the Union Hotel with its loathsome smells and damp halls had given way under the administration of the Sanitary Commission to the clean, airy barracks and tents of this new building. The latrines and dead rooms were no longer to be found next door to rows of sick and wounded men. Food was wholesome and edible, not the half-petrified meat and watery soups she had first been obliged to serve. There were plenty of medicines and bandages now and a number of women much like herself, in long white aprons and clean caps, to administer them.

The worst time for her had been after the transports from the Peninsula began arriving filled with the wounded and dying men from the battles of Seven Days. It was the first time she had seen suffering on so huge a scale and it all but drove her back to Southernwood. But she persevered and found that she even gained strength from the experience. After that she never quailed before any hideous wound and there was no despicable chore she could not carry out; never again would she allow herself the luxury of self-pity now that she knew what real distress was.

Once she moved from the terrible Union Hospital to the new one outside the city a deep contentment took hold. She was contributing a valid service to the cause of the war in surroundings that came closer to meeting the needs of an army medical department than ever before in history, and she knew she was good at her job. The courtesy and respect she received from all the men with whom she worked attested to that, from the lowliest wounded private to the officer recovering from typhoid to the hard-pressed doctors in the wards. The gratitude that lit up the faces of the men when she appeared and the grateful letters from mothers, wives, and sweethearts thanking her for her kindness to their menfolk were all proof of her abilities. She was happier than she had ever been in her life and there was nowhere else she would rather be.

Her only disappointment—when she allowed herself to think of it—was that Ethan was not there to witness her accomplishments. She knew he took a skeptical view of her abilities and it was only out of a sense of kindness that he had helped her come to Washington. Now that he was serving with the Army of the Potomac, he spent most of his time campaigning in Virginia and only occasionally came to the city. She had seen him once or twice so far, and since she was reluctant to talk about her achievements she guessed he knew nothing of them. It saddened her a little because of all the people in the world, he was the one she most wanted to be proud of her. But that was a foolish hope at best. What mattered was that *she* knew she was doing a good job. Ethan, after all, had far more important matters to concern him.

Picking up her pen, she dipped the point in the inkwell and pulled a piece of paper toward her. She did have an idea that might help Jesse. It was farfetched, considering relations between the two families, but it just might work. She began filling the paper.

In early May 1863 the beleaguered Union army suffered another crushing defeat at the hands of Lee's Army of Northern Virginia. Chancellorsville was a brilliant victory for the Confederacy and another bitter loss for the Federal Army of the Potomac, now serving under their fifth commander in over a year and a half of fighting.

Though there was no cause for ringing bells and hanging banners, the Ladies' Aid Society of Sing Sing refused to allow any discouraging talk or slackening of effort. Rolling up their sleeves, they went to work harder than ever, raising money, sewing clothes, rolling bandages, and writing cheerful, encouraging notes for "the boys." The prime mover behind this determined optimism was Emily Deveroe, assisted and abetted by her right-hand advisor and assistant, Jesse Whitman.

Corrine's suggestion to bring in her mother to help Jesse had proved to be the best solution to the problem. After years in which Fade's wife and his sister had pretended to themselves that the other did not exist, Emily took matters in hand, sailed into Matilda's kitchen, seized the Bible from Jesse's hand to thumb through it, read aloud a few well-chosen passages, and decreed in the strongest words possible that it was as good as stabbing the Union through the heart to hold back his knowledge and his talents from those who, though mere women, were endeavoring to serve their country. Whether from shock or surprise or because of Emily's forceful personality, Jesse Whitman was moved to leave his corner to oversee the work being done by the Ladies' Aid and to share his firsthand knowledge of the kind of articles that would be most useful to soldiers in the field. Emily, having wrung from him a reluctant agreement to attend the group's next meeting, left nothing to chance; she called at the farmhouse herself to take him to the meeting in her carriage. Neither of them really knew why she succeeded when all else had failed, but the project proved to be something Jesse needed and provided a renewed contact with people that was as beneficial to him as any medicine in the world. The ladies of the village treated him with a matter-of-fact courtesy that almost made him forget at times that he was crippled, and because they relied on his expertise, he began to think that his frightful experience might yet serve some useful purpose after all. Jesse laid it to the intervention of God, but Damaris summed it up for her father: "Once Mother makes up her mind to save you, the Devil himself couldn't carry you off."

"I do think it's the most dispiriting thing in all the world that this terrible war should come just at this time," Winnifred said, frowning over the flannel shirt she was stitching. Damaris looked up from her own work and thought what an attractive young woman her sister was becoming. With her honey-blond curls, the long lashes contrasting with her pale skin as she peered closer to her work, and her full, gracefully shaped mouth, Winnifred had emerged from her schoolgirl cocoon into the freshness of womanhood right before their eyes.

"War! It's all the boys can talk or think about, not to mention those who have gone away. And no one wants to spend money on parties or balls when so much is needed for the war effort. Why did I have to be born just at the wrong time?"

"Be happy you were born a girl or else you might be off fighting yourself," Damaris said, turning her gaze to her one-year-old son, who was waddling on the grass near her chair. Hopefully there would be no wars when Freddy was seventeen!

"Even that would be better than sitting home sewing all the time," Winnifred answered, unconvinced. "Anything would!"

"You'd better talk less and work more. Mother will certainly be angry if those five shirts aren't finished in time for the meeting tomorrow. Come back, darling," she called to her son, who was following the meandering path of a very large ant headed for the orchard. "Freddy dear, come to Mama."

Glancing around, Freddy noticed that his progress had carried him a little farther from the secure orbit of his mother than was comfortable. He dropped to all fours and began crawling leisurely back, considerably hampered by the tails of his long dress. Damaris went and swooped him up, tucked him in her arms, and carried him back to her bench. Laughing and crowing, Freddy did not protest until she sat down, whereupon he insisted he be allowed back on the ground to begin the process all over again.

"Bother!" Winnifred exclaimed. "Just because Mother can run up ten shirts in one week she thinks we are all so capable. I hate sewing. My fingers are too big for the needle and I'm always sticking myself. I'll never get this thing finished."

"Here, give it to me." Damaris had nearly finished her week's quota and she could see that her sister's impatience and irritation were only hampering her efforts. "You write another of your cheery notes to tuck in the pocket while I finish it up for you. This is really terrible needlework, Winnifred. I think Mother should find something else for you to do in place of the kind of fine stitching that's needed here. Perhaps you could make some of those little kits."

"Damaris, you're an angel. Suggest it to Mother, won't you. I'd be ever so grateful."

Looking up, Damaris saw that her mother and father were walking arm in arm along the garden path toward them. "Suggest it yourself, why don't you. Here she comes now."

"Oh, you know she pays no attention to anything I say. But she'll listen to you."

"That's certainly not true," Damaris exclaimed. "She never listens to *anyone* except, occasionally, Father."

Bending over the flannel, she wondered at the irritation in her voice. Her mother was demanding, that was true, but she had almost single-handedly run up a record for the Ladies' Aid Society that was the envy of the other villages in Westchester. She drove, cajoled, argued, at times even shed a few tears in order to draw more work from the already overburdened and more money from those who could still afford to give anything at all. Damaris knew almost better than anyone that Emily's contribution to the war effort had been invaluable. She wished she could give her mother credit without struggling with her own impatience and resentment, but it seemed to rise to the surface no matter how hard she tried to prevent it. And somehow the sight of Emily and Fade walking arm in arm pricked at her own sense of discomfort. Her father was the only person to whom her mother was vulnerable. He could control her highminded ways when no one else in the world was able to, and yet Emily seemed to love him the more for it. Sometimes she wished her own husband was that strong. Wesley was so . . . so accommodating. He loved her so much, would do anything for her, had put her on a pedestal and set his world revolving around her. And she, beast that she was, instead of gratefully accepting this adoration and respect, often wanted to fling it in his face and make him stand up and fight her!

"Hello, my darling child," Emily called, and Freddy, hearing a beloved voice, went scuttling straight toward her. She picked him up, dandled him in her arms while he bubbled with laughter, then kissed him soundly on his pink cheeks.

Damaris reached over to move her large wicker sewing basket so her parents could join them under the ancient ash tree.

"Damaris, you really ought not let Freddy crawl around on the grass with bare legs," Emily said, settling down with the baby in her lap. "He'll catch some terrible chill for sure."

"For heaven's sake, Mother, it's as hot as can be. How could he catch cold in this weather?"

"All the same, it's not healthy. And look, he's got grass stains all over his pretty dress. Ah, my poor baby, how shabbily your mother takes care of you."

Gritting her teeth, Damaris concentrated on her stitches.

"Damaris is a fine mother, Emily," Fade said, throwing his daughter a smile. "That has to be the healthiest boy in ten counties."

"And the most doted upon," Winnifred added languidly.

"And the most darling," Emily said, bouncing her grandson on her knees. "Is that the last of your sewing, Damaris? The meeting is tomorrow and we want to pack up the boxes to be shipped."

"I'm aware of that, Mother. Mine are done, but I'm helping Winnifred finish up hers so she can compose another of her charming notes to tuck into the pockets."

Emily frowned at her youngest. "I'm not sure I approve of that. The shirts are more important than any letter, for when a man is cold and wet it's not a few words from a stranger that will keep him warm."

"My letters warm the heart," Winnifred answered with spirit.

At Fade's muffled chuckle Emily glared. Winnifred had always shown a disturbing lightness of mind.

"If you'd ever stood for hours in a pouring rain or had to sleep on the frozen ground in a winter's blizzard, you'd know that it isn't the heart that needs warming—it's the backside! I trust that you will finish your own quota in the future, and on time too, young lady."

Winnifred wilted under her mother's severe gaze. "Yes, Mother."

"You might consider giving her something to do that does not require such careful work," Damaris said warily. "Perhaps those little kits the soldiers like so much. Anyone can make them."

"Every young lady should know how to make fine stitches. Winnifred, you simply must practice a little more. I don't like to see you give up so easily."

"But if I'm not good at it . . ."

"Then you must learn to be good at it through constant practice. Look at Corrine. The things she has learned to do in the hospital—things she never in her wildest dreams imagined: cooking, scrubbing, tending wounds, even assisting in the surgery on one occasion. How long do you think she would have lasted if she had not continued always to work at making herself proficient?"

"But Corrine wanted to do all that. I hate sewing!"

"I've had a letter from Corrine," Fade broke in, glad of an excuse to turn the conversation. He pulled it from an inside pocket. "She says she saw Ethan recently. He was visiting the city and took her to supper."

Damaris's needle jabbed the cloth in her hand. What did she care? Ethan was less than a memory to her now.

"He's still with the Ninth New York and he's seen a lot of fighting: Antietam, Fredericksburg, Chancellorsville—some terrible battles. He told her how at Antietam they were bandaging men's wounds with corn husks before the relief supplies sent up by the Sanitary Commission finally arrived."

"All the more reason we must work harder," Emily cried.

Even Winnifred seemed impressed. "He went through all that and he wasn't hurt? He's a very lucky man."

"Yes he is, considering the horrible casualties in those battles. He told Corrine he's seen so much suffering now that nothing affects him anymore. The most mangled bodies are just another patch-up job. But he does get furious and upset at the bureaucratic bungling that keeps food and supplies from the field hospitals where they are so desperately needed. And, of course, like everyone else, he grumbled a lot about the do-nothing generals who can't seem to get the best of those Rebels."

With a sudden movement Emily set her grandson down on the grass. "They need a few women running things down there," she said briskly. "They'd get the job done in short order. Damaris, you are mangling that poor shirt, and look, you've pricked your finger and are getting stains on the cloth. Give it to me. I'll finish it up. My goodness, sometimes I think nothing would ever get done around here if it wasn't for me!"

One of the most bitter disappointments for Corrine since coming to Washington was the fact that she had missed doing service on the hospital ships during the engagements on the Peninsula. The ferries and tugs the Sanitary Commission had outfitted to care for the sick and wounded during the three months that McClellan had tried vainly to take Richmond from the sea had saved many lives and introduced an entirely new concept for caring for soldiers in war. Corrine loved nothing so much as to hear Katherine Wormeley, Helen Gilson, and Mrs. William Griffin, who had been on board, tell of their adventures. When she listened to their stories, she felt as though all her work in the hospitals in Washington was simply routine, contributing very little to the salvation of the Union.

Thus inspired, Corrine was one of the first to volunteer her services when rumors reached Washington in early July 1863 of a terrible struggle being fought on the hills around a sleepy Pennsylvania town called Gettysburg. Reports pouring in from the battlefield told of twenty-two thousand wounded and dying men, the stragglers and the exhausted from both armies, lying exposed to the sun in a twenty-mile radius around the village. Both the Sanitary Commission and the Christian Commission launched frantic preparations for a relief unit to be immediately dispatched. A train filled with food, clothing, tents, stoves, and medical supplies was hastily thrown together in Baltimore. Attached to it were coaches for women who had volunteered to serve alongside the Negro contraband units. Corrine was one of the first to leave Washington to join that train, determined to overcome any objections to her youth with the hard facts of her service and experience. She met with few objections, however, for in the face of so great a need someone who had already proved herself a valuable nurse with a serious dedication to her work was worth her weight in gold.

It took twenty-four hours for the train to complete what normally would have been a two-hour trip. Because the railroad had been torn up and bridges destroyed, there was confusion all along the way, particularly at every rail crossing. The roads were thronged with weary, perplexed men seeking food and rest and finding none.

Stepping off the train two miles from the battlefield, where the railroad ended, the stench struck Corrine like a blow. The warm drizzle dampening the air did nothing to dispel the odor of decomposing bodies. The train itself was met by a horde of wounded, limping, famished men who had been left behind by the army and had heard relief was on the way. Corrine, along with the other women and Negroes, went immediately to work; they pitched two large hospital tents, set up a stove on which to start supper, and prepared clean beds for the most seriously wounded. Corrine quietly threw herself into these chores and it wasn't until the next day, when someone from Washington recognized her, that she was pulled out and sent up closer to the battlefield to assist the regular army nurses with the worst of the casualties. There she found several young women who, like herself, had been accepted for service in spite of their obvious youth and attractiveness.

For a week Corrine labored, losing all consciousness of time. Up at dawn, in clothes still damp from the dew, she worked all day until she dropped utterly exhausted on her cot at night. The seven days merged into a montage of blood, bandages, hot soup, iced lemonade, milk punch, and medicines. She directed the distribution of clothing and clean towels; she registered the names, towns, and units of scores of men, the living and the dead; she dealt with the pitiful relatives seeking sons, husbands, or brothers among the city of white tents and the hastily dug gravesites. She subsisted on a diet of potatoes and onions, hesitating to eat anything that might better serve a wounded soldier. She had never worked so hard or felt so well in her entire life.

On the morning of the first day of her second week at Gettysburg she was serving milk punch to some of the amputees in one of the tents near surgery when she looked up to see Georgiana Woolsey coming down the aisle toward her. Georgy, as she was known, besides having a friendly good nature which endeared her to all, was one of the most experienced and respected women with the commission. Corrine was relieved to think she would have her help during the long day ahead.

"Miss Whitman," Georgy said, tying her apron around her waist. "How are things over here?"

"Pretty good," Corrine answered. "We've handled nearly two thousand men so far and managed to send most of them along to their appropriate stations. Of course, these young gentlemen are going to have to put up with us for a while longer."

Lifting the corner of a sheet covering a sleeping soldier, Georgy peered at it closely. Like most of the women with the commission, she was a stickler for cleanliness.

"I think we've done a little better over by the railroad terminal. Nearly four thousand men have gone through there this past week. But not many of them suffered as severely as these. What are you giving out?"

"Milk punch."

"That's good enough. We've put a contraband cook to work making ginger panada in tent number three. They'll enjoy a bit of that later on, I should think."

Walking along between the cots, Georgy paused now and then to study some of the cards that noted the names of the men and their injuries, shaking her head over the most traumatic.

"Well, at least some of the chaos has been cleared away," she said almost to herself. "My guess is it will be another two weeks before we can leave this town. With all we've done there are still people lying about everywhere wondering where they should go next."

The man Corrine had been serving drifted off to sleep.

Picking up a tray she had set nearby, she started back to the
kitchen for more punch, thinking there were still nearly twenty
men in this tent alone who, because of the loss of arms and
hands, were unable to feed themselves. If one or two more
women showed up, they might get through them all in the next
hour.

"Oh, Miss Whitman," Georgy called as Corrine neared the
flap of the tent. "I meant to tell you—I came across a relative
of yours yesterday."

"Relative? Here?" Corrine paused, thinking of Jesse. But
of course he was at home, in no condition to be back in the
army. And she knew of no one else who had joined unless it
was one of Jesse's brothers. But surely her mother would have
written her of that.

"Yes, Surgeon Slade. He's your brother-in-law, isn't he?"

"Ethan! But I thought he must have gone back to Virginia
with the army. He's working here?"

"Not exactly working. He caught a ball through the shoulder
in that last engagement. Lay in a ditch for nearly two days
before he was found and brought in. By then it had begun to
putrefy and he was out of his mind with delirium from a fever.
He's better now, though. Are you all right?"

Corrine had turned as white as the milk in her hand. The
tray tottered, and seeing it about to go, Georgy jumped to take
it from her.

"Here now, I didn't mean to startle you so. Sit down a
moment. Catch your breath."

"No, no, I'm all right," Corrine stammered, regaining control. "It was just a shock, that's all. I had thought Dr. Slade
was gone from Pennsylvania by now. I never thought he would
be hurt . . ."

"Even surgeons are mortal, you know. We've lost many a
one in the battles of this war. Here now, let me keep this tray.
I'll serve the milk and you can go along back to the railroad
and see for yourself that he's all right. I think it might do him
good to see you as well, judging from the way he talked yesterday."

"But there are still so many men left to serve. I couldn't go
now."

"Nonsense. A lot of good you'll be to any of us worrying
your head off. Besides, Katy and Mary should be along in a

while to help. If we can't handle breakfast for twenty men between the three of us, then we don't deserve to be here at all."

Corrine made an effort to curb her excitement. "You're sure?"

"Certain. He's in tent number thirty-three, near the supply wagons. Hurry along, for we'll certainly be needing you in an hour when surgery starts."

Corrine did not even take the time to say thank you. Still wearing her apron and cap, she ran from the tent and started at a brisk pace down the white canvas-lined rows toward the railroad stop a mile and a half away. Ethan here! And wounded! She could hardly believe it—it was so unlike him to ever be in need. Her damp skirt hampered her long strides, but she pushed on, her breath racing. And he had asked for her. Actually asked for her! Her heart pounding, she almost broke into a run, then caught herself. She would be no good to anyone if she wore herself out like this so early in the day. She continued on, a small smile teasing the corners of her delicate lips.

✤ Twenty-one

THE SPECIAL relief squadron worked for three weeks on the fields of Gettysburg, dispatching nearly sixteen thousand men, who were fed, rested, cared for, and sent on to their various destinations. When the ladies of the Sanitary Commission finally packed up and marched to their train back to Washington, they were escorted by two army bands playing "Three Cheers for the Red, White, and Blue." Behind them they left four thousand men still in the hospitals on the field.

Corrine left with the first contingent, escorting the hospital car in which Ethan was returning to Washington. Although she felt some guilt about abandoning the hard-pressed regular army nurses, he had pleaded with her so to go with him that in the end she gave in. It had not taken too much urging since, as she admitted to herself, it was such a delight to have him want her so badly.

From the first moment she had appeared at his bedside, he had clung to her hand, reluctant to let her out of his sight even to perform her duties on the other wards. It was uncharacteristic of Ethan to need anyone, and she was both surprised and delighted it should be her. The suffering he had gone through and his close brush with death seemed to have changed him, to have shattered his self-confidence. She didn't quite understand it and she was careful not to speak of it, but in her secret heart it was like a dream come true. Feeling sure this uncharacteristic dependency would not last, she was all the more determined to enjoy it now.

Ethan himself did not understand why this small, quiet, capable girl was suddenly so important to his well-being. He thought it had something to do with the easy familiarity of their friendship. They had been children together, and she was the very embodiment of home and easier days. But it had a lot to do, too, with the way she handled herself. She never talked too much; she was there with whatever he needed almost before he felt the need; she seemed to sense his every wish—when it was time to rest, when he would like a letter written, what kind of food would make him stronger, what would ease the searing pain in his shoulder and arm. Most of his experience in field hospitals had been with nurses commandeered from convalescing soldiers, and he had not spent much time around the few women who were working in the field. If Corrine was typical he had to admit they were a vast improvement over the men.

He brought this up one day as they sat on the grass outside the hospital, where he had been convalescing. Corrine had brought out a chair for him while she sat on the ground working through a large basket of scrapped linen.

"I would never have believed it," Ethan said, watching her brisk fingers, "but you women have very nearly turned the army on its ear. You have changed forever the ancient ways of waging war, for certainly no one ever before gave a thought to caring for soldiers in the way you have done. They were supposed to care for themselves, unless they were fortunate enough to have a wife or girl friend along to help them."

"Miss Nightingale started it, I believe," Corrine answered,

"and there have been some wonderful women in this country working like the devil to implement her ideas. And some fine doctors too."

"I heard that Mrs. Bickerdyke with the western army is called General and that when she speaks the officers tremble."

"The men speak of us as angels," Corrine said, smiling at him, "but that's out of gratitude, I'm sure. I must say, however, that I have never been treated with anything but respect and good manners by all the men I've worked with. All those fears about women, especially young women, moving among men were completely unfounded. They are too grateful for our care."

They sat in silence for a moment and when Ethan spoke she looked up, surprised at the feeling in his voice.

"Did you know that you have a special name among the men?"

"Why, no. Do I?"

"Yes. They call you the dove."

"Dove! I cannot imagine why, unless it is because of my chattering and scolding."

"On the contrary . . ." He paused, wanting to explain that the name was inspired by her gentleness and quietness, but he was reluctant to embarrass her. "Corrine, I want you to know— that is, I'd like to say, I cannot really put into words how much it has meant to me . . ."

Could this really be him—this tongue-tied, stammering yokel who couldn't find a way to say thank you to a woman? He, who had never before felt at a loss for words that would charm. Tears sprang to his eyes and he cursed himself for having become so weak and foolish. This was what illness could do to a strong man—reduce him to a crying, stuttering wreck.

But for once Corrine did not notice Ethan's discomfort. Her eyes were fixed on a gentleman who was making his way briskly down the walk toward them. Her gaze had first been caught by his dapper appearance—the brown plaid trousers under a fawn-colored frock coat, the cane and gloves in one hand, the brown silk hat on his head. Then she saw him smile as he waved a free hand in their direction and broke into a hurried run.

"Ethan, I believe that's Wesley! Can it be possible?"

Twisting around in his chair, Ethan recognized his brother

and, giving a cry of genuine delight, tried vainly to stand. Before he could manage to get to his feet, Wesley was there, pulling him up in his strong embrace.

"It *is* you! How good to see you, Wes! I can hardly credit my eyes."

"Ethan. Let me look at you," Wesley said, holding his brother at arm's length. "Oh dear, forgive me, I've hurt your bad shoulder in my enthusiasm. My, my, you've lost some weight."

More distressed by Ethan's appearance than he wished to show, Wesley helped get him settled back in his chair, gave Corrine a quick hug, then stretched out on the grass beside his brother's chair.

"He's looking very well now, Wesley," Corrine said, resuming her place. "You should have seen Ethan when they first brought him into the hospital. It took two days just to get the grime off."

"That's what two days in a ditch will do for you. I don't recommend it. What brings you to Washington, Wes?"

"Why, you do, of course. I'd have been here sooner but I went to Gettysburg looking for you. It took me a while to learn you'd already left."

"You came just to see me? Didn't you know I was all right?"

"Well, we thought so, but once we heard of your wounds, nothing would do but that I must be dispatched to go and make sure that you were expected to recover. You have the combined forces of two full families wringing their hands over you."

"That really was not necessary."

In spite of Ethan's words, Wesley fancied he was pleased to see him and to know of his family's concern.

"How in heaven's name did you come to lie in a ditch for two days, Ethan? I should think a surgeon would be so important that he couldn't possibly be missing for so long. Especially if that battle was as bad as the papers say it was."

"Oh, it was as bad, all right."

"But weren't you in a field hospital?"

Ethan stirred restlessly at the painful memory. "No, I hadn't yet got to the hospital. How I wish I had. I might have at least been spared this bad shoulder, though there is no guarantee of that. Many a doctor has been shelled along with his patient while he was in the process of amputating. That's the kind of war we're fighting."

Corrine said quietly, "Ethan won't tell you, but I happen to know he was hurt while trying to save some of the wounded near Cemetery Ridge."

"Dashing around half-cocked like a damn fool!"

Corrine shook her head. "It was bitter fighting, nearly hand to hand. He was very brave."

"And very foolish. My own officers told me to get back behind the lines to the field hospital, but I didn't want to leave until I could bring away with me some of the fellows who needed help. Stupid!"

"I agree with Corrine," Wesley said, realizing how much he wished he could have been there himself. "It was extremely brave of you."

"Well, I'll have a long time now to reflect on my bravery and the fact that it will be months before I can use this arm to help patch up these poor fellows again. It was a silly waste. I should have listened to those officers."

"Come now, Ethan," his brother chided. "No one could ever tell you anything, you know that. And I would wager you saved someone's life out there while you were risking your own."

Ethan shrugged. The truth was he couldn't remember whether or not he had succeeded in dragging anyone out of the line of fire before he was hit himself. All he could see now was the long period of enforced idleness before him which might have been avoided had he been less headstrong.

"What was it like out there?"

Ethan turned away without answering, so Corrine tried to explain what Gettysburg had been like when she got there two days after the battle. Wesley listened as she described the stench, the wounds, the grime and blood, and the cleaning up they had tried to do; then he sat silently for a moment contemplating the two of them.

"I think you are both quite wonderful," he said with great feeling. "I don't know any other two people in our families who could have faced all that you both have faced and handled it half so well."

"Oh, I think Mrs. Whitman could," Ethan said casually. "And she'd probably have Bobby Lee surrendering his army to her as well."

"And Damaris could," Corrine added, "if she had been free to come."

Wesley smiled good-naturedly and picked up his silk hat. "I stand corrected on both counts. Now that I know where you are, Ethan, I shall go and see if I can get a room at Willard's. Then I'll have a bite of supper at Mr. Harvey's Oyster House and come back before dark. Would you join me, Corrine?"

"Why, I—"

"No, Corrine has to see that I get my supper," Ethan broke in. "You can manage on your own, brother. Don't carry off my other good arm."

Corrine colored. "Thank you, Wes, but perhaps I'd better stay on and see to my duties here. Perhaps in a few days, when Ethan is well enough, we can all go out together."

Trying not to show his surprise, Wesley said lightly, "Of course. I wouldn't think of taking you away from your work." He rose with easy grace. "I plan to stay in the city for at least several weeks, so there will be plenty of time later on."

"Is Damaris coming down to join you by any chance? I'd love to see her," Corrine said.

"No. I tried to talk her into accompanying me, but she felt she was needed at home with the baby. To tell the truth, I hated going off without her but Freddy needs her more than I, as she said. She made me promise to give you both her love, though."

He took his leave with no further comment. But as he boarded one of the new horse-drawn railroad cars to Willard's Hotel, he couldn't help wondering at the way his brother had clung to Corrine and his obvious reluctance to let her out of his sight. This was certainly a side of his brother that Wes had never seen before, and perhaps it was a positive one. Ethan could use the influence of a good woman. Damaris would be so pleased.

Wesley's suspicions were well founded, for before he left Washington, Ethan confided in him that he had almost made up his mind to ask Corrine to marry him.

"I'm not sure myself why," he said in his laconic manner, "except that I've come to respect her and lean on her in a way that I've never needed any woman before."

"I think it's wonderful, Ethan. She's a lovely girl, sound and true. She'll make you a fine wife..."

"But?"

"Well, I confess she's not the type of young woman you've been drawn to in the past. But then you never wanted to marry any of those women either."

Ethan's expression was veiled as he said, "Only one."

But Wesley was too intent on his own thoughts to pick up on Ethan's unguarded comment. "On the other hand, it's probably good that she is so different. A wife should be."

"You make it sound as though my lady friends have all been drawn from the brothels south of Pennsylvania Avenue!"

"No, no. Not at all. But they have usually been what I would call spirited fillies. However, that doesn't signify. What matters is that you've found someone you want to spend the rest of your life with and she's a fine young woman. And she's always been a special pet of Papa's, you know. I'm very happy for you, Ethan."

"You think she'll accept me?"

Remembering the long, lingering looks Corrine cast on his brother when she thought no one was looking, the way she colored when he paid her the slightest compliment, the unquestioning manner in which she rushed to fill his every wish, Wesley was able to reply without the slightest hesitation: "I don't believe you have a thing to worry about."

"Well," Emily said, laying down the letter from her daughter and looked at Fade over her round spectacles. "I would never have believed it, but it looks as though I'm going to have Ethan for a son-in-law after all. Two Slades! My heavens, we couldn't have planned it better if we'd tried."

"She's very happy—you can read it between the lines. I'm glad for her." Knocking his pipe on the edge of the hearth, Fade concentrated on searching out his tobacco case. "I thought you were reconciled to Wesley long ago."

"Oh, I was. Who wouldn't be—he's such a good-natured thing. But I've always had a special fondness for Ethan and I confess I'm happy to think that one of my daughters got him. But Corrine! Who would have ever thought!"

"What about Corrine?" said Damaris from the doorway. She had just entered the hall, back from a walk with Freddy. Standing there holding him in her arms, her cheeks still flushed from the September winds, her black hair framing her face, Fade thought she looked as beautiful as he had ever seen her. Her lips were parted in the faintest smile as she looked at her parents—who were obviously filled with great news—and waited to share in their delight.

"It's Corrine, my dear," Emily said, reaching for Freddy. "She and Ethan are going to be married. Isn't that an amazing turn of events?"

The color drained from Damaris's face and what would have become a smile turned into a grimace. "Married!"

"Yes, here's her letter. Come and read it. He's been quite dependent on her since he was wounded, you know, and I suppose he decided he liked having her about. She is a dear."

"When?"

At the tone of her voice, Fade looked up sharply. "Damaris, are you all right? Sit down and catch your breath. You look as though you've been playing too hard with that child. He'll run your legs off if you aren't careful."

Damaris moved on stiff legs to the nearest chair and perched on the edge. "When is this marriage taking place?"

"No, no, my darling, you cannot have Grandma's black beads. Here, Freddy, take this key. See how it jingles." Emily, engrossed in dangling her key ring before Freddy's outstretched hands, gestured toward the letter lying on the table. Damaris's eyes flew to it but she carefully avoided reaching out.

Fade said, "There's no date set yet. It will probably be in Washington, Corrine says, and will be very quiet. Neither of them wants any fuss, so thank heaven I don't have to finance another large affair. With Ethan still recovering and the war going full steam, it wouldn't be appropriate anyway."

"I should think they would want to wait until the war was over," Damaris said in an icy voice. "After all, Ethan's still with the Army of the Potomac and there's no end in sight yet. It would make much more sense."

"That makes more sense to me too, Damaris," Emily said, bouncing her restless grandson on her lap. "But Corrine says Ethan insists it be soon. He refuses even to consider waiting more than two months and would have it be sooner if she'd agree. You know how love is—it can never wait."

Jumping to her feet, Damaris fled from the room, throwing back some comment about changing for dinner.

Fade followed her to the door and noticed that she headed for the porch, not the stairs. Sauntering down the hall, he looked after her, his expression one long question as he saw her pause on the veranda, clasp one of the columns, and lay her head against it. He did not like this at all. Surely Damaris could not still have any feelings for Ethan, not after two years of marriage and a fine son like Freddy. And yet he remembered how close the two of them had been during those years of her girlhood. Nearly everyone in both families had expected them to marry. He supposed it would be difficult for her even now to see him wed her own sister.

He walked toward the veranda to speak to her and offer her his support, but before he got there she was gone, flying across the grass to the edge of the hill overlooking the river, her wide skirt billowing behind her.

By the time Wesley returned home, Damaris had schooled her emotions to such an extent that she could listen to the supper conversation centering on the coming wedding without betraying by so much as a twitch of a muscle how much the idea still galled her. As they sat down to dinner a week later she was so preoccupied with her own thoughts she failed to notice that her husband was unusually reflective and withdrawn.

Wesley had returned from Washington to find a situation developing in his law office that he felt powerless to do anything about. The owner of the firm where he had worked for many years had taken on a bright young apprentice who, in Wesley's absence, had been given several responsibilities which up to then had been Wesley's. The loss of work was bad enough, but even worse were the small rumors he kept hearing that Mr. Walker had it in mind to groom this young man as his successor. All the way home and through a quiet dinner, Wesley turned this information over in his mind, trying vainly to see it in a light that would make it a little less painful.

After supper he sat brooding in the parlor, pretending to concentrate on his book, unable to shake off the sense that he had somehow failed. It did no good to remind himself, as he had all week, that his comfortable inheritance did not require him to work at all, or that the branch of the law at which he was most proficient—real-estate titles and boundaries—was sometimes exceedingly boring even to him. This new fellow was so young and so clever, so filled with enthusiasm and energy: anyone would pale beside him.

Across from him, Damaris plied a needle through one of Freddy's shirts, lost in her own thoughts. Emily, on the sofa against the rear wall, worked at her endless stock of army shirts. And Fade, on the opposite end of the couch, leaned close to the lamp as he tried to make out the small print of his newspaper. Wesley studied his wife's profile, the shadows her eyelashes cast on her creamy cheek as she stared down at her darning. She was looking especially lovely tonight, with her burgundy silk skirt spread out around her, her hair parted in the center and sleeked back into a chenille snood. A fine cameo clasped the white lace collar at her throat. Should he tell her about his problem, ask her opinion, share his disappointment? He could pretty well guess what she would say:

"You must fight back, Wes. Stand up for your rights. Insist that Mr. Walker return the work you had started and show this upstart young man that he cannot push you around. You've put in enough years there. *You* ought to be the one to step into Mr. Walker's shoes."

The truth was he had no stomach for pushing himself forward like that. He shifted in his chair, uncomfortable even to think of it. He had always hated competition: he had learned early on that with Ethan as his principal competitor, he was never going to come in first anyway.

Glancing again at Damaris, he thought, as he had many times before, his marriage to her probably represented the only time in his life that he had bested Ethan.

Looking up, Damaris caught his intense look and smiled at him. "You're very quiet tonight, Wes."

"I was just thinking, how would you like a game of backgammon? It's been ages since we played."

"Oh, why not? Might as well."

Fade folded his newspaper and said, "If you young people are going to start one of those long games, I think I'll just go on up to bed. I'm feeling a little tired this evening."

Looking up at him over her glasses, Emily jabbed her needle into the linen cloth. "Have you been riding again, Fade? I thought you looked strained when you came in for supper. You know the doctor told you not to take any strenuous exercise."

"Now don't fuss over me, Emily. It was just a short canter."

"With God knows how many gallops and jumps," Emily

said in exasperation. "Why won't you take care of yourself? You're not a young man anymore."

"When I get tired I rest. To hell with the doctor."

While Wesley set up the game table in front of the fire, Damaris pulled out the backgammon board and began arranging the counters.

Laying her sewing on top of a basket at her feet, Emily rose and took her husband's arm. "I'll go up too. I feel a little sleepy myself. Now don't be up too late, you two."

They played an uneven game as the French clock ticked its soft accompaniment, with an occasional staccato snap from the fire. Between plays Wesley watched his wife, enjoying the sight of her. He was thinking how the soft light in the room accented the planes of her face when she looked up and caught him studying her.

"Wesley, I think you are letting me win!"

"My dear, you always win. I don't know why you should say that."

"Because tonight I'm playing the worst I ever played and I'm still beating you."

"I have to admit it's been work to keep from giving you a thorough trouncing for a change," he teased.

"Then you should not have resisted. It is no game at all if you don't take advantage of the opportunity to win. How many times have I told you that?"

"I know. But you looked so sad it seemed like adding insult to injury to make you lose to a player so much poorer than you."

"Oh, Wes!" Catching on to his mischievous tone, she laughed and swept up the counters. "You're right," she said. "I should have died of shame."

"I thought as much."

"Now that that's out of the way, however, we must play one more game, and this time you must beat me if you can. I insist."

"Very well. But you've got to promise not to get angry and start throwing things."

"I promise."

They set up the counters, bent over the board once more, and played the best game of the evening. Damaris lost, in spite of her halfhearted attempts to win, and feeling somewhat better about himself, Wesley put the board away. Then, linking his arm through hers, he led her up the stairs to their bedroom.

Closing the door behind him, Wesley thought that perhaps his problems at the office were not really so important after all. He watched Damaris as she moved to her dressing table, and then he set down the lamp and walked over to her. Gently he slid the net from her hair, allowing it to cascade in a dark cloud around her shoulders. Bending, he kissed her lightly on her full lips, then slipped his arms around her, pressing her body against his. As she pressed her face into the soft folds of his shirt, he caught the scent of lavender water and soap. Lifting her hair, he traced a line along her neck with his fingers. She stirred in his arms and Wesley gave a deep, throaty laugh.

"I thought I could get you interested."

"You know me too well. And I was just thinking how tired I was."

"But not now," he said, trailing kisses along her cheeks.

"Mmmm. Just give me a moment."

He left her only long enough to take off his clothes and turn out the lamp. Then, slipping in between the sheets, he found her waiting, her body eager for him. Searching out the warm moist places that he knew so well, the firm nipples of her swelling breasts, he sighed with exquisite delight. To hell with Mr. Walker and his young apprentice. Nothing in life mattered except being here with Damaris. She was his home, his destiny. Without her he was nothing. With her he was complete.

Damaris lay on her back, studying the canopy over the bed long after Wesley's even breathing told her he was asleep. She felt immeasurably comforted. It always amazed her how the touch of a man's hands and the exhausting act of love could restore one's self-esteem and make the world seem right again. After so much time together she and Wes knew just what to do to pleasure each other. She knew he would be gentle, restrained, comfortable, and familiar. If the thought sometimes came whispering that never with him would she experience the kind of wild passion and unrestrained earthiness she might have known with Ethan, well, what of it! The two men were different and it was no use comparing them. Besides, she rather suspected that Ethan was not going to find that with Corrine either.

Turning onto her side, she snuggled against her husband's

body, her arm draped over his solid waist. He was here and he was hers and he loved her. What more could she ask?

The wedding was a quiet one in late November, with only the parents of the bride and groom looking on and Wesley standing up for his brother. Damaris was ill with a terrible cold and so begged off, and Winnifred, though she was dying to go to a garrisoned town as lively as Washington, stayed at home to be of service to her sister. By Christmas they were all settled back into their old routines and Damaris had decided that her initial dismay had been a momentary reaction and now she was quite able to handle the situation. The long, glowing reports of Ethan's devotion to his new wife helped to solidify her indifference.

Her equanimity lasted until spring, when Corrine and Ethan came home for their first visit. She heard the carriage arriving, and straightening the wide bow under Freddy's chin, she took him by the hand and started down the stairs just as everyone came into the front hall. Corrine, in a dull brown dress and a tiny bonnet, the familiar wisps of hair like cobwebs around her brow; her father, in his greatcoat, taking a carpetbag from Ethan's hand; Emily fussing around Corrine, her long paisley shawl slipping from her shoulders; Wesley removing his gray felt hat, smiling in welcome; and finally Ethan, in a black frock coat, taller and more gaunt than she remembered.

All kinds of thoughts raced through her mind: everything is different now—let him love Corrine; let him show me only courtesy and the easy familiarity of a sister. They have all said he is devoted to his wife—let it be true; help me not to care!

Then Ethan moved away from the others, walked to the bottom of the stairs, and stared up at her. He said nothing, only continued to stare at her. And from the look in his eyes Damaris knew nothing had changed. Nothing at all.

Corrine and Ethan were to stay at Southernwood nearly two weeks. There were many visits between the Slade and Whitman families, occasional excursions into the village, frequent calls on friends in the neighborhood, and every day there were long meals together followed by quiet evenings in the parlor. Corrine often sang; Damaris and Emily sewed. The game table was brought out and the men played whist or five-card draw. There was such an easy intimacy among the family members that

Damaris began to think her imagination had deceived her and
that Ethan would not make things difficult. The only unpleasantness during the entire visit was caused by Garret's presence.
Claes had evicted him from Agatha's old house in the village,
and he had taken up temporary residence at Southernwood.
Yet even he (for once) kept his drinking to a tolerable degree
and seemed in a more mellow mood than usual.

The newlyweds would be leaving Monday, and on Saturday
evening, Emily gave them a party—a modest affair out of
deference to the war. The doors to the parlor and dining room
were thrown open, making one long room, a small orchestra
was brought in, and there were quadrilles and contra dances
for the young people as well as a few more sedate ones for
their parents. The ladies wore flowers in their hair and jewels
around their wrists and necks, and the men put on their best
formal evening dress. Claes, who was now a master's mate in
the Federal navy, was home, as was Stephen King, now with
the Ninth New York Zouaves. For Damaris it was like stepping
back a few years to the sumptuous balls her parents and the
Slades had given before the war and she enjoyed it thoroughly,
even going so far as to allow Freddy to stay up long past his
usual bedtime so he might enjoy it as well. It was nearly eleven
o'clock when she finally carried him upstairs and tucked him
into his cradle. Kissing him gently on his forehead, she lowered
the gas lamp to a soft dim glow and was turning to leave the
room when she saw Ethan standing in the doorway.

"Did I startle you?" he asked softly, stepping up to the
cradle. "I saw you leave with the boy and had an impulse to
watch you put him down. Somehow I never imagined you as
a doting mother."

Damaris took a few steps back, so that the corner of the
bed was between them. "One tends to get that way just having
a baby to care for. Especially one as satisfying as Freddy."

Ethan looked down at the sleeping child with an expression
of concentrated intensity. "He is a fine boy, Damaris. I don't
think I've mentioned it to you. You and Wesley must be very
proud."

Lovingly she smoothed the soft curls away from her son's
damp brow. "We are so very happy with him. Especially Wesley. Being a father rather suits him, I think."

"I can see that. He's sometimes a little silly, in fact, but I don't blame him. I'd probably feel that way myself."

Keeping her eyes on Freddy's face, Damaris fought down an uncomfortable sensation. Her imagination was playing tricks on her; she was reading things into his innocent words. "Perhaps we'd better get back to the party," she whispered, "before we wake him up."

Ethan straightened and walked to the window, pulling back the curtain. "Oh, I don't think anything will wake him right now. It's such a lovely evening. Look at those stars," he said. "The moonlight on the river reminds me of yards of silver chambray gauze draped over black gossamer satin." He went on almost as though talking to himself:

> "So I have seen behind some sable cloud,
>   Its skirts just tinted with a silver hue,
>   The queen of planets veiled in lovely gloom..."

"'Serena,'" Damaris said, recognizing the lines.

Turning, he smiled at her. "I don't think I've had such a feeling of perfect peace in months."

Thinking of the horrors Ethan must have witnessed these last years, Damaris scolded herself for being so silly as to question his motives in following her to Freddy's room. She stepped to the other side of the window, speaking softly and gazing out at the night.

"Has it helped, being home? You look better, you know, than when you came. You're not as restless and you smile more."

"The wounds of the body heal faster than those of the spirit," he said, smiling. "Being here in this peaceful place among my family has helped a spirit which, I confess, had taken rather a battering."

Ethan had mentioned few particulars of the war during his stay at Southernwood. It was one of those bonds between him and her sister that excluded all the others because none of them had experienced the war or could even imagine what it was like. Appalling casualty lists and broken men like Jesse told them something, but, Damaris suspected, no one could really understand unless they saw it for themselves. It occurred to her that now, in this quiet room, he might share with her some of the intensity of those scenes, and though she would not ask him to, she waited, hoping he would speak of them himself.

Turning to face her, Ethan leaned against the window frame and crossed his arms over his chest. "I would have thought you'd have another on the way by now."

The change of subject was so abrupt that Damaris had to stop and think what he was talking about. "Another?"

"Another baby. You had the first one so quickly that I thought you were set to have one a year, at least. What are you waiting for?"

All the sympathy she had been feeling for him melted away. Flustered, she turned and muttered, "There's plenty of time." Then, getting hold of herself, she added, "We thought Freddy should have some time to be the baby of the family. Why saddle him with competition right away?"

"Oh. A sensible solution."

"Besides, everything is so unsettled with the war and all. Father has been taking a beating with the economy the way it is. Unfortunately, he does not have investments in the things that are now in great demand. We were forced to sell a bit more of our land last fall just to keep the Dolphin yards going."

Ethan answered her almost absently. "The war should be over soon. Gettysburg was a disaster for the Rebels, and coming as it did right on the heels of Vicksburg, they will be forced to give up sooner or later. Everything is against them. We can only hope that it won't drag on for three or four more years, butchering men and throwing the country into upheaval."

Through all this talk of war she could feel his eyes burning into her. After a long pause, he spoke again, his voice low and full of emotion:

> "...when fancy's pow'r
> Wakes the loved shade of some departed hour..."

Damaris caught her breath. "Serena" again. Relentlessly he went on, staring at her:

> "Breathes in regret's dull ear a soothing strain,
> And almost bids past joy be joy again."

With an effort Damaris broke the spell, forcing herself to sound nonchalant as she said, "I forgot to ask Corrine what you plan to do once the war ends. Are you going to stay in Washington?"

Even in the dim light she could see the startled look that crossed his face at the mention of her sister. He turned to stare out at the night again. "I don't know. We haven't decided."

"I'm proud of Corrine," Damaris went on. "She seems to have done very well at what must have been a terribly difficult job, especially for someone of her sensibilities. I confess I didn't think she would stay with it."

"She's an excellent nurse," Ethan murmured.

"It all worked out very well, didn't it?" Damaris said, unable to keep an edge out of her voice. "Well, we really ought to get back," she added, starting for the door. Reaching out, Ethan stopped her with a firm hand on her arm.

"Damaris . . ."

"Please, Ethan," she said, trying to pull free. It happened quickly then. Pulling her swiftly to him, one arm closed around her shoulders, while he tilted up her chin with his other hand and pressed his lips down hard against hers. Struggling to pull free, she twisted under his stubborn embrace, filled first with panic, then with outrage. When he finally eased his grip, she jerked away and slapped him.

"How dare you!"

"Damaris . . ." The look of surprise and disappointment on his face was almost comical. Clearly he had not expected her to react this way.

"You haven't changed at all! How dare you touch me? I'm your brother's wife. You're married to my sister!"

Recovering, Ethan stepped back, rubbing his cheek and laughing at her. There was just a little too much outrage in her reaction. She cared more than she wanted to. "My apologies," he said.

"Have you no sense of decency, no—"

"Stop it, Damaris. I wanted to know if you still had any feelings for me, that was all. You're a very beautiful woman, and here in the moonlight I was carried away. Put it down to 'past joys.'"

Damaris moved quickly to the door. But she paused, her hand on the knob, and forced herself to consider what he had said. Her anger and guilt were nearly washed away in the flood of old feelings that came surging to the surface. But she must be sensible. She must not give way.

Speaking quietly, she said, "The past joys are gone, Ethan. Gone forever. You ought to know that better than I. I love Wesley and I love Corrine and I won't hurt them."

"You loved me too, once."

"That was long ago. It is dead now and it must stay dead. I will appreciate it if you will respect that."

There was a long pause before Ethan answered. Approaching her but careful to keep his distance, he said, "I love Corrine too, Damaris, and she is my wife. But I shall never love her in the same way I loved you. You might as well know that. However, I'm not a complete cad, and I will respect your wishes. This won't happen again."

This was the worst of all.

She felt the tears well behind her eyes. She looked up at him and wanted to weep, to lay her head against his shoulder and feel the comfort of his arms around her. But she could not take that step because she knew it would be fatal. Throwing open the door, she ran from the room, down the hall, and into her bedroom, needing a few minutes alone in which to regain her composure.

Why had this happened? What use was it to reawaken these old emotions when there was no way to give expression to them? She wanted to be a good wife and a good mother. She did not wish to hurt Corrine, who was, she knew, almost unable to believe her good luck in having gotten Ethan for a husband and completely blind to his clay feet. There was not the slightest doubt that Ethan would turn to some other woman eventually, but it could not, must not, be her. And yet the memory of his embrace caused her searing pain. How many times had she dreamed of feeling his arms around her again? Yet when at last she did, she could not respond. How cruel life could be.

Splashing some lilac water on her face, she dried her eyes and smoothed back her hair. She would go back downstairs and never let anyone see by so much as a flicker of her eyelids how disturbed she was. Especially Ethan!

The wide center hall was a blaze of light after the darkness of her bedroom. Lilting strains of a waltz from the small orchestra in the parlor gave a gay obligato to the confused chatter of the guests moving back and forth through the open doorways. The dark formal attire of the men was in sharp contrast to the shimmering colors of the women's dresses which billowed over their wide hoops as they walked.

When she reached the foot of the stairs, Damaris ran into her mother and Garret. Emily was attempting to convince him to go upstairs to bed. Damaris tried to slip around them unnoticed, but Garret, spotting her, grabbed her arm, beseeching her to tell Emily that he was actually stone-cold sober and ought to be left alone.

"Really, Uncle Garret, you cannot expect me to mediate between Mother and you," Damaris said halfheartedly, not liking at all the way her mother was staring at her.

"Corrine would. Come on, Damaris, be a good girl and—"

"Stop it, Garret," Emily said sharply. "I don't care what Damaris thinks, I won't have you making a scene at my party. If you go upstairs to bed now before you reach the last stages of inebriation, we might all avoid the usual unpleasantness."

"I don't want to go upstairs, and if you force me to, I'll make a scene just to annoy you. I'm sober enough to do it, too, and to do it right. You can't push me around this way."

"Why don't you take a bottle of whiskey up with you, Uncle Garret," Damaris said soothingly. "You've often said you don't like parties or young people, so the quiet of your room might just suit you." Motioning to the butler, who was standing in the hallway, Damaris had him bring over a bottle of good Kentucky bourbon, one of Fade's treasured holdovers from before the war. Recognizing its quality, Garret clasped it to his chest, smiling at the thought of his brother-in-law's fury when he learned of its fate.

"Good girl, Damaris," he muttered. Damaris, anxious to get past both of them, started for the supper room. She had taken only a few steps when Emily caught her and pulled her around the stairs, demanding, "What's the matter with you?"

"Don't worry about the bourbon, Mother. I'll explain to Papa and I'm sure once he knows his good whiskey helped send Uncle Garret quietly off to his room, he'll think it well worth the price."

Emily's eyes narrowed as she looked searchingly into her daughter's face. "I don't mean that. What's wrong with you? Are you ill?"

"Ill? Of course not. I'm fine."

"You look just fine to me," Garret said with a smirk, stepping up beside them. "Jes' fine to me."

"It's not Freddy, is it? He's not got a fever from being up so late?"

Damaris tossed her head in exasperation. "Good heavens, Mother. Of course not."

"Musn't let precious Freddy get sick."

"Garret!" Emily snapped. "Go upstairs and stay there or, so help me, I'll pour that bourbon on the ground while you watch."

"Fade wouldn't like that. Wouldn't like that at all!"

"I'll do it anyway if you don't go."

Grumbling, Garret turned away and started up the stairs. Damaris would have fled then, but Emily had a strong grip on her arm. "You cannot pull the wool over my eyes," Emily said. "I know something has upset you. Are you going to tell me what it is or not?"

Damaris jerked her arm away. "Mother, let me alone. I'm perfectly all right."

Emily could see she was getting nowhere, so she stepped back. Whatever was wrong, Damaris was not about to discuss it now. Perhaps later. Relieved, Damaris started to move past her mother. Just then, Ethan descended the last few steps. Damaris paused long enough to look straight up at him and then, without acknowledging his presence, disappeared into the dining room. Emily did not miss the look on her daughter's face, nor did she fail to notice how Ethan's scowl turned to a polite smile when he spotted Emily watching.

"Nice girl, Damaris," Garret said from the landing. "Good girl. Sensible girl."

Emily glared up at him. "Oh, go to bed!"

Two days later, on a cloudy overcast Monday, Ethan and Corrine left Southernwood to return to Washington and the war. Damaris stood on the veranda holding Freddy in her arms and waved good-bye to them, grateful that they were leaving. Since their confrontation in the upstairs bedroom, Ethan had treated her with easy, almost formal respect. Now she could try to forget and go back to being the contented wife and mother she fancied herself to be when Ethan Slade was not around to disturb her.

It was nearly three months later that Emily received a sad letter from Corrine describing in terse words how she had suffered a miscarriage almost as soon as she had realized she was pregnant. Ethan, she said, was almost more disappointed than she, something that did not help to ease her feeling that she had let him down.

Poor dear, Emily thought, overwhelmed with pity for her daughter. I shall write to her at once and remind her that I suffered the same ordeal soon after my marriage, yet eventually bore three healthy children. Perhaps it will comfort her a little.

Twenty-two

THE WAR dragged on for one more year. When word came of Lee's surrender at Appomattox on April 9, 1865, joy erupted in the form of spontaneous celebrations all over the country. Banners, flags, and bunting hung from windows in every village and town. Services of thanksgiving were held in packed churches, while in countless homes toasts were given to the Union and the brave men who had preserved it.

Then, six days later, all that joy turned to grief when President Lincoln was killed by an assassin's bullet. Although Westchester was heavily Democratic and many of its newspapers had been outspoken in their criticism of "honest old Abe," the President's death brought forth an anguished sorrow sharpened by feelings of loss, horror, and waste. Now that he was beyond the range of mortal vulnerability, Lincoln was recognized as the astute moral force that had held the nation to its course.

These were Damaris's thoughts as she stood beside Wesley and Winnifred in the crowd grouped around the railroad tracks,

now draped with black bunting, and watched the sad procession
of the train carrying the body back to Springfield for burial.
When she saw Jesse hobble up on his crutch to stare at the
dark windows of the car, when she thought of merry, silly
Stephen King buried somewhere near Petersburg, and of all
the men who had died or been left crippled for the rest of their
lives, this last death seemed only the most tragic madness of
the whole tragic war. Yet these men had preserved the nation
and done away forever with the evil of slavery. For such a
cause surely no price was too dear.

She felt Wesley's arm firm around her shoulders and gratefully leaned against him, the tears streaming down her cheeks.

One morning some weeks afterward Damaris walked into her
father's study to find him poring over a desk littered with
papers. She had been worried about him for a while, and at
first she thought perhaps he was experiencing the same feelings
of depression and despair she had felt after Lincoln's death.
But such melancholy was uncharacteristic of her father. Like
Wesley, Fade was inclined to take heart in the orderly routines
of everyday life and to leave the more complicated issues to
the politicians. When he brooded and became withdrawn as he
had these last weeks, she suspected the reason was more practical than philosophical. A few well-placed questions revealed
that her suspicions had been correct.

To Damaris's astonishment, Fade seemed almost glad to
share his concerns with her.

"I hesitate to tell your mother, you see. It's her inheritance,
and I dread having her think I have mismanaged it."

"But, Papa, you have always managed very well. Mother
has said so many times. I don't understand."

"I don't understand it completely myself," Fade said, shifting the papers on his desk. "Some of it, of course, is because
of the war. But I ask myself over and over—what have I done
wrong? The problem, you see, is that your mother thinks I can
do anything, when the truth is I was never brought up around
the halls of business and what I've learned has been strictly on
my own. She refuses to remember I was a common sailor before
she married me. What did I know of finance and investment—
I, who thought a second mate's share was a fortune?"

"She says you have a head for business. In New York, when
you were first married—"

"Oh yes, I was enterprising enough then," he interrupted. "But it was a far cry from the 'empire' I was suddenly thrust in to run when we came back from St. Louis. She thought I could do it—I thought I could do it. Well, it seems I can't, and I don't know how to tell her, after all these years."

Damaris pulled her chair closer to the desk. "What exactly is wrong, Papa? Describe it to me."

"It would do no good." Fade shrugged. "You're a woman. You wouldn't understand half of it."

"Perhaps not, but try to explain it anyway. I've always wondered exactly why it is we are able to live so grandly when so many other people are not."

"You may very soon be living like all the other people. In the simplest terms, what we take in is less than what we put out. I was able to deplete some of the debt last year when I sold those ten acres for Mr. Webster's grand country house, but our business interests keep sliding downward and I continue to be forced to borrow to meet my commitments. The yard has not made a profit since the first year of the war, the river traffic has fallen off so that the docks, mills and warehouses have all been affected and the Clipper ships have all been sold abroad—thanks to these damned Confederate cruisers."

He turned in his chair to stare out the window, brooding. "It's not so much my own failure that bothers me as it is the loss of Emily's inheritance. I wouldn't have her lose a penny of it through my blundering, and now she's in a fair way of losing it all."

"Now, Papa," Damaris said sharply, sounding much like her mother. "You must not let despair pull you down. How long has it been since you took over Mother's fortune—twenty-five years? It's still here after all that time and I'm sure it will go on a lot longer. There must be reasons for what has happened."

"The Deveroe interests were rather slack when I took them over," Fade said, almost as though explaining to himself. "Old Josh had wasted a lot on bad speculations and then Garret had all but run through what was left, spending half of it and selling the rest. And after I took over, things seemed to flourish for a while. But now . . ."

"Don't you think the effects of the war are partly to blame?" Damaris asked. "I mean, even I can see how prices have nearly doubled in four years."

"Well that's certainly true," Fade answered. "Here, look at this." Digging around in the pile of papers that littered his desk, he pulled out a column clipped from a local newspaper and handed it to his daughter.

Damaris held it to the light and read aloud. "'Butter was twenty-three cents a pound before the war, now it is sixty. Pork was twelve cents, now thirty. Cotton cloth jumped from fourteen cents a yard to thirty-three; tea from fifty cents a pound to a dollar and a half. Flour was eight dollars a barrel, now it is twenty dollars.' Well, you see. That's just what I meant."

"And agriculture has suffered terribly," Fade said, leaning forward in his chair. "Farmers are not bringing their produce to the docks as they used to. No one needs packets and market sloops any longer to carry their goods into the city. Now they go by rail. That damned, heathenish railroad!"

"But aren't wages better than they used to be?"

"Oh, they're better but not enough to keep up with prices. A man who earned a dollar an hour before the war can earn a dollar and a half now, but that won't pay these increases." He frowned. "And yet, some men have done well in spite of everything. A rich shipbuilder like William Webb can still afford to build a fine estate in which to spend his weekends."

"But surely the war was good for some industries."

"Oh yes, the Starr Arms in Yonkers and Mr. Owens's mills in Owensville. The firearm factories in the Bronx did well too. And the railroad, much as I detest it, has encouraged these starched-shirt millionaires from New York to build their country homes out here. Unfortunately, none of these are businesses in which we have interests, thanks to my lack of foresight."

"What about the Peekskill ironworks?"

"It's not done badly, but our share is too modest to be of much help."

"Papa, you blame yourself too much. Nothing is to be gained by that. I think you would do better now to consider which industries will flourish now that the war is over. If the county continues to grow—"

"I don't know why it should when there are not enough jobs now for the men returning from the war. Heaven knows what we'll do if we get a new influx of foreigners."

"Which, considering the past, is very likely to happen. What a shame Deveroe Enterprises never invested in the railroad."

"I'll give Garret credit—he always believed we should go that way. But I detest them so. Vile, smelly, ugly black monsters! Ruining the countryside, fouling the air, shattering the peace with their ear-splitting belches. Ugh!"

"Papa, I fear you are a romantic, and as near as I can tell, that is not a quality which makes for hard practical business sense."

Fade stared at her for a moment, and then a grin trembled on his lips. "I fear you are right, my saucy daughter."

Damaris leaned across the desk, her eyes alight with enthusiasm. "I'm not really clever about these things, but I would like to be. Teach me, Papa. I'd like to learn all about Deveroe Enterprises. It's a challenge to look ahead and try to decide what the future will be like and how we might make it profitable for us. Who knows, perhaps I have a talent for it and can be of some help to you."

Fade studied her thoughtfully. "Perhaps you might—you're certainly intelligent enough. But no, a woman's place is in the home; the grubby details of business are best left to men."

Throwing up her hands, Damaris flounced back in her chair. "Oh, Papa, surely you don't believe that! Why, I know many women of great talent. What a waste to keep them straightlaced in the home, cooking and sewing, when they might be useful outside as well. Look at Mother, the wonderful way she organized the Ladies' Aid. Why, she did her part to help win the war as surely as General Sherman or Jesse. I want to help you. I can hardly bear to think of my whole life passing, while I do nothing but care for Wes and Freddy and attend church socials and charity meetings. Please let me help, Papa."

"I grant you your mother could have probably run this business better than I, but she wisely retired and let me do it. It's a man's world, Damaris. Women don't belong there."

"What nonsense! Look how the army howled when women like Dorothy Dix and Mary Safford wanted to wade in and use their talents to improve the conditions of the army hospitals. And now, four years later, Corrine says that every proposal they fought for has been accepted as routine. What would have happened if they had believed women ought not to interfere in the military's business?"

Fade rubbed a finger along his chin. "Well, that's true . . ."

"At least let me try," Damaris went on. "If you don't like

my advice, then ignore it. What harm can it do?"

Fade reached out and began stacking the papers before him in a neat pile. "All right, all right. If it will amuse you, go ahead and study the ledgers, visit the yards, and make your recommendations. But you must promise not to be hurt if I pay no attention to them."

She sat back, her eyes shining. "Here," he said, handing her a tall red leather book whose frayed edges showed evidence of much handling. "Start with this."

"Is it the household ledger?"

"No, your mother has that. This is the overall account book for Deveroe Enterprises. It should give you a good picture of the total problem."

If he had handed her an autographed copy of St. Paul's Epistle to the Romans, Damaris could not have taken it more reverently. "I'll need it back by tomorrow morning," Fade said, trying to hide a smile.

"Then I'd better get busy," she said, darting to the door, already determined to forget lesser things and spend the rest of the day concentrating on this exciting new challenge. He watched the door close behind her, chuckling to himself. It wouldn't hurt anything to allow her this amusement, and God knows, had she been a son, he would be overjoyed to see such a display of interest in his work. Let her play with it for a while. In two weeks time she would go on to some other project. Meanwhile, he would go ahead and explain his problems to Emily. Somehow they didn't seem so insurmountable now.

To Fade's surprise, Damaris did not lose her enthusiasm for everything connected with the Deveroe interests. In fact, she amazed him by the depth of her knowledge and perception. For Damaris the experiment had been one of the most satisfying experiences of her life. She had grown up around the Dolphin yards and knew them well: the smell of raw wood, the cacophony of saws and hammers, the hot ovens steaming planks to be shaped into pliable contours, the intricate fashioning of a vessel from newly laid keel to gracefully sculptured hull. But now all at once she was filled with a curiosity about how it all happened. How was a contract won and worded? How much profit could be expected after the costs of labor and materials? How could overhead be reduced and higher profits encouraged?

What improvements could be made to modernize the work? She became a familiar figure at the dock, where the lumber yard and mill had been steadily losing money as the river traffic slowed. She studied maps of the area, wondering why the farmers no longer filled the winding roads from Connecticut and the northern regions of the county, their wagons overflowing with produce for the New York markets. She talked Wesley into taking her on a brief swing through the upper sections of the county to visit some of the farmers and there discovered that most of them were converting their fields to pasture land for dairy cattle in order to sell milk to city residents.

"And that milk is carried into the city by railroad, of course," she explained later as she and Wesley sat in the parlor enthusiastically describing their trip to her parents. "The trains can get it there before it spoils. It's not the only answer, Papa, but it is certainly part of the reason our markets have fallen off."

"Well, I knew it was happening but I had no idea of the extent. I thought it was high prices."

"Papa, I know you don't really want to believe this, but I think the future of market sloops is very dim."

"Oh you do, do you?" There was an edge to his voice which made her hesitate, but she was too involved to draw back now.

"Yes I do. The railroads are not going to go away. On the contrary, they are going to grow. There will be more of them all the time, and they are bound to capture most of the river business because they are so much faster. I think we have to ask ourselves how they will change the county and then try to turn that to our advantage. Look at the village of Mount Vernon. We talked to John Gordon, who runs a store in the town, and he told us that fifteen years ago there was nothing there but trees and woods. It was the railroad that made the village. Now they are having something of a real-estate boom. These rails carry people out to Westchester as well as carrying goods into New York."

"It seems you've become an expert on railroads all of a sudden. In fact, you seem to be quite an expert on all kinds of subjects!"

"Now, Papa, don't be vexed. The truth is I went everywhere I could go where I thought there was something to learn, and I talked to everyone who would talk to me. Surely that ought to be of some help."

"It depends on what you infer from all this newfound knowledge," Fade said cautiously.

"Oh, she has some ideas. You may be sure of that!" Wesley said. "She nearly talked my ear off the whole trip."

Damaris smiled at her husband. "Wes was so good-natured, Papa, to tag along with me to all these places I wanted to visit. I could never have had so good a trip without him."

"All right, let's hear it," Fade said, filling his pipe. "I am in a state of trembling expectation."

Emily, who was sitting on the sofa and working at her tatting, said nothing but waited with interest for her daughter to speak. Damaris's expression was so animated. She was clearly enjoying this exercise of wits and perception. Fighting down a little envy, Emily realized that her bright, restless daughter was thriving under this challenge. If Fade belittled Damaris or treated her efforts with contempt, Emily would certainly give him a piece of her mind later.

"I had two thoughts," Damaris began, leaning toward her father. "It's quite useless to try to talk you into investing in the rails—"

"Quite. I haven't the money anyway and, besides, I hate them."

"Right. However, there's no reason not to invest in the dairy farms, is there? Why couldn't we own some of those herds and the machinery it takes to process the milk? If only the land around here was suitable for grazing, I'd say convert Southernwood's fields to pasture land. But since it isn't, why not look for a small operation already in existence in North Salem or Croton Falls and take it over?"

Making an obvious stab at patience, Fade said, "You'd have to have somebody to run such a place. What do we know about dairy farms?"

"Nothing. But I have one or two ideas about that too. Meantime, since the yards are our first asset, I think we should begin to face the fact that the river traffic is never going to be what it once was."

"I remember saying that to my own father years ago, Damaris," Emily interjected. "And yet look how long it has survived. Don't look for its demise too soon."

"Oh, it will go on awhile, I suppose," Damaris said, turning to her mother, "but in the end it has to fail. The railroads are too extensive and growing every day."

"I suppose next you'll suggest selling the Dolphin," Fade said.

"No. But I overheard Mr. Oakley talking with Benjamin Jenks on the docks a few weeks ago and they said something that stayed in my mind. Market sloops are not the thing, but packets are going to be popular for a long time to come. Mr. Oakley feels that the only way to combat the railroads is to build up a popular fleet of sidepaddle steamers, and I think he may be right."

"He told me as much," Fade grumbled.

"It's worth considering, Papa. Why not get some of the other rivermen whose pockets have been hurt by the railroads together and see what can be done about it. A concerted effort by all of you would do more than any one small business could."

"I suppose next you'll be telling me to build iron-clads," Fade muttered.

"Well, certainly the war proved they could be successful. You must admit that by now, Papa."

"Damaris!"

Emily leaned forward and put her hand on her daughter's arm, as if to say: Please don't get off on that tangent again. Then, turning to her husband, she said, "Forget the iron-clads, my dear, and think of what Damaris just said about paddle steamers. The Dolphin has been building them off and on for years. It would do no harm to concentrate on them if there really is a market. Many people still prefer to travel by river rather than on the rails. Esthetically there is no comparison between them. And it would keep the yards in the family, where they have always been."

A gentle knock at the door announced the new housemaid Cora, carrying a tray with tea and biscuits. Temporarily distracted, Fade thought how galling it was to hear such things from his daughter. Yet at the same time he was pleased to see her so involved. Perhaps he should give her suggestions a fair hearing. As the door closed behind the maid, Emily laid her tapestry frame aside and sat down in front of the table to pour.

Fade turned back to Damaris and said, "I'm interested to hear which dairy experts you would hire to run our new farms."

Reaching for a cup of the steaming tea, Damaris could not look at her father as she replied, "I had thought of Jesse for one. He may be crippled, but he knows everything about farming and he certainly needs useful employment now. He's very quick, and once he decided to learn everything there was to know about milk processing, he'd be an expert in short order."

Fade stirred his tea laconically. "Mmmm. And the other?"

Damaris raised her cup to her lips and sipped the hot tea, then sat back. "Uncle Garret," she said deliberately.

Setting down his cup with a loud clatter, Fade stalked from his chair to the mantel. "Now I know you have lost your senses, Damaris!"

"Even I am aghast at that," Emily exclaimed.

"I told you that would be their reaction," Wesley said quietly, taking the cup and saucer from his wife.

"It's not such a wild idea if you will only stop and listen," Damaris cried. "All my life the only positive thing anyone has ever said about Garret was that he had a good head for business."

"Which he totally wasted!"

"But you've never given him a chance. All he ever does is live off Deveroe Enterprises and waste his time drinking and causing mischief. Perhaps if he had some useful employment he might yet make something more of his life."

"Did he put you up to this?" Emily asked, her expression stony.

"Of course not. He doesn't know anything about it."

"I don't believe you. It was his idea, wasn't it?"

Even Damaris was surprised at the hostility in her mother's voice. Her father's reaction was only a little less intense.

"Enough!" Fade cried. "Until now I thought your ideas had some merit, Damaris, but this is beyond all. I think we'll drop the whole subject."

"But, Papa, that's not fair!"

"Listen to your father, Damaris," Emily snapped. "He makes all the decisions about the business in this family, and I assure you that neither he nor I will ever consider allowing Garret anywhere near it."

"I don't understand either of you. Why shouldn't he have a chance?"

"He had his chance once."

"My dear," Wesley interrupted, "I think I hear Freddy upstairs. He's probably waked from his nap. Why don't we go up since we've seen so little of him these last two weeks." He took Damaris's arm and pulled her to her feet.

Anxious as she was to see her son, Damaris was reluctant to have what might have been her triumph turn to disaster. Quickly she tried a compromise.

"Well, if you don't agree about Uncle Garret, Papa, will you think about some of my other ideas?"

"Yes. There is merit in them, I don't deny."

That was some consolation at least.

The following month Fade invited several of the prominent river men of the area to Southernwood to discuss possible solutions to their joint economic problems. When he took the unheard of step of asking his daughter to listen in on the meeting, Damaris knew that her suggestions had not fallen on deaf ears. The gentlemen gathered around Fade's dining-room table, smoking Cuban cigars and sipping Spanish sherry, included the owners of most of the local lumber mills, shipyards, and docks, as well as the captains who ran fleets of sloops and schooners that carried passengers and freight between Westchester and New York City. Each of them depended in some way on the Hudson for their livelihood, and there was not one who hadn't been adversely affected by the growth of the railroads. They all shared a concern for their future.

By the time they left, Damaris, who spent the entire time quietly listening in a corner, had convinced Fade of her tactful ability to function in such company. She also had the satisfaction of hearing her opinions vindicated by the businessmen of the area. To a man they agreed that in order to survive railroad traffic they would have to make a joint effort to convert market sloops to passenger packets and to provide more runs at swifter speeds and cheaper rates than ever before. It was all Damaris could do to keep from saying, I told you so.

"Oh dear," Wesley said later when he joined his wife and her father in the parlor, "I suppose this means there will be no holding her back now. Watch out, Mr. Whitman, or she'll have you dancing to her tune before you know what has happened."

Although Fade answered with a lighthearted deprecating remark, Damaris could see he was proud of her. She had kept her place and had not tried to push herself forward—something her father would have immediately resented. And her opinions had been supported by men he respected. Whatever happened now, she felt sure Fade would encourage her involvement in the business. She looked forward to the future with anticipation, certain that her father would encourage her to stand beside him more and more. It was an exciting and satisfying thought.

The first shadow was cast over her enthusiasm a few days later, when she ran into Robert Slade just as she was emerging from Barlow's on Main Street. Loaded down with several boxes, she didn't see him until she careened into him, knocking his stovepipe hat off and into the mud. Smiling and apologetic, Robert helped her carry her boxes to the gig waiting near the blacksmith's, his cheeks reddening from the exertion. Wheezing a little, for he was far too gone in weight, he told her that they had had a letter from Ethan with the grand news that he and Corrine were thinking of moving back to the area.

"It would be wonderful to have them both living nearby, now wouldn't it?" Robert gasped.

"Yes, it would indeed. I wonder that Corrine didn't mention it," Damaris murmured, keeping her aplomb.

Driving back toward Southernwood, she mulled over this piece of news, trying to assess her reactions honestly. She didn't like it. Given a choice, she would have preferred to have Ethan two hundred miles away. But surely she was older and wiser now and too involved in her new interests to care much whether he was around or not. There was really no reason to worry about the magnetic effect of Ethan Slade's presence. She only hoped he didn't make a point of pursuing any other woman in the area and thus break her sister's heart. In any event, she had better things to think about.

Damaris was very surprised when Garret stopped her in the upstairs hall one evening after she had put Freddy to bed and invited her into Fade's study for a private word.

"They're expecting me downstairs," Damaris said, leaving the door open as she entered the room.

"This won't take but a minute," Garret answered, sidling around to lean against the window sill, his arms folded across his chest. Damaris sat perched on the edge of her chair, ready to flee at the slightest provocation, and avoided his eyes. Though Uncle Garret often tried to give the appearance of a dull-witted drunkard, his alert, crafty eyes did not fit the picture at all.

"I want to thank you," Garret began, his mouth sliding into its customary crooked grin.

"For what?" she asked, bewildered.

"For suggesting to your parents that I would make a good manager for the dairy factories."

"How—" She bit back the question. After all, she wasn't really surprised. Garret always knew everything that went on at Southernwood, though no one had ever figured out how. "I thought it a good idea," she muttered.

"Which fell on deaf ears."

Damaris stirred uneasily in her chair, wishing she could leave. In spite of the fact that Garret was sober, the intensity of the look he fastened upon her was disconcerting. She could never figure out what thoughts lay behind those dark, disturbing eyes, but she suspected they were not quite as dull as he tried to make people think.

"The truth is," he went on, "I would be very good at running a factory, even one that merely processes milk. I could make it work for you even better than Jesse, who, in spite of his abilities, is only half a man."

Immediately Damaris bristled and Garret perceived he had made a mistake. "Oh, he'll be very good," he said quickly, "but so would I. It was perceptive of you even to suggest me."

"Why don't they trust you?" She could not believe she had actually spoken the question aloud. But she had wondered about it so often, and since he had brought up the issue, she thought she might as well ask.

Garret waved a hand idly and looked away. "Oh, it was a matter we differed on long ago. Emily was well taught by my father to believe I could do nothing right. I suppose she feels that giving up that idea now would be like betraying old Josh, and she would never do that. Anyway, it's all water over the dam."

Damaris laid her hands on the arms of the chair as if to rise. "Well, Uncle Garret, if you'll excuse me..."

"No, don't go yet," he said quickly. "I want to ask you to do something for me. Something especially for your old Uncle Garret."

The blatant insincerity in his voice disgusted her. "What is that?"

"I want you to try again. Make another attempt at convincing them I deserve a chance. I'm not blind, you know. I can see that Frederick's blundering has put us all in pretty bad straits."

"Papa only did what he thought best. How could he know the way things would turn out?"

"Very proper of you to defend him, but if he had looked beyond his nose he could have seen that the railroads were bound to kill river traffic. They have only just started. In twenty years the river will be dead. In forty there won't be a boat on it except pleasure crafts and a few fishermen. I could have helped him avoid this if he had ever allowed me a voice. But he's far too much under the spell of my beloved sister for that!"

Stifling an urge to jump to her feet and protest, Damaris instead sat very still, waiting, for Uncle Garret was talking sense, confirming her notion about him.

"You're a very clever girl," Garret went on, "and I have a suspicion that as the years go by, with your father's help, you may be the power behind Deveroe Enterprises."

"That's just nonsense. Papa would never—"

"Papa won't live forever. It's incredible to think of a woman being groomed to take his place, but I suspect Fade has enough imagination to try. And you have enough of your mother in you to do admirably. I want to help you, that's all. And make no mistake—I can be of help."

"Really, Uncle Garret, this is a ridiculous conversation. If my father won't allow you a voice in the family business, I can do nothing about it. He still suspects that my own enthusiasm is temporary and that it will fade with the first new interest that comes along, and I don't know myself but that he may be right."

"I don't think so," Garret said carefully.

"And in any case, why should I alienate Papa by trying to foist on him someone he wants no part of? I would only be doing both you and myself a disservice."

Garret looked at her intently, his eyes narrowing. "You may be doing yourself a disservice not to try."

"What do you mean?"

One corner of his mouth lifted. "Nothing. Only, let's suppose that there was a secret which we two shared. You and I against the rest of the world. Maybe one other person somewhere, too, but he's not involved in this."

Damaris felt the blood leave her face. She gripped the arms

of her chair, fingernails digging into the cloth. "I don't have the slightest idea what you are talking about."

"It's just a supposition," Garret purred. "Let's just pretend that there was something we two wanted at all costs to keep the world from knowing. In a case like that, wouldn't it behoove you to be a friend to me?"

"I cannot imagine any secret on this earth which the two of us would share. Really, Uncle Garret, you must have been dipping into the Kentucky whiskey again. Now, if you'll excuse me, I really must get downstairs."

She was already at the door when he spoke sharply again. "I understand Ethan and our dear Corrine may come back to Mount Pleasant to live."

Damaris paused, momentarily paralyzed.

"How lovely for us all. Who knows, perhaps they will end up living here at Southernwood as you and Wesley did. Then we'd all be under the same roof. One big, happy family . . ."

She heard no more. Running from the room, she dashed down the stairs and into the front hall. She paused there for a moment, listening to the sounds of laughter coming from the back parlor, where her parents and Wesley were waiting for her. Then she threw open the door and walked into the welcoming warmth and light.

At least company would keep her from thinking. She'd think about Uncle Garret later in the dark and quiet of her bedroom. Somehow that suited him more.

🌹 *Twenty-three*

AFTER WORRYING long and hard about her uncle's veiled threat, Damaris finally came to the conclusion that the best thing for her to do was to withdraw quietly from all associations with Deveroe Enterprises. It was not an easy decision to make or carry out. She felt like a bird poised for flight who suddenly had its wings clipped. Deep within her she knew she could help her father and perhaps contribute something very special to her family's future. She was certain she had talents and abilities as yet undeveloped. Now they would have to shrivel and die, never seeing the sun. Now she would have to content herself with running a house and caring for a family and somehow find satisfaction within those limitations.

Hard as it was, she was determined to do it. Uncle Garret certainly suspected there was something between Ethan and herself, and after all this time she could only surmise she had spoken her question aloud that Christmas Day before Freddy's

birth. Garret's devious, fertile mind would fly with such a
suggestion and it would never be possible to deceive him or
convince him he was wrong. Furthermore, though she did not
understand the origins of the bitterness between her parents
and Garret, she could not ignore its depth of feeling. It would
be useless to attempt to convince them that it was better to use
Garret than to allow him to decay. And, considering the fact
that he had already tried to blackmail her, perhaps they were
right.

She did not announce her decision to Garret or in any way
indicate that she even remembered their conversation. She simply lost interest in the business, pretending to become engrossed
with a new Ladies' Commission Committee to enlarge the
Campwoods meeting grounds and plan a series of Great Revival
meetings there. Her father shrugged and muttered that it was
no more than he had expected, while her husband seemed
relieved that she had more time for Freddy. But her mother
was more difficult.

"It shows a decided lack of character, Damaris, to be flighty
and shallow in one's interests," Emily chided her. "Part of
maturity is the ability to see something through."

"Oh, Mother, please don't lecture me."

Emily made a clucking noise and shook her head. "I expected better of you. You have a keen mind and good instincts.
I could see you at Fade's right hand, even groomed to take his
place. What a victory that would be for women everywhere."

"That was your hope, never mine."

"Nevertheless, I am very disappointed in you. I have to say
it. Very disappointed indeed."

Damaris bore her mother's censure with bad grace, feeling
so keenly her own loss. Yet as the months went by, she was
more concerned with Garret's reaction. She avoided him almost
to the point of rudeness until she realized one day that he was
laughing at her and had no intention of seeking her out. After
that she breathed a little easier. She was not sure whether he
had backed away from his threat because he realized she no
longer had any influence on the business or because when it
came right down to it all he really had were some nasty suspicions. But it did not matter. All that mattered was that he
left her alone.

When Emily found a small, neat house in the village for
Garret, Damaris was filled with relief and expected that her

life would now fall back into its usual dullness. Then, all within the space of a week, they received word that Ethan and Corrine were coming back to Westchester and, at Corrine's insistence, hoped to live at Southernwood until they decided where to settle next, and Uncle Garret found some impossible inconvenience in his new house that made it absolutely untenable.

"Why couldn't Corrine take the house in the village?" Damaris suggested cautiously to her mother. "If it was so perfect for Uncle Garret, why shouldn't it do for them? They'd still be very close."

Emily barely paused in her work of counting and stacking the patchwork counterpanes she had removed from the press. "Why, I couldn't suggest such a thing. Corrine wants to come home, and I want her here. I'm just glad Ethan does not object to living with his in-laws."

"She could still see you every day. And how do you think Gabrielle Slade is going to feel about both her sons living at Southernwood?"

"That is the least of my worries." Putting down a pile of neatly folded quilts, she turned to face her daughter. "I didn't want to tell anyone this, but perhaps you at least should know. Corrine has just suffered her second miscarriage. She was only two or three months along, but she is dreadfully disappointed and depressed. She needs her mother at a time like this."

"You just want to baby her!"

"Damaris, you have a healthy son. You ought to be more understanding of Corrine's feelings. Besides, Garret says that house has dry rot."

"You always babied her!"

"She never had your strong constitution. You ought to be ashamed of yourself, Damaris, begrudging your sister the comfort of a place in her own home. Especially when you have so much."

Feeling thoroughly guilty, Damaris turned away and busied herself refolding the light blankets. How she wished she could tell her mother that although she did feel pity for Corrine, the order of her life would be threatened by the presence of her sister and brother-in-law in the same house. The thought of Ethan so near, of Freddy more a Slade every day of his life, and suspicious Uncle Garret hoping for some small sign that would betray them—it was too much. If only she had been able to stay involved in the business she might have kept busy and preoccupied. But she had been denied even that.

It was just too much.

When Wesley had to journey across the county to inspect some
boundary problems near Purdy's Station two weeks later, Damaris went with him, ostensibly for the ride but actually to see
firsthand how Jesse was managing the nearby milk factory.
During the week they were gone, Wesley was kept busy searching titles and walking boundaries while Damaris immersed
herself in learning all the minutiae of processing and shipping
milk. She found Jesse a willing teacher, eager to help her learn
the details he had mastered so well. Damaris had the consolation
of knowing that at least Jesse's life had been greatly enhanced
by her idea of placing him in charge of the newly acquired
farm and factory. Over the years he had learned to compensate
for his missing leg and hand with a crutch and an iron hook,
and he managed to be everywhere and know everything that
was going on. Quickly familiarizing himself with the intricacies
of raising dairy cattle and keeping them healthy, he had made
it his business to learn all he could about the new processes of
containing milk and shipping it by rail into New York. Already
the factory was turning a profit. Jesse's life had been further
enhanced by his having had the good fortune to meet and marry
a quiet, unassuming girl, daughter of the man who owned the
adjacent farm, who saw his worth at once and did not hold his
deficiencies against him. Damaris thought she had not seen
Jesse look so contented since that long-ago day when he marched
off to sign up with the New York Seventeenth Volunteers.

Ethan and Corrine arrived at Southernwood during the week
she and Wesley were gone. Damaris arrived home to find them
both very quiet and withdrawn. Ethan, particularly, barely spoke
to her, or anyone else for that matter. He was up early and
gone most of the day, and Damaris saw so little of him that
she decided there would be no problem after all in having him
around. Corrine seemed terribly sad and depressed, but Damaris put that down to her recent loss. Certainly she had never
known anyone who wanted a baby so badly. It was a shame,
really, yet not something to go into the depths over. Corrine
was very young and still had lots of time to have a family.

As large as Southernwood was, with three families living
under its roof, it seemed to grow smaller every day. The first
week they were all together, they were scrupulously polite and

thoughtful. By the end of the second week, tempers flared on occasion but were generally held in rigid control. During the third week, the undercurrents of anger and tension began bubbling to the surface more and more often.

Ethan maintained an icy politeness with the family but went out nearly every evening to visit friends or one of the taverns in the village. Damaris, while relieved to find that she was rarely thrown into contact with her brother-in-law—indeed he had barely said more than ten words since his arrival—struggled to keep her temper down whenever her mother launched into a lecture on how she was raising her son the wrong way. Wesley was his usual good-tempered self, yet instead of helping matters, his pleasantness only served to make his wife wonder if he was not a rather shallow person. Emily, who had so looked forward to having all her children together under one roof, soon found that her ideas on how they should conduct themselves were not going to be kindly accepted. She was particularly disappointed by Ethan, who pointedly ignored every suggestion she made concerning his future. And she had made several, all of which she knew to be excellent.

"I cannot understand why Ethan doesn't pursue that partnership with Dr. Meade in Tarrytown," she said to Fade one night. "I've already sounded the gentleman out and I know he would consider it favorably. It is such a fine opportunity."

"Perhaps he wants to make his own plans. Meade is a country doctor in many ways, while Ethan, with his war experiences, must be far beyond him. Besides, I can't see Ethan being happy living in a backwater town like Tarrytown for the rest of his life. He has larger ambitions. He always did."

Emily pulled the brush through her long hair, staring not at her own reflection in the mirror but at her husband's. "Corrine would love it and surely that should count for something. And the area needs a good, knowledgeable young physician who knows all about the newer techniques. Our own Dr. Sayre still refuses to give chloroform to women in childbirth. Mary Ackerman was in labor nearly thirteen hours while he stood over her saying it was better to be awake and suffer through it. Too bad he can't have the experience and see for himself! Fade, are you listening to me?"

Her husband looked up at her over the edge of the report he was leafing through. "I've heard every word."

Swiveling on the chair, she turned and looked at him directly. "Then help me to persuade Ethan. Talk to him yourself. Make him see what a pleasant future this would mean for all of us."

Fade smiled at her, thinking what a handsome woman she was for all her years. As always, Emily was never so vibrant and animated as when she was planning someone else's life.

"No. He must decide for himself."

"But—"

"Let the boy alone, Emily."

She knew that tone of voice. Turning back to her mirror, she gave up any hope for help from him. She'd simply have to find a way to convince Ethan herself.

The very next day Emily made a point of pulling Damaris aside for a quiet conversation.

"I'm very worried about Corrine," she started.

"Why? She seems fine to me."

"Then you haven't used your eyes. She mopes around in a blue melancholy, barely saying a word to anyone. And she's lost weight and is terribly pale. I don't know what to think."

"Now, Mother, you said yourself she was bitterly disappointed about losing her baby. Give her time to get over it."

Emily twisted her ring, a sure sign of preoccupation. "It's more than that, I just know. I think she fears that Ethan will take her away again now that she has come home. He has this wonderful opportunity to begin a practice here in the next village, but he won't even consider it. Talk to him, Damaris."

"No! That I refuse to do. Ask Wesley to talk to him—he's his brother."

"But the two of you were always so close."

Damaris carefully avoided looking at her mother. "That was long ago, Mother, and is certainly not true anymore. Besides, I don't think you should attempt to influence Ethan. He won't appreciate it and you'll only drive him to do exactly the opposite of what you want."

There was some truth in that, Emily realized. "Very well then, talk to Corrine. I want her nearby so I can care for her. I'm truly worried about that girl's health, Damaris, and the thought that he might take her far away again is almost more than I can bear. Promise me you'll talk to her, please."

"Oh, very well, although I really don't think she'll tell me anything she hasn't told you. We are not that close anymore either."

Yet as it turned out, it was not her sister with whom Damaris broached the subject but Ethan. She had no wish to talk to him at all, but one rainy afternoon as she was putting on her waterproof cloak to go to the village for a Ladies' Planning Commission meeting, she looked up to see him descending the stairs wearing his greatcoat and a tall black hat. When he found out where she was headed and offered to drive her, she did not refuse, telling herself that one break in the careful distance she had set between them could not do much damage. And, after all, her mother had asked her to speak to him.

It was clammy and damp inside the chaise and the soft rain was barely audible on the calash roof. They rode in silence for so long that Damaris began to think Ethan was no more eager to talk to her than she to him. Mentally she went over the sentences she could use to open a conversation devoted solely to Emily's request, and yet the first thing she said startled her almost as much as him.

"Ethan, have you been avoiding me since you came home?"

He turned toward her and gave her a long look, then said, "Yes, now that you ask."

Damaris lowered her gaze in embarrassment. "It's not necessary. We all live under the same roof, temporarily at least, and we are all adults. Can we not be friends as we once were?"

When he did not answer, she muttered, "I want you to enjoy your stay . . ." then, thinking how foolish that sounded, added, "that is, I am perfectly contented now and I assure you I hold nothing against you."

"How very kind."

"You needn't be sarcastic!"

"Look, Damaris. You told me very firmly that the past was dead and you'd prefer me to respect that. I'm only trying to carry out your wishes. Can't we leave it at that?"

"Well, yes, but—"

"Am I to gather that you've changed your mind?"

"Of course not. It's just that—"

"Very well, then. Where would you like to be set down? At Barlow's or Tompkinson's?"

"Neither. Talcott's Hall will be fine. That's where we hold our meetings."

"You really ought to try to get Corrine interested in your revival plans. She needs something to occupy her mind."

Feeling thoroughly put down, Damaris did not reply and both of them sat in silence for the rest of the ride. During the meeting Damaris struggled to try to keep Ethan out of her thoughts. Rather than disrupting her life, he was sincerely trying to abide by her wishes, and in doing so was showing more integrity than she had ever given him credit for. She ought to be happy, but instead she was upset. Why this brooding sadness, this feeling of loss?

Suddenly she understood. She had wanted to be the one to turn her back on him. Instead it was he who was giving her up. And that was much harder to bear!

To Damaris's surprise, Corrine readily accepted her invitation to join the Ladies' Planning Commission committee. Corrine herself was at a loss to explain her sudden attraction right now to any kind of religious activity. Perhaps, she hoped, by serving God in some small way she might gain something of His comfort and help for herself. So she began accompanying Damaris into the village several times a week, making placards and posters, collecting linens and extra clothes for those families who were staying overnight, arranging kitchen schedules, planning extra programs for the younger children, and even playing the piano for the church choir rehearsals.

Damaris congratulated herself on her good work until she went searching for Corrine one afternoon only to find her sister sitting in a small, secluded private chapel. Corrine was bent over in her chair and Damaris assumed she was praying. But when she laid her hand lightly on her sister's shoulder to break her repose, Corrine turned a white face toward her and Damaris was startled to see huge tears spilling from her red and swollen eyes.

"Why, Corrine, what is the matter?"

"Nothing. It's nothing!"

Damaris, her heart full with pity, hugged her sister close. To her surprise Corrine did not pull away but rested against her, giving way to deep sobs.

"My poor dear," Damaris murmured. "What could have hurt you so? It will be all right. You'll have other children. I just feel it in my bones."

"It's not that," Corrine sobbed. "It's Ethan. I don't know

what to do, Damaris. I just don't know what to do."

"Ethan!" Damaris stiffened, suddenly wishing to hear nothing more. But the words came pouring forth along with Corrine's tears, both having been held back for so long and now finding release.

"He hates me! He's sorry he ever married me! I thought I could make him happy. I tried to give him the children he wants so badly. If I can't even do that, he has no reason to care for me."

"Corrine, this is nonsense. Ethan is a doctor. I'm sure he understands that it's not your fault about the babies. You're his wife and he loves you."

"No, no. He doesn't like me at all. I'm not witty or vivacious like other women. I'm not even pretty. I don't blame him for . . . I don't blame him!"

A chill clutched at Damaris's heart. "Blame him for what?"

"For turning to that other woman. She was so attractive and so full of charm. Everything I'm not."

Gripping her sister's shoulders, Damaris sat her down and looked deep into her eyes. "What are you saying, Corrine? That Ethan became involved with another woman? Who was it? A prostitute? If it was, that is not so unusual. Men do it all the time."

Corrine pulled out a handkerchief and wiped her eyes. "Not a prostitute. It was a woman we knew in Washington. Her husband was on the hospital board and she was Ethan's patient. We had been to her house many times. I don't know when the affair started, but eventually everyone in the city knew about it. I was so ashamed I stopped going out in the street, afraid to look our friends in the eye. It was terrible!"

"How dare he! The least he could have done was to be discreet!"

"I think he tried, but it went on for so long and she was so brazen about it. I tried to tell myself that he had found something with her I couldn't give him but, Damaris, I never knew what it was! If only I did, perhaps I could . . ."

Her sobs overcame her and she fell into her sister's arms again. Damaris held her comfortingly, all the while wishing she could strangle Ethan for hurting her gentle sister so badly. He was nothing but a roué! That was all he had ever been.

"What should I do, Damaris?" Corrine whispered, trying

valiantly to stem her tears. "I pray for God's guidance but answers never come and I don't know what to do."

Fighting down her own distaste and anger, Damaris searched for the right thing to say. "You don't have to do anything. After all, he came home with you, didn't he? That shows some kind of loyalty on his part. And one affair, horrible as it may have been, is better than running around with women all over the place. Ethan was probably infatuated. This woman was probably a temptress who could draw any man into her net. You never had a chance against her, Corrine, nor would I or any other respectable woman." *But I would have torn half her hair from her head and enjoyed doing it.*

"Do you really think so?"

"I'm certain of it," Damaris said soothingly. "I am sure Ethan loves you and feels very badly about what happened. When you have that baby you want so much he'll see more clearly the error of his ways. Now dry your eyes or Mother will surely know you've been crying and she will not rest until you tell her everything."

"I don't want to do that. I'm too ashamed. I didn't even want you to know."

"Well, you have to share your troubles with someone or you'll go crazy. Come on now. Let's go home."

Suddenly Corrine threw her arms around Damaris and hugged her warmly. "Oh, I wish I had your strength. You handle things so well."

I don't! I don't, she wanted to scream. But she said nothing and returned her sister's hug. Even as she wanted to strangle Ethan Slade, the thought of him with another woman, a stranger and a temptress, was like a knife through her heart.

"I do think Ethan could have used better judgment," she said angrily to her husband that evening in the privacy of her bedroom. "I shall never forgive him for hurting Corrine."

Wesley walked in from his dressing room, pulling at his blue satin tie. "My dear, you must know by now that Ethan has no self-control when it comes to satisfying his whims. He never did. However," he added, stepping back into the room, "in all fairness I must say women always made it very easy for him. I fancy if I had half his appeal and half the temptations he has had, I might do the same."

"That's not true," Damaris said, flouncing into the chair

before her dressing table, her silk negligee swirling around her ankles. "You would never treat me like that, you know you wouldn't."

Wesley walked over to her and kissed her shoulder lightly. "That's because I had the good fortune to win the only woman I ever really wanted. Ethan's trouble is he never wanted anyone that much."

"Don't make excuses for him, Wes. He's behaved like the worst kind of cad. Can't you talk some sense into him—make him see the proper way to behave?"

"No! I can't and I won't. Blast these cuff links. I can never get them unfastened. I told you last Christmas you should have taken them back. Shoddy work, that's what it is."

"Here, let me do it." She concentrated on the gold pins in silence, finally working them loose. "There. Now the other one."

"Try not to worry about Ethan and Corrine," Wesley said in a gentle tone. "They must work out their own lives. Ethan has many fine qualities, but he was always so attractive and lively that he learned right from the cradle he could have his own way with very little effort. I don't think it has made him a better person or a happier one, but it is far too late now for him to learn anything different."

Damaris sat back and looked up at him. "Oh, Wesley, you are too understanding by far. What Ethan needs is a good caning, and the way he's going some outraged husband is certain to give it to him. I should like to do it myself."

"What's the use of discussing it?" Wesley said testily, returning to the dressing room. "Let them work it out."

"You always defend him because he's your brother. Why won't you admit he's wrong?"

"Why does it bother you so much? Give Corrine all the support and sympathy you can, and leave the rest to the two of them. Really, Damaris, it is an unpleasant subject and I'd prefer to drop it."

"It won't go away just because you sweep it under the rug!"

How he wished Corrine had never confided in his wife. He hated these scenes. Damaris always got herself upset, then wound up by making him feel it was all his fault. He did not understand Ethan and never had, but why should his brother's actions upset his life?

Damaris heard the door close and realized that Wesley had

gone into his adjoining bedroom, shutting her out. With an exclamation, she turned in the chair and found herself staring at her own reflection in the gilt mirror: angry eyes, downturned mouth, and dark lines of contention on either side of her nose, etched down and out toward her chin. She looked and felt ten years older than she had that morning. Dropping her head into her hands, she fought to understand why she was so angry. For Corrine? Yes, but that was not the whole of it. At Wesley for refusing to face the gravity of Ethan's conduct? Yes, but Wesley's optimistic view of people often aggravated her. At Ethan for marrying her sister only to betray her? Yes, but that was no surprise. The two of them were never really suited and people don't change that easily.

Raising her head she looked once again at her dark eyes. The truth was she felt Ethan had betrayed *her* in turning to that woman. If he was going to go behind Corrine's back it should be to her he turned, and no one else. The thought of him in some other woman's arms stirred into life feelings she had thought were dead. Damn him! Why did he have to come back!

This would not do. Opening her robe so that the lacy edge of her gown exposed the curve of her breasts, she turned down the gas lamp and went to knock softly at Wesley's door. She would be gentle and pliant, and she would spend the night in her husband's arms. And she would squeeze every thought of Ethan Slade from her mind if it was the last thing she did.

Her efforts worked that night, but as the days went by she grew more and more convinced that for every small victory there were two setbacks. She didn't speak to Ethan, barely looked at him, and made sure they were never alone together. Since he made no effort to seek her out, this was not difficult to do. The problem was trying to control her own thoughts and emotions, and Ethan intruded far too much on those.

However, as the week of the Great Revival drew near it became easier to forget him in the press of activities. The well-known evangelist Reverend Albert Winston Littlefield had been booked to lead a week of prayer meetings and Bible study, and interest in the revival was so great that a record crowd was expected.

On the Tuesday afternoon before the first meeting, which was to be on Friday night, Damaris was counting linens in the utility closet at the campground when Ethan appeared and asked her if she knew where Corrine was.

"She was helping Winnifred in the kitchen, but it is possible she went with Mrs. Oakley into the village for more supplies," Damaris said, taken aback. "In any event, she ought to be back soon. Why don't you wait there?"

He made to leave but then stopped, looking at her intently with a wry smile. "What a sight you are! Your hair straggling in every direction under that cap, that huge apron pinned up over your skirt. All you need is a broom in your hand to make Cinderella!"

Embarrassed, Damaris smoothed down her skirt. "Well, we've all been working. What do you expect?"

To her dismay he leaned against the door frame and folded his hands over his chest, prepared to stay. "The comical thing is that none of you would think of doing these things in your own home. But here, in this rustic, flea-ridden, primitive outpost you work like Trojans. All for the Lord, I suppose."

She reached down for a stack of towels on the floor. "It is not flea-ridden! There's not a surface in the place that hasn't been scrubbed with carbolic acid."

"It's still primitive," he answered, looking around. "Why do you do it, Damaris? You never struck me as the religious type. Have you been touched by the flame?"

Scowling, she placed the towels on a shelf and began sorting through them. "Perhaps I've changed," she muttered.

"Not that much."

His eyes seemed to look right through her. In the confines of the closet, she could feel the current of physical longing between them. Unconsciously she moved away against the back wall.

"The revival is sponsored by St. Paul's, as well as the other churches in town," she said briskly, "and the Ladies' Commission offered to help. Besides, I've heard Reverend Littlefield is a great preacher. We expect many souls to be saved under his influence."

"Are you suggesting I should come?"

She flushed at the irony in his voice but there was a mischievous glint in the look she gave him.

"Well, I'll say this for the place," Ethan went on, "it's very beautiful and a wonderful romp for children. When I came up

I found Freddy racing across the grass, laughing like a little leprechaun. Nothing would do but I must give him a ride on my shoulders. I indulge him too much, I'm sure."

"He's fond of you," Damaris murmured.

"Yes, I like to fancy he is. And he helped put me in a better humor, at least. When I left the house I was ready to strangle your mother, but now I think I can go back and face her with only a little less grace than usual."

Damaris moved a stack of neatly folded towels to the shelf above. "What's she done now?" she asked absently.

"Invited Dr. Meade for tea, on the provision that I be there too. I guess she thought if she threw us together I'd be so enthralled by his boring tales of small-town physic that I'd immediately agree to throw in my lot with him. I used to think Emily had better sense."

"It's only because she wants the two of you to stay nearby," Damaris said lamely. "Try to see her point of view."

"It's because she likes to order the lives of everyone around her!" Ethan said bitterly. "Well, she shan't manage mine, and the sooner she realizes it the better! I've already written to the Pennsylvania Hospital in Philadelphia and am waiting now to hear their reply. It's a long shot, but if they want me I will certainly go."

She looked up sharply. "How does Corrine feel?"

"Corrine wants what I want."

"Oh . . ."

The towels she held slipped from her hands and fell to the floor. "Here, let me," Ethan said, springing to retrieve the linens and shaking them back into some kind of order before holding them out to her. The touch of his strong fingers on her arm as she reached for them was like an electric shock coursing through her body.

"Thank you," she muttered.

Stepping back, he picked up the whip he had thrown down. "Well, I must go find Corrine. Don't work too hard."

He was nearly through the door by the time she spoke. "Ethan!"

Turning, he waited.

"Be patient with Mother. She means well."

"Yes. I'll try to remember that."

Then he was gone, leaving her in a state of confusion and distress.

A few minutes later Freddy came running to her, out of breath and with his clothes delightfully disheveled. "Mama, Uncle Ethan gave me a ride on his shoulders all the way across to the brook!" he cried, his eyes alight with pleasure. "Now he wants me to ride back in the gig with him and Aunt Corrine. Can I, Mama, please?"

"No. I want you to stay here and go back with me. You'll see Uncle Ethan later at supper."

"Oh, please, Mama. He even said he'd let me take the reins and drive Darcy. Please, Mama, *please!*"

Damaris smoothed the hair back from his face. Why not? It was foolish to resent the affection her son felt for Ethan. If he and Corrine were really going to move to Philadelphia, it would not matter for much longer anyway.

"All right, my love. Go ahead."

"Oh, goody," Freddy cried, and went flying off without a backward glance. Damaris stepped to the door just in time to see Ethan sweep Freddy up over his head before depositing him into the carriage.

Let them go soon, please God. Let them go soon.

In the days that followed, Damaris found that even the feverish last-minute preparations for the revival could not clear her mind of her own obsessions. The more she tried to forget about Ethan, the more he was in her thoughts. Something had been unleashed by the strong current of physical attraction that had passed between them at the campground, and to her consternation, she found that every time he was around she longed to reach out and touch him; she ached to have him take her in his arms. At first she told herself this was the last thing she wanted and it was only some perversity of hers that made her torment herself with thoughts of Ethan. But finally she faced the terrible truth: she wanted this man.

It was wrong, it was horrible, it devastated her pride and her integrity, but it was true. He had a lure she was unable to ignore and the fact that she knew he was unfaithful to her sister, rather than causing her to turn away in disgust, had only enhanced his attractiveness. What was wrong with her anyway? Was she simply an evil person? Did she lack character or moral fiber? Was Ethan a sickness she was just too weak to resist, or was he the great passion of her life? Certainly there was more of passion than love in her feelings for him, and with each passing day she grew less able to deny it. She became nervous and preoccupied, with dark half moons under her eyes, and both her parents and her husband began to worry about her health.

"You never smile anymore," Wesley commented, trying to mask his concern with a casual tone. "You've been working too hard on this blasted revival. I'll be glad when it's over and perhaps we can get away for a few days. It would do you good."

Damaris shrugged and drew her misery more closely around her, shutting out everyone. How she was going to occupy her time once the Great Revival was over she couldn't imagine. But she would find something. She'd have to.

Reverend Littlefield arrived in Sing Sing on Friday afternoon.

"He's very small, isn't he?" Winnifred whispered to Damaris and Corrine as they stood together among the crowd waiting to welcome the famous evangelist. "I thought he'd be a big man."

"He has a big reputation," Damaris whispered back, "and that is what we need to make this week a success."

As soon as he stepped on the deck, they learned that what Albert Littlefield lacked in stature he more than made up for in imposing looks and a booming voice. With a barrel chest and a large head, bald at the top but overgrown with white sideburns and whiskers and a fringe of longish strands at the back, his most striking features were a pair of faded blue eyes that reflected the piercing intensity of the mind behind them. Nature had given him such a resonant baritone that it was impossible for him to render the smallest, most inconsequential observation without drawing the attention of everyone around him.

"My brethren," he boomed, gesturing with his arms to include the whole of the village in his embrace, "in the joy of the Lord, I greet you all!"

Having at first quaked a little at his fierce Old Testament visage, Damaris quickly realized that when he relaxed into a smile, his features softened and warmed. There was joy in him as well as seriousness, and as she stepped forward, one of several prominent citizens to take his warm handclasp, Damaris began to feel that the Great Revival was sure to be an outstanding success.

This year, with the planning that the women had put into the revival, and with the dynamic presence of Albert Littlefield promising a special kind of program, the Whitman and Slade families, with the exception of Ethan, decided to stay at the campground rather than travel from their homes every day, as they had in past years. The program, which began at 6:00 A.M. with early morning prayer and did not draw to a close until the end of the nightly revival near 11:00 P.M., was so full in between that they would have spent most of their time there anyway.

The ten-by-twelve tent, sectioned off into a small sitting room in the front, a bedroom with cots, men on one side and women and children on the other, and a small area at the rear where an iron cookstove stood on a wooden platform, was certainly more crowded than anything this family was accustomed to. But when the section flaps were rolled up during the day to throw open the whole tent, it presented an airy, pleasing appearance.

For Freddy, the entire excursion was a lark. For Fade and Wesley it was a welcome change from the routine of their working lives and a pleasant opportunity for visiting with friends. Fade saw more of his own family during these two-week meetings than at any other time of the year. The women were kept busy with the business of trying to accommodate a huge crowd of people smoothly and efficiently. Corrine, who was on the committee handling the restaurant tent, was constantly occupied, and by the third day Emily had dropped her other concerns in order to help her. Because the largest part of her job was finished once the families were settled in, Damaris had the most free time. She attended the constant prayer meetings and Bible classes with fervor, hoping to find release there from the constant clamor of her own emotions, but the wonderful old gospel hymns she had sung since childhood only served to reinforce her feelings of guilt for desiring her sister's husband and not appreciating her own. Moreover, Reverend Littlefield's thundering word, rather than comforting her, seemed to hammer home the need for black hearts to be washed in the blood of the lamb. Every night at the evening revival she watched as people came forward to be counted among the faithful who had thrown off their coils of sin and turned to a new way. It was with sadness that Damaris realized she could not join them, that she did not want to throw off her obsession with Ethan.

One balmy evening when the two weeks were nearly over,

Damaris rose with the congregation to sing the familiar words of the sermon hymn. It was a rousing old song that seemed to speak especially to her since the whole of her life had been spent along the banks of the beautiful Hudson:

> "In that far off sweet forever,
>   Just beyond the shining river,
>   When they ring those golden bells for you and me..."

Her voice rang out clear and pure as the words of the song filled the tent, a plaintive lament for some perfect home. The music ended and, feeling some contentment, she resumed her chair. A man suddenly appeared, taking the empty seat next to her, and with a start of surprise she saw that it was Ethan. She had only encountered him briefly once or twice during the past week and she thought she had her feelings for him under firm control. Now, however, she found she could barely keep her mind on Reverend Littlefield's impassioned words, so conscious was she of his physical presence. When the sermon finally ended and the crowd rose to sing again, Ethan shared her book, holding the page in one hand, leaning toward her as he peered down at the fine print. But this time there was no consoling hymn about a life to come. It was deadly:

"Yield not to temptation, for yielding is sin," they sang, while Damaris tried fiercely to concentrate on the words.

> "Each victory will help you, some other to win;
>   Fight manfully onward, dark passions subdue,
>   Look ever to Jesus, He'll carry you through."

The voices around her carried forward swells of feeling. Damaris glanced up at Ethan and met his gaze. A devilish grin pulled at the corners of his mouth, and she blushed and hurriedly looked away.

> "Ask the Savior to help you,
>   He is willing to aid you, He'll carry you through."

They sat down and he was so close that she could feel his arm brushing against her sleeve. His hand lay on his knee, and she stared at the long fingers, the thin scattering of hairs under his cuff. She longed to reach out and grasp it and place it on her breast. Like a searing shaft of light she suddenly knew that she wanted this man more than anything else on earth and that all her efforts to deny it were a mockery. And, what was worse, she was going to have him if it cost her everything else she loved.

Such a terrible realization! She swayed, reeling forward so that Ethan had to reach out and catch her to keep her from falling. For a few moments she leaned against him, feeling the strength of his arms.

Damaris lay awake most of the night, tossing around on her cot as though it were a bed of nettles. The next morning she drew Wesley aside.

"Did you mean it when you said we could go away once the meeting is over? Because I would like to take a trip. A long trip, just the two of us."

"Of course, Damaris. You've worked entirely too hard on this revival. Ethan told me you nearly fainted last evening at the prayer meeting. A trip will do you good."

"Can we go really far, Wes? I thought I'd like to see something of the deep south. Florida, perhaps."

"The south is still in poor condition and I doubt if we'd be made welcome there. Feelings still run very strong, you know."

"But not in Florida—it was barely touched by the war. I hear people are moving to it in great hordes, homesteading land that just a few years ago belonged to the Indians and the alligators. It sounds so exotic and different. I'd love to see it."

"It's very far. I had thought something closer. Boston, perhaps. Or one of the western cities."

Those were too close. Slipping her hand through his arm, Damaris leaned against him, pouting ever so slightly. "I had my heart set on Florida. Please, Wes."

He smiled down at her and patted her hand. "If that is what you want, that is what it shall be. But we'd better bring plenty of netting!"

She was satisfied. Florida was a long trip away and a long trip back, with any number of places to visit in between. It would be new and different and perhaps it would take her mind off her problems and help her regain her equilibrium. It was certainly better than staying here, where she knew she could not win the battle to leave Ethan alone.

"Thank you, Wes," she said gratefully. "You're very good to me."

"When would you like to leave?"

"Right away. The sooner the better."

🌸 *Twenty-four*

THEY JOURNEYED south to a land scarred by war and reeling under economic devastation. Traveling by railroad to Baltimore, they went from there to Gettysburg, where they took time to wander around the battlefield, trying to imagine where Ethan had lain wounded and where Corrine's hospital tents had been set up. The railroads south of Washington were still undependable, and it was with difficulty that they continued down the coast aboard a variety of hired chaises, steamboats, and an occasional stage.

It was a relief to reach Charleston after a trip along the bad roads of the Carolinas, where weeds choked fields that would once have been white with cotton, grim testimony to the war's destruction. Wesley wanted to linger in the town, but Damaris had her heart set on Florida so they pressed on, traveling by boat to Savannah and from there to St. Augustine.

This old city was like a different world. Although Florida had been one of the Confederate states, it had escaped most of the ravages of war and the natural beauty of its unusual landscape could still be enjoyed. Damaris found the city of St. Augustine a fascinating blend of Spanish and English cultures, so different from any place she had ever seen before that she wandered gawking through its narrow streets and old fort. Before the war Florida had been well on its way to developing the same kind of plantation-centered, cotton-growing society as its neighbors to the north, but all that was changed now. Pensacola, far to the east, and Key West, far to the south, were its principal cities, but to venture on to either meant a long and difficult voyage, either across a wide swath of jungle wilderness or down six hundred miles of coastline. They were wondering whether or not to try either one when Wesley ran into a friend from New York in one of the local saloons and heard about Mrs. Harmon.

"Her husband owned Galatia, one of the largest plantations on the St. John's river. He was killed in the war and now, since her Negroes are dispersed and no crops in, she has begun opening her house to tourists. I was told she would gladly rent us a room for several weeks so we can get a good rest before starting home. What do you think?"

"I think it sounds wonderful. To tell you the truth, I'm a little tired of traveling. But are you sure you want to?"

Wesley lounged in his chair, absently waving a palmetto-leaf fan in front of his face. "Why not? After all, you're the one who has been dragging me around the country. I'd love to sit on a veranda and sip bourbon through a straw all day."

She smiled at this image since it was so unlike him. "Well, you never seemed to mind—"

"My dear," he interrupted, laughing, "I didn't mind. I told you this was your trip and I'm only along to escort you wherever you wish to go. The question now is whether you wish to go to Galatia."

Damaris moved to him, leaned down, and, slipping one arm around his neck, laid her cheek against his. "You've been so patient with me, Wesley, and I do appreciate it. If you think you won't be too bored, I'd love to go. We've found such poor hotels all along the way, perhaps this will be a pleasant stay for a change."

He reached up and stroked her other cheek. "Good. I'll see to the arrangements at once."

For Damaris, the days they spent at Galatia were like an exotic dream. It was a pleasant, rambling house set far up on the low banks of the St. John's River, surrounded by a lush growth of spreading live oaks dripping Spanish moss. Mrs. Harmon was a handsome woman who ministered to their comfort with southern gentility, even though underneath her gracious manner they could sense her embarrassment at having to receive payment for what it had once been her pleasure to offer free.

Their favorite pastime was to take a boat and spend long, slow hours exploring the river and its surrounding pine barrens, hammocks, and swamps. Wesley fished from the boat with exquisite leisure while Damaris searched the dark waters for glimpses of fish or maybe an alligator and watched the flight of flocks of egrets, ibis, and pale green wild parakeets. She was enthralled with the huge cypress trees, the palms and sweet gum, and the vivid tropical flowers. They ate with relish native dishes of sweet potatoes, rice, and pork, biscuits or cornpone, and grapefruit shortcake. They fought the mosquitoes and the heat, which, to their surprise, was truly terrible. Damaris, encased in petticoats, crinolines, corset, long sleeves, voluminous skirt, bonnets of ribbons and straw, stockings, and slippers often came near to fainting from heat prostration. She soon learned to retreat during the hottest part of the afternoon to her bed, where, with a minimum of clothing, a large palmetto fan, and a cool drink, she made it through until teatime. Nor were the insects easy to take. They flourished in the wild, warm, untamed climate and fought a perpetual battle with intrusive humans over who was going to survive. Most often, she felt, they won.

As their departure for the long trip home grew imminent, Damaris found that the sense of having existed in some world suspended apart from time and trouble was heightened. One sweltering evening they walked down to the river's edge to watch the crimson sun dip behind the dark rim of the forest and she was overcome by the beauty of it and a feeling of sadness that she must soon leave it forever.

"Will you be happy to go home, Wes?" she asked almost tentatively, for she wanted him to feel the same enchantment.

Wesley was too busy watching an eagle gliding above the blue-black treeline to notice her melancholy. "Oh yes, I suppose so," he answered absently. "It will be good to see Freddy again. I have to admit I won't miss this heat."

Damaris felt a little disappointed that he could see only the mundane when she was so filled with the magic of the place.

"It has been unusually hot today."

"Old Joseph says there's a storm coming."

"Now, how would he know?"

"He reads the signs. Mrs. Harmon says he is the best darky she knows for predicting the weather. He says that smoke refused to rise all day and the bats have been flying too close to the ground. Those are sure indications of a storm coming."

"Perhaps it won't break until after we've left."

They turned back to the house, where they joined the other guests on the veranda, sitting and talking long after night descended. The glow of the smudge pots on the lawn keeping the insects at bay glimmered like eyes in the black night, but the heat went on, enveloping them like a heavy blanket of air. Damaris felt drained and weary from the heat and the oppressive sadness of leaving, so she left Wesley to his visiting and went upstairs to bed. It was so hot that she peeled down to her shift, tossing restlessly under the netting.

She was awakened by the wind moaning eerily outside her window. The room was dark. She reached out with her hand and realized she was alone in the bed. The wild, cold air streaking through the open windows at first seemed refreshing after the heat of the day. But then the murmur of the wind crescendoed to a cry, then a shriek. Lightning crackled like flame and thunder came crashing down on the roof of the house like the roar of a battleground. In one sudden moment a sheet of rain unloosed its torrents over the house, spilling through the windows as the wind ripped the netting from its frame and snatched at the covers on the bed.

Where was Wesley? Running to the window, Damaris pulled frantically at the louvered shutters, but they eluded her grip. The rain soaked her light garments and fell in puddles at her bare feet. Fighting the strength of the wind, she managed to pull the shutters closed just as the door opened behind her and she caught a glimpse of Wesley, holding a candle in his hand. The candle was blown out immediately, but when he heard her call and saw her silhouetted in the lightning flash at the window, he threw it aside and hurried over to help. By then the worst of the storm was shut out, although they could still hear it beating against the house as if in a frenzy to enter.

Damaris had never been so glad to have her husband near. Throwing her arms around his neck, she strained against his body.

"Damaris, you're soaked," Wesley cried. "There's not a dry thread in that gown. Come here and let me get it off you."

Leading her to the bed, he began peeling the cloth from her wet shoulders. She clung to him wildly, all her senses heightened by the fury of the storm and her relief at having him near. He tore away the last of her wet shift and she pulled him down beside her.

"Don't leave me, Wes," she moaned, digging her fingers into his shoulders and twisting underneath his body. "Don't leave me."

"Never, my darling. I'll never leave you."

The storm raged as they turned and tossed on the damp bed, but they ceased to hear it.

The next morning the sun shone brightly on a pristine world where only the litter of broken branches across the lawn gave testimony to the violent storm. Damaris woke feeling warm and refreshed, stretched languidly, and leaned over to kiss her husband's shoulder before slipping out of bed. Wes stirred in his sleep as she replaced the light coverlet over him. Dressing quietly, she went downstairs and walked to the river's edge.

The memory of last night filled her with happiness. It had been a long time since either of them had allowed such intense feelings to sweep them away, and Damaris now realized it was something she had long needed. Perhaps that was the real reason Ethan haunted her as he did. Ethan always held the promise of heady excitement, while with Wes everything had become familiar and ordinary over the years. But now she knew it did not have to be so. They must simply work at having this experience more often. Then surely she would be able to break Ethan's hold over her mind and heart.

Her contentment lasted until the voyage home was half over, but then with each day it became more evident that her old problems were just waiting to haunt her in Westchester.

Had this long trip really accomplished anything, Damaris wondered as she stood on the deck of the schooner. For a little while it had drawn her closer to her husband, but now, as the thought of resuming their life at Southernwood grew more real, she felt in her bones that it was not going to be enough. She was grateful for Wesley's companionship and patience. But the excitement they'd shared the night of the storm had not been repeated and they had easily slipped back into their old comfortable, placid relationship. Her disappointment led her to dread the simple affectionate gestures her husband constantly bestowed upon her. She became rude and short with him, moody and more depressed with every wave that thrust them closer to the shores of the Hudson. And he bore all her unpleasantness with such stoicism that she ended up wanting to goad him into a rip-roaring tide of insults. She was ashamed of herself for treating this good man so shabbily, yet day by day she had less control over her reactions. Soon she would be home again, living under her mother's domination, facing Ethan every day, trying to force down the desire she felt for him. She knew she would not be able to deny her need much longer. She wanted Ethan and she knew of no way to drive that desire from her heart.

Neither confronting it or avoiding it had worked. Now she no longer cared about hurting Corrine or Wesley or about her good reputation. She was going to take what she wanted, and if she was lucky, perhaps once she did, she would discover she wanted it no more. That was her only hope.

"It has been such a comfort having Ethan and Corrine here all the while you were gone," Emily said to her eldest daughter, handing her a cup of tea across the table in the back parlor. Damaris looked around, thinking how familiar and dear the old room was with its heavy drapes and comfortable furniture, its polished wood and framed landscapes.

"Corrine was a treasure with Freddy. It's only because of her that he did not grieve for the two of you the whole time you were gone. And it did her good too. Wait until you see the change in her."

"When they weren't on the porch to meet us, I thought perhaps they had already moved to Philadelphia," Damaris said, stirring her tea laconically.

"No, Ethan drove her to the village for a meeting of the Ladies' Commission, but they should be back for supper. They have not decided what they want to do yet, and since Ethan has been helping one day a week at the dispensary, I have not given up hope that he will decide to stay. Wesley, you are looking very fit. Travel must agree with you."

Settling back on the sofa, Wesley laid his arm across the back, his fingers resting on Damaris's shoulder.

"Actually, I'm exhausted. Your daughter led me such a dance. We must go everywhere and see everything. It will take me a month to recover."

"You were just as enthusiastic as I," Damaris said irritably.

"I can see that it did you both good," Emily interceded. "Travel always does. I remember so well my trek westward when your father was so ill. I always hoped to go back, but somehow it hasn't happened."

Damaris, in the first flush of pleasure at returning to her well-loved home, could barely contain her eagerness to see Ethan again. That evening, when she walked into the dining room to find Corrine already at the table and Ethan standing behind her, the surge of feeling she experienced left her knees weak and trembling. Jumping up, Corrine threw her arms around her sister, giving Damaris a warm hug, while Ethan strode forward and placed a soft kiss on her cheek. Damaris only hoped her face had not betrayed her. During a meal interspersed with lively conversation about the trip, she stole many a glance across the table at her brother-in-law, drinking in every detail of his appearance. There was that same air of grudging tolerance about him that made her certain he was still only marking time in Westchester and had every intention of getting away eventually. He showed his restlessness in the way his dark eyes darted around the room and the manner in which he played with the food on his plate, consuming more wine than food. Even while she made an effort to carry her part of the conversation, Damaris's mind toyed with the delicious anticipation of being alone with him. Perhaps if she told him how she felt it would be enough. Then she saw Corrine's sad, preoccupied expression, her pale face bent over her plate, and shook herself. What was she thinking of! What kind of a person was she!

Damaris's hand wavered as she reached for her wineglass, nearly spilling it. Glancing up, she saw Uncle Garret watching her as though he were reading her thoughts, and a chill touched

her spirit. Hopeless as the attempt might be, she must try to
overcome this obsession. In the end she would be a better
person for it.

Her determination lasted until the next morning, when she
saw Ethan leaving the house and quickly decided she needed
to go into the village. The ride was pleasant and their conversation easier and more spirited than she would have expected.
She knew she was flirting with him and it was obvious he
realized it too. But he discreetly kept his distance and acted
the gentleman.

In the days that followed, Damaris's frustration grew. The
more she sought Ethan out, the more he seemed to avoid her.
The more she openly encouraged him, saying with her eyes
what she dared not speak aloud, the more distant he became.
Her conduct was so openly aggressive that she felt both Emily
and Garret watching her, and even Wesley began to make
guarded comments about her close friendship with her brother-
in-law. Yet not one gesture or inappropriate word passed between them and Damaris consoled herself with the thought that,
think what they may, she had done nothing wrong. Of course
that was more to Ethan's credit than her own, but it still left
her with the consolation that whatever her true desires, her
conduct was beyond reproach.

On a bright, crisp morning three weeks later Damaris was
standing at the door to the veranda buttoning Freddy's jacket
when Winnifred came bounding down the wide stairway in a
flurry of skirts and petticoats.

"Oh, going out, are you?"

"Yes," Damaris said. "Freddy wants to show me his pony."

"Mama is going to watch me ride," Freddy said, his eyes
alight with excitement. "You come too, Aunt Winnifred. I'm
very good. Mr. Rufus said I ride better even than Mama did
at my age."

"I shall have to speak to Mr. Rufus," Damaris replied,
fastening the last button on her son's brown velour riding coat.

"It's such a beautiful day I'd love a walk," Winnifred said.
"Just let me get my coat and I'll go along with you."

They set off down a path lined with crisp dried leaves,
Freddy bounding on ahead and the two sisters following se-
dately.

"He does ride well, you know," Winnifred commented, drinking in the clear air that was tinged with the autumn smell of apples and burning leaves. "Rufus told me that over the summer he improved marvelously. Last spring he was so frightened of the horses he screamed when they tried to place him in the saddle."

"All the same, five is very young to be riding a pony. I wish he had waited awhile."

"You can blame Ethan. The whole time you were gone he took him in hand, working with him every day, gentling him along until he got over his fear. After that, it was easy. Freddy dotes on his Uncle Ethan and wanted to please him."

Damaris pulled the ends of her shawl across her chest. "I haven't seen Ethan working with him since we got back."

Winnifred shrugged. "Well, he certainly did while you were away. Look at the apples on those trees. They seem nearly overwhelmed with fruit."

"It's a good harvest this year," Damaris replied lightly, her mind filled with an image of Ethan teaching her son to ride.

Winnifred waved her arms in a sudden burst of joy. "Oh, it is a good harvest. And a beautiful autumn. What a lovely place Southernwood is sometimes."

"You seem unusually enthusiastic," Damaris said, smiling at her sister. "And brimming to the ears with good feelings. I suspect there is a young man involved."

Winnifred chuckled, beaming. "That's true. Can I tell you a secret?"

"Please do."

"I'm engaged. Oh, no one knows it yet, not even Mother and Papa. But they will soon. And I'm so happy that sometimes I want to burst out singing and dance around all over the place!"

Winnifred's high spirits were infectious and Damaris found herself filled with happiness for her. "And who's the fortunate gentleman? Or can I know that yet?"

"Oh yes. You might as well, since before long everyone else will too. It's Claes Yancy."

Damaris was astonished. "Cousin Claes?"

"The same. Why do you say it like that? Don't you like him?"

"Why, of course I do. It's just that I seldom see him, he's away on his ships so much. And I never thought of him as the

romantic type somehow. He's just always been Cousin Claes.
I had no idea you two were so close."

"We've been good friends for a long time—like you and
Wesley were. But the last time he was home, well, he told me
he loved me and he... well, he kissed me, and oh, Damaris,
I knew right then and there it was him I loved. So we were
promised and now I've had a letter that he will be home next
month and he intends to speak to Papa. And I'm so happy I
can barely stand it!"

Damaris gave her sister a sidelong glance. Winnifred was
not an especially pretty girl. She was the only one of the sisters
to inherit the round plainness of the Whitman women rather
than the Deveroes' sleek good looks. But her lively spirit gave
her a vivaciousness and animation that lit up her ordinary face
and made her unusually appealing. Small wonder that Claes
was attracted to her, since he had always been shy and retiring.
Damaris only hoped that Winnifred knew her mind. It was not
always so good to rush into marriage with someone just because
you had grown up together and they were familiar and dear to
you. As Damaris cast about in her mind for a tactful way to
express this warning, she looked up to see Garret standing on
the walk ahead, obviously waiting for them.

"Oh dear," Winnifred muttered, spotting her uncle at the
same time. "It's too nice a day to have to deal with him. Let's
take the other path."

"Damaris my dear," Garret said in an unctuous voice, bearing down on them. "I've barely had a moment to see you since
you got back. How propitious to find you here."

"Too late," Damaris whispered to Winnifred. "We're on
our way to the stable, Uncle Garret," she said in a louder voice.
"Freddy is waiting for us."

"Well now, you won't mind if I walk along with you, will
you? Thought I'd try to get someone to drive me into town."

"No, of course not," she muttered as Garret fell in step
beside them.

"My goodness, look at that Freddy. He's already reached
the yard. I'd better go and catch him before he gets in the way
of the horses," Winnifred said, seizing the first excuse she
could find to escape. As the youngest of the girls she had always
seemed like a flighty child to her uncle and he had never even
tried to disguise his contempt for her. And now he had inter-

rupted her first joyous revelation of her engagement. In her dislike and annoyance she wanted only to get away from him and could spare not a shred of pity for her sister who was throwing her pleading looks.

"He'll be all right, I'm sure," Damaris said.

But Winnifred was already speeding ahead of them. "I'll just make sure," she called back over her shoulder, skipping down the path.

"That child is a flibbertigibbet," Garret groused. "She never walks, she runs. Like a steam engine going full blast all the time. She wears me out!"

"She's not a child any longer, Uncle Garret, in case you haven't noticed."

"She'll always be a child! Hasn't got half the sense her older sisters had at her age."

Damaris wondered at that, trying to remember when her uncle had ever shown any respect for her judgment. It was a long walk to the stable and they were not yet halfway there. She watched with dismay as Winnifred disappeared down the path and reluctantly slowed her step to match her uncle's sedate pace.

"I've been hoping to have a talk with you," Garret said.

An ominous chill began working its way through her breast. "It won't do you any good to ask me to speak to Papa. I'm not involved in his business anymore."

"Oh, it's nothing like that," he answered in a pleasant voice. "I quite realize you have separated yourself from all those things. No, no, it's nothing like that at all. Have you quite recovered from the rigors of your trip?"

Caught a little off pace by the abrupt change of subject, Damaris muttered an innocuous reply, all the while wondering what could be behind Garret's sudden interest in her, for he seldom bothered with anyone unless he wanted something from them. He went on chatting aimlessly as they neared the stable and Damaris began to wonder if her suspicions were unjust.

"You're not anxious to see your sister leave Southernwood, are you?" he asked.

"Why, I don't know. I haven't thought about it."

"Your mother certainly isn't. Dear Emily has done everything but demand that Ethan set up practice in the village, never realizing that her bossiness only makes him more determined to resist her."

That was exactly what she had told her mother, Damaris recalled.

"You'd like to have him around, wouldn't you?"

"What do you mean?" she said sharply.

"Oh nothing, nothing at all. By the way, do you know my little house in town? On Center Street. Yes, it still is my house, although I haven't felt like moving there. In any event, I'm quite agreeable to the idea of giving it over to Ethan and Corrine. It would be quite suitable for them, actually. It's got three bedrooms, all furnished; a lovely parlor, with one of those imposing round tables made from the whole side of an oak; and quite a large kitchen—yes, the kitchen is very adequate. Don't you agree it would be the perfect house for them?"

"I've never seen the house. Besides, it's not my concern."

"Well now, it does seem as though you might do your mother the service of helping her in her little schemes. You have more influence with Ethan than she ever could. Why not encourage him to stay? Show him around the house. Show Corrine too," he added quickly. "The door is always open. You've only to walk in."

"Really, Uncle Garret, I can't think why I should bother. Ethan would resent my interference as much as he does Mother's."

"Oh, but he is so fond of you. And Wesley. And he loves Freddy like a son."

She was finding it difficult to breathe. And yet her uncle's words were innocent, could mean nothing. Was she reading too much into them? "Why don't *you* show Ethan and Corrine your house," she snapped, "since you're so anxious for them to have it. I assure you I don't care what they do."

"Don't get upset," Garret said smoothly, smiling at Damaris's obvious agitation. "It was only a thought. I assure you I don't care one whit where they live. Well, there's Forbes taking the gig out. I suppose I can get that ride into town after all."

To Damaris's relief, at that moment Freddy came darting from behind the stable gate, running toward her, anxious to drag his mother into the yard.

"But don't forget," Garret added. "If you change your mind

the door is always unlocked. Oh, and by the way, it might be better not to mention anything about my offer to Emily. She's got a suspicious nature, my sister, and she's very sharp. Always sees more of what's going on than you want her to. If you have any secrets, you can't keep them from her."

Abruptly Damaris hurried away from him to meet her son and take his hand.

"Hurry, Mama, the pony's all saddled," Freddy cried, pulling her toward the gate.

"I'm coming, love," she answered. Garret, for all that his wits were dulled by drink and laudanum, still had some powers of perception. He certainly knew Emily inside and out. But how well did he know her? Later. She'd think about that later.

For several days Damaris tried to put Garret's suggestion from her mind, dismissing it as the crazy idea of a sour old man. But try as she might, pictures crowded her mind, images of herself showing Ethan around the small house, where they could be alone. It was such a seductive idea that once she knew the opportunity was there, it latched on to her thoughts with a grip she could not shake, tormenting her with its promise, tempting her with its challenge. It did not help that Emily pulled her aside one afternoon a week later, saying sharply, "I want a word with you, Damaris."

"Not now, Mother. I've got to draw up the treasurer's report for the Ladies' Commission. The meeting is tomorrow, you know, and—"

"That can wait," Emily said with the decisiveness of a drill sergeant. "Sit down," she said, closing the door behind her.

Damaris was filled with an unreasoning fury. "I'm not ten years old, Mother! Don't speak to me this way."

"Then don't act ten years old. I can't believe my eyes. I didn't want to speak openly about this, but your behavior has left me with no alternative."

"What behavior? I've done nothing wrong."

"You know very well what I mean," Emily said, standing over her daughter, arms folded across her chest. "Following Ethan Slade around like a . . . a bitch in heat!"

"Mother!"

"Well, it's the truth. You've barely a civil word for your sister or anyone else in the house. And poor Wesley—I don't know how he puts up with your scoldings and contempt. The only time you are pleasant is when your brother-in-law walks into the room and then, oh, but what a flirt! It's disgraceful to watch!"

Furious, Damaris flounced to the door. "You don't know what you're saying. I won't listen to this."

"Yes, you will. I'm your mother and I have the right to tell you when you're behaving like a child."

Damaris paused, her hand on the doorknob.

"Listen to me, Damaris," Emily said in a more reasonable voice, walking up to her daughter and laying a hand on her shoulder. "I once hoped you'd marry Ethan and I was very sorry when you chose not to. I think he would have suited you better than Wesley, who is too easygoing by far. But that's water under the bridge now. Ethan is your sister's husband. Put him out of your mind. Adultery is a sin that no pure-minded woman even touches upon in her thoughts."

"Mother, you don't know what you're talking about. Besides, you've said often enough that you want Corrine to live nearby. Did it ever occur to you that perhaps I'm only trying to make that possible?"

Emily shook her head. "Whatever it is that you're about, it isn't any concern of mine. I'm afraid for you, Damaris. You were always far too willful for your own good."

"Oh, thank you!"

"Forget him, Damaris."

Damaris turned and fled the room.

That evening, finding Ethan alone on the back porch, Damaris told him about Garret's house and offered to show him around it if he would drive her into town the next day. To her surprise, he agreed.

Although Ethan would have been the first to admit that he had not the slightest interest in seeing Garret's house, his curiosity was piqued by Damaris's invitation. He had been wary of her since she returned from her trip with Wesley. She had behaved outrageously, flirting with him openly, but as long as she did it only when the others were around, he didn't take it seriously. He was unable to believe that she had really changed her mind. But now her intention was plain: she wanted to be alone with him. This was an opportunity he wouldn't pass up for the world.

For the trip to the village Damaris wore a new bonnet she
d bought in Charleston, the ribboned brim showing to best
vantage the way she had slicked back her hair into a fall of
rls that framed the sides of her face. She smelled faintly of
esh violets, and her lavender print dress had deep ruffles on
e wide skirt and a tightly fitted bodice with a pointed lace
rtha that set off the pink tones of her complexion. Feeling
etty and looking pretty, she did her best to draw Ethan under
r spell, laughing and chatting all the way to the village. He
oked on, smiling his wry smile, and she knew full well he
as charmed.

arret's house was an attractive place, with huge mounds of
ue-black mountain laurel framing a white gate that led to a
rrow yard. It had a dollhouse quality, from the small porch
the high peaked roof elaborately trimmed with gingerbread
namentation.

"It has some charm, don't you think?" Damaris said gaily
he swung her down from the chaise.

"It seems very small," he remarked, tucking his whip under
s arm and pulling off his gloves.

"Oh but it's larger inside than it looks—at least so Uncle
arret says."

Slipping an arm through his, she led him up the path to the
orch. The door was unlocked and the rooms smelled musty
d stale, with that forlorn emptiness of unlived-in houses. It
as completely furnished, from the faded turkey carpets on
e floors to the heavy chairs and sofas under white dust covers.
ven the kitchen had its full complement of pots and pans,
rooms and mops. Damaris enjoyed herself, inspecting every-
ing, lifting the covers, opening drawers, and pointing out
very detail.

Taking his hand, she led him up the stairs to the bedrooms,
ill chatting deliberately and all the while feeling the warm
nticipation growing within her. The largest room, little more
an half the size of hers at home, was made still smaller by
s massive oak furniture. The bed had a headboard that reached
lmost to the ceiling, while across from it stood a huge black
resser covered with a slab of marble that could have graced
sarcophagus. The heavy drapes darkened the room, but Dam-
ris made no effort to open them. In a dancing motion that set

her wide skirts swirling she swept her arm around the room.

"Here now, isn't this pleasant? It's all you need to make charming home."

Abruptly she came to a stop next to him, so close that the tight bodice of her dress pressed against his chest. He looked down at her, and she deliberately faced his direct gaze.

She expected him to say something, to ask her why she had brought him here or what she wanted from him. Instead, he placed his hands on her shoulders, dug his fingers into her flesh, and pulled her to him, kissing her on the lips, long and hard.

Letting her arms slide around his neck, Damaris gave way completely to the surge of feeling that swept over her. *I love you, I love you,* she thought, and a voice dimly answered, *No love. Nothing but lust, pure and simple, and oh, so good!*

When he finally released her, she caught at her breath, not wanting to let go of him. He stepped back and she quickly pulled the ribbon of her bonnet free and threw it on the bed. Then his arms were around her again, crushing her to him, his hands sliding up her waist to cup her breast.

"Ethan! Ethan. Oh, my dear . . ."

But Ethan did not answer. He was already joyfully embarked on her seduction. With his lips he explored her face and neck while his insistent hands dug at the buttons of her dress and forced their way to her yielding flesh. Damaris moaned with pleasure.

"Hello! Hello!" a voice called brightly from below.

"Oh my God!"

Panic, confusion. Cold reality draining away hot passion.

"Hello. We're here to see the house. Damaris?"

"It's Mother! My God, what's she doing here?"

Frantically Damaris clutched at the buttons of her dress while Ethan turned away, trying to regain his composure. Recovering before Damaris, he walked to the door and called down: "We're upstairs. Just looking over the bedrooms." Glancing back at Damaris, who was by now nearly buttoned, he whispered, "Corrine's with her. I'll go ahead and hold them."

Damaris was pale as death and nearly as cold. The thought that they might have walked in ten minutes later almost made her faint.

"Don't forget your hat," he whispered and then he was gone.

Struggling for control, Damaris grabbed her bonnet and retied it, looking at her reflection in the tarnished mirror over the dresser. Pinching her cheeks to bring back the color and hoping her voice would not betray her, she stepped into the hall and looked down at her mother and Corrine, who were standing at the foot of the stairs talking to Ethan.

"I thought Corrine might like to see the house too," Emily said, smiling innocently at her daughter, "and since the meeting got out early, I brought her over. How fortunate to find you here."

"Yes, isn't it?" Damaris muttered.

"Ethan, perhaps you could drive Corrine back with you since I must stay and meet with some of the ladies of the guild. She is looking a little weary to me and it would be better for her to get home, don't you agree?"

Descending the stairs, Damaris tried to avoid looking directly at her sister. "Do you like the house?"

"Well, I haven't seen too much of it yet," Corrine answered, "but it seems nice. I think I should like living so near the village. What do you think, Ethan?"

"It's adequate," he answered indifferently.

"Let me show you around, Corrine. There are some advantages you don't see until they are pointed out," Emily said, taking her daughter's arm and beginning the same kind of animated tour Damaris had given less than half an hour before.

In the hallway Ethan stood next to Damaris listening to Emily's chatter as she and Corrine moved through the downstairs rooms. "Do you think she knows?" he whispered.

"It's hard to tell with Mother. But it would be just like her to suspect something."

Stepping out of sight of the women in the kitchen, Ethan drew her to him. "I must see you," he said, gripping her arm.

Damaris was very conscious of her mother's voice down the hall. "I want to," she whispered, "but I don't know how."

"Meet me somewhere. You can slip out, can't you? Say you have a headache and are going to your room."

"But where? It's too dangerous at home. And if we come back here again, someone's sure to see."

"There is an empty workman's cottage beyond the stable. It's secluded, especially at night. Will you meet me there?"

"When?"

"Tomorrow. I won't be home this evening. Tomorrow, about midnight."

"Damaris," Emily called, "I can't get this pump handle to work. You're so clever about these things—come and explain it to Corrine."

"Of course, Mother," she answered, then whispered to Ethan, "I'll be there."

Emily had told the truth when she said she had several calls to make, but one of them had not been planned until she found Ethan and Damaris in Garret's house, both looking so obviously flustered and guilty that she would have to be blind not to suspect what they were about. Although she was deeply concerned over Corrine's health and wanted desperately to keep her nearby, she was forced to admit that under the circumstances Corrine's health would be more hindered than helped by living at Southernwood or even in the village. She wanted to shake Damaris until her teeth rattled, but that was no answer. The girl had too restless a spirit and too little to occupy her and, just as she'd done as a child, she fell into mischief. But this was beyond mischief. This was a kind of destructiveness that must not be allowed. So with a heavy heart Emily had her groom drive her to Tarrytown to the imposing granite pile that William King called home and, as luck would have it, found him in his library.

King had made his money in real estate early in life and then retired on his fortune, devoting himself to the sedate life of an entrepreneur. At one time or other he had been on the board of nearly every significant charitable institution in New York City and had headed endless committees sponsoring everything from the new opera house to relief for immigrants. He had never quite gotten over the death of his dandified son at Petersburg late in the war and by now had quietly disassociated himself from many of his former offices. But Emily knew that he still retained his place on the New York Hospital board.

"I'm here to ask a favor," she said in a businesslike manner, settling uneasily into a comfortable chair opposite her host. "You have served so long with the hospital, surely you must have contacts among many of the best medical institutions in the country."

"You might say so, yes," King agreed, stroking the fine hairs above his thin lips. He had known Emily Whitman for years and had always admired her good figure and handsome features. She was a little more aggressive than he liked, but she was also intelligent and very charming when she wanted to be. It was so unusual for her to be asking anything of him that he was already prepared to help her out.

"Do you think you could manage to have my son-in-law appointed to the staff of one of the medical colleges in Philadelphia? He's a fine doctor, as anyone who looks at his war record can see. And he has always wanted some kind of teaching position. It would mean a lot to him."

"Well, I don't know, Emily. Most of these fellows have worked their way up within those institutions for years. And he's rather young."

"Yes, but he's had a unique experience in the field, unlike your average physician. Surely that would be of some use to an institution that is always looking for new methods and better ways of doing things. And it doesn't have to be permanent, at least not at first. He could be a visiting lecturer, couldn't he?"

"What about our own medical houses? Wouldn't New York be more suitable? I might have more influence there."

Emily's expression hardened. "No, I don't think so. Ethan has his heart set on Philadelphia for some reason."

"Ethan Slade is an intelligent man with some excellent experience, although he is a little too unpredictable in my view. However, I will do what I can. The chairman of the board at the University of Pennsylvania Hospital is a very old friend. He'll consider him for my sake."

"Do you think it could be soon? He's so anxious to go and is so restless knocking about here."

"That shouldn't be too difficult. I'll ask my friend to invite him down to look the place over. He'll want to meet him anyway."

Emily sat back in her chair, smiling grimly. "Thank you, William. Thank you more than I can say."

"No problem, my dear. I'll get the letter written this evening."

Damaris spent all the next day wavering between spells of guilt and expectation. She was sure her emotions must be apparent to everyone else in the house. As the afternoon wore slowly on toward evening, she began to wonder if she would ever be able to escape from the rest of her family long enough to meet Ethan or if she would even have the courage to try.

It was a relief after supper to hear her father ask Wesley to join him in a game of chess. Pleading a headache she went upstairs at ten, slipped into a light cotton gown without a hoop, and turned down her lamp, just in case anyone looked in. Around eleven she heard the others come up. Wesley stepped into her room and smoothed the covers around her, then closed the door and retired to his own room.

By the time the distant chimes of the hall clock struck half past eleven, the house had settled into a sleepy stillness. She waited nearly twenty more minutes, then rose and put on her wool cloak, stopping only long enough to listen at her husband's door for the sounds of his quiet snoring. Mindful of every creak on the carpeted stair, she made her way carefully to the side door that opened on the veranda. It was very dark, but she dare not light a lantern. Her hand was on the polished brass lock, ready to slip back the rod, when she heard someone softly speak her name behind her. Twirling around, her heart racing, she looked straight into the black, questioning eyes of her father.

"Damaris, what on earth . . . ?"

"Papa! I . . . I was just going out for a little air. I couldn't sleep . . ." Her voice trailed off, sounding hollow and unconvincing. "What are you doing up so late?"

"I was restless so I went out for a long walk. Just as I was coming up the drive not ten minutes ago I saw Ethan slip out this same door. What is going on here?"

Damaris tried to make her tone light. "I suppose restlessness is catching tonight. We are all affected by it." Through her own anxiety she noticed that her father did look strained and tired, although the anger and suspicion in his eyes worried her more. "You shouldn't exert yourself so, Papa. You know how the doctor told you not to take strenuous exercise."

But Fade would not be put off so easily. "Never mind about me. I'm a lot more concerned about you right now, Damaris. Don't tell me you were going out to meet that young man!"

She moved away from the door, slipping her cloak off from around her shoulders. "Oh, Papa, why should you jump to such a conclusion as that? I couldn't sleep, that's all. Now that you're here, we can sit and have a glass of Madeira together. That will do as well as a walk."

She started past him toward the back parlor, sick with disappointment and chagrin. Reaching out, Fade clutched her arm, searching her face angrily.

"Don't try to deceive me, Damaris. I can read you as clear as day. You were going to meet Ethan, weren't you? Emily told me she suspected—"

Furious, Damaris tore her arm from his grasp. "Oh, Mother! She's always seeing things that aren't there. Especially about me."

"That's not true. I heard about your little escapade at Garret's house, but I wouldn't believe you could do anything so stupid. Now I'm beginning to wonder if perhaps I'm not the one who is naïve. My God, Damaris, he is your sister's husband!"

Groaning, Damaris turned away from his shocked eyes. It grieved her to disappoint and anger her father, yet her own longings were so strong that she almost did not care. To have Corrine thrown up to her at that moment was like putting a match to tinder.

"Always Corrine! Poor Corrine! Well, what about me? What about my needs, my wants? I love Ethan. I always have."

Fade fought to control his emotions. For the first time ever, he wanted to slap his daughter's lovely face. Spitting out his words, he dug his fingers into the soft flesh of her arm.

"I never thought to hear such selfish, stupid words from your lips. You are Wesley's wife, or don't you remember? You'd be making a whore of yourself, bringing down scandal and ruin on your whole family, on your mother and me! Did that thought ever occur to you?"

His words fell on her like searing flame. She must not cry! She fought to hold back the hot tears. She would not cry!

"Papa, I love him."

"This is not love. It's nothing but lust. Passion, if you will. He was always bad for you, Damaris. Always getting you into scrapes that caused you nothing but pain and disgrace. Leave him alone, Damaris. Stay away from him!"

"No!"

"You are not going out there tonight if I have to wake the

whole house to stop you. He'll be gone soon. Emily went to see Mr. King just today and he thinks an appointment to the University Hospital in Philadelphia can be arranged very quickly. Good riddance, I say."

She looked pleadingly at her father, her eyes liquid with unshed tears. "Then why can't I have these few moments? It's not fair."

"For God's sake, Damaris, use your wits. If Ethan gets involved with you he may not want to leave when he gets the chance. And he must go. It will be better for everyone if he does."

Fury and disappointment drowned all discretion. "You never liked him! This is all Mother's fault. She never wanted me to have anything I wanted. She is always standing in my way."

Her father stepped back, his face gone suddenly white. "Damaris that is unfair. How can you talk so of your mother?"

"Well it's true. She was always against me. All she ever cared about was you and Corrine."

"I won't have you speaking this—"

"I hate her! I hate her!"

"Damaris . . ."

As she watched horrified, Fade froze, an expression of startled shock fixed on his face.

"Papa, what's wrong?"

Seconds passed, seconds in which all her anger and resentment dissolved as Damaris realized her father was stricken. Then he pitched forward even as she reached out to catch him, his weight carrying them both to the floor.

"Papa! What is it?"

Fade tried to answer her, but his throat would release nothing more than a choked gurgle. He let go of her arm and clawed at his collar. Even as she stared into his face, laying him down on the carpet, she could see the glaze that quietly, irrevocably covered his dark eyes, like a night cloud slipping over the moon.

Damaris, frantic now, slipped her arm underneath his head and tried desperately to lift him. She screamed, her anguished voice echoing through the long hallway and up the stairs: "Mother! Mother, come quickly. It's Papa!"

Fade's head hung limply as his daughter cradled him in her arms. His eyes rolled back, and through the slit of half-opened lids there was only a ghastly sliver of white.

A door slammed upstairs and Emily's startled face peered over the railing.

"What's the matter?"

"Mother," Damaris sobbed. "Help me. Papa's hurt!"

🌸 *Twenty-five*

SOME IMAGES sear themselves onto the mind, never to leave. It seemed to Damaris, looking back, that many such pictures drawn from the space of only a few days would intrude upon her memory for the rest of her life.

Emily, her dark blue dressing gown spilling around her on the floor, clutching Fade's head to her breast, weaving back and forth, nearly incoherent: "Oh, he can't be dead! Please God, don't let him be dead! Please, please..."

Fade's swarthy face against the white linen, the pillow's lacy edges vividly intricate.

The doctor's dispassionate voice. "It's a stroke, Mrs. Whitman. I'm very sorry but it looks as though much of the brain has been destroyed. He may live for a few days or a few years, but he'll never be the man you knew again."

Damaris herself, sick with guilt and grief. "But Papa's so strong. He can't be dying. It's not possible!"

Wesley, quietly supportive, filled with a concern for his wife that made her want to rail against him. "Why don't you lie down and rest, Damaris. You look exhausted."

"I don't want to lie down. Let me alone!"

Emily again, dark splotches beneath her eyes, her face drawn and lined, her eyes constantly inflamed from weeping, keeping a ceaseless vigil by her husband's bed.

"Mother, please go and stretch out on my bed. You cannot keep this up forever. I'll watch Papa for a while."

"I'm all right. What if he wakes up and I'm not there? He opened his eyes once last night and it seemed as though he knew me. I don't dare leave."

It was Matilda who finally got Emily away from Fade's bedside. In her competent way, Bible in hand, she lifted her sister-in-law from her chair and helped her to a cot that had been set up in the room. Whether from exhaustion or despair, Emily let herself be led. After that, she and Matilda shared the round-the-clock care Fade required.

Damaris longed for a moment alone with her father to whisper her remorse and beg his forgiveness, but since the presence of her mother and her aunt made this impossible, she gradually came to feel relieved that she was not called upon to wait by his bedside. That inert figure on the bed was not the same person she had known and loved. Vital, cheerful, soundly sensible, Papa had been the touchstone in her life. He could not be more surely gone now had he died that terrible night. And it was all her fault!

Because of her grief and guilt she found it easy to ignore Ethan, who skulked around Southernwood, carefully avoiding her and keeping away from the house as much as possible. When a telegram finally came inviting him to visit the University of Pennsylvania Hospital, he was packed and gone almost before the rest of the family knew what had happened.

Damaris was relieved to see him go. She had all but put him out of her mind when Corrine sought her out one rainy afternoon to tell her that Ethan had been invited to serve as a visiting lecturer at the hospital and that she would be leaving to join him as soon as their father's situation allowed for it.

"Are you pleased?" Damaris asked, wondering at her sister's reserved demeanor. "Is it what you wanted?"

"I guess so. I want to be with Ethan. I feel I belong with him no matter what comes."

"Even after the way he's treated you?"

Corrine's expression was veiled. "I'm his wife. Nothing can change that."

Once her words would have cut sharply, and Damaris wondered that she felt them so little now. "Yes, and so you must be with him. I hope this move will be a happy one for you, Corrine. I truly do."

And she meant it, since with the two of them gone her life was bound to be easier. Perhaps someday she might even manage to forget how her passion for Ethan had destroyed her beloved father.

For two long months after his mind had all but ceased to function, Fade Whitman's body lingered on. It was long enough to make his release almost welcome when it finally came. Not even Emily, who felt as though part of her very soul was dying, would wish him to go on like that any longer. In the end, with his sister, wife, and three daughters surrounding his bed, his hand still tightly clutched in the hand that had held it through so many years, Frederick Whitman's spirit broke free for other realms, leaving behind a gray room filled with the bitter grief of the five women in the world who had loved him most.

Fade was buried in the small cemetery near the old meeting house on the post road near the graves of Josh and Morna Deveroe. Nearby, a weathered granite stone marked the resting place of Richard Deveroe, Josh's father, and the twisted, worm-damaged gray branches of a dogwood dipped silently in the wind.

His family was somewhat surprised to learn that Fade had made a will. He had never talked of death or seemed concerned about the future and, having seldom suffered from any illness, gave the impression he never intended to fall victim to one. Yet at some time he must have faced the possibility and taken the precaution of setting his business in order. The personal property which Emily had bestowed on him was carefully divided among his children. The bulk of Deveroe Enterprises belonged rightfully to his wife, and to her they returned. Small gifts went to faithful servants and to two of the men who had worked as foremen in the yards for many years. From his own funds he left modest gifts for his own family—Matilda, Jim, Jesse, and even Florrie. There was only one startling legacy: subject to

Emily's agreement, the care and guidance of Deveroe Enterprises, particularly the Dolphin yards, was left to the direction of his daughter Damaris, whom he was sure would manage them with talent and intelligence.

No one was more surprised than Damaris herself, and yet she welcomed the opportunity as a way of making some small amend to her father. She expected her mother to immediately veto the idea, but Emily, almost prostrate with grief, seemed not to care who took over the business. Not a few eyebrows were raised when the news spread around the village, and more than one of Fade's colleagues shook their heads over their sherry cobblers and prophesied the imminent destruction of a fine old family concern. Though no one ever voiced this opinion to her face, Damaris was aware of it, and though she would not admit it to anyone, she rather feared they might be right.

"Will you mind very much?" she asked Wesley, who had already expressed some concern that her time would be severely limited.

"Of course not, if it's what you want. I admit the idea seems terribly avant-garde, but your father believed you had a talent for business and I suppose this was his way of offering you the opportunity to discover whether or not you really did. What about your sisters, though? Are their feelings injured?"

"I don't think so. Corrine can hardly wait to leave and get back to Ethan, and Winnifred's only fear is that we'll be bankrupt before she has her wedding. But, Wes, I'm not sure I can handle it. It's rather frightening to think that everything depends on me. Why, even when I was helping Papa, he made all the decisions. What if I fail?"

"You won't. You've got too much of your mother's determination about you. You'll do splendidly."

"Oh dear. I hope you're right!"

There were butterflies dancing in her stomach the first morning she walked into Fade's old office at the Dolphin yards, but she was careful not to let her nervousness show. Ignoring the skeptical glances of some of the old hands, cheerfully greeting a few who had known her as a child and were obviously still seeing her that way, politely asking Robert Manning, Jr., who had taken over as foreman after his father's retirement and had worked with Fade for many years, to help her learn her way around, she made a determined effort to charm them all, hoping they would overlook the fact that she was untrained, unskilled, and a woman.

At first she believed she had succeeded, for everyone was polite, courteous, and helpful. In the space of a few weeks, however, she began to think otherwise. Some of the laborers were openly skeptical. Others ignored her, going about their work just as they'd done for years. A few took advantage, lolling around on the job, suddenly unproductive, ignoring her advice or admonitions. She began to realize that money came in and went out without her knowledge, and the suspicion that someone else might take advantage of that fact frightened her. She knew she was floundering and she knew the men around her knew it. The more helpless she grew, the more they seemed to challenge her.

"Why won't they listen to me? Why won't they obey me?" she railed to Robert Manning.

"Because you're ignorant and you're female," he answered with a rare piece of candor.

"I can have them fired. In fact, that's what I will do. I want you to fire everyone who's not doing his rightful day's work."

"Pardon, ma'am, but these men are skilled workers. Who are you going to find to replace them? That contract for the paddle steamer we're building is the only contract we've got right now. Do you want to be left with a half-finished packet lying about? Word'll be around in no time that Dolphin is going to rack and ruin."

"But they ought not to want that either. After all, they stand to lose their jobs if the yard folds. Why don't they realize that and make the effort to put out a decent product?"

"Begging your pardon, ma'am, but it's a question of authority. They simply don't think you know anything about running a shipyard, and they don't think you have the gumption to let them go. Truth is, you're in no position to fire anyone."

Leaning her head in her hands, Damaris stared at the incomprehensible figures covering the papers on her father's desk. Though she hated hearing Manning's words, she had to admit he was right. She knew a little but not enough to step into Fade's shoes; and unless she began learning—and soon—she would never make a success of running this business.

"Can you help me?" she asked softly.

Robert frowned at her. "I'd like to, Miss Damaris, but truth is, I never knew half what your Dad knew. He gave me orders and I carried them out. I kind of depended on him to know if they was the right ones or not."

Damaris drummed her fingers on the tabletop. "There's my cousin Jesse," she said, looking up. "I could bring him in from the dairy farm in Purdy's Station. He's very knowledgeable and he learns fast. He'd help me, I know he would."

"Jesse Whitman is a good man. I hear he's done wonders over there in Purdy's."

"He has, that's true. In fact, I hate the thought of taking him away from there, since it's the only business in the whole company that's making money right now."

"That might not be wise to change, considering."

"Then what am I to do, Robert? I've got to have someone."

Manning rubbed the stubble of whiskers on his square chin. "I been with the Deveroes a long time, Miss Damaris, and my pa before me. I heard him say more than once that old Josh was a bright one when it came to building ships, and the only one he ever saw that could touch him was his son Garret. 'Course that was back before Garret took so to drink and all. My pa was fond of him when he was a lad and used to hang around the yards all the time. Said he was bright as a penny and his own pa never could see it."

Damaris groaned. "Oh no. Surely there must be someone else."

"T'was just a thought," Robert drawled. "Probably he's too far gone in whiskey now to help anybody."

"Whiskey and God knows what else," Damaris muttered. Pushing her chair away from the desk, she rose and moved to the window. It looked as though half the men were standing about aimlessly in the yard while a few worked with dispirited motions at the saws and hammers. Clucking softly to herself she turned back to Robert Manning.

"Well, it's worth a try. I've heard all my life that Uncle Garret had a talent for business. Perhaps it's time to give him the chance to prove whether he does or not." If, she thought to herself, I can only get Mother to agree!

"Do you really think it will work?" Wesley asked later that evening when she told him of her conversation with Manning. "After all, if they won't take orders from a woman, what makes you think they'll take them any sooner from a drunkard? And Garret's reputation is pretty well known in this area."

Throwing back the covers, Damaris crawled in beside her husband on the plump feather mattress. Since her involvement with the company filled so much of her time and interest, she had taken to sharing his room. It was a comfort she relished more every day.

"He will have to straighten up, that's all. And I suspect he may want this opportunity enough to make the effort. This might prove to be the only thing that has ever helped him."

"That would be a miracle," Wesley answered, turning down the gas flame and drawing his wife into the circle of his arms.

"It's Mother I'm the most worried about. I did broach the subject with her this evening, and I expected to get a flaming reaction. But she only looked at me with that vague expression she wears all the time now and made some comment that Garret was undependable. It was not what I expected at all."

"She's still grieving. I suspect she doesn't really care what happens to anybody who is left in the world, now that her beloved Fade is gone."

"I know. He was her whole life for so long. It won't last, you know," she said, snuggling down next to Wesley. "Mother has too much vitality and is too strong-minded to wither away. She'll come back, but I just may be able to sneak Uncle Garret under the door before she wakes up and realizes it. Who knows, if he does a good job, she may have to admit it wasn't such a bad thing after all."

"Let's hope it turns out that way," he answered, not at all convinced.

"Look at this wood." Garret ran a bony finger along a beam of raw oak. "Half of it was cut before it was mature and nearly all has been improperly salted. You'll have dry rot before you can start using it next spring."

Unsure whether to be defensive or dismayed, Damaris bent to inspect the huge logs as though she could see the same things Garret saw.

"But Mr. Wilkerson has supplied the Dolphin for years. Why would he sell me defective lumber?"

"Because he probably figured you wouldn't know the difference—and he was right."

"But someone must have known. Surely Robert Manning . . ."

"You'd think so, wouldn't you? I'd have him on the carpet for this and quick!"

Glancing around, Damaris noticed that the men working nearby were visibly straining to pick up every word. "Let's go inside, Uncle Garret," she said, steering him back toward the office. Glaring at the men, Garret followed her inside, settling on a straight-backed chair near Fade's expansive oak desk, eyeing a decanter near the window but not asking for a drink. Damaris did not offer it.

"All right, Uncle Garret," she said briskly, sitting down opposite him. "You've been over the whole yard and you've examined the books. What do you think?"

"I think it's obvious that if you don't get some good advice you are going to fail—as they are hoping you will."

"But I trusted Robert . . ."

"Women! What has trust got to do with anything? You want to put the fear of God in him and all the rest of that scurvy lot. What do you care if they like you or not? They liked your father, didn't they, and I wonder how long they've been cheating him."

From under his narrow lids Garret examined his niece sitting primly upright in her chair. She looked very businesslike in her neat dark blue dress with its high collar showing a tiny edge of ruffle caught with a cameo at her throat. Her hair was pulled back into a wide woven chenille net that looked severe but not unfeminine. Although he was as surprised as everybody else that his brother-in-law had entrusted her with so awesome a responsibility, he suspected Fade had seen some untapped abilities there. She had intelligence and spirit and was willing to learn. Had she not been born a woman, she would already have this place humming. It was just as well she had, however, since that disability made it natural for him to step in and help. How many years had he brooded over just such an opportunity?

Damaris felt her uncle's eyes on her and, stirring uncomfortably, stared at the faded rug. Certainly she had never liked him, she had much reason to fear him, and the idea of working alongside him was repugnant. But she needed his expertise, he had the advantage of being one of the family, and he would have the natural authority she lacked until she learned enough

to take over herself. Yet in spite of his knowledge, she trusted
him as little as she now trusted Robert Manning. After all, he
had once been so anxious to get back into the family business
that he had tried to blackmail her. Could she really expect to
get more help from him now than from the others?

He broke into her thoughts: "This is a trim little yard and
could be made to turn a profit again. Fade brought in a few
innovations, but there are better ones now which could save
some money in the long run."

"Such as?"

"Steam derricks, for one, and steam-powered saws. Donald
McCay's been using them for years, as has every yard in New
York."

"But they're all much larger concerns."

"Still, no reason why we can't turn their ideas to our advantage. Invest in some good equipment. Get rid of the dead
wood out there who have kept their jobs for years because they
were old friends of your father's. Give me free reign to stand
over them and make them earn their day's wages. Let me search
out a good draftsman who'll make plans we can work from—
this last lot was the shoddiest effort I've ever seen. I'll see that
you are sold good lumber and that it's used properly. If we do
better work, we'll get more contracts."

"It all sounds so simple."

"It's not simple. It's a matter of teaching people that they
can't fool you. You want to make a go of this, don't you,
Damaris? I mean, it's not the kind of challenge you want to
let slip through your fingers, is it?"

"No, it isn't."

"Well, they all expect you to fail. Give me half a chance
and we'll show them what we can do."

"Do you think the yard can be prosperous again, considering
the state of river traffic?"

"No, frankly I don't. The future lies with the railroads, as
I've always said, and river packets are on their way out. But
they've a few more years to go. Make a profit on them and
invest it in the rails—that's my advice."

It seemed to Damaris she could almost hear her father's
outraged response. But Fade was gone now and it was up to
her to save what he and her grandfather had built for Freddy
and any other children who came along.

"All right, Uncle Garret," she said, looking him straight in the eye. "You obviously know a lot I don't, and I want you to teach me everything. In return you can be my chief assistant, with the final decisions made by me and the ultimate responsibility mine. You can have any salary you want—within reason—and in return I make only one absolute condition. No drinking on the job. What you do the rest of the time is your own business, but I won't have you stumbling about down here. Is that agreeable?"

Garret smiled his narrow lopsided smile. "How generous!"

"I know you mean that sarcastically, but that's beside the point. I'm determined to show them all that I can run this family's affairs as well as any man, but to do so right now I need your help. If you give it to me I won't be ungrateful. What do you say?"

He was already out of the chair, pulling off his coat. "I say, let's go to work, my darling niece!"

It was several weeks before Emily finally lifted herself from the fog of her grief and realized that Damaris had hired Garret as an assistant. By that time he had proved such a valuable help that even she was impressed and she reluctantly agreed to consider his new activity as something in the nature of an experiment, especially when Damaris assured her that the first morning he walked in reeking of whiskey his new role would be automatically terminated.

To everyone's surprise, Garret turned up sober day after day, and although the manner in which he drove the yardhands did nothing to endear him to them, production and efficiency increased so much that even Damaris began to have some respect for him. Every day she learned some new detail of the business, and as her knowledge increased, so did her assurance.

At the beginning of the summer she and Wesley made a tour through the county with Garret, visiting the ironworks at Peekskill in which they still owned a small interest and the dairy farm at Purdy's Station as well as a newly acquired one near Somers. With an embarrassed Mr. Wilkerson they examined every detail of the Middle dock lumber yard and sawmill, agreeing in the end to sell out their interest and put the money into the proposed New York, Westchester and Boston Railroad. Garret was also anxious to get his hands on the records covering Southernwood's vast acreage above the Hudson, but Damaris, knowing how her mother would resent his intrusion, refused to allow it.

By the fall Garret had found a young man recently graduated from an apprenticeship with Grinnel in New York who was, he believed, a talented draftsman and an innovative designer as well. A slight man with a studious face, nearsighted from close work, Jim Casey bent to his new job with a driving ambition. By November they had contracts for two new packets and plans under way for a small merchant whose design utilized some of the sleek lines and narrow hulls of the great clippers.

A year after Fade's death, Casey hovered with a mallet and gouge over his models and the yardhands went searching the woods for trees to fell. Meanwhile, the women at Southernwood turned to the preparations for Winnifred's wedding in March. Even Damaris, feeling that some of the pressure was finally off and reveling in the satisfaction of her work, was able to turn aside briefly to share her sister's happiness over the long-desired union with their cousin Claes.

Damaris had worried that Ethan might show up for the wedding and was relieved when Corrine came without him. It had been more than a year since she had seen her brother-in-law, and often in the dark of night when she was unable to sleep for mulling over some concern or other at the yard, he would intrude into her thoughts, causing her to wonder if now, with all that her new life involved, he would still have the power to make her act as foolish as she had before. She was not sure she still really wanted him, but she was glad she would not have to confront him just yet.

"Oh, I do wish Mother would let me run my wedding my own way!" Winnifred cried angrily, flouncing down on the sofa across from Damaris. "She has her hand in everything I do— what to wear, what foods to prepare, what flowers, what colors, who to invite—it's driving me crazy!"

Working her needle into the canvas, Damaris bent over the frame. "She did the same thing with mine."

"Yes, but I'm older than you were then. Why can't she respect that? Speak to her, Damaris. She'll listen to you."

"Nonsense. She'll do exactly as she pleases no matter what I say. Why don't you let her go ahead? She has excellent taste."

"I can fancy you doing that! It's my wedding, and I want it my way. We've waited so long, what with Papa's death last year and that long voyage Claes had to make around the Cape. Sometimes I wish Mother had stayed in her blue melancholy. At least then she didn't bother anybody."

"No, that wasn't like her at all. She's beginning to come out of it now, so we may as well get used to her bossing us around again. It's a healthy sign."

"That's easy for you to say. You stay so busy all the time and have so much authority of your own at the Dolphin you don't mind her domineering ways. But I have to put up with it all day and all night too."

Damaris gave her sister an indulgent smile. "Well, you'll soon be married and gone away. Then you can have a turn bossing poor Claes around."

Winnifred's expression softened at the thought. "Yes, he's such a dear he shall probably end up as henpecked as Wesley."

"I beg your pardon!"

"Aren't you glad we don't have to wear those huge, cumbersome crinolines anymore?" Winnifred went on, not even hearing Damaris's outraged response. "My dress is going to be so lovely, though I won't be able to sit in it with all the yards and yards of train. Mama wants me to wear some oldfashioned design with a full skirt all around, but I won't do it! It's my wedding and I should be allowed to wear what I want."

Tuning out Winnifred's chatter, Damaris concentrated on her needlework, which she found restful after a long day at the yard. Wesley henpecked? What an absurd idea. That showed how little Winnifred really knew him.

The wedding went off smoothly, with Winnifred looking beautiful in a dress of white chambray gauze trimmed with white satin folds and blond lace and Claes smart and distinguished in his new captain's uniform. The only distressing note of the whole affair was provided by Corrine, who arrived thin and pale and showing obvious signs of ill health. She stayed on for nearly two months after the wedding, allowing Emily to indulge and pamper her to her heart's content, and by the time she returned to Philadelphia her coloring had improved and she had gained a little weight.

"I'm so concerned about her," Emily confided to her eldest daughter. "She's not at all well, and no one seems to know what's the matter. Here's her husband teaching young men how to be doctors and he can't even help his own wife!"

"Perhaps he's one of the things that's wrong with her."

"Oh, I don't think so. She said that since they moved away he has been as considerate and pleasant as never before. She wants a child so badly and is just distraught over her inability to carry one to term. I believe that is behind much of her poor health."

"Perhaps. Why don't you go and stay with them awhile, Mother? Now that Winnifred is gone and Freddy is in school most of the time and I'm away so much, you have the time for visiting. It would do you good."

Emily looked away, her heart aching that Fade was no longer there either to occupy her time. "I don't think so. Someone has to keep things going smoothly here with you giving so much of yourself to that shipyard and all those other things. And who knows what Garret might do without me around to keep an eye on him."

"For heaven's sake, Mother, I ought to be able to control Uncle Garret by now. He's worked with me over a year and has caused no trouble at all. In fact, he's been a great help."

"You don't know him as I do. He's just biding his time, pulling the wool over your eyes."

"Give me a little credit. By now I think I would know if he was out to cause trouble, and he's done nothing to make me think so. On the contrary, he appears to have the interest of the business uppermost."

"And what would you know about it? You're still only a child to him. That you trust him so much only proves my point."

Damaris glared at her mother but said nothing.

The truth was, it was Emily who still treated her like a child—that was the problem. If she managed to work her way to a position on the board of directors at the New York Stock Exchange, she'd still be only a child to her mother!

🌸 *Twenty-six*

STANDING AT the office window looking down into the yard, Damaris could hardly believe that nearly seven years had passed since her father's death. She could not resist a swell of pride as she watched the shipwrights and laborers swarm around the bulky frame of the new propeller, *Marianne,* which would go sliding into the Hudson in two days and the half-built frame of a sloop commissioned by Captain Acher of Sparta. All the distinctive ambience of a boatyard seeped through the closed windows to penetrate the room: the sharp *boink* of the hawsing beetle that the calkers were using; the pungent odors of tar and oakum; the rhythmic ear-splitting noise of Garret's steam derrick; the red clouds of saw dust.

She had one humiliating failure behind her. The New York, Westchester and Boston Commuter Railroad had finally been organized just in time for the panic of 1873 to send it into the hands of receivers and thus it had not proved to be the pot of gold they had all been hoping for. In fact, they lost a good deal of money when the scheme was finally abandoned. But the milk farms grew even more prosperous, and as long as the Dolphin yard continued to go well, they remained solvent.

And the Dolphin was going well. Garret had done a good job, and Damaris was almost to the point where she would no longer have to rely on him. She could sense respect from the men she dealt with now, from the merchants, who supplied the needs of the yard, to the yardhands and foremen, who accepted her orders without reservation. Even her family friends, many of whom were successful businessmen in their own right, now treated her more with admiration. She had consciously set about achieving this by always maintaining the feminine look they so professed to admire and by never appearing domineering or dogmatic when she was around them. It had paid off and she was proud of her achievement. She fancied her father would have been proud of her too.

"Forbes has brought the gig round, Mrs. Slade," said Robert Manning, poking his head through the door. "Whenever you're ready."

"I'm coming now, thank you, Robert," she answered, tying her bonnet. "I won't be here the next two days, you know. Have to go tour the milk factories. But everything will be ready for Thursday's launching, won't it?"

"Oh yes," the foreman answered, opening the door for her. "Cradles in place and greased, deck all calked. We'll be ready on time, no need to fear."

"If anything unexpected comes up either with the launching or with Captain Acher's sloop, see Mr. Garret. He'll hold things down while I'm away."

"Very good, Mrs. Slade. Enjoy your trip."

Damaris nodded, then swept down the narrow stairs and out of the building. As she stepped up to the carriage, she was startled to see Emily lean forward from inside and reach to push open the door.

"Why, Mother, what on earth brings you down here?"

"I just came for the ride and to get out in the air a little. I knew Forbes was picking you up so I asked him to bring me along as well. It vexes me so, you know, dear, that you never have time for me anymore. And when I do see you, you are always so preoccupied you never pay the least attention to my needs."

"Oh, Mother, you sound like Wesley!" Damaris settled back on the creaking leather seat across from her mother, noticing absently that Emily looked rather handsome this afternoon. Although she still wore black most of the time ("just like Queen Victoria," Damaris often chided her) and the years had pulled the corners of her shapely mouth downward into a permanent pout, with her thick gray hair and her fine eyes she was still an imposing woman. Damaris had once suggested that perhaps she might consider marrying again, but Emily was so outraged by the suggestion that she never mentioned it again.

"Well, my dear," Emily went on, "it's only natural that a husband would resent his wife devoting so much of her time and energies to so unnatural as a profession and ignoring her own family."

"I don't ignore my family!"

"You do, Damaris, you do indeed. And you ignore me as well."

With an exasperated sigh Damaris made an effort to change the subject. "You're looking very well today. Is that dress a foulard silk? It's quite becoming."

Emily shook her head, refusing the compliment. "I don't feel at all well. But then I never do of late. I felt better while Corrine was here on that last visit, but since she went home, I don't know, nothing seems to perk me up. It's very discouraging."

"I've told you many times, you need something to occupy your time. You'd feel better if you stayed busy. Why don't you go to the Ladies' Temperance Union meeting next Tuesday? They need someone to help organize their next campaign and you'd be perfect for the job."

Emily waved a gloved hand. "Those old biddies. Why should I waste my time?"

"It would do you good, Mother. You can't go on grieving forever."

"All right, all right. Stop pestering me, Damaris. I'll get out again when I'm ready."

The carriage lumbered slowly along the rutted road, the two women inside swaying with its uneven rhythm.

"I had a letter from Corrine today," Damaris said. "She's asked me to let Freddy go down there to stay with them when school is out. I don't quite know how to answer."

"She's so fond of him, and Ethan is too—why not let him

go? It might lift her spirits to have him there. Will he want to go?"

"Oh, I'm sure he will. And I doubt that Wes would object; he never can refuse the boy anything he wants."

"Freddy's twelve years old now—plenty old enough to be away from home. But I confess I shall miss him. He's my only grandson and the only grandchild I ever see much of at all, with Winnifred's little Miranda living so far away. What's the use of being a grandmother when you can't enjoy having the chicks around!"

"I suppose it would be all right," Damaris muttered more to herself than her mother. How to say she did not relish the idea of Ethan and Corrine having so much influence over her son? That it was especially galling to see Ethan growing closer to the boy every year.

"Damaris, you haven't heard a word I've said," her mother broke in.

"What? Oh no, I was thinking of something else."

"You ought to do something about that bonnet. It's most unbecoming and makes your face look hard and sallow. I'd take it right back to the milliner and demand my money back!"

"But I like it. I think it's very pretty."

"You wouldn't say that if you could see yourself in it."

Sinking into her seat, Damaris wondered what had happened to the pleasant contentment she had felt earlier standing at her office window. It had turned to gray, like the evening darkening around the carriage. What a pity.

Since Wesley had no objection and Freddy was delighted by the prospect, Damaris consented to her son's visit to Philadelphia. One month turned into two and it was nearly time for school again when he returned to Southernwood, full of enthusiasm for the Quaker city and especially for the University Hospital, where his uncle had shown him through every corner. It was with a terribly serious tone of voice that he announced his first evening back, "I've decided to be a doctor like Uncle Ethan. He's already started teaching me how."

Since Damaris had decided Freddy was the natural person to step someday into the shoes she now occupied and Wesley, for his part, was already planning how he might be educated to the law, both of them received this news with barely disguised dismay.

"Don't worry about it," Wesley said later to his wife. "In a year or two he will have outgrown the whole idea. I remember when I was his age all I wanted was to be a seine fisherman like Jesse."

"You're probably right," she replied. What she could not say was that the influence of Ethan Slade in this sudden enthusiasm for medicine worried her more than anything else.

The insistent clanging of the bells in the tower of Trinity Church pulled Garret reluctantly awake. Like a man drugged, he looked around the shabby little room and tried to remember where he was. Slowly he became aware of the clatter of horses' hooves and the jarring noise of iron wheels on the paved streets outside his window, while far in the distance the persistent chiming of a fire bell screeched a shrill obligato.

Where else would such a clamor drag a man from his sleep but on the streets of New York? Staggering to the window, attempting to keep upright while his head went reeling around the room, he yanked the dusty, worn, gold-fringed drapes across the white scar that was the daylight. How had he got here, he wondered.

It came back in scudding pieces. Yesterday's meeting with Benjamin Wells & Company to sign the contract for a pilot schooner to slide down the ways next year. Visits to the Stock Exchange and the merchant houses. An interesting tour of Howland & Aspinwall's yard to see what was probably one of the last of the great clippers slowly rising from its keel.

And then last night! He had been very well behaved during the entire visit—until last night, when he had succumbed to the lure of a sleazy barroom in a cheap porter house on Fair Street.

His hand shaking, he dug through his portmanteau until he found his flask of brandy, turned it up to pour out the dregs, then downed it. He staggered back to bed, and pulling the covers up around him, he waited for the drink to take effect. What a way to wake up on a Sunday morning! Some part of him felt a little disappointed that he had slipped out of the regime of respectability he had imposed on himself for so many years. But maybe it was time to give up this attempt at respectability anyway; it was costing too much. He would spend the better part of the day trying to regain control of himself so as to arrive at the Dolphin tomorrow morning sober and industrious—and for what? To help a silly woman feel she could do a man's job in a man's world! It wasn't worth it.

Draining the last of the brandy, he threw the empty flask across the room and, unsteady on his feet, managed to get up, dress, and drag himself to the hotel dining room where he put some solid food in his stomach. Afterward, feeling better, he bought a copy of the *Herald Tribune* and a cigar and found a spot in the men's smoking lounge to wait for the five o'clock boat back upriver.

"Good afternoon, Mr. Deveroe," said a smooth voice. Looking over the edge of his paper, Garret saw a distinguished-looking gentleman in a shiny black frock coat looking down at him. Every bit of his attire—the fashionable cravat with its diamond stickpin, the high starched collar, the pale gray silk hat—looked expensive. Impressed, Garret lowered the paper.

"I see you do not recognize me," the gentleman said in a pleasant voice. "Jonathan Healey of Benjamin Wells. I met you at the signing yesterday."

"Oh yes, of course," Garret answered, although he had no recollection at all of seeing this imposing face among the group around that table.

"May I join you for a moment?"

"I suppose so," Garret said ungraciously. Healey was well aware that Mr. Deveroe would have preferred to read his paper in solitude, but he pulled up a leather armchair nonetheless, seating himself opposite Garret and laying his hat, gloves, and cane on the table with a flourish.

"You look as though you've been to church," Garret could not resist saying.

"I was this morning, yes, and I thought I might see you there. When I did not, I excused myself to look for you. I take it you do not go to church."

"Not when I can help it. Those damned bells woke me this morning from a sound sleep. Should have known not to take a room so close to the end of Broadway, but I'm fond of this old hotel. Been coming here for years."

"Yes, there are some fine newer ones uptown. The St. Denis at Broadway and Eleventh Street, for example, is one of my favorites."

"You do look a little out of place here, now that you mention it."

Healey gave him a direct gaze and smiled thinly. "But you do not."

Garret's face flushed in sudden anger. Resisting the urge to jump up from his chair and turn his back on this dandy, he waited, wondering what the man wanted.

As though reading his mind, Healey settled back, crossing one leg over the other, and said, "I know a little about your position, Mr. Deveroe. For the past several years you have been the guiding hand behind the Dolphin yards, allowing your niece, Mrs. Slade, to take most of the credit for putting the place back on its feet."

"You seem to know a lot."

"Oh, it's common enough knowledge. What does any woman perceive about running a business? I fancy it was your expertise that made the Dolphin healthy again and I like to see a man given due credit for his accomplishments. You strike me as a man of great talent, Mr. Deveroe, a man I should like to do business with."

Garret had the uneasy suspicion he was being buttered up. "What kind of business?"

Healey coughed discreetly. "I've been with Mr. Wells for many years," he began, "and have the honor of his implicit trust. Mr. Wells has a large enterprise in New York and for some time now he has been thinking of broadening his base, so to speak. Deveroe Enterprises is a modest concern, comprising two milk factories and farms, several interests in manufacturing concerns, and, of course, the Dolphin, a small yard with a fine old name and not much else."

"You make it sound rather shabby."

"That is not my intention. No, no, it's a respectable enough enterprise, but quite limited compared to the concerns here in New York. Benjamin Wells is a great merchant house—its flags fly on ships coursing the seas of the world. Why, one cargo of jute and sugar from the Philippines would buy and sell your entire business."

"So what do you want with me?"

"Mr. Wells has expressed an interest in buying up the entire stock in Deveroe Enterprises. He would make you a very generous offer and in return would take over the management of both the milk farms, hoping to expand them."

"The manufacturing concerns?"

"I can only say that if he follows past procedures he would probably sell his interests to buy more stock in the railroads. Mr. Wells is very partial to railroads."

"And the Dolphin?"

Hooking a thumb in the pocket of his vest, Healey reared back and stared benignly down on Garret. "Mr. Wells feels that Hudson River shipyards have seen their best days. After a suitable time he would probably resell or close it."

With careful deliberation Garret folded his paper and spread it across his lap, all the while mulling over this unexpected offer. He had a sudden longing for an energizing drink to help clear his mind. "Why come to me with this?" he said angrily. "It's my niece who holds the power at Deveroe, no matter who does the work. She'd be the one to talk to."

Healey ran his fingers across his silk hat. "Your niece is a woman, and women are apt to operate more on a basis of sentiment and emotion than sound business sense. Mr. Wells feels you are the likely one to handle such a transaction, and in return he wishes me to assure you that he will find a place in one of his other concerns commensurate with your skill. And, I need not remind you, Mr. Wells has a great number of concerns."

"Still, Damaris—my niece—she'd have to know and approve. And so would my sister. Between them they own ninety percent of the company. You're asking the wrong person."

With one smooth motion Healey placed his hat under his arm and rose from his chair. "A man of your talents ought to be able to bring them around, I should think. After all, if your niece should fail . . ."

"What does that mean?"

"Why, nothing. It is merely to say that it would not be the first time a woman took on more than she could handle and was eventually forced to give way to someone else. Now, I must be getting along, Mr. Deveroe. I trust you will consider Mr. Wells's offer and convey it to your niece—if you feel that is wise. I shall be in touch. Good day, Mr. Deveroe."

"Good day," Garret muttered, watching the debonair figure wend his way toward the door.

"And be damned to you," he added under his breath. Opening his paper, he tried to read it but saw none of the words, for his mind was racing. For over six years now he had been sober and industrious, helping his niece and earning a modicum of self-respect. And for what? She could dismiss him any time she chose. And no doubt she would, too, when she felt sure enough of her own abilities. But as Healey had implied, he was in a position to bring down his niece if he so chose. Better do it to her before she did it to him. It might even be fun putting his mind to the challenge.

He laid the paper in his lap, struck a match to the end of his cigar, and puffed it into life. His eyes narrowed as he watched the modulations of the smoke. It was something to think about!

While Garret was bending over his desk at the Dolphin yards the next morning reexamining the Wells contract, Damaris and Wesley were bouncing over the rutted roads leading to Purdy's Station and the Deveroe dairy farms.

"This is one of the few occasions when I get to see you," Wes said, driving the horses with a sure hand.

"Now that's just not true," Damaris protested as the familiar irritation roused by comments of this sort swelled within her.

Wesley, who was not anxious to begin an argument on what promised to be a pleasant occasion, softened immediately. "An exaggeration, then. But I'm glad I was able to come with you. It's been a long time since we had a trip together. Remember that time we went to Florida? That was such a pleasant experience. I wish we could do something like it again. Perhaps Europe . . . I've always wanted to see it, and nowadays if you haven't been to Paris or London you're not considered an educated gentleman."

"You know I could never be away from the business for that long. I'd lose all the ground, and it has taken me so long to make gains. I don't really trust Uncle Garret. He'd like nothing better than to get me out and take over everything himself."

Wesley fussed with the reins, not answering. It seemed to him that the more successful Damaris became in taking her father's place, the more distant she grew to her family. Nor was she the same woman he had loved and married. Her mind was always full of details and plans for Deveroe Enterprises— things no respectable woman should have to bother with—and there was little left for his concerns or Freddy's. He didn't like to think about it, but Damaris seemed to be growing more brittle and hard every day. But then why shouldn't she? What she was doing was unfeminine and unnatural. He had tried to hint at this before and had gotten only an angry response. Better not start that again. Peace was more important.

Damaris chewed over Wesley's comment, nurturing a sense of aggrieved injustice. Underneath her husband's dissatisfaction with her success was, she suspected, a little jealousy that she had done so well while he remained a lesser partner in Mr. Walker's law firm. He was just too easygoing to ever try to make more of himself. But why should it be unnatural for her to run a successful business just because she was a woman? It was unfair!

By the time they reached Purdy's Station, Wesley's refusal to argue had worked its effect and they enjoyed looking over the beautiful farms, inspecting the milk factories, and visiting with Jesse and his wife in their modest but pleasant house. Seeing her cousin productive and contented, Damaris was filled with a sense of self-congratulation. It gave her great satisfaction to know she had improved his fortunes, along with her own.

One morning two weeks later, Damaris was at her desk at the Dolphin when Robert Manning ushered a well-dressed gentleman with a trim white beard and mustache into her office, introducing him as Mr. Healey from Benjamin Wells & Company. Damaris assumed this imposing man had come to discuss plans for the new pilot schooner, and with characteristic graciousness she set about putting him at his ease before getting down to business.

Healey, for his part, noting her neat, trim appearance and charming demeanor, was impressed. He had expected either a shifty feminine version of Garret Deveroe or a flinty, hard-edged masculine creature with an overbearing manner. Surreptitious glances at this lovely woman in her black silk over-dress, with her lustrous hair swept back in a chignon, her fine, direct eyes, left him both surprised and confused. Garret had insisted that the first step must be to offer Damaris the choice of accepting or refusing Mr. Wells's proposal, and since he felt sure she would refuse, that would leave him free to pursue the matter his own way. Although Healey had thought it was probably wiser to work the whole arrangement behind her back, he had reluctantly agreed to go along with Garret's plan. He put Wells's proposition to her with a minimum of preparation, not bothering to smooth the way as he might have done were he dealing with another gentleman.

"I would never consider such a thing," Damaris said, trying not to let her voice betray how insulted she felt. "This is a family business and has been so for nearly one hundred years, since my great grandfather, Richard Deveroe, put his first sloop on the Hudson. Nor would my mother consider it, and she would have to agree with it. I cannot even understand why Mr. Wells should wish to be bothered with us. We have had some success, but we are only a small firm. He is practically a merchant prince and certainly a millionaire."

"Well, madam, you must realize that he achieved his position by constantly expanding his holdings, adding to those that made a profit and purging those that didn't."

"Of course," Damaris said silkily. "Shipping milk into New York has become a very lucrative business and our dairy farms have been most successful."

"That is true."

"And Mr. Wells has an interest in the railroads, does he not?"

"He does."

And he would like nothing better than to control both aspects of the trade, she thought. Over my dead body!

"But what would he do with a small shipyard like the Dolphin? Surely it could not be in his interest to run such a small concern as this when there are so many great yards right in New York."

"I cannot speak for him," Healey said smoothly, "but it is likely he would eventually close it. The future of shipping is not along the Hudson. Surely you can see that."

"They have been saying that for years now—even when my father was running this place—but the boats are still out there. Besides, I would never consider selling to anyone who would close down the Dolphin."

Healey brushed at some invisible speck on his knee, thinking that her feminine appearance was not at odds with her ability after all. She was as sentimental and foolish as all women.

"You will please go back to Mr. Wells and tell him that we absolutely and unconditionally refuse to consider his offer," Damaris said, rising and offering Healey her hand. "Please also tell him we are flattered and honored and very sorry."

Healey bowed over her fingers, thinking what a lie that was. She was not the least sorry. Now that this foolish piece of business was done with, perhaps Garret Deveroe could set about doing things his own way. He had no doubt at all that he would succeed.

After debating for two days whether or not to tell Emily about Mr. Wells's offer, Damaris finally decided she must. All the way home in the carriage she tried to find the right words, knowing that however she put it, her mother would find something wrong with the way she had handled the matter. She entered the hall, removing her brown velvet basque coat and handing it to the waiting maid, then walked to the back parlor, where she knew she'd find Emily at her usual afternoon tea. Stepping across the threshold, she recognized Ethan sitting across the room next to the hearth, holding a delicate cup and saucer on his crossed knees, and for a moment her heart seemed to stop. Confused and flustered, she stood staring at him, unable to say a word. Setting down the cup, he rose and crossed the room to give her a brotherly hug.

"I can see I've surprised you," he said, smiling at her. "I should have sent some warning ahead, but to tell the truth I wasn't sure I could get here at all."

Recovering, Damaris hugged him gingerly and sat down on the sofa next to her mother.

"I confess it is a shock to see you here. It's been so long . . ."

"I know. I wouldn't be here now, but I was sent to New York Hospital for a conference which ended earlier than planned, leaving me with two extra days. I decided at the last moment to take advantage of that and come here to see my family. Mama was happy enough to put me up in Tarrytown, and Corrine would never forgive me for being this close and not going to see her family too."

Damaris only half listened, her mind in a turmoil. Ethan was a little heavier, a little more distinguished in dress, and even more self-confident in manner, but he exuded the same vitality and earthiness she remembered so well.

"And how is Corrine?" she murmured.

"As well as can be expected considering the uncertain state of her health. She speaks so often of home and all of you, especially Freddy. How is the boy, anyway? I hope I can get to see him while I'm here."

"He'll be home very soon now," Emily said, "and he'll be so excited to know you're here. You must at least stay for supper, Ethan, or you'll have no opportunity to visit at all. He's so fond of you, you know."

"As a matter of fact, I did hope to take him shooting with me tomorrow, Damaris, if you'll allow him to miss a day of school. What do you think? He's a clever boy and not likely to suffer from one day away."

Concentrating on her cup, Damaris said, "I think you should ask Wesley. He's more concerned with Freddy's schooling and he knows the schedule at the military academy better than I."

"Oh, of course. I forgot that running a business probably leaves you little time for such matters."

Damaris looked up sharply and Ethan added hastily: "But it suits you very well in every other way. I've never seen you looking better."

When Wesley and Freddy came home they were both so delighted to see Ethan that it was easy for her to sit silently on the side, saying little. To her surprise, Wesley agreed to let Freddy go with his uncle the next day, saying only that he wished he could join them. But then Wesley could never refuse his only child anything.

Ethan brought Freddy home the following afternoon and stayed to take supper with them. Damaris bore the rest of his visit with fortitude, forgetting about Healey's offer in her effort to remember that Ethan meant nothing to her anymore. Thankfully, his visit was a short one and once he was gone she quickly regained her lost equilibrium. Back in her placid routine she recalled Healey's offer but decided not to tell her mother about it after all. What would be the point? Emily would never agree to it, and she herself had already turned it down.

It was nearly two months after Ethan's visit that Winnifred descended on Southernwood, her tiny three-year-old, Miranda, in tow, ready to sit out the three months of her husband's voyage to Australia on his new clipper, *Windward*. Though a wife and mother now, Winnifred seemed as flighty as ever to her older sister. But her liveliness served to brighten up the house, which with Freddy gone so much now, had grown to be a very quiet place. To Damaris, Miranda seemed completely undisciplined and untamed, running up and down the halls squealing and laughing, breaking into every unlocked cupboard or drawer, and destructively handling everything that was not nailed down while her mother looked on, unperturbed, indeed almost charmed. Trying to be fair, she finally admitted that she had not been around a small child since Freddy was this age. And yet she could not remember that he had been that wild. But then, she reasoned, no mother, looking back, ever did.

By the fourth week of their visit, Miranda had everyone in the household cowed yet somehow under her thumb as well, and even Damaris had begun to enjoy herself. Winnifred turned out to be a pleasant companion and, with Garret's urging, Damaris began taking days away from the office to accompany her sister into the city to visit the shops, a luxury she had not allowed herself since becoming so involved with the business.

Early one afternoon the sisters were sitting in the elegant dining room of the St. Nicholas Hotel having lunch when their conversation got around to children.

"That Miranda," Winnifred sighed. "She's so...so busy all the time. She wears me down. Sometimes I think I won't live until she's eleven."

Damaris hesitated. It seemed a grand opportunity to point out some of the defects of Miranda's upbringing, but on second thought she decided to let it pass. After all, Winnifred might have plenty to say about Freddy, and she would just as soon not hear it. Besides, they were having such an enjoyable time together, why spoil it?

"Mother used to say the same thing about you," she pointed out, congratulating herself on her excellent judgment.

Winnifred giggled. "Yes, I did used to run her quite a race. But I've settled down, don't you think? It must be Claes's influence. He's so serious, you know."

"Perhaps when you have another," Damaris offered, "things will change. A little competition could go a long way toward settling Miranda down. I hope you won't wait too long."

"I don't want to wait at all. We both want a houseful of children, but I'm afraid the family prospects don't favor it. I mean...well, look at all of us. Claes was an only child, Mother and Garret were only two, you have only one, and Corrine none. It's very depressing to come from such an unprolific family when all around you people are having more than they know what to do with."

"But that's just fate. It's in the hands of the gods. You've had one, why shouldn't you have some more? Mother did."

"But you didn't," Winnifred bubbled on. "Did you want only one child?"

"Why, no, I don't suppose so. I always expected to have more, but somehow it just didn't happen. Certainly we never did anything to prevent it."

"Why, I never supposed you would," Winnifred said in a shocked voice. "It is just the way we Whitman women are made. I declare it's very depressing."

"You really shouldn't worry so," Damaris replied. "There's nothing you can do about it anyway, so why not just let nature take its course."

"But didn't you ever wonder why? I mean, did you just say, 'That's the way it is,' and not try to find an answer? I've read everything, taken every kind of herb and powder known to man, talked to every doctor—"

"Why, that's terrible, Winnifred," Damaris broke in. "It's . . . it's degrading!"

"No it's not at all. It's fascinating. Take your own case, for instance. You've probably thought all these years that it is your fault that you never had another child. But perhaps it isn't at all. Didn't Wesley have the mumps years ago? They know now that when young men catch the mumps it can sometimes leave them . . . well, unable to father a child. So you see, it may not be you at all."

"That can't be true," Damaris scoffed.

"But I assure you it is. One well-known example is the father of our country—George Washington. He had mumps as a young man and he never had a child, though his wife had two by her first marriage. Of course, in your case," Winnifred went on, waving her fork in the air, "that can't be the proper explanation because you did have Freddy. But it's an interesting idea nonetheless."

Catching hold of the edge of the table, Damaris stiffened her arms to steady herself. She was trying desperately to remember when it was that Wesley had had the mumps. Certainly it was long before they were married. But what about Corrine? She had no children either. Yet Corrine had certainly been pregnant more than once. She had just not managed to carry them to term.

"What's the matter, Damaris?" Winnifred was peering closely over at her. "Is there something wrong with the salmon? Mine is not as good as usual."

"No, no. It's all right. I was only thinking that worrying so much about another child may actually prevent you from having one."

Winnifred sighed. "You're probably right. And it doesn't help either to have a husband who's sailing around the world months at a time!"

Twenty-seven

"I DECLARE, there are so many millionaires moving into Westchester that if you laid them end to end you'd never have to step on the gravel!"

Throwing down her copy of the Sing Sing *Republican,* Emily reached for her cup of coffee and took a large swallow, feeling the heat all the way down her throat. Across the breakfast table Damaris dabbed her fork at her plate of steak and eggs while Wesley wolfed down his breakfast and reached for more.

"It's been happening for a long time, Mother Whitman," he said between swallows. "In the long run it should be good for us—bringing in business and jobs and all that."

"But they gobble up all the land with their great big houses and they clutter up the roads with their engraved barouches and fancy chaises. They're all newcomers! They have no right to be here."

"What do you think your grandfather was when he first built this house?" Damaris said. "The people who lived here then probably called him a newcomer."

Emily glared across the table at her daughter, annoyed that Damaris was always so quick to disagree with her. "Yes, but we've been here now for seventy years. They're taking over everything while we're left behind. And such fortunes! Why, some of them commute by yacht! I'm told Mr. Gould arrives from the city at his private dock every evening."

"Mother, I think you're just jealous that they don't invite you to their parties. Be grateful they don't. We could never afford to return the invitations in the same manner."

"That's not it at all, Damaris, although it's just like you to twist my meaning. I declare, you never understand anything I say. We may not have the piles of money these people have, but we have an old and respected name. Certainly that ought to count for something."

"Ahem." Wesley coughed discreetly, seeing another argument coming. "I think as you meet more of these newcomers, Mother Whitman, you'll find they have a great respect for the antiquity of your name. A veneration, in fact."

"Well, so they should. Deveroe was a great name in New York when old John Jacob Astor was still selling furs and long before John Thompson opened his first tobacco shop."

"But, Mother, your name is Whitman now and ours is Slade. Perhaps they are not aware of the ancestral line."

Emily's eyes flashed angrily at the mention of Fade's family. "Then they ought to be!"

"Excuse me, I have some things to do," Damaris muttered, pushing back her chair to leave the table and so avoid another argument. Since Winnifred's departure, it seemed as though the quiet gloom of the house left her mother with nothing better to do than provoke these contentious discussions. Damaris often wondered if Emily was in some unconscious way seeking to liven things up a bit. Whatever the reason, she did not want to think about it so early in the morning.

"I declare, I cannot talk to that girl anymore," Emily said to Wesley as the door closed behind her daughter. "She never takes anything I say in the way it is meant, and no matter what innocent comment I make, she gets offended. It's this unnatural life she leads."

"I'm afraid I must agree with you," said Wesley, who usually made it a point never to take sides. "She grows more preoccupied every day. I often feel, as you do, that whatever I say comes out wrong and offends her when it was never my intention to do so."

"I'll tell you frankly, Wes, I believe that one of the reasons we have been ignored by most of these new people is because of Damaris. They don't know what to think of a woman trying to fit into a man's world and they are naturally prejudiced against her. It was the worst thing Fade ever did to leave her with this responsibility and I wish she would admit defeat and give it up."

"But she's handled it very well. We ought to be proud of her."

"Pooh. Proud that she ignores her husband and son, to say nothing of her mother—that she makes our good name a laughingstock?"

"Oh, I think that is an exaggeration."

"That's all you know. If you were not so henpecked you would do something about it yourself. Make her act as a woman should and turn the business over to Robert Manning or someone who can run it as it should be run."

Wesley rose stiffly. "Damaris can make her own decisions," he muttered, trying not to let Emily see how much her words hurt him. Mother Whitman, as she grew older, seemed to feel she had the right to say anything that flew into her mind. It was one of those changes that had come over her since her husband's death and made her seem so different from the woman he remembered as a youth. "I must get into the village," he added. "See you at dinner."

Emily saw the door close behind him and looked around at the empty room. How she longed for the noise and vitality that Miranda had brought to the old house. Even Winnifred's flighty silliness was preferable to the deadly quiet that was Southernwood with Damaris and her family away most of every day.

Leaning her arms on the table, she dropped her head into her hands. God, after all this time how she still missed Fade! Would this terrible emptiness never leave her? Would the anguish and the hurt never slacken, never become bearable? She had offended both her daughter and her son-in-law before breakfast was over and she had done it almost intentionally, knowing that she spoke the truth and not really caring how they took it. In all fairness, there was no one else to run the family business except Garret, and God forbid that should ever happen. And Damaris had not done badly in a man's world. She simply did not belong there. As for Wesley, well, he *was* henpecked. Perhaps if he was confronted with that fact often enough he'd do something about it.

And yet, to be honest with herself, she had to admit she was difficult to live with. For too long now she had allowed her grief to sap her strength, turning on herself and those she loved best all the energy she ought to be using in better ways. How many times had Damaris tried to tell her that? And in her heart she knew Fade would say the very same thing if he were here.

Very well, then. She would try to do something about it. She would find some outlet—the Ladies' Temperance Union or the Charity Relief Society. She had served well enough in the past and there must be some worthy cause that still needed her time and talents. She would go into the village today and call on Mrs. Brandreth, the distinguished doctor's wife. She would know what to do.

With a new purpose and a feeling of great self-righteousness, she went upstairs to change her clothes.

Everything seemed wrong, Damaris thought during the carriage ride to the Dolphin, and she wondered how she was going to put things to rights. Briskly ascending the stairs, she knocked on Manning's door and asked him to step into her office. A couple of taps on the glass partition brought Garret forth, and she faced them both.

"Sit down, please. We've got some things to discuss."

She saw how Garret watched her with hooded eyes. He's not to be trusted, Damaris reminded herself, and briefly toyed with the idea of sending him packing since he was of so little use anymore. Yet some sense of gratitude for his former help led her to humor him along and include him in these discussions. Besides, the problem today was one he had created.

She pulled up a straight-backed chair and sat on the edge, leaving room for the great swath of bustle on the back of her skirt. Women's fashions were designed for the drawing room, not a dark, cramped little office with scruffy chairs and dusty windows.

"Charlie Houston was up to the house to see me last night," she announced. "He asked for his past wages and told me in no uncertain terms that he would never set foot in the Dolphin again."

"Cantankerous old bastard. He'd better not!" Garret mumbled.

Damaris stared at him contemptuously. "He was the best shipwright we ever hired, Uncle Garret. Why you had to go and pick such a quarrel with him is more than I can tell. And to insult him as you did..."

"He insulted me! I'll be damned if I'll take that from a common laborer!"

"He was a master shipwright. Just how do you think we are going to replace him?"

"It's even worse than that, Mrs. Slade," Robert added in his slow drawl. "Four of the apprentices went with him, or at least they didn't report in this morning. There's one more may not show up either. Mr. Casey is fit to be tied."

Damaris threw up her hands. "Really, Uncle Garret, you might have had more consideration for the business. This on top of everything else! Captain Acker's complaining because the wood for his sloop shows a low impregnation of metallic salts."

"Interfering old—"

"The premium on our insurance has been allowed to lapse."

"I'll see that it's taken care of today."

"The repairs on the steam derrick have dragged on for nearly two weeks, and the load of wood we should have had a week ago has still not arrived. If it doesn't get here soon, the keel for Mr. Wells's schooner will be late getting laid. And even if it comes, how are we going to replace Houston and his men?"

"Don't upset yourself, Mrs. Slade," Manning said smoothly. "We've often had wood arriving behind times, but we usually get caught up."

"Not without these men we won't."

"I have a few people in mind," Garret offered. "My contacts at the New York yards are worth something, you know. There are plenty of fellows down there who'll come upriver if we make them an attractive enough offer. In the end we'll be glad to have seen the last of Charlie Houston. He was always a troublemaker."

"We can't afford too attractive an offer without sacrificing all our profit. I suppose I have to leave this to you, Uncle Garret, but I'm telling you straight—you'd better do a good job of it and quickly. I won't tolerate shoddy work, not even from you."

"May I remind you, my dearest niece, how only two months ago you were saying you wanted to run the business yourself and then a month later you were off visiting with your sister, asking me to take care of things for you. You can't have it both ways, Damaris. Make up your mind now. Do you want me here or not? If you don't, I'll just leave right now."

Although her common sense told her that this was the time to tell him to leave, her fears held her back. She had depended on him for so long, and she was not really sure that she could handle everything without him.

"Yes, I want you here. But you must watch your temper and not drive away men we need so badly. That was a mistake, which you must surely see. Go down to the city and bring back the tradesmen we need. Meanwhile, Robert, I want you to help me correct Captain Acker's wood and get off a telegram to the lumber company. We must get that keel laid by next month at the very latest."

Garret slipped from the room and went back to his own office, working through a stack of papers on his desk. He knew he ought to feel some satisfaction about Damaris's being so upset, since most of the things that had upset her were of his doing. It was a slow business, though, trying to sabotage the yard so that ultimately she would fail so badly she'd be forced to withdraw in his favor. Too slow a business. A stubborn woman like Damaris would hang on to the last inch—if she didn't guess what he was up to before that. There had to be a quicker way.

One of the letters on the bottom of the stack arrested his hand. It was the unpaid insurance premium, and he pulled it out, intending to leave it on Manning's table. Then, thinking better of it, he folded the paper and slipped it into his coat pocket.

While Garret was away in the city, Damaris received an elegantly engraved invitation asking her and her husband to a small supper party at the home of Benjamin Wells and his wife.

Such an invitation was the envy of every matron in lower Westchester, and curious and not a little wary, Damaris accepted.

A week later, she and Wesley set off in the barouche, both of them dressed in their best elegantly understated clothes.

The Wells's imposing mansion of Sing Sing marble was situated in an area south of Tarrytown that was studded with grand new homes. A long winding drive led them to a front door wide enough for a carriage and four to drive through. In the main hall *faux marbre* walls and statues on pedestals suggested a baroque splendor. A butler in full livery ushered them into a white and blue French drawing room laced with gilt, where they were greeted by a tall, graceful woman draped in Belgium lace. With an air of grave formality she introduced them to her husband, Benjamin Wells.

Damaris had often wondered about the rich upstart who wanted to buy out Deveroe Enterprises, and she fancied he looked her over with some of the same curiosity she felt. Well over six feet tall, he was a man who exuded power, and his look of elegance suggested attention to every detail, from the emerald stickpin in his white satin cravat to the high gloss of his patten shoes. His iron-gray hair was worn long with sweeping sideburns that flowed naturally into a very thick mustache, but his eyes, of a surprising light blue, seemed to pierce right through her. Mrs. Wells introduced them to several other people in the room, and Damaris was relieved to see that some of them were old friends she had known for years.

Benjamin Wells made no mention of her place at Deveroe Enterprises or to any other business concern, but she fancied there was a grudging interest underneath his gentlemanly politeness. She sat two places down the table from him at supper, and she noticed that the only remarks he addressed to her were in the nature of safe subjects: the new buildings going up all over the city, the state of the arts, the new bridge to Brooklyn that was being built, and the beauties of the Hudson—anything, in short, that would not compromise her identity as a woman.

The richness of the house and the food was almost overpowering, and when she and Wesley left, she was still mystified as to why they had been asked there. However, Damaris did not have to wait long for an answer.

Monday morning, as the blocks were being put into place

to lay the keel of his pilot schooner, Mr. Wells showed up at the Dolphin yards.

"I do wish I had known you planned to visit us," Damaris said, showing him to the only comfortable chair in her office. "I might have at least brought some better wine from home. However, I can offer you a little Portuguese sherry. Would you like some?"

"No thank you," Wells answered, almost filling the room with his presence. "It's a bit too early in the morning for me. I'll be honest with you, Mrs. Slade. I do not quite know how to conduct matters, dealing with such a lovely woman in a place like this."

"I can appreciate that, Mr. Wells. My father supervised the work of the yards from this office for many years and my grandfather before him. Perhaps if you remember them you may not find it so difficult."

"Perhaps," he said, studying her intently. "I like to drop in unannounced, you know. Keeps people on their toes."

"I suspected as much."

"I admit, however, that I'd heard things. Rumors, innuendo, the usual gloomy prophecies."

"What kind of rumors?" she asked, startled.

"Oh, that tradesmen refuse to deal with you; that your work is inferior because you don't know what you are doing. That you are about to go under."

"But that's absurd. Why, you yourself gave us this contract."

"Yes, but that was when your uncle was at the helm. I understand now that he's leaving."

Damaris raised an eyebrow and then replied firmly, "My uncle has been helping me for some time now, Mr. Wells, but I assure you that at no time was he at the helm. My father left this yard and all the rest of Deveroe Enterprises in my hands, and I intend to keep them there. In any case, Uncle Garret has no intention of leaving the yards in the near future."

Wells's eyes reminded her of winter ice on the Hudson. "I admire your courage," he said. "You are obviously a woman of spirit. But if you have any sense of business, you can also understand why I must reassure myself that my investment is safe."

"Of course. Why not come with me now and tour the yard? That should do more to convince you than any words of mine."

"I'd be honored to."

When he left an hour later, Damaris felt sure that both her hard-earned expertise and her new self-confidence had impressed him. Not once had he mentioned buying her out. Perhaps she had laid that idea to rest along with his concern over his investment.

She was pretty sure she had made another kind of impression on Benjamin Wells too. He had looked at her with an admiring eye that was almost flirtatious. It both pleased and intrigued her.

It was an easy matter for Garret to let himself into the Dolphin yards using his own key. He slipped through the gate, pulled it closed, and left the padlock open. Then he felt his way across the cluttered yard toward the storage shed.

Stumbling over one of the long timbers strewn about the ground, he fell forward against a barrel of nails and knocked it over. Muttering curses, he pulled the barrel upright and leaned against it until he could get his bearings in the dark. His cursed legs were trembling, and his hands too, because of the whiskey. He probably should not have had any, for he needed all his wits and strength for this job. On the other hand, without it he'd never have had the courage to come here at all.

Better get on with it, he thought, inching his way toward the shed. Every inch of this shipyard was familiar from his childhood and he knew that if he stopped to think about it too long, sentiment might interfere with what he had to do. That must not be allowed to happen. The future was what mattered now, not the past. *His* future. The past was nothing much anyway.

He found the kerosene without any trouble. There was only a small amount, stored far from the lumber, but he judged there was enough for his purposes.

Making a tour along the walls, the newly laid keels and the newly completed Acher sloop, he soaked enough boards to be sure the fire would spread. With satisfaction he noted the brisk, snapping wind—that should give momentum to the blaze once it was started. When he had finished, he set the can down near the gate and almost slipped through, then decided that was leaving too much to chance. To be really effective the fire would have to engulf the sheds too.

Leaving a thin trail from the nearest wall into the largest

shed, he dribbled a line down the middle along the shavings that littered the floor. The kerosene ran out nearly two-thirds of the way down. Upending the can, he splashed out the last drops and threw it aside. Then, working quickly, he struck a match, dropped it on the floor, and watched as the flames swept down the building and out toward the walls.

It was a beautiful sight: a long, undulating snake of fire flaring against the dark. He watched almost mesmerized before he realized he had better get out of there. Running toward the door, it occurred to him how slow-witted he had been to strike that match inside the shed instead of at the gate.

Old Josh's voice roared in his head:

Imbecile! Dolt! Trust you to mess up even this. Can't you do anything right!

This place reeked of Josh Deveroe.

He watched, amazed at how quickly the flames fanned out across the shavings and sawdust that lay inches deep on the floor. With a cry Garret saw himself suddenly standing in a lake of fire. It licked at his feet and caught at the kerosene that had splattered on his trousers, flashing into flame.

Frantically he beat at the fire that erupted around his feet and legs, hopping toward the door. Heat and smoke rose up like a wall in his face. He heard his father's voice again, thundering through the flames.

Why can't you be sensible like your sister? She'd never botch a job this badly.

I hate my sister! I wish she'd die!

The light from the fire was blinding, making it difficult to find the door. Careening sideways, he stumbled into a stack of hand-hewn timbers neatly piled on a frame, knocking them loose. The searing pain in his singed legs made it difficult to think. In agony he reached out, clutching at one of the timbers, but it rolled away and clattered to the ground, dragging him down with it. As he fell onto the burning floor, his coat caught fire and he screamed in terror.

His mother's gentle voice broke through the crashing timbers and her sweet face crystallized before him, her black hair vivid against the gold flames, her sea-green eyes brimming with sympathy.

It's all right, my darling little boy. Mama will make everything all right.

* * *

Damaris sat across from Wesley in the parlor, listlessly picking at her tapestry frame and wondering why her husband seemed so unaware of the attraction other men felt for her. Poking her needle into the canvas, she studied him quietly as he lounged in his favorite chair, his glasses perched halfway down his nose, his chin jutting forward as he peered down at the evening paper. Wesley had put on weight these last few years and was beginning to look almost pudgy. His jowls hung loosely, and his heavy frame was soft from lack of exercise. Instead of struggling against time in an effort to keep his body youthful, he was starting to show the settling of middle age, she thought, going along placidly, as he had always done, savoring the pleasures of eating and drinking with no thought of the consequences.

"Damaris, you can't see a thing in that light. You'll ruin your eyes." Emily rose from her usual spot on the sofa at the rear of the room and turned up the gas lamp on the table next to her daughter's chair. Damaris, who had been enjoying the dim light, started to protest, then changed her mind. Why did her mother have this ability to drive her crazy with the smallest motion, Damaris wondered. Why must she always treat her like a child? Why could she never understand that sometimes Damaris wanted things *her* way no matter if they made her blind, ignorant, selfish, or a babbling idiot!

In truth, she and her mother were cut from the same cloth. They were too much alike, and poor Wesley, easygoing and good-natured, was pulled back and forth as though between two strong magnets. No wonder he never asserted himself. Her father had been able to do it, but then he'd had more backbone. And, whatever her faults, Emily had always adored him enough to respect him for it. Perhaps, Damaris thought, that explained why she herself did not feel the kind of attraction for Wesley that she felt for Ethan. When it came right down to it, she did not really respect her husband. He was too easy to dominate.

"Excuse me, Mrs. Whitman. There's a gentleman to see Mrs. Slade."

"At this hour?" Emily looked up at Cora, who stood in the doorway.

Damaris turned in her chair to catch a glimpse of one of

the young apprentices from the yard standing in the hall behind Cora, almost attempting to push his way around her. From the look on his face she knew something was wrong.

"Mr. Manning sent for you, ma'am," the boy cried, looking at Damaris. "There's trouble at the yard and he thinks you should come right away."

"What kind of trouble?"

"It's a fire. It's bad and it's stubborn and they're having a time trying to keep it in. He said to bring you down as fast as possible."

"My God! I'll be there at once." Throwing aside the frame, she was already at the door.

"I'll get the carriage ready," Wesley said, dashing after her into the hall and grabbing for his greatcoat. "Wait for me here."

"No, I'll meet you at the stable," she cried, running for her hat and cloak.

Try not to panic, she told herself. But a fire in a shipyard, with timbers everywhere, rope, tar, varnish, sails—it would go up like tinder if it spread.

"I'm going too," Emily cried, dashing up behind Damaris. By the time they both had their coats, one of the servants was waiting with a lantern to guide them down the path to the stables. There they found Wesley, struggling alongside the groom to get the horses in place and ready to hand them up. Cursing the wind, which was blustery and cold, Damaris clung to the ribs of the carriage as it moved to the post road, where they could strike out with some speed. As they passed through the village she could hear the bells of the fire alarm and catch an occasional glimpse of a reddish glow above the trees. It streaked so high that her heart sank, knowing no contained fire would make such a nimbus of flame.

It was all they could do to get the carriage and the frightened horses through the crowd that had gathered around the Dolphin's outer fence. A melange of fire wagons with water pumps and long hoses stood near the entrance, where men and women were milling about, watching with eager faces as the holocaust spread and the jets of flame leaped high above the fence. Damaris, almost jumping from the carriage, ran toward the gate, but John Coleman, one of the firemen from the village, held her back.

"You can't go in there, Mrs. Slade. It's too dangerous. The whole place is going."

Looking up, Damaris saw leaping threads of flame behind the old office window. The second story of the building was filled with the fire, though it had not yet come through the roof.

"The sheds, the mold loft?" she cried.

There was a crack like the sharp snap of a rifle, followed by the sickening roar of timbers shattering and falling inside the yard.

"It's all going," Coleman answered grimly. "We tried to confine it to the shed where it started, but it spread in the wind. I'm sorry, Mrs. Slade."

Damaris clutched at his coat. "But can't you do something? Can't you save anything?"

"We tried, ma'am. Now all we can hope for is to keep it from going any farther than this yard."

Damaris turned and searched the crowd frantically. Feeling a steadying hand on her shoulder, she turned to see Wesley standing beside her and leaned against him to keep from sinking to the ground. She fought back her tears, too proud to give way to them in front of all these people. Next to Wesley, Emily stood gazing at the burned buildings, tears streaking unashamedly down her cheeks. Beyond Emily, Damaris spotted Robert Manning, staring at the yard with bleak despair on his soot-stained face. His shirt tail was straggling over his trousers and showed signs of having been singed and torn. He looked over at Damaris, and the whites of his eyes stood out vividly against his dark skin.

"It wasn't just the wind," he muttered. "A fire like this takes more'n wind. It takes the hand of man."

Damaris hardly heard his babbling as she clung to Wesley's arm. The Dolphin, pride of the Deveroe family for seventy years, was burning away into nothingness and there was no way she could save it. With the valuable buildings, timbers, and equipment would also go the frames of two ships and all the profits they represented. Feeling suddenly sick, she turned and buried her head against her husband's shoulder, more grateful for his presence than she'd ever been before.

They stayed until morning, when, weary and heartsick, they finally returned to the house for breakfast. Two hours later Damaris was back, looking over the blackened ruin that had been the Dolphin yards.

Almost nothing had been salvaged. The magnitude of the destruction was almost more than she could take in, so sudden and all-encompassing was it. What had been a successful, well-stocked shipyard yesterday was now a smoking, desolate pile of charred wood.

Yet worse was to come. Even as she picked through the rubble Robert Manning called her aside to a spot where John Coleman and two other men stood near a shapeless mound covered by a thin tarpaulin. Apologetically Coleman informed her that they had found evidence that a fire had been deliberately set and that the arsonist, trapped in the rapidly sweeping flames, had paid for his crime by dying in the ruins. His body lay there among the rubble.

Damaris stepped quickly back, averting her eyes. If only she need never know.

Obviously embarrassed, John Coleman turned his hat in his hands. "I'll be counting on you, miss, to inform your mother."

"What do you mean?"

"I'm that sorry, Mrs. Slade, to have to be the one to tell you, but that there body is Garret Deveroe and t'was his hand that set this fire, as God is my witness."

"I knew it," Robert Manning cried. "I knew it was a man's hand that done it, and it don't surprise me at all to know it was Garret. He was always a mean—"

"Hush!" Damaris snapped. She couldn't really believe it was possible that her uncle had done so despicable a thing.

"Are you sure? He was supposed to be in New York."

"Yes'm. But if you want to identify the body . . ."

"No! My husband will do that later."

"It grieves me, Miss Damaris, that this could happen to a yard that has been here so long."

"Yes," Damaris muttered. "I think I'll just go on home now and inform my mother and then send Mr. Slade down."

Robert Manning followed her outside, still muttering about Garret's infamy. Damaris felt too stunned to quiet him or even to answer his questions about what should be done next. However, just as she was about to step up to her chaise, she remembered the insurance.

"You did pay it, didn't you, Robert?" she said, turning her anxious eyes on him.

"Why, no. Mr. Garret told me he would take care of it."

"Merciful heavens! What if he didn't?"

"T'would be just like him. Though I'll be darned if I know why he should do any of this. None of it makes any sense, 'cept that he got what he deserved."

Damaris rode back to the house overwhelmed by a sense of loss. Of course the insurance had not been paid up, or why would Garret have set fire to the yard? With no insurance and everything gone, they were ruined. There would be no way to recoup this loss, no way to rebuild, no way to return to Wells and Captain Acker the advances invested in their boats. Even if she sold the dairy farms and other stocks, it would never be enough to start over.

No one would grieve over Uncle Garret, especially after what he had done. Under other circumstances she might have felt sorry that he was dead, but now she felt only rage. All the time she had congratulated herself on masterminding his redemption he had been working to bring about her ruin. Now she doubted that she would ever be able to forgive him—not even in death.

It took Damaris a week to get up the nerve, but in the end she put on her best bonnet and black watered-silk dress, curled her hair, splashed on her favorite scent, and had Forbes drive her to Tarrytown to call on Benjamin Wells. He greeted her warmly, ushering her into a cavernous room dark with nearly black oak paneling broken at intervals by shelves crammed with neat ranks of leather-bound books.

"I was so pleased to receive your note, Mrs. Slade," he said, pulling forward a large leather chair. "Please make yourself comfortable. Is your chair too close to the fire?"

"No, no, it is all right, thank you."

"Won't you share a glass of this sherry with me? It's a fine old vintage—a little dry, but excellent."

"Thank you. I should enjoy it."

Handing her an exquisite crystal goblet, he sat down opposite her and leaned forward, resting his arms on his knees.

"Let me say how very sorry I was to hear of your loss. Such a blow that must have been. Too bad . . . too bad."

Damaris nodded, afraid to speak of it for fear of bursting into tears. And that was one thing she was determined not to do here. "It was a loss to you too," she finally murmured.

"Yes, I am conscious of that, of course. But nothing compared to yours."

Deliberately she set her glass down on the table next to her chair.

"Mr. Wells, I won't mince words with you. The loss of the Dolphin yards was irreparable to my family's concerns, especially since the insurance had been carelessly allowed to lapse. I have discussed this state of our affairs with my mother and my husband, and we have concluded that under the circumstances we have no choice but to consider your offer—that is, if you are still interested in making it."

She fancied she saw the slightest smile play on his lips. "My dear lady, I am indeed interested."

"I won't pretend that this is not the last thing we wanted. My father had three daughters, but I have a son and it was my hope to hold the family concern together until he was of an age to carry it on. However . . ."

"The best laid plans, madam. That is one of the very first maxims a good businessman learns."

"Well, it is of no matter now. We have a large number of debts and we are anxious above all to hold on to our family home, Southernwood. Therefore, the wisest thing seemed to be to sell everything outright and invest what is left in something that will provide at least a modest income."

"You are very candid, Mrs. Slade. That is another lesson a good businessman learns at the beginning: never reveal all your cards too early in the game."

Twisting her hands in her lap, Damaris looked away from his intense stare. "I suppose I must admit I am not all that good at handling a business. My father had some faith in me and I wanted very much to justify it. But I have failed, and I believe the best thing now is to withdraw with some semblance of dignity."

"Surely you cannot blame·yourself for a devastating fire that was deliberately set."

"No, but I do blame myself for allowing the insurance to lapse. I knew about it and did not follow through. I let my uncle handle it when I knew how untrustworthy he was. A good businessman would have done better."

"Yes, that is true. But then that's always the trouble with a family business—relatives are kept on the payroll who would never be hired anywhere else. To tell you the truth, madam, I know what you have been up against and I think you've done a magnificent job. I expected you to sell out long ago. You stepped into your father's shoes not knowing anything and with all the prejudices of being a woman against you, yet you handled yourself very well indeed. Even now, had it not been for this unforeseen calamity, I doubt very much you would be sitting here at this moment."

His words were like balm to her hurt pride, and she stared down at her glass, hoping her tears didn't show.

"Well," Benjamin Wells said, leaning forward in his chair, "let's be practical for a moment. I shall have my lawyers draw up a contract for a very suitable sum—and not a 'modest' one either—in return for which the entire holdings of Deveroe Enterprises will become part of Wells and Company. The Dolphin will probably not be rebuilt; shipping on the Hudson is on its way out anyway. In another twenty years the only shipyards worth owning will be in New York City, and there won't be nearly so many of them as there are today. At the same time, I cannot help but feel that what you have accomplished is most impressive and shows a talent quite beyond the reach of most women. If I can devise some way to use that talent for the good of Benjamin Wells and Company, would you consider the opportunity worth your time?"

Surprised, Damaris looked him full in the face. "You mean you want me to work for you?"

He smiled at her. "Well, not exactly for me," he hedged. "Let me explain by telling you a story about a little boy named Eugene. Some years ago I had a fellow working for me in one of the Eastchester quarries. He was a fine quarryman and it was my hope to see him move up to the position of stonecutter and so improve his lot. Unfortunately, demon rum was his undoing and I finally had to let him go. He had four small children, and later, when he was caught stealing and sent to jail in White Plains, his friends told me of his family's plight. His wife, alas, was as intemperate as himself, and by the time the matter was brought to my attention, the four young children were so undernourished as to be almost unable to walk. The mother and younger babes were sent to the almshouse but the two older children—a boy nearly three and a girl of four—I proposed to help. The Benjamin Wells Home for Destitute

Children was born of that effort. It is a modest affair that has
only been in existence two years."

"I've never heard of it."

"Few people have. Very recently the boy, Eugene, who was
always difficult to control, fell from a two-story window and
died. That prompted me to take a long, hard look at the charitable institution with the thought of even closing it. However,
I found much that was good there, including the valuable assistance it has given several of my own employees. What it
needs is a strong hand at the helm, guiding it along a better
course. I set about reorganizing, establishing a board of directors, and making a wide appeal for funds from among my
friends. We are now in a position to expand our little home
and eventually take in children from all over the country. I feel
sure you are aware of the need."

"Indeed yes. From time to time we have had to seek such
assistance for some of Southernwood's people."

"Then you understand what we are about. We want our
home to be a place where improvident children can find shelter,
sustenance, and good moral training. Too often today's paupers
are tomorrow's criminals. If we can save these young sinners
from a wasted life, think what an achievement that would be."

"Your sentiments do you credit," Damaris murmured, wondering where all this was leading.

"That brings me to my point. We need a person of excep-
tional skills to develop and guide the expansion of the home,
and I think you might be just that person."

"Mr. Wells, you do me too much honor," Damaris exclaimed. "Are you sure this is what you want? It's not necessary, you know. The sale is quite complete without it."

"Quite sure."

"But I may not be the right person at all for such a responsibility. It would require extraordinary patience, not to mention
gifts."

Wells reached over and took her fingers. "Madam, your
warm heart will be as balm to those broken lives. And as for
your gifts, I myself can attest that it was you who kept Deveroe
Enterprises from me long beyond the point at which I planned
to own it. Will you consider it?"

Embarrassed, Damaris reclaimed her hand. His offer was
tempting beyond her highest hopes, for the thing she most

dreaded about this terrible sale was the enforced idleness it would bring her. Absently she watched the play of blue light streaking through the stained-glass windows. Then she said mischievously, "Of course I had hoped to be in your New York office . . ."

He laughed. "I can see that I had better watch my step or you'll be after replacing me." Reaching for the decanter, he refilled her glass. "You accept, then?"

"Yes, on consideration that I first talk it over with my husband"—a mere formality, since Wesley would never stand in the way of anything she really wanted. "I confess I would welcome something to keep me occupied and busy now that I no longer have to worry about the Deveroe interests."

All at once she felt more lighthearted than she had in days. Not only would she be doing something constructive, but this time there would be others to share the responsibility. It seemed as though she would have the best of both worlds.

"I'm very pleased," he said, studying her intently. "That should take care of everything."

"Oh, there was one other matter," Damaris said, picking up her glass. "Your generous offer almost caused me to forget that I wanted to ask you something. I would hope that my cousin Jesse Whitman could remain with the farms in Purdy's Station. He is very capable, as you probably know, and would give you good service. I do hope you will consider keeping him on."

Wells turned the glass in his hand as though his mind was not really on what she was saying. "We shall be expanding those farms, but there is always need for a good foreman. I see no difficulty in retaining your cousin."

Damaris ran her finger lightly around the rim of the glass. "Thank you. You are an easy man to do business with, Mr. Wells."

He raised his glass to her, a satisfied smile on his lips. "May I say I have never completed a business transaction with so lovely and gracious a competitor."

❧ *Twenty-eight*

BENJAMIN WELLS was as good as his word. The substantial settlement he offered for Deveroe Enterprises, coupled with the more than generous salary Damaris received as director of the home, ensured the end of financial worries for the family for years to come. When Freddy turned seventeen and finished school, Damaris and Wesley took him to Europe. They claimed it was a combined birthday-graduation present, but in truth it was a trip they had longed to make for many years. Damaris was especially happy, for it was her first real vacation since her long-ago trip to Florida with Wesley. After all the years at the Dolphin, followed by another four years of dealing with the depressing details of countless broken lives on the one hand and the spasmodic charity of egocentric rich matrons on the other, she had felt overwhelmed by the need to escape it all. At least for a time.

The trip was all she had hoped it would be. There was so

much to see and do, so many places to visit that she had only read about before, so much pleasure to be gained from the company of her husband, who was always eager to accommodate himself to her wishes, and her son, who was as thrilled and fascinated with everything they saw as she herself. How could she not enjoy it? They were gone nearly four months, and when they finally sailed through the Narrows into New York Harbor she was happy to be home after a trip that had been perfect in almost every way.

Emily greeted them at the dock, waiting in a hansome cab standing among a sea of horses and carriages. It was Freddy who spotted her, weaving his way through the assorted conveyances and animals, a large portmanteau held over his head.

"Wait until you see what I brought you from Venice, Grandmother," he cried, climbing into the cab to plant a wet kiss on Emily's cheek. She hugged him warmly, delighted to have him back.

"You must have grown another inch while you were away! But you're as skinny as ever. My goodness, I thought surely the excellent food in France would have fattened you up a little."

"I'll run back and get Mother and Dad. Don't go away now."

Emily laughed. "That's not likely, is it? We'll be lucky to get out of this crowd and back to the hotel by six o'clock tonight!"

One look at her mother told Damaris that something was wrong, but she did not broach the subject until the two of them were alone later that evening. After a light supper in the dining room of the Fifth Avenue Hotel, Wesley took Freddy off to sample a cigar in the men's barroom and the two women went upstairs to their suite. Relieved to let out her corset laces and slip into a silk robe and soft slippers, Damaris settled into a comfortable chair and asked her mother how she had found Winnifred and Corrine. To her consternation Emily burst into tears.

"Why, Mother! For heaven's sake..." Damaris cried, kneeling swiftly beside Emily's chair.

"It's Corrine. She's so very ill, Damaris. I didn't want to tell you of it like this, but I just can't help myself. I cry all the time."

Stunned, Damaris put her arm around her mother's shoulders and tried to comfort her. "I had no idea. Why didn't you write me?"

"No, no. There was no need to spoil your trip, especially when you'd looked forward to it for so long."

"Well, what's the matter with her?"

Emily wiped at her eyes with her handkerchief. "No one seems to know. She's just wasting away. She was always slight, but now she must not weigh a hundred pounds. Her skin is like parchment and all her bones show. She puts a brave front on things, but I watched her. She can hardly go up a flight of stairs without stopping for breath."

"But Ethan is a doctor, for God's sake. Are you saying *he* doesn't even know what's wrong with her? What about his hospital? Can't they treat her?"

"She won't allow him to help her. I don't know what's between them, but I suspect it is an old hurt. In fact, I suspect she wants to die. If that is true, I don't think I will ever be able to forgive Ethan Slade!"

"She's not going to die, is she?" Damaris whispered.

"Yes! Yes she is, the way she's going now. Unless somebody does something to convince her to get help, she is certainly going to die and very soon. Oh, Damaris. Go to her. Talk to her. Convince her she's only hurting herself to get back at him!"

Abruptly Damaris rose. "I can't do that, Mother. Besides, if she won't listen to you, she's certainly not going to pay any attention to me. I cannot believe Ethan would allow this to happen."

"What does he care," Emily said bitterly. "He's got his busy life and all the prestige that goes with it. And though Corrine would not tell me so, I suspect he has his lady friends as well. I think that is what has hurt her the most, that and her disappointment over not being able to bear a child. She had this idea fixed in her mind that things would have been different if they'd had children, but I think she is dead wrong. Nothing would change Ethan!"

"Well, she certainly tried hard enough. He can't fault her for that. She must have had three miscarriages at least."

"Yes, and that is probably the cause of all her ill health. Oh, Damaris," she cried, breaking out into fresh sobs, "it breaks my heart to see her like this and know we may lose her. I can't bear it!"

Damaris, who was having her own trouble assimilating this news, sat on the edge of the chair and laid a steadying arm around Emily. "Come now, Mother. She's not gone yet. We'll think of something. Insist that she come up here to stay with us. Then perhaps between the two of us we can get her into the city and to one of the excellent physicians here. It's not hopeless."

Emily leaned against Damaris, more grateful than she had ever been for her daughter's strength. "Do you think it would really work?"

"It's worth a try."

"Damaris, you don't know how happy I am to have you home again."

Damaris turned away so that Emily could not see her face. She had not been on American soil twelve hours yet and already her gay, lighthearted trip was fading away under family troubles and concerns. And such a miasma of emotions! She was flattered and pleased by her mother's compliment, yet distressed at her worry and grief. She could barely tolerate the idea of Corrine being sick unto death, so conflicting were the feelings it aroused in her. She loved her sister and could not bear the thought of losing her at so young an age. But Corrine dead would mean Ethan free. Excitement flamed into life at the thought, and determinedly she pushed it from her mind. It was too terrible to even consider. But it fluttered there, in the background, corroding the contentment she had so cherished during her long trip abroad.

There was only one answer: she must see Corrine—not in Philadelphia, with Ethan around, but at Southernwood. Somehow she must get her up there. But how to do it?

"Freddy!"

Emily looked up. "What?"

"Freddy could do it," Damaris cried, turning back to her mother. "I'll have him write and ask Corrine to come. We'll think up some excuse or other why he can't go down there. She hasn't seen him in nearly half a year and I'll just bet she'll jump at the chance to visit him."

"Oh, Damaris, do you think it will work?"

"I'm sure of it, Mother. I'll have him write the letter to-

ight—no, in the morning, after I've thought of the right things
o say. It will work. It's just got to."

Catching some of Damaris's enthusiasm, Emily began to
brighten. "Let me think for a moment," she said, "and I'll tell
you just how to word it."

Freddy's letter was soon dispatched and Damaris went back to
her work at the Wells Home with the specter of her sister's
illness hovering over everything she tried to do. By the end of
her first week back, she felt as though she had never been
away. By the end of the next week she began to suspect that
her obsession with Corrine's health had more to do with Ethan
than with her sister. If Corrine was truly ill, it was almost
certain that she and Ethan would soon meet again and perhaps
the old feelings would be fanned back into life.

Though living with her mother was often trying and her
work at the home often seemed to weigh her down—for it was
terribly depressing to see so much misery, especially when it
involved young children—she had gotten on well these years.
She had her husband and her son and her beloved Southernwood. Surely the old ghost of a hopeless passion would not
have the power to disrupt the order of her life after so long a
time.

On a brilliant Sunday in October, Damaris came out of church
on Wesley's arm to a world bright with the glassy crispness of
fall. Slipping her fur muff over one hand, she leaned closer to
her husband and whispered: "My goodness, but Reverend Abbott went on for a long time this morning. I thought he would
never end. And so dull!"

"Poor old fellow is about in his dotage . . . Ah, good morning, Mr. Wells. It's a fine autumn day, isn't it?"

Benjamin Wells lifted his tall silk hat. "Fine indeed, Mr.
Slade. Good morning, Damaris. May I say you almost outshine
the brilliance of the foliage in that lovely gown."

Damaris nodded her thanks for the compliment. She had
been hoping to avoid Wells after church, sure he would raise
some issue or other about the home. It was his habit.

"That hat has the look of Paris, I should say."

"You are right." Damaris brightened. "How clever of you.
I brought it back with me from our recent trip."

"Oh, my good wife has dragged me through the Parisian shops often enough to make me something of a connoisseur. It is very becoming."

Wesley gave her a gentle tug in the direction of their carriage, also hoping to avoid any serious conversation. Every time they were around Benjamin Wells it meant some new worry for Damaris. Besides, there was something disturbing in the way the man always looked her over.

To Wesley's consternation Wells fell in step beside them. "I have a pressing problem, Damaris my dear, which must be faced, and since it is a rather complicated one I thought to stop by the home tomorrow morning. Will you save some time for me?"

"Of course. May I ask what kind of problem?" she asked, filled with dismay.

He was obviously reluctant to say too much. "It concerns something that was brought to my notice by Mrs. Weeks about that young Howland child. I'm sure it can be cleared up in a few moments' conversation."

"Mrs. Weeks."

"Now I must go have a quick word with Reverend Abbott. Wonderful sermon today, don't you think? See you tomorrow, my dear."

With a wave of his hat he was off, leaving them at their carriage. Wesley helped Damaris up, then sat beside her, acutely aware of the cloud that now hovered over her. With a flick of the reins he set their pacer smartly down the street toward the post road.

"Mrs. Weeks!" Damaris muttered. "That meddling old busybody. Wouldn't you know she'd go to Mr. Wells with her tales. She's never approved of the way I handle things."

"Isn't she the wife of the banker who lives in Irvington?"

"Yes, and a member of the board whose sole aim is to make my life miserable. I suspect she has a relative or a friend that she'd like to see take my position and she wants to drive me out. I'm sure that is what's behind all this. The Howland child is only a means to an end."

Wesley raised his hat to Dr. and Mrs. Brandreth, who were standing in front of the Union Hotel, and turned the carriage onto the post road.

"What's wrong with the Howland child?"

"I told you about her. She's the little girl whose parents tried to give her away. When she came to us she did not weigh thirty pounds although she was four years old. Now that she's clean and healthy and strong, her worthless parents have decided they want her back. Probably because she would be of use to them."

As they left the village behind, the road grew empty, allowing them a fast, easy pace.

"But surely Mrs. Weeks would not want to return her to such a home."

"Oh, but she does. Somehow they have convinced her it was all a misunderstanding and they actually love the child dearly. What a lie! Either Camilla Weeks believes them or she is just using this as an excuse to question my judgment. At any rate, I dread having to fight out the issue with Mr. Wells. He almost always sides with his rich friends."

"That's because he depends on them for the money to run the home. Try not to worry about it, Damaris. It will only spoil your day."

"Oh, Wes. How can I not worry about it!"

"It will all work out in the end. Perhaps it's time you began to lessen your involvement in the home anyway."

"You sound just like Mother."

They rode on in silence, Damaris brooding over the next morning's confrontation.

"By the way, dear," Wesley said, breaking into her thoughts. "I ran into Robert Manning yesterday in the village and he asked me if we had any work for him up at the house. He's had a difficult time since the Dolphin burned down, and he desperately needs something steady. I told him I'd mention it to you."

"All he knew was how to build boats," Damaris said. "Yet he had worked at the Dolphin all his life. I suppose we ought to be concerned."

"Exactly. I thought you might want to help him out."

"But, Wes, you could have hired him. You know as much about the estate as I do."

"Oh, I wouldn't think of doing such a thing without first consulting you. It should be your decision."

"No, it really ought to be Mother's. As a matter of fact, I think the present farm manager is about to leave and largely because of her. He says she is driving him crazy, half the time telling him to do things the way he wants and then, when he does, running in to change everything. Robert might be able to take over when he leaves, although it is not the kind of work he knows best."

"Why don't I tell him to stop around and talk to you, then?"

"You talk to him, Wes. I have enough to handle with all this trouble at the home."

Wesley focused his gaze intently on the road ahead. "I'd really prefer not to do that, Damaris."

"Oh, very well. There ought to be time some evening this week when he could sit and talk with Mother and me. He might as well know right away what he'll be dealing with."

"That's my girl," he said, snapping the reins over the bay's back. "Now get along, horse, or we'll be late for dinner."

By the end of that week Damaris had hired Robert Manning and calmed Benjamin Wells. Camilla Weeks was a thornier matter. That formidable matron was not really worth the aggravation she was beginning to cause, Damaris felt, and more and more she found herself wondering if she should not just give up the battle and resign her position at the home. Perhaps she had served long enough in this difficult and demanding job. She was still mulling over the problem when she arrived at Southernwood on Friday. She climbed out of the carriage to hurry up the stairs and out of a cold mist that spelled the end of autumn. As she was reaching for the door, it was thrown open and Emily rushed out onto the porch carrying a letter in her hand.

"What's wrong?" Damaris said, taking in her mother's obvious distress.

Emily thrust the letter at her. "It's from Ethan," she cried. "He says Corrine cannot come up here. Oh, Damaris. He says she is dying!"

From the moment she read Ethan's letter until the moment she stepped off the train in Philadelphia, Damaris carried about with her the feeling that this could not be happening. Surely she would see Corrine welcoming them, standing in the doorway, glowing with that quiet happiness she always exuded when she was around her family. But Damaris was also terribly worried about facing Ethan. It had been so long. How would she feel? Would the past be easily forgotten, buried by the concerns of the present?

Ethan met them at the station, scowling and reserved, but with something about him that still recalled the shining youth of her girlhood. He treated her with such polite indifference that Damaris wondered why she had ever worried about seeing him. Wasting no time on small talk, he ushered them into a rather large hansom cab.

"And how is my daughter?" Emily asked anxiously, not at all reassured by his grave demeanor.

"A little better, I think," Ethan replied, sitting between Freddy and Wesley on the crowded seat. "But you'd better be prepared for a shock when you see her. She's changed very much these last few weeks."

"Oh dear..."

Ethan balanced his hat on his knees and listened absently to Emily's chatter, trying vainly at the same time to keep his eyes off Damaris sitting opposite him. She was looking particularly beautiful in her elegant velvet traveling suit and an exquisite hat that had the unmistakable look of Parisian fashion. She glowed with good health: her figure, more mature now, was so well rounded and solid, her hair so lustrous, her eyes so full of life. When he thought of Corrine waiting at home...

Glancing up, Damaris caught his devouring stare and colored, looking as quickly away as he did. So there *was* something still there, she thought. But it must not be allowed to surface. As if in tacit agreement with her, Ethan, though she darted infrequent looks his way, did not so much as glance at her again.

Yet any disquiet she felt over Ethan was quickly forgotten at the first sight of her sister's wasted body. Corrine looked like an old woman. She had lost much of her beautiful hair and her skin had the appearance of old parchment.

"I can't stay in this house," Damaris cried to Wesley once they were alone and she could give vent to her tears.

Placing a comforting arm about her shoulders, he held her against him. "We don't have to. They have only two spare rooms. We can give one to your mother, and Freddy can stay in the other. Ethan particularly asked if Freddy could stay here since he cheers Corrine so much."

"But I want him with me!"

"Come now, Damaris. Don't begrudge your sister the only small comfort that is in our power to give her. For Ethan's sake, too, I would like him to stay. They both need him right now."

"But it's so depressing for him. Are you sure he won't mind?"

"I've already asked and he's agreed. He's as fond of his aunt and uncle as they are of him, you know, and he says he wants to do what he can to brighten up Corrine's last days. I'm proud of him for that."

She wished she could be proud, too, but in fact she was a little jealous of the way Ethan and Corrine had once again taken over the boy's affections. As she had many times before, she wondered if Ethan suspected that Freddy might be his son. Miserably she clung to Wesley as the only steady support in her life, hating herself for feeling an old bitterness at a time like this. To see Corrine so broken and ugly by illness was terrible. She didn't want her sister to die! God knows she didn't!

"Don't cry, Damaris," Wesley went on soothingly. "We'll find a place nearby so you can spend some time here every day. And when I have to go back to New York, if you want to stay on longer, perhaps Freddy can join you then. Will that be all right?"

"Yes, yes," she said, wiping at her eyes. "Thank you, Wesley."

"Dry your tears now, before Ethan comes back. I have a feeling it would unnerve him greatly to see any of us break down. You must not give way in front of him or Corrine. Who knows, maybe she'll get a little better now that she has her family around her."

Wesley's words proved almost prophetic, because for a time Corrine did improve. Freddy spent hours with his aunt, reading to her, playing cards when she was up to it, regaling her with tales of his European trip, and his efforts were like a tonic to Corrine. On the days when Ethan carried him off to the hospital, an excursion he loved above all others, Corrine wilted and drooped visibly. Then the fatigue and apathy that had been so apparent when they arrived seemed to grip her again. They had been there one week when it became obvious that not even

Emily's considerable strength of will was going to save Corrine.

In all that time Damaris saw little of Ethan and only once had a short time alone with her sister. That particular afternoon Freddy had carried Corrine to a chair near the window so she could feel the sun on her face for a little while. Emily then took her grandson off downstairs, leaving the two sisters alone. Corrine was sitting back, eyes closed, savoring the warmth of the sun through the window, and Damaris was bent over a shirt she was attempting to mend. After a few comments about everyday matters, they lapsed into silence and Damaris thought perhaps Corrine had fallen asleep. Concentrating on her sewing, Damaris was startled when her sister spoke. She looked up to see Corrine watching her intently.

"Seeing you sitting there like that takes me back to my days at the Union Hospital during the war," Corrine said, a small smile playing about the corners of her pale lips.

"Why, I thought you girls never had time for such mundane things as mending with all the nursing you had to do."

"The washing and mending were for afterward, when all you wanted to do was drop into bed. You know, I didn't realize it then, but those were the happiest years of my life. I never worked so hard or felt so well."

Damaris wanted to push aside the air of finality about those words, try to convince Corrine there were good years still to come. But that was foolish and false. Her sister had nothing if not the courage of true honesty. She deserved better than a cheap effort at deception now.

"Have you not been happy with Ethan?"

Corrine turned back to the window. Finally she said, "Yes, at times. Especially when we were first married and living in Washington. Then, well, I don't know what happened. I suppose I failed him somehow."

"More like he failed you," Damaris muttered.

There was another long pause while Corrine rallied her strength to answer. "Perhaps he has. Yet he's been good to me in his way. I worry about him a little now . . ." She struggled for breath. "He is always looking for something that he expects to find just around the next corner, something that will make him really happy. But he never finds it. I don't know if he'll be able to handle the truth, when it finally comes to him, that there is no such happiness waiting for him, that happiness has to come from within himself and he does not have it."

Distracted, Damaris pricked herself with the needle. The pain she felt in her finger only accented the other pain she felt.

"Take care of him for me, Damaris."

"Oh, Corrine!"

"He needs someone and I won't be here to—"

"Stop it, Corrine," she cried, jumping up. "Stop worrying about Ethan. He has ten times the strength you do. Take care of yourself!"

She could see at once that she had upset her sister. With huge dark eyes, Corrine watched as Damaris shook her finger angrily in the air, trying to hide the real cause of her distress.

"What have you done? You've hurt yourself."

"Yes. I stuck the needle in my finger. It's nothing at all, but it hurts like the very devil at first."

Wearily Corrine fell back against her chair. "I remember during the war my fingers were pricked all the time. It was one of the hazards."

"You know I was never very good at sewing. You could always make my work look shabby, you did everything so well."

Corrine smiled weakly. "Well, you were better than Winnifred!"

Picking up the shirt, Damaris settled down in her chair again. She could hear her mother talking to Freddy as they came up the stairs. In a moment she would enter the room, bearing another cordial that was sure to give Corrine back her strength.

"That's not saying much! Poor Winnifred. She struggled so hard and she could never make her stitches look like anything. Remember the times she used to throw her sampler down and stomp on it?"

Damaris was relieved to see Corrine close her eyes and smile at the pleasant memory. The tense moment was safely by and it would not come again. They would go on, not exactly pretending, but not saying the dreadful words that would bring death too close. She wanted to weep but she could not, must not.

"Here, my love," Emily said, pulling up a chair near Corrine's. "Freddy, bring over that little table, please dear. That's right. We'll set it down right here beside you, Corrine. Come along now, I'll help you drink it. This is going to do you a world of good . . ."

* * *

On the night before Wesley was to return to Southernwood, they were awakened in the early hours of the morning by a summons from Freddy, who had run the block to their lodgings. Corrine was suffering a sudden and devastating coughing spell. Throwing on their clothes, they rushed to Ethan's house to find that, drowning in her own phlegm, she had died in Ethan's arms just a few moments earlier.

Damaris stayed in the bedroom only long enough to pull her mother, distraught and near hysterics, away from the inert body of her daughter. With only a glance at Ethan, she left him to Wesley and Freddy and gave her whole attention to her mother, whose relentless sobs had something of madness about them. For an hour Emily clung to her, crying until it seemed she could have no tears left, then crying some more. This outpouring of grief, terrible as it was for Damaris, seemed to help Emily, for as dawn came she was able to put on her clothes, comb her hair, and turn her attention to preparing her daughter's body for burial. She flatly refused to allow anyone else to touch Corrine.

Worn out from lack of sleep, choked by tears that would not be released, Damaris wearily trudged downstairs to the kitchen to make herself a cup of tea. At first she thought the room was empty, but then she saw Ethan slumped over the table, his head on his arms. When he heard her footsteps, he lifted his head. Though his eyes were black and empty, Damaris saw no suggestion of tears.

"I didn't mean to disturb you," she said softly.

"It's all right. I was just looking for a place to light and I found this." He didn't appear to be aware of what he was saying.

"Let me fix you some tea," Damaris said, moving to the stove in a brisk, businesslike manner. "Look, the kettle is already hot."

She began rummaging around in the cabinets, searching for a cup.

"I think I'd rather have whiskey," Ethan muttered.

"Nonsense, this will be better for you. How do you like your tea? Strong, as you used to?" Foolish question.

Without answering, Ethan rose from the table and stared at her. "Damaris..." There was so much sorrow in the way he said her name.

"Oh, Ethan. I'm so sorry!"

She went and put her arms around him. He did not hold her or respond in any way except to lay his head on her shoulder. She gently stroked his hair, caressed his cheek. And still her tears would not come.

"There you are, old fellow. I've been looking for you everywhere."

Looking up, Damaris saw Wesley standing in the doorway. Moving forward, he took Ethan from her and led him to the door. "Come along, it's bed for you. You need some rest. How's Emily, Damaris?"

"She's better now. She's getting dressed and then she'll take care of Corrine's . . . body."

Wesley paused a moment, looking over at her, his arm around his brother. "Are you all right?"

"Yes. I just wanted to make some tea."

"Good idea. Make me a cup, too, will you. I'll just get Ethan to bed, and then I'll join you. There's a dear."

They were gone, leaving her to search for the teacups.

They took Corrine's body back to Westchester and buried her near her father and grandfather. The old cemetery at the Presbyterian meeting house was almost too full now for new graves, yet Emily jealously, stubbornly, held on to the area that the Deveroe family had marked as its own as far back as Richard Deveroe's death in 1810. She had always thought there was just room left for her eventually to lie next to her beloved Fade, and never had she dreamed that one of her own daughters would precede her there. She would be the next Deveroe to claim that precious ground, for it was unthinkable that either Winnifred or Damaris, the one so full of life and the other so strong, should go before her as Corrine had done.

Ethan returned with them, and Winnifred arrived with noisy eight-year-old Miranda for the sad private services at the foot of the hill. It was a dismal gray day with the sky dripping tears to match those of the sad group of mourners at the bleak graveyard.

Once back at the house, Damaris had fires laid in both downstairs parlors and copious amounts of food and punch set out for the steady stream of friends and neighbors who dropped by to pay their respects. Among the most welcome were Jesse

Whitman and his wife, whom Damaris had not seen for nearly two years. Once again she was impressed with Jesse's quiet inner strength. She felt great satisfaction at having prevailed upon Mr. Wells to keep him on at the Purdy's Station farm.

It was a difficult afternoon for Miranda, who, sensing that the adults around her were distressed and preoccupied, exhibited her anxiety by demanding attention and giving way to loud complaints when it was denied her. Her distraught mother was too overcome with grief to cope with her young daughter. Winnifred knew Corrine had been very ill, but she had not let herself believe she would really die and now the whole weight of her sister's death opened up vistas of terror and loss that she had never dealt with before, not even when her father died. Her answer was to cling to Damaris.

Damaris found her sister's emotional needs very draining, but she was more worried about their mother. Emily tottered on the edge of hysteria, clutching for a handhold to keep herself from drowning in agony. It wouldn't take much to push her beyond reason, Damaris feared. How could she herself hold on if her mother fell apart before their eyes?

When at last the terrible afternoon was over and the last visitors had taken their solemn faces out the door, Damaris looked around the parlor and sighed with relief. It was quiet now, since Winnifred had finally taken Miranda upstairs and Emily had agreed to lie down and try to rest for a while. Seeing Wesley moving quietly around the room behind her, Damaris thought she could not have gotten through the day without him. Suddenly she remembered Ethan, and asked Wesley where he was.

"He's left," Wesley told her, stacking some of the empty cups and dirty plates on a tea cart for the parlor maid to take away.

"When did he leave?" she asked in surprise, assuming he must have gone back to his parents' house for the night.

"He spoke to me only very briefly because there were so many people to talk to. But he said he could take no more and was going back to Philadelphia. He promised to keep in touch, but he wasn't sure what he was going to do next."

"Back to Philadelphia! So soon!"

"You can understand how he feels. This is not his home anymore. It was Corrine's, and now that she's gone, he finds only pain here. I didn't try to hold him back. I wanted to be with him longer, but I realized it was selfish of me."

"Well, it was selfish of him to leave. He's not the only one who's suffering!"

"Yes, but we have each other and he has no one now."

She turned her back on her husband and stared down at the dying flames in the fireplace. She had longed to comfort Ethan and now he was gone. He hadn't even said good-bye.

🌹 *Twenty-nine*

EMILY AWOKE from a drug-induced sleep feeling as though her head were three times its normal size and full of cotton wool. Groaning, she staggered across the room to the washstand and poured out a little cold water to bathe her forehead. The icy shock of it hurt her skin but soothed the dull ache in her head a little.

After Fade's death she had been surprised to learn that grief could be a physical thing. That was what it was like now. When she thought of Corrine lying in a coffin underneath the earth, a cutting, twisting pain gripped her body. Losing a child, even a grown child, is the most terrible thing a woman can go through, she thought, for no matter how old she is, the mother wants to comfort and protect her baby from suffering and harm. Gladly, willingly, she would have died in Corrine's place if only God had allowed it. She would happily have taken on her daughter's death rather than have to bear this suffocating, paralyzing pain.

There was no use now trying to pull herself up, force herself to get out and get involved. She no longer had the heart. She could not understand what possible reason the Lord could have for leaving her here—a useless, crotchety old woman no one needed or wanted.

She stared at her reflection in the looking glass, pressing her fingers against the sides of her face, stretching back the skin. Where was the woman she used to be, the woman who would have once found her way out of useless grief and searched for something constructive to keep her busy? Where was the face of the young girl she had been, the vibrant, youthful face that Fade used to take between his hands and cover with his kisses? Why wasn't he here now? He would have helped her bear this terrible pain and kept her going, for his sake if not her own. He would have told her she was making Damaris's life miserable, for surely she was, and that she must get hold of herself. If he were here, she could confess to him that Damaris was almost an affront to her now: Damaris with her health, her iron will, her opinions, her constant "Mother, do this" and "Mother, do that."

Why did Fade have to die? Why did Corrine have to die? And why did she have to live?

God, how old she looked! Her hair, once so thick and lustrous, was thin and anemic-looking, a sickly shade of steel gray. Her skin was pockmarked with brown age spots, and where it was not puffy it was veined and inflamed. She was ugly—an ugly old woman who had outlived her usefulness— and she hated herself. Throwing on some clothes, the darkest, most depressing she could find, and with her hair half-combed, she went downstairs to face breakfast and the family when she would have preferred to drug herself with laudanum and sleep away the long hours of the day.

Looking up from the table where she sat sipping her coffee and glancing through the pages of *Harper's Bazaar,* Damaris saw her mother coming through the doorway and recognized the dark contentious lines set on her face.

"Oh dear," she muttered to Wesley. "Watch out. It's going to be another one of those days!"

Damaris had hoped that with time her mother's grief would diminish and her disposition improve, but she could see no sign of either. Since Corrine's death six months before Emily had dropped all her former activities, refusing to find comfort in anything, Damaris thought, and turning all her energies into making those around her as miserable as she was. Every day she seemed to grow more complaining and judgmental, constantly dwelling on her own health or lack of it and the many grievances she suffered at the hands of her family.

At times Damaris feared that she herself was growing more like her mother under the weight of Emily's demands. Problems at the home now seemed twice as difficult to deal with than ever before. It irritated her beyond measure that Wesley was always ready to escape to the quiet of his law office, leaving her to handle all the problems of Southernwood alone; that she and not Winnifred should have to bear the burden of living every day with their difficult mother. Even Freddy irritated her. He had so many interests and activities that his very patience with his grandmother the rare times he was around her was almost an affront. And he still clung to his dream of living and studying with his uncle in Philadelphia. For now, Ethan's whereabouts were unknown so there was no immediate danger of Freddy's fulfilling that dream, but Damaris was determined it would never happen. Even with Garret dead, she had no intention of encouraging the bond between Ethan and Freddy.

Often Damaris debated moving away from Southernwood, but she could not bring herself to leave the house and land she loved so dearly. And so she stayed, quarreling with her mother, resentful of her patient, long-suffering husband, irritated with her son, and wondering where Ethan had gone and what he was doing, hating herself for remembering that he was now free and she was not.

"Damaris, I want you to drive me to the cemetery this afternoon," Emily said as she sat down at the breakfast table. "I have some biennials that I'd like to transplant near Corrine's and your father's graves."

Damaris set her cup down sharply on its saucer. "But, Mother, I stayed home today to do some things for myself. Besides, look at the weather! It would be foolish to go out on such a blustery day. You'll catch a cold and be sick. And the plants will probably die anyway."

Emily's jaw was set in the familiar lines of defiance. "Why

must you argue with me whenever I ask you to do something? This is the time to transplant young hollyhocks, Canterbury bells, and English daisies, and frankly I don't care if I catch a cold and die. Perhaps then you'll wish you had on one occasion done something I asked without complaining."

"Now that's not fair," Damaris bristled.

"Damaris has a point, Mother," Wesley said in his level voice, laying down his newspaper. "It would be better to wait a day."

"I don't want to wait! Any other day Damaris won't be home."

"Perhaps you could ask one of the stablemen to drive you."

"That's not the point, Wes," Damaris said testily. "I am always running around carrying you here or there, Mother, and you never give me credit for it. I wait on you hand and foot."

"You most certainly do not! You spend all your time taking care of Mr. Wells's charity, and whenever I ask you for the smallest favor I always get some kind of petulant excuse. Of course I could ask one of the servants to do it, but I particularly wanted you to go with me. You never visit your sister's grave and you should."

"Really, Mother, what earthly use is it to go stand and stare at a mound of earth? Corrine is not there, nor Father either."

"It's as much of them as is left to us."

"Damaris, Mother, please..." Wesley broke in. "Surely this subject can be handled without an argument. I'll drive you, Mother Whitman, if that would make you happy."

"I did not ask you, I asked Damaris."

Damaris could feel her irritation expanding uncontrollably into real anger. "You don't really want me to go with you, Mother, you just want to make sure I pay my respects to the dead. Why can't you let me do things my own way?"

"I only wish with all my heart that I could drive myself. That's the worst thing about getting old—you're so damnably dependent on ungrateful children."

Wesley folded his paper, obviously anxious to escape from the unpleasantness that had erupted. "Well, I must be going. You're quite sure you don't wish me to drive you, Mother?"

Damaris turned on him. "She's already made it clear that she's determined to make me do it. Go on, escape to your law office and leave it to us to work out."

Wesley leaned over and kissed Damaris lightly on the top of her head. "All right, dear," he said softly. "See you later."

Damaris angrily watched Wesley leave. She knew she would end up driving her mother down to the cemetery and have to stand in the wind for a half hour while Emily went through her ritual of bereavement. Both of them would probably end up with the ague. And in spite of that, the next time she opened her mouth, her mother would find something wrong with whatever she said. That was all there was to her life now and she simply could not see how she was going to bear it for the years to come.

"You should not have spoken so harshly to Wesley, Damaris," Emily murmured.

"Oh, mother, please . . ."

Damaris buried her nose in her magazine. How could she say that she knew Wesley did not deserve her sharp words? How could she explain that she did not know what demons made her behave so badly to such a patient, long-suffering husband whose love for her was unquestionable? Overcome with guilt, Damaris laid the magazine aside, leaned her elbows on the table, and stared down at her plate.

Watching her, Emily could sense exactly what she was feeling; she had often felt the same way herself.

"Forgive me, Damaris. I was bad-tempered and short just now and I really did not mean to be. I meant to ask you very kindly if you would drive me to the cemetery, and if you had something else to do I had every intention of accepting it graciously. I don't know what comes over me sometimes and I know you get the full blast of my dissatisfaction."

Looking up into her mother's drawn face, Damaris could see she meant every word. And she was grateful to her, even though she knew the same scene would be played out again tomorrow and the next day.

"It's all right, Mother. I'll drive you down. It's just that I find the cemetery so depressing and it doesn't mean the same to me as it does to you. But if you are set on going, I'll take you."

"Thank you, my dear," Emily answered, gripping her arm. "You really are good to me and I don't know what I'd do without you."

The trip to the cemetery was not too bad, since the wind had dropped a little by afternoon and a sullen sun even managed to sneak a glance now and then at the gray world. This must have been a very peaceful place once, Damaris thought, looking around at the weathered stones, but now with the post road so near it was anything but. Carriages, wagons, chaises, and buggies rolled by incessantly, breaking the sleep of the dead with their rattling harnesses, iron-rimmed wheels, and heavy-footed horses. After nearly an hour, she drove back up the hill, a quietly subdued Emily beside her.

As they turned through the gates and wheeled along the drive skirting the hill toward the house, Emily said, "Tomorrow you can help me carry down one of those young rose bushes from the garden. It should add a nice touch by summer."

A stone lodged itself somewhere in Damaris's chest. "Mother, you know I cannot drive you down there again tomorrow. I have to be at the Wells Home."

There was a long pause before Emily spoke again, her voice sullen. "There are other people working there, Damaris. Surely they can get along without you. You give far too much of your time to that place, to the detriment of your family, I might add. I wish you would give it up."

"I've already cut down on the time I spend there. Isn't that enough? I don't want to give it up altogether. It's my work and I've done a good job of it. I'd go mad sitting around Southernwood day after day. It wouldn't hurt you to have something to occupy your time instead of moping about that cemetery day in and day out."

Emily's eyes flashed. "Don't start that again. When will you understand that I want to be at the cemetery and I don't want to be part of some foolish ladies' crusade? No amount of urging on your part is going to make me go back to them."

"Very well, but at least allow me the right to fill my days with something that matters."

She could see the gables of the barn above the trees at the bend. Thank heaven, Damaris thought with a sigh. Maybe she'd be able to escape to her room for an hour of quiet before tea time.

Emily went on muttering to herself. "What could matter more than your family? Than your mother? It was that shipyard that started you on all of this. Once it burned down, I thought you'd ease up, but no! You had to go and take on some other chore almost as demanding. I declare . . ."

Damaris tried not to listen. How she wished her mother would give her credit just once for a job well done instead of always dwelling on how it took her away from her family. She brought the horse smartly up in the stableyard and climbed down eagerly.

Inside the front hall, she handed her hat and coat to Cora, the parlor maid, while Emily, the weight of her grief stronger now than her irritation with her daughter, went straight to her room. Damaris was about to follow her up the stairs when Cora leaned closer and said quietly, "Mr. Manning is waiting to see you, ma'am. He said I was especially to ask for you and not Miss Emily."

Frowning, Damaris turned this over in her mind. Robert Manning. That meant another set of problems. "Are you sure he did not wish to see Mr. Slade?"

"No, ma'am. He was very particular. He said I was to ask if you'd have a word with him direct you returned from the cemetery."

Struggling with her impatience, Damaris went to the tiny room under the stairs that served as a home office. Robert Manning was lounging in one of the Windsor chairs, but he jumped to his feet when she entered.

"What is it, Robert?" Damaris said shortly, pulling out a chair. "I'm very tired and I don't have much time."

Robert held the chair for her, then stood back, running a hand through his lanky hair.

"Sorry, Miss Damaris, but there's a few problems come up on which I need the benefit of your advice."

Reaching into the pocket of his trousers, he pulled out a long piece of paper and resumed his seat, spreading it out on his knees. Damaris felt her heart sink.

"Aren't these things you can handle yourself?" she asked. "You're the overseer, after all. You must start making decisions on your own."

She could see at once that she had wounded his pride. "Now, Miss Damaris, you know I was a boatman all my life and a good one. I know everything there is to know about a shipyard, but I'm still learning about seeding and plowing and working fieldhands. You got to help me some. 'Specially since when I do make a mistake, seems your ma is right on to it."

Reaching over, Damaris took the paper from his hands. "Well, if you're frightened of Mother, you must learn to speak to my husband. He has more time to give to this than I do and certainly he knows as much about it."

"I do ask him, Miss Damaris, but seems like he always tells me to speak to you."

Pursing her lips, she ran her eyes down the page. Practical matters, all of them, involving orders, crop rotation, and discipline among the workers. This was going to take an hour at least.

"I see Sven Gunderson's name mentioned three times. What's the problem?"

Robert's long, knobby fingers clenched around the arms of the chair. "That fellow!" he cried. "Of all the Swedes you brung in here to work, Miss Damaris, he's the worst. Gives me more trouble than ten other men. Always talking back, telling me what I ought to be doing and ought not to do. Thinks he knows more about farming than any man since Adam."

Damaris suspected that he probably did know a great deal, or else Manning would have fired him long ago. "Is he drunk?" she asked. "Aggressive? Picking fights?"

"No, none of them things. Just loud-mouthed and smarty. 'Tween the two of us, I think he's after my place. I would take it as a favor if you'd speak to him yourself, Miss Damaris. He causes the other men to think less of me."

"Come now, Robert. I can't run your hands for you. You must earn their respect yourself."

"You could back me up."

"Well, I don't think I should. You try to work things out with this Gunderson yourself, and if you cannot, I'll consider speaking to him. But I'll tell you frankly, I don't think my rushing in to help you does much to solve the problem. Now, let's go over the rest of this list."

They were almost at the end of the page when Damaris heard a commotion in the hall. Recognizing Wesley's voice, she sighed with relief and leaned against the back of the chair, thinking that with any luck he could take over for her. The thought had no more than crossed her mind when the door flew open and Wesley came flying in, still wearing his greatcoat and hat, a piece of paper clutched in his hand and a broad smile on his face.

"Damaris, I've had great news. I finally heard from Ethan. He's been traveling all this time and he's coming home."

He thrust the letter at her and she turned it over, looking at the sweeping pen scrawls that covered it. All thought of Robert Manning and his petty little problems fled her mind.

"Ethan? But when will he arrive?"

"In just a few days. He's been traveling through the west these last months, but he's in New York now. How good it will be to see the old fellow again! This is great news, isn't it?"

She laid the letter aside, then folded Manning's list and handed it back to him.

"We'll have to finish the rest of this some other time, Robert. I think you have plenty to work with for a while and I'm feeling a little tired."

"Of course, Miss Damaris," Robert answered, replacing the list in his pocket. "I don't want to trouble you any more than can be helped. I'll just go along and leave you to talk over the happy news about Mr. Ethan."

As the door closed behind him, Wesley took his wife's hand and pulled her to her feet. "You do look tired, Damaris. Come along now. Put all this business aside and rest for a while. There's a fire in the parlor and we'll have your shoes off and your feet on the grate while I fetch you a nice glass of sherry. Then I'll read Ethan's letter to you. How does that sound?"

"Lovely, Wes. Lovely."

And it was.

Ethan arrived within the week, looking tan and fit, leaner than the last time she had seen him, and much improved in spirit. She had waited for him to come, wavering between great anticipation and dread. Then, at last, there he was. Emily greeted him with noticeable coolness, and Damaris knew she was still blaming him for Corrine's illness and death. But Wesley's delight at seeing his brother, Freddy's joy at being with his uncle, and Ethan's own evident pleasure in this family reunion all weighted the scale on the positive side.

He was changed—Damaris could see that at once. There was a firmness of purpose about him that she had not seen since the war days. And though he was scrupulously polite and formal when the others were around, she suspected from the unguarded way she caught him watching her that something was lurking at the back of his mind. There was an undercurrent between them just waiting for the right time to surface. She knew it and Ethan knew it, and she only hoped it was not apparent to anyone else, particularly her mother. Damaris's own solution was to avoid being alone with him, a policy she succeeded in carrying out very well. It did not make her happy, but she maintained her discretion, knowing it was the wisest course. She hoped he did not plan to stay long and that he would come and go without disrupting all of their lives.

Yet she did not reckon on Ethan's determination. On the third day after his arrival he showed up at Southernwood during the late morning, when Wesley and Freddy were both in the village and Emily had been called to help nurse a neighbor with a sick child. Damaris hesitated when Cora told her Ethan was waiting in the parlor, but she knew she could not send him away. The best she could do was reach for her hat and shawl and ask him to walk with her through the orchard. That way, at least, they would not be alone.

She began making excuses for the other members of the family, but he interrupted her almost at once.

"I know where they are. Who do you think suggested your mother as a nurse?"

"You didn't! Now how did you manage that?"

"Mama asked me to look in on the Willard child, and while I was there, I mentioned Emily's talents for home remedies. I think Mrs. Willard was far more ready to trust someone like your mother than a doctor like myself. She told me she would send off a message first thing this morning, and I felt sure Emily would go unless she had changed even more than I thought. She was always good about things like that."

"Mother has changed," Damaris said thoughtfully, scuffing the leaves from her path. "Yet in spite of everything, she still loves to be needed."

"As for Wes and Freddy, they told me they had some business in town this morning. Now you see what lengths I will go to to get you alone."

He looked down at her with such hunger in his eyes that Damaris, trying to ignore the fluttering in her chest, had no idea how to respond. Without waiting for her to sort through the possibilities, Ethan took her arm and led her over to a weathered stone bench under the ash tree.

"Sit with me, Damaris. What I have to say to you cannot be said strolling along a walkway."

"Oh, dear . . ." She sat down, a terrible sense of dread growing within her. She was afraid and excited at the same time.

Ethan did not touch her—in fact, he was careful to keep a polite distance between them. Nor did he look at her as he spoke. "Since Corrine died I've been doing a lot of thinking. That's why I left Philadelphia—there just seemed to be so much to sort out. We did not have much of a marriage, Corrine and I. I suppose I hurt her quite a lot."

"Yes, you did."

"Candid Damaris," Ethan said ruefully. "Well, that's over now and that's not what I want to talk to you about. The point is, we each tried at first to be what the other wanted, but somehow we failed. And one of the reasons we failed is that we were never truthful with each other. As I went vagabonding around these last months I became aware of two overwhelming facts: that we might have solved some of our differences if we had ever faced them honestly; and that much of our lives were wasted in living with them unsolved. I look back now, Damaris, and I'm very jealous of all those years gone for nothing. I want them back. I want to be happy and I am absolutely unwilling to lose any more time from my life hiding from the truth."

"Oh, Ethan." A part of her wanted to get up and run away. He is going to strip away all your life's defenses, she thought. He's going to tear away the protective cover and lay bare the ache underneath. He is going to destroy you.

But she could not move. Reaching over, Ethan took her hand in his, and she was acutely conscious of his warm flesh.

"I realized that there are two things I want in my life. Two things that are rightfully mine—should always have been mine—and that I intend now to claim. You and—"

"No! No, don't say it." She started to jump up, but he caught her arm and held her there beside him.

"You and Freddy."

"No!" She turned on him furiously. "You have no claim on either of us. I am Wesley's wife and Freddy is his son. We both belong to him."

Undaunted, Ethan went on in a level voice. "Freddy is my son. Do you think I haven't known it all these years? Do you think I could ever forget that afternoon on the hill? That I haven't longed for it over and over again all this time?"

"You don't know anything! *I* don't even know."

"Come now, Damaris. If you had borne three or four other children, I would believe that. Neither of us could be sure. But all these years you never conceived again."

"I did. I had two or three miscarriages."

"That's a lie. Corrine told me you were never with child after Freddy. There's only one answer."

She went on, hardly aware of what she was saying. "No there isn't. Perhaps I had another lover beside you. Two or even three. You can't be sure Freddy's your son even if he isn't Wesley's. He could be anybody's!"

"I know you better than that. Why not other lovers over the years and other children, then? Why did you never allow me to make love to you again even though you love me as you do?"

"I don't love you!"

"Yes you do. You always have, and we both know it. We should have been together from the beginning, Damaris, and it was only because of my foolishness and your pride that we weren't. All those years—wasted."

She felt all her strength crumbling as she fought to hold back the tears that choked her. Reaching out, Ethan took her in his arms, pulling her close against him, and gladly, willingly, she let him hold her tight. After a few moments he began lightly to stroke her neck and shoulders, sending a delicious warmth through her body. His hand moved restlessly over her back and his lips brushed her cheek. The exquisite warmth of his touch blazed within her and, beyond caring about anything else, Damaris gave way to his embrace, clinging to him, crying half in joy, half in anguish: "Oh, Ethan. I do love you. I've always loved you . . ."

Her words were lost on the wave of feeling that overcame them both. All the passion they had pushed down for years came bursting forth as strong and sweet as it had been eighteen years before. Taking her face between his hands, he covered it with kisses, and willingly, joyfully, she returned them. When she finally remembered they were outside where they could be seen by anyone, she tried to pull away.

"Let them look," Ethan said carelessly. "The world will have to know soon anyway."

His words brought cold reason rushing back. "Ethan, what are we thinking of? This cannot be. I'm married."

His fingers dug into her shoulders. "Then you'll have to become unmarried."

She looked around, trying to be sure that the foliage of the trees hid them from the view of any of the gardeners. "Think what you are saying! I can't deprive Wesley of his whole family in one blow. I can't hurt him like that. He's a good man, Ethan, and he's been a good husband and father. I do love him, though not the same way I love you. You cannot undo all these years in one moment."

"I don't want to hurt Wesley either, but why should he have what is rightfully mine? I want you, Damaris, and I want Freddy. I need you both. I want us to live together, to share the years that are left. Wesley has already had so many, why should he have all the rest?"

"Ethan, you are talking foolishness. I can't divorce Wesley and I'd rather die than tell him that Freddy is not his son."

"Come on, Damaris. Wes is not stupid. He must know."

"No he is not stupid, but he is very good at not facing unpleasant truths. If such a thought ever entered his mind, he would push it right out again."

"Come away with me, Damaris. If you won't divorce him, then come and live with me anyway. We'll be happy together, I know we will."

"Oh, Ethan. How can I do that? You said you knew me well enough to know I would not indiscriminately take a lover. How can you think I could bear the scandal of such a life? It would cause Wes and Mother such pain."

Abruptly he released her and sat back down on the bench. Now he was angry with her, she thought miserably.

"Very well, then," he said bitterly, "if you won't come to me, at least give me my son. He wants to study medicine. Let him come to Philadelphia and live with me. I deserve that much of him, Damaris."

"No! He would end up caring more for you than for Wesley. I won't have you taking him away from us, Ethan, even if you are his natural father. It is Wesley and I who have raised him to be the boy he is, and Wesley is devoted to him. I won't let you destroy that."

"You needn't be so afraid. He wants to go with me, but he

won't leave without your consent. You sound as though you fear my influence on the boy."

"Perhaps I do," she answered stiffly.

Ethan leaned forward, resting his arms on his knees. "Don't answer me now, Damaris. Perhaps you need time to think about what I've said. I'll be around another day or two. When I leave, I want you to go with me, or if you refuse, I want your permission to take Freddy. I hope and pray that I'll be able to take you both, but I must have at least one of you. It's only fair."

Her resolution began to waver. "Oh, Ethan. I wish I could. I wish it with all my heart."

He took her hand and placed it on his lips, whispering, "Come riding with me tomorrow. We'll go back to the hill we loved so much."

"No!" Pulling her hand away, knowing her misery was written on her face, she answered softly, "No, not until I come to a decision. If I choose to go with you, then you shall have all of me there is to give. But until then I belong to Wesley. I nearly jeopardized that tie once, Ethan, but I will not jeopardize it now, not unless I mean to break it for good."

"You will consider breaking it for good?"

It was a long time before she could whisper, "Yes."

When Damaris left him she did not go straight back to the house. Instead she wandered through the orchard and the gardens, around the orangery and out beyond the fields to where the trees marked the beginning of the woods and the bare patches of ground on the edge of the hills looked out over the river, shining like silver in the afternoon sun. She was dismayed and transported in turns. The thought of going off with Ethan, of living with him, sharing his bed, lying hot and satiated in his arms, made her heart sing. But when she thought of Wesley left behind, of Freddy and her mother, of the disgrace and hurt she would bring upon them all, her joy turned sour. What to do: be selfish and let her own desires and needs take precedence, or do the moral, the right, thing and stay at Southernwood? As the sun slid toward the gray hills across the river, she finally went inside, no nearer to a solution than before.

They were all gathered around the supper table when she entered the dining room, all but Ethan, who had gone back to his parents' house. Damaris took her place at the table and looked at her family, none of whom seemed inclined to talk. Emily was picking at her food, preoccupied with her own thoughts. Wesley glanced up to see Damaris looking at him, smiled, and resumed his ruminations. Freddy stared down at his plate. He was probably trying to figure out how to get her to allow him to go off with Ethan to study in Philadelphia.

Damaris began to toy with her food, wondering if anything in her demeanor betrayed her conflict, and was startled when Emily said, "The hem of your skirt is very dirty, Damaris. You haven't been tramping about the fields, have you?"

"Yes, I did go for quite a long walk."

"And I suppose you did not wear a coat either. How many times have I told you you'll catch your death of cold if you're not careful."

"I was warm enough."

"So you say, but I saw myself this afternoon what carelessness can do. That Willard child would not be about to die of pneumonia if her mother had taken the proper precautions. And I told her so, too."

"That must have made her feel a lot better!"

"Well, it's the truth, and sometimes the truth has to be spoken."

"I hope you did not go out walking alone, Damaris," Wesley said, looking up from his plate. "You know I don't like the idea of you tramping about these woods unattended. It isn't at all safe."

Suppressing a sigh, Damaris said, "Nonsense. Who's going to bother me?"

"Why, you never know whom you'll meet," Emily said.

"For heaven's sake, Mother, I only went for a walk and I never even left the grounds of Southernwood. This is a ridiculous conversation."

"Yes, you always think everything is ridiculous unless you raise the issue," Emily bristled. "Then it's all wise and very important."

Damaris clanked her fork down on the table and twisted her hands in her lap. "Leave me alone!"

"Let her be, Mother," Wesley interrupted. "Can't you see she doesn't feel well? Probably got a chill out there in the woods."

"Just as I said!"

"I did *not* get a chill," Damaris exclaimed. "Why can't either of you ever ask me anything about what I saw or how I felt or what it meant to be there? Why must I always be chided for not wearing a coat or for going out at all?"

"I can see you are in one of your moods," Emily said patiently, "and nothing anyone says will be satisfactory to you. I only wish you had seen the suffering I saw this day. If you had, you would not be so quick to get upset over such trifles."

"Wesley," Damaris cried, seeking his support.

"Well, dear, your mother may be right. You do sometimes let small issues grow large in your mind. Seeing someone else's suffering often helps one put things in a better perspective."

Damaris looked across to her son, but he only gave her a faint smile and shrugged.

For Damaris, the moment took on great significance. She was about to sacrifice her one chance for happiness in order to spend the rest of her life as a target for the ill humor and indifference of these people. There was not one of them sitting there with her who had the faintest notion of what she was feeling or the great choice that lay before her. She could run off right now and join Ethan and they would all sit there, puzzled and hurt, asking "why."

She made one last tentative reach for help. "Wesley, could I please talk to you after supper?"

"I'm sorry, dear," Wesley said, spooning sugar into his coffee cup, "but I promised John Acker I'd go to a meeting of the village board. Can't it wait until tomorrow?"

"It's very important."

"But Damaris, what I'm doing is important too. Why can't you ever see that? You do have a tendency, my dear, to think that your concerns matter more than anything else."

Taken aback by his uncharacteristic irritation, she stared at him. Suddenly she heard footsteps in the hall and her heart gave a leap. Perhaps Ethan had returned.

"Damaris has always showed a tendency to put her own concerns first," Emily muttered. "Corrine was the only one of my daughters who was truly selfless."

"Excuse me, miss," Cora said from the doorway. Damaris looked up expectantly at the maid.

"It's Mr. Manning. He says he's had a problem with that

Gunderson fellow and he especially needs to see you."

Throwing down her napkin, Damaris jumped from her chair and started for the door.

"Shall I put him in the parlor, miss?" the startled maid cried as Damaris rushed past her.

"Put him any place you please," Damaris snapped, and fled the room.

Her mind was made up. Emily, Wesley, Robert Manning— they could all go to the devil as far as she was concerned. She was going away with Ethan.

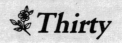

Thirty

WHEN DAMARIS heard the carriage drive off, she knew that Wesley had left for the village and began filling her portmanteau with the things she wanted to take with her. There was no joy in the task. Fighting down tears, she selected and discarded ruthlessly, denying herself the things she most wanted. She was so preoccupied that she did not hear a soft knock at the door and was startled when she looked up to see Emily framed in the doorway, staring at her.

"What's going on here, Damaris? What are you doing?"

Instinctively, Damaris thrust the dress she was holding behind her.

"Mother! Why, nothing. I'm just pulling out a few things I want to store away."

Emily walked over and touched one corner of the dark green sarcenet. "You're putting away your best dress that was only finished last month? It's barely been worn."

"It . . . it doesn't fit right. I don't really like it."

"Why, you loved it and it looked beautiful on you. I declare, Damaris, I don't understand what has come over you. You are not acting yourself at all. You flounced off without facing that Manning fellow and now he's brooding about downstairs. Why don't you take care of him?"

"It's your house, Mother. Why don't you take care of him?"

"I would never have hired him in the first place. He doesn't know the first thing about running a farm. Besides, you always handle things like that."

Yanking a frothy lace petticoat out of the press, Damaris bunched it into a ball and threw it on the box. "I can always count on you, Mother, to point out my mistakes. Well, Manning may have been the wrong man to hire, but someone else will have to straighten it out. I'm sick and tired of trying to run the Wells Home and Southernwood at the same time."

"You know Manning pays no attention to anything I say, and I haven't the strength anymore to argue with him. I'm not at all well."

"Then he'll just have to wait until Wesley gets back."

"Wesley! He's so namby-pamby, he'll just feel sorry for the man and tell him to do whatever he thinks best. Then he'll come running to you again."

"Please, Mother. I have a headache. We can talk about this tomorrow."

Emily hesitated for a moment, then said, "Very well, dear. We'll talk about it in the morning. But for goodness sake, leave all this sorting to your maid."

Damaris almost pushed her mother out the door. "I will. I just wanted to get it started."

"In the morning. Don't forget."

Damaris closed the door, locked it, then leaned against it, vastly relieved that Emily had left without asking a lot of questions. I shall just have to be more careful, she thought, and returned to the task at hand.

Damaris did not go down to breakfast the next morning until she was sure Wesley had already left. As she went through the hall she could hear Emily talking to one of the maids in the pantry but she managed to slip by them without being seen. Throwing on her coat, she hurried out onto the porch where she ran into Freddy. He was just coming back from a morning ride, looking vibrant and full of life in his riding coat and high boots, his hair tousled by the wind and his face flushed with the chill of the morning.

He gave her a quick kiss on her cheek. "Morning, Mama. Feeling better today?"

"Why, what do you mean?"

"Well, you were not yourself at all last night at supper. But then none of us were, I expect. What a glorious morning, though—enough to lift the blue devils from anyone's spirits. We should all be back in good humor by dinner, don't you think?"

"If we're around you long enough we will be," Damaris said teasingly.

"I've had a glorious canter with Uncle Ethan. He's down at the stables now and says he'll be up at the house in a few moments and could we scare him up some breakfast."

"Of course. I'm sure breakfast is still laid out. Why don't you ask Cora. I'm just going for a short walk."

He was already on his way. "It'll do you good. Enjoy the air. I'll see that Uncle Ethan's fed."

Once the door closed behind him, Damaris hurried down the steps to the walk and toward the orchard. If she could catch Ethan before he got to the house, they might have a few moments of privacy. She was halfway there when she saw him standing near the bench, waiting for her. He opened his arms and she ran into them. Crushing her in his embrace, he pulled her down on the bench, kissing her long and hard.

"You're going to come with me. I can tell," he murmured.

"Yes, yes. I'm sick of this place and these people. I'm sick of having to carry the burden of it. I'll go with you, Ethan, anywhere you want. Just take care of me and love me and make me forget the hurt I'll have caused."

"When? Tonight? Tomorrow? And Freddy—does he know?"

"No. He mustn't know yet. Give him a little time. He'll come to us eventually, I'm sure of it, but it would be too cruel to Wesley for both of us to go away at once."

His eyes darkened. "I suppose, but I had hoped to have you both. Can you leave with me tonight?"

"So soon?"

"It's better this way. Make the incision quick and fast. It's cleaner and it hurts less. Besides, I don't want to give you a chance to change your mind." He crushed her lips to his again, and his hands restlessly explored her breasts and her back. She was on fire, consumed with such a hot longing for him that she could barely contain it. She wanted him to throw her on the grass and take her right there.

"Oh, Ethan. Love me. Love me."

"I shall love you as you've never been loved before. We were meant for this, Damaris. It's right. It's ours."

Abruptly she pulled away. "My God, what am I doing? Not here. Not now."

Reaching for her again, he pulled her back, refusing to allow her out of his arms. "Tonight, then. I'll have a carriage ready. Meet me . . . where? At the stable? Would that be safe?"

"No, no. I can't do that. I can't just walk out and leave Wesley to discover I'm gone. We have to tell him, Ethan. We have to tell him what we're going to do."

He dropped his arms and sat back. "You can't mean that!"

"Yes, I do. I owe him that much." She could not keep the anguish from her voice. "You said we belong together, that we've always belonged together. Very well, I agree. But you must explain it to Wesley, make him understand. Perhaps he won't be so badly hurt that way."

"Surely you don't think he's going to give us his blessing? You can't be that naïve, Damaris."

Damaris gripped his hands. "No, I know better than that. But at least we will have been honest with him. We won't be sneaking away like cowards. Please, Ethan. Do this much for me, at least."

"And what about your mother? Is she to be in on this farewell scene too?"

"No. I'll ask Wesley to tell her after we've left."

For a moment she thought he was going to get up and walk away. But to her relief, after studying her face a moment, he pulled her into his arms again, smoothing back her hair.

"All right. If that's how you want it, I'll face my brother with you. I'll come by tonight, directly after supper. You be ready to leave afterward."

"I will. I promise. We will be happy, Ethan, won't we?"

"We'll be happy. Just keep remembering that we belong together."

* * *

She clung to his words throughout the long day. They helped her bear the strain of Emily's suspicion, though she died a little each time she imagined confronting Wesley that evening and each time she saw her son, laughing and happy, never suspecting that his world was about to be turned upside down. She wondered over and over whether she would really be able to walk out into the night with Ethan and leave behind the life she had so painstakingly built over the years.

Somehow she got through supper. Wesley's problem with the town had been resolved and he came in full of his old good humor, relieved and ebullient. Kissing Damaris lightly on the cheek, he sat down at the table and began piling food on his plate with enthusiasm. She could hardly stand to look at him.

Though Damaris barely spoke during the meal, she had the feeling that everything she did betrayed her plan. She caught her mother's intense, watchful gaze on her several times, but Wesley and Freddy were engrossed in a political discussion and seemed not to notice anything unusual. When at last the difficult meal was finished—her last with her family—she started from the room, intending to go upstairs and sit by herself until Ethan arrived. Wesley caught up with her at the foot of the stairway.

"Damaris, dear. Must you go up? I had hoped we might have a game of backgammon in the parlor."

She could not look him full in the face. "I'm sorry, Wes, but I really don't feel like it. I have a frightful headache."

He laid a gentle hand on her shoulder. "Then you must rest awhile. Can I bring you something? Hartshorn drops, or a cool cloth for your forehead?"

Why must he be so nice to her now? She would have preferred last night's neglect and irritation to this kindness.

"No thank you. Nothing. Just a little rest will do it, I'm sure."

"Damaris, I . . ." Embarrassed, he went on: "I just wanted you to know I felt very bad about last night. I'm sorry I was short with you and that I had to leave you here to deal with Manning alone. I was so concerned about working things out with the board that I neglected the person who means the most to me."

"Wesley, please . . ."

"When I thought back on it, I felt beastly bad about my irritation. After all, you're worth twenty village boards to me. You're everything in the world."

She choked back a strangling sob, then threw her arms around his neck and hugged him. "Dear Wes. You're such a good man."

"I'm not good. But I do love you. I just wanted to be sure I told you so tonight. You go and rest now."

Upstairs in her room, she leaned against the door and gave vent to her tears. She was never going to be able to do this! She would have to catch Ethan before he saw Wes and told him she couldn't go through with it, that he must go away without her.

No! It would mean giving up forever her dream of leaning on someone stronger than herself, of knowing what it was to be completely possessed by passion, to give over her life to the strength of an all-consuming love. It would doom her for the rest of her days to the boredom of mundane, ordinary relationships. This was her only chance to follow her dream, and she must take it. She would take it!

She was too restless to lie down even for half an hour. Striding up and down her room like a caged animal, she mentally crossed off the minutes as they dragged by, checking her portmanteau once again, laying out on the bed her dark blue traveling dress and hat, brushing her cloak, counting the money in her purse. Her taut nerves jangled at a sudden sharp rap on her door. Before Damaris could answer, it was thrown open and Emily came into the room slamming it shut behind her. The gas lamp was very low, but she could see her mother's expression clearly enough to realize that a storm was about to break over her head. Deliberately Emily turned up the lamp, letting the bright light stream into all the dark corners of the room, illuminating the clothes laid out on the bed.

"You little fool! What do you think you are doing?"

Damaris raised her arm as if warding off a blow. "Mother, I didn't ask you in and I'm telling you now to get out."

"I will not get out. Someone has to talk sense to you. You thought you were fooling everyone, didn't you? Well, I'm not blind. When you left this morning I knew you were up to something and I watched you from the window. When I saw you kissing that man, Damaris, I could hardly believe it. You can't mean to run away with Ethan!"

There was no use pretending now. Angrily Damaris faced her mother and said, "Well, I do mean to, and tonight. And there is nothing you can do about it."

"We'll see about that! I'll stop you if I have to tie you to the bed. I won't let you throw your life away like this."

"You can't stop me, Mother, and I'd advise you not to try. I've thought it through and my mind is made up. Ethan loves me and I love him. We were meant to be together and should have been from the start."

"Poppycock! He'll ruin your life just as he ruined Corrine's."

Damaris felt her fury rising and she had to fight to keep her voice down. The worst thing that could happen now would be to bring Wesley and Freddy upstairs.

"If I had married him in the beginning he would never have had the chance to hurt Corrine. But it won't be like that with us. I know it."

"You don't know anything, you foolish girl. Can't you see how basically selfish Ethan is? He doesn't want to make you happy; he simply wants something his brother has always had. He doesn't know how to love anyone. He never did."

"That's not true. I don't want to discuss this now, Mother. Please go away and let me alone."

"Never! I won't let you do this, Damaris. I won't let you hurt your husband and son this way. Not to mention me."

In a blind rage, Damaris turned on her. "Oh, of course, that's the unpardonable sin. Hurting you! That's all you ever think of—how everything affects you. Well, I'm doing this for me—*me!* And I don't really care how anybody else feels about it!"

Stunned at the near hatred in Damaris's eyes, Emily automatically stepped backward, struggling to keep her temper under control. She knew what she was trying to deal with here was too significant to let her own emotions get in the way, and yet in spite of that knowledge, an unreasoning anger clutched at her. How could Damaris be so blind, so stupid! To give up all that she had, a good husband and a good home, for a man not worth half of either—it was beyond comprehension.

"Damaris, you're making a terrible mistake. You'll be

wretched and unhappy. How long do you think this great passion will last? Not more than a year at best. Then he'll be off trying to assuage his restlessness with some other woman and you'll be left with your life in shreds. I won't let that happen! I won't let a daughter of mine disgrace herself so!"

"It's my life!" Damaris said wildly. "If I want to throw it away, that's my decision. For God's sake, let me make my own choice for once!"

"That wretched man—I've seen him ruin everything he's touched. Every time he's around you he changes you. He destroyed Corrine and now he's trying to destroy Wesley through you and Freddy. What right has he to act like he does toward Freddy, playing on his affections and interests until the boy almost adores him more than his own father."

"Every right."

Emily barely heard her. "The arrogance of it," she went on. "Coming here like this and talking you into leaving with him. Acting as though Freddy was his son instead of his brother's."

"Freddy *is* his son!" The words were out almost before she knew it.

Caught up in her indignation, Emily very nearly missed their meaning. Then her mouth dropped open and she stopped, staring at Damaris.

"What do you mean?"

"Just what I said. Freddy is Ethan's son. Not Wesley's."

Her mother's face went white. Behind her intense stare Damaris could almost see her thoughts racing: When? How? Turning away from that startled, horrified look, she walked to the bed and leaned her head against the post.

"Ethan and I were lovers—once, just before he went away to war. I meant to break off my engagement right then and marry him, but he left so suddenly and without any word. I was young and proud and deeply hurt, so I went ahead with the wedding. I knew I was pregnant almost immediately, but I thought perhaps . . ."

Emily lowered herself very carefully on to the edge of the bed.

"If Wes and I had ever had any other children perhaps I would never have known. But we didn't—we can't. I know that now and I know that Freddy must be Ethan's."

Her mother's voice was barely audible. "Does Wesley know this?"

"I don't know. Ethan knows, though, and wants to claim Freddy as his. If Wesley ever did suspect, he would die before he would put it into words."

"Oh, Damaris. And you've lived with this all these years?"

"Yes. But it never seemed very important. Freddy is himself, not his parents. And siring the boy is not what makes a father. Wesley raised him, cared for him, taught him, supported him. He's far more of a father than Ethan, though Ethan believes he has some claim on the boy now."

Emily studied her daughter's profile, seeing her clearly for the first time in years: the almost classic lines of nose and chin, the thick lashes downcast on her pale cheeks, the sensuous curve of her full lips, the thick black hair that waved away from her face and was caught in a lustrous chignon at the back of her willowy neck. Damaris was a beautiful woman, full of warmth and vitality, and she wanted to reach out and grasp life and all it had to give. Emily knew what that was like. Long ago, so long ago as to be almost past recalling, another young girl in this same house had struggled with these same longings.

Absently she looked down at her own worn hands and smoothed the folds of her skirt. She still felt the same way she had a few minutes ago, yet she knew now that she must find a better way to express herself. This woman, Damaris, with her deep feelings and old hurts, would not be bullied or shamed into staying with her family. Emily felt a cold knot of fear in her chest, as she realized for the first time that Damaris might very well leave them.

Damaris raised her head but still could not look at her mother. "So you see, Mother, he does have a hold over me. I was his before I was Wesley's and I love him still. I want to go with him. I want this life he is offering me."

"Oh, Damaris," Emily said gently, "I know something of what you are feeling. Don't you think I remember what it is like to want a man so badly that nothing else in life matters? From the first moment I set eyes on Frederick Whitman I wanted him in just such a way. And it never stopped, that longing. But it was not just for his body; I loved his character and soul as well. Can you truly say you feel that way about Ethan?"

Damaris forced herself to face her mother without flinching. "No. But then I'm not sure what love is. I don't think I could ever love anyone the way you loved Papa. I'm too selfish."

"Then what you really feel for Ethan is passion, not love. Do you think it will survive the routines of everyday life? It seems glamorous now to think of running off and living with him, but would it be so much better than your life here?"

"Yes. It would have to be."

In the sudden silence even the quiet ticking of the small clock on the mantel seemed to resound through the room.

"Is life here so dreadful, then?" Emily said quietly.

"Yes it is," Damaris cried in anguish. "You make it so, every day of your life. 'Damaris, do this, do that! Damaris, everything you do is wrong; everything you do is for yourself alone! Don't ask me anything, ask Damaris, she'll handle everything!' I'm tired of it all. I'm tired of your complaints, your demands, Wesley's dependence, Freddy's constant praise of his Uncle Ethan. I want someone to love me just the way I am. Someone who will occasionally say 'You did that well, Damaris' or 'You're a good person, Damaris.' All I've *ever* had from you is criticism!"

Her voice broke on a sob. To her horror, the tears came flooding and, clinging to the bedpost, she choked them back. When Emily reached up and put her arms around her, Damaris could hold the tears in no longer. Falling against her, she laid her head on her mother's breast and cried like a child.

Emily wanted very much to comfort her, to murmur the words one croons to a hurt child. Instead she stroked her daughter's hair back from her forehead and gripped her tightly. You meddlesome old nag, she told herself. This is one time you'll keep your mouth shut!

They talked for a long time after Damaris stopped crying. Listening to her mother, Damaris finally heard the common sense behind her words, while for the first time in years Emily really listened to what her daughter had to say.

"I've been a difficult person to live with," Emily admitted. "With Fade's death and then Corrine's, I fell into a bad habit of taking out my misery on you because you were the most convenient scapegoat. I'm sorry, Damaris, and I promise I'll try to do better. But don't leave us, please. We love you. You're the touchstone in all our lives."

The lamp fired gold flecks in her mother's dark eyes. How old she looks, Damaris thought. How tired.

"But, Mother, I get so weary of all of you looking up to

me. I need someone to lean on too sometimes."

"Then we shall all of us have to do a better job of sharing the burdens. I think the first thing for me to do is to take myself off for a nice long visit to Winnifred. She'll just have to put up with me, that's all. A tiresome mother ought to be shared among her children."

Damaris almost demurred the point, then decided it was just too true.

"Who knows, perhaps you'll miss me a little if I'm not here and then we'll appreciate each other more when I return. Meanwhile, you and Wesley can begin to work some of your problems out. You were happy together on that trip to Europe, weren't you?"

"Oh yes."

"Then perhaps with a little time to yourselves here in this house you will find that same happiness. Only..."

"Only what?"

"I'm talking as though you've decided to stay. Do you want to stay, Damaris? Because if you don't, I won't try to keep you from going."

Damaris could not answer. Rising abruptly, she walked to the washstand and, dampening a towel, wiped it across her eyes. She stared for a moment at her reflection in the mirror, as though trying to look beyond the white face, the drawn mouth, the shadowed crescents underneath the eyes, to what lay inside.

"Part of me wants to run to him, Mother, but another part of me does not. That part realizes he would be no more be happy with me than he was with Corrine, and that ultimately I would not be happy with him. I'm not sure that the pleasures we would share would make up for all the hurt I'd cause and the guilt I'd feel as a result of it."

Emily breathed a small sigh of relief. "My dear, that's very wise of you."

"But I'm not sure either that I can endure watching him leave this last time without me."

"If you know that we'll all try to make things different here, won't that help you get through it?"

"And Ethan? What's to become of him?"

"I think you should let Freddy go to Philadelphia and study with Ethan, Damaris. Give him that much of the boy. I have a suspicion that is what he really wants and that ultimately it would make Ethan happier than running off with you. It allows everyone to win with the least amount of hurt."

There was a soft knock at the door followed by Cora's muffled voice from the hall: "Pardon me, Miss Damaris, but Mr. Ethan has arrived. He is downstairs with Mr. Wesley and they asked if you would join them."

Damaris's eyes flew to her mother's. "Yes. All right. Thank you, Cora."

"Ethan is here?"

"Yes. We were going to try to explain to Wes. Now I don't know what to say."

Emily walked over to her daughter, smoothed back her hair and straightened her collar. "There. You look presentable again. You'll do the right thing; I know you will, Damaris. Perhaps if I came with you . . ."

"I'd really prefer that you didn't."

Damaris could see the struggle in her mother's eyes. At length Emily turned away. "Very well. I'll wait up here."

Damaris gave her mother a quick embrace, grateful for this new understanding between them. Taking a deep breath, she left the room and went downstairs.

She entered the parlor to find Wesley and Ethan sitting tensely quiet on either side of the room. Easing herself down on the edge of the sofa, she absently twisted her wedding ring.

"My dear," Wesley said quietly, "Ethan tells me we have something to discuss. Do you know what he's talking about?"

Damaris could not look at either man.

"Well," he went on, crossing his legs and smoothing the fabric of his trousers over his knee, "who wants to start?"

Ethan coughed and stood up, leaning on the mantel. "I think Damaris should be the one."

Damaris glared at him. She took a moment to compose herself before turning to her husband. "The truth is, Wesley—"

"Excuse me, ma'am," Cora interrupted, peering around the door. "I'm sorry to disturb you again, but it's Mr. Manning. He's asked me to tell you that he's been waiting in the kitchen for nearly an hour and if you could give him a few moments before you get settled here he'd be most grateful."

"Oh, for pity's sake," Damaris exclaimed, falling back against the sofa. "I can't face Robert Manning right now. Tell him it will have to wait until morning."

"It's about that Gunderson fellow again, isn't it?" Wesley

said. "He's been pestering you about him for days."

"Probably. I don't know what to tell him. Why doesn't he take care of it himself? It's too much!"

She could hear the faint note of hysteria in her voice, and it made her all the more grateful when Wesley stood up and laid a sympathetic hand on her shoulder.

"Don't worry about it, dear. I'll handle Manning. This has gone on long enough, and it's time it was settled one way or another."

Damaris stared up at him in surprise. "Do you mind?"

"No. You stay and keep Ethan company. We can continue this discussion when I get back."

He went out quickly, closing the door behind him. There was a long, uncomfortable silence during which Damaris knew Ethan was watching her, waiting for her to speak. Instead, she rose and walked to the window, pulling back the drape to look out into the night. In spite of her brave words to her mother she still felt torn. She wanted to do the right thing, and for the most part she felt willing to renounce Ethan. Yet there was still that glimmer of a cherished dream that she did not want to give up.

Outside she could see the moonlight falling on the bronzed lawn, touching it with magic. It was April now. Soon the grass would be a brilliant green and the white lilacs and wild dogwood would lay like cotton strewn across the verdant lawn. The orchard would be a sea of pink and white blossoms and the tulips and wisteria and day-lilies would bloom in a riotous frenzy of color. The old borders of Southernwood would fill the air with their fragrance and the river would be a deep periwinkle blue sprinkled with silver dust.

Year after year the seasons took their endless turn. She knew them all intimately: the feel of them, the look of them, the glory and despair of them were part of her very blood and spirit. How could she think of leaving her home to go away with Ethan?

She heard Ethan come up behind her, felt his strong hands on her shoulders, the light touch of his lips on the nape of her neck. Moving out of his embrace, she turned to him and cried, "I can't go with you, Ethan."

Even in the dim light she could not mistake the anger and disappointment that darkened his eyes.

"But you said . . ."

"I know what I said. And part of me wants desperately to go with you. But another part of me wants just as desperately to stay."

Ethan stepped back, clenching his hands as if to keep himself from choking the life out of her.

"Why are you doing this?"

"There are so many reasons." Damaris struggled to keep her voice calm. "I can't betray Wesley like this. We've shared too much; we've created a home, and a family. To give that up would be to give up the best part of me. And there's Mother, and Freddy. If I leave I would lose them forever. And I'd lose Southernwood, Ethan. And my work. So many people depend on me; I can't hurt them now."

"And what about me? Does it occur to you how you're hurting me? I can make you happy, Damaris, deliriously happy. I can give you everything you'll never find at Southernwood: excitement, passion . . ."

Damaris studied him as he stood before her, scowling at her even as he tried to convince her of his love. His figure was tall and assured, the square-jawed face still strikingly handsome, the eyes dark and compelling. Even as desire stirred to life within her, she saw too his arrogance and pride. Ethan loved only himself; any hurt she caused him would be to his vanity, not his heart. She smiled sadly.

"Perhaps you could, for a time. But I could never forget all the pain I would cause. Besides, you don't really love me, Ethan. You want me, but you don't love me."

"That's not true!"

"Isn't it? Then tell me honestly that you would give up everything you've worked for to follow me into exile."

He walked abruptly to the other side of the room and stood drumming his fingers on the mantel.

"Well . . . after all, I've got a career, a reputation. And a lot of people depend on me, too."

Damaris felt the tears gather behind her eyes. It was no more than she expected.

"I suppose this means I cannot have Freddy either," Ethan said bitterly.

"No. There is no reason why Freddy cannot stay with you while he's studying at the hospital in Philadelphia. All I ask is that you don't attempt to destroy the ties he has to Wesley and me."

She was surprised to see the faintest glimmer of a smile soften the scowl on Ethan's face. So, Emily was right: it was Freddy he really wanted all along, not her. Her one brief hope that he might renounce the boy to win her was extinguished forever as she watched a satisfied expression settle over Ethan's face. Something within her died with that hope, and yet, to her surprise, what she felt most was simply relief.

"Perhaps I should go."

"Perhaps you should. I'll explain to Wesley that you were called away."

"You know I won't come back. I won't ask you again."

"I know."

He threw his coat over his arm, then picked up his hat and riding crop. "I'll be going back to Philadelphia early tomorrow morning. I think it's best we don't see each other again. Write me when to expect the boy."

At the door he paused with his hand on the knob, looking back at her. Damaris met his eyes, though her own were so filled with tears she could barely make out his tall figure.

"Good-bye, Ethan."

Without answering he jammed his hat on his head and stalked into the hall, slamming the door behind him.

Her knees began to give way. Resting one hand on a nearby table, Damaris poured herself a glass of port and downed it in one long, searing swallow. Clutching her glass, she looked around the room. So many small, familiar things seemed to leap out at her. There was the old sofa, worn with the imprint of her mother's body: how many evenings had Emily sat there sewing, peering at her stitches through the round glasses perched halfway down her nose? Her father used to sit at the opposite end, straining toward the lamp to read the fine print of his newspaper. There was the gold chair in front of the fireplace where Wesley smoked his pipe, his feet resting on the brass fender; and her own chair, opposite, where she had spent so many hours listening to the crackling of the fire interspersed with the quiet conversation of her family.

Family. They were a family, she thought, seeing that image clearly for the first time in weeks. The loss of any one of them meant that a piece of the whole was torn away. Didn't she still feel the pain of her father's empty place? How would she react if Emily were suddenly gone? Or Wesley? And how much would they suffer if she were no longer there?

Groping her way to the sofa, she sank down onto it. She felt as though a cloud was passing from in front of her eyes. She was almost surprised to realize how much she loved Wesley. For nearly all her life he had been at her side. He was her husband, her lover, her friend. Could Ethan have become all the things to her his brother had been? Whatever she might have found with Ethan, could it ever have replaced all she'd been prepared to give up?

And she loved her mother, too, in spite of their problems. Tonight they had faced some of the things that made their relationship so difficult and had agreed to try to change them. Perhaps it would make a difference.

When Wesley came back a few moments later he found her still sitting on the sofa, staring at the faded Wilton carpet.

"Well, that's taken care of," he said brightly. "Robert Manning won't bother you again for a while. I advised him to fire Gunderson. The man is not worth all the trouble and contention he causes and there are plenty of other good farmworkers about. Robert seemed relieved just to have someone make the decision for him."

"I'm so grateful you took care of that, Wesley. I really did not feel up to facing those petty problems tonight."

Wes gave a satisfied little laugh. "Why, it wasn't half bad. In fact, it gave me quite a feeling of accomplishment. I told Robert that the next time he has a problem he should bring it to me before bothering you with it."

She didn't answer. She did not have to look up at her husband to know that he was standing there, studying her silently. She was not surprised when he spoke:

"Where's Ethan?"

"He had to leave."

"Oh. What about our talk?"

"It wasn't all that important. He only wanted to ask us if Freddy could live with him while he's studying medicine in Philadelphia and I agreed. I think it's what the boy wants too. Was that all right?"

"Of course. Freddy will be good company for Ethan now that he's alone."

Alone. Ethan alone. When she might have been with him . . .

Her throat closed and the tears spilled from under her lashes, running silently down her cheeks. She covered her eyes with her hand. She felt Wes sit down beside her on the sofa, and she was grateful to feel him lay his arms around her shoulders, drawing her against him. There was comfort in the gentle touch of his fingers stroking her hair and strength to be drawn from the familiar lines of his firm body.

Yes, this was where she belonged. And though he said nothing, his loving gestures made her wonder if he did not know what he'd almost lost and in his own quiet way was thanking her for coming back to him. It was a long time before she was able to speak.

"Do you remember, Wes, how when we were children we used to take the punt through Sparta brook? Remember how the trees were so dark and the water so gentle and quiet?"

"I remember it very well. And how Jesse was always pointing out that actually there was quite a lot of life going on underneath that peaceful surface."

"Remember how I was always following after Ethan and getting into trouble with Mother? And how Corrine was always afraid of the shadows and you always tried to encourage her?"

"Poor Corrine. But you were wonderful. You weren't afraid of anything. I loved you even then. I cannot remember a time, Damaris, when I didn't love you."

She pulled away, facing him, and cried, "Wesley, I'm afraid of the shadows now. Help me as you used to help Corrine." She gripped his hands. "I need that help, Wes. I need you."

"I've always been here, Damaris, and I always will be. We'll drive away those shadows together, you and I."

With his fingers he tipped her chin and lightly kissed her lips, still wet with her tears. Slipping her arms around him, she nestled her head against the comfortable hollow of his neck.

Yes. This was where she belonged.

MARYHELEN CLAGUE'S SWEEPING, TWO-VOLUME SAGA OF PASSION, PRIDE, AND DESTINY

Set against the beauty and romance of 19th-Century Westchester County, *Beyond the Shining River* and *Beside the Still Waters* is a monumental saga of the Deveroe family... men and women whose triumphs and tragedies, courage and love built them into a great dynasty.

_____	06484-0	**BEYOND THE SHINING RIVER**	$3.95
_____	06273-2	**BESIDE THE STILL WATERS**	$3.95

Prices may be slightly higher in Canada.

Bestsellers you've been hearing about—and want to read

___ **GOD EMPEROR OF DUNE**   06233-3-$3.95
   Frank Herbert

___ **19 PURCHASE STREET**   06154-X-$3.95
   Gerald A. Browne

___ **PHANTOMS**   05777-1-$3.95
   Dean R. Koontz

___ **DINNER AT THE HOMESICK RESTAURANT** 05999-5-$3.50
   Anne Tyler

___ **THE KEEP**   06440-9-$3.95
   F. Paul Wilson

___ **HERS THE KINGDOM**   06147-7-$3.95
   Shirley Streshinsky

___ **NAM**   06000-4-$3.50
   Mark Baker

___ **FOR SPECIAL SERVICES**   05860-3-$3.50
   John Gardner

___ **THE CASE OF LUCY BENDING**   06077-2-$3.95
   Lawrence Sanders

___ **SCARFACE**   06424-7-$3.50
   Paul Monette

___ **THE NEW ROGET'S THESAURUS IN**   06400-X-$2.95
   DICTIONARY FORM
   ed. by Norman Lewis

___ **WAR BRIDES**   06155-8-$3.95
   Lois Battle

___ **THE FLOATING DRAGON**   06285-6-$3.95
   Peter Straub

___ **CHRISTMAS AT FONTAINES**   06317-8-$2.95
   William Kotzwinkle

___ **STEPHEN KING'S DANSE MACABRE**   06462-X-$3.95
   Stephen King

Prices may be slightly higher in Canada.

Available at your local bookstore or return this form to:

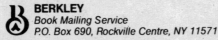

BERKLEY
Book Mailing Service
P.O. Box 690, Rockville Centre, NY 11571

Please send me the titles checked above. I enclose _____ Include 75¢ for postage
and handling if one book is ordered; 25¢ per book for two or more not to exceed
$1.75. California, Illinois, New York and Tennessee residents please add sales tax.

NAME _____

ADDRESS _____

CITY _____ STATE/ZIP _____

(allow six weeks for delivery)   **1D**